THE MYSTERIOUS BOOKSHOP

presents

THE BEST
MYSTERY
STORIES
OF THE YEAR

2022

THE MYSTERIOUS BOOKSHOP

presents

THE BEST MYSTERY STORIES OF THE YEAR 2022

INTRODUCTION BY
SARA PARETSKY

FOREWORD BY
OTTO PENZLER

THE MYSTERIOUS PRESS
NEW YORK

THE MYSTERIOUS BOOKSHOP PRESENTS
THE BEST MYSTERY STORIES OF THE YEAR 2022

Mysterious Press
An Imprint of Penzler Publishers
58 Warren Street
New York, NY 10007

First edition

Interior design by Maria Fernandez

Library of Congress Control Number: 2022906585

Hardcover ISBN: 978-1-61316-348-1
Paperback ISBN: 978-1-61316-349-8
ebook ISBN: 978-1-61316-350-4

10 9 8 7 6 5 4 3 2 1

Printed in the United States of America
Distributed by W. W. Norton & Company

CONTENTS

Bonus Story

The Best Mystery Stories 2022 Honor Roll

FOREWORD

If you stick around long enough, things accumulate. I'm not a writer, but I have somehow amassed more than seventy books to my credit, mainly as an anthology editor. (I do not include the twelve children's books I wrote under pseudonyms.) Although real writers wrote the overwhelming percentage of the material contained in those anthologies, I nonetheless have a proprietary pride in them, however minimally I deserve to take credit. I refer to them as "my books" and the contributors as "my authors."

The Mysterious Bookshop Presents the Best Mystery Story Stories of the Year, which made its debut in the autumn of 2021, is largely a continuation of a series of which I was the editor for twenty years and the same criteria for selecting stories apply to the current iteration as they always have.

As a reader, you know what makes stories good enough to stand out from their peers: narrative drive, characterization, clarity of vision and execution, literary style. If authors make me believe that the people who populate their stories are genuine, force me to wonder what they will do and what will happen to them and have those events be compelling, and say it all in a way that I haven't heard it said before, they have me in the palm of their hands.

While the great age for fiction magazines has passed, a lot of mystery stories continue to be written. The first reader for *Best Mysteries*, my friend and colleague Michele Slung, the fastest and smartest reader in the world (and I *never* engage in hyperbole except when I talk about Mickey Mantle or Tom Brady), looks at and reads about three thousand stories a year. They can be found in consumer magazines, such as *Harper's*, *The New Yorker*, and *Playboy*; mystery magazines, such as *Ellery Queen Mystery Magazine*, *Alfred Hitchcock Mystery Magazine*, and *The Strand*; short story collections (all written by the same author) and anthologies (written by various authors); electronic magazines (e-zines), such as *Thuglit*, *Tough*, and *Shotgun Honey*, though they often disappear after a short time; and literary journals, such as *Ploughshares*, *The Kenyon Review*, and *Texas Quarterly*.

After Michele culls the nonmysteries and the stories that clearly have no chance of being named among the best, I read the several hundred remaining tales, trim that list to fewer than fifty, and the guest editor makes the final selection, leaving the twenty that we regard as the best of the year to be memorialized between the covers of *Best Mysteries*. Like every "best" list, this really means the stories we liked the most.

To be selected for the volume is clearly an honor and one of the best parts of my job is hearing from authors who are thrilled to have their stories recognized and appreciated. A tiny handful of writers have declined to appear in the book. More than a decade ago, T. Coraghessan Boyle turned me down, saying that he was wasn't a mystery writer and didn't want to be identified as one. A couple years later I had dinner with him and a few other authors and I berated him for his decision and he swore he'd be happy to accept if I ever picked one of his stories again. I never have—not out of petulance but, sadly, he's never written another mystery.

At this point, I should say that I define mystery very liberally as any work of fiction in which a crime, or the threat of a crime, is central to the theme or the plot. This allows me to embrace detective stories (which is the first kind of mystery that comes to mind for many people), thrillers, crime fiction, and suspense.

Following this guideline, Sara Paretsky, the guest editor for this year's volume, and I made the final selections for the book, with an honor roll of ten stories that also were distinguished and carefully considered.

It would be impossible to adequately thank Sara Paretsky for her work on this volume, of which we both are proud. As most mystery readers know, she is one of the most significant figures in the history of American crime fiction. With her series character,

V. I. Warshawski, introduced in 1982's *Indemnity Only*, the hard-boiled female private detective became a popular protagonist in detective fiction, spawning countless imitators.

Raised in Kansas, she received a degree in political science at the University of Kansas before moving to Chicago in 1968 and went on to earn a PhD in history at the University of Chicago, followed by an MBA from the University of Chicago Graduate School of Business.

Warshawski, who has appeared in more than twenty books, is a tough private investigator who isn't afraid to get into a physical fight (and usually wins) but is also a woman who pays attention to the way she dresses and sings opera along with the radio.

Thanks also are extended to Lee Child, who was kind enough to be the guest editor of the first edition of this series.

While I engage in a relentless quest to locate and read every mystery/crime/suspense story published, I live in terror that I will miss a worthy one, so if you are an author, editor, or publisher, or care about one, please feel free to send a book, magazine, or tear sheet to me c/o The Mysterious Bookshop, 58 Warren Street, New York, NY 10007. If the story first appeared electronically, you must submit a hard copy. It is vital to include the author's contact information. No unpublished material will be considered for what should be obvious reasons. No stories will be returned. If you distrust the postal service, enclose a self-addressed, stamped postcard and I'll confirm receipt.

To be eligible for next year's edition of *The Best Mystery Stories of the Year*, a story must have been published in the English language for the first time in the 2022 calendar year. I am being neither arrogant nor whimsical when I state that the absolute firm deadline for me to receive a submission is December 31 due to the very tight production schedule for the book. Sending submissions early is better than sending them later. If the story arrives one day past the deadline, it will not be read. Sorry.

Otto Penzler
February 2022

INTRODUCTION

"There are eight million stories in the Naked City," says Mario Richetti, one of the assistant DAs in Carolyn Wheat's *Dead Man's Thoughts*.

The protagonist thought differently. "I disagreed. 'There are eight million *clients*,' I corrected him. 'There are three stories.'"

The lawyers agree and come up with two: *I found it in the street*, and *He's lying*. The assistant DAs are called away by their boss before we learn what the third story was. I've always guessed: *It was that other person*.

Several years ago, my dinner partner at a garden party was a psychoanalyst. As we reached the dessert course, he excused himself, stepped away, then came back, leaned over, and said in a low voice, "You are a sociopath. You need help."

At the end of the evening, he sought me out and apologized for his comment. "You didn't tell me you wrote mysteries," as if it were my fault that he mistook my witty badinage for the revelations of a criminal.

I gave what I hoped was a Mona Lisa smile and said, "They always tell you to write what you know."

I was afraid he might give me a bill, since he had offered a professional diagnosis, but he merely scuttled off to the safety of his spouse.

Write what you know. This has always seemed strange advice.

Some crime writers know poisons, guns, rifles, machetes, knives, hacking, fraud, accelerants, telekinesis, forgery, but most of us rely on research and imagination.

What good writers know are emotions. Everyone has felt fear. Everyone experiences narcissistic wounds, and fantasizes about revenge. Most of us have been in love, and some of us have felt rejected by the object of our devotion. Perhaps the willingness to follow those emotions into the tortured minds of characters like

Carrie or Buffalo Bill could be a sign of sociopathy to an analyst. For the writer, it could be a way of cauterizing a psychic wound.

Long before I was a published writer, I turned one of my own rejecting objects into a desiccated old man in a trench coat who stood on the Michigan Avenue bridge over the Chicago River, trying to stick his hand up the skirts of passing young women. He was truly disgusting—I think he didn't even bathe—and in the middle of the night, when my insides were twisting with longing and rage, I'd reread the story. *So there, Fred Barnacle*, I'd think. *This is how you're going to end up.*

Cass Jameson, Wheat's protagonist, is partly right—there aren't a lot of different stories. But there are seven-plus billion imaginations which keep rethinking those stories and coming up with new ways of telling them.

Fashions in stories change as do subjects and language. We all admire Conan Doyle, and Anna Katharine Green, but contemporary writers would lose their readers if we used language as ornate as theirs.

Poe, who knew horror and madness in the depths of his soul, wrote short stories whose imagery remains with us one hundred eighty years later.

Montresor's wounded narcissism in *The Cask of Amontillado* makes him a more chilling monster than Hannibal Lecter. I'm sure with the passage of time we will have many stories built around COVID, but I challenge any writer to surpass *The Masque of the Red Death*.

At the same time, the African Americans in Poe's stories, whether enslaved or free, speak and act in a way that is unbearable. Their speech is always in a crude dialect meant to show a limited intelligence. Characters like Jupiter in *The Gold-Bug* always put the needs of a white person ahead of their own.

While it's painful to read stories like this, or Dorothy L. Sayers's casual anti-Semitism, we also get something more than an entertainment from them. Popular fiction opens a window onto the culture of the epoch in which the stories were written.

The stories in this collection include a range of voices that we wouldn't have found twenty years ago, let alone at the dawn of the short story. They'll tell readers of the future what was on our collective minds in 2022.

These stories include writers experimenting with narratives outside their own life experience, and those are a welcome addition. If we can't imagine places we've never been, lives we've never lived, then we'll be stuck in that worst of all literary genres—the novel of political or religious dogma. I don't know how many trees were cut down to produce *Spring in the Victory Collective Farm* by Stalin's favorite writer, Gribachev, or the saccharine novels put out by the Religious Tract Society, but these instructive works never found many readers even in their target markets.

In this collection, you may find words that engage you or enrage you, but they won't bore you. Our main hope in putting this collection together is to entertain you, perhaps show you worlds you yourself hadn't imagined, or bring you the comfort of a world that you long to inhabit.

Sara Paretsky
Chicago
February 2022

Doug Allyn *has twice been an Edgar Allan Poe Award winner, and the record holder in the Ellery Queen Mystery Magazine Reader's Award competition. "Doug Allyn is one of the best short story writers of his generation—and probably of all time. He is also a novelist with a number of critically acclaimed books in print."* Ellery Queen Mystery Magazine.

The author of twelve novels and more than one hundred forty short stories, Allyn has been published internationally in English, German, French, and Japanese. His most recent novel, Murder in Paradise *(with James Patterson), was on the* NYT *Best Sellers list for several weeks. More than two dozen of his tales have been optioned for development as feature films and television.*

Allyn studied creative writing and criminal psychology at the University of Michigan while moonlighting as a guitarist in the rock group Devil's Triangle and reviewing books for the Flint Journal. *His background includes Chinese language studies at Indiana University and extended duty with USAF Intelligence in southeast Asia during the Vietnam War.*

Career highlights? Sipping champagne with Mickey Spillane and waltzing with Mary Higgins Clark.

KISS OF LIFE

Doug Allyn

What could be sweeter than a day at the beach? Lounging with my ladylove on a king-size terry towel in the Vale Dunes, mid-July, mideighties, midsummer breeze riffling the whitecaps on Lake Michigan. And just when I thought the day couldn't get any better—

"Maybe I should go topless," Marcy said.

Which captured my attention for a split second—but then reality set in. We've been dating a year, and Marcy is a walking contradiction, a CPA who got through college on a gymnastics scholarship, cute as a bug, tough as a combat boot, with wiry swimmer's muscles on a squared-off frame. A tight cap of brown curls, and gray eyes that constantly glitter with mischief . . .

Which meant . . . *Damn.* Her offer was too good to be true.

"I'd second the motion," I offered, "but this isn't a nude beach, babe. You'd get busted (pun intended) and hauled off to jail. As your lawyer, I'd happily bail you out, but . . . Where's this coming from?"

"A hundred young hot-bodies are scampering around the beach, practically starkers, and you're paying no attention to any of them, *or* to me. You keep staring off down the shore."

"Guilty," I admitted. "There's a woman down there, maybe a hundred and fifty yards? The tall brunette, just beyond the park on one of the private beaches."

"The one wading out into the surf in the see-through bikini?"

"That's her," I said. "She's been sitting on a sand dune in street clothes for some time, staring out over the water, and—something seems *off* about her."

"Off how?"

"I don't know. It's a beautiful day, but she seems to be under her own personal dark cloud. She was staring out at nothing for a long time, then suddenly stood up and started shucking her duds, down to what she's wearing now. Then she waded out into the surf."

"It's called swimming, Ray—"

A kid screamed, snapping our attention back to our beach. A kid, four or five years old, was being dunked by his older sister.

"Hey, you little twerp!" Marcy yelled at the girl, shaking her finger at them. "Knock it off!" And when I glanced back down the shore, the dark-haired woman was gone. Underwater, I guessed. Had to be. She was too far out to have made it back to shore, so I watched, idly waiting for her to surface . . . Only she didn't freaking surface. And she'd already been underwater for too long and—*holy crap!*

"Call nine-one-one!" I yelled at Marcy.

I was already up and sprinting down the beach, trying to keep my eyes fixed on the area where the woman vanished. And as I ran, the detail that bothered me in the first place suddenly registered. Her suit definitely wasn't one. I grew up in Valhalla, on Michigan's north shore, and spent every summer day of my childhood on this beach. I've seen a million suits, from grandma prim to teenybopper outrageous, but her bra and bottom looked odd, because they weren't a suit at all. She'd stripped to her lingerie and—damn it! The window for her air supply was already closing fast when I veered out across the shallows, splashing through the surf, driving hard for the area where I'd last seen her—there!

For just a moment, I glimpsed a pale white disturbance between two swells. A body? Maybe. It had to be. Her time was almost up when I began my sprint and she hadn't surfaced since. If the shape wasn't her—

Plunging into the surf, I knifed through the waves, swimming as hard as I could toward the ghostly outline—and slammed into her body, head first! I was stroking so fiercely I slid clear across her form, pushing her under. Not that it mattered. She was drifting with the waves, already beginning to sink. Which meant she'd inhaled water, and could be dead already. I didn't see any air bubbles around her nose or her mouth, her eyes were open and unresponsive—damn it!

Squirming around behind her, I hooked my left arm under hers, lifting her head above the surface, just in time to catch a breaker full in the face. I shook it off, but the woman didn't react at all. She was inert, dead weight now. Shifting her body around to get my left arm under her torso, I started kicking hard for the beach, hauling her with me, fighting to keep her face above water.

I risked a quick glance shoreward. Marcy was on her cell, giving directions to an ambulance. Then she tossed her phone aside and raced into the surf, coming out to help.

She met us at a sandbar where the lake was only chest-deep, and together we hauled the woman to the shore, lifeless as a sack of cement.

Easing her facedown on the sand, I tilted her jaw to open her airway, then compressed her lungs, once, twice. Some water burbled out of the corner of her mouth, but Marcy was holding a finger against her carotid to check for a pulse. She shook her head. No heartbeat.

We rolled her over and I started CPR as best I remembered it, pumping her chest for twelve strokes, then blowing air into her mouth to inflate her lungs. Her lips felt ice cold, with no more life than a bronze statue. I could taste secondhand booze.

Her lungs deflated, technically exhaling, but I felt no other response. Not a gasp or even a shiver. Dead as a headstone. *Damn it!*

I ran through another compression series, then pressed my mouth on hers again, huffing away, forcing air into—she bucked beneath me, lurching upward so violently our foreheads banged together in a head-on collision!

I actually saw stars. She snapped bolt upright, her slim frame jerking like she'd been zapped with a cattle prod. Then she spewed, spraying my face and chest with lake water, snot, and everything she'd eaten for a week, a phlegmy mess streaked with bloody foam from her lungs.

I shook off my stunned surprise to the sound of applause. We were surrounded by a ring of bystanders, mostly kids, wide-eyed and grinning. And I realized the woman's bra had slipped down around her waist. Marcy tugged it back into place as the EMT bus came rolling up the beach to us. Two uniformed medics scrambled out, and I rose and backed away, giving them room to work.

Wading into the shallows, I knelt, splashing water up into my face to rinse away the dreck, then I trudged back to the ambulance, leaning against it to catch my breath. Marcy came trotting up. She'd pulled on her own saffron sunsuit and had the woman's clothes in her arms.

"Found these on top of the dune," she said. "Didn't see a purse." She placed them at the foot of the metal gurney, then put both hands on my shoulders, scanning my face.

"Ray? Are you okay?"

I nodded. It was all I could manage; my bell was still ringing from the head butt. I'm in fair shape for a thirty-year-old attorney who spends most days behind a desk—muscle and bone and not much more—but I was definitely running on fumes now. I turned my face up to the noonday sun, content just to be alive and breathing. Marcy fetched my beach clothes—baggies and a T-shirt—and I pulled them on over my trunks.

One of the EMTs tapped my arm, a guy I knew from Merchant's League hockey. Kraniak? Krawchek? Something like that.

"Mr. Beaumont? The woman's conscious, but she's not talking. Do you know her name?"

"No."

"What about drugs? She has tats on her arms that mask her veins. Do you know if she's using?"

"No clue, pal. I tasted booze on her lips, but that's it. I've never seen her before. I saw her wade into the surf and disappear, went after her. That's really all I can tell you."

"She's in her underwear. Was it a suicide attempt?"

"No idea."

"Roger that. She's asking for you, though."

"What?"

"She's asking for the guy who saved her. That's you, right? We're going to transport her to Samaritan. It would help if you can get her name, we can call ahead for her records."

"No good deed goes unpunished," I groaned, straightening up. I circled to the rear of the van. The woman was on a metal gurney now, pale as death, her lips bloodless. A good-looking woman, midthirties, short dark hair, trim and fit. Pretty.

"Hey," I said, kneeling beside her. "How are you doing?" Dumb question. Her gaze locked on mine a moment, as if memorizing my face.

"Ma'am? Can you tell me your name?"

She closed her eyes, perhaps the only answer she could manage, then gestured with her fingertips for me to come closer. I leaned in to hear better and—*wham!* She nailed me! Slapped my face so hard that my head snapped halfway around.

"Oookay, guess we'd better go," the EMT said quickly, suppressing a grin as he and his buddy loaded the woman hastily into the ambulance. "Sorry about that, Mr. Beaumont."

"No good deed is right," Marcy cracked, also grinning, enjoying this way too much. "Are you okay, Ray?"

"I'm just ducky," I mumbled, dabbing at the blood drooling down my chin. "And I'm definitely done with good deeds for today."

But I was wrong about that.

We were in my summer runabout, a '63 Corvette convertible, headed back to Marcy's apartment, when my phone hummed. I frowned at the caller ID. Valhalla Police, Chief Marge Kazmarek. I switched on.

"This is Ray Beaumont."

"Ray, it's Chief Kaz. I'm calling from Samaritan Hospital. The woman you saved? She's asking for you."

"We've already talked, Chief. I've got a fat lip to prove it."

"The medics told me what happened, but she seems more together now. I wouldn't ask if it weren't important. The medic says it could have been a suicide attempt. If a victim's a danger to herself, we can hold her for observation, but she's demanding to be released, and wants a lawyer."

"And you gave her *my* name? Thanks a lot, Marge."

No comeback from Chief Kazmarek, and suddenly my alarm bells started going off.

"C'mon, Chief, what is it you're *not* telling me?"

"Her name," Chief Kazmarek sighed. "Her driver's license says she's Terri Prinz. But she claims to be Mrs. Leo Stefano."

I blinked. "The labor boss? I thought he was dead."

"Missing, presumed dead as Jimmy Hoffa and almost as famous. Walked out of a Detroit bar last year, hasn't been seen since. The FBI, DEA, and organized-crime units have been digging up baseball fields and barnyards all over the country looking for him. But that's Leo Senior. The lady claims she married Leo Junior a few weeks ago in Mexico. You know young Leo, right?"

"Sort of. His family has a summer house on the shore. I used to hit parties there back in high school."

"You and every other underage kid in Valhalla. And from what the lady says, Leo Junior hasn't grown up much. In any case, I gave her your name and she's asking for you. If she's a potential suicide I can't cut her loose. But she claims it was an accident, that she caught a bad wave, and she seems—well. Rational. What's your take?"

"I really don't know, Marge. I didn't actually *see* what happened, I saw her walking out, when I looked again she was gone. Sorry."

"Then talk to her, Ray, please. You two saved her, but I think she might still be in trouble, especially if she's Leo's latest wife."

"Are you sure she is? I haven't heard anything about Leo getting married again."

"Nor have I, but if I order a psych evaluation, she'll be in custody for forty-eight hours, and she's already threatening to sue."

"You understand that if I talk to her, our conversation will be privileged, Marge. Lawyer, client. I can't be your snitch."

"Just clear up the confusion. I'll owe you one."

"On my way," I said, wheeling the Vette around in a tight U-turn.

"Where to?" Marcy asked.

"Samaritan Hospital. Our vic wants a lawyer."

"Terrific," she grinned. "Think she'll smack you again?"

"Probably," I said.

Samaritan Hospital is a Vale County showcase, five stories, a snow-white facade of sprayed concrete, a tiered entrance à la Frank Lloyd Wright. It was built to impress wealthy tourists and the nouveau riche newbies who've quadrupled the north shore's population over the past decade. Internet money, mostly. If you can do business online, why not move your laptop to Valhalla? Summer beaches, hunting in the fall, skiing in winter, skydiving year round if you're crazy enough.

Leo Stefano's family moved up here from Detroit back in the nineties, one step ahead of an indictment for labor racketeering that faded after the old man disappeared. In the meantime, the family put down serious financial roots in Vale County. A bank, a hardboard plant, and a trucking firm, fully unionized, of course. International Brotherhood of Gangsters. And if my victim was really Leo Junior's wife . . . ?

My day was about to get a lot more interesting.

Valhalla PD Chief Kazmarek was waiting for me at the Samaritan admittance desk. Marge is a queen-size woman, wide as a semi, nearly six feet tall, gray hair tightly permed as a Brillo pad. She was in her tan summer uniform, no badge or name tag necessary. Everybody in Valhalla knows Chief Kaz. We rode the elevator up to the third floor together.

"The detention wing?" I noted. "Do you think she's mental?"

"I don't know what she is, Ray. So far, all she's given us is a name, Terri Lee Stefano, which doesn't match her driver's license, which says Prinz. We need to clear that up, for openers. If she's a walk-away from a funny farm, hooray for us, problem solved. But to run that down, I'll need to verify her name."

"I'll do my best." Which was all I could promise. The only sure thing about head cases is that *nothing*'s sure about head cases.

The detention suite had a patrolman just outside the door and bars on the windows. It was a white room, acoustic-tiled ceilings, gleaming tiled walls, white sheets. Terri Lee whoever was a color match for the decor, pale as a wraith. Her face and lips were bloodless, her eyes looked bruised, with blue circles beneath them. Only her hair had color, dark as a deep forest. Her face was fine boned, almost patrician, but showing some mileage lines around her eyes and at the corners of her mouth. I mentally revised her age upward a tad, to forty. Older than Leo by a few years, but still, a fine-looking woman. Chief Kazmarek pointedly took up a post by the door, out of earshot, effectively giving us the room.

I eased down on a white plastic chair beside the bed. Terri didn't notice me at first. She was awake, but her eyes were focused on something a long way off.

"Hey," I said. "I'd ask how you're doing, but the last time you smacked me in the mouth."

She turned to face me, slowly, looking me over. Clear-eyed and dead serious.

"The chief said you wanted to talk to me?" I prompted.

"Not you, necessarily," she said. "I'm in a situation here. I want to leave, but that Nazi with a badge wants to hold me for observation. I need a lawyer to make that go away. The chief said you could help me."

"I'm not sure I should. What really happened out there?"

"When I slapped you? Sorry about that, I was groggy—"

"Stop right there, lady," I said, waving her off. "No games, or I am *so* out of here. From now on, I get the truth and nothing but, or I'm gone. So, straight up, when you waded into the lake, were you trying to end your life?"

"Of course not. Why would you think that?"

"You were dressed in street clothes, staring out at the water a good half hour before you stripped to your skivvies and marched out into the surf."

"You've never gone swimming in your underwear? You must lead a dull life. Why were you watching me, anyway? Trolling for a date?"

"You looked . . . troubled, to me. You still do. Before law school I did a tour in Afghanistan. I've seen a fair number of desperate folks up close and you definitely looked the part. So here's the deal. If you like, I'll be your lawyer long enough to get you out of here, and anything we discuss will be protected by attorney–client privilege. But if you want my help, you'd better tell me exactly what's going on."

"God," she sighed. "If you knew that, you'd have thrown me an anchor. Look, maybe wading out there was—a lame decision. I was upset at the time, and ready for"—she shrugged—"whatever comes next. But since you blew up my big plan, I've been rethinking things . . ." Her voice was fading. I was losing her.

"Listen up, Terri," I said, leaning in, trying to pull her back from the darkness. "As an attorney I've dealt with the aftermath of suicide. It may seem like an easy way out, but the ones you leave behind are saddled with the ache of it forever. It's always a bad choice. If you're jammed up, let's talk it through. We'll figure things out together, starting at square one. What's your real name?"

"Terri Lee Stefano, née Prinz. I'm Mrs. Leo Stefano."

"Since when?"

"Since . . . three weeks ago. We were married on a wild weekend in Cancún."

"That sounds like Leo. How did you two hook up?"

"In Vegas. I was a showgirl till my boobs started drifting south. I could see the Dead End signs ahead, so I took some classes and became a croupier. I was dealing blackjack in a casino, Leo won big at my table. Burned the house for seventy-six grand and change."

"Wow," I whistled. "That's a lot."

"Not to Leo, he's a whale, and a degenerate gambler. The pit bosses know he'll lose it back soon enough. But after his big win, he took us all out to celebrate—me, the other players in the game.

He chartered a plane, flew us down to Cancún. We partied non-stop for umpty tequila sunrises, and three days later, Leo and I woke up in bed. Married."

"Married how?"

"In a church, with a priest, and the other players as witnesses. The whole enchilada."

"So it was legal?"

"Totally legit, all properly notarized. I know, it sounds like a madcap, romantic fling out of a movie, but Leo and I have both been married before, so in the cold, sober light of our hangovers, we naturally considered calling the crazy thing off, getting a divorce or an annulment."

"Why didn't you?"

She took a deep breath. "Because I was desperate to change my luck and my life. So I basically screwed my new husband into rolling the dice to see if it could work out."

"And was Leo sober at any point in these—negotiations?"

"Sure. That first morning after. Since then, not so much."

"Okay. It started out as a fling—"

"Excuse me," Chief Kazmarek said, stepping in. "Mrs. Stefano? Your husband's downstairs. With your daughter."

"Oh my God," Terri groaned. "Don't let them see me like this—"

But it was too late. Leo Stefano bulled past the patrolman at the door into the room. I hadn't seen him since high school. Leo was a jock back then, hardbodied and handsome. He was running to suet now, with the permanent flush of a steady drinker. He was dressed for the links, a U of M golf shirt and matching Bermuda shorts. Deck shoes, no socks, and he wasn't alone. Two cronies trailed him in, a slick in a tailored suit, slim, trim, and Black, carrying a leather-cased laptop that probably cost more than a Ford Focus.

His white pal was strictly muscle, the size of a building, leather jacket with an OTR Union flag on the shoulder, black denims, work boots. A face like a pimento loaf, odd bits of stuff dotting it. Both men stayed back, watching, as Stefano stalked to his wife's bedside, looking more annoyed than concerned.

"What the hell is this, Terri?" he demanded, gesturing at the room. "What happened?"

"I was swimming," she said, meeting his gaze straight on. "I caught a bad wave and swallowed half the lake. This gentleman was kind enough to haul me out."

"Ray Beaumont, Mr. Stefano," I said, offering my hand. "You played ball with my brother Cooper back in the day."

He gave me a vague nod, the reek of secondhand scotch rolling off him like aftershave. He ignored my outstretched hand. Maybe he didn't see it. Maybe he did.

"I remember you." He nodded sourly. "The hockey player, right? A thug sport."

"Sometimes," I conceded.

"So thanks for helping out, Ron—"

"It's Ray, Mr. Stefano. Ray Beaumont of Beaumont and Deveraux, attorneys at law. Your wife has retained me as legal counsel."

"What? You hired a freakin' lawyer?" Leo scoffed, turning on Terri. "Terrific! Let's start the damn dance, honey. It's not my first rodeo. But if you think I'm paying this schmuck a damn dime, you're wrong. She hasn't got a cent of her own, pal. Hope you like working for free."

I let it pass. He was half blasted and looking for a scrap. And the way my day was going, I was tempted to give him one. But not here.

"So where are we, Chief?" Stefano demanded, turning on Marge. "Is my wife free to go?"

"I'd rather—rest here a bit," Terri said. "Is Jolene with you?"

"Out in the hall," Leo said. "Didn't think she'd want to see her drunk-ass mom in this shape."

"I'm not—"

"We'll talk at the house," Leo snapped. "How about it, Chief?"

"She's a patient, not a criminal, Leo. She's free to leave, but she did have a close call—"

"I'm the one paying the bills!"

"She's not your property," I put in, "and as her lawyer—"

"My lawyer is the fella with the briefcase," he said, jerking a thumb at the pair by the door. "I didn't hire you, and I'll burn my damn money before you see a red cent."

"Actually, burning money is a federal offense, Mr. Stefano," the stud in the suit offered.

"One you could beat by taking a Breathalyzer," I finished.

"Are you calling me a drunk, you smartass shyster!" Leo lunged at me, taking a wild swing that I sidestepped easily. Seizing Stefano's upper arm, Chief Kazmarek used his momentum to swing him completely around, then marched him out the door to turn him over to the sentry out in the hall.

"Take him home," Marge snapped at the cop. "Don't let him get behind the wheel."

"Relax, Mr. Stefano," the suit called after him. "I've got this."

Marge followed her patrolman out to the elevators, making sure Leo took one.

"Mr. Beaumont, is it?" the suit said, handing me his business card. "Can we talk?"

I scanned the card. "Jervis Cleveland, of Howe, Hepner, and Walsh, attorneys at law," I said. "Offices on Cadillac Square, Detroit. I'm impressed."

"You should be. Our firm represents the OTR Brotherhood, the long-haul truckers' union. I'm a union business agent, but I primarily function as a—legal janitor. Messes are my specialty."

"If Leo's your client, you've got a full-time job."

"Actually, to be clear, Mr. Stefano *isn't* my client, the union is. Mr. Stefano holds his father's seat on the commission, but he also holds a good many opinions that aren't shared by the union hierarchy."

"Such as?"

"Leo considers himself a crown prince, entitled to the wealth and influence his father left when he—went missing. Which brings us to our immediate problem, Mr. Stefano's new and *very* inconvenient marriage."

"You've lost me. Why would the union give a rip about Leo's love life?"

"Whom Mr. Stefano marries isn't the problem. But a contentious divorce? That could be another matter."

"A divorce judge would demand to see Leo's finances, which could also open the Union's books—"

"A situation we'd prefer to avoid," Cleveland finished. "All I need from you is a simple number, Ray. Name the cash settlement that will get your client on a plane to Vegas to obtain a quiet annulment that will resolve this travesty."

"I have no idea what that number would be, nor any indication that my client would be interested. She isn't looking for a payoff, Mr. Cleveland, she's hoping to salvage her marriage."

"Perhaps you can make her see reason. We're offering a hundred thousand up front, but off the record?" he added, leaning in. "We can easily double that offer. And how you choose to divide the funds is strictly between you and your client."

I didn't answer, eyeing him curiously.

"I see I've captured your attention," he said, stifling a smirk.

And I realized he had no idea what could happen next. I was only half a word away from punching his lights out. I looked away instead, clamping down my temper. For the moment.

"And *if* I can put Terri on a plane for, say . . . a hundred grand? I can pocket the rest? Keep the change, so to speak?"

"A hundred thousand is hardly a gratuity."

"No, it sounds more like a bribe, one I'm required to report to the Bar."

"And I'll swear you mistook my meaning. Be reasonable, Ray. The situation is a shambles. We're offering your client a way to cash out."

"By throwing her marriage under the bus?"

"This honeymoon isn't headed for happily ever after, Mr. Beaumont, it's on the fast track to the Dumpster. The only question is '*qui bono*'? Who will benefit? Why not you, for example?"

"Pass," I said.

"But—you will inform your client of our offer?"

"Absolutely. The full two hundred. But don't get your hopes up."

"Hope has nothing to do with it. Money talks. Our offer stands for twenty-four hours."

"And then?"

"And then it doesn't," he snapped, annoyed. "This matter's going to be settled, Beaumont, with your help or without it."

"Without it, I'm thinking. And if bribing me was Plan A? I hope Plan B is a little smarter."

"I think you'll like it less," he said grimly, turning away. "We'll talk again."

He paused at the door for a word with the bodyguard, then headed out, slamming the door angrily behind him.

"What was that about?" Terri asked, knuckling her eyes.

"Cash," I said, crossing to her bedside. "A union lawyer is offering you a serious payoff if you'll agree to an annulment."

"You mean Leo—?"

"The offer isn't from Leo. The union wants to protect their books from a divorce judge. They're offering two hundred grand, but I can probably get that bumped up."

"If I was in this for money, Leo's worth a lot more." Terri sighed. "Why do they want an annulment, anyway? Leo's been married twice, he's probably got a lawyer on speed dial."

"An annulment could be settled quietly, in Vegas. Maybe you should consider it."

"It's not that simple. I'm not the only one involved—"

"Mom?" A tall girl in a flowered summer dress, with a candy-striped beach bag over her shoulder, was paused in the doorway. Slim as a whip, and with a short, boyish hair style, she could have been Terri twenty years back. "Are you okay?" she asked, hurrying to her mother's bedside, taking her hand. "Sweet Jesus, what were you thinking?" She gently but firmly twisted Terri's wrist, pointedly scanning her tattoos.

"It was just an accident, Jolene," Terri said, wincing. "I'm not using."

"Take it easy there," I said.

"What?"

"You're hurting her wrist."

"Who the hell are you?"

"Ray Beaumont, her attorney."

"The guy who saved her, right? So you're after a cut of her action now?"

"He's a friend, Jolene," Terri said weakly.

"Gee, maybe you should marry him, Ma. If you weren't already married to some guy you barely know. And here we are again, hooking up in a hospital."

"Lighten up," I said.

"Screw yourself, sport! You're not my dad, whoever he was, so back the hell off! Look, Ma, if this was about our big argument,

I'm sorry I said all that crap. When we get hot, we both say things we don't mean, but I'm not a kid anymore. I'm seventeen, and you can't make these monster decisions without giving me a say. It's not fair."

"You're right, we should have talked first," Terri said evenly, her eyes locked on her daughter's. "But it's not that simple anymore. Is it?"

"For Pete's sake, let's not start fighting all over again," Jolene said, straightening up, looking down at her mother, the resemblance between them so close they could have been sisters. "But look where you are, Ma. Play it smart for once. Get yourself together, then head home to Vegas and sort things out there."

"No, not quite yet," Terri said, turning away, facing the white tiled wall. "I need to rest my eyes a minute. . . ."

Her voice faded out. Her daughter stood there a moment, looking down at her—

And I had a sudden, odd flash. Déjà vu.

I'd seen that look before. Somewhere. Couldn't place it, or recall it clearly, but I'd seen it. The memory was crouching in the shadows—

"Can we talk?" the girl asked, heading for the far corner of the room without waiting for a response.

Terri was drifting off, so I joined her daughter, who wheeled to face me, fierce and fearless, a teenager making the jump from sneakers to heels.

"That old-lady cop said you saved my mom's life. Thank you for that. But Terri is—" Jolene looked away for a moment, deciding what to say next. "Look, she tries hard, she really does, but Mom's got problems you should be aware of."

"Such as?"

"She's a junkie," the girl said bluntly. "She claims she's not using now, but I've heard that before and here we are again. She goes to work on an ordinary Friday night, then calls me from freakin' *Mexico* to say she's married, for God's sake. Then I get a text saying 'Come up to Michigan, honey, we'll be one big happy family.'" Jolene shook her head with a *Can you believe it?* look that only a teenager can pull off.

"So I quit my job and fly up, but when I get here, Mom and Leo are fighting like cats and dogs, for crissake!" She turned away a moment, getting a handle on her anger. Then faced me again.

"Honestly? Was she trying to do herself in out there?"

"I don't know, miss. Has she done anything like it before?"

"Hell, shooting speed is slow-motion suicide, but she always had an excuse. Needed crank to keep dancing, then needed 'ludes to calm down. Before long, she was stoned twenty-four/seven."

"You checked her arms. Did you see any fresh tracks?"

Jolene hesitated, reading my face, an uncomfortable experience. This was one tough kid. "No," she said, "not this time, but she's quit before. Then something happens and she's back on the spike. I love my mom, but I've paid my damn dues, growing up in strip joints, always on the move to the next town, the next club. I changed schools like you change shorts, always the new kid, getting jumped by bullies, getting busted for fighting back—"

"It must have been rough."

"It was. So am I. And normally I'd figure it was Terri's just in another scrape, and we'd move on, but this time Ma may be in real trouble."

"What trouble?"

"Two guys have been tailing us. Blacked-out SUV, shiny as a new dime. A Cadillac, maybe, I don't know cars."

"Do you know who they are?"

"Nope, but I know *what* they are. Muscle. Like the goon I passed on the way in. Who is he, anyway?"

"He came with Leo's lawyer."

"Well, the two who've been tailing us aren't lawyers, they're thugs from Vegas."

"Why do you think so?"

"Are you serious? Leo hits Ma's table for seventy-five grand, and two days later she marries the guy? If you ran a casino, would you get all warm and fuzzy about the happy couple honeymooning on your money? Or want it back?"

"Leo Stefano doesn't need to scam casinos. His family's loaded."

"Maybe Ma's bosses don't know that. All I know is, people who rip off casinos have terrible luck. Their cars blow up, they go hiking in the desert and don't come back. Terri needs to go home to Vegas and straighten this out."

"*She* needs to go? Not you?"

"Hey, I just got here, pal. Leo's got a beach house, big bucks. I'm in no hurry to get back to the strip clubs I grew up in. I've been sorting out Terri my whole life. You can take a turn. And good luck with the goons in the Caddy." She headed out without looking back, which was just as well. I was still trying to place the déjà vu of her earlier look.

Couldn't.

Out in the corridor, the leather-jacketed union goon fell in step with Jolene. Huge guy, the size of a football lineman.

"Something you want, big fella?" she asked.

"You," he said simply. "I'm Cooch. I'll be your driver today."

"I don't want a driver. Leo loaned me a car."

"What you want ain't on my list of things to worry about, girl. You're a looker, but that can change in a New York second. Understand?"

Jo looked him over more carefully, then glanced up and down the corridor. The nurse's station was deserted, the elevator at the end stood open and empty.

"You're late," she said drily.

"What you talking about?"

"My ma's in showbiz, so we move a lot. Every new town, every new school? Somebody tries to jump the new kid. Mostly, it's a bad move. For them."

"This ain't high school, girl," Cooch said, seizing her upper arm with a grip like a C-clamp. "My boss wants you on ice while he seals a deal with your ma. After that, happy trails."

"Okay, okay, don't bruise the merchandise," Jolene said, pulling her arm free, then slipping it through his. "I get it, I'm with you for now. Which doesn't have to be a bad thing," she added. "I like big guys."

"You're a little strange, you know that?"

"So my counselors keep telling me," Jolene sighed, falling into step. "So where to? Someplace with a bed, I hope? Can we get ice cream after?"

Out in the parking lot, Cooch marched her to a mud-spattered Chevy pickup. Opening the passenger door, he thrust her into the bucket seat.

"Don't make me chase you, eh?"

"Why would I?" Jo asked, as he slid behind the wheel. "This is the most excitement I've had since I got here. Where are we going?"

"No place, yet. Your ma's hooked up with some lawyer. We're gonna send him a message."

"With this?" she asked, reaching for the sawed-off shotgun snugged between the seats. He slapped her hand away.

"Mitts off, girl."

"No problem." She shrugged. "But possession of a chopped shotgun is a five-year felony."

"What do you know about guns?"

"I know it doesn't take Superman to pull a trigger. Is it loaded with buckshot or slugs?"

"Why?"

"Wondering if the message is to scare him off or blow him away?"

Cooch eyed her curiously. She wasn't a bit scared. More like . . . turned on. Up for some action.

"How about I show you what message," he said, firing up the truck, pressing the tab that rolled his window down. "Better cover your ears."

I eased down on the chair at Terri's bedside. Her eyes were half closed and I guessed I'd only have a minute or two before exhaustion carried her under.

"Your daughter says you're being threatened," I said flatly. "What's going on?"

"Two thugs with tattoos stopped me in a parking lot. Claimed to be working for a casino, but more likely Leo hired them to spook me."

"Why would you think that?"

"Because they want the same thing Leo wants. Me, out of the picture."

"Maybe you should take the hint, Terri."

"Have you ever bet ten grand on the turn of a card, Ray? I do it every night, and I'm betting I can turn my freak show of a marriage into something worth saving. Leo may not know it, but he needs me. He's a boozer with a gambling jones, and I've dealt with the same problems. I can help him straighten out, give us all a better life. Jolene's been through so much, I owe her this chance."

"By staying with a man who wants you gone?"

"Most of Leo's guff comes out of a bottle. It's not terminal."

"Walking into a lake can be."

"Look, I had a dark moment. Haven't you ever had a moment like that?"

"It wasn't just a moment, lady, you were gone. Stone-cold dead. If I'd been a few seconds later—"

"But you weren't. You gave me the kiss of life."

"What?"

"That's what the EMT called it. The kiss of life. Like the kiss of death, only backward. And I'm grateful for this second chance, Ray, but I've got my head on straight now. I won't need any more kisses, I just need . . . rest a bit. Then I'll check out of this place, sit down with Leo, and . . ." She was asleep before she finished the sentence.

"Ray?" Chief Kaz spoke from the doorway. "Buy you a coffee in the cafeteria?"

"My girlfriend's waiting for me in the lobby," I said, following her to the elevator.

"Assuming she's still there, she can wait a bit longer," Kaz said. In the elevator, she hit the stop button between floors to buy us privacy.

"Let's clear the air, boyo. For openers, is your client a danger to herself or others?"

"She's—in a tough situation, Marge. But she seems rational about dealing with it, which doesn't mean she's not at risk. She and Leo got married after a wild weekend. From his attitude, I'm guessing the honeymoon's over."

"If we send her home, will she be walking into the surf twenty minutes later?"

"I don't think so. She's hoping to make her marriage work."

"To Leo Stefano," she said, shaking her head. "Which is a separate problem. Leo. He's not the party animal you knew back in the day, Ray. His father was a labor racketeer, and Leo's following in his wing-tip footsteps. He beat a kid nearly to death a few years ago."

"What happened?"

"You were still overseas at the time. Leo was shooting pool against a local hotshot. He was loaded and losing, and kept doubling down, trying to catch up, until the tab was up to thirty thousand. The kid demanded his money, Leo slammed him upside the head with a beer stein, then kicked him half to death when he hit the floor. Collapsed a lung, ruptured his spleen."

"What came of it?"

"Nothing. A union shyster paid off the kid and the witnesses, but Leo's risky business now, mean as a snake with a backache."

"Where does that leave my client?"

"Possibly at risk, if things don't work out with him. But it's not illegal to have bad taste in mates. If she seems rational to you—?"

"She does."

"Then when she's medically cleared, I'll cut her loose." Marge hit the elevator's start button, and we headed down.

But as we slowed to a halt, I heard a heavy thump, then another, in the distance. The chief's eyes locked on mine.

Gunfire! On instinct, we both flattened against the side walls as the door slid open to—chaos!

In the lobby, people were screaming, streaming in all directions. Marge rushed to the security guard who was cowering behind the admittance desk.

"Active shooter!" he yelled, waving his pistol. "He's in the parking lot! Get down!"

"Red light!" Marge called over her shoulder as she raced past him. "Don't shoot me!" Drawing her weapon, she edged up to the front door, then slipped outside, weapon at the ready.

"Marcy!" I shouted, looking wildly around.

"Over here!" she called back, much calmer than I was. She was crouched behind a tiled column. I sprinted to her side.

"Are you okay?" we said together, then "I'm good," again in unison, both of us grinning at the insanity of it.

Outside, the chief was edging along the wall, her weapon in a two-hand hold, scanning the lot.

"What happened, Marcy?" I demanded.

"I heard some bangs from the parking lot. Firecrackers, I thought, but then somebody yelled gunfire, and everything went nuts. Cars started peeling out all over the place."

"Okay," I nodded. "Stay here—"

"Not a chance," she said, hovering near my shoulder as I edged out the front doors to Chief Kazmarek.

"Marge?" I said carefully, making sure she was aware of our approach. "What happened?"

"Somebody fired off a couple of rounds, then took off. Isn't that your Corvette?" She pointed to my '63, parked near the rear of the lot. I trotted out to it. Two ragged patches were torn in the driver's door and front fender, shredding the paint and the fiberglass.

"Shotgun, didn't penetrate," Marge noted, kneeling to inspect the damage. "Who's ticked off at you?"

"Leo Stefano, obviously."

"Leo left half an hour ago with one of my officers," Kaz pointed out, "and he was so loaded I doubt he could hit a barn with a baseball bat."

"Marcy, you said cars were peeling out? Did you see anyone near mine?"

"It was craziness, Ray, like a demolition derby."

"How about a black Cadillac?"

Her shrug said it all.

"Who owns the Cadillac, Ray?" the chief asked.

"When I find out, I'll let you know," I said. "If you're through with me, Chief, I'd like to get Marcy home and get my car out of range."

"The damage is superficial. Go ahead," Marge nodded. "Bring it by the station later and we'll photograph it. And Ray? I'm sorry about all this. Thanks for helping out."

I didn't bother to answer.

I was so steamed about the damage to my car that I didn't spot them right off, but I must have caught a glimpse, because I kept checking my rearviews with a growing sense of unease.

"Is something wrong?" Marcy asked.

"You think? We rescued a woman who didn't want to be saved, I got punched out for my trouble, now I've got a client who's at risk or unbalanced and people are using my car for target practice. Otherwise, things are fine as wine."

But even as I said it, I realized I was already too late. The minivan behind me turned off, and the car I'd glimpsed earlier moved up in its place. A black Cadillac Escalade, shiny as a new dime. Following us? I made a quick left without signaling.

The Escalade made the same turn, but stayed back, making no attempt to tailgate us or run up alongside. Definitely trailing us, though. I could make out a driver and a shotgun-seat passenger, but no details. The windows were smoked.

Marcy caught my look. "Do you know those guys?" Marcy asked, swiveling in her seat to look back as I pulled over.

"Jolene said Terri had a run-in with two goons in a black Cadillac. I'm guessing that's them."

"Should we call the chief?"

"Not yet. Stay in the car and keep your phone handy. If things go south, dial nine-one-one."

My golf clubs were behind the seat. I snaked a nine iron out of my golf bag, then turned to face the Cadillac.

The Escalade slowed to a halt directly behind us, idling in the middle of the street. Even with its tinted windows rolled up, the heavy thump of rap music echoed across the sleepy neighborhood like jungle drums beating out a warning.

They'd picked a poor place for a showdown, a quiet suburban neighborhood, cookie-cutter homes, lawns neatly mowed. Up the block, kids were playing soccer in a schoolyard. Lots of witnesses if trouble came.

And it was coming.

Two men climbed out. Thugs, Jolene said. It was an apt description. Both were pushing forty, in matching sunglasses, black T-shirts, jeans, and boots. One was a First Nations brave, complete with a Mohawk haircut. His partner was a copper-skinned Black man, with his skull shaved smooth as a bullet. Mohawk was wearing a motorcycle-chain belt and looked bad to the bone.

His partner was more compactly built but just as hard. Chinese characters tattooed on his neck, and a razor-cut goatee.

"Mr. Beaumont?" he called. "My name's Raven. Can we talk?"

"I keep office hours. Call for an appointment."

"We'll only need a minute of your time, and I promise you won't need the putter."

I shrugged, but kept the club. He got the message. Raising both hands, palms forward, he did a slow pirouette to show he was unarmed, then nodded at his bud, who did the same.

"I'm Beau Jean Raven, my large friend here is Tommy Pachonka. We work for TCA, the Tribal Casino Administration out of St. Regis, New York. Here's my card." He cautiously handed me a business card that confirmed what he said. His name, phone, mailing address, even his picture.

"Asset management?" I noted. "Which means . . . ?"

"Collections," Pachonka said with a smile that never reached his eyes. "Write a bad check, cancel a credit card, we'll be around to see you."

"Not me, I don't gamble. I'm guessing your beef is with Leo Stefano."

"We've got no problem with Mr. Stefano," Pachonka said. "He's a valued customer. We'll hate to lose him."

"Why should you?"

"Which brings us down to it," Raven said. "We have information which could be of considerable value to your new client, Terri Stefano."

"What makes you think she's a client?"

"Information's our business, Mr. Beaumont, and business is good. There's only one catch. We'll need your word that the intel stays between us. No one else."

"I'm an officer of the court. If you're talking about a crime—?"

"Not a crime," Raven said quickly, "a situation."

"How does it involve my client?"

"Her new husband, Leo Stefano, is almost bankrupt. By the end of the month, he'll be flat broke."

"Nonsense. The Stefanos are loaded. They practically own the trucker's union, plus real estate, a hardboard plant, and a controlling interest in the Vale State Bank—"

"All of which Leo has put up as collateral for a series of shaky loans. He's flushed away a small fortune to finance his gambling habit, Mr. Beaumont. His lawyers have stalled us as long as they can, but the TCA is about to haul him into court for bad checks, hundreds of them. He'll walk out so broke his lawyers will have to file suit to get paid."

I cocked my head, reading Raven's eyes. People lie to lawyers every day. White lies, black lies. Sometimes clients lie when the truth would serve them better. A good liar can be so convincing, Solomon himself couldn't read them. I certainly can't. But I've gotten pretty damn good at recognizing the truth when I hear it.

And Raven was telling me the truth.

"Okay, say you're right," I conceded. "Why tell me?"

"Because adding a new wife to the mix could stall our case for months. It's my understanding that Stefano wants an annulment and is willing to pay for it. Tell your client to take the money and run. While she can."

"That sounds like a threat."

"Not from us. We mean her no harm, but that doesn't mean she's not at risk. We're collectors, Mr. Beaumont, we came here to offer Leo Stefano one last chance to avoid bankruptcy, by setting up a repayment program. He wasn't interested."

"What happened?"

"At first, he blew us off. Claimed he was flush again, that he'd scored a big win in Vegas."

"That part is true," I said. "He won seventy grand plus."

"He could win seventy ten times in a row, and it wouldn't make a dent in what he owes," Pachonka put in.

"So where does the threat come in?"

"I left Leo my business card," Raven said. "Two days later, he called me, but not about a repayment plan. He wanted to hire us. To make his new wife go away."

"Run her off, you mean?"

"Or run her over," Pachonka grinned. "'Whatever it takes,' the man said. 'Just get her gone.'"

I mulled that for a moment.

"You took the job. Didn't you?"

"Absolutely," Raven said, with a feral grin. "Said we'd do the deed for ten large, and we'd get as ugly as he wanted. We have him on video paying us the ten to rough up his wife. At the foreclosure hearing, he'll cough up his last nickel just to stay out of prison."

"If you've got things all sewn up, why tell me?"

"Because the Council hates news stories about customers losing at our casinos. We'd rather keep this on the down-low. So how about this? We'll *give* you a copy of the Stefano video. Use it to negotiate a sweet deal for your client. But in the end, she has to agree to the annulment and walk away."

"I can't promise she'll do that. She's well aware that Leo's halfway off the rails, but she desperately wants this marriage to work, for her daughter's sake as much as her own."

"Her daughter's most of her problem," Pachonka said flatly.

"What does that mean?"

"Sorry, that's outside our wheelhouse, Counselor," Raven said. "Do we have a deal?"

"Not quite. Here's a counteroffer, guys. I'll sit on your info for now, but in return, you'll stay clear of my client and her husband. Give her the chance to work things out."

"It'll never happen," Pachonka scoffed.

"She gets to try, or you two can tell your story to the local law." I nodded at Marcy, who began dialing.

"No need for that," Raven said quickly, raising his hands in mock surrender. "You win this round, Counselor. We'll back off, but not for long. The clock's running on this. Are we clear?"

"Crystal."

"Then I wish your client luck. She'll need it, especially with her daughter."

They climbed back into their oversized SUV and roared around my Corvette, burning rubber to jack up the drama, running the stop sign at the end of the block.

I watched them go, wondering what he meant by that crack about Jolene.

"This isn't the way to Leo's beach house," Jolene said.

Cooch ignored her, speeding along the rural two-lane, heading into the Black River hills.

"Hey, big guy, he lives on the freakin' beach. This isn't—"

He backhanded her, hard, snapping her back in her seat.

"Reality check, kid," he snapped. "Leo Stefano's got a big house on the freakin' beach. You and your ma live in a low-rent trailer park forty miles outside of Vegas, and you're both getting on the next plane back there."

"You're making a mistake. Leo wants me with him, he said so."

"Was he wearing pants when he said it?"

"He wasn't wearing anything. We were in a hot tub."

"Here's another reality check, honey. In that situation, guys will say anything to close the deal."

"No, he meant it. Take me to his place, he'll tell you himself."

"Girl, I'm taking you straight to the airport, unless you want to see another trick I can do with a shotgun—"

Jo grabbed the steering wheel, jerking the pickup off the road onto the gravel shoulder, sending it fishtailing wildly out of control. Yanking her hands off the wheel, Cooch slammed the girl back against her seat, then matted the brakes, wrestling the truck to a halt, rocking broadside across the center line.

"You crazy bitch! You could've killed us both!"

Jolene didn't answer. Raising the shotgun she'd snatched off his lap, she cocked the hammers. She needed both hands, but it was pointed directly at him.

"Take me to Leo's house, big guy. Right now. Or get out and I'll drive myself."

"You can't even hold that thing, you little—" He grabbed the gun muzzle, twisting it out of her hands.

In the closed cab, the shotgun blast roared like the end of the world!

"What was that about?" Marcy demanded, as I climbed back in the Vette. "What did they want?"

"They're casino collection agents. They offered to trade information that could help Terri score a serious settlement, but only if she's willing to quit her Looney Tunes marriage."

"What kind of information?"

"This guy—" I handed her his business card. "—Raven, claims Leo's all but bankrupt, but he tried to bribe them to rough Terri up—" She was staring at me. "What?"

"Has it occurred to you that we're in way over our heads, Ray? We rescued the Stefano woman, if that's even her name, and now your car's been shot up, we're being pulled over by thugs. Maybe you should give this situation a second thought."

"What second thought?"

"Good point. When people say 'on second thought,' it indicates that they've actually had a *first* thought, and you haven't. From the moment you saw her walk into the water, all you've done is react."

"Maybe I should have considered my options while she drowned?"

"Don't be an ass," she snapped. "You saved the woman—"

"*We* saved her, actually—"

"Fine, good for us. But this isn't about a good deed anymore. You're crossways of a labor racketeer, the trucker's union, and casino thugs—"

"You're right," I said, waving off the rest of her argument. "I should never have involved you in this. I'll take you home—"

"The hell you will! That's not what I'm saying!"

"Okay, what *are* you saying, exactly?"

"Good lord, Ray, what do you think I do all day?"

"Um—you're a CPA. You—keep books?"

"I manage the accounts of five corporations, including your Uncle Gus's lumberyard, and roughly a hundred and seventy private accounts. Some are mom-and-pops, others are substantial holdings."

"Got it," I said. "You're saying I should marry you for your money." Which won me a smile, at least.

"No, I'm saying that before we get any deeper into this, you need to deal me in."

"In—to what?"

"Everything. The collector, Raven? Or Leo Stefano. If you want to know who's for real, give me twenty minutes online and I can tell you. Can we do that?"

"Uh—sure. Should we—?" But she waved me off, already focused on her smartphone.

I've got a phone. Nearly every American from second grade up has one, but Marcy's focus was so total that I instantly realized she was on a different level. Five minutes in, she tossed me Raven's business card.

"Raven's legit," she said, already turning back to her phone. "He's employed by the Tribal Casino Administration out of upstate New York. Owns a house in St. Regis, two cars, a boat, and an AKC registered Labrador Retriever . . ."

I started to congratulate her but she'd already refocused on her phone. So I left her to it, circling the car slowly, to kill time, and to think. About what she'd said. And what it meant.

Marcy was right. I'd blundered headlong into a dicey situation. I'd put her at risk, and she was steamed at me, because—Okay, I wasn't entirely clear about that part. But whatever had tripped her trigger, she didn't want out.

She wanted further in.

And it dawned on me that our relationship might be moving onto new and uncertain ground. Marcy Quinn was lovely, fun, and scary smart. We'd been seeing each other for nearly a year of very good times, and lately I'd sensed things were getting semiserious. Which might be a good thing. Or the opposite.

Because I had no idea how she might feel about that. Was I a serious contender for happily ever after? Or just a boyfriend she dated while she waited for Mr. Right?

I truly hadn't a clue.

Marcy snapped her phone shut.

"What?" I demanded.

"Your First Nation friends are absolutely right," she said flatly. "Leo Stefano is financially stretched past any hope of recovery. His savings and investments are gone, credit's maxed out, his home is triple mortgaged, car and boat leases all overdue. He'll crash and burn in a matter of months."

And I'd heard enough.

I dropped the Vette into low gear and peeled out, as Marcy strapped herself in.

"Where are we going?" Marcy asked, bracing herself against the passenger door.

"To talk to the guy who started this mess by marrying a blackjack dealer. I'm going to get a cash offer to get Terri out of this while we still can."

"But you said she doesn't want out."

"She doesn't know the truth. When she does, if she still wants to book passage on the Titanic, I'll wave goodbye from the pier. This started out to be a day at the beach, and we've been in the crazy world of Leo Stefano ever since. And one way or another, we're getting off at the next stop."

I didn't mention Chief Kaz's warning about Leo's temper. Down deep, I was *really* hoping he would take another swing at me without a cop at hand to break it up. I'd make it the biggest mistake of his miserable life.

But Leo didn't take a swing at me.

He didn't answer the doorbell either.

I hadn't been to the Stefano beach house since those high-school beer busts, but the place was still an eyeful. Built with lumber money a century ago, the Stefanos had updated it, converting the carriage house to a five-car garage, adding tennis courts to the backyard, plus a putting green, overgrown now. Back then it was a posh palace, but it was showing its age now. Peeling paint, a sagging roof above the *Gone With the Wind* front porch.

I hammered on the door, hard, but no one came and there was no sound from within. The front door had leaded-glass panels with sidelights, rippled with age. Marcy pressed her nose up against one of the panels.

"No lights. I don't think anybody's home." I tried the knob. Locked.

I stalked off, following the flagstone walkway that circled the house.

"Where you going?"

"Around to the beach. Maybe he's swimming. Or a back door is open."

"And what? We just break in?"

"Hey, his wife nearly drowned, somebody shot up my car, and thugs in Cadillacs are dogging us. We're way past common courtesy, Marcy. I want a word with this idiot."

At the rear of the house, the porch expanded into a patio large enough for garden parties, with a spectacular view of the dunes and the breakers. The deck was an extension of a glass-walled library/rec room within. Its French doors were open, so I edged inside.

"Hello?"

No answer. Sofas and love seats all faced the beach where I'd first seen Terri. Two gleaming brass-barreled telescopes on wooden tripods offered close-ups of the young hard-bodies swimming or playing volleyball if you were inclined to watch, and who wouldn't be?

The interior walls were floor-to-ceiling bookcases, filled with pristine volumes, probably purchased by the linear foot. I doubt they'd ever been read.

Aside from the sofas, the only practical piece of furniture in view was a massive desk at the rear of the room, probably assembled where it stood. It was much too large to fit through a doorway. A marvelous creation, with hand-carved moldings and intricately detailed lion's feet.

A desk to die for, apparently.

Leo Stefano was seated behind it. Or at least, I think it was Leo. The build was right, and he was still dressed for golf in the U of M togs he'd worn at the hospital. Still, it was difficult to be sure. Most of his face was missing, erased above his jawline, blood and brains sprayed all over the bookcase behind him and the pressed-metal ceiling overhead. Crimson goo was dripping down on the shoulders of his golf shirt, congealing into strawberry puddles on that marvelous desk.

"Sweet Jesus," somebody said. Me, I guess. Marcy was at my shoulder, but she didn't say anything at all. Just nodded slowly, taking in the God-awful tableau. Shocked to silence, I thought.

Then it hit me.

"The girl," I said. "Terri's daughter said she was living here. *Jolene!*"

There was no answer. Edging gingerly around the blood, we searched through the house, calling her name. But we found no one else. Living or dead.

Terri sensed someone near her bedside before she opened her eyes. She expected to see Ray Beaumont, but it wasn't. The African-American lawyer in the three-thousand-dollar suit who'd come with Leo was in the plastic chair by her bed, watching her.

"What—?" She coughed. Her mouth felt like it had been scoured with steel wool. He just watched, without speaking. "What do you want?" she managed.

"It's not what I want," he said, leaning in, "it's what you want, more than money, more than being Mrs. Leo, more than anything in this world."

"What are you talking about?"

"Your daughter, Terri. Right now she's with a friend of mine, partying like it's nineteen ninety-nine. According to her records, she has a nose for coke, and so I'm guessing she's already high as a kite—"

"You son of a *bitch!*"

"Easy, lady, I'm not done," he said, glancing at his watch. "Later today, she'll be found in a crack house during a drug raid, stoned out of her mind, with enough coke and paraphernalia on her to earn a fifteen-year fall. Possession with intent, second offense. With her juvy record, she'll disappear into the system like spit on a griddle.

"Or . . . my associate can put Jolene on a plane to Vegas, first class, with an open charge card to a fifty-K account. You'll get a second fifty when you file for an annulment, and another hundred the day it becomes final. No police involved, no jail time, but no more negotiating either. This is a one-time offer, ma'am. Do the smart thing. Take it."

He placed a cell phone on her pillow as he rose to go. "Text me in an hour, yes or no," he said, looking down on her like a sympathetic uncle. "You can start a new life in Sin City, with serious bucks. Or see your daughter once a month on visiting days for the next decade. Assuming she lives that long. Most Pittsfield inmates are violent offenders."

He patted her hand, then turned and walked out.

Terri stared after him, stunned, then glanced around the sterile white room for help, or comfort, or any trace of mercy.

But there was nothing.

Stifling a groan, she eased out of the bed and padded barefoot to the room's narrow closet, looking for her clothes.

"When you went through the house, did either of you see a gun?" Chief Kazmarek asked.

I glanced at Marcy, who shook her head. I did the same. "We were looking for the girl, Marge. We tried not to disturb anything, but . . ." I shrugged. We were sitting on a bench at the end of the patio, watching cops search through the beach house like ants on a jam jar. Marcy looked a bit green and I certainly felt that way.

"Did your people find a gun?"

"We found a hundred of them," Marge said. "Leo has an arms collection, everything from skeet guns to AK-47s, complete with illegal bump stocks and fifty-round drum magazines. But nothing seems to be missing or out of place. There's no question about the murder weapon, though. A shotgun, almost certainly sawed off. Maybe a *lupara*. Leo has several in his collection."

"So whoever capped Leo probably shot up my car?"

"Too soon to say, Ray," Marge said. "We're still trying to sort out what happened. Did you see this?" She held up a glassine envelope, smeared with blood, that contained a checkbook.

We both shook our heads.

"It was on Leo's desk, in a puddle of gore," Chief Kaz explained. "Thing is, there's blood on the *inside* as well, on a check dated today. The techs think he was writing a check for ten grand when someone shoved a gun in his face and—Bang. Did you see anyone leaving when you arrived? Maybe on the beach?"

"When no one answered the buzzer, we walked around to the beach side, found him, and called you."

"And where was your client during all this?"

"What do you mean, where was she? In the hospital."

"Actually, she's not. At some point after we left, she found her street clothes, took the service stairs down to the parking garage, and walked out. She didn't call you?"

"The only people I talked to were the casino goons I told you about. They claim Leo owes them big, so they should definitely be persons of interest in this. Terri wasn't with them, but they could have grabbed her up since. You need to find them."

"I've got an APB out for Mrs. Stefano *and* the two collectors. A neighbor confirmed that they've been cruising the area, parking on the street to watch Leo's house, and they were definitely at the hospital earlier. We have them on CCTV, cruising the parking lot."

"Any chance *they* shot up my car?"

"Unfortunately, the security cams were blocked by an EMT bus. We can't be sure of what happened. My officers are still interviewing witnesses, but there was a lot of confusion."

"Maybe we can ask them personally," Marcy said, cocking her head, listening. "I think I hear them coming."

Then I heard it too, the deep thump of an amplified rap track that rose from loud to thunderous as the black Escalade pulled up beside the coroner's bus. Raven and Pachonka stepped out, hands raised, to show Chief Kazmarek they weren't armed. Two coroner's aides were rolling Leo's corpse out to their bus. Raven lifted the shroud as he passed. His eyes narrowed, but that was all.

He quickly introduced himself and his partner to the chief, and handed her a legal folder. She scanned it quickly.

"You're investigators," she said, still reading, "from New York?"

"Licensed to operate in the lower forty-eight, and Puerto Rico," Raven said. "You'll also note federal firearms licenses for the weapons in our vehicle, and a permit to monitor police-band radio. We picked up your all-points alert on us and came to check in."

"Hopefully, to say goodbye," Pachonka added. "We collect from deadbeats, not stiffs. The headlines would write themselves."

"You came looking for Leo Stefano, and now he's dead," the chief noted. "You've got some explaining to do."

"A picture's worth a thousand words," Raven said. Reaching into his vehicle, he came out with a laptop. He flipped it open, showing the screen to the chief.

"Reality TV," Raven explained. "We're wired for surveillance twenty-four seven. Dash cameras, body cams, rearview cams, high-def panoramic cams, with directional mikes and night vision."

"I don't follow," Marcy said.

"When we show up to arrange a repayment schedule, the first thing most deadbeats do is dial nine-one-one with a bogus story about how we threatened or assaulted them," Pachonka put in. "Having everything on video solves that problem. In Leo's case, it was a game changer, because we got him hiring us to mug his wife."

"Do you have any idea what happened here?"

"Not exactly," Raven said. "We can only legally film our marks in public places, not in their homes. But we do have something for you."

He tapped a few keys, changing the picture to a scene I instantly recognized. It was a still photo, of Leo's driveway, showing a police car, with Leo Stefano exiting the vehicle. The screen flickered, and the prowl car was replaced with a muddy Chevy pickup, then another flicker and the truck was replaced by my Corvette, with Marcy and me knocking at the front door.

"We placed a motion-activated camera in a tree across the street," Raven explained. "It only takes single shots. I already ran the pickup's plates. It belongs to a Charles Couture, Detroit address." Cooch's license photo flashed on the screen.

"He's the Union goon who was with Leo and his lawyer at the hospital," I said. "Was he in the vehicle?"

"The driver exited on the far side," Raven said. "Didn't get him."

"Or her," Marcy offered. "I saw him leave. He was with a tall blond teenager."

"Terri's daughter," I said. "Did she go willingly?"

"She seemed to be okay," Marcy said. "They were arm in arm."

"We'll find out soon enough," Chief Kaz said grimly, tapping her smartphone to life. "I'll switch our APB from Raven's vehicle to Couture's, and . . ."

Her eyes darkened as she scanned the small screen.

"Charles 'Cooch' Couture has been in the system a dozen times," she said, still reading. "Assault with intent, felony firearms, resisting arrest, arson. A regular Boy Scout."

"What about the girl?" Marcy asked.

"The girl?" I echoed, surprised.

"They looked awfully cozy together."

The chief shrugged but tapped in the query, her eyes widening as it came back. "Jolene Prinz has also been a guest of the state," she said, frowning. "She just finished up a four-year bit at McClure in Nevada."

"For what?" I asked.

"I can't access that. She's a juvenile, her records are sealed."

"A minor would only draw four years for a violent felony," Raven pointed out.

"We've got to find them both, Cooch and the girl," I said.

"We wish you luck," Raven said. "We're due back in New York, if we're free to go. Chief?"

"We're good, Mr. Raven, and thanks for the input."

The two collectors stalked back to their Escalade, fired it up, and rumbled off. I could feel the thump of the bass line long after they vanished.

"Are we done too?" I asked. "I should get Marcy home."

"Of course. But if your client contacts you—?"

"You'll be the first to know," I said. "And you owe me one, by the way. A big one."

"What's up with you?" Marcy asked. We were in the Vette, headed back to her apartment. "You haven't said two words since Raven showed us that video."

She waited for me to explain, but I had trouble finding the words. Because it had nothing to do with words.

"The girl, Jolene? I only talked to her for a few minutes, but as she was leaving, she gave her mom a look. And I got a jolt from it. *Déjà vu*. I knew I'd seen that look somewhere before. And I had. In Afghanistan."

"I don't understand. Somebody in Afghanistan—?"

"Not somebody. Some*thing*. In the Sulaiman Mountains, tribal leaders hunt with falcons, peregrines mostly, magnificent birds. I saw one up close once. This local sheik was showing her off. She was perched on his glove, had talons like switchblades. And when he removed the hawk's hood, her eyes immediately locked on mine. It was like staring into . . . I don't know. Nothing. The abyss. The raptor didn't see me as human, or as anything, really. Her decision-making process was limited to prey or not-prey. Attack or don't. It took her all of a nanosecond to decide I wasn't a viable target, then her gaze flicked around our little circle, looking for something else to kill.

"Terri's daughter had that look. She looked at her mom the same way that falcon looked at me. With one difference. There was no decision to make. Prey? Not prey? The girl made that call a long time ago."

"Is Terri in danger from her?"

"I think anyone who crosses her might be in danger. Why?"

"If Jolene was involved in Leo's death, she's in serious trouble and knows it. And the only friend she's got here is Terri."

"But Terri's on the run, with no car. She doesn't know anyone in this town—"

"Except you," Marcy noted, as my phone hummed. I didn't recognize the number.

"This is Ray."

"It's me," Terri breathed. "I'm in trouble. I need your help."

"Where are you?"

"I'm—not sure. In a park a few blocks from the hospital, some kind of street fair going on? We're at a gazebo—"

"I know the place. You said we."

"Jolene called me and—"

"It's okay, stay put, both of you. I'm on my way."

"No police! Jolene says—"

"I'll come alone. But if Cleveland or Cooch show up? Dial nine-one-one. I'll be there in ten, tops." I rang off and gave Marcy my phone. "Call Chief Kaz, tell her what's happening."

"You promised no police."

"And I lied!" I snapped, dropping the Vette into gear and flooring it, blazing through traffic like a NASCAR driver on

Sunday. I half hoped we'd get pulled over, but you never see a cop when you need one.

"At the park, you stay with the car, wait for the police," I yelled over the wind blast. "Keep an eye out for Cleveland's goon."

"What if he shows? You could end up as dead as Leo."

I started to argue, then didn't. She was absolutely right.

We rolled into the Vale Municipal Park lot ten minutes later, and were lucky to find a parking space. The North Shore Flea Market was humming like a beehive. Seven hundred vendors under candy-striped tents and awnings, pandering to ten thousand tourists, most of them gabbling on phones as they strolled the paths between booths full of crafts and collectibles.

I ignored the crowd, totally focused on the two women in summer dresses seated at a picnic table under the gazebo in the center of the park. I drifted toward them, edging between the shoppers, trying to look calm, cool, and collected. I wasn't. I had my eyes peeled for Cooch, or his boss. Didn't see either one. Maybe Jolene had given them the slip. I sure as hell hoped so.

My phone hummed. Chief Kaz. I ducked into the shadow of an antiques tent to take the call.

"Ray? We found Charlie Couture, dumped in a ditch on the road to the airport. Blown nearly in half, maybe with the same shotgun he used on your car. We didn't find a weapon. The girl may still have it."

"She's just a kid—"

"Not anymore, if she ever was. I called in a favor, got her juvy record unsealed. It's a horror story, Ray. Torturing animals, abusing other children, finally convicted of assault with intent on a high-school counselor. She was last seen with Couture, which makes her a person of interest in this. If you know where she is—"

"I'm looking at her," I said. "And she's looking at me. I'm at the street fair, at the gazebo. I'd better go."

"Ray, wait for us—"

But I couldn't. Jolene had seen me, and had probably already decided whether I was a threat. Or not. Game on. I walked toward them.

She'd been carrying a canvas shoulder bag at the hospital. I didn't see it now. Or a weapon. Maybe she'd ditched it. Maybe not.

At the gazebo, I eased down at the picnic table, facing Terri and her daughter.

My client looked rough. Haggard from her near-drowning, her hair was stiff and lank from the lake. She was a handsome, athletic woman in her prime who looked like a death-camp survivor.

Jolene, on the other hand, looked perky as a tourist, if you ignored the spray of crimson across her bodice. She seemed unaware of the bloodstain, but I doubt that it would have mattered much to her. She scanned my face with the same predatory look I'd noted before. The feather touch of her gaze felt like fire ants crawling on my skin.

"If you're ticked off about your car, that was all Cooch," Jo offered. "It was supposed to send you a message."

"He couldn't text?"

"He had a shotgun. Scared the bejesus out of me when he touched it off."

"I'll bet it did. Where is it now?"

"I have it," she said calmly. "Places I've been, foster homes, juvy jail? You'd best get dangerous straight off, because somebody always comes for fresh meat. Leo was like that. He marries my mom, but as soon as I show up, he came after me. He molested me. I had a right to defend myself."

"You might have trouble selling that version. Leo was at his desk when they found him. Armed with a checkbook."

"But that was *after* he forced himself on me. He tried to buy me off. It was adding—" She frowned, searching for the words. "Insult," she said, with a smile cold as a winter sunrise. "He added insult to injury. First he assaulted me, then—" She stiffened, looking beyond me. I didn't turn. I could guess what she was seeing.

"You promised no police, sport," she said icily.

"C'mon, Jolene, you're a smart girl. You knew they'd find you, it's sooner rather than later, that's all . . ." I broke off, realizing why I hadn't seen the beach bag. It was on her lap. And her right hand had snaked below the table into the bag for the gun.

I broke into an instant cold sweat. Thought about diving across the table but knew I'd never make it. If the gun was in her hand?

She'd blow me in half.

I only had one chance now.

"Listen to me," I said carefully, forcing myself to an ice-cold calm, trying to sound reasonable, matter of fact. "The story you just told me? Any good attorney can sell that. An underage girl kills a child molester with his goon's gun? Hell, they'll give you a medal."

"Listen to him, honey," Terri said.

"Shut up, Ma!" Jolene snapped. "You always say the same stuff! Make nice with social workers, yes sir, no sir the cops! It doesn't matter. I still end up in the hole. Women's prison or a psych ward."

Both hands were below the table now, and I guessed she was holding the weapon or sliding it out of her bag.

"The gun's the wrong move," I said quickly. "With the right judge, a sympathetic jury, you'll get off with minimum time. You've been inside, you know you can survive. But only if you give it up peacefully. They're small-town cops, Jo. They don't want to kill you, and you don't want to be dead."

"Please listen to him, Jo," Terri pleaded. With her tears streaming mascara down her cheeks, she looked like a crying clown. But if her mother's tears had any effect on Jolene, it didn't show.

She was eyeing me instead, mulling her options. One of which was blowing me away for bringing the police.

Beyond her, I could see patrolmen encircling the gazebo, quietly herding the crowd back. Jolene must have seen them too, and knew her world could end in the next few seconds.

Along with mine.

But not today. Giving me a thin smile, she laced her fingers behind her head, and rose slowly from the picnic table, letting the beach bag slide to the ground, her eyes locked on mine the whole time. Then she knelt, and waited to be handcuffed.

But her facial expression, that icy smile? It never wavered. It was like locking eyes with a stone statue.

Jolene didn't say goodbye, to me, or to her mother. Terri watched two policewomen lead her daughter off in cuffs in icy silence. Not for the first time, I guessed.

When I offered her a lift, she accepted without a word. Marcy gave me a dark look, then backed away and caught a ride with Chief Kaz. I had a hunch I'd hear about that later, but maybe not. With Marcy I'm seldom sure about much. Mostly that's good, but this time, probably not. Our relationship, love or something like it, was changing. For better, for worse, we'd see.

In the car, neither Terri nor I spoke. She looked utterly spent, and had a right to be. She'd traveled an immeasurable distance this day, literally to hell and back. And yet here she was. Alive and breathing. I'd hauled her out of the surf and gave her the kiss of life. But I wasn't sure I'd done her any favors.

Time to find out.

She stiffened in her seat when I turned off the main drag, into the Vale Beach entrance, glancing the question at me without asking.

I didn't respond, just followed the driveway into the empty parking lot and pulled up facing the lake and the beach, deserted now as twilight settled silently over the dunes.

I shut down my Corvette. And waited.

"What are you doing?" Terri asked. "Why are we here?"

"Time to settle up," I said flatly. "This is where I first saw you, and saved you, and I apologize for that."

"Why?"

"Because we both know it's not what you wanted. You wanted to be gone. I hope you've changed your mind about that, but if not? At the end of this conversation, if you want to wade out and go under forever? I won't stop you."

"You're angry with me."

"Damn straight. Slapping my face was the only honest thing you've done all day. You've been lying to me, and to Chief Kaz, and worst of all, lying to yourself. All that guff about making your marriage work, to give your daughter a real home? A total crock and you know it. Marrying Leo may have begun as a madcap fling, but bringing Jolene up here wasn't. It was sheer desperation."

"She'd been locked away for four years. She needed a new life."

"And she found one. Yours. She saw Leo's mansion and his money, and wanted it for herself. You hoped staying married to Leo, giving her a fine home, would be enough. But it wasn't, because she didn't want to be part of a family. She just wanted to take what you had, including Leo."

She flinched as though I'd struck her. "She's only seventeen," she stammered, "she doesn't know what she wants."

"Actually, she does, and she knows how to get it. You can't control her anymore, Terri, if you ever could. You may love her with all your heart, but you're too street-smart not to see what she is."

"You promised you could save her!"

"And maybe I can. I can plot a plausible defense, her youth, Leo's abuse of parental authority, hire a team of mental-health professionals to testify for her. And if we catch the right jury, she might get off with minimal time.

"But then what? She's a sociopath, Terri, or worse, and you know it. That's why you kept moving. Not for your career, but because of the jams Jolene got into in school, the people she hurt—"

"You don't understand—"

"You're right, I don't. I've never had a child, so maybe I can't. But this time was different. Something happened that was so bad it sent you out into the surf. What was it?"

"I—found Jolene in the hot tub, no swimsuit, no—anything. Waiting for Leo. We fought. She said I was a flop as a mother, a flop at everything. And she said—"

Terri broke off, swallowing hard, remembering. I waited.

"She said I was old, and in her way, and she wished I would die," Terri said, swallowing. "It all seemed so hopeless that—but it doesn't matter what she said, or how I reacted. I'm all she's got. I have to help her."

"To do what? Kill again? She's a predator, Terri. And down deep, you've always known it."

Her lips narrowed into a tight white ring around her mouth. But she didn't argue the point. Which said it all, I suppose.

"Why did you bring me here?" she asked at last.

"It's where I found you. But I didn't bring you here to bust your chops. As your lawyer, I'm obligated to offer you the very best counsel that I can."

"And what would that be?"

I swiveled in my seat to face her.

"Run," I said.

"What?"

"Run like a scalded dog, Terri. Take Cleveland's offer and leave here. Go back to Vegas and restart your life."

"And—abandon my child?"

I hesitated. Knowing the answer she so desperately wanted would be a lie. But truth has its limits too. "You nearly died today. If you stay, it will happen again, and who will help Jolene then? If you go, you'll be able to help her, from a safe distance. But not—"

"If I'm dead," she finished, nodding slowly, absorbing what I'd said. And what I hadn't.

We sat in silence for a time, then she leaned over and kissed me fiercely on the mouth.

"What was that for?"

"The kiss of life," she said with a wan smile. "I'm giving it back. Whatever happens now, you're off the hook, Ray. You've done your best. From here on, it's my wreck of a life, my choice to make." She turned away to open her door, but I grasped her arm.

"Damn it, I mean it, Terri. I won't save you again."

"I know," she nodded, "it's okay. It's my call. It always was."

She slid out and stalked off across the dunes in the fading twilight, her arms folded tightly across her chest. A quarter-moon was inching slowly above the far horizon, lighting a silvery lane across the gentle swells, a shining path to forever.

It was so achingly beautiful, I thought she might just take it straightaway. But she didn't.

Instead, she climbed a nearby dune and sat down, looking out over the surf, hearing its siren song as she mulled over a truly God-awful set of choices, looking as lost as when I'd first seen her. And I already knew how that played out.

But I meant what I said. I started the car and backed slowly out of the slot, to leave her alone with her thoughts and the night and the moonlit bay. And her decision, whatever it was.

I'd promised not to interfere a second time, and I flat-ass meant that.

When I said it. *Damn it!*

But it wasn't that simple. Maybe I'm just not wired that way. Or maybe it's the nature of the kiss of life.

Or any kiss.

They can only be given. We can't take them back.

So I wheeled the Vette around in a full circle, and pulled back into the same parking slot and shut it down. To wait.

The headlights had played across the dunes as I turned, but if Terri noticed, she gave no sign. She kept on staring out over the water for what seemed like a lifetime. Then, finally, she shivered, and nodded to herself. And slowly rose to her feet.

And I stopped breathing.

Because I had no idea what she would do.

None at all.

The question comes up at every seminar and signing. Where do you get your ideas? We trot out the usual suspects: the nightly news, scholarly research, serendipity, even the occasional dream. But this story is a reminder of how little we truly understand the creative process.

I was at a cocktail party, a celebration of my family attorney's fiftieth year of practicing law. It was a hometown night, a lot of smiling faces I hadn't seen in years, catching up, swapping lies, slapping backs. A fine revel. But as I was shouldering through the crowd in search of a fresh drink, I overheard a snatch of conversation—"I gave her the kiss of life and—"

And what? What the hell is the "kiss of life," if that was actually what he said. I turned back, trying to pick up the rest of the story, but totally struck out. Couldn't find the speaker, or the conversation, and in a roomful of lawyers, my question earned some very odd looks.

But the truly odd thing about it? I knew I'd just been given the title of my next project, though I had no idea what it would be. God, I love this game.

Colin Barrett *is from County Mayo, Ireland. In 2009 he was awarded the Penguin Ireland Prize, and in 2014 his debut collection of stories* Young Skins *was published and awarded The Rooney Prize, The Frank O'Connor International Short Story Prize, and The Guardian First Book Award. In 2018 he was announced as the Rolex Arts Initiative Literary Protege, mentored by Colm Toibin. His stories have appeared in* The Stinging Fly *magazine,* The New Statesman, The New Yorker, Harper's *and were read on Radio 4.* "Calm With Horses" *was adapted for a feature film, released in 2020.*

A SHOOTING IN RATHREEDANE

Colin Barrett

Sergeant Jackie Noonan was squaring away paperwork when the call came in, just her and the gosling, Pronsius Swift, in Ballina Garda Station. The third officer on duty, Sergeant Dennis Crean, had run out to oversee the extraction of a Renault Mégane that some young lad—sober, apparently, just a nervous nonlocal negotiating the cat's cradle of back roads around Currabaggan—had nosed into a ditch a half mile out from the national school. The car was a writeoff but the lad had got away without a scratch, according to Crean, and he was a lucky lad, because Noonan knew the roads out that way and they were wicked: high-ditched, hilly, and altogether too narrow; scantily signposted and laced with half-hidden, acutely right-angled turns that it took only a second's inattention to be ambushed by.

Noonan was at her desk drinking coffee as black as a vinyl record from a battered silver cafetière and transferring a weekend's worth of writeups from her notebook into the central computer system. The weekend had been unremarkable but busy: a dozen or so minor traffic infractions, a fistfight between stocious teen-age cousins outside a main-street chipper late last night, and a callout this morning prompted by what turned out to be a man's duffle coat snagged in the weir gates of the Moy river, which was enthusiastically mistaken for a body by a band of visiting American summer students and their professor taking an early constitutional along the quays.

The notes, executed in Noonan's irredeemable *ciotóg* scrawl, were the usual hassle to decipher, their transcription to the computer an activity of an order of tedium that Noonan nonetheless found strangely assuaging. So absorbed was she in this task that she started in surprise when the phone on the main desk rang out.

"Pronsius," she commanded, without looking away from the screen.

The phone continued ringing.

"Pronsius!"

Noonan glanced up. Pronsius wasn't at his desk. He wasn't in the room.

Noonan made her way over to the main desk. She snatched the handset from its cradle.

"Ballina Garda Station, Sergeant Noonan speaking."

"There's been a shooting," a voice, a man's, declared.

"A shooting?" Noonan repeated just as Pronsius appeared with a mug in his hand. Pronsius Swift was twenty-four, out of Templemore less than three years, and an aura of adolescent gawkiness clung to him yet; he was tall but disposed to stooping, with an emphatic aquiline bump in his conk, jumpy eyes, and a guileless shine coming off his forehead. Even the chevrons of premature gray in his crewcut served only to emphasize his prevailing boyishness. When he heard Noonan say "a shooting," he froze in place and stared at her with his mouth open.

"When you say 'a shooting'—a shooting as in someone's been shot with a gun?" Noonan asked the man.

"What other kind of shooting is there?" the man said.

"Hang on, now," Noonan said. Keeping the cordless handset to her ear, she returned to her own desk, sat back down, and retrieved her pen and notebook.

"How many people have been shot?" she asked.

"Just the one."

"The person shot. A man or a woman?"

"A man."

"Is he dead?"

The man on the other end of the line sighed.

"He is not. He's out there now in the back field. He's in a bit of a bad way."

"How badly injured is he, in your estimation?" Noonan said, raising a finger to catch Pronsius's attention, then pointing at the phone on his desk, meaning *Call the emergency at Castlebar General.*

"He took a serious enough hit. But what it was was a warning shot. I want it on record I was in fear for my life and my son's life. I was not aiming at him at all. He broke onto my property. I was in fear for my life and was only trying to warn him off."

The man was outside, on a mobile, his voice dipping in and out amid the ambient scratch and crumple of the elements.

"I need your name," Noonan said, and when the man did not immediately answer she added, "It's important that you answer my questions now, please."

"Bertie. Bertie Creedon," the man said.

"Where's your property located, Mr. Creedon?"

"Rathreedane. I'm on the far side of Rathreedane."

"You're going to have to narrow that down for me."

"Take the Bonniconlon road as far as Mills Turn. Do you know Mills Turn?"

"I do," Noonan said, dashing down *Mlls Trn* in her notebook. "Where am I heading from there?"

"Take the third road on the left after Mills Turn. Keep along *that* road a mile and a half until you come to a farm with a yellow bungalow and a '92 Fiat motor home up on bricks out the front."

"Yellow bungalow, '92 Fiat motor home, up on bricks," Noonan recited as she wrote. "OK. I have you, your young fella, and the fella's been shot—is there anyone else to account for on the property?"

"That's it."

"And the injury. How many times was the fella shot?"

"Just the once. By accident. Like I said."

"Where on his body did he take the hit, can you tell?"

"In his . . . in his middle. His midriff."

"What kinda gun was he shot with?"

"A shotgun."

"Double barrel?"

"Double barrel."

"And that's your gun, is it?"

The growl of a throat-clear, sounding almost gratified, came down the line.

"It's legally registered and I'm lucky I have it."

"As far as you can determine, is the man bleeding badly? I don't want you to go prodding at him but it's important to stop the bleeding if you can."

"The son's after going inside and emptying the press of every last towel. We've the wounds stanched as best we can."

"That's good, Mr. Creedon. Keep the pressure on the bleeding. We are coming right out. The ambulance is on the way too. What I would ask is that you render your gun safe if you haven't already done so—"

"What happened to this fella is on him," Creedon interjected with renewed conviction. "He was on my property, he was in the act of committing a crime, and I was in fear for my life and my son's life. I want that clear."

"OK. We will be there in fifteen minutes, Mr. Creedon. Just heed what I said about the gun. Let's take the gun out of the equation altogether," Noonan was saying, but the quenched noise of the disconnected line was already in her ear.

Noonan dropped the handset on her desk.

"Did you catch all that?" she asked Swift.

"Ambulance is dispatched," Swift said.

"Let's beat them to the draw," Noonan said.

Noonan and Swift were on the road when they got Crean on the squad-car radio.

"Shots fired, man down, firearm still in play," Crean summarized after Noonan had given him a rundown of the situation.

"That's the size of it," Noonan said.

"I'm wondering if we shouldn't just put a shout in now to the Special Response Unit," Crean suggested.

"Fella's done the shooting rang us of his own volition. I asked him questions, he answered them. He's not lost his reason."

"You can't rely on reason with a firearm in play."

"Just let us put our feet on the ground out there, get the lay of the land. No cause to escalate yet."

"I'm the other side of Ballina and I'll be out to you as soon as I can. But, Noonan, ye get out there and there's a hint of *anything* off, I need ye to withdraw and hold tight."

"I hear you."

"Good luck," Crean said, and signed off.

They were a couple miles out from Mills Turn when they ranged into the wake of a tractor towing a trailer full of sheep. Noonan got right up the trailer's arse, siren *wapwapping*, but the stretch of road they were on was not wide enough for the tractor to let them pass.

"Come on to fuck," Noonan said as the trailer weaved from side to side ahead of them. Sheep were packed thick into it, stamps of red dye smudged on their coats like bloody handprints, their snouts nudging in anxious query between the gaps in the trailer's bars. Once the road opened out, Noonan gunned the engine and streaked by the tractor.

As instructed, they took the third left after Mills Turn and found themselves on a single-lane road through Rathreedane. Rathreedane was nothing but flat acres of farmland, well-spaced houses set off the road at the ends of long lanes, and cows sitting like shelves of rock in the middle of the fields, absorbing the last of the day's declining rays. Where the hedgerows dropped low, those same rays, crazed with motes and still piercingly bright, blazed across Noonan's line of sight. She flipped down the visor. She considered the gosling. Swift was quieter than usual, his gaze trained out the window and one knee frantically joggling.

"That is some incarnation of sun," Noonan said, talking just to talk, to draw Swift out of his introversion. "Haven't seen a sun like that since Guadalajara. You know where Guadalajara is, Pronsius?"

"Is it the far side of Belmullet?"

Noonan smiled.

"Technically it is. Visited there a few years back. Unreal how beautiful it was. The light just lands different."

"The world is different everywhere, I suppose."

"It is. We went there for an anniversary. It was Trevor's idea. Trevor's the traveler," Noonan continued. Trevor was her husband. "Enjoying the place you get to is one thing. But Trevor has this thing for the travel itself: the luggage and the security lines, the time zones, the little trays of food with the foil lids you peel back that they give you on board, and even, these days, having to drag a pair of mewling teenage boys everywhere with us. Trevor gets giddy at all of it, somehow. Me, I could live a long, happy life never going through a metal detector again. You ever been anywhere exotic, Pronsius?"

"I been the far side of Belmullet."

"Good man."

"Ah," Swift said. "I've no interest, really. Wherever I am, that's where I like."

"A man after my own heart."

Presently they found the residence, a low bungalow off a gravel lane, the red galvanized roofs of farm buildings visible at the rear of the property. An enormous, rickety white motor home was stranded in the grass at the front.

"Now we'll see what's what," Noonan said.

She cut the siren and turned through the concrete posts of the gateless gate. The squad car bounced and lurched as it passed over the rattling bars of a cattle grate. Next to the motor home, there were pieces of outdoor furniture and what looked like a little fire pit dug out of the ground, empty wine bottles planted in the moat of ash surrounding the pit. Scattered elsewhere in the grass were bags of feed, a stripped-down, rusted-out engine block, scraps of tarp, scraps of lumber, metal piping, plastic piping, bits and bits and bits.

"Look at all this shit," Noonan said.

"Steady on," Swift said, nodding ahead.

A man had come around the side of the house. He was holding something to his head and his other arm was raised, palm forward.

Noonan killed the engine and got out of the squad car, keeping her body behind the door. Swift followed her lead on the other side.

"This the Creedon residence?" Noonan asked.

"It is, surely," the man said.

He was pressing a stained tea towel of blue-and-white check to his temple. The stains looked like blood.

"I'm Sergeant Noonan, out of Ballina Garda Station. This is Garda Swift. You Bertie Creedon?"

"Christ, no."

"You'd be the son, then?"

"That's more like it."

"What's your name?"

"I've no say in it but every cunt that knows me does call me Bubbles."

Bubbles looked to be in his early thirties. He was stocky, his head shaved close. He was in a faded gray T-shirt with "QUEENS OF THE STONE AGE, ERA VULGARIS" printed on it in a disintegrating white script. There were dark, wet daubs of blood flecking his forearms like tracks left by a bird.

"We hear there's been a spot of bother," Noonan said.

"There has."

"That knock to the head part of the bother?"

"A little bit, all right," Bubbles said, and lifted the towel away from his temple to let them see. There was an open gash above his eyebrow.

Noonan whistled.

"I wager that needs stitching. I understand there's another man in a bad way here, too, is that right?"

"There is, yeah."

"That his blood on you?"

"Some of it, yeah."

"Can you take us to him?"

"I can."

"Get the emergency kit," Noonan said to Swift. Swift popped the boot, took out a bulky, multipocketed bag, and handed it over to Noonan.

"Lead the way," she said, sliding the kit's strap over her shoulder.

Bubbles cleared his throat.

"This situation here. You have to understand, my father was in fear for our lives."

"We'll be sure to take that into account."

Bubbles led Noonan and Swift down a short dirt track into the yard at the back of the property. The yard was covered in matted, trampled-down straw. Noonan watched Bubbles step indifferently into a cowpat the size of a dinner plate, his boot heel leaving an oozing bite mark in the pat's crust. The air was thick with the heavy, grainy-sweet redolence of fodder and shit. Through a window cut out of the galvanized facade of a shed, cows blinked their stark, red-rimmed eyes as if roused from sleep.

"That's where we caught him, brazen as you like," Bubbles said, gesturing at the large, cylindrical oil tank mounted on a bed of brick next to the cowshed.

"He was thieving oil?" Noonan asked.

"Such a stupid thing to be at," Bubbles said. "There's nothing left from the winter gone and it won't be filled again for months. Who's going to have a full tank of oil in the middle of summer?"

They passed a final row of sheds and came out into an open field. Fifty feet ahead of them, a short man was standing over a second man lying on his back on the ground. On the horizon, Noonan could make out the low, blunted serrations of the Ox Mountains.

"Bertie Creedon?" Noonan called out to the standing man.

"Aye," Creedon said, not taking his eyes off the man on the ground, his shotgun tucked at an idle diagonal under his arm.

Noonan kept walking toward Creedon at an even clip, not hurrying, taking care not to break stride. When she was a handful of paces from him, he finally looked at her. Creedon had watery blue eyes, cheeks latticed with broken blood vessels, a head of wind-blown, thinning yellow hair, and a set of small, corroded teeth. He did not react as Noonan gripped the barrel of the shotgun, brought her second hand to the butt, and transferred the weapon into her embrace as firmly and gently as if she were taking possession of a newborn. She checked the safety, broke the gun, slipped the ammunition from the chamber, and pocketed the cartridges.

"All right," Noonan said.

She handed the gun off to Swift, took a second look at Creedon to make sure he wasn't considering anything, then addressed her attention to the man lying in the grass. The man was young, lanky enough by the sprawl of him, his dark hair sticking to his pale forehead in strings, and for a moment Noonan did not recognize him, his features crushed into anonymity with distress. It was only when his eyes, screwed shut, burst fearfully open—they were blue, but a deeper, more charged blue than the farmer's, phosphorescent almost—that his face turned into one Noonan knew.

"God above in Heaven, is that you, Dylan Judge?"

Dylan Judge groaned in assent.

Dylan Judge was from Ballina town. He was what you would call "known to the police." In his early twenties, he had already run up a decent tally of minor convictions: breaking and entering, drunk and disorderly, possession. Judge was one of those prolific, inveterately small-time crooks who possess real criminal instincts but no criminal talent. He was opportunistic, impulsive, and undisciplined, requiring little in the way of convincing—and not even much in the way of incentive—to be roped into an under-handed scheme, so long as the scheme did not involve much effort or forethought. Noonan kneeled down in the grass next to Judge and slid the emergency-kit bag from her shoulder. She tore open a pack of nitrile gloves, worked the gloves over her hands.

"Do you remember me at all, Dylan?"

"Yeah, yeah," he muttered vaguely.

"It's Noonan, Sergeant Jackie Noonan, out of Ballina. And that there is Garda Pronsius Swift."

"Pronsiusssss," Judge repeated with a faint sneer.

"It's a name that draws attention to itself, all right," Noonan said as she began scanning Judge's wounds. There was a mess of hand towels plastered over his groin and tucked in under his backside; the towels, along with his jeans, were plum-dark with blood. From the amount of blood, Noonan could tell he was in a very bad way. She unpacked the gauze, the trauma shears.

"You remember the last time we met?" Noonan asked. "We were chasing a consignment of cigarettes and wound up at your house."

"Ye stormed into the gaff at all hours," Judge said with genuine recollection.

"We thought we had you, Dylan."

"And ye were out of luck."

"That time, we were."

It must have been a little over a year ago. They'd received a tip considered credible that Judge was sitting on a significant quantity of cigarettes smuggled down from the North, so they got a warrant and raided his place, in the Glen Gardens estate. Technically not even his place, because there was only the girlfriend's name on the lease, if Noonan remembered correctly. They raided the house at dawn and made Judge, his girlfriend, and their little daughter stand outside in their pajamas in the chill gray light while the Guards turned the place upside down. Noonan remembered the girlfriend: five foot nothing, stick thin and incensed, unceasingly effing and blinding while a saucer-eyed and gravely silent little girl, no more than three or four years old, sat up in her arms watching the Guards troop in and out of the house. Not a peep out of this fella that Noonan could remember, Judge just skulking meekly behind his raging *beoir*, eyes on the ground. His entire demeanor had read guilty as sin, but the raid somehow turned out to be a waste of time. All they found was a half-dozen cartons of cigarettes under a tarp at the back of the property's suspiciously empty shed, nowhere near enough to hang an intent-to-sell charge on.

"Are you still with that young one, Dylan? That little one with the mouth on her?" Noonan asked. She wanted to keep him awake and talking.

"Amy, yeah? Same bird."

"Such language out of her, this tiny thing stood there in her fluffy slippers, and the little beaut good as gold up in her arms. What age is your girl?"

"That's Amy's kid."

Gingerly, Noonan removed the towels covering Judge's groin. Judge gasped.

"That's OK, that's OK," Noonan said. "It doesn't matter a whit whether she's yours or not, so long as you treat her well."

"I treat her like a queen," he slurred.

"I bet you do. Bear with me now, Dylan," Noonan said. She slipped off Judge's runner, lifted the cuff of his pant leg, and with the trauma shears drew a clean slit from his ankle up to his hip, then peeled back the panel of the jean. She could make out several raw black punctures where the buckshot had gone into his thigh. His skin was stained with drying blood and there was fresh blood oozing steadily from the wounds. Noonan continued cutting, delicately tearing away his T-shirt. His abdomen was completely sodden with blood and there were big ugly perforations in the flesh of his stomach, as if he'd been gored. A malign smell began to gather beneath Noonan's nose. It took her a second to recognize it as the smell of human shit.

"How's it look?" Judge croaked.

"Like you got shot."

"Ah, fuck, am I gonta die?"

"I reckon if you were going to bleed to death, you would have done so by now."

There was little Noonan could do but keep Judge calm and conscious. Steadying her touch as best she could, she began tearing gauze into strips and placing the strips over the worst-looking wounds, watching as each swatch of material was immediately soaked through with a fresh bloom of red. She picked back up one of the towels and pressed it against his abdomen. In close, she heard a faint, insistent noise. There, down in the grass under Judge's head, a racing, paper-thin beat was escaping from an earbud.

"What's the little girl's name?" Noonan asked, but Judge did not answer. His eyelids were heavy and fluttering, like those of a child fighting sleep. His lips were colorless, stuck to his teeth.

"Come on now, Dylan," Noonan asserted, tapping his cheek with her fingers. "Ambulance'll be here any second. Come on. They're going to pump you full of the good stuff. Pharmaceutical-grade narcotics and no fucking about."

Noonan thought she saw a smile, a brief flicker on Judge's lips. A few feet away in the grass were a couple of plastic jerricans, a length of hosepipe sticking out of one of them. There was a small amount of urine-colored oil in that can. The second can was empty. Noonan wondered where it was Judge might have been heading, and then she saw it, at the far edge of the field, the squat, muddy white body of a quad bike parked in the declivity of what must have been a boreen or a back lane.

"See that?" she said to Swift. "The getaway vehicle."

She thought about what Bubbles had said in the yard: that summer was the stupidest possible time to try to rob oil out of an oil tank. Noonan had grown up in the countryside. There had been a tank out the back of the house that was filled every autumn, just before the cold weather set in. Although there was always a sitting-room fire going, use of the radiators was strictly rationed. The goal was to try to make the single tank of oil last the whole winter. And so Jackie Noonan's house had been a cold house. Noonan remembered her mother roaring at her and her siblings to put on a jumper whenever one of them dared voice a complaint about the cold. She remembered the single-glaze window above her headboard in the bedroom she shared with her sisters Maureen and Patricia, the brown-putty smell of the flyspecked sill and the clear ache in the tips of her fingers when she touched her hand to the thin glass on winter mornings.

She was holding Judge's arm, two fingers pressed to his wrist. His arm was an alienly cold weight. He was still breathing but she wanted to feel the tick of his pulse under the skin to assure herself it was there. With her other hand, she was keeping a towel pressed against the worst of the bleeding. Beneath his head, she could still hear the tiny, tinny *ttt ttt ttt* of his headphones. The miasmic smell of human shit seemed to be getting stronger. She felt as if it were working itself into her pores, coating the back of her throat. Noonan believed that Dylan Judge was going to die if the ambulance did not arrive very soon, and probably anyway.

"They're here," Swift announced.

Noonan looked up and saw three figures jogging across the field. Sergeant Dennis Crean led the way, followed by two paramedics toting a scoop stretcher. Just as he was about to reach them, Crean stumbled and his jog turned into a sudden hobble.

"Shite!" he exclaimed.

"You OK?" Noonan asked.

"I'm after going over my ankle."

The paramedics dropped down into the grass next to Noonan and Judge.

"We have it now," one of them said.

Noonan got to her feet and stepped back. She brushed her brow with the back of her gloved hand and felt the cold slickness of blood on her forehead.

"That's Dylan Judge," she said to Crean, who was grimacing and testing the weight on his foot.

"Are you kidding me?" Crean said, squinting coolly at Judge's white, unconscious face.

Crean had played rugby for Connacht when he was younger. The rim of his left ear was baroquely gnarled, his nose coarsely flattened from repeated breaks. These historical injuries, combined with Crean's big belly and bull neck, suggested vigor and capability. Noonan could hear the sound of air being expelled in a slow, pronounced jet through the crushed passage of his nose, a noise she had always found reassuring.

"Judge was in the middle of robbing the oil tank in the yard when these two interrupted him," she said.

Crean lifted his foot, rotated it carefully in the air, and put it down.

"Who shot him?"

"Bertie here, the senior of the two, is claiming he did," Noonan said when neither man spoke.

"I did not mean to," Creedon said.

Crean chuckled coldly at that.

The paramedics were preparing to move Judge. They had strapped him to the stretcher and placed an oxygen mask over his face. Crean touched Noonan on the elbow to indicate that she should stay put. He joined the paramedics, exchanging a couple of hushed sentences with one of them before they lifted the stretcher and began making their way toward the yard.

"Is he still alive?" Noonan asked when Crean came back over to her.

Crean's grunt was equivocal.

"I reckon he was just about to go as you got here," Noonan said.

"That's not your call to make. That boy isn't dead until they say he's dead."

Crean addressed the Creedon men.

"Walk us through what happened here," he said.

"We'd been away at the Mart in Balla," Creedon said. "Only we came back earlier than usual this afternoon, because the young fella was supposed to have football training tonight. We got in and Bubbles went out to the yard to check on the animals."

"That's when I saw him, brazen as you like, straddling that tank like he was up on a horse," Bubbles said. "He'd his back to me. Before I could stop myself, I called out *Hey!* But he didn't pay me a blind bit of heed."

Bubbles pointed a finger at the side of his head.

"The fella had headphones in! Sat up there in broad daylight, listening to music, having the time of his life. So I rang the oul fella on the mobile and told him come out quick, there was an intruder in the yard, and that's when this fella turned around and saw me. He was down in a flash, a length of rebar in his hand from God knows where, and before I knew it he'd hit me a clout on the head."

"I came into the yard and that's what I saw," Creedon said. "This fella stood over my son with a steel bar in his hand and my son's head pumping blood. To see your child like that, the shock of it. He saw me and started running for it."

Noonan looked back toward the yard, then down at the rumpled patch of grass where Judge had been flat out on his back.

"He was running away from you when you shot him?" she asked.

"Do you understand I had the fear of God in me? I didn't know where he was going or what he was going to do. I didn't know how badly my son was hurt. I was afraid he'd be back to finish the job with something worse than the rebar for all I knew. It was a warning shot."

"If he was running in *that* direction, *away* from you, how'd he end up taking the shot to his stomach?"

"The rush of it—it all happened so fast," Creedon stuttered.

"But he was running away from you?"

Creedon shook his head. "I don't know what to tell you, it was all a confusion. I was in awful fear for our lives."

"You're telling me you weren't aiming at him?"

"I swear on my life I was not!"

"You took an awful fucking chunk out of him for a fella you weren't aiming at," Noonan said.

"He came here," Creedon said, pointing angrily at the ground. "He came here!"

The farmer turned toward the worn-down, darkly glinting peaks of the Ox Mountains to compose himself.

Crean unclipped a pair of handcuffs from his belt and sprang them open.

"Garda Swift," he said, "can you please place these on Mr. Creedon."

"I will come willingly," Creedon said.

"This is how we're doing it, Mr. Creedon," Crean said as Swift took the cuffs from him. "There's a forensics team on the way, and once they secure this scene we're going to run you and your son here down to the station and get everything on record. The cuffs are for your own security. Pronsius, you can cuff him from the front."

Swift drew Creedon's arms together in front of his waist and clicked on the cuffs.

"Come here," Crean said to Noonan, walking a dozen paces off into the field, still tentative on his ankle. Noonan followed.

Dennis Crean was forty-nine years old to Noonan's forty-five. He had made sergeant eighteen months ahead of her—later in his career relative to her, but before her chronologically—and so, by the dictates of the informal but binding hierarchy that exists inside any official hierarchy, Crean was considered her superior, despite sharing the same rank. Nobody had ever put it that way to her, nobody had ever had to, least of all Crean, who was impeccable in his behavior toward Noonan. He was always careful to solicit her opinion and often deferred to her judgment. He gave her any amount of latitude and agency in her duties. But still Noonan could never quite forget that that latitude and agency were only ever granted, and only ever his to grant. Noonan knew it, Crean knew it. She had made her peace with this arrangement a long time ago, and she tried not to hold it against Crean. If it weren't him, it'd just be another fella, and probably one less considerate. Crean was fair-minded, decisive, and dependable. He was a good policeman.

"How's the ankle?" Noonan asked him.

"I'll live. Are you OK?"

Noonan took off her cap. Navy, with the gold badge of the Garda crest set into the black band above the cap's peak. Noonan rotated the cap in her hands and placed it back on her head.

"It's been a long weekend," she said.

Crean was gazing off down the field.

"They're very presentable all the same, aren't they?" he said, nodding at the Ox Mountains.

"They are."

"That's the thing about Mayo. I find it's very presentable from a distance. It's only up close it lets you down."

Noonan managed a smile.

"The family will need to be told," Crean said. "Can you handle that?"

Noonan nodded.

Crean studied her for a moment, rooted out a pack of disposable tissues, and offered them to her.

"Your forehead," he said. "You can't be showing up to the family's door with that poor fucker's blood all over your face."

The forensics team arrived, as did Inspectors Burke and McElroy over from Castlebar. Crean and the inspectors escorted the Creedon men to Ballina station. Noonan and Swift detoured back to the station so that Noonan could clean up, change shirts, and double-check the address they had on file. The house in the Glen Gardens estate was under the name Amy Mullally. Noonan rang the listed number but got no answer and decided against leaving a message. She rang home, told Trevor she would be late.

"How are you now?" Noonan asked Swift as they idled in traffic in the town center.

"I'm OK," he said. "I mean, you know."

He did not complete the thought, smiling dumbly and gazing out at the streets of Ballina as if he weren't quite sure they were there. It was darker now, the street lights throwing down their harsh yellow dazzle.

"That the first death you seen on the job?" Noonan asked him.

"It's not been called yet."

"No. But was it?"

"There was that lad topped himself in the shed in Easky last Christmas."

"I mean a death where someone else has done the killing."

"There was a couple of gangland shootings up in Dublin, after I'd just come out of Templemore. Only saw the aftermaths, though. Never saw a fella dying in front of me like that. You?"

Noonan shook her head.

They were waiting on a light at the entrance to the Tesco car park. A pack of teenage boys was crossing the road. There were five of them, moving in addled formation. They were dressed interchangeably in branded hoodies, some in tracksuit bottoms, some in jeans. They were clean-faced and dark-haired. They so resembled one another, at least at a passing glance, that they might all have been brothers. As they moved from streetlight to streetlight, Noonan watched their bobbing, intent, vociferating heads and smiled, because the thing about boys was that they only had the one haircut. That haircut changed every couple years, but whatever it was they all had it. Noonan remembered that for a while—ten, twelve, fifteen years ago?—it had been the peroxide-blond highlights; every strutting little gangster coming up had the peroxide-blond highlights. The style now in vogue was tight at the sides, with just enough hair on top to brush forward or to the side. Her own sons wore that style, and each of these boys did too. For an idle moment, Noonan's attention dwelled on the lad trailing the group, the tallest and palest, not speaking but sunk in his thoughts and seemingly indifferent to the animated cross-talk of the four in front. He looked up and caught Noonan's eye. Without thinking, Noonan raised two fingers from the steering wheel in that immemorial gesture of laconic country salute. The boy's face, benignly blank, compressed into a sudden snarl as he hocked a thick pearl of phlegm into the gutter by the squad car and kept on walking.

"Did you see that?" Noonan said to Swift, watching the boys recede in the rearview mirror.

"See what?" Swift mumbled.

Noonan swerved the squad car onto the curb, unclipped her seat belt, and jumped out onto the pavement. She came right up behind the boy, grabbed a fistful of his collar, and shoved him against the parking-lot wall so forcefully that her own hat went twirling to the ground.

"What was that, now? Have you something you want to say?" Noonan roared into the boy's face.

The boy looked at her, startled, a muscle jumping in his clenched jaw.

"Hey, he didn't do nothing," one of the boy's friends blurted.

"Shut up," Swift said to the friend as he arrived on the scene.

"Well?" Noonan asked the boy.

"Tell me what I did," the boy said.

"You know what you did!"

The boy said nothing. The muscle in his jaw stopped jumping.

"Pick that cap up," Noonan said.

The boy looked at the Garda cap on the ground, looked back at Noonan.

"Pick. It. Up."

Noonan released him from her grip and the boy reached down and picked up the cap. As she snatched it from his hand, he skittered out of her reach and straightened his rumpled top.

"You can't just be grabbing people for no reason," he said, brave and indignant now that Noonan had let him go.

Noonan looked at Swift, at the boy's friends. She stepped up to the boy.

"You know well what you did," she said. "And you know *I* know. Have some fucking respect for yourself."

She put her cap back on, nodded at Swift, and turned on her heel.

"What the hell was that about?" Swift asked when they were back in the car.

"Let's get this done," she said, putting the car into gear.

There was a large oval green at the center of the Glen Gardens estate. Several teenagers were punting a ball around beneath the lunar glow of the park lamps, and a couple more were sprawled in the grass spectating, a little nest of bags and soft-drink bottles next to them.

"See that?" Noonan said. "Any money there's drink in them bottles."

"Want to ruin their night?" Swift asked.

"Tonight, they're off the hook."

Once they'd persuaded Mullally to let them come in, Noonan got a glimpse inside the sitting room as they passed down the hall. It was bathed in the light of a TV, and the little girl, longer-limbed now, was curled in a chair staring at an iPad. Mullally brought them through to the kitchen. She was still perilously skinny, her hair up in a pineapple, the tendons in her neck flexing like high-tension wires when she spoke. Noonan gave a careful, broad outline of the events at the farm: Judge's apparent scheme to rob the oil tank, the residents confronting him. She said that he had been shot and was not any more explicit about his injuries beyond describing them as extremely serious. This time, Mullally did not shout or rant. She absorbed what Noonan told her without interruption. She did not debate or refute the narrative Noonan laid out. All she asked was if Dylan was going to die. Noonan reiterated that he had been taken to Castlebar General, and that that was as much as they could tell her right now.

Noonan and Swift stayed put while Mullally rang her mother, who came over to look after the daughter. Mullally agreed to let Swift accompany her to the hospital.

Back at the station, the inspectors' unmarked Focus was parked out front. Noonan picked up the cafetière from her desk and brought it into the station's poky little kitchen. Crean was in there, mugs laid out on the counter, meditatively watching the kettle rattle to a boil.

"Castlebar's finest in with those two?" Noonan asked.

Crean came out of his thoughts, cracked a faint smile.

"They have me fetching the tea while they work their magic," he said, pouring the water from the kettle into the mugs. "Did you talk to the family?"

"The girlfriend. Swift is gone with her to Castlebar General."

"The two will want your report the second it's done."

"I'm getting on that right now," she said, waving the cafetière at him.

Crean stood back so that Noonan could access the counter. He watched her refill the kettle, rinse out the cafetière, and dump in a couple spoonfuls of instant coffee.

"You know, there's bags of beans you can get for that thing," he said. "Ground, whole, vanilla, real fancy stuff."

"I know. I see them every time I'm in Tesco."

"And you never bother with them?"

Noonan considered the cafetière, its chipped silver handle and scratched glass body. It was Trevor who had bought it for her years ago, under the characteristically generous misapprehension that it might inspire in her an enthusiasm for something more than the cheapest of cheap coffee.

"I just never got around to it. Every time I see the fancy stuff in the supermarket, I think, Ah, next time, and the next time I think the same."

"Word came back from the hospital," Crean said.

"OK," Noonan said.

"Judge was just out of surgery when I spoke to them. Doctors said it'll be touch and go the next couple of days, but it's looking like he might pull through."

"Are you kidding me?"

"I am not."

The kettle came to a boil. Noonan placed her tailbone against the lip of the counter.

"The fucker," she said, relieved and appalled. "Oh, the rotten little fucker."

"I reckon you might just have saved that rotten little fucker's life."

"Stop," Noonan groaned. "When we were over at the girl-friend's house, giving her the lowdown, the whole time in the back of my head I kept thinking how Judge had just about done her the favor of her life, getting the guts shot out of himself."

"My condolences on his survival," Crean said.

"I was sure he was a goner."

"So was I when I saw the state he was in. But as of right now Dylan Judge remains in the land of the living, thanks to you."

"Thanks to me," Noonan said with a shake of her head.

She filled the cafetière with hot water and brought it back to her desk. She knew the report would take her some time. She had decided that what she was going to do was get down the most crucial details quick, by hand, then go back and flesh the events out on the computer. She sat down and opened her notebook, reread the litter of harried notes she'd jotted down over the course of Bertie Creedon's phone call.

SHOOT
1 MAN
BERTY CREEDN
RATHRDN
MLLS TRN
3 LEFT
YELLOW H
92 FIAT
SON
1 SHOT
DUBL BRRL
BLEED

She poured a cup of coffee, turned her notebook to a clean page, and began to write.

Much of the material that became the story "A Shooting in Rathreedane" was originally included in a much longer text I was writing. The particulars of the crime committed were different in that work, but the characters of Jackie Noonan and Pronsius Swift were always there. When that material got cut for structural reasons, I had a suspicion I could make a solid story out of it and I also just did not want to lose the character of Jackie. By American standards, the typical Irish police officer is woefully under-armed and, as I reworked the material, I wanted to see how Noonan and Swift might deal with a violent crime. I was intrigued about how things might play out in a crime story where the more typical type of confrontation was impossible. If only one character has a gun, and nobody else does, a certain porousness and flexibility and unpredictability has to enter the narrative. "A Shooting in Rathreedane" is the resulting story.

Jerome Charyn *began his saga of twelve crime novels featuring Isaac Sidel with* Blue Eyes *(1975) and completed it with* Winter Warning *(2017), where Sidel, once a murderously honest police inspector, becomes president of the United States. A Guggenheim Fellow, Charyn was named Commander of Arts and Letters by the French Minister of Culture in 2002. His novels and graphic novels have been published in over twenty languages, including Russian, Japanese, Korean, Turkish, and Greek.*

WHITE CHOCOLATE
Jerome Charyn

1

I liked the waterfall. I could see it from my office window, its fullness, its graceful flow—a melody that rebounded in my bones. We had very mild winters, and I could hear the lulling whish of water most of the year. It salvaged my soul. Ice came in January and left in January. I was the only lawyer in town, and so I represented every damn person who was up to mischief. But I couldn't bear wife-beaters, and I left them to dangle on their own. It was amazing how busy I got. I trekked to the courthouse twice a day. Our prosecutor was inept and couldn't deal with my strategies or my eloquence. I never lost a case. The mayor had to import prosecutors from other parts of the county. And they still lost. I had what our preacher called the gift of tongues. It was more than that. I cared about my clients; I really cared. And to the mayor's small army of desperado prosecutors it meant just another afternoon in court.

So I was pissed off when Cousin Fred called. The town was rampant with cousins. It was like one big incestuous family tree.

"Mother stole the child," he said.

"Elmer"—that was his name. "What the hell are you talking about?"

"She stole Lucy's child right out of the clinic crib."

"Elmer," I said, "start making sense. Mother wouldn't steal her own child's child."

"Well, she did."

We didn't have a real hospital, just a clinic, and doctors were on loan to us. According to Elmer, Mother fell in love with the baby, like a fellow human might fall in love with a cat, and took the little boy, her own grandson, from the nursery despite the clinic's outcry, and drove him back to the farm in her Cherokee. The sheriff was called in—he was also a cousin of mine. But he wouldn't drive out to the farm, even if he had half a dozen deputies. He might not have returned with a paycheck in his pocket, and he knew it. The town may have elected him, but Mother took care of all the bills. Mother Smyth owned the town. The waterfall sat on her property. I paid my rent to her, and she was my own mama. But tribal relations meant little to Mother. Her Christian name was June. I had seven sisters and brothers, and this little boy, Josephus, was her sixth grandchild. He hadn't been christened yet, hadn't had water sprinkled on his little bald pate. Mother snatched him right out of the crib. She was known for her craziness, but you couldn't call it that. She was master and mistress of a town she herself had dubbed Smyth Falls. We were just an appendage to another town until Mother appeared and seized the landscape for herself.

I went to see Sissy first. None of the tribe was close. That's how Mother raised us. Our father had been a brutal man who couldn't match wits with Mother. He copulated with her, and she had him sit in jail after his drunken fits. She walloped him with a frying pan during his rages. He didn't live past forty. She'd sucked all the vitals out of Papa Jed. He should have run into another county, but none of us did. I managed to get four years out of the Baptist college across the wooden bridge. I had to work like a dog to pay my tuition. And I found an online law school that took me in. I studied with Harvard professors in a festival of classes on video and passed the state bar. The professors were like ghosts visiting us from another planet.

So I went to see Sissy. She kept staring at the empty crib. "I can't believe my eyes, Wash." That's my name. It's short for Washington Smyth. "Do you think she wants ransom money?"

"No," I said. "It's sheer perversity, Sis. She's too old to have another child. She must have looked into little Joe's blue eyes and decided that she had to have him for herself."

"That's mighty selfish. Don't I have any recourse?" Sissy asked. It's not as if she had a husband or a boyfriend to protect her. Sis must have slept with every stray rattlesnake in the county.

"Couldn't I hire you, Wash? Couldn't I take her to court? You are my brother."

"Sister Lucy, we have to make an appeal. No frontal attack would work."

"Well," she asked, "will you appeal to her for me?"

Sis was thirty-five. She's managed the affairs at Mother's hardware store on North Main since she was sixteen. That's the only occupation she's ever had. Her salary and all her other resources came out of Mother's purse. She was beholden to the Smyth clan. All my brothers and sisters and cousins were, except for me. The online law school made all the difference. I could throw dust in Mother's face, defy her, without ever leaving town.

2

I drove to the farm in my Cherokee. Mother had a kingdom of cows. She had eleven barns, a plant with electric milkers, and a creamery that produced the best ice cream on the planet. Mother Smyth's was celebrated in the Southwest for one of its unusual flavors—Clotted White Chocolate. It amused me that white-chocolate ice cream had also been a preferred flavor of the Russian royal family.

Mother hadn't touched a cow's teat in years. Bankers and brokers had come all the way from Dallas to seduce Mother into listing her brand on the stock exchange. That's the only time she ever came to my office. She knocked all my other appointments aside, but there was confusion and terror in her eyes.

"Wash," she said, "they promised to write me a check for ninety million—write it blind."

Oh, we were in my element now, not hers. I wasn't back in the family cradle on the farm.

"Mama, do you need that ninety million?"

"No," she said with a smile, half the terror gone.

"You'll be saddled with a board of directors, and pretty soon you'll have plenty of stock, but Mother Smyth's won't belong to Mother Smyth. You'll need permission to enter your own barns."

I wrote the letter for her, refusing the bankers' proposal. She kissed my hand for the first and last time. And that's when I found a Cherokee under my office window, the exact same model as hers.

"To my son Wash," she wrote, "who saved me from a fate worse than death."

An orphan, she'd come from Illinois to live with an uncle when she was five and helped take a windswept five-cow barn and build it into a dynasty of barns. She hated school because the other children had mocked her homespun dresses. And she stopped going to class before she was eleven. She managed her uncle's farm by the time she was thirteen. And she began to own property in her dead mother's name. That's why the enterprise was called Mother Smyth's. Soon she owned bits and pieces of the town. She shunned the town's schools as the town had shunned her. And she scorned the education of her own children. None of my brothers or sisters ever got past the tenth grade, and none felt deprived. I was different. I came along last, the youngest of the brood, not counting Ethan. And I had to fight Mama tooth and nail to finish high school. I applied to the Baptist college on my own, against Mama's wishes, and earned my keep shoveling cow shit. I studied at night in one of Mama's barns. And now I had to plead for Sister Lucy.

My eldest brother, Lucian, who ran Mother Smyth's, was reluctant to let me near mama.

Lucian was never kind—kindness wasn't a commodity in the Smyth clan. Lucian walloped me more than once while I was growing up. He was more like a surly uncle than a brother. He was sixteen years my senior, and had his own children to worry about. They were all homeschooled. Mama paid for their private classes and music lessons. Lucian could deliver epic monologues about clotted white chocolate, but he'd never heard of a single philosopher; Lucian wouldn't have cared that Wittgenstein washed his dishes in the bathtub and loved to sit in the first row at the movies.

"Wash," my brother said, with his menacing charm, "can't you stay out of this? I haven't seen Mama happier in years." He was six feet tall and always seemed about to lurch. He had a lot of hair on his face and reminded me of the Wolfman; this Wolfman was worth five million.

"But she stole her daughter's child right out of the crib," I said.

"So what," Lucian said, growing less and less tolerant of me and my journey to the farm. "The boy's a little bastard. He's better off with us."

"That's not for you to declare."

"Well, I'm declaring it," Lucian said. He would have broken my bones if I hadn't passed the bar. He was frightened of my law degree. I was Counselor Smyth at the courthouse, the bane of prosecutors. Lucian was wary of titles such as Washington Smyth, Esquire. I'll bet he was still prepared to break my bones.

I couldn't have gotten through that impasse if Mama hadn't heard the arrival of my Cherokee.

"Lucian, is that Wash? Let him in."

So I climbed onto the porch with its familiar splintered railing and entered the big house.

Mama never believed in niceties or the usual signs of wealth. The couch was fifty years old. The lamps had been there since she was a child. She didn't have to suck up to any of the ice-cream wholesalers. Mama had her brand—Mother Smyth's Clotted White Chocolate ice cream sold itself.

Her eyes had gone bad. And she was sitting in a darkened corner with the baby in one of my old cribs that a farmhand must have brought down from the attic.

"Wash," she said in a plaintive voice, "have you come to rob me of my blood and joy?"

She was nearing sixty, and she'd worked every damn day of her life. She wore a denim shirt and overalls like a man. Her face had a rough, masculine edge, but her brown eyes, even in the dark, had an uncertain, wavering softness.

"The sheriff won't come. But you'll sue me. And it's a case I might not win."

"Mama, you took your own daughter's child. You have to give him back."

"Why?" Mama asked. "Sissy can always have another child. I'll give her the hardware store. It's worth a million—retail. She's a whore, Wash. The boy is better off with me. I'll make him a millionaire before he's five."

She grew nervous when I didn't answer. "You were always like that. You never cried as a baby, not once. It's not natural."

"And it's not natural to steal Lucy's child."

She could have had the sheriff arrest me on some ridiculous charge. She had all the power, and I had none, even with my law degree.

"Don't I deserve another baby?" she begged.

"Yes, Mama. If you can't adopt one, I'll find one for you."

She began to sob. I had never seen my mother cry, not at my father's funeral, nor at the funeral of my stillborn brother, Ethan. She loved that boy, born dead. She rocked him in her arms for days, wouldn't let the undertaker near him.

She must have had Little Ethan in her mind when she drove down to the clinic. "I didn't come to the nursery to steal," she said. "And then I looked into the boy's blue eyes. He smiled at me, grabbed my finger. And it was worse than a lightning bolt. I stood there, Wash, shivering for half an hour. Meeting your father, hah! That was nothing, no more than measuring the worth of a prize bull."

Mama came out of the corner. "I wanted to win you over, Wash, have you on my side. I failed. I lost you a long time ago."

No one at the farm said goodbye. I rode away in the Cherokee I got from Mama.

3

I was a strategist, told you so. I ran for mayor, and I won without any help from Mama and her brand of clotted ice cream. My cousins voted for me and not Mama's candidate, the deputy sheriff. It was Mama's first defeat in forty years. But she came to my swearing-in at Town Hall. She had the clan congratulate me, and then Mama got down to business.

"You know I pay your salary, Wash."

"I'll work for free."

"You still won't get back Little Joe. That child adores his new mama."

She'd brought the blue-eyed boy to my installation, carried him near her heart, in a cloth cradle that was really a bandanna slung around her shoulder. Lucian must have constructed it for her. That sling tore at me, because Sister Lucy was standing right there, looking at her own child in Mama's arms. There was nothing but defeat on her face. Her shoulders slumped, and her head whipped back and forth, like a candidate for the asylum.

"Mama," Sis pleaded, "can I hold the baby for half a minute?"

"No," Mama said with irritation in her voice. "I like to hear his heartbeat. It comforts me."

Lucian started to escort Sissy out of Town Hall, but I stopped him in his tracks.

He glowered at me with his own blue eyes. "Don't interfere, little brother. Mama's uncomfortable around Sissy and her whining song."

"Well, big brother," I said. "This isn't the farm. Town Hall is my dominion. Sissy stays."

Mama left with her entire clan. And a fancy trial lawyer from Dallas visited me next afternoon. He didn't feel that he had to be polite to a small-town mayor. "We'll plead negligence," he said, "that she's unfit to be a mother. I'm sure I'll find plenty of witnesses. And if I can't, I'll buy whoever I can. You can't plead for her now that you're mayor. You can't even sit at her table. I'd rather not bring this to trial. Your little sister would lose custody of that child forever. Right now we're in no-man's-land. Mother Smyth hasn't moved to adopt. I wouldn't force the issue, son."

I didn't like his custom-fit suit, his cuff links, his tie clip, his manicured fingernails.

"And I, Counselor, might resign, and whittle you down a peg in open court. Go on back to Dallas, and don't you ever threaten me again."

I was boastful, yes, but we'd never have won in court, not while Sissy gave birth to a fatherless child and Mama had her millions to pound away at Sis and me and buy whatever expert witnesses she wanted. So I had to wait until the dust settled a bit. The sheriff may have been elected, but I had the power to fire him and all his deputies. And I made him aware of that. "Sheriff Tom, if I catch you spying, you're dead." He wasn't sure what to do. I was a Smyth, after all, Mother's youngest living son.

The town prosecutor was feckless, and I couldn't rely on him. I sat in my office and had one consolation. I could still hear the faint whish of the waterfall, even if I couldn't see the water from my window. I hired a new secretary, Cousin Alice, who was more loyal to me than to Mama's clan. I couldn't count on the district judge. Mama had contributed to his election campaign. I had to go deep inside the well at Town Hall and examine every single one of the local ordinances. I was frustrated at first and had to dig deeper and deeper until I uncovered a forgotten ordinance from the county Board of Health. Mother's milking plants were inspected at regular intervals, but not the trucks that delivered her bounty of ice cream.

There'd been an outbreak of salmonella a hundred miles from here. An entire crop of avocados had been contaminated. The pickers of the crop had all used a suspect toilet facility. So I petitioned the Board of Health.

Gentlemen: As mayor I am not at all concerned about the milking plants at Mother Smyth's. But the delivery trucks are another matter. The trucks have not been inspected and may contain a bacterial reservoir. I do not want to have a similar outbreak of Salmonella in Smyth Falls . . .

It was cruel of me, I know, to use the mayor's seal of authority to plot against my own mother. But we were in the middle of a war, and I had to take advantage of whatever was at my disposal. A team of inspectors descended upon the farm, and that team did find a bit of contamination in two of the trucks. Mother Smyth's was shut down for a month while every one of its facilities was tested for salmonella. I don't know how many millions Mama lost. Mother Smyth's Clotted White Chocolate ice cream wasn't in such demand after that inspection. Sales dropped by ten percent. I was blamed, of course. It hurt my pocketbook, too, since I was one of the minority owners.

Cousin Alice quit. Lucian had threatened her, I imagine. And then Lucian's anger clotted his judgment. He entered Town Hall with a loaded twelve-gauge bird gun. Everyone scampered, even the sheriff and his men. Lucian marched right into my office. I sat behind my desk and stared into his blue eyes. He'd expected me to flinch, what with his finger on the trigger of that bird gun.

"Wash," he said, "do you know how much you cost us with that sneak attack of yours?"

I sat there with my tape recorder running. "Brother Lucian, it was no sneak attack. We've had an outbreak of salmonella."

"But not at our farm, damn you. Mama had palpitations. She could die on account of your dirty tricks. I'd walk carefully, Brother Wash. You might never reach home."

The sheriff stood near the door with his deputies.

"Sheriff Tom," I uttered in a soft voice, "arrest that son of a bitch."

"He's your big brother, Mayor Wash," the sheriff said.

"He still threatened me and brought a loaded bird gun into a government building. Cuff him," I said.

Tom and his deputies cuffed Lucian and led him to the little jail one flight below. As mayor, I was also chief magistrate of the town. I didn't even bother to set bail. I let Lucian sit and had the sheriff drop off the bird gun at the farm.

I didn't have to wait very long. Mama appeared with little Joe wrapped in a blanket.

That cloth cradle was gone.

She did look kind of skeletal for a woman with such a hefty build.

"Wash, I never meant to keep him. I had one of my seizures."

"Mama, you never had a seizure in your life."

She frowned at me. There was nothing as baleful as one of Mama's frowns. It could rip right through the corduroys I'd worn since college.

"It was a seizure, I said. You never lost a child, Wash. I stared into the little boy's blue eyes and I saw my own Little Ethan come back to life. Hell, I was borrowing the boy. Sissy can have him back. But I don't want Lucian to sit in the dark."

"Mama, the jail has more light than a firecracker."

And I realized how much I still loved her, despite the fact that she'd killed my dad with her frying pan. We had the same stubborn streak. I released Lucian in her custody. I hadn't even charged him yet. Then it all came to me like one of Mama's lightning bolts. I must have been six or seven, and she wasn't a monarch yet. She had her barns and milkers but not her creamery.

"We're gonna make ice cream, Wash. What flavors do you like best? Butterscotch? Pecan? Cherry vanilla?"

"White chocolate," I said. I liked the majesty of it, the contradiction. I'd first read about the exotic charm of white chocolate in a child's history of the Romanovs. The tsar was trapped with the royal family inside the cellar of a house in Yekaterinburg. They lived in that cellar, suffered in that cellar. But Alexei, the tsarevich—the bleeder, the hemophiliac—had a passion for white chocolate ice cream. And as the Bolsheviks approached, Alexei said, "I would like my last dessert, please."

The servants brought the family bowls of white chocolate ice cream made in their own little creamery.

The Bolsheviks arrived in the middle of that repast. They didn't waver. They shot the tsar, the tsarina, and the tsarevich, and the family's four daughters—Anastasia, Tatiana, Olga, and Maria, who all had diamonds sewn into their bodices. The diamonds deflected the path of the bullets, and the four princesses didn't die during the first volley. So the Bolsheviks stabbed them to death. I couldn't forget that tale. It haunted my childhood with its totemic flavor—white chocolate.

Mama made a mint on one of my memories. She had Lucian, and I returned Little Joe to Sissy.

"It's a miracle, Wash."

"No, it's not," I said.

What pleased me most was that purr of the waterfall, like a soft heartbeat I can still hear from my window.

I suppose that one day I'll marry some lost cousin of mine, right in Smyth Falls, and Mother will come to the wedding in her overalls, with perfume to mask the oppressive odor of cow shit. Lucian and the others will come along. Sis will be welcomed back into the fold with her blue-eyed baby and some new rattler she met at a bar near the edge of town. I'll dance with Mother and she'll say, "I'm proud of you, son. You're settling in."

It's the sound of the waterfall that keeps me sane. Mother and Lucian have their electric milkers and their cascades of ice cream, and I have my bride. But it's funny. Even in my dreams she doesn't have a face. There's nothing, nothing under her bridal veil.

I didn't have a story in mind. Just a whim. A matriarch of a small town is so insanely powerful that she steals her own grandchild—a baby boy—out of a hospital crib and claims him as her own. And then the story began to construct itself. What Mother Smyth did was monstrous, but who would take her on? She owned the police, paid the sheriff his salary. Still, I found a protagonist, one of her sons, Wash, the only lawyer in Mother Smyth's town. But somehow, as a reader of my own tale, I began to root for the matriarch. She had looked into baby Joe's blue eyes and couldn't help her own criminality. Perhaps it was because I was a man without much of a patrimony, who had never had a son to buy or to steal.

Michael Connelly *has published thirty-six novels and one book of journalism. His books featuring characters Harry Bosch, Mickey Haller, and Renée Ballard have hit the top of bestselling charts around the world. His books have been turned into the films* Blood Work *and* The Lincoln Lawyer *and the long-running streaming show* Bosch. *He lives in California and Florida.*

AVALON

Michael Connelly

S earcy always watched the first Express come in. He'd take his morning coffee up in the break room and sit at the table by the window. There was a view straight down the pier and if he leaned toward the glass he could take in the whole horseshoe of the harbor going all the way over to the casino. There was even a set of binoculars on the windowsill if needed.

Searcy's own office was a converted cell on the first floor and was, therefore, windowless.

He was at the table, coffee in the mug he'd brought up from his desk, reading the transcript of his grand jury testimony on the Gallagher case when the 7:10 came in from Long Beach. He set the prep work for the trial aside and trained his observation skills on the passengers disembarking and walking down the pier to the island.

It was usually too early for tourists. Mostly it was workers, craftsmen and domestics coming over to do a job. In early, then back to the mainland on the 4:10 return. Sometimes it brought people in who were hard to read. He called them the strangers. Watching the strangers was an exercise. It kept his skills sharp.

A few of the arriving passengers he recognized. Housekeepers that worked up at the Mount Ada or the Zane Grey or other hotels. There were also men carrying toolboxes or pulling equipment on two-wheeled luggage haulers. One man had a collapsible table saw on a two-wheeler. He was a carpenter Searcy knew was putting in a new floor at a house up on Falls Canyon by the high school.

There were also a few tourists who made the early trip to get a whole day in. They were revealed by their cameras and Jimmy Buffett shirts.

One man caught Searcy's eye because he wasn't dressed like a tourist or a craftsman. He carried no bag of any sort as he made his way down the pier with seeming purpose. He wore dark pants and a blue button-down shirt beneath a green windbreaker he had unzipped after the biting winds from the crossing were no longer an issue. Searcy wondered if he was a gambler who mistakenly thought the casino was a gaming house. There were a few of them every day.

And then Searcy's mild curiosity about the man in the green windbreaker changed in one moment.

There was a tourist walking next to the man. He was made obvious by his shorts, black socks, and the camera hanging from a strap around his neck. The tourist was walking with his eyes up, staring at the cathedral-like mountain that rose behind the town. It was a beautiful sight, especially to the first timers to the island. The tourist wanted a photo and removed the cap from his camera without taking his eyes from the vista he hoped to capture for posterity.

He fumbled the cap and it dropped to the pier's wood planking and started to roll on its side. It was heading to the edge and a twenty-foot drop to the water below. But the man in the windbreaker made a move, leaning down without missing a stride and swiftly grabbing the cap before it could go over the edge. He did it fluidly. Like a shortstop scooping up an infield dribbler and tossing it to first base, the man in the windbreaker flipped the lens cap back to its owner, who caught it easily and then thanked him. But by then the man in the green windbreaker had moved on.

All that was mildly interesting to Searcy—one stranger doing a nice turn for another—until he saw the front right flap of the windbreaker flip open while the man was scooping up the lens cap. That was when Searcy saw the gun tucked into the waistband of the man's pants.

Searcy left the transcript and coffee table and immediately moved from the break room down the stairs and to the dayroom. Mary Emmet, the substation clerk and dispatcher, was at her desk and Randy Ahern, a uniformed deputy, was at the shared desk filling out a report. Matt Rose, the other deputy on duty, was out in the field. Searcy took a two-way out of the charging station and grabbed the key to his golf cart off the hook. That drew Emmet's attention.

"Heading out?"

"Got a nine-twenty-five off the boat. I'm going to check him out."

Searcy clipped the radio to his belt.

"Suspicious person?" Ahern asked. "You need help?"

"I'll let you know," Searcy said.

He went out the front door of the substation and unlocked the bicycle lock on the golf cart assigned to him. He looked around for the man in the green windbreaker and didn't see him at first. He then saw the courtesy cart from the Zane Grey on Crescent heading into the roundabout. Searcy could see the green jacket. He backed out and followed.

The Zane Grey cart took the first right off the roundabout onto Casino Way. Searcy hung back so as to not be noticed following. He knew where they were going anyway. They cruised past the Tuna Club and then the Catalina Yacht Club before taking the left onto Chimes Tower Road. In three minutes the cart pulled into the adobe-style hotel's parking lot. Searcy slowed to a stop and watched from afar as the man in the green windbreaker got out of the cart and went through the doors into the lobby.

Searcy thought about what to do. The man in the windbreaker had not acted suspiciously other than the fact he was carrying a firearm. He could be one of the few people in California with a concealed-carry permit. Maybe he was retired law enforcement. He had that demeanor in his purposeful walk. But he carried no bag. That made him a day-tripper—a day-tripper carrying a gun. Searcy's instincts told him that this was more than a 925.

Emmet's voice came up on the rover asking for a status check. Searcy radioed back that all was good and that he was still engaged. He watched the Zane Grey for another five minutes, in case the stranger came out, and then drove into the front cart lot when he did not.

The lobby and front desk area of the boutique hotel was the former living room of the famed writer who had lived on the island.

The man behind the desk was Jerry Daniels, a born and raised islander Searcy had known since he first came to the substation as its sole detective five years earlier.

"Nick," he said with a smile. "How are you?"

"Doing good," Searcy said.

He moved closer to the front desk. It was chest high and he leaned over the top to speak confidentially.

"You just had a check-in?" he asked. "The man in the green windbreaker?"

"Uh, yeah," Daniels said. "Mr. Christov."

"Christov? What was the first name?"

"Uh, Maxwell."

"Can I see the registration form he filled out?"

Searcy expected no pushback from Daniels when he asked the question. No talk of search warrants or protections of civil liberties. Avalon was a small town on a small island. Only an hour by Express ferry from the mainland but a world away in civilities. The locals went along to get along. That meant they cooperated with the lone investigator assigned to the LA County Sheriff's Department substation.

Daniels handed Searcy a one-page printout of the registration form. Searcy studied it and saw that Christov had paid in cash. There was no credit card information, but he had listed an address on Fairfax Avenue in Los Angeles.

"Did you check his ID?" Searcy asked.

"He showed it to me—it's required," Daniels said. "But I don't remember what—"

"Did you check the address against what he put down here?"

"Yes, I did that."

"Okay, and he's staying two nights? Did his luggage come separately?"

"No, there was no luggage. And the first night was last night. He had to pay for last night to get into a room this early. So he's technically only staying one night."

"Was it a reservation or did he just show up?"

"No reservation but I think he called from the boat—somebody did—and asked if we had anything available."

"He say anything about what he's doing here?"

"Uh, no. I mean, I didn't ask. A lot of people come here, you know, to just lay low. I don't really ask them their business."

Searcy heard his name come up on the radio.

"Just a second," he said to Daniels.

He turned away from the counter and responded on the radio. "Go ahead."

It was Emmet. She told Searcy that Deputy Ahern was requesting an investigator at the Trading Post on Metropole. Searcy said he would be there in fifteen minutes. He clipped the radio back on his belt and returned to the front desk.

"Which room is Christov in?" he asked Daniels.

"He took the Purple Sage suite," Daniels said. "Harbor view. It's all we had available."

"Okay, you've got my cell number, right?"

"In my phone, yeah."

"If he goes out, text or call me, okay?"

"Uh, sure. You going to tell me what's going on?"

"Hopefully nothing."

Searcy turned away. Daniels called after him.

"Hey, I thought the Gallagher trial has started," he said. "Aren't you supposed to be overland for that?"

"Just jury selection this week. I'll go over Sunday, testify Monday, maybe Tuesday."

"Must be exciting. Big case and all."

"Well, big around here, I guess."

"Only murder I remember ever happening. Unless you count Natalie Wood as a murder."

"Not officially. Anyway, I gotta go. Somebody needs me at the Trading Post."

"Okay, I'll call ya—if I see him go out."

"Thanks."

Searcy took the golf cart back down to the basin. Along the way he used the radio to ask Emmet to run a wants and warrants check on the name Maxwell Christov. It came back negative. Searcy knew he would do a deeper dive on the name later, when he got back to the sub. He turned onto Metropole and a half block up was the Trading Post. One of the other sheriffs' carts was parked outside.

The Trading Post was a shop that sold tourist knickknacks and T-shirts in the front and basic convenience store items in the back. Inside, Searcy found Ahern with the store's manager, Todd Helvin. They were waiting silently. Ahern had only been working on the island for eight months and had not established many relationships.

Catalina was always seen in the department as an R and R posting—that was R and R as in redemption and recovery. An assignment to the substation in Avalon usually followed an on-the-job injury or a scandal or an internal political fuckup. Searcy had been assigned to Catalina five years earlier while recovering from injuries incurred while making an arrest in a domestic dispute. While he had gotten into a wrestling match with the husband, the wife came up behind him and stabbed him in the back.

Searcy knew Ahern had come in from the jail division, where scandal was always rife, usually from use-of-force complaints. Over the five years Searcy had been at the substation several jail deputies had been rotated in and out of Avalon for R and R reasons. But Searcy had not yet gotten the story about Ahern because the stories were basically all the same and didn't really concern him.

What did concern him was that Ahern had brought his jail persona with him to the island. In the jail, everybody was accused of something and the high majority were most likely guilty of the offense and rightfully behind bars. Jail deputies had to walk with a don't-fuck-with-me bearing and menace. More than once Searcy had seen him employing that persona with islanders and tourists. It wasn't a good look and it didn't go over well with the locals. Searcy was aware that many of the islanders referred to Deputy Ahern as Deputy A-hole.

"What've we got?" Searcy said as he approached the two men.

"Shoplifting," Ahern said. "He's got it on video."

Searcy paused in midstep for a moment. A shoplifting report hardly needed a detective.

"What was taken?" he asked.

"A can of beer," Ahern said.

"Are you fucking kidding me, Ahern?"

"Hold on, hold on. It's not what was taken, okay? It's who took it. Show him, Mr. Helvin."

Helvin led Searcy behind the checkout counter where there was a screen quadded into feeds from four surveillance cameras. Three of the cameras were located over the front door, checkout counter, and the rear of the store where the cold case lined the back wall. The feeds were live and Ahern could be seen on the third camera checking his phone.

Helvin pointed to the fourth feed where it was obvious the camera was located inside the cold case. It was actually a walk-in refrigerator that allowed Helvin to stock the cold cases from behind.

"He didn't see this camera," Helvin said. "They never do."

"Go ahead and play it," Searcy said.

Helvin rewound the playback almost an hour and started playing it. On the playback, Helvin was busy checking out a customer when a boy of about sixteen entered the store, backpack over his shoulders, and proceeded to the cold cases in the back. He wore a hoodie and baggy cargo pants. He went to one of the cold cases and opened the door. His eyes followed his right hand as he reached up to the top shelf to grab an orange juice container. At the same time his left hand reached to a lower shelf and grabbed a can of beer. As he turned away from the case to his right he slipped the can into an open side pocket of his backpack.

The maneuver was clearly seen on the feed from inside the case. On the camera feed from outside the case, the sleight of hand was unseen. The kid was good. He just hadn't scoped the fourth camera.

"You know who that is, right?" Helvin said.

"Ricky Galt," Searcy said. "The city manager's son."

"That's fucked-up," Ahern said. "Kid needs a beer on his way to school."

"I didn't see it until after he bought the orange juice and left," Helvin said. "After he was gone I started thinking. I'm down a six-pack or two a week on Bud and that kid comes in, gets orange juice five mornings a week. So I look at the cameras and . . . called you guys."

Ahern came over to the other side of the counter and looked at Searcy.

"What are you going to do?" he asked.

"Go up to the school," Searcy said. "Yank him out of class, scare him."

"That's it?"

"What would you want me to do? Haul him down to the sub, have his dad come in?"

"Well, not much lesson in what you're going to do."

Searcy looked at Helvin.

"You want him to come sweep the store out after school every day?" he asked.

"I might lose more beer that way," Helvin said.

Searcy nodded. He had thought so. He looked back at Ahern.

"I'll handle it," he said. "You can get back out there."

"Roger that," Ahern said.

He walked out of the store, leaving Searcy and Helvin.

"A-hole," Helvin said.

Searcy didn't respond.

"I hear that a bunch of people are going across next week to watch the trial," Helvin said.

"I figured they would," Searcy said.

"And you know Ricky Galt was in the same class with Jamie Gallagher, right?"

"I know."

"Maybe that's where all this started. The drinking, I mean. Something like that . . . go easy on him."

Searcy was annoyed by Helvin's last remark. If he wanted to go easy on the young thief he should have handled the incident on his own and not called in the sheriff's department.

But he said nothing about that.

"Is it possible to get a copy of that fourth camera feed?" he asked instead.

Searcy took the cart up Sumner Avenue, then passed by city hall and the office of the city manager, before cutting over to Falls Canyon Road. At the high school he followed procedure and went to the security office where he asked John Bozak, head of security, to take Ricky Galt out of class for an interview.

That process took nearly twenty minutes and then Bozak set them up in a small office alone. No introductions were needed. Searcy had interviewed the kid once before. It was the morning Jamie Gallagher's nude body was found floating in the harbor.

"You missed the fourth camera," Searcy said.

"What?" Galt said.

Searcy opened the video app on his phone and started to play back the surveillance footage Helvin had emailed him. He slid the phone across the desk so Galt could watch it. The edges of his ears got red as he did so.

"That's fucked-up," he said.

"Yeah," Searcy said. "You gotta stop doing that."

"I will."

"The stealing *and* the drinking."

"One time, what's the—"

"Mr. Helvin says he's been coming up light at least a six-pack a week."

"One can a day, what's the big deal."

"Come on, Ricky. You're sixteen years old, drinking on your way to school. You've got a problem and there are ways to deal with it. Do your parents know?"

"No, and they don't have to."

"If you do something about it."

"I said I'll stop."

"You might need help stopping. Most alcoholics do."

"I'm not an alcoholic, okay? I just . . . don't like thinking about what happened to her. With everybody talking about the trial and his lawyer trying to act like he's the victim and she was the bad person . . . like she rowed out to his big fucking yacht uninvited."

"Look, what you are going through is totally understandable. I have some of that too, and I have to go testify against the guy next week. You're just not going about it the right way. Talk to your parents. Tell them you need to see a counselor. It will then be a private thing and you can talk about Jamie and the drinking and everything. It will help. You do that and this little thing goes away."

Searcy held up his phone with the video feed cued up and ready to play again—to the kid's parents if necessary.

"Okay, okay, I'll tell them," Galt said.

"Good," Searcy said. "Shoot me a text and let me know."

Searcy knocked his fist down twice on the wood desktop like a gavel—end of discussion.

Sitting in the cart outside the school, Searcy called the Zane Grey and talked to Daniels.

"How's our guy?"

"What guy?"

"The guy in the green windbreaker—Christov."

"Oh, I don't know. Still in his room, I guess. At least I haven't seen him."

"Okay, let me know when he makes a move."

Searcy drove back down to the basin, passing by city hall again. Only Emmet was in the sub. She told him that Ahern and Rose were out and about on routine patrol. Searcy sequestered himself in his windowless office and opened up the search window on the National Crime Information Center. He put in the name Maxwell Christov and the Fairfax Avenue address he had to go with it. Through the federal database he would get a nationwide search of criminal records and warrants. The search Emmet had conducted for him earlier had only a local reach.

The kickback from the search was immediate. His running the name had drawn an FBI flag and a request to contact an agent named Alex Cohen at the Las Vegas field office. Searcy made the call and was immediately put through to Cohen.

"Deputy Searcy, I was just about to give you a call," Cohen said.

"Why is that?" Searcy said.

"Because like you, I got the alert when you put the name Maxwell Christov into the NCIC database. It says you are LA County Sheriff's Department. Can I ask where you work and where you encountered Christov?"

"I'm a detective assigned to the Avalon substation. I encountered Christov here this morning. Who is he to you?"

"You encountered him how?"

"I observed him acting suspiciously."

Searcy had decided not to give up the gun unless this agent started giving up information.

"Where is Avalon located?" Cohen asked. "Is it South LA?"

"Close," Searcy said. "There is an Avalon Boulevard in South County but the town of Avalon is on Catalina. An island. We're twenty-five miles off the coast. About four thousand people live here full-time and a million tourists come visit each year."

"I've heard of Catalina and I don't need the tourism pitch. Christov is there?"

"Got off a boat this morning."

"And you found that suspicious?"

"That's not what I thought was suspicious. But I'm not going to tell you what that was until you start to fill in some—"

"I'm assigned to an organized crime task force here in Vegas. Does that make it clear enough for you?"

"Okay, this guy is OC. He still might be a tourist over here."

"Did you confront him, speak to him?"

"Agent Cohen, I get that he's OC, but you don't put an NCIC flag on every person with ties to organized crime. What's so special about this guy?"

There was a long pause while Cohen apparently decided whether to engage further.

"What is the name of your supervisor?" Cohen finally asked.

"I'm pretty autonomous out here," Searcy said. "But I report to a lieutenant at the Hall of Justice. His name is Turner, but if you think calling him is going to—"

"Maxwell Christov is an alias used by a contract killer. If it's the same Maxwell Christov, then he is most likely on your little island to kill someone."

That hit Searcy like a jolt, and he was embarrassed that he had danced the local/federal tango with this guy.

"It's him," Searcy said. "He caught my eye because he was carrying a gun when he got off the boat."

"Do you know where he is right now?" Cohen asked urgently.

"He checked into a hotel this morning. The Zane Grey. I have someone there who's supposed to let me know if he leaves. And I think I might know who his target is."

"Who?"

"Me."

"What are you talking about?"

"I arrested a man last year for murder. The trial goes next week and I'm a witness. The main witness."

"What was the case?"

"We have yachts from all over the world come in here all the time. There was a sixteen-year-old girl—a local kid. She went to a party on this guy's sixty-five-foot boat. She got roofied and raped. Her body was found floating in the harbor. It took the homicide unit three hours to get their shit together and get out here on a helicopter. Meantime, I traced her movements to the boat and went out there to secure evidence. I talked to the guy and arrested him when he made incriminating statements. I wasn't expecting it and wasn't recording. At trial it will be my word against his."

"And if you're not there to testify . . ."

"Exactly."

"What's the defendant's name?"

"Rory Stanfield. He's thirty-two years old. He supposedly made his money in software. I don't know of any connection to Las Vegas."

"Doesn't need to be one. Christov—we think his real name is Eric Reece—is an equal opportunity killer. Not associated with any organization though many have hired him. Anybody who can get to him can hire him."

Searcy felt his body heat rising. He glanced through the open door of his office into the front room. Ahern and Rose were still out on patrol. Only Emmet was out there and she would put up no resistance to an intruder with a gun.

"What should I do?" he asked.

"I need to hang up and get the Los Angeles FO moving on this," Cohen said. "I'll head them your way. You sit tight and take all precautions. If you can, see if he is still at the hotel. My guess? He's probably waiting until darkness. If we get out there earlier, we'll take him at the hotel. You live on the island or commute?"

"I live here."

"Wife? Kids?"

"No, alone."

"He probably knows all of that and is waiting for darkness. We have some time."

"All right."

"Let me go and I'll get back to you as soon as I set things in motion. You're armed, right?"

"Yes."

"Good."

Cohen disconnected and Searcy was left in his office by himself, thinking about how a stranger had come into town to kill him.

"Mary?" he called.

"I'm here," Emmet responded from the dayroom. "Call Ahern and Rose in. No delays."

"Something up?"

"Just do it."

He would keep the two deputies close while the FBI mustered. Searcy knew he had to inform Lieutenant Turner of what was going on, but he called the Zane Grey first.

"Daniels, it's Searcy, is Christov still in his room?"

"Far as I know. I haven't seen him."

"I'm going to see if he answers. Put me through."

"You sure?"

"Just do it."

Searcy knew that the call could serve to spook Christov and let him know he had aroused suspicion, but he would bluff his way out of the call.

There was no answer. After twelve rings he hung up, then called the Grey's main number again.

"He didn't answer."

"Well, hmm, you want me to check his cart?"

"What cart?"

"I told you. He rented the Riders of the Purple Sage suite. It comes with use of a private golf cart. I gave him the key when he checked in."

"Damn it, you didn't tell me that. Yes, go check and see. I'll wait."

Searcy could hear Daniels put the phone down on the desk. It was a long forty seconds before he came back.

"It's gone," Daniels said. "He not here."

Searcy knew the Zane Grey was known for its colorful golf carts.

"What's the cart look like?" he quickly asked.

"It's got a yellow body and the roof is blue-and-white stripes like a beach towel," Daniels said.

"Okay, if he comes back call me. But be discreet. This guy's a killer."

"*What?*"

"You heard me."

Searcy disconnected. He leaned back in his chair so he could pull the gun off his belt. He checked the action and returned it to the formfitting holster. He had to think a moment to recall when he had last fired the weapon. It was seven months earlier at the academy for annual qualifying.

He got up and went out into the dayroom. Ahern and Rose were nowhere in sight. He looked at Emmet.

"Did you call those guys in?" he asked.

"I put out the calls," Emmet said. "Rose is coming in from Descanso and Ahern hasn't responded."

"Try him again."

Emmet picked up the radio mike on her desk and put out the call to Ahern. Searcy paced in front of her desk while they waited for Ahern to respond.

He didn't.

"Keep trying," Searcy said. "I'm going up to the break room for coffee."

Searcy bounded up the stairs, but he wasn't going for coffee. He wanted to get to the window that gave him a full view of the harbor and business district.

He was at the spot less than a minute when he spotted the golf cart from the Zane Grey. From the angle of his second-floor position, it was easy to pick up the blue-and-white-striped roof. The cart was parked illegally alongside the seawall on the south side of the pier. He grabbed the pair of binoculars that had sat on the windowsill since his first days at the sub and scanned the crowds of tourists on and around the pier.

People were lining up to board the 2:10 Express going back to Long Beach. There were people fishing, posing for photos. He was looking for the green windbreaker but didn't see it.

He heard steps behind him and turned to see Rose enter the break room. He was in uniform with his short sleeves tailored to the middle of his impressive biceps.

"Searcy, what's going on?" he asked.

"Need you here," Searcy said as he turned back to the window and raised the binoculars to his eyes again. "Where's Ahern?"

"I don't know. Mary can't raise him."

Just then Searcy thought he caught a glimpse of the green windbreaker. A man had just moved across the five-foot boarding bridge onto the Express and then disappeared from view behind the boat's cabin structure. It had happened so quickly Searcy wasn't sure what he saw. Had it been the stranger? Was Christov or whatever his name was leaving without his kill?

This didn't make sense.

They were then joined in the break room by Mary Emmet.

"I can't get Ahern on the radio," she said. "I'm getting worried."

It hit Searcy then. He may have had it wrong. He turned to Rose.

"Rose . . . you transferred in from jail division, right?" he asked.

"Right," Rose said. "Why?"

"Did you know Ahern there?"

"No. We had some overlap but I didn't know him in there."

"But you talked to him when he got here, right? Shared experience, all of that."

"Yeah, we talked. What's going on?"

"What happened? Why'd they send him out here?" Rose glanced at Emmet and then back at Searcy.

"Uh . . ." he began. "He didn't really—"

"Mary," Searcy interrupted. "Go back down and keep trying the radio."

Emmet looked at the two men. It was clear she knew she was being dismissed so they could talk.

"Go," Searcy said.

"Okay," Emmet said. "But I don't think his radio is working."

She left the room and went down the stairs. Searcy looked at Rose.

"It's important," he said. "No bullshit—what did he tell you happened?"

"He just said he fucked up the wrong guy."

"He had to have said more. You didn't ask? Who was the wrong guy?"

"He didn't say, like, a name but he said it was up at Wayside. This kid came in to do a bullet on a probation violation. He had a smart mouth and his old man was getting money in to him so he could buy up protection. He mouthed off to Ahern—kept calling him A-hole—and he got tired of it. One day at yard time he diverted the kid's protection and he went out there naked. A couple of bangers set on him and fucked him up good. Lesson learned except he got brain damage. Permanent brain damage and one of the bangers said it was Ahern who put them up to it."

It was the kind of story Searcy had heard coming out of the jail for years.

"So they didn't fire him," Searcy said. "Instead they sent him out here."

"I guess till things sort of blew over," Rose said.

"Except they didn't," Searcy said.

Searcy left the break room and went down the steps. Emmet was standing behind her desk in the dayroom.

"Nothing," she said. "He's not answering."

"Run the locator on his cart," Searcy said.

Emmet sat down and pulled up an app on her computer. All the sheriff's carts were LoJacked with GPS. After a few moments she got a location.

"Avalon Canyon Road. By Sky Summit. Why would he go up there?"

Searcy and Rose rode up together. Up past the high school, the city hall, and the golf course. At the top there was an open view off the back of the island with the misty Pacific seemingly going on forever. They first saw Ahern's cart parked in the rough off the side of the road. They followed a hiking trail and fifty yards in they found his body. He was face down in the rocks, two entry wounds in the back of his head. It looked like maybe he had been forced to his knees before he took the shots.

Rose got dizzy and had to drop to a knee with one hand on the ground for balance.

"If you're going to puke, move away from the crime scene," Searcy said.

"I'm not going to puke," Rose insisted. "I knew the guy, all right?"

Searcy pulled his phone. He called Cohen at the FBI first.

"I was wrong about the target," he said. "It was somebody else. Divert your helicopter and everything else to the harbor in Long Beach. Your hitter is on the Express that left here a half hour ago. It'll dock over there in twenty."

"Got it," Cohen said. "We'll redirect."

"Let me know if you get him."

"Absolutely."

Searcy disconnected and then called in the murder to his own department. They told him a homicide team would be on the way shortly.

The assignment was simple: A stranger arrives in town and disrupts the fabric of the community. My initial reaction was to think of Jack Reacher and Lee Child. They want a mini-Reacher story. I decided to go the other way and have the protagonist part of the town and have the stranger be, well, a stranger—a villain. So next it was a question of location. I usually write about Los Angeles and that is hardly a town where strangers would get noticed. A thousand or so arrive every day. So I decided on an island; Catalina, just off the coast of LA, and the town would be Avalon, a place where most people arrive by boat. I was all set to go. I just needed a story. Raymond Chandler—at least I think it was him—said that if you are stuck writing a story just have a blond come through the door with a gun. I decided on a stranger getting off the boat with a gun. I was good to go.

Susan Frith *writes from Orlando. Her fiction has appeared in* Briar Cliff Review, Cleaver, Emry's Journal Online, New Madrid, Sycamore Review, Zone 3, *and more. She has recently completed a novel about a lactation consultant swept up in a cult that's also a goat farm.*

BETTER AUSTENS
Susan Frith

We tend to go light. Cozy mysteries. Bodice-rippers. Meet-cutes. A classic now and then, but nothing requiring a hankie. Given how demanding our jobs are, we all want an escape when we read. The whole work-life balance thing.

This Sunday finds our book club gathered in Gretchen's sunken living room, sipping Pinot Gris and discussing *Fifty Shades Darker*. We've spent most of the hour going around about which character annoys us more, Anastasia or her controlling partner, Christian.

"I'd tell my daughter to run—even before I saw the sex dungeon."

"Well, Anastasia's an idiot."

We're Mothers, all of us, and I'm a grandmother too. One of the best things about the job is how I can be home in time to watch my grandkids after school, since very few executions take place between 3:00 and 6:00.

Eventually, we get into shop talk. Specifically, last meals. Alana had one the other day who kept a lump of chicken pot pie between gum and cheek to savor till the end. Another slipped into the afterlife on a cinnamon cloud, muffin crumbs falling from his lovely mouth. That's how Natalie describes it. We squirm in our seats, thinking those weren't crumbs.

It's a fine line we walk—as Mothers, as Executioners.

Changing the subject, Gretchen reminds us it's Dominique's turn to pick the next book.

Dominique's been quiet until now. (A retired English teacher, she seems to think she's above it all.) "To be honest with you, ladies, I'd like to see us elevate these discussions," she says. "Let's do *Mansfield Park*."

It's hard to miss the dig. I feel badly for Gretchen after she put together such a nice spread for us—very clever with the wordplay, Domination Dip and so forth—but I'm also disappointed. "You know, there are better Austens out there."

Dominique plucks a black-licorice whip from its serving bowl and studies me coolly. "My turn, my choice."

There are no scheduled procedures on Monday, which I prefer, coming off a weekend. Instead, Covely-Bell's sponsoring a scholarship breakfast at one of the local high schools. I dress up in my silk-crepe blouse with the red poppies, black slacks, and shiny but sensible pumps. For these occasions they like to have a couple of us Mothers front and center. Gretchen's there too. We joke about how our outfits nearly match. I ask if she's picked up her copy of *Mansfield Park* yet.

"No, I'm not ready to be *elevated* like Dominque."

As we laugh the caterers scurry around us in the cafeteria, stacking napkins in a spiral, filling cups with juice, setting out berries and Danish. So much Danish.

Before executions were privatized, we were looking at seventeen percent unemployment in the region. We're lucky that Covely-Bell—Executions with a Mother's Touch™—chose to open its seventh branch here. They're a full-service operation, with set-up, clean-up, personnel, procurement, billing, transport, and catering all under one roof; it adds up to a lot of jobs. They're big on giving back to the community too.

Today our outreach director announces five more college scholarship recipients. "Each of you embodies our company's values of cleanliness, compassion, and efficiency," he tells them. "Just like our Mothers do."

The students clap politely. Gretchen and I smile and nod. I look past their sweet, blemished faces to the petrified blob of peanut butter that's been stuck on the ceiling in the corner since my son was a student here. The decor's no different, and yet everything's changed.

⊙━━━○

On my lunch break I find *Mansfield Park* at the bookstore. It's got an updated cover, with two women standing back-to-back in Regency gowns and fur hand-warmers. Too bad priggish Edmund Bertram can't hold a candle to Mr. Darcy. I add a new bookmark and a small sack of chocolates to my purchase, because self-care is so important.

Our branches are named after different words for mother: Madre, Mere, Ahm, Majka, Mzazi, Manman, and so on. I work in Covely-Bell's Moeder facility, built four and a half years ago. Not the newest or largest, but it's got a pretty atrium with peace roses planted around a trickling fountain. A soothing Mary Cassatt print takes up the back wall. It's one of those paintings with a naked child peering over the shoulder of her mother, dressed in angelic white.

We're conveniently located next to the penitentiary, where I have an afternoon meeting with a new client named Richard Fitzgerald. I'm sitting behind a desk in the private visiting room when the guard brings him in. Late twenties, large brown eyes, and an unpresumptuous chin. "I'll be your executioner," I tell him. I hand him my business card and one of my truffles, which he tosses to the floor, foil wrapper and all.

Undaunted, I open his information packet and pull out a fluorescent-yellow paper that lists his execution date, two weeks from now, along with last-meal options. We give them plenty of choices these days—Tex-Mex, Italian, Chinese, and now, Caribbean. "You don't have to decide yet," I say. "It's a big decision—kind of like picking which book to pack on vacation."

"Funny, I don't give a damn about this menu or your stupid vacation."

On we go.

While I take his measurements (height 180 cm; skull, front to back, 175 mm; side to side, 146 mm), I tell Richard a few things about myself, about my hobbies and grandkids, and how long I've lived in the area. (Some Mothers skip the chit-chat, but I'd like to think it helps make an awkward situation a little less so.)

His face softens all of a sudden. "Are you Zach's mom?"

I almost drop my tape measure. Not many people ask about Zach these days. "You know him?"

"We were good friends in school," he says. "I went by Ricky Benson then. Took my mom's last name after we moved away end of my senior year."

I pat his skinny arm. "Of course—Ricky! I remember you now, and your sweet mother too." We were neighbors. She knocked on my door one Saturday to say that Ricky's dad had left them, and could her six-year-old hang out with mine while she collected herself? That day, the three of us made a giant batch of oobleck—oozing blue goop from cornstarch, water, and food coloring—because distracting Ricky was more important than the shine on my kitchen floor. Mothers are resourceful.

Ricky tells me his mom died a few years back, after a fight with pancreatic cancer. "What's Zach up to? I always meant to look him up."

"He lives somewhere else now." After a moment I add, "He's in good health."

Ricky doesn't press me. He asks about the book in my bag.

I roll my eyes. "*Mansfield Park* is not one of the better Austens in my opinion, but someone in my book club is dead-set on reading it."

"Read some to me."

I've received requests for prayer, for help contacting loved ones, for sex even (I'm a young-looking sixty-two. And no, that's not in my job description). But none of my clients has asked me to read Austen to them before.

About thirty years ago, Miss Maria Ward of Huntingdon, with only seven thousand pounds, had the good luck to captivate Sir Thomas Bertram, of Mansfield Park . . . and thereby raised to the rank of a baronet's lady, with all the comforts and consequences of a handsome house and large income.

I look up, remembering the fidgety kid he was, sure that Ricky's already bored, but he nods for me to go on. I skip ahead. *Few young ladies of eighteen could be less called upon to speak their opinion than Fanny.* That would be Fanny Price, the underprivileged niece of the Bertrams, brought to Mansfield Park to help look after her fragile aunt. Fanny gets the room without the fire. Fanny has no horse to ride until cousin Edmund insists on one for her. Things aren't always fair for Fanny.

My butt starts to feel numb on the metal folding chair, and I remember the paperwork we still have to complete. I show Ricky our disclaimer that while we make every attempt to create a quick and comfortable execution, there may be rare mechanical or operator errors, unforeseen delays that lead to unwanted pain or panic, etc. . . . etc. . . . He signs it with barely a glance.

"Will you come back and read more?"

This is not the way we typically do things. I'm scheduled three visits with each client: an introductory session, a midpoint check-in after they've moved into their special cell at Covely-Bell, and the execution itself. But he's Zach's friend, so I tell him I'll see what I can do.

Tuesday I've got an execution first thing. I oversee the setup, which is easy-peasy thanks to Covely-Bell's step-by-step instructions. This one was supposed to go a week earlier, but he's so short they had to custom make his restraints. He's been fairly reserved since the day I met him, but as soon as we step within the powder-blue walls of the chamber, he's crying on me. Some of my colleagues have a no-nonsense approach. *You get what you get and don't get upset.* Me, I try to show the kind of love I'd show my own. "Oh, honey," I say. "This is going to hurt me more than it hurts you." Mothers are all so different.

Afterward, I pull out my box of cream-colored stationery and write a letter to the family to reassure them that their loved one was provided a dignified death, courtesy of Covely-Bell. I let them know when his remains will be made available (if desired), reminding them that thanks to Covely-Bell's negotiations with the state, no more than two immediate family members can be executed in a three-year period. (The benefits of public-private partnership.)

A plaque on my desk states that I'm an Exemplary Employee, with seventy-five out of seventy-five executions completed. (The number's higher now.) I've never asked to recuse myself from a case, though we're allowed up to five passes a year, using a simple check-off form. (Excuses include A. Soft Eyes. B. Friend or

Relative. C. Excessive Crying. D. My Birthday Week.) But if I don't do it, someone else has to take the job, and I don't like to make extra work for others.

I'm a professional, but sometimes an image lingers. I'm watching the grandkids bounce on the trampoline this afternoon, and I can still see it. The short man trembling, pleading.

My son's ex arrives fifteen minutes late from work to pick up the grandkids, and I'm short with her (which, unfortunately, is nothing new). The boys ride off, waving. They're starting to ask questions.

Ricky has been moved to the preparation cell inside Moeder, which is a considerable upgrade from his previous accommodations. There's some classy wainscoting on the walls, a few Monet prints to brighten things up, and a higher thread-count for the sheets. I visit him on my own time since it would be frowned on during work hours. He looks surprised to see me pulling up a chair outside his cell.

"I figured I'd be reading the book anyway," I tell him.

Ricky smiles. "You know, I always liked coming to your house."

New acquaintances enter the lives of the Bertrams at Mansfield Park. Henry Crawford is plain but has very good teeth and lots of money. His sister, Mary, is pretty in a way that the snobby Bertram sisters find nonthreatening. She's quite curious about Fanny's social status. To his credit, cousin Edmund stalls to avoid her nosy questions before finally acknowledging that Fanny's never been to a ball.

Oh, then the point is clear. Miss Price is not out.

Ricky leans forward. "Whatever happened to that children's book you were writing?"

"Never published." I wish he hadn't brought this up.

"That's too bad. I remember you reading us one of the chapters. I mean, I'm no expert, but it seemed pretty good to me at the time."

"It's a vicious market," I say, eager to get back to *Mansfield Park*.

You might be wondering what I do at work when I'm not conducting executions. Paperwork, and plenty of it. Meetings, evaluations, product testing. The occasional on-site visit to observe best practices at Covely-Bell's other facilities. But so much waiting and sitting goes into this job, and that's why they've built an indoor track for the Mothers. We circle it again and again, at least an hour a day, practicing our mindfulness. Sometimes we nod to each other in passing. We never speak.

The Bertrams and their new friends decide it would be great fun to put on a play at Mansfield Park while Sir Thomas is away on business. Edmund and Fanny disapprove of the play-acting—killjoys that they are. *To think of the licence which every rehearsal must tend to create.* Indeed. Eventually, even those two get dragged into the production. Fanny, who's in love with Edmund, who's smitten with Mary Crawford, must suffer in silence, watching the couple practice their lines together.

"It's hard to be sympathetic," I say, "when she does so little to help her own situation."

Ricky snorts. "What would you have her do? It's not like she's got any money or power."

"She could start by being less meek." More like Eliza Bennett, I want to add. But that's another Austen, and we must continue reading if we have any hope of finishing.

My grandsons draw a chalk castle in my driveway and soon they're arguing about who's allowed to stand in the biggest room. When yelling leads to shoving, I call them back in the house and make them mop the kitchen floor. *Rules are rules.* It's better for them to learn this while they still have time.

The Moeder branch is surrounded by protestors when I come to work the next Monday. They're all kids cutting school, since no one over eighteen would be caught at an event like this. A Covely-Bell security officer escorts me through the crowd, but that doesn't keep a girl in a gray hoodie from spitting on me. Her sign reads: *Bad Moeders! How can you live with yourselves?* While rinsing the spit out of my hair, I stare into the restroom mirror and remind myself what a good mother is: someone who'd do anything for her son.

I pay the official visit to Ricky so he can select his last meal. He checks the box for Chicken Cacciatore, and I tell him he made a good choice. (I always say this.) "Don't forget to pick a dessert. The chocolate-chip cookies get rave reviews."

"They won't be as good as the ones you used to make."

It occurs to me that Ricky could be playing me. Maybe he's only pretending to have fond memories of coming over to my house, only pretending to be interested in *Mansfield Park*. There was a scandal here last year when a Mother tried to fake three executions scheduled in the same week. Employees from four different departments were involved in the cover-up, and two of the clients actually escaped, but the Mother wasn't so lucky. I will tell you this: Mothers don't like to execute other Mothers. They gave me the rest of the day off.

I keep reading to Ricky.

"Do you remember the accident?" he asks me a couple nights later.

"Scared me half to death."

Ricky fingers his bumpy scar, which is the size of a pen cap and mostly covered by the hair hanging over his forehead. Zach's was even larger. The surgeon who stitched them both up left in bits of windshield glass on purpose.

"She wanted to remind us how dumb we'd been."

"I know."

"I guess I didn't learn my lesson."

"Stop," I say. "We're not supposed to discuss what you've done." It's against company policy. "If you like, I can put in a request for the chaplain to visit."

Ricky says he's not religious.

Covely-Bell employs psychologists to help with the regrets. They show us all we're doing for the greater good. They provide us with medications and meditations and interest groups to help us unwind. I considered gardening, rock-climbing, volleyball, and sushi-making, but I chose the book club, because I've got a soft spot for stories. The club's been okay, but just because you work with a group of people doesn't mean you get along. Though there's one thing we Mothers can agree on. It's better if we don't know why.

The gentlemen joined them; and soon after began the sweet expectation of a carriage, when a general spirit of ease and enjoyment seemed diffused, and they all stood about and talked and laughed, and every moment had its pleasure and its hope. Finally, it's Fanny's turn to shine. Sir Thomas decides to throw a ball for her and her older brother, a midshipman on leave from the Royal Navy. Better yet, Edmund has reserved two dances. Fanny's beloved brother leaves the next morning, and Edmund's on the verge of proposing to another. But one can still experience happiness in the present.

"Where are they holding Zach?" Ricky waits until the end of Wednesday's reading session to ask. "I hear Ahm's pretty nice," he goes on. "Another friend of mine was sent to Mzazi."

"Does it matter?"

"They're using you."

"You're entitled to your opinion."

I've been a model employee. After all I've done for Covely-Bell, it's possible they'll let Zach go. Maminka, Mutter, Induk, Okaasan. Whatever they're called, Mothers live with uncertainty.

My Thursday execution gets postponed at the last moment, hung up on a judge's orders. I cross it off my planner, but I'm sure it will be rescheduled. Covely-Bell has an excellent legal division. For his last meal, this man requested borscht like his grandma made, and the caterers went to considerable lengths to obtain the recipe and ingredients. Next time he won't get fresh. He'll get canned.

The night guard makes kissing noises as I walk past. He thinks I'm sweet on Ricky—why else would I be visiting a man I'm unrelated to on my own time? I've learned not to care what anyone thinks.

Somehow Fanny catches the eye of Henry Crawford. No one can understand why she won't accept his marriage proposal, least of all Sir Thomas. *I hope you're sorry and you will probably have reason to be long sorry for this day's transaction.* As far as he's concerned, she's thrown away her only decent choice.

Fanny's uncle thinks he knows what's best for her, but he's blind to all the other problems in his family, including the fact that his eldest son has drunk away half his fortune—money that should be coming to Edmund.

"How long you gonna keep doing this?" Richard asks. "I mean what if something happens to you? What if you get sick?"

"I take very good care of myself."

He keeps pushing. "You're not a young woman."

"Not old either."

"You don't even know where he is now, do you? Doesn't that tell you something?"

"We can't continue like this." I shut the book and walk away.

The following afternoon, I call up Manman. That's the last place where Zach was held. I ask to speak to my son, and they tell me that this is not possible. Down the hall, Zach's old bed squeaks as my grandsons jump up and down on it.

I ask about the status of his case. I tell the operator about my commendation from Covely-Bell. She says they have many Mothers calling—more than they can process at the moment. But she'll submit my request. I plead with her, asking for a transaction number, a name, anything to document my call.

"Your request has been noted." (They always say this.)

Alone in Zach's bed that night, I read about how Fanny is sent back to her small, grimy childhood home for an extended visit. Sir Thomas hopes she'll gain a new appreciation for the benefits she enjoys at Mansfield Park, that she'll regret her choice to throw away her best chance at a settled, respectable life. Just as predicted, she's miserable.

I run my hand across Zach's sheets. He used to be scared of the dark—constantly stalling at bedtime, asking for *one more story*. One night I suggested that he read to his stuffed-animal friends. I found him asleep soon afterward, surrounded by bear and goose, probably a dozen animals, each with its own book. A fortress of stories to protect him.

I return to Richard on his final night. His tray of Chicken Cacciatore sits outside his cell, half-eaten. "I don't know what you expect from me," I tell him, "but this is all I can offer. It's all we have." I go back over the pages he missed, reading quickly to make up for lost time.

Eventually, Edmund writes to Fanny, begging her to come back to Mansfield Park. He needs her to bring comfort to his mother, who's distressed by family troubles and scandal. (And, just maybe, he needs her too.)

In Fanny's absence Mary Crawford has proved to Edmund just how shallow she is. With her out of the way, Edmund eventually falls in love with Fanny, but the romance takes place off the page. *It must have been a delightful happiness!* Must have been?

Richard's staring at the wall when I finish.

"It's not a proper happy ending at all," I say. "The love story gets hardly any play." Austen spends twice as many words on everyone else's issues—this one's exile, that one's reform. I suppose I should be more understanding because endings are hard. I could never reach a good conclusion to my children's novel. That's why I stopped writing years ago.

"Maybe," says Richard, "it wasn't Austen's point to make us happy."

"But that's my point in reading Austen."

Unsure of how to say goodbye, I slip the book through the bars and leave it with him.

I arrive home to a message from Gretchen, letting me know I was missed at book club. I leave it unopened and look up my old copy of *Pride & Prejudice*. I lie in Zach's bed with it, skimming the pages until I find my way back to Pemberley House.

The next day I rise early to go with Ricky. The guard's keys jingle, breaking the silence as we walk through the halls. He locks us in the chamber, so it's just the two of us and the surveillance camera. "It's time," I say, and try to keep my voice from shaking.

I secure Ricky in his chair. "You were always so polite when you came over." I tighten the straps across his shoulders and waist. "Please and thank you and all that." The arms and legs come next, followed by the head and neck. It's important for the head to be still. "You were a good friend to Zach. A good boy." I brush the stray hairs away from his forehead and kiss his scar. "This is going to hurt me more than it hurts you."

To activate the drone requires a few simple steps. I'm halfway down my checklist when Ricky calls out to me, the distance forcing him to shout.

"You said there are better Austens!"

I walk halfway back to hear him better. *"We should have read Pride & Prejudice."*

"What's so great about it?"

"Mr. Darcy's more interesting than Edmund. And Eliza Bennett's way livelier than Fanny."

His hands and feet wiggle impatiently. "But what happens? If you don't tell me now, I'll never know."

I stare at Richard's feet. "He was such a jerk, Darcy was, insulting Eliza at the ball, acting so grumpy, but she didn't understand who he truly was. And Eliza, she's got this great spirit about her, especially the way she stands up to Lady Catherine—that's Darcy's aunt. She tried to keep them apart." I'm rambling.

"Quote me something from it."

I squeeze my hands together. "I don't know, Ricky."

A sweat has broken out across his forehead. He holds up an index finger. "One line. That's all I'm asking."

It's a simple request, but I'm drawing a blank. "This whole thing is timed," I say. "They need the chamber for the next—."

Ricky shuts his eyes, which lets me walk back to my spot, to the dark line on the floor where I always stand. I could pass this job on to someone else. I could fill out the form and Gretchen would do it. Or Alana. She owes me. I could walk out the door and not look back. But Mothers abide.

Once I hit the button, I remember Darcy's perfect answer to Eliza asking when he first fell in love with her: *I cannot fix on the hour or the spot or the look or the words which laid the foundation. It is too long ago. I was in the middle before I knew that I had begun.*

The drone whirs overhead, and Ricky can't hear what I'm saying. Maybe he's retreated to Mansfield Park. What a shame, I think, that there's so many books and we can't possibly share them all.

*I wrote "Better Austens" inside my stay-at-home "coffee shop" during the first summer of COVID, while our country waited for leaders to concede that a pandemic might be a problem (and also, that Black lives do matter, as do democratic principles). It was then that the idea of an escapist book club for moms who are executioners took hold of me. (I suppose it was the writer's equivalent of a COVID dream.)

While I chose to wrap in mystery what specific circumstances led to the execution economy in my story, I clung to the notion it would be mothers we expected to carry out this unpleasant work, to put a brave face on things, and to assure us that in the end, everything will be OK.

Tom Larsen *was born and raised in New Jersey and was awarded a degree in Civil Engineering from Rutgers University. Tom is the author of six novels in the crime genre, all available on Amazon.*

Larsen's short fiction has been published in Alfred Hitchcock Mystery Magazine, Mystery Tribune, Sherlock Holmes Mystery Magazine, *and* Black Cat Mystery Magazine. *His nonfiction work has appeared in four volumes of the anthology series,* Best New True Crime Stories. *He and his wife Debby recently returned to the Pacific Northwest after living for six years in Cuenca, Ecuador. While in Ecuador, Larsen published several articles on Ecuadorian history and culture in the country's largest circulation English-language periodicals:* Cuenca Highlife, Cuenca Dispatch, *and* Cuenca Expats Magazine.

EL CUERPO
EN EL BARRIL

Tom Larsen

1
Manta, a port town on the Pacific coast of Ecuador
(pop. 250,000)

Sergeant Orlando Ortega studied himself in the mirror and liked what he saw. He wasn't a classically handsome man. The wide face and fleshy nose he had inherited from his indigenous ancestors made sure of that. But if ever there was a man born to wear the uniform of Ecuador's *policía nacional*, it was Orlando Teodoro Ortega Jaramillo. The khaki shirt fit him like a second skin. The olive-green trousers were the perfect length. His wife ironed them before every shift using starch made from a tiny bit of ground yucca root mixed with water. His black shoes, although the soles were worn, were polished to a high gloss.

Ortega swiveled right and then left, examining the red, yellow, and blue Ecuadorian flag on his right sleeve and the *policía nacional* patch on his left for any imperfections. He passed a finger along the epaulet on his shoulder, which displayed his newly granted sergeant's stripes.

With the three stripes had come assignment to the Detective Division where Ortega would be driver, gofer, and general flunky for *Capitán* Juan Delgado, newly transferred from Cuenca, high in the Andes Mountains. Ortega's phone call to a colleague up there had resulted in little information, only that *El Sapo Gordo*—the fat toad—was an arrogant prickly sonofabitch. Ortega was welcome to him, and *buena suerte.*

The sergeant squared his shoulders and checked his watch. A half hour until his first meeting with the new boss. His cell phone buzzed, indicating that a text was coming through.

Body found in Paseo de los Sacerdotes.

Capitán Juan Delgado was not your typical *Ecuatoriano*. In addition to his size—nearly six feet and two hundred twenty-five pounds—the captain had no patience for the little niceties that were staples of Ecuadorian society. *How are you today? How is the family?* Who cares?

Delgado's indifference to society's norms is perhaps what made him a good detective. Many were the suspects who melted beneath the murderous glare of this swaggering behemoth. Many provided a full confession just to get away from the penetrating gaze of those coal-black eyes, deeply inset below a protruding brow. Were they all guilty? "They were guilty of something," Delgado was fond of saying, his jowls quivering with what passed for laughter.

His attitude didn't, however, endear him to those who served under him, alongside him, and least of all those above him in the organization. Which was why he was right now sitting in an uncomfortable chair that made a squeaking sound every time he shifted his bulk. Across the desk from him sat Osvaldo Ruíz, the provincial commander of Zone 4, which included all of Manabí province, of which Manta was the largest city. Even having strategically adjusted his chair to be several inches higher than the guest chair, Ruíz had to look up to make eye contact with the captain.

"I trust that you and your wife have located suitable accommodations," Ruíz said, his thin fingers rolling a silver pen back and forth on the polished teak desk in front of him.

"My wife has decided to stay in Cuenca, for now," Delgado responded. *As you well know*, he might have added, but didn't.

"Hmm, yes." Ruíz said. "It's difficult for a woman to leave her family behind, isn't it?"

"I suppose." Delgado inserted a sausagelike finger behind the collar of his dress-blue uniform. The captain wore the uniform only half a dozen times a year, at official functions or on occasions such as this one, and it chafed every time.

Sensing the captain's discomfort, Ruíz adjusted his own tie, even though it didn't need it, and got to the point.

"You realize of course that I didn't request your transfer to my command?"

Delgado grunted in response.

"No," Ruíz went on. "I am the junior commander in all of the organization. So, when they wanted to find a place to stick you, well . . ."

Once more Delgado grunted, drawing a sharp look from the commander.

"In fact, Captain, I am the youngest man to obtain the position of provincial commander. Ever."

"Yes, sir. I knew that. Congratulations." Delgado was genuinely impressed with the man's accomplishment. He himself had once been a rising star, destined for great things. *If only*—he cut the thought short, shaking his head side to side to clear his mind. What was, was, and he wouldn't change a thing he had done in his thirty-five years with the top law enforcement agency in the country.

"I didn't get to this position," Ruíz said, "by tolerating insubordination." He imagined his face taking on a stern expression, but to the captain he was a joke.

"There will be no insubordination," Delgado promised, trying in vain to adjust his expression to show that he had been surprised by the implication. "And, of course, your solve rate will increase dramatically."

"Yes, there is that," Ruíz said. "Your results in Cuenca have been most impressive."

The commander sat back and said nothing for a few moments, during which time Delgado was silently thankful for the dark blue of his uniform shirt, which concealed the sweat stains beginning to form at his armpits. *Mierda*, he would surely perish if he had to spend much time in this coastal heat and humidity.

"Well, Captain," Ruíz said, standing suddenly and extending his hand. "Welcome. I look forward to watching you in operation."

"Thank you, sir." Delgado struggled to extricate himself from the undersized chair and saw a brief smirk flash across the commander's face.

"Now." Ruíz clapped his hands together once. "Let me show you your office."

The captain brightened as much as was possible for a man of his temperament. He had liked the cool and airy feel of his old office in Cuenca, but the building itself had been built in the nineteen-thirties and was badly in need of an upgrade. The building they were in was no more than five years old, and the commander's fourth-floor office featured floor to ceiling windows that gave a great view of the harbor and the sparkling Pacific Ocean beyond. Delgado was so eager to see his new office that he nearly collided with Ruíz, who stopped suddenly and pointed out the window.

"See down there?" Ruíz said. "Just to the south of the hospital?"

It took Delgado only a second to locate the squat, flat-roofed, two-story white stucco building with the letters UPC painted in blue. The captain had begun his career in a Unidad Policía Comunidad building, so he knew what his immediate future would be like. He would be assigned a battered metal desk in one corner of a large windowless room. A pair of ceiling fans would succeed only in stirring up the variety of smells—all of them unpleasant—coming from two small jail cells in the opposite corner.

When he looked at Ruíz, he saw that the smirk was back, and this time it didn't go away.

Realizing that he had slumped a bit in disappointment, he brought himself to his full height and prepared to leave the office.

"Just a minute, Captain." Ruíz looked up from the text he had been reading. "This may be your lucky day."

"Sir?" Delgado said.

"A body has been discovered near the Maria Auxiliadora Church. Sergeant Ortega will pick you up downstairs in five minutes."

"Yes, sir." Delgado headed for the door, feeling the commander's self-satisfied sneer like the lash of a whip across his back.

2

Had Sergeant Ortega not been belted in, he might have leaped up from the seat when the captain's right hand slammed the roof of the squad car. He fumbled with his phone to keep it from flying out the window, and to conceal from his new boss the fact that he had been deeply engrossed in a game of Candy Crush. He needn't have bothered. Delgado had watched him for a full twenty seconds before he made his presence known. In that short time, the captain felt he knew everything he needed to know about the young sergeant.

Delgado had to execute a complicated maneuver in order to wedge himself into the compact Chevy. Bowing his head as if in prayer, he hunched over and deposited his massive butt onto the seat, and then, leaning so far to the left that his head was almost in the sergeant's lap, he pulled his legs in and finally swiveled around and arranged himself in relative comfort.

"Does this thing have air-conditioning?" he demanded.

"Yes, sir." Ortega responded.

"Turn it on, then." The captain rolled up the window on his side and motioned with his free hand that Ortega should do so as well.

"Yes, sir," the sergeant repeated. In his nervousness, as he rolled up the window with his left hand, his right hand accidently activated the car's radio, filling the small space with Pitbull's "Don't Stop the Party" at full volume.

Delgado formed his right hand into a fist and bashed the radio button, cutting off the singer in midlyric. Flipping on the AC switch only brought a rush of warm stale air. The captain glared at Ortega as if it were somehow his fault. Finally, the sergeant found the right control and the small cab quickly began to cool.

Mierda, thought Ortega, *It's barely ten in the morning. What is this fat toad going to do when it gets really hot?*

The sergeant put the car into gear and flipped on the light bar.

"Turn that goddamn thing off," Delgado roared. "We're not in a parade."

Ortega turned off the lights. He drove three blocks and then activated the turn signal, indicating a right turn.

"No! Turn left!"

"But the crime scene is in that direction," Ortega said, realizing as he said it that he had already committed an unpardonable sin—contradicting the big man.

"But my apartment is this way. I need to change clothes." Delgado had already stripped off his tie and unbuttoned the top buttons of his uniform shirt.

"Yes, sir." In his five years with the National Police, Ortega had never uttered those two words so often in such a short amount of time. He yanked the wheel to the left and tromped on the gas pedal. After a brief hesitation, the Chevy's little engine responded and they careened onto the side street, narrowly missing a vendor hawking fresh mangoes and pineapple from a wheeled pushcart. Delgado shook his head side to side. Ortega wasn't sure if it was a comment on his driving, the car's performance, or the captain's disgust with his new situation.

They pulled up in front of Delgado's building, a nondescript, four-story yellow concrete structure. Twenty minutes later, during which time Ortega, at the captain's instructions, had procured a Styrofoam cup of weak Nescafé with milk and two cheese sandwiches from a local *panaderia*, Delgado returned to the car, dressed in a wrinkled green woolen suit with a yellow tie, loosely knotted.

The fat pig will roast himself in that material! Ortega already knew better than to express himself, even in an edited version of his thoughts. They drove along in silence, except for the chewing and slurping sounds from the captain.

3

"*¡Madre de diós!*" the captain exclaimed as they turned into the narrow alley. "Who taught these clowns to secure a crime scene?"

Three patrol cars were parked diagonally against the rear of a concrete block building from which came the smell of roasting chickens. A half dozen cops leaned against their cars, checking their phones. A small crowd of onlookers pressed against the yellow crime scene tape that extended from the rear door of the chicken joint to a small green dumpster, which was full to bursting with a week's garbage. Less than a foot behind the tape sat a blue plastic barrel, from which the lower part of a man's legs extended. Delgado assumed they belonged to a man due to their size and musculature. One foot was shod in a cheap red tennis shoe, while the other was completely bare, exposing the pink sole of the man's foot.

A small boy had ducked under the tape and was posing in front of the barrel while his mother took a photo with her phone. Given what a struggle it had been for Delgado to get into the small car, it was amazing how quickly he exploded from it.

"Get away from there!" His voice echoed off the concrete walls on both sides of the alley. The onlookers, as well as the patrolmen and women, stared at him for a few seconds, as if they had never encountered such a strange beast as this. The blaring horn of a city garbage truck as it attempted to enter the crowded alley and retrieve the overflowing dumpster was simply too much for Delgado to bear. He tore off his suit jacket and tossed it onto the seat of the squad car, revealing that the back of his white shirt was already soaked through with sweat. He loosened his tie even further and charged the approaching truck like an enraged bull.

"Back up!" he bellowed. The driver, rattled by the approach of this screaming *gigante*, ground the gears until he found reverse.

The truck lurched backward into Calle 103, the beep of its back-up alarm quickly drowned out by car and truck horns, angry shouts, and some inventive curses from the startled drivers.

"Ortega!" the captain shouted. He threw his hands in the air in exasperation and then waved an arm, taking in the entire length and breadth of the squalid alley. "Fix this!"

4

Exhausted from his fit of activity and rage, Captain Delgado sat on an overturned plastic bucket and watched as Sergeant Ortega took control of the situation. The sergeant chased the onlookers away and ordered all the police cars, including his own, moved out to the main street. He then strung crime scene tape from building to building at both ends of the alleyway and stationed two cops at each end. He and the remaining two cops took up positions about two meters in front of the blue barrel and stood with their legs slightly apart and their hands folded in front of them, waiting expectantly.

Not a bad job, Ortega, Delgado thought as he hoisted himself to his feet. It occurred to him that the sergeant resembled his eldest son, physically and in the way he carried himself. He brushed that thought away quickly. Juan Carlos had moved to Quito to attend university and never returned, for which the boy's mother would always blame her husband.

Delgado crossed the alley about halfway and then stood motionless, except for his head, which swiveled slowly side to side as he focused in on various quadrants of the crime scene. After a while he nodded as if satisfied, and strode over to the blue container, which held . . . well nobody knew for sure, did they? That was why they needed him.

The exposed pair of legs belonged to a skinny black man who had been essentially folded in half and stuffed into the barrel. That much was obvious. There was no way he could have ended up in this position accidentally. *So, was it murder, or was this just the way they disposed of their dead here?*

The man's eyes and mouth were open wide, his face frozen in a horrific expression of . . . of what, exactly? Anger? Fear? No. Surprise. The poor soul had been truly astonished to find himself being murdered. *Yes,* the captain decided, with that energized feeling he always got, *it was murder.*

"I wonder why they took his other shoe?" Ortega mused aloud.

"Well, Sergeant, I think you may have solved the case."

"What?"

"Oh, yes," Delgado said. "Alert all patrol cars to be on the lookout for a one-legged man, wearing a red tennis shoe, size . . . about forty-three, I would think."

"You're making a joke," Ortega said, his eyes narrowed, and his jaw clenched like a petulant child. Sarcasm was another of the captain's traits that his countrymen found less than endearing.

Delgado regarded the man for a minute, his own expression softening.

"Yes, Sergeant," he said, the gentleness of his voice surprising both him and Ortega. "I was making a joke."

"Gloves!" Delgado demanded, and the sergeant hurried off to get his kit from the trunk of the squad car. The captain began his examination. The body was shirtless and wore only a pair of loose-fitting white cotton trousers that appeared to be stained with, among other substances, splotches of blood. Delgado doubted that it was the victim's blood. The splotches had soaked into the fabric and had dried long ago. He supposed it could be fish blood: Manta was a fishing port, after all. Maybe the blood was from a cow or a pig. Maybe the victim worked in a butcher shop or a slaughterhouse.

"Looks like our man is a fisherman." Sergeant Ortega appeared suddenly at the captain's side, handing him a pair of blue propylene gloves.

"What makes you think he's a fisherman?" Delgado asked. "Enlighten me."

Ortega hesitated for a moment, sensing another joke was being made at his expense, but his desire to impress his new boss was too strong. "See those thin scars across the first finger on his right hand? That's where the fishing line cut into his skin as he pulled in baitfish. They drop a small net off the dock, see, and after an hour or so, they pull it in full of sardines and other small fish. Sometimes, if they're lucky, the net can be very full. And of course, very heavy."

"Who says an old dog can't learn new tricks," the captain mused.

"Not me, sir."

The captain almost smiled.

"Well," Delgado said, "there are no visible clues to the cause of death." He rolled up his sleeves, reached into the barrel, and grasped the front of the dead man's trousers. "Let's see if we can find out more about this man." Grunting as he made a swift upward jerk, he quickly searched the man's pockets and retrieved two items that seemed promising.

From the victim's front right pocket came a cheap cell phone and an even cheaper cloth wallet.

"Looks like he was a cautious man," Ortega said.

"What makes you say that?" After a quick scan of the victim's rear pockets, Delgado released his grip and the man slid back into the position in which he'd been found.

"He carried his wallet and cell phone in his front pocket, making it harder to be pickpocketed. Lots of thieves in this town, you know."

"Interesting," Delgado said. "The man took great care to guard a cheap phone and a two-dollar wallet but let *somebody* get close enough to him to stuff him upside down in a barrel.

"Did you call DINASED yet?" he said. DINASED is the forensics examination arm of the National Police, well known for their cavalier attitude and general incompetence.

"No, sir. We weren't sure it was a crime scene."

Delgado's muffled grunt could have meant either *Good job* or *How could you be so stupid?* But he didn't seem angry, so Ortega, still smarting from the captain's mockery, took that as a good sign.

"Go ahead, then. Call them. See if they can get off their delicate behinds and come down here. We'll have to get the final word from them, but the rigor has completed its rigid stage and is just beginning the flaccid stage, so I think the man's been dead for ten, twelve hours. That puts his death last night, probably sometime after midnight. Of course, he could have been killed elsewhere and dumped here anytime after. Nobody around here reported anything odd last night. From say, midnight on?"

"No, sir. I checked."

Delgado mumbled something that, to the sergeant's ears at least, seemed as if it might be a compliment.

"I just noticed, sir," Ortega said. "There's a security camera over there. Right above the back door of the restaurant."

"Hmm. You're right, Sergeant." Delgado had, of course, clocked the camera as soon as he had entered the alleyway, but he knew that the odds that it had recorded anything were extremely low. Most businesses, small ones like this chicken joint at least, would mount a cheap camera connected to absolutely nothing as a deterrent. Still, in a murder case, you had to follow any lead, no matter how unpromising.

"Have one of the patrol officers check it out," he said. "What time was the body found?"

"A *mototaxi* driver flagged down a patrol car at about eight-fifteen this morning."

"Where's he now? The driver."

"He took off, sir. He had to take his passenger to the airport, he said."

"Is that right?"

"That's what he said. But I think—"

"You think, what? You think he just didn't want to talk to the police?"

"Yes, sir. That's probably it. People in this town don't always trust the cops."

"I'm not sure I blame them." Delgado turned his attention to the items he had extracted from the victim's pockets.

5

The wallet was the kind of cheap woven item that you could buy for a couple dollars on any street or along any highway in Ecuador. This one, though, had presumably been made in Colombia. Delgado might have mistaken it for Ecuadorian because the Colombian tricolor flag exhibited the same colors—yellow, blue, and red. Even the proportions were correct—the top yellow band twice as wide as the blue below it and the red below that. The seals of the two countries, of course, were different, but nobody was going to waste time weaving a complicated thing like that into a cheap

.tourist item like the one he held in his hand. It was the white lettering that told him where the wallet hailed from: COLOMBIA.

"*¿Él es un Colombiano?*" Sergeant Ortega examined the man more closely, as if he might have missed some key identifying mark.

"*Venezolano,*" Delgado countered, holding up the national identity card that he had found in the wallet. The man's name was Aquiles Eduardo Jaramillo Ochoa. He had been born the eighteenth of August 1984, making him thirty-five years old, and he was single. The card held no more relevant information, and the captain tucked it back into the wallet. A small piece of paper bearing the seal of Ecuador's Ministry of Migration showed the man's entry into the country about a month and a half earlier.

The wallet also contained an American five dollar bill along with a few Peruvian *soles*, and nothing more. Ecuador had adopted the US dollar as its currency when the *sucre* crashed in the early days of the twenty-first century, so that was not odd, and if the man was a fisherman, it seemed likely that he might have visited Ecuador's southern neighbor at some point. Delgado pocketed the five and left the Peruvian money in the wallet.

He powered up the phone, and a message on the screen announced, "*Nuevo mensaje de voz.*"

"Check his voicemail." Delgado handed the phone to Ortega.

Ortega entered #99, activated the phone's speaker, and they heard a man's voice, faint and distorted, say: "*This is what happens to scum that comes here from outside to take our jobs and our women.*"

"He's not from around here," Ortega said, almost to himself.

"Of course not, he's from Venezuela."

"No. I meant the dude on the phone message. He's not a *Costeño.*" Ortega paused, but the captain said nothing, merely looked at him expectantly.

"The way he draws out the words, pronounces all the syllables. And he doesn't drop the last vowel. He's definitely not from the coast. I'm not sure that means anything," he said finally, his face downturned from the captain's relentless glare.

"Could mean something, I suppose," Delgado said. "Now, get a tarp and get two men to lift this body out of there."

"Before DINASED arrives?"

"Yes, Sergeant. Before DINASED arrives."

"Yes, sir." Ortega turned to go carry out his orders, but Delgado stopped him.

"That one there." He pointed to a patrolman whose tight-fitting uniform showed that he possessed good upper body strength. "And her." He indicated a young patrolwoman whose uniform showed off impressive attributes of her own. It would be entertaining to watch the two of them struggle with the dead weight of the fisherman, and Delgado was a man who took his entertainment wherever he found it.

But his enjoyment of the performance was dampened somewhat by the troubled look that he saw on Ortega's face.

"Something bothering you, Sergeant?"

"Well," Ortega said, embarrassed. "I understand, you know, that Venezuelans are coming here and taking our jobs, working for practically nothing, but . . ."

"But, what?" Delgado seemed truly curious.

"But I don't understand how you could hate them so much that you would . . ." He trailed off and waved a hand toward where the two cops were still struggling to remove the body from the barrel.

"No." Delgado shook his head. "This isn't a hate crime."

"It's not?" The sergeant's mouth dropped open.

"No." Delgado turned and began to walk toward the main street.

"Where are you going?"

"To dinner." Delgado patted his stomach and raised a hand to signal a passing *mototaxi*.

"What am I supposed to do?"

"You're a detective, Sergeant," Delgado said over his shoulder. "Detect!"

6

Captain Delgado sat on the small balcony of his fourth-floor furnished apartment, sipping from a tumbler of scotch and watching with only mild interest as the sun dropped into the ocean, briefly lighting the sky with a combination of gray, pink, and orange hues. The ever-present traffic noise seemed to diminish for a moment, as if in respect for nature's light show, but quickly resumed. Streetlights flickered and then shone steadily. Lights from fishing boats, container ships, and oil tankers pierced the sudden darkness.

Delgado wore only a pair of green striped boxer shorts and a ribbed cotton undershirt with narrow straps. His white dress shirt hung over the railing to dry after a quick washing in the bathroom sink. For Delgado, eating was a contact sport, and his evening's dinner at a seafood place on the *malecón* had left his shirt stained with garlic sauce and red wine.

It had never occurred to him before, but now he wondered how his wife always got those stains out with such ease. Maybe he should call Teresa and ask. He decided against it. A sea change had occurred in their relationship, and he didn't yet fully understand it. He had been . . . was *hurt* the right word? Certainly, he had been astonished at the calm matter-of-fact way in which she had told him that she would not be going with him to Manta.

"You have a choice, Juanito. You have enough years in service to take your pension."

"And do what? Drive a taxi? Become a security guard at the bank?" Even as he responded he had been aware of the first inklings of change.

After a few more drinks, he decided he *would* call Teresa. He missed her, damn it. They'd been married longer than he'd been a cop. Unfortunately, he'd been a better cop than a husband. *If you're such a great cop, then why are you stationed here in the ass-end of nowhere?*

He drained the last swallow of scotch and tossed away the plastic tumbler, which bounced off the concrete wall of the building, spun a few times on the balcony floor, and finally lay still.

Away to hell with all this maudlin crap. He got up and retrieved his cell phone from the table in the tiny kitchen.

"Hola?" Teresa's voice sounded far away, farther than the actual distance between Cuenca and Manta.

"Hola, Teresita,"

"You haven't called me that in years."

"Haven't I?" He supposed she was right. "How are you?"

"I'm fine. Have you been drinking?"

"A little. Not too much"

"Maybe it's the connection. You sound different, Juanito."

Delgado heaved a thunderous sigh, but Teresa said nothing.

"I miss you, Teresita."

"I miss you too," she said after a pause that seemed to last forever.

"Maybe you could come down for the weekend."

"Maybe," she agreed. "Have they given you a case?"

"Yes, a murder."

"Hmm."

"What?"

"You know. You know that when you're involved in a case, a murder especially, you're impossible to be around. I don't want to spend seven hours on a bus, just to sit and wait for you to come home."

"They have flights now, direct flights, you know."

Teresa's sigh was every bit as profound as the one Delgado had just released. "You are missing the point, *mi cariño*," she said. "Purposely, I suspect."

"What do you want me to say, Teresa? Do you want me to say that I'll change? That I'll be a better husband? That I won't take my job so seriously?"

"I don't want you to say anything that isn't true." There was frost in her voice, and Delgado knew from experience that the conversation was, for all practical purposes, finished.

"You've changed," he said quietly.

Her laugh reminded him of when he first met her, at the bus stop in front of their high school. He tried to remember the last time he had heard that laugh, and the thought made him sad.

"Yes, Juan. I've changed. People do, you know. Some people."

He had no answer to that, and the silence between them became uncomfortably long.

"I have to go," Teresa said finally. "By the way, your son would like you to call him."

"Juan Carlos?" Delgado was surprised, not having spoken to his son for at least two years. "Why?"

"Call him and find out."

"I love you," Delgado said, but she had already hung up.

7

Long after Delgado had gone to sleep, and after Sergeant Ortega had finished "detecting" for the night, he joined his friend, Wilson Escovedo, another sergeant in the national police, on the road heading out to the airport.

They had chosen the time and location carefully. The last flight out was a little after midnight, so they arrived at their post, a hundred meters from the airport entrance, around eleven. They stood back from the road behind a concrete abutment and watched the oncoming traffic carefully.

"There," said Wilson after fifteen minutes of waiting.

He pointed down the road where a small pickup truck with one burnt-out headlight approached. They waited until the truck was within fifteen meters, and then Ortega stepped out into the road and held up his hand.

The truck bed was stacked high with cardboard boxes. The driver had driven this road hundreds of times, so he knew the drill. By the time Ortega reached him, the driver had his license and registration in his hand.

"What is the problem, Officer?"

Instead of answering, Ortega stepped back and studied the man's papers carefully. He pretended to be consulting his cell phone, which in reality showed only a picture of his wife.

"Did you know that you have one headlight that doesn't work?"

"What? No! I didn't know." The driver started to open his door, but Ortega stopped him.

"It's very dangerous, you know, to be driving this road at night without all of your safety equipment working properly."

"I know, sir. Believe me, I'll have it fixed first thing in the morning, as soon as the parts store opens."

"I'm afraid I can't allow that." Ortega looked truly sorry. "You'll have to park over there." He pointed to a gravel turnout behind the abutment. "In the morning, you can come back and pick it up. Then, be sure to have it repaired before you drive again at night."

"But," the driver protested, "these boxes have to be on the last plane to Quito, in thirty minutes."

"I'm afraid that will be impossible." Wilson had stepped out of the shadows and stood at Ortega's elbow. Ortega checked his watch and nodded his head in agreement.

"But, Officers, if I leave these boxes out here in the open all night, they'll be gone in the morning. And, I'll lose my job."

Ortega appreciated the man's attitude. He didn't plead, he didn't yell or swear. Visitors from other parts of the country, or especially from out of the country, often did one or both. He and Wilson stepped to the side of the road and pretended to have a hushed conversation.

Returning to the side of the pickup, he said: "My partner and I understand your problem, and we'd like to help. But . . ." He raised his shoulders to show that it was out of his hands. "There is the matter of the fine. Forty percent of a basic salary. One hundred sixty dollars." He shrugged again to show that even he thought that was a lot.

"Hmm." The driver did a passable impression of someone deep in thought. "Perhaps we could take care of it here," he said. "I don't have that kind of money with me, but perhaps a deposit?"

"How much?"

"Well, let me see." The driver took out his wallet and opened it, showing a lone ten-dollar bill.

"Stop wasting our time!" Wilson threw his hands in the air. Everyone knew that if you drove these coastal roads at night, you had to carry at least a twenty for situations just such as this.

"Wait, wait!" The driver dug into a small pouch on the seat next to him, carefully shielding it from the view of the two officers. "I just remembered. I might have more."

The driver handed a twenty through the window. Ortega grabbed it as well as the ten from the man's wallet. A penalty for trying to be too cute.

"I'll need your license too."

"Of course." The driver handed it over without complaint.

"Tomorrow," Wilson said, "Get the light fixed and go to the UPC station on Avenida 14. You can pay the rest of the fine and your license will be returned to you."

"*Gracias, Señores.*" The man started the truck and pulled away.

Ortega examined the license under the streetlight. It was, of course, only a laminated copy. Real licenses had a chip in them. A replacement cost about eighty-five dollars, so most experienced drivers carried only a copy. He tossed the license into the bushes.

"How many more?" Wilson asked, stretching his arms and yawning.

"One more should do it," Ortega responded. "Then I'll have enough to buy that crib that Diana saw at Bebé Mundo."

"I told you that you could use José's. He's way too big for it."

"I know, but it's our first. Diana wants everything to be special."

They stood for a while in silence, watching the oncoming traffic.

8

The next morning at eight A.M. Delgado again performed the difficult task of inserting himself into the small car.

When he had settled in, Ortega handed the captain a small paper bag splotched with grease.

"What's this?"

"Empanadas. Cheese, and I think one has chicken filling. My wife made them for you."

"So, you told her I like to eat."

Ortega ducked his head in embarrassment, but he couldn't keep a smile from forming on his expressive face. "It did come up," he said.

"Your wife is a good cook," Delgado said as he attacked the still-warm doughy treats. "Is she a fatty?"

"What? No! She's not!" Ortega seemed to get bigger and appeared ready to take on the big captain in defense of his young bride.

"Calm down, Sergeant," Delgado said around a mouthful of empanada. "I was just making a joke."

"I don't like anyone making jokes about my wife. Even you, sir."

"Fair enough." Delgado brushed his hands together, filling the air with crumbs. "Tell me, now, Sergeant. What do we know that we didn't know yesterday when I left you?" He watched the sergeant struggle with himself. He still wanted to be angry, but he was also bursting to reveal what he had learned.

"I started thinking," Ortega said, "if the victim was a fisherman, he would have to be a member of the union."

"But he wasn't a citizen."

"That's right. So, I called around and finally reached the union president. He confirmed that Jaramillo would not have been allowed to fish legally."

"Surely, though, there are illegal fishermen in these waters."

"Exactly! Córdova, he's the president, wouldn't come out and admit it, but he came close."

"Well, I think our second order of business today should be to meet with this esteemed union president."

"Yes, sir," Ortega agreed. "We have a meeting with him at ten o'clock. But what's first, then?"

"Hmm?" Delgado appeared to be deep in thought.

"You said that meeting with Córdova was our second order of business. What's first?"

"Our first order of business, our very first order, is to get us a decent vehicle." He squirmed a little in his seat to emphasize his point. "Where is the motor pool?"

Ortega smiled. "It's a block or two from the stadium, on Avenida 113. But it won't do you any good. The new commander has put a hold on spending. He's doing an inventory of all the vehicles in the fleet, and for the immediate future, we're supposed to stay with whatever car's been assigned to us."

An hour later, after a quiet conversation between Delgado and the head of the motor pool—a stocky little man in grease-stained coveralls—Ortega piloted them back onto the street behind the wheel of a 2012 Kia Sorento. The rear bumper was missing, the steering was loose, and the mini-SUV had a dent the size of a large coconut in the right front fender, but the interior was roomy enough and smelled strongly of pine-scented air freshener.

"How did you do that?" Ortega's eyes were wide.

"I promised him a sack of your wife's empanadas every morning for the next two weeks."

"What? No!"

"Oh, yes." Delgado fished in his wallet and handed Ortega a twenty dollar bill. "For flour and . . . whatever." He waved a meaty hand in the air. "Let me know when this runs out," he said.

At first, Ortega looked as if he might not take the money, but twenty dollars at the *mercado* would buy enough flour to last him and his wife a couple months. In the end, he stuffed the bill into the breast pocket of his uniform shirt.

The Fisherman's Union office was in a white stucco building just outside the port entrance. Painted around the front door was a series of blue waves with white foam at their tips. A school of bright yellow tropical fish covered a big portion of the front wall, along with smaller paintings of a variety of other fish.

The interior was spotless, all gleaming white tile. Rather than smelling of fish, as Delgado had feared, the place smelled of ammonia and disinfectant.

They found Francisco Córdova, the illustrious president of the *Unión de Pescadores*, at his desk in a small office off the main entryway. He stood to greet them, and Delgado noticed the thin scars on both the man's hands. *So he was a fisherman before he got this cushy job.*

Córdova was a thin man, but his royal blue pullover shirt showed off his powerful upper body, built through years of hauling in nets full of fish. After they had turned down offers of coffee, tea, and water, he ushered the two policemen to a pair of chrome and black vinyl chairs and took his own chair—also chrome and black vinyl—on the opposite side of a battered wooden desk which seemed out of place with the rest of the furnishings.

"The sergeant tells me that you are new to our town. What do you think of—"

"Do you know this man?" Delgado showed him the picture of the dead man's ID card that he had captured on his phone.

Córdova shot a surprised look in Ortega's direction, but the sergeant avoided his gaze. He studied the image on Delgado's phone carefully. Or seemed to. Delgado was not convinced.

"No," Córdova said, sliding the phone back across the desk. "I don't recognize him."

"And yet, Señor Córdova, your eyes flicked up to me, over to the sergeant, and back down."

"What the hell does that mean?" Córdova started to rise from his chair, but the captain motioned him to sit back down.

"Maybe nothing," Delgado declared. "How many members are there in your union?"

"About two thousand, more or less." Córdova seemed to be struggling to understand the quick change of subject, and Ortega seemed just as lost.

"Do all of them live here in Manta?"

"No, our members come from all over Manabí Province. Well, the coastal region anyway."

"You have addresses for all of them. No?"

"Our members are not always good about notifying us when they change addresses." He gave them a small shrug and a smile. "But, yes, we have basic contact information for all of our members."

"And . . ." Delgado sat forward and Sergeant Ortega followed suit. "If you gave us the information, we—"

"We don't, as a matter of policy, give out our members' contact information." Córdova smiled and shrugged once more to show that his hands were tied.

"But this is a murder investigation." Delgado leaned farther forward and seemed to grow even larger. Ortega leaned closer as well, but he was no match for the captain.

"So, you *will* give us the list if we ask for it."

"I don't understand why you would want such a list."

"Because, sir, if I were to give such a list to Sergeant Ortega, he could visit each and every one of them."

"For what purpose?" It was Córdova who spoke, but Ortega appeared just as puzzled.

"Ortega could tell us, for example, which of your members live in wooden shacks with dirt floors and which of them had managed to obtain more suitable accommodations for themselves and their families."

"I see."

"Do you?" Delgado leaned back in his chair and Ortega mimicked his movement. "I read an interesting article recently in *Vistazo Magazine*. Do you know it?"

"I'm familiar with it. We may have a copy or two in the waiting room."

"What the article said," Delgado went on, before Córdova had finished speaking, "was that there is not a single fisherman in the area—ones who own their own boat, of course—that has not been offered ten thousand dollars, at a minimum, to take a shipment of drugs to Mexico or the United States. And the way that you can tell which one has accepted that offer, is what kind of home they live in."

"I'm not involved in any of that!"

"Oh, no?" Delgado's face showed surprise "What, then? Guns? Liquor? Girls? You're involved in something, Señor Córdova. No one takes a job such as yours for the salary."

"I see," Córdova said, and this time it appeared that he really did see. "Could we speak privately, Captain?"

"Sergeant," Delgado said, his eyes still fixed on Córdova. "Go wait outside."

Ortega got up without a word and left the room, his shoulders sagging, and his fists clenched, like a small boy who had just been dismissed from the adult's table.

9

"How much?" Córdova's face narrowed and his eyes seemed to gain focus, like a fox with a fat little rabbit in its sights.

"It's not 'how much?' It's 'what?'" Delgado watched as the man's eyes lost focus for a second.

"What, then?" Córdova quickly regained focus. "What do you want? I'm already protected, by the way."

"Protected? From what? Sharks?" Delgado pretended to be confused. "Oh. I see what you mean. You think I'm one of those cops who would not say no to a *mordida*—a little bribe."

The expression on the union president's face morphed quickly from suspicion to confusion.

"You're not wrong, you know," Delgado said. "I take my opportunities as they come. But in this case, I need information. See, I don't care if every *drogadicto* in the entire United States blows his brains out with heroin, or cocaine, or whatever. But there are plenty of people who do. Important people." He paused and his eyes bored into Córdova's until the man looked away. "And some of those packages of drugs have your fingerprints on them."

"You don't know that."

"Oh, I know. I may not be able to prove it, but give me, uhm . . . twenty-four hours, and I'll have all the proof I need."

"What exactly is it that you want, Captain?"

"Now." Delgado clapped his hands together. "Now we're getting somewhere." He stabbed his index finger down on his phone, which was still lying face-up on the table. The screen had gone dark, but now it brightened, and the image of Aquiles Jaramillo stared up at them.

"I need information about this man. That's all. I know you have it. I could see when we first showed you the photo that you knew him. And I knew from the first that you are the type of man who doesn't do anything unless it benefits you." He lifted his finger and pointed it directly at Córdova.

"How does me giving you information on this man benefit me?" Córdova said—the words of a man who knew he had been bested but wanted to delay the inevitable.

"It benefits you," Delgado said, standing up and placing both fists on the edge of desk, "because you get to keep your job. Simple as that." He waited, but he didn't have to wait long.

"*Bueno,*" Córdova said. "This is what I know."

Delgado exited the building and stood for a moment, observing his new assistant. Ortega sat motionless behind the wheel of the SUV, staring straight ahead.

Mierda, Delgado thought, *he looks just like Juan Carlos.* He replayed in his mind his conversation the previous night with his wife. She had, without saying so directly, told him to contact their son and make amends. The implication, it seemed to him, was that this was a test that he had to pass if she were to ever consider coming back to him.

Maybe it's time that I changed my ways, he thought. *Be more sensitive to other people's feelings.*

But by the time he had walked the fifteen meters to the waiting car, all his good intentions had blown away like leaves before an autumn wind.

"You're not my partner, Sergeant," he said as he got in the car and buckled up. "You are my assistant and my driver. That's it."

"Yes, sir." Ortega put the car in gear, set his hands at ten and two, and drove to the parking lot exit. "Where to?"

Delgado consulted the piece of paper he had torn from Córdova's desk pad. "Calle 12, a few blocks off of Avenida 24." He examined the sergeant's stoic profile for a few seconds, his own expression a combination of amusement and sadness. Then he sighed once, turned on the air-conditioning, and stared out the window as Sergeant Ortega navigated the streets of Manta.

10

"While I was waiting, I got a text from the DINASED investigator," Ortega said after a few minutes of silent driving. "Do you want to know what they found?"

"Tell me," Delgado responded. He had little faith that the lazy *pendejos* from the forensic team had found anything of interest, but the young sergeant's barely contained excitement intrigued him.

"They found," Ortega said breathlessly, "that the man in the barrel had suffered a heart attack. That's what killed him."

"A heart attack? How old was this man? Thirty-five, maybe?"

"According to his *cédula*, he will . . . would have turned thirty-six in February."

"Thirty-five," Delgado mused. "And by all outward appearances he was in good shape."

"That's right. Odd, don't you think?"

"Your face is very expressive, Sergeant. Did you realize that? For example, I can tell from your expression that there's more to this story. Isn't there?"

"Yes, sir. Would you like to hear what else they said?"

"I can hardly wait."

"Well, Lopez, that's the DINASED investigator. Do you know him?"

"No, Ortega. I've never met him." Delgado's small reserve of patience had been exhausted. "And, I can live the rest of my life quite happily without ever meeting him. Now tell me what the man said!"

"Yes, sir." Ortega stiffened. "They found a small puncture wound in the man's left side, a few centimeters below his armpit. They figure it was from a—"

"Syringe!" Delgado completed the sentence. "They injected some chemical, directly into the heart. Do they know what was used?"

"No, sir. They said they'll have to do some tests and they would get back to us in a few days."

"A few days? Sure, and I'll win the *lotería* today. Doesn't matter, though. There are probably a dozen different chemicals that would cause a heart attack—strychnine would be my guess. It's enough for us to know how it was done, and that it was indeed a murder. Anything else?"

"They said that the phone"—Ortega indicated the cheap cell phone that sat on the console in a plastic evidence bag— "had been wiped clean of prints. It had a Claro SIM card, and Lopez said we could access their database to find who it's registered to."

Delgado knew it would be a waste of time. Either the phone would be registered to the victim, or to a fraudulent account. Still, it would give this young *currante*—this eager beaver—something to do while he, Delgado, solved the crime.

"Okay," he said. "Let's interview this . . ." He glanced down at the paper. "Roberto Aguilar, see what he has to say, and then you can go back to the office and start making phone calls."

"Yes, sir." Ortega sped up a little in his excitement. Delgado wondered how long it would take for the sergeant to become a jaded, corrupt imitation of a policeman, like all the rest.

11

Córdova's information turned out to be accurate. Roberto Aguilar, after fishing all night and successfully handing off his catch to a broker from Guayaquil, was relaxing in an orange hammock in front of his house, a cold bottle of pilsner beer in his hands. Like most fisherman, Aguilar never left his fifty horsepower engine with his boat. It leaned against a porch column with a length of rusted chain securing it against thievery.

Ortega and Delgado exchanged glances as they approached the house. While not luxurious in any way, it was a sturdy concrete structure. It showed only minimal cracking from the devastating magnitude 7.8 earthquake that had occurred a few years earlier, its epicenter less than forty kilometers to the north. The man was married, Delgado surmised, because an array of colorful flowers adorned the second-floor balcony, their leaves glistening from a recent watering.

So, Delgado thought, *Señor Aguilar is one of those who has successfully made the journey north carrying a shipment of drugs. Maybe he's done it more than once.*

Delgado instructed Ortega to park the SUV blocking one lane of the narrow street. Traffic would have to slow down to get around it, ensuring that within minutes the entire neighborhood would know that Roberto Aguilar was being questioned by the national police.

Aguilar took a swig of his beer and watched them approach with a suspicion born of a lifetime living on the edge of the law. He was a muscular man with a slight beer belly and wore only stained white basketball shorts with blue piping and a pair of pink flip-flops. He sat the bottle on a plastic table next to the hammock but made no move to get up.

"You know this man." Delgado showed him the image on his phone, his expression making it clear that he was making a statement, not asking a question.

"So?" Aguilar stretched his arms out, yawned, and then laced his fingers behind his head.

"So, I want to know everything you know about him."

Aguilar managed somehow to shrug with his hands still behind his head. "I don't know much," he said. "His name's Andres something." He pantomimed deep thought for a moment and then took his right hand from behind his head and snapped his fingers. "Andres Morocho," he said, and resumed his relaxed posture.

"No. His name is Aquiles Jaramillo," Delgado said, drawing another shrug from the man in the hammock.

"Well, then I guess I don't know him after all."

Aguilar was reaching for his beer bottle when Delgado grasped the edge of the hammock and yanked hard. The fisherman was launched into the air and landed atop the plastic table. The table collapsed and Aguilar hit the concrete floor amid a pool of beer and shattered glass. He had lost one of his flip-flops and his shorts slid down several centimeters, exposing more of his butt crack than anyone wanted to see.

Despite the hard fall, he came up swinging, but Sergeant Ortega, moving quickly, grasped him by the back of his shorts, spun him around and slammed him against a concrete column that held up the second floor.

"You need to show the captain the respect he deserves," Ortega said, his breath coming hard and fast from the exertion.

Aguilar mumbled something that sounded like an agreement. Ortega spun him around to the front and pushed him down hard onto a wooden bench next to the front door. Before he could gather his wits, Delgado was on him, holding his phone right in front of his face.

"You see? His name is right there. Aquiles—"

"Okay. I see. But he told us his name was Andres."

"Tell me why you killed him," the captain demanded.

"What? No! He's dead?" Aguilar looked truly shocked at the news, but Delgado remained unimpressed.

"Stop lying!" He pressed his face close to the smaller man's. Aguilar tried to recoil. Who wouldn't? But Sergeant Ortega had twisted his arm behind his back and was applying steady upward pressure, while grasping the back of his neck with his other hand and forcing him to hold still.

"I didn't kill him," Aguilar said, his voice barely audible. "I . . ."

"You what?" Delgado and Ortega spoke in unison.

"I tried to help him."

"How? You tried to help him, how?" Delgado inched even closer, and Aguilar screwed his eyes shut.

"I gave him a job."

"Is that right?" Delgado stood up, breathing hard. "Did he have a work permit?"

The sound that escaped Aguilar's lips was somewhere between a cough and a bitter laugh. "You know the answer to that," he said.

"Yes," Delgado agreed. "I do. So it wasn't so much that you helped him as you helped yourself, by hiring an illegal and paying him a fraction of what you would have to pay an Ecuadorian."

"Then arrest me for that. But I didn't kill anyone!"

"No," Delgado said. "I don't think you did. At least, not Jaramillo."

"What?" This time it was Aguilar who spoke in unison with Ortega. The sergeant relaxed his grip momentarily and that was all the bigger and more powerful fisherman needed. He shook loose from the startled sergeant and started to rise, but Delgado's hand on his shoulder stopped him.

"Sit down! I'm not done with you."

"But you said that you knew I didn't kill Andres."

"Aquiles." Ortega corrected him.

"Whoever!" Aguilar said. "I told you the truth. Why don't you leave me alone?"

"Because." Delgado leaned in once more. "You have information. Just like Señor Córdova, the illustrious union president.

And, like Córdova, you have something to hide, so to keep your little secret, you will tell me what I want to know, and then I will leave you alone."

"What secret? Because I hired a foreigner? What's that? A fine? Ten percent of a basic salary? Forty dollars?"

"No, Señor Aguilar. I don't care if you hire a foreigner. But ..." He rubbed his hand over the shiny teak trim around the front window. "How did you afford this fine house, I wonder?"

"Our old house was destroyed in the earthquake a few years ago. Nothing left but a pile of sticks. My son was nearly killed."

"That's a very sad story," Delgado said, his face showing that he didn't find it sad at all. "But it doesn't answer my question. You own your own boat, I assume?"

"Yes." Aguilar seemed to know that he was walking into a trap.

"How much do you earn? After you buy bait, and gas, and after you pay your crew?" Delgado smiled nastily "Even if your crew *is* full of illegals."

"No!" Aguilar shouted. "Only Andres. The rest are all Ecuadorians."

"Stop avoiding my question. How much do you make? Thirty dollars a day? On a good day."

Aguilar slumped back against the wall. He held a hand up as if asking for time to think. Surprisingly, Delgado obliged. He took out his wallet and handed Ortega ten dollars.

"We owe this man a beer," he told him, nodding his head in the direction of a small *tienda* on the corner. "Get a couple for us too." He drew a white handkerchief from the breast pocket of his jacket and mopped his brow.

12

"My sister's husband died at sea two years ago." Aguilar took a deep pull from his beer before continuing. "It's been difficult for her. She has three kids, from six to ten. She met Andres . . . whoever, a few months ago and things started to look better for her."

"Wait a minute!" Delgado held up his hand like a traffic cop. "Your sister met this Venezuelan and her life started to improve? Financially, you mean?"

Once again Aguilar seemed to sense that his own words had tripped him up. He looked down at his feet in sullen silence.

"You can see why I'm confused," Delgado said, although he didn't appear confused at all. "Tell me if I'm wrong, Señor Aguilar, but most of these *Venezolanos* that come here? They're desperate, aren't they? If they weren't, why would they travel thousands of miles on foot?"

Delgado took the man's shrug as agreement.

"Then how did this particular Venezolano have the financial means to help your sister?"

"Wait a minute!" Aguilar stood up, surprised that no one tried to stop him. "Does Renata know? Does she know that he's dead?"

Delgado shrugged. "Probably not. The sooner you give us what we need, the sooner you can go and tell her."

Aguilar looked at him as if seeing him for the first time. "You're a coldhearted sonofabitch," he said, and spit on the ground near the captain's shoe.

"So I've been told," Delgado agreed. "Now . . . how did Aquiles Jaramillo make his money? Enough money, I remind you, to help your poor sister and her three little brats."

Aguilar seemed to want to take offense at the captain's description of his nieces and nephew, but Delgado offered so much to be offended by that it didn't seem worth it.

"Surely, not by working for you," Delgado said.

A silence fell over the little gathering as Aguilar tried to work out his problem. *Everyone in the neighborhood knew how he had earned the money to buy his house. No one cared, least of all the police. This one appeared to be a different animal. He wanted something; they all did. But not money—not this one. He wanted information. What would it hurt to give it to him? Aquiles was dead.*

"If I tell you what I know, you'll only use it to find my friend's killer?"

"Of course."

"And, you'll forget about this? My house."

"Of course."

"All I know is that Aquiles was working a deal with some guys down at the port."

"A legal deal?" Ortega asked.

"What do you think?"

"What kind of deal? Who with?" Delgado said.

"I don't know, and I didn't ask."

"Call the narcotics task force." Delgado's words were directed at Ortega, but his eyes remained fixed on the hapless fisherman.

"Wait," Aguilar protested. "You promised you wouldn't—"

"And you said you would tell me everything you know," Delgado countered. "I'm a patient man, but I have my limits," he said, drawing an amused look from Sergeant Ortega.

Aguilar lifted the beer bottle to his lips, but Ortega grabbed it before he could take a drink and set it down on the bench with enough force that foam spewed from the neck.

"Answer him!" Ortega demanded, and it was Delgado's turn to look amused.

"You need to get your monkey under control," Aguilar mumbled in a last-ditch attempt to save face.

Ortega raised his hand, preparing to deliver a backhand slap, but Delgado moved with surprising speed to stop him.

"Okay, okay." Aguilar raised his hands in surrender. He took a moment to catch his breath and then he told them everything he knew. The strange case of Aquiles Jaramillo became stranger still.

As Captain Delgado headed for the car, his stomach rumbling like far off thunder, Ortega lingered behind. He made grunting monkey sounds and then tipped over the beer bottle, drenching Aguilar's shorts with the foamy liquid. The fisherman jumped up and raised his eyes and his hands to the heavens. Receiving no answer, he sighed, and went inside to change clothes.

13

The decor in Chifa Ming Yuan, a Chinese restaurant on Calle 24, consisted of faded red brocade covering the walls, faux gold dragons on nearly every flat surface, and the mandatory fish tank containing a half dozen carp swimming listlessly back and forth in the green-tinted water. Although it was nearly one thirty, the middle of the lunch rush, the staff outnumbered the customers. The restaurant owner, a slight Asian man with a wispy black mustache, peered hopefully through the plate glass window that faced the street.

Delgado and Ortega sat at a table near the kitchen. The table, designed to seat four people, overflowed with food—crab puffs, two kinds of fried rice, sweet and sour chicken, barbecued pork with wasabi, breaded shrimp, and a steaming platter of egg rolls. Delgado ordered a big bottle of Tsingtao beer, and Ortega stuck with water.

"Dig in," Delgado said, stuffing a cloth napkin into his shirt collar. "I'm buying."

Ortega looked up in surprise. He had assumed that the older, higher paid officer would buy their lunch. Would he be expected then to buy lunch the next time? Since they found that his wife was pregnant, she had taken to giving him a single five-dollar bill each morning and expecting change when he got home. His appetite, no match for Delgado's at the best of times, flagged even more.

The sergeant picked at his food in silent frustration. He was eager to discuss what they had learned from Roberto Aguilar, but there never seemed to be an opening. Delgado attacked his food as if it had offended him, chewing and slurping with gusto. At one point, the tip of his tie dipped into the sweet and sour sauce. The captain frowned, dunked it in his water glass, dried it on the tablecloth, and went back to eating.

Finally he was done. He pushed away his plate, broke in half one of the wooden chopsticks they had been given, and used the jagged end as a toothpick. He sat back, loosened his belt, belched mightily, and signaled for another beer.

Ortega wasn't sure if this was merely a rest period, but he used the opening he had been given.

"Should we call for backup when we go to the warehouse?" he said, pushing away his half-eaten plate of food.

"We're not going to any warehouse." Delgado reached for the last breaded shrimp and popped it into his mouth.

"What?" In his shock and surprise, Ortega spoke louder than he intended, causing the sad little owner to momentarily look away from his vigil. "What about what Aguilar said? The warehouse?"

"Aguilar is a liar."

Ortega couldn't have been more shocked, and it showed, drawing a smile from his boss. "Why didn't we keep working him, then? We had him!"

"No, Sergeant. We didn't have him at all."

"Okay." Ortega spread apart his hands in frustration. "You'll have to explain that. What am I missing?"

"It's not so much that you missed something," Delgado said. "In fact, it was your comment about the voice on the phone that we found with the body. Do you remember, you said that whoever left that message wasn't from this area?"

"Yeah. So?"

"So, it started me thinking. Not only the man on the phone wasn't from here on the coast, he was an educated man."

"You could tell his level of education just from his voice?"

"Of course." Delgado took a big swallow of beer before continuing. "That and more. Do you remember the rhythm, the cadence of his voice? He's a man who is used to being listened to. So, just from those two things we can figure that he's a businessman, maybe a lawyer, or—"

"A doctor!" Ortega nearly upended his water glass in his excitement.

"Why a doctor?"

"Because," Ortega said, his words coming in a rush. The way Jaramillo was killed. Someone injected him with some type of poison—"

"Strychnine, I think."

"Okay. Strychnine, whatever. The point is that whoever did it was a professional. He knew that the breastplate protects the heart, so he had to go in from the side." He lifted his arm to show where the puncture wound had been found on the victim. "And, he had access to a long enough syringe to reach the heart from that angle. Not something you can buy at the local *farmacia*."

"Good work, Sergeant." Delgado dipped a piece of barbeque pork in wasabi and popped it in his mouth.

"Thank you, sir," Ortega said modestly. "But you already knew it was a doctor we were looking for, didn't you?"

Delgado didn't seem to hear the sergeant speak. In fact, he seemed to be somewhere far away.

"My son is a doctor," he said quietly. "Or he will be when he finishes his residency."

Ortega had no idea what to say to that.

14

"How many doctors do you think there are in this town?" Delgado continued to clean his teeth with the broken end of the chopstick from the restaurant.

"Thousands, I suppose." Ortega started the engine of the small SUV. "But I've been thinking."

"Is that right?"

"Yes." Ortega released the clutch and pulled out in traffic. "I was just thinking, we know that whoever killed Jaramillo was a doctor. Or at least had medical training. But he's also a criminal. Right?"

"Yes, Sergeant. He's a murderer."

"No, that's not what I meant." Ortega wanted to take offense at the captain's sarcasm, but he was too excited. "He was a criminal before he murdered Jaramillo. Don't you think?"

"Hmm." Delgado tossed the broken chopstick out the window. "That makes a certain amount of sense, actually."

"Yes, exactly." Ortega crowed with excitement. "We know, or we're pretty sure that Jaramillo was involved in something illegal. That's why he had money to help Aguilar's sister, when all the other *Venezolanos* are broke, begging on street corners, or stealing whatever isn't nailed down."

"So, then, you think that this doctor we're looking for was involved in something shady with Jaramillo."

"It makes sense, doesn't it? He was able to get close enough to him to stick a needle up under his arm like he did."

"He could have had help, I suppose. Someone to hold the man down, while he poisoned him."

"I suppose," Ortega said, "but you yourself said that Jaramillo had a surprised look on his face. Like he had no idea he was going to be killed until the moment it happened."

"But, just for the sake of argument, Sergeant, let's assume that you're right. How does that help us in our investigation?"

"Well . . ." Ortega could barely contain his excitement. "We're not going to find a shady doctor like that working at any of the legitimate hospitals or clinics. Are we?"

"Then, where do you suggest we look?"

"There's a small clinic on a side street off of Avenida 103. They perform abortions." The sergeant's disgust showed clearly on his face. "And, they . . . you know, if someone gets shot or stabbed while committing a crime, you know, they can't go to a regular hospital."

"Does it have a name? This clinic?"

"Not officially. They call it the Hankook Clinic, because it's housed in a building that used to be a store where they sold those Korean tires."

"Okay, then. That's where we'll go. But first, we need to go back to the station. I assume you have a set of civilian clothes there. We'll want to not advertise ourselves as cops."

"Yes, sir." Ortega veered off onto a side street, ignoring the angry shouts and blaring horns. He could barely conceal his excitement. His first plainclothes assignment.

"So, this underground clinic," Delgado mused, "operates with impunity? I mean, you know about it, so it has to be common knowledge among the police. Yes?"

Ortega hesitated before answering, looking for the accusation in the statement. But there was none. Delgado was just asking a question, policeman to policeman.

"Well," he said finally. "You know how it works."

"Yes, I do, Sergeant. Yes, I do. And, do you get a taste of that? The *mordida*?"

"No," Ortega said immediately, and then grinned. "I'm too low on the food chain for that."

"Have patience, Sergeant. You'll get there."

15

Captain Delgado stayed in the car while Ortega went inside to change clothes. If it were up to him, he'd never enter the squalid little cop shop.

Something was nagging at him. It took a while but finally it clicked into place. The voice on the cell phone had said: "*This is what happens to scum that comes here from outside to take our jobs and our women.*" At the time, he had dismissed it as a red herring. The killer wanted them to think that Jaramillo had been murdered because he was Venezuelan. But he had said, *take our jobs and our women.* It was common knowledge throughout the country that Venezuelans, desperate as they were, would work for next to nothing, but he had never heard anyone specifically accuse them of being homewreckers.

So had the murderer, in his attempt to be clever and throw them off the scent, slipped up and exposed the true motive for the crime? Delgado examined his new theory carefully, searching for holes in it. By the time Ortega came sprinting back to the car, his mind was made up.

"Go back inside and change into your uniform," Delgado said, without explanation.

Ortega, dressed in black slacks, a blue and yellow T-shirt of the local soccer team, and thick black sandals, opened his mouth to speak, but decided against it. He turned and trudged back into the building as if he had just been sentenced to a long prison term. Delgado didn't notice. His mind was somewhere else.

16

"Where are we going?" Ortega spoke in short, clipped tones, staring straight ahead with his hands tight on the wheel.

"Aguilar, the lying fisherman. He gave you his sister's address. Yes?"

"Yes."

"And you wrote it down?"

"Yes, of course."

"Then, Sergeant, that's where we are going."

"Yes, sir." Ortega pulled his notebook from his breast pocket, consulted it briefly, and put it back. He signaled a right turn and kept his eyes straight ahead.

Delgado watched Ortega as he drove and sighed quietly. He wasn't an insensitive man, as many had accused him of being. He just, when he had a crime to solve, gave not one thought to anything but that. People's feelings be damned. Once again, he had the feeling that he was watching his own son.

Ortega pulled the SUV to a stop on Calle 115 in the Three Kings Barrio. "That should be the house right there." He pointed to a ramshackle wooden structure next to a hardware store that took up most of the rest of the block.

The house had been painted turquoise at one time—the weathered planks on the exterior showed faint traces of the color. Kids' toys, remnants of plastic bags, and a worn car tire were scattered across the rusted tin roof. Aguilar had told them that Jaramillo was able to help his sister financially. Apparently, his financial assistance fell short of providing adequate shelter for her and her three kids.

"I don't understand why we're here," Ortega said. Again, he wanted to remain angry at Delgado for taking away his chance to work in plainclothes, but his curiosity was too keen. "What was his name, the fishermen's union president?"

Delgado said, "Córdova. He lied to us. He sent us to Aguilar because he assumed we would find the connection between the fisherman and Jaramillo sooner or later. But then, for whatever reason, he didn't warn Aguilar that we were coming. You saw that the man was truly shocked when we told him that Jaramillo was dead."

"I didn't see a cell phone on the porch," Ortega said, "which is kind of odd in itself. Fishermen are never far from their phones.

They're always gabbing to one another about the weather, the tides. Or where the baitfish are running."

"Maybe it's broken," Delgado mused.

"I suppose." Ortega didn't seem convinced.

"Sometimes, Sergeant, and very rarely, luck is on our side. When it is, it's better not to question it."

"But how does that help us? Aguilar would have likely told his sister by now that Jaramillo is dead. So, it won't be a surprise to her when we show up asking questions."

"Not we, Sergeant. You."

"Me?"

"Yes. I've been told"—the captain allowed himself a tight smile—"that I lack a certain delicacy when dealing with the ladies."

Delgado laid out the plan. The sergeant was dubious but kept it to himself. He got out of the car, straightened his uniform, and headed off down the street.

Delgado sat and watched the sergeant stride away. He fidgeted in his seat for a while and then took out his phone.

"Call your son," Teresa had told him, so he did.

"*Mande.*" The voice coming from the phone was like an echo of his own voice, only younger, clearer, and stronger.

"Hola, Juan Carlos."

"Hola, Papi." Whatever else he was, Juan Carlos was polite.

Delgado had carefully scripted in advance the first few lines of the phone call. So far, so good.

"How are you, son?"

"Why did you leave Mami?"

What was this? Two sentences in and we're already off script.

"I didn't leave your mother," Delgado said indignantly.

"But, she's in Cuenca and you're in Manta. No?"

Juan Carlos could sound maddeningly reasonable while ripping you a new one. *He should be a lawyer instead of a doctor*, Ortega thought, with a mixture of pride and sadness.

"She could have come with me." He heard the weakness in his argument even as he was making it.

"In that heat?"

"I suppose you're right."

That stopped the interrogation, if only for a minute, as Juan Carlos struggled with this new concept of his father admitting that he was wrong.

"What I meant," he said finally, "when I asked you why you left Mami . . . What I meant was: Why did they send you there? What did you do?"

"Ah." Delgado's first instinct was to lie, but he knew intuitively that that was the wrong way to go in this instance. "Why do you want to know?"

"It's important to me, Papi. Okay?"

"Of course, son." Delgado took a deep breath and then let it out. He told his son the story of his fall from grace. He told him how, frustrated at his inability to gain a solicitation of murder conviction against a wealthy and powerful Cuencano businessman, he had systematically set out to destroy the man's reputation, resulting in his losing his business as well as his marriage.

"Oh." *Was that the sound of respect in his son's voice?* "I thought it might have been . . ."

"Might have been, what?"

"You know, taking bribes or something like that." Suddenly Juan Carlos reverted to the tongue-tied eight-year-old that his father remembered so fondly.

"No, son," he said gently. "It was nothing like that." *How could it be when he always kicked a little upstairs to the commander?*

17

Ortega was a bundle of nervous energy as he walked the half block to the home of Renata Vasquez. He was excited for the chance to question the woman on his own—his first solo interrogation ever—but his brain roiled in confusion. They had gone to see the fishermen's union president, who directed them to Roberto Aguilar. He in turn told them about a warehouse down by the docks where Aquiles Jaramillo was, according to Aguilar, involved in something sinister. But then Captain Delgado had changed his mind and said that they weren't going to the warehouse, they were now in search of a doctor—one who would no doubt be up to something sinister himself.

And then, in the time it had taken him to change clothes, the old toad had decided that this woman, this Renata Vasquez, was the key to it all. He couldn't shake the feeling that the captain was setting him up for another embarrassment.

He had nearly reached the house before he noticed the woman sitting on the green plastic chair in front. She wore a faded blue dress and her dark hair was a tangled mass of knots and curls, as if she had just awoken. The sergeant noticed that she had nice legs, and the shapeless dress couldn't completely conceal her curves, which in his opinion were also quite nice.

When he got closer and saw the expression on her face, the sergeant suddenly felt the weight of his inexperience. Was it grief for her loss that he saw, or had a lifetime of crushing poverty etched a permanent frown on what had probably once been a pretty face? He squared his shoulders and approached the woman, who remained motionless, only her dull brown eyes tracking his movements.

"Señora Vasquez?" he said politely.

"Is this about Andres?"

"Aquiles? Yes. I'm afraid it is. So, you know?"

"I know that he's dead. Murdered, they say." Her voice changed neither in pitch nor volume.

"Yes," Ortega said in his best official manner. "We believe he was murdered."

"Why?" There was no force behind the question, no expectation that she would receive a satisfactory answer.

"We . . . I am hoping that you could help to answer that."

"Me?" Her voice rose several octaves and her facial expression showed genuine surprise. Perhaps she had never been asked to help in anything of significance.

"Yes, ma'am." Ortega took his notebook and a worn stub of a pencil from his breast pocket. "What was your relationship with the deceased?"

"He was my man."

"Your man? You mean, your boyfriend?"

She nodded once, and then three more times, as if convincing herself.

"How long have you known him?"

"Two months?" Time seemed to be a difficult concept for her.

"And you were aware that he was Venezuelan?"

"Of course I was aware! Is that why they killed him?"

"We don't think so."

"Then, why?" Her face collapsed in grief, and the tears started to flow.

Ortega pulled a clean white handkerchief from his pocket and handed it to her. She took it without comment and dabbed at her eyes. This was the moment for which Delgado had instructed him to be on the alert.

"If you can get her crying, then bear down," the captain had told him. "Use your boyish charm. If I talked to her, she'd clam up from the start."

Feeling like a complete horse's ass, but afraid of what the captain would say if he came back with nothing, he went on the attack.

"Who were you seeing before Jaramillo?"

"What?" She squinted at him through her tears. "Why is that any of your business?"

"Because, Señora, we believe that is who murdered your boyfriend." Ortega wasn't sure that he believed it, but the captain did, and that was enough.

"Raúl?" she said. "No! He wouldn't!"

Ortega held his pencil in readiness above his notebook. "What is Raúl's surname?" he said.

"Oh, no!" Señora Vasquez shot to her feet, and Sergeant Ortega saw the pretty young women that he had suspected was behind the lifeless mask. Her eyes widened, the tears stopped as suddenly as they began, and her face contorted in rage. "No!" she shouted. "You're not going to shake down Raúl, just because he has money."

She turned and entered the house, slamming the battered wooden door behind her. A mixture of dirt, dead leaves, and coconut husks, dislodged by the slamming door, showered down from the roof onto Ortega's shoulders.

18

If the captain was surprised to see the sergeant's normally impeccable uniform stained and wrinkled, he didn't show it.

"Well?" he said. "Anything?"

"Not much, I'm afraid." Ortega gave himself a last brushing down and then slid in behind the wheel.

"But, something? Right? I can see from your face that you've got something."

Ortega took a quick look at himself in the rearview mirror, wondering what it was about his face that gave his inner thoughts away.

"Like I said, not much. All I really know is that her former boyfriend is named Raúl, and—"

"Raúl?" the captain interrupted. "Raúl who?"

"I don't know. She wouldn't tell me his last name. I think the first name kind of slipped out. What I do know is that this Raúl character has a lot of money."

"She said that? So, he's rich. How rich?"

"She didn't say. She wouldn't say. Like his first name, I think that bit of information just popped out, and then she closed the vault."

"Okay," Delgado said, rubbing his hands together. "We're looking for a wealthy man named Raúl. Not much to go on, but I've solved cases with less."

"Wait a minute!" Ortega said. "Who has a lot of money? Doctors, among others."

"So, we're looking for a doctor named Raúl. And we know that a doctor figures in the *Venezolanos*'s death somehow. That's definitely something."

"There's more, though." Ortega reached for his cell phone. Switching it on, he typed rapidly, scrolled for a few seconds and then read the entry he had pulled up, at first to himself and then aloud.

"From *El Tiempo* three years ago: 'Raúl Uligheri, a cardiac surgeon at the Jaramillo Zambarano hospital in Manta, was sentenced to five years imprisonment and the loss of his license to practice medicine.'"

The article went on to explain that the ex-doctor had falsified documents and committed other irregularities so that he was able to move preferred patients—ones with plenty of money—up on the waiting lists for heart transplants. Essentially, he had been convicted of selling vital organs to the highest bidder.

A later article dated about six months ago said that Uligheri had been released early from prison due to overcrowding. A crowd of nearly two hundred gathered at the prison in Guayaquil to protest—relatives who claimed that the ex-doctor's actions had resulted in the death of, or permanent harm to, a loved one.

"There are no more recent articles," Ortega said. "Nothing about where Uligheri might be now."

"We don't need them," Delgado declared. "We know from Señora Vasquez that he's in Manta. And we know that he's not working at any legitimate hospital. Not with that conviction hanging over him. But Señora Vasquez told you that he has a lot of money. What does that tell us?"

"It tells us that he's working at the Hankook Clinic."

"Right. The underground clinic that's such a secret that half the police force knows about it."

"Is that where we're going then?" Sergeant Ortega looked as if he might levitate up out of his seat from sheer excitement. "Shall I go back to the station and change clothes again?"

"No," Delgado said, and Ortega slumped visibly. "No time for that. We have to assume that his ex-girlfriend has warned him that we're on his trail."

"Why would she though?" Ortega wondered. "He's her ex. And he might have killed her new boyfriend."

"A woman like that. Who knows what she might do?" Delgado turned away and looked out the side window, leaving the sergeant to wonder: *A woman like what?*

19

"Shouldn't we have backup?" Ortega asked nervously as he piloted the SUV around the traffic circle on Calle 12. "They have guards. They're armed, you know."

"So are we, Sergeant," Delgado replied.

"Yes, I know." Ortega seemed to be having trouble swallowing as his hand went to the butt of the revolver that he carried on his hip. Delgado saw that it was a .38 caliber Taurus revolver, a cheap Smith and Wesson knockoff made in Argentina.

"Have you ever fired that thing?"

"Of course. I scored a ninety-five on the range just last week."

"I meant," Delgado said, "have you ever fired it in the line of duty?"

"No." The palms of Ortega's hands were suddenly sweaty on the steering wheel. He removed them from the wheel one at a time and rubbed them on his uniform pants.

"Well, this may be your lucky day."

The captain went back to studying the passing scenery, and Sergeant Ortega dried his hands one more time.

The Hankook Clinic was at the end of a two-block dead-end street off Avenida 103. Seen from the street, the two-story structure could have been anything—an abandoned office building, a seldom-used warehouse. All the street-facing windows had been covered over with white paint, making it impossible to see inside, and the front door was secured with a thick chain and a big brass padlock. Ortega stopped the SUV a half block before the clinic to avoid the cameras mounted on the front of the building.

"How do you get in there?" Delgado wanted to know.

"See that dirt path, there between the building and the big concrete wall? You walk down there. There are cameras all along the path, and when you get around the corner, to the back of the building, it looks like the front of a regular clinic. There are no signs or anything, but there's no mistaking where you are."

"Seems as if you know your way around the place pretty well," Delgado said with a leering grin. "Maybe you brought a girlfriend or two here to, you know—"

"No! Absolutely not!" Ortega took his hands from the wheel and it looked for a second as if he might attack the bigger man.

"Okay, Sergeant. Calm down." Delgado's grin faded quickly. They were about to head into a potentially dangerous situation, and he couldn't afford to have the sergeant's mind distracted by righteous anger. "I'm sorry," he said. Ortega nodded tightly, but Delgado waited until the sergeant's breathing had returned to normal before he spoke again.

"That's the only way in?" He indicated the narrow dirt path. "No rear entry?"

"No. The property is completely surrounded by those big walls. And, look." He pointed to the top of the wall.

"Razor wire," Delgado muttered. "The same in the back?"

"All the way around."

"Hmm. And the backyard. How wide? How much room between the building and the wall?"

"Maybe two or three meters. Not much room."

"Grass? Dirt? What's the surface?"

"I think it's all concrete. It's kind of broken up and uneven."

"How many men? Armed men? Where do we run into them?"

"There are usually two. One has a sawed-off shotgun. The other, I think, just has a pistol. They have a room toward the front of the building where they watch the video feed."

"So, if we go charging down that path, they'll be ready for us long before we reach the backyard."

"Yes." Ortega worked his tongue side to side, trying to summon up some moisture to his parched lips.

Delgado pursed his lips in frustration and then pointed to the chained up double glass doors in the front of the building.

"Where is this command center, relative to those doors?"

"Just a little to the right of the doors. It was a big supply closet, I think, but they've got it set up with state-of-the-art surveillance equipment." He allowed himself a brief smile. "The guards even have uniforms, but I don't think they're legitimate."

"No, probably not." Delgado cocked his head and regarded his young sergeant thoughtfully. "Now, don't get all upset again, Sergeant, but you do seem to have a pretty extensive knowledge of how the place is set up."

"My former superior officer, Captain Reinoso, was the one who . . ."

"The one who provided them protection," Delgado finished for him. "What happened to him?"

"He retired about six months ago. You're his replacement."

"So then, do I get his piece of the action? Sort of an inheritance?"

Ortega squirmed in his seat, clearly uncomfortable with the direction the conversation was taking.

"Oh, this is going to be good, I can tell." Delgado rubbed his hands together. "Come on. Give it up. Who gets the bite now?"

"Ruíz."

"Ruíz?" It took a lot to surprise the jaded old detective, but Ortega had succeeded. "The provincial commander?"

Ortega couldn't keep himself from smiling, but Delgado's next words wiped the grin from his face.

"You knew that this operation is protected by our boss? My boss! The one who has the power to send me to someplace even worse than this hellhole?"

Ortega nodded.

"And you didn't bother to share that bit of information with me?"

"I couldn't find the right time." Ortega looked down at his hands and then looked up, making direct eye contact with the captain. "And I didn't think it would matter."

Delgado sighed heavily and opened the car door.

"You're right," he said, "it doesn't."

20

"Don't try this in forward gear," Delgado advised as he started the engine. "Something will poke a hole in the radiator, and you'll be dead. Maybe literally."

The captain and the sergeant had traded places in preparation for their assault on the Hankook Clinic. Delgado dropped the shift lever into reverse and backed about fifty meters down the narrow street. He executed a reverse U-turn and adjusted the mirrors in readiness.

"Buckle up, Sergeant, but be ready to bail out of here as soon as we get through that door. Stay low and try to keep the car between you and the guys with the guns. Okay?"

"Okay," Ortega agreed.

Delgado studied his junior partner's face and had an uncharacteristic moment of regret. Who was he to ask this young man, a father-to-be no less, to risk everything like this? It wasn't the fact that they might both lose their lives—Ortega had made that decision the moment he first put on the uniform. But they were about to cross their commander, a powerful and ambitious man. There wasn't much that Ruíz could do to Delgado, really. What could be worse than where he was now? But Ortega had his entire career ahead of him.

The captain shook his head briskly from side to side. *Get yourself straight, Juan*, he told himself.

"What are we waiting for?" Ortega's question jolted Delgado out of his reverie.

"What, indeed?" He mashed the gas pedal to the floor and the SUV rocketed off down the street backward. At a point just short of being even with the double doors he cranked the wheel hard to the left. The car shuddered as the tires struggled for traction. They bottomed out once as the car jumped over the curb, and a second time as it took the one step up to the front-door landing. By the time they crashed through the doors, the SUV had blown two tires and the engine had begun to smoke.

Sergeant Ortega was out of the SUV before it stopped moving, his .38 out in front of him. The two guards had seen their approach on the video monitor but had only time to get up from their chairs. A sawed-off shotgun leaned against the wall, too far from them to do any good.

"On the ground!" Ortega yelled. The two guards hesitated, not with any idea to fight back, but rather they were stunned by this turn of events. Delgado struggled with his seat belt, but finally freed himself and burst out of the car.

"You heard him!" Delgado yelled. The guards hit the floor.

A man wearing green scrubs, a mask, and a surgeon's cap rushed out of an adjoining room.

"What is going on here?" he demanded.

Even with all the chaos surrounding them, Delgado and Ortega both recognized the voice that they had heard on the dead

Venezuelan's phone. Ortega was the first to react. He pivoted to train his revolver on the new arrival.

"Raúl Uligheri, you are under arrest for the murder of Aquiles Jaramillo."

21

Sergeant Ortega sat at his new desk in the UPC building reading the report on the arrest of Raúl Uligheri. He was not a fast reader, and he struggled with some of the bigger words. At times he had to consult the dictionary that he found in a drawer. The report contained not a single mention of Captain Delgado or his part in the case. The name of the arresting officer was of course Sergeant Ortega, and the investigating officer was listed as none other than Osvaldo Ruíz, the *Comandante* himself.

It was as if the captain never existed, and at times it seemed to Ortega that the whole escapade had been a dream. But what a dream it had been. He felt again the thrill of blasting through the front door of the Hankook Clinic, and the feeling of power when he leveled his pistol at Uligheri and placed him under arrest.

Uligheri, it turned out, had moved up from performing illegal abortions and providing medical assistance to criminals. He had graduated to harvesting human organs. Renata Vasquez who, as Ortega had suspected, was quite a beautiful woman beneath her drab exterior, would lure unsuspecting men to a secluded location with the promise of sex.

Then Aquiles Jaramillo, who turned out to be the originator of the scam, would disable the prospective lover, either with the drug scopolamine or by injecting them with a strong sedative, supplied of course by Dr. Uligheri.

The scheme began to unravel when Jaramillo and Renata Vasquez began an affair while she was still involved with Raúl Uligheri, at least according to Raúl. It didn't show up in the final report, but Ortega smiled as he remembered Renata's characterization of her relationship with Raúl Uligheri.

"He spent money on me," she said. "He gave toys and candy to my children. That was the only reason I was with him at all." She made a face. "He smelled like antiseptic all the time. It was never serious between us."

The disgraced doctor disagreed. He had confronted Aquiles Jaramillo, but the younger man laughed in his face. After stewing about it for a few days, Uligheri set up a meeting with Jaramillo in the alley behind the chicken joint. There, he injected strychnine directly into the Venezuelan's heart. Death was almost instantaneous, and the doctor had been able to upend the skinny fisherman into the blue plastic barrel where he had been found, the look of surprise and shock frozen forever onto his face.

The phone call had been a last-minute idea. As Delgado had suspected, the doctor bought a SIM card at a local tienda, inserted it into his phone for the one call, which he had hoped would cast suspicion away from him, and then tossed the card into the trash.

Ortega signed the report in the space allotted for the arresting officer and got up to put it in the mail pouch that would go in the morning to the commander's office for his final signature. His phone buzzed with a text from his friend and fellow sergeant, Wilson Escovedo.

Airport Road in one hour?

Ortega sighed and rubbed a hand across his face. His star was rising quickly in the department, but the baby was due in less than two months and they still needed so many things.

See you there, he texted his friend.

22

Juan Delgado waited in the terminal for his eleven-forty-five P.M. flight home to Cuenca. He hated flying, but the only other option was to spend seven hours on a bus. The overnight bus, it seemed, was always full. Ecuadorians, being thrifty people, would rather spend ten dollars on a bus than twenty-five on a hotel room for the night. The thought of a night spent trapped in a tin can full of squalling babies and snoring *campesinos* was more than he could bear.

At heart, Delgado was a practical man. If he were to admit the truth, he should have left the force when they exiled him to this backwater hellhole. But he felt that he had made his point. He'd solved the murder of Aquiles Jaramillo quickly. Wasn't that what he was paid to do? The higher-ups liked their murders solved with a minimum of fuss, but that had never been his style.

Delgado remembered with great satisfaction rocketing through the front door of the Hankook Clinic behind the wheel of the unmarked SUV.

The meeting with Ruíz had been short. Delgado had composed and printed out his resignation letter in an Internet *cabina* near his temporary apartment. He had laid it on the *comandante*'s desk along with his badge. Like all members of the national police he had purchased his own service revolver, so he kept that.

Ruíz didn't seem surprised at the captain's opening move. In fact, he seemed more interested in how Delgado had circumvented his policy and obtained the SUV than anything else. The commander was a young man with big ambitions, and the wily old captain played on that. In the brief conversation that followed, there was no mention of the fact that Ruíz had been accepting money in exchange for allowing the clinic to operate without interference. There was, however, the very clear indication that there should be no retribution against young Sergeant Ortega.

"Ortega is a good man," Delgado said. "You should count yourself lucky to have him."

The commander nodded his agreement, and it was done. Delgado was a free man. A free man with no job and a meager government pension.

He reread the text he had received earlier from his son.

"I'm getting married in June. I hope you and Mom can make it."

Had Delgado been in front of a mirror he might have wondered what the strange look was on his face. It was a smile.

*When I retired from my "real job" in 2014, my wife and I sold everything and relocated to Cuenca, Ecuador, where we lived for six years. We had contracted with a driver to meet us at Guayaquil Airport and take us on the four-hour trip through the Andes to Cuenca.

Emilio turned out to be the perfect individual to introduce us to our new home. He was friendly, knowledgeable, and his English was great, having lived in Minneapolis for ten years.

As a writer I am always looking for new characters, and Emilio's journey intrigued me. What would it be like to leave your home at the age of twenty-one and travel to a frigid northern city where you knew no one and didn't even speak the language? And what changes would you find when you returned?

Emilio was the inspiration for my Ecuadorian PI Wilson Salinas, whose first story appeared in the July 2017 issue of Alfred Hitchcock Mystery Magazine. Wilson needed a nemesis, so I created Capitán Ernesto Guillén of Ecuador's policía nacional. I made the captain an overbearing, bungling, corrupt tub of lard—a bit of a stereotype I admit. Then I began to wonder: what if he was still overbearing, fat, and corrupt, but was in fact a skilled investigator. Thus began my second series set in Ecuador—The Capitán Guillén Mysteries.

I had a lot of fun with Guillén, especially having him banished from Cuenca for various offenses and sent to some coastal backwater town. As a fat man, Guillén loved the cool springlike weather in Cuenca and hated the hot and humid climate on the coast.

I did some readings and book signings in the seaport town of Manta and thought that it would be a fantastic location for a mystery. For the purposes of this story, I changed Guillén's name to Juan Delgado and the rest is history.

We are back home now in the Pacific Northwest, to be nearer to our family, but I will always have a warm place in my heart for Ecuador and its people. I dedicate this story to them.

Sean Marciniak *is a former crime reporter, and his nonfiction has appeared in* The Wall Street Journal, The Dallas Morning News, *and other newspapers. Somewhere in the colon of the Internet, you might find a news story he wrote about Senator Orrin Hatch, his patriotic music albums, and the senator's biggest fan—a dude from East Texas who bought more than a thousand copies of a single Hatch album. Marciniak hopes to have similar fans one day. His own creative works—short stories—have appeared in* Mystery Tribune, J Journal, *and elsewhere, and have been nominated for Pushcart, PEN America, and other awards. When he's not writing, he's trying to catch up on sleep, raise a family, and figure out witty things to say on Twitter (spoiler, it never happens; see @sean_marciniak).*

OCTOBER IN KAUAI

Sean Marciniak

Our plan to run away had imploded. All the money was gone, every last Bitcoin.

"That was three thousand dollars' worth," Kayla said. "How does it just disappear?" We were both fifteen, and three thousand dollars had been a fortune to us.

"It's complicated," I lied. "It's not so easy to explain." Also untrue.

She closed her eyes, she shook her head. I knew what she was thinking. She was thinking of the hundreds of hours we'd logged at the supermarket, making birthday cakes for strangers.

I remember we were sitting on the roof of Kayla's house, north of downtown Schenectady, under an October sky. The low valley splayed before us, a sea of rooflines penetrated by church spires and antennae, and the General Electric sign with its fourteen hundred light bulbs, scripting the company name atop the factory. It was after supper, the light fizzy, when neighbors settled in to watch their game shows and test their aptitudes. Kayla chewed the end of her dark hair.

"So you got hacked," she said. Not a question. Her jaw flexed against her olive skin, her neck corded. She'd never trusted in digital currency but, in just a year, the value of Bitcoin had doubled—and so had our savings.

I watched a light bulb flicker out in the GE sign. "We didn't get hacked," I said. "That had nothing to do with anything."

"It was Francis then, wasn't it?"

Francis was what we called my dad.

I nodded.

Since the department put him on leave, Francis had spare time to take an interest in my life. He learned about my job at Price Chopper, and took an old push-button calculator and guesstimated my earnings. It was only a matter of time after that. At the precinct they'd called him "the juicer." His proficiency at interrogation, at squeezing confessions from the Schenectady locals, was the subject of local legend. It was part of the reason, too, he was on leave.

"Hey," Kayla said.

I looked over.

"We'll start over. I'll open a Trustco account that he can't touch." She reached over and laid a hand on my forearm.

I drew my elbow back and away. "Christ," I said. Under my sweatshirt there were fresh, second-degree burns, new since the morning.

Kayla took a breath, then swept her hair up and tied it into a knot. "Let me see it," she said, her black eyes still and resolved. I rolled up my sweatshirt, past the yellow and purple marbling of old bruises, and showed her. The four parallel burns were each an inch long, raised and glossy.

"Jesus," she said. "What is this?"

"It's nothing."

She leaned in and studied the marks, unafraid. Then pursed her lips and blew warmth across my skin, moving her chin back and forth. The fine hairs on her forehead caught the last of the day's light. I parted my mouth to say something.

Kayla looked up. "Tell me," she said.

I shook my head—shook it of everything I couldn't say.

He'd been cleaning his fingernails with the tine of a fork. Francis was always grooming himself. Combing hair with an old-school black comb, de-linting jackets with a shaving razor.

Swallowing two rolls of breath mints a day. The house was a dump but Francis walked out of it each day in shoes polished to reflect the sky above, with a shaved jaw, with immaculate fingernails. Inside the home he looked like you'd expect. A caveman, hair at different pitches and yaws. Gritted canines. It was no different that morning. He asked me about the money, where it was, how much, his words tight, the fire danger high. So the truth came quick. Because, shit no, I didn't want him screwing a thumbnail under my jawline again. Or holding my head to the table and pressing a Q-tip deep into my ear canal.

After I finished talking, Francis broke from his manicure and regarded me. The skin around his eyes gathered itself, a new idea born.

"You should be ashamed," he said. He stood, fork in hand, and crossed to the stove and turned one of the knobs below the General Electric insignia. His body shielded the stovetop, so I couldn't see at the time that he'd pressed the fork to the coil. "I've had little gangbangers in the box," he said, "not even out of middle school, who won't talk no matter what you do to them. But you"—he checked the stovetop—"that was a lot of money you had. It's okay with you, huh, that people can just take things from your pockets?"

Kayla didn't need to know any of this. I rubbed the heel of my sneaker against the roof, loosening grit from the shingles.

"He spent it all on Amazon," I told her.

She blinked. "What?"

"You can buy things on Amazon with Bitcoin. We're getting almost twenty packages tonight. He'll sell them on the hill for half of what they're worth."

"Koshe," she said. "I don't care about that, okay? I care about your arm." Her hand found its way around my shoulders. "Hey, look at me."

I couldn't. Our money had been for tickets—for me, for Kayla, and our best friend McNally. The plan? One-way flights to the tiny Hawaiian island of Kauai where, we'd read, there were secret tunnels on the old sugar plantations, leading to secret valleys. Hidden waterfalls and clandestine swimming pools. We were blessed with the idea that something was possible just because we could think it. But when I revisit what we believed, what motivated us, I don't think it was stupid. Even still. We were seeking something we'd lost so early in our lives. That sense of wonder.

"Koshe, I'll tell McNally, okay?"

I nodded. McNally was like my brother, and I was fed and watered at his house a couple times a week.

"You focus on Francis," she said. "On getting him back. It's time you did this."

She was driving at something in particular. In August he'd come home with an iPhone and asked me to set it up. It wasn't store-bought—it had to be jailbroken—and I found myself erasing photos and texts belonging to a kid who went to Schenectady High. In configuring the device for Francis, I built a back door into it, which meant there was a portfolio of deplorable things on the menu here. Planting stolen credit card numbers. Filling his camera roll with photos of adolescents. But at the end of the day, I could think up whatever I wanted. Even Kayla knew the cops wouldn't arrest Francis. Evidence would vanish, leaving just me and him alone at a kitchen table.

Below our feet, beneath the asphalt shingles, Kayla's mom yelled at her dad. It was a full-on holler, her mom's voice husky, maybe a word or two away from tears. Her dad yelled back, so it went. Kayla put her head on my shoulder and began to sing. It was an Italian song she'd learned from her grandmother. I don't recall the words or the melody, just her voice. Her low register, the static in her tone, as though filtered through an old radio grabbing signals from a distant land.

Kayla cleared her throat. "Let's get out of here," she said. "There's something I want to tell you."

The walk to the railroad bridge took us through the neighbor-hoods and into the pine forest. The wind died at the tree line and it was only us, the steal of our footsteps over bedded needles, the scent of pitch.

She had something to tell me, she'd said.

My feet lost touch with the earth and I felt it—transcendence. Transcendence over the endless gray days we faced, the milky light from an estranged sun, a winter that lasted into May. None of that would affect us, we had each other. There'd be no need for Kauai.

We arrived at the abandoned railroad tracks and followed them to the bridge. It was an old iron warhorse of a bridge, built the same time as the Erie Canal, spanning a deep ravine. At the edge of the hollow, where the ironwork projected from the falling ground, we found the trapdoor and eased it open and climbed into the chamber below. Workers had used it to access the railroad trestles but that was long ago. This was a forgotten place. Not even the seniors had found it. A hundred feet below in the belly of the ravine, they smoked dope and fondled each other.

I closed the top hatch while Kayla turned on her iPhone's flashlight and lit the kerosene lamp.

The cast of the small fire danced across the walls. Kayla had etched drawings into the iron plates with a slotted screwdriver, her lines silver and shiny. She preferred the bold style of the graphic novel, but it wasn't superheroes populating the walls. The protagonists were small figures dwarfed by big places. One man adrift in a rolling ocean. A young woman diving across the face of a mountain. Maybe that's why she picked Kauai. It was part of an archipelago that had the audacity to stretch fifteen hundred miles across the Pacific Ocean. In a corner we kept rolled posters of the Nā Pali coast.

In another corner we'd stowed sleeping bags, patched with duct tape. I shook them out. Kayla reached up to hang the kerosene lamp on a hook, and the waistband of her panties flashed from above her blue jeans. We weren't boyfriend and girlfriend, but I'd spent the whole summer riding my bike past her home.

I zipped together two sleeping bags and we pulled off our boots and fit ourselves in. Kayla smelled of scented soaps and lotions, an intoxicating confusion of lavender and cocoa butter. This was all something new. It'd started in July, when she'd traded in her boy T-shirts for halter tops. I think McNally and I both noticed, though it wasn't something we spoke about. It wouldn't have been okay if we both liked her.

"What did you want to tell me?" I said. It was all I could do not to squeak.

Her body tensed.

"So," she said, and a giggle escaped her. Which was a strange thing, because Kayla wasn't the sort who giggled.

"This just kind of happened," she said, her eyes dancing. "I gave McNally a blow job."

She seemed giddy, like she was excited to tell me. Like this was something I wanted to hear.

And all I could think was, McNally? The hygiene issues aside, there were a thousand reasons it shouldn't have been him. He was uncircumcised. The missing link between Sapian and Neanderthal, a kid with a loop of cartoon music playing in his head. What connection could she have with him? With his apple-pie family. A dad who favored talk of mortgages and airline points, a mom who fretted over the DNA test results of her pets.

I looked away, blinking back salt water, wondering what signs I'd missed, wondering what would become of me. Kayla and McNally were my only friends, and they were evolving. Me? Not so much, apparently.

God knows what humiliations I would've suffered next if the trucks, growling and diesel-fueled, hadn't rolled up overhead. An old road followed the railroad tracks, with no sanctioned access, and only two kinds of people drove this route at night: cops, and robbers. Kayla and I sat up together in the shared sleeping bag. She unzipped the bag, stood, and snuffed the kerosene lamp. I stood too and took her hand. In the dark we held our breath.

There were two vehicles, pressing the gravel flat. One engine died, then the other, then the tick of cooling engines. A door opened, followed by boots, crunching through the dirt and rocks, until the bridge clanged under the stranger's weight and his soles came to rest on the trapdoor, feet from our heads.

There was only one other way out of our chamber. A small door led to the undercarriage of the bridge, a skeleton of iron girders that crossed and angled to the far side of the ravine. I wasn't a Mensa candidate, but monkeying our way through the trestles in the dark, I knew, wasn't a solid idea.

The man standing above us took a husky inhale—God, it sounded like his mouth was at our ears—and threw something into the ravine. There was a grunt as it left his hands, the whisper of rip-stop nylon under quick, violent friction. A few moments later we heard the sound of something breaking through canopy branches, then pinwheeling through piles of leaves and knocking across rocks.

A slow clap followed from the access road. "Bravo," another man called.

The man above us huffed. "Enough," he said. "Wipe it down, then we go." His voice was big, his accent shaped in the Eastern Bloc.

The trapdoor whined as the man shifted his weight and he stopped short, as if aware for the first time of his footing. He must've leaned over. I heard panting at the gaps around the trapdoor, then a tentative knock, as if to test for solidity. Of course he found none.

We waited. We squeezed each other's hand.

"It's done," the other man barked.

A long second passed, the universe choosing among outcomes, and the big man's heel turned against the iron trapdoor. His footfalls clanged over the bridge and onto the gravel, ten steps, maybe a dozen. Vehicle doors opened and closed, and one truck pulled away.

Kayla and I sat down, side-by-side, fingers still interlaced. I tapped out sixty seconds on the softer flesh between her knuckles and, hearing no more noise above us, I whispered, "Let's go see."

The abandoned truck rested there like a creature asleep on the earth. A rhino or other large ungulate. Ten, maybe fifteen feet tall, a shade darker than the trees behind it. I climbed from the iron chamber to my waist and picked up a chip of gravel and flung it at the vehicle. The ding carried far into the cold night.

I waited.

Nothing moved inside the truck. Nothing crawled from beneath. I waited a minute more. "C'mon," I told Kayla, and helped her from the bridge, clasping the small bones in her hand. I thought of McNally at home at this moment, not here, not helping, sunk into a leather couch, mesmerized by the Superman movie he'd insisted on seeing.

The moon was nowhere in the sky but when my eyes adjusted, I knew dead-on what we were dealing with. This thing sitting twenty yards away had the unmistakable boxy shape of a UPS truck. With the proper squint, I could pick out the yellow shield on the side, the riveting too. My first thought was that nothing alive sat within the truck. My second thought was that the great category of un-alive things included thousands' worth of UPS packages.

"Let's go," Kayla said. "This is someone else's problem."

But I wasn't having it. This was our find. Our treasure. Kayla might've had marathon make-out sessions to go back to but I had nothing. Not even a place to sleep that night. Staying with Francis wasn't doable anymore. And my mom? She'd married another cop and moved to Tampa, which seemed a lot like Schenectady but with bigger bugs.

I circled the truck and approached at the back corner, then sidled up its length, along the yellow pinstripe to the passenger door. It'd been fixed open and I stood at its edge, listening, until there was only the low-toned tinnitus in my ears and the thrum of blood pushing through my chest.

Dread. Most of all I felt dread, fueled by the thought of dead body, slumped around the next turn. Francis once made me watch a video from evidence, of boys who'd made a pipe bomb and blew themselves up. I thought of their hollow eyes and purpled, open lips.

But Kauai.

White sand.

Twisting, thousand-foot waterfalls. Utopian communities hidden in the jungles on the island's northwest coast, welcoming all so long as they had love in their hearts. Kayla and McNally and their love would be background music, overcome by bigger notes.

I steeled up and shoved my head around the corner to look. Keys dangling from an ignition. More importantly, no body.

Rinse and repeat, stepped into the cab, turned on my phone's light, and forced myself to look into the maw of the cargo area. No body. Just packages. Hundreds of packages. My face lost its rigidity, my lips slackened, and for the first time in weeks I smiled. Because the thought also occurred to me that maybe, just maybe, all the packages Francis made me order through Amazon Prime were sitting there, just feet away.

That we could be made whole.

"It's clear," I called.

Kayla dashed across the gravel and hopped up into the cab and beheld what fell within the oval of my phone's light. "My God," she said.

"Un-effing-believable."

"Hold on." Kayla turned around and lifted her camera into optimal selfie position. "Say cheese," she said.

I rounded on her. "Are you serious?"

It was too late. The camera flashed, a blinding one-two assault of strobes. My mouth dropped open, but I never got to say "stop." In that single barbaric stab of her thumb, she'd exposed us. In the photo's metadata was our geolocation, the ESN of her mobile phone. The time, the place.

"Please don't post that," I said.

"Dummy, we haven't done anything wrong." There was an eye roll. "I'm just going to send it to McNally."

Eye rolls, selfies, trading texts. What was next? Pigtails? Cherry chapstick? I meant to run her through the science of cell towers and metadata, but what I said was, "Put the goddamn phone away," sounding . . . like Francis.

"What did you say?" She knew exactly what I'd said, but was giving me a chance to refine history.

"I'm sorry." I started to say more, but she held up her hand.

"Let's just get what we need and go. We'll talk later."

She made a flashlight of her device and shined it across the insides of the truck. Shelves on either side, the packages labeled, ordered. All bar codes facing out.

"What if—" But she didn't finish. She'd arrived on my thought about Francis's purchase order. "C'mon," she said.

The packages were arranged by street addresses. It was much like finding a book by author in the library, our eyes dancing across the names, then zeroing in. And I had to read the labels twice but there they were, eighteen packages occupying the lower shelf at the truck's rear, all bearing my name. Jack Kosciuszko.

Kayla looked at me, gave me a kiss on the cheek.

But happiness in Schenectady has a short half-life.

The tap of fingernails on metal paneling broke the moment, because those fingernails didn't belong to us.

Two members of the senior class choked our exit to the cab, and there was nothing in that doorway I liked.

"If it isn't little Kayla and her skinny friend," said Posy Sayles. She held a bag of chips in her hand and blew a crumb from her lip. Her cousin, Shane, rested both hands against the stainless-steel panel over the exit, leaning in and bending at the elbows.

They were well on the other side of puberty, and they looked like L.L. Bean models—tall, fair-haired, limby, blue-eyed. Dimples and good teeth. But they weren't the sort to preen before catalog test shoots. They were the sort to spend Tuesday nights smoking weed in the belly of the ravine and, if the study hall rumors had it right, mess with each other in ways frowned upon in the Bible. The sort to tag team freshman girls in the school's boiler room.

Posy stepped first but Kayla was quicker. She blinded them with her phone's flashlight, meanwhile scouting the back of the truck for something useful. I tried the rear door handle—it was locked, immobilized.

"Shine that fucking thing somewhere else," Shane said, his hands raised before his eyes.

Attached to the rear corner of the truck was a small black box, disemboweled, wires poking in scattered directions. And below that one of those tiny crowbars, the sort they call a cat's claw. With the ease of a marionette Kayla dropped down and palmed the tool and stood back up.

"This is ours," she said, brandishing the claw.

"Oh no, sweetie," Posy said. She dropped the bag of chips and closed the distance between them and took hold, too, of the cat's claw. "Shane," she said, looking over her shoulder, "are they making good decisions?"

A butterfly knife appeared from the pocket of his jacket and in two flips and a twist the knife split and rejoined, the blunt halves latched, the blade catching every last photon in the truck.

Posy was a full foot taller than Kayla, and looked down into her. "She's pretty, don't you think Shane?" Posy's grin was easy, her eyes glassy, her smell a blend of autumn leaves and cannabis. With her free hand she took Kayla's jaw in her hand and angled it this way and that. Her fingers were long and they scrolled up the sides of Kayla's mouth and formed her lips into a pucker.

Kayla looked out the corners of her eyes, her pupils tremoring, seeking me out. But I couldn't move. This was something she didn't know about me, not for sure. That my move was to play dead, go stiff and belly-up like an opossum. So many times, with Francis over me, nostrils flaring, fists raised. To stay still was to survive, and I leaned out of Kayla's periphery.

In that moment it was understood—by me, by Kayla—why McNally was the proper choice. I thought again of McNally watching superhero movies. I thought too of all the ice hockey games Kayla and I had watched him in, half the size of other players but muscling them out of the lower slot, diving in front of pucks, chips of ice flying. McNally, with his oversized knuckles and his under-evolved threshold for pain, would've done something that night in the truck. He offered the best chance of survival in this world we knew, and whatever affection stretched between Kayla and me was woven only from sympathy.

Shane spoke. "Get rid of the kids," he said. "This isn't the time for your sick shit." His eyes, bloodshot and rounded, flitted around the cargo hold. He leaned back into the cab and eyeballed the open door.

Posy gave a little up-down look to Kayla and, maybe satisfied to find inferiority, pushed her face away. Kayla stumbled back into the rear of the truck, the roll-up door rattling.

Shane beckoned us forward with his knife. I took Kayla's arm and we side-stepped around his cousin and up toward the cab. From his back pocket he withdrew a device, something akin to a fat TV remote, and shoved it into my gut. "Here's your consolation prize," he said. "You're going to keep it in your locker, and I'm going to bed-check you. Got it?"

When I didn't answer, he told me to nod.

I nodded.

"Now split," he said.

Kayla and I parted ways at her house and I took the city bus back to Mont Pleasant. Blue lights flickered through curtains along Erie Boulevard, the residents enchanted by loud-talking men on infomercials armed with kitchen knives, sawing through nails and aluminum cans.

The plan had been to stay at McNally's, two streets from my house. I'd stashed my backpack and a sleeping bag in his boat, which sat up on a trailer, ready to be winterized, at the side of his house. McNally's bedroom light was on when I got there, his curtains backlit and amber.

He'd made a mess of my phone, with bubble-after-bubble of texts. "Koshe, lemme know when you're here." "WTF, where is everyone?" I pictured him in his clean clothes, laundered with scented soap and fabric softener. A functioning house. A good family. He only would've come to Kauai out of loyalty, not need. Loyalty and, apparently, blow jobs. So no, I didn't want to see him, I didn't want to see anyone. That image of Kayla, that wild-eyed look of hers—imploring me to *do something*—wouldn't quit my mind. I tried to reimagine what'd happened with different running commentary. Just run-of-the-mill bullying. More bark than bite. But each time things replayed, the voice-overs rendered things cleaner but the images got worse. Posy with a hand on Kayla's mouth, her throat, her thigh, between her legs. Until I wasn't sure exactly what happened. Kayla hadn't said a word to me the entire walk home, just a quick goodbye at her house, then the back of her head.

McNally's golden retriever eased from his doghouse in the backyard and ambled up to the fence at the end of the drive. He pressed his muzzle through the chain link. "Hey Buster," I said, and reached over the fence and rubbed the hollow behind his ear. The dog pressed into my hand. Loyal, brave, which was all that mattered. I glanced up at McNally's window, then pulled my arm back over the fence.

The boat's canvas top was secured with a square knot, easy to loosen. I slipped under the fabric and into the boat, where I pulled my laptop from my rucksack and connected it to one of the 12-volt batteries that McNally's dad kept under the seats.

The screen's blue light washed the underside of the canvas and the waxy vinyl of the boat seating. While the laptop chirred, I unfurled a sleeping bag and unpacked my toiletries. This was an old routine.

A baby-wipe, taken from the supermarket, to clear the day from the corners of my eyes. A dry-brushing of the teeth, the taste of metal along my gums.

The screen blinked on, the desktop materializing. I exhaled the day. Just the four corners of the computer display remained—no fourteen-foot fishing boat, no tattered Kmart sleeping bag, no trainwrecked night. Here was the place I kept my superpowers. Here was Clark Kent on the threshold of a phone booth, and from the other side I'd emerge into a world where I could pass through boundaries, move through people's lives, with nothing more than the gentle shower of keystrokes.

First I hijacked the neighbor's Wi-Fi. About fifteen percent of the world doesn't change its network name, which defaults to the make and model of the router being used. Ms. Kowalski, who lived next door, fell into this fifteen percent. Knowing her equipment, I put in the manufacturer's default password (also unchanged) and, bingo, I was online. Koshe-1, world-0. Next came the anonymous remailer, then Tor. Layers and layers of protocol, leaving me without an IP address, without fingerprints.

On the school's server, where I had root privileges, I looked up Posy and Shane, their grades, what teachers said about them in emails. There wasn't much—the cousins operated with impunity under their shield of dimples and frontier good looks. To the extent incrimination existed, it blew back on our educators. The younger history teachers, a group of men with goatees who coached football and lacrosse, had interesting things to say about my female classmates, including Kayla. Talk of turning "bro-downs into ho-downs." Ending sentences with poetries like "plunging in to the hilt."

I found, too, emails about me, sparked by Francis's headlines. *Schenectady "River Rat" police unit under investigation. Hamilton Hill community demands dismissal of SPD sergeant.* The emails about me circulated among a group of teachers I liked. People who did decent things. Who hosted book clubs, who put together fundraisers for Third World refugees. Some had seen the bruising, some had kept me after class. They'd speak in gentle tones and make meaningful eye contact, but to tell them anything? I pictured them in a room with Francis, the men with their thin necks and prominent Adam's apples. The women with their conflict-free clothing, who grew teary about police brutality affecting other races. Their support was fair-weather. One punch to the nose, one rock through a window, one small brandishing of the .38 he kept on his ankle—that's all it'd take. Good causes were plentiful, these samaritans would find another.

The temperature had fallen, my breath condensed into a cold steam. A soft rain pattered against the canvas overhead. Fuck it, I told myself, and took screenshots of the history teachers' bro-down conversations. My fingers blurring across the keyboard, I placed the image captures in an email from a dummy account, populating the recipient field with the email addresses of the superintendent and the Schenectady Gazette. My cursor hovered over the send button.

This wasn't something I'd done before. Prior to that night, when I got into systems, it'd been enough to be somewhere forbidden. The thrill was in the trespass.

I hit send. I did it before my brain fully locked on to the idea. I don't know what I'd sought—power, maybe justice—but I realized that, whatever I'd set in motion, it chanced only at solving the wrong problem. This plot didn't end with goodnights from Kayla.

I sat up and the little gadget, the one that Shane had saddled me with, fell from the yawn of my sweatshirt pocket and clunked across the boat's floor. It was a funny little thing. Like a television remote but chubbier. The exterior was badly damaged, the screen cracked, the UPS logo above it scuffed. I imagined its being tossed from the bridge, landing in a pile of leaves only feet away from Posy and Shane with their hands in each other's pants.

It was dangerous to have—Shane's gesture was no accident of generosity. If he came under fire for stealing UPS packages, he'd narc on me. The device would be in my locker, it'd be my problem.

The Internet called it a DIAD. One gigabyte of memory, expandable to thirty-two with a micro SD. Equipped with GPS. With each specification learned, it felt less and less like kryptonite and more like a tool. More like a little handheld computer that UPS drivers used to collect signatures and record the delivery of packages. And more like the key to solving the UPS truck mystery, which I had to get out ahead of.

Now, because the device had GPS capabilities, I didn't even want to think about turning it on, having imagined a team of UPS tech support in a situation room, waiting for it to ping concentric circles on a digital map. I bounced into a couple chatrooms to see about disabling it, and one of my contacts from Europe emailed me, saying he could help. László had been a UPS driver in Hungary—I hadn't realized UPS existed outside America—but he walked me through the DIAD, knew what wire was what and, within twenty minutes, we powered up the device without SWAT descending on McNally's driveway. László also sent over pirated UPS software, which I used to download information from the device.

It came spilling across the screen. Hundreds of lines of data. A thousand tiny puzzle pieces washing across a proverbial kitchen table, each with a purpose that, with diligence, would amount to a comprehensible whole. And what the data showed after assembly was a complete list of packages delivered that day. The times, the locations, where the packages had been stowed on the truck.

Including the truck's last recorded delivery.

That last package had been destined for Alpaus, a small hamlet north of the Mohawk where Kurt Vonnegut lived while working at the GE factory. But looking at a map, it was easy to see why the truck disappeared there. The area was wooded, there were fewer witnesses. You didn't have to be a criminal mastermind to figure it out, just the son of a police sergeant.

For a while I followed the truck's route using Google Street View, moving in circles, going nowhere. It was when I stopped focusing on where the truck had been, and focused instead on why it'd been taken, that things jelled. Because wouldn't someone steal a UPS truck for its packages? Maybe one package in particular? But to know this, I'd have to go back to the truck—to see what was missing, but never recorded as delivered. The stupidity of it aside, the crime scene wouldn't have been preserved. Shane and Posy no doubt had looted the hell out of it.

Except for one thing.

Kayla's selfie, the photo she'd taken inside the back of the truck. A digital record of what had been.

It was after midnight but I texted her all the same. I asked for the selfie, and for her forgiveness. An ellipsis appeared on my screen, almost immediately, and I had a quick thought that maybe I'd been too hard on myself. That maybe everything was cool between us. Kayla and McNally would be a thing, okay, but I could sit with them at the lunch table. Tag along for a movie.

She only sent the selfie. No words, no emojis, and I thought of how she handled asshole customers at Price Chopper. Efficiently. Curtly.

In the photo Kayla was playful, with an over-pronounced lip pout. Then there was me, sour, my mouth midopen in complaint. A total fucking tool. But ah, the background, divided into twelve million individual pixels, hundreds dedicated to each label on each package. Zooming in, I started cross-referencing these against the electronic manifest.

Ultimately I'd been making things harder than they needed to be. Because on the top shelf over Kayla's shoulder, there was a small gap in the assemblage of boxes. Like a missing front tooth. Package 1Z789475849934234, weighing 16.5 ounces. Missing but never delivered.

It was three o'clock in the morning. I noted the relevant address, gathered the sleeping bag over my shoulders, and fell into a dreamless sleep. Just screens of cyan code scrolling over a dark window. Humanless, solvable.

The missing package was addressed to a duplex, shelved on the street among many similar duplexes. Families on top, families on the bottom, constructed when the City's great-great-grandparents came from Poland, Italy, and Ireland. The house I'd come to see had off-white paint that matched the sky, a patchy lawn, wind chimes. Nothing special.

I must've walked by a half-dozen times, milking a candy bar, wondering what to do, when I thought to check the garbage for clues. Two metal cans huddled against the side of the home, in an area that cops called the curtilage—a place where they could search trash without a warrant. I finished the candy bar, folded the wrapper, and strolled over to the cans and lifted one of the lids. Torn bags of cement occupied the top strata of garbage.

A curtain twitched above my shoulder.

I looked up. Tattered lace, darkness beyond. It'd been subtle, maybe figmental, but it'd been enough for me. I walked away, didn't look back, aiming for the street corner, burying my face in my phone, thumbing through email, looking at news, appearing inconspicuous. Another meatball teenager.

I probably would've ended up back at McNally's except my obsessive refreshing of Google News picked up the missing UPS truck. Missing, too, was the driver, and a thumbnail picture showed him and his wife smiling, both with bad teeth. Crimestoppers offered a reward of five thousand for information leading to the driver.

Five thousand dollars. I could repay Kayla and McNally twofold. All I needed was credible information, legally obtained.

I turned around.

I studied the porch for signs of kidnapping or murder. Like stained garden tools, jugs of Chlorox bleach. But there were only the wind chimes, tinkling sound across the street, and a welcome mat, embossed with bowling pins and a ball.

My knock died against the hardwood door. A television yammered inside, the words blunted. I rocked on the balls of my feet, deciding, deciding, when a man answered. He wore navy coveralls, and wasn't looking at me but over my shoulder. A big man, muscular, well over six feet, each limb twice the width of a normal extremity.

"Sorry," I said. "I have the wrong—"

"Voitec, let the boy in." A granny hobbled up from behind, tall as a broomstick and a hundred pounds wet. "Don't mind him," she said, her voice reedy, each word crackling. "Come in, we don't get many visitors."

Five thousand dollars. That's what I told myself.

It was sweltering inside, the air practically wavering above the wall heaters. The granny wore a sweater, and she bunched the knitting around her neck as Voitec closed out the chill and locked the door. Sweat beaded at his hairline, and he mopped himself with a rag. The faint scent of plums and alcohol drifted through the foyer.

"Voitec," the granny said, "take the boy's jacket."

"I'm okay."

The granny shook her head at me. "Give him your jacket."

And I did. Passive, compliant, I unrolled myself from my coat and handed it to Voitec, who stuffed it into a closet jammed with winterwear.

"His shoes too," the granny said.

There was no part of that I liked. The granny wore Reeboks, and Voitec wore boots—the heavy steel-toed kind. The granny watched me noticing things.

"Come, follow me. You are safe here." Her eyes were round, clear, and blue. "I have made fresh babka and I think you will enjoy it. Now, please take off your shoes."

I took them off but left the openings wide, easy to slip into. She thanked me and took my hand, her grip dainty, papery, and led me to a kitchen. A blond woman sat at a round, laminate table, smoking a cigarette, watching a thirteen-inch television on the counter. A baby monitor, one of the old analog kinds, lay on its side by her elbow. The TV vibrated with the sounds of a pro wrestling match, two three-hundred-pound men, their shoulders juiced and oiled, poking fingers into each other, spraying personal space with spittle.

"You like this?" the granny said to me, pointing at the screen. She eyeballed the woman at the table. "Bah, I remember Ivan Putski, the Polish Hammer. He could take the handle of a sledge-hammer in one hand and touch the stone back to his nose. But this, today, is what children like. Razzle-dazzle."

The young woman's eyes were dully fixed on the TV, the cigarette burning in her hand. A trickle of smoke disappeared against the tired white of the ceiling. She was older than me, in her twenties or thirties. Bruises covered her arm, fresh ones, still black-and-blue. A dark blotch curled under her jawline too, ashen under her makeup. There was something familiar about her.

I scanned the kitchen. Bowling trophies littered the top of the refrigerator. A two-gallon jug of plum brandy anchored the counter, next to a picture of the last Polish pope. And the walls bore photos of family members—school portraits, family groupings. But it was a void, an absence, that caught my eye. A rectangular lull in the photography, the wallpaper there darker. A picture had been removed, someone edited out.

The granny took the cigarette from the woman at the table, took a drag, and placed it back in the woman's hands. "What's your name?" she said to me, the smoke dribbling from her mouth.

"Koshe."

The granny turned to Voitec and said something in Polish. My own babcia spoke Polish to me as a baby, so the sounds and rhythms were recognizable. The meaning was not. Voitec nodded and opened a door. It led to a basement and he disappeared into its depths and shut the door behind him. At the threshold a layer of fine, gray dust plumed across the linoleum, imprinted with his footprint.

"Koshe?" the granny said. "That's not a name. Your given name."

"Jack . . . Kosciusko."

The woman at the table turned to look at me. She took a pull from her cigarette and exhaled. The injury to her jaw prevented her from making an "o" of her lips, and the smoke filtered through a jumble of gritted teeth, gray in color. That's when the recognition kicked in. Those mismatched teeth. She was the UPS driver's wife.

The granny, her eyes steady, moved between me and the room's exit. "Your people are buried at the St. Adalbert cemetery. On the left side, nineteen rows back."

"Yes ma'am." It was true, all the dead Kosciuskos in Schenectady were buried in the Polish cemetery she'd named.

"You are related to Jan Kosciusko," she said. That was a second cousin of mine, a night janitor at the middle school. "And your father," she said, "is Francis Kosciusko."

"Yes."

"A good man," she said, and studied me from her wide-set, blue eyes. I thought of a cat's stare, curiosity mixed with heartlessness. "He'd been strong," she said. "It's too bad."

I moved toward the door. "I really need to get going," I said, and went to pass her.

She grabbed at my sweatshirt, latching onto my forearm, closing over the burns. Her hand was pure bone and leather, each finger a claw. Black dots bloomed across my field of vision—I yelped. The granny looked surprised.

"Boy, roll up your sleeve." She released my arm.

I did as told, and her eyes traveled my skin. Over the bruising. Over the burn marks too. The woman at the table watched us, and our eyes met for a moment. I found sympathy there, but no offer of help.

"Come," the granny said. "Let's get you some ointment, away from this." She waved at the pro wrestling program and led me back into a room with thick carpet. Glass cases lined the walls, filled with porcelain angels. A small cardboard box with a shipping label sat on the floor, its flaps splayed, its bubble wrap disturbed.

She showed me in.

"I have to go," I said. "I've got the wrong house. I was looking for the McNally place."

"Sit." She placed a hand on my arm, over the burn marks, enough pressure for me to pay attention. I realized, then, there was no ointment in that house. That wounds in this house would heal on their own, or they wouldn't. The granny stared into my eyes. "You're a nice Polish boy, yes?"

I agreed.

"Our people," she said. "Do not sing."

I started not feeling well.

"We take care of our own problems. Consider my granddaughter—" the granny looked back toward the kitchen—"poor thing, kicked and smacked for so long. She's a stupid girl, she cannot choose men, but she is mine. Only mine to hit. No one else's."

She released my arm. "Please sit."

I lowered myself onto a couch.

"Now," she said, taking a seat beside me, "you are not a stupid boy. You are a smart boy, a boy who is good at figuring things out. Tell me, then, what brings you here? Not a pledge drive, you are too old to be a Boy Scout."

I said nothing.

"If you'd like," she said, "I can call Voitec." She nodded at the branding on my forearm. "We can make a place setting. A spoon, a knife."

I thought on this.

I told her everything.

About the DIAD, about finding the UPS truck. About the missing package, about the electronic manifest. As I spoke I found myself turning my arm and body away from her, my movements paced in millimeters. Her grip had cracked some of the scabbing, the burns wet at the fractures.

The granny seemed to take each thing I said like it was a piece that would or would not fit together. At times she'd stop me, not to ask questions but to process what I'd said, and when I finished, she sat for a minute. A clock ticked from the wall.

One of her glass cases sat ajar, and the porcelain angel inside still had a price tag affixed. Its hair was blond, its face pitched down in shame. Its wings had scales. I'd been to enough Roman Catholic masses to recognize the angel that fell.

"And this interests you?" she said. "Information on a computer, when you have so many packages in the truck?"

Her phone buzzed then, and she produced it from a fold in her dress. An off-market kind, with the Jelly Bean operating system and an origin in a Wal-Mart Supercenter. It was a burner, pre-paid, cheap. I'd used them on occasion. So did drug dealers and, according to my dad's friends, Schenectady's organized crime. The granny checked the number on the screen.

"What kind of phone is that?" I said.

Her arctic eyes lingered on the display, then unstuck themselves. She looked back and called over her shoulder in Polish. The only word I understood was "Voitec."

"How did you buy it?" I started to rise but thought better of it. My mouth, however, was on a tear. "Look, you can't buy them with a credit card. The phone's ESN is matched to your credit card, and the carrier receives the data when it pings off the cell towers. And you shouldn't make calls with it in any sort of pattern, and definitely don't use it near times and places when you use your other phones. The police pick up patterns, and they can use it. . . ." Half of this I knew from my dad's work. Some came from the Internet, and the rest I made up.

"Boy," she said, "I am not a fool."

I just kept talking. "The analog baby monitor," I said. "The one in the kitchen. You need to upgrade to digital. The analogs work on 43 to 52 hertz frequencies and anybody with a police radio can listen in. And do you use computers?" I segued into IP addresses and the use of Tor. I mentioned access to the Deep Web and Silk Road.

That caught in her ear. Silk Road. It'd made its way into conventional wisdom in recent years as the Amazon.com for contraband. The granny rubbed a thumb under her chin.

Voitec darkened the doorway, new concrete dust on his coveralls. He said something in Polish and his voice—it was the first time I'd heard it—was a dead ringer for the one on the railroad bridge. A voice that could vibrate the soil. Behind Voitec was another man with a thin mustache and a 1970s haircut. Thinning at the top, combed back straight, and ending above his neck in a cascade of greasy curls. The porcelain angels, so many of them, watched me from their glass prisons.

Voitec and the granny fell into discussion. The Polish came fast, submachine-gun-like in intensity, until the granny threw up a hand and said, "Well then, see what he knows."

The big man knelt down on the carpet and began asking me questions. Technical questions about cell phones, Tor, the Silk Road, the Deep Web. What I didn't know I fabricated. He asked me too about the Schenectady police department's computer network, and I'd seen enough manuals to fake my way through a few sentences.

Voitec stood. "Ciocia Ursula," he said, "Chłopiec zdaje się znać jego gówno." I knew what this meant, my babcia had said it about me as a child. *The boy knows his shit.*

The granny nodded, her mouth and lips thin, but softened. She turned and looked at me, but spoke to Voitec. "He is a good boy. His arms are a mess, but does he tell the police?" she said. "He will be a helpful boy."

Her eyes landed on me. "You live on Holland Road, yes?"

I nodded.

"You will bring me that UPS computer, yes?"

I nodded again.

Voitec pulled papers from his pocket and started flipping through them. It took me a second to realize he was counting off twenties, the money gray in the low-wattage, yellow light of the room. I lost count after he hit fifteen, and at some point he stopped and folded the wad and pressed it into my stomach. "Stan will take you for the device. You will come back tonight," he said. The brandy in his mouth had soured. "We have work for you."

It was night when we left, and Stan didn't talk much on the drive out. I tried to chat him up but he told me to shut the fuck up, and turned up the radio. An AM feed, the Buffalo Sabres a score behind in the second period. I felt the lump of cash in my pocket and counted the edges. Forty edges, eight hundred dollars. Equal to a hundred hours of slicing bologna behind the Price Chopper deli counter.

Stan aside, entering this world held promise. It was full of capable associates, full of chances. A chance of never having to endure another white-eyed look from Kayla, reflecting back atrocities I was impotent to cure. There would be an old me, left behind on the receding side of this night.

Back on Holland Road, Stan put the car in park and told me to get the fuck out. I'd stashed the DIAD in the safest place I knew—under a loose step on Francis's back porch. Only a damn fool would trespass on our lot. Neighbors didn't even park at the curb in front of the house. So when I went around back and found the step dislodged, the inside of it empty, there was only one place the DIAD could've been.

I closed my eyes. My insides were pins and needles. Go in, get the DIAD, I told myself. A member of my new family sat outside in an idling vehicle, within earshot of a holler. Go, I told myself. Don't stay a coward, don't let the cement set.

So I went.

My dad's head sat in relief against the snowy static of a television that was not a flatscreen, the bunny ears at errant angles. He was passed out on the couch, his feet extended under a coffee table. He wore a flannel shirt, unbuttoned, the flaps tucked under his back, his chest and stomach exposed. I'd never looked at my father before, not like this. I'd only seen him in glimpses, snapshots of Francis in various states of rage, various states of dominance. Under the flicker of television that night, his stomach rose and fell, his body hair matted, wisps of old beer and sweat curling from his pores. He was built like the Polish Hammer, his muscles shaped and hardened from manhandling people. But his hands rested on a mound of a belly, the fat subcutaneous, buried and cradling his organs.

The coffee table bore a take-out container, half-full of cold noodles, and a Styrofoam cooler filled mostly with water. A handful of ice cubes and Busch Lite cans bobbed at its surface. And then the DIAD, lying amid a crowd of twelve-ounce cans. I reached for it, my hand trembling.

Francis's eyes opened. "The fuck you doing?"

I grabbed the DIAD.

"You spineless little shit," he said, his voice awakening. "Put it back." Francis tried to get up but he fell back into the couch. He slumped forward and swiped at the cans on the table until he found one that didn't move, then tipped it back and emptied it into his mouth.

The house was dark and, from where I stood, I could see through the front window and across the yard to the street. My friend Stan sat at the curb in the Bronco. Layered in the foreground, I saw a faint reflection of myself. Skinny, pale, a body subsisting on candy bars and processed meats. There were no romantic illusions I'd beat my dad head-to-head. But I had a group now. A gang.

"I've got friends now, Francis," I said. I thought of what the granny told me, about my dad losing his power. "You'd better watch yourself."

But my voice was thin.

Francis scoffed. "*I've got friends now, Francis,*" he said in falsetto, bobbling his head. His eyes cracked back open and found me. "Look, shit stain. Tomorrow I'm going to find your *friends* and break their fingers. Then I'll find you, and beat your hide until it scars, into something serviceable. Toughen you up. And don't," he said, "bother hiding. You can't hide in this town, this is my fucking town. I mean, who the fuck do you think you're dealing with? Huh? Francis Fucking Kosciusko."

By this time he was standing over me, shadowing me.

But I hadn't gone in without a plan. That backdoor into Francis's iPhone allowed me that menu of options. Stolen credit cards. Pictures of adolescents. But what I chose to do was sync my father's phone with mine, and what I did was, hand in pocket, press a certain button on my phone that told Francis's mobile to call the Schenectady police chief's home number. Only I monkeyed with the software so that Francis's phone showed the opposite—that the chief was calling him.

My father's phone was on the table, vibrating against the surface, rattling aluminum cans. He picked it up and took a look. "Don't you go anywhere. Don't—"

"Hello? Francis?" The police chief, growling and tired, came on the line. Francis's eyes screwed up, wondering how this happened without him accepting the call.

I made my move. Out the living room, through the kitchen, out the back door in a burst. My head spun, my knees didn't quite work. The world was spinning on a new axis, but going farther wasn't necessary. Entrance to our basement was through one of those sloping, bulkhead doors, and I circled back and slipped into the bowels of the house. Never would he imagine I'd do such a thing and, there in the dark, I'd wait behind the oil tank, while things settled.

Overhead my father finished with the chief, then stomped through the kitchen. The storm door swung open and he called my name. Then again.

But not a third time.

"You're not fit for this world," he yelled to the neighborhood. "It's going to crush you, just you wait." The storm door clattered shut and his footsteps carried him back to his couch. The springs groaned under his weight and, within minutes, he was snoring.

I pictured Francis. His face. His pronounced brow, his broad nose. How, I thought, had I turned out so different? And yet his nose was my nose. His ears, tinier than you'd think—they were my ears. And I pondered the choices he'd made, the choices I was making. I thought about the granny, about trading masters, about the things I'd be doing in my new life. Jobs involving the Silk Road and ninety-pound bags of cement. I thought on what this meant, about disqualifying myself from all that was good. Maybe Kayla was already lost to me but, soon, all the Kaylas of the world would be too.

The DIAD, though slick with sweat, remained within the stranglehold of my fingers. With my other hand I reassured myself there were forty bills in my pocket.

I closed my eyes. I decided something.

In the basement I situated myself at our workbench in the glow of my phone's flashlight. The soldering iron took a minute to heat, and finding the coil of lead wire took a minute more. Next I opened up the DIAD and removed the battery and located the disconnected wire. With the soldering iron I liquefied the end of the lead, a dewy metallic drop forming, which broke away to seal the gadget's circuitry back in place.

A new energy hummed inside. I opened my laptop and set it on the workbench and ran through my usual protocols. Things happened fast, my fingers dancing across the keyboard. A machine executing commands. Through a voice-over-Internet service I ordered a cab to Norwood—two streets away, with a straight shot to the highway. I called the airline next. The woman at the desk was in a quiet place, her voice worn. Five hundred and eight-six dollars, she told me. And yes, I could buy it at the counter. I confirmed my ID was still in my wallet and re-checked the airline's policies online, confirming minors could buy tickets.

By the time I emailed the FBI, I was feeling right again. I bounced the email through the server of a local public library, pretending to be an anonymous neighbor of the granny who'd seen a body carried in, along with four ninety-pound bags of cement. They could find the empties in the trash bin at the side of the home. They could find the UPS truck at the railroad bridge, and tire tracks belonging to a second vehicle in the dirt turnout at the main road. Maybe a Ford Bronco. I cc'd Crimestoppers—I'd figure out later how to collect their reward, anonymously, and wire it to Kayla and McNally. Lastly, a call was made to Schenectady PD, to report that a sketchy-looking dude in local gang colors loitered at the thirteen-hundred block of Holland Road in a running SUV, outside the home of Francis Kosciusko. "Frankie?" the dispatcher said. I hung up.

Standing on an upside-down bucket, I peered at Holland Road through the freckled glass of a tiny basement window. A handful of flurries sifted under the street lamp. The tailpipe of Stan's Bronco dripped water onto the asphalt.

He saw things before I did, but it was too late for him. High beams swung down the length of the street from both ends. The V8 engines of the police cars roared, though still no sirens. As they neared, the patrol cars threw the neighborhood into a disorientation of blue and red light. I hoisted my backpack over a shoulder and slipped out the back, then over the chain link.

Before we left the Schenectady city limits, I told the cabbie to make one quick stop. At Posy's house I got out and popped the battery into the DIAD and placed the device behind the garbage cans alongside her garage. In the curtilage. Elsewhere, in a faraway UPS control room, concentric circles radiated outward from a single dot under my feet, I was sure of it.

"What was that about?" the taxi driver said when I got back in.

"Nothing," I told him. "A computer game I borrowed from a friend." The driver rubbed his jowls. He shook his head at the nerdiness of it.

I recall little after that. A quick memory of passing highway, the General Electric sign receding. The quiet curb of the Albany airport, just one or two milling around on a late Wednesday night, bundling themselves against the wind over the hardscape.

Because I was done with Octobers. The endless gray skies, the endless gray lives. I was headed to a better place. And I can tell you this. The water here in Poipu is warm, the sea turtles will swim within inches of your fingers. The tunnels are real, so are the secret valleys of Hanalei. The Milky Way writes itself across the sky, the light from a billion stars arriving just now, carrying only the image of what once was. Most nights I sit on the beach under starlight and thumb my way through songs on a ukulele. I know that looking into the sky is looking into the past, a reminder of worlds never conquered, and it's only during these moments when I dare revisit the industry that made this dream.

In high school I worked at Ellis Hospital in Schenectady as a mover of people and medicines, which gave me authorized and unauthorized access to most corners of the one-hundred-thirty-year-old hospital. There's nothing like sitting on the roof of the building and watching the sun set over the skyline. The church spires. The General Electric sign that unspools across the top of the factory. It is not an energizing vista. It's like the sun gives up on the city day after day. But it is a city replete with people that will make you laugh until you choke, a city of devastating stories, and a city rich in grit. Oh, the grit. I wrote this story as an homage to this place, and this story got rejected thirty-two times before it saw daylight. The story was too long. It wasn't literary and it wasn't genre fiction but it wasn't not either. Read that a few times, it'll make sense. I think. But the story found a home and plenty of life and I'm grateful to those who saw something in it. And it makes me smile that there's a badass, stylized version of my grandmother, herself born and raised Schenectadian, in the third act of the story. Rest in peace, Granny! You're welcome!

Stefon Mears *was raised by lawyers, and the two decades–plus that his father sat on the Private Defender Panel for San Mateo County gave Mears a distinct view of crime and criminals. Best known for his space fantasy* Rise of Magic *series, Mears has published twenty-one novels so far, including the* Cavan Oltblood *high fantasy series, the* Telepath Trilogy, *the* Spells for Hire *urban fantasy series, the* Edge of Humanity *urban fantasy series, and a number of standalones in different genres. Mears's short pieces have appeared in more than twenty professional magazines and anthologies, and a dozen collections. Look for him online at http://www.stefonmears.com, as well as Facebook and Twitter. Sign up for his newsletter at stefonmears.com/join, or his Patreon at patreon.com/stefonmears.*

GUN RUNNING ON VACATION

Stefon Mears

1

JON

It all started with a colossal fuckup. And I was looking at him. Derek. My best friend for ages, and partner in crime for the past decade. Might as well have been brothers. We were close enough, and we looked the part. Both tall, lean, blond, and mean.

Well, Derek was the mean one. He had the OC pedigree. I had the head for money. Yeah, I could handle myself, but Derek's bad-boy streak made me look strictly G-rated. By all rights, he should have had a facial scar or an eyepatch. Some kind of warning not to push too hard.

Didn't look mean right now. Had that hangdog, I-know-I-fucked-up look I'd seen way too many times over the years. Shoulders slumped, head hanging forward, lips pulled in tight.

And this fuckup, this was the worst of all.

Of course, part of the reason for that is that I was hearing the worst possible news in the most beautiful place on earth. A beach just outside a little town called . . . well, let's just say it's called San Fernando. It's down in Baja, on the Sea of Cortez, and you can probably figure out its real name if you try hard enough. But you won't hear it from me. Not after the way things went down.

The April sun was blazing that day, at least to two boys from the Pacific Northwest. Barely noon, and so hot already that I could feel my sunblock melting down my face. So bright my sunglasses needed sunglasses.

But the place was worth it. Explained why people liked the beach so much. Lots of toasty sand, and blue-green water—not the vicious, dark blue of the Pacific or the Sound, both of which were what I knew best. Here it was more green and inviting.

And so warm. Nothing like the icy death trap of ocean water up around Washington and Oregon. The water here was like wading into a warm, welcoming, armpit-deep hug that gently rocked me.

And it seemed we could wade forever. We'd wandered out into the water while talking—before we got to Derek's news—and even a good hundred yards from the shoreline, the water still wasn't touching our shoulders.

Even smelled salty and clean here, which surprised me. Didn't have the kind of decay odor I usually associated with my infrequent youthful trips to the shore.

Not to mention the peaceful beauty of the chaparral and desert behind us, or the exquisite beauty of some of the other tourists, both American and Mexican, frolicking back by the waterline.

All this. And Derek had to go spoil it.

"You lost *all* our money?" It was the third time I'd asked the question. I still didn't want to believe it. Wanted to think this was some stupid joke. *Ha, ha. Just a little vacation humor.* Poor taste, but better than the alternative.

But no matter how many times I asked the question, Derek's answer didn't change.

Slow intake of breath, nostrils flaring. Grimace. Nod.

"No, you son of a bitch," I said, loud enough that Derek winced.

I had to stop and check to make sure we were alone out here. Seagulls squawking overhead. Laughter back at the shore where the smart, reasonable vacationers were having fun on the crowded beach. Fishing boat motoring by a few hundred yards farther out.

Right here, just the two of us.

I lowered my voice anyway.

"No, you son of a bitch. Don't you just nod at me. You say the words."

"Yes, Jon," Derek said, eyes still downcast. "I lost all our money."

"Let me get this straight," I said, then needed a shaky breath to hold my temper. My knuckles were aching to do something unconstructive. "Not only did you go find a poker game last night, which we have both agreed you're not supposed to do. You *suck* at poker."

I gave Derek a chance to deny that, if he had the guts. But he didn't. Maybe that meant he'd finally learned his lesson? Either that, or he had a plan. And I was angry enough to assume the latter.

"Not only did you do that, instead of a rendezvous like you *claimed* you had," I continued, "but you took *not only* your walking around money. *Not only* your share of the vacation money. But *all our goddamn money*?"

Derek started to nod. Checked it. Said, "That's right, Jon. The buy-in was—"

I held up a warning finger and cut off that excuse right away, then shoved that hand back into the sea to keep from doing anything else with it.

Ten thousand dollars should have been more than enough for a freaking vacation. And this idiot . . .

I clenched and unclenched my fists under the water. Took a slow breath.

"So you're saying the sixty-odd bucks I've got in my wallet is all we have until we get back to the States?"

Derek nodded.

I shook my head.

"That's not going to cover enough gas and food to get to San Diego, Derek." San Diego was the closest city where we had cash stashed in a safe deposit box. And right then, it might as well have been in outer Mongolia. "Not to mention what we'll have left on the hotel bill over and above our deposit."

That part was my fault. I liked late night room service garlic fries. But compared to what he'd done . . .

Another slow breath. My heart was pounding with the kind of driving tempo my fists were requesting.

My fists would have to wait. At least until I heard his plan.

"So?" I said.

Derek looked up at me. Eyes narrowed.

"Let's hear it. There's no way you take the heat without bitching, even when you're entirely in the wrong. Not without waiting until I lose enough steam that you can tell me your solution. Out with it. And you better hope it's good enough that I don't drown you right the fuck here, which we both know I should do."

Derek could take me in a fight. We both knew it. That he chose not to point this out only told me I really wasn't going to like this plan.

I didn't. Oh, I let him finish before I started in on him, but this . . .

"Derek," I said, once he laid out the particulars, "do you remember the little agreement we made back when we started working together?"

"Yeah, we—"

"We were very clear on who we are, and what we do. We steal cash from the outfit boys before they can stash their ill-gotten gains in overseas accounts. And what do we *not* do?"

Fire in Derek's eyes now, but I was fine with that. I was sick of being the only angry man in this conversation. He shot back what I wanted to hear, but he did it in his most sarcastic tones.

"We don't move drugs. We don't move guns. We only touch cash."

"And what is this brilliant solution of yours?"

"*Necessary!*" Now it was Derek's turn to check his volume. "Look, you smarmy bastard. I fucked up and I know it. But we can't pull our usual moves here. We can't exactly spend months studying the ins and outs of the local rackets, can we? Not to mention that we don't speak enough Spanish to do it right. Not down here. But that gun shipment is *tonight*. We get paid *tonight*. It's a one-time thing."

The finger he held up to emphasize his last words at least suited his tone.

"A one-time thing set up by the guy you lost our money to? And you think you can trust this? How do we know the job is the only thing being set up tonight?"

"You have an alternative suggestion?"

"Yeah. Let's steal our money back. Or at least enough to get us back to the States. Sounds like this guy's OC, or whatever the equivalent is down here. At least he's a good target, and then we skip across the border ASAP."

"Oh, this coming from Mr. Cautious? Mr. Study Twice, Rob Once?"

"Well, we're kind of pressed for time, aren't we?" I tapped my chin. "And let me think. Whose fault is that again?"

"Look," he said, trying for something like a calm, if angry, tone, "this guy, he's Hector Fucking Cruz. If he just wanted us dead, he'd kill us. He's a major player down here."

"Why do you know that?"

"Doesn't matter," he said over my disagreement. "Anyway, I already said we'd do it. And he has our names."

"Fuck you," I said, shaking my head. Derek gave my real name to some gun runner? And I was supposed to just *accept* it? "Maybe I'll just call Uncle Sal and have him wire me enough to get home."

Derek caught the singular pronoun there. He also knew the only way Uncle Sal would send me money is if I came home without Derek. Probably wouldn't even wire me money, just a single, nonrefundable plane ticket or something.

Uncle Sal didn't know what Derek and I did for a living, but he suspected it wasn't on the up-and-up, and he blamed Derek for that. Hell, he blamed Derek for my dropping out of business school too. For a lot of things.

And Derek, he didn't have anyone willing to wire him money. Not after that trouble at the docks a few years back.

Derek held up his hands like I'd pulled a gun on him.

"Whoa," he said. "Look. It's a good gig. A transfer between branches of a drug cartel. So regular their security is lax. We slip in, lift one particular crate. The delivery boys won't know it's special, so they won't miss it until delivery is complete. Might even be days before they discover it's missing. Anyway, we drop that crate off, get paid same night, and we're home free."

I just stared at him. Didn't have to say why.

Derek shrugged, but had the grace to look guilty. "He had my name already. I couldn't not give him yours."

"Why did you give him your . . ." We both had fake IDs. Top of the line. There was no reason to give anyone our real names. Not unless . . .

Slow breaths. Just keep clenching and unclenching those fists. Anything to keep from using them.

"You didn't just lose our money, did you." Not a question. My tone was flat with certainty. "You let him front you when you ran low."

"Another five grand worth."

I shook my head. Started to turn back toward shore. Ready to let him dig himself out of this one. Maybe he gave my name, but if I never showed up for the crime, it was just hearsay.

But Derek dropped the big one.

"You owe me."

Now Derek and me, we'd covered each other's asses many times over the years. So for him to say those words, we both knew what he meant.

Derek was the reason my father was no longer around to beat me. As of back when we were both fifteen. First guy Derek ever killed. First body I ever helped hide.

"Fine," I said, and sighed as I turned back to look at him. My best friend. My brother in all but blood.

My next words tasted bitter. I had to say them though. Derek was still gambling more than he could afford, and with the wrong people. Now he was handing out our *names* . . .

"I'll do this. But then I'm out."

2

MARIA

I stretched my arms, languorous, feeling like a cat in a sunbeam. Trying to milk the last of that setting sun.

The sun wasn't more than a fat, red-orange sliver now, over the mountains in the distance, and the crowds were off seeking their dinners. Only a few remained out here, anywhere near me. A couple sharing a towel that wasn't big enough for two. Two kids with a rubber ball and the happiest collie on earth. Playing and splashing as the tide came in. Their laughter as constant as the break of the waves.

This morning was racing ATVs across the chaparral. But I'd spent most of this afternoon—my final day on assignment down here in Mexico, and the only day I got any playtime—here on the beach. Stretched out on the big red towel that matched my bikini.

Felt weird, having the sun set behind me while I stared out across the water. I grew up around Malibu where the sand was more white-brown than the yellow-brown down here, and where the sun set over the ocean.

I wasn't at the ocean though. I was on the wrong coast of Baja for that. This was the Sea of Cortez. Little too green for my tastes, but it felt warm enough whenever I felt like getting a dip instead of baking my skin an even darker shade than my Salvadorian heritage blessed me with.

Went through enough suntan lotion today that the coconut aroma even flavored the fish tacos I'd snacked on a few hours ago.

The thought of fish tacos made my belly rumble. I checked my phone. No messages, and I still had time before I had to report for tonight's op.

With a sigh I slipped my feet back into my flip-flops and stood. Shrugged into my white floral cover-up that hung to my knees and put at least a little netting between my bikini and onlooking eyes. Enough for beachfront decency, anyway.

I shook the sand out of my towel, slipped my bag over one shoulder, and sauntered back toward the asphalt a few hundred feet away.

The street bordering the beach was filled with parked cars, even now. Only a dozen or so cruising for a parking spot. I wrinkled my nose and pretended I couldn't smell their gas, but already my sense of my idyllic afternoon was shattered.

Not more than a few hundred feet from where I'd been stretched out, and here was humanity. For better or worse. Mexican and American pop music pushed its way out of the sprinkling of restaurants, both the open-air Mom and Pop places and the indoor, sit-down types. And mixed in among the restaurants, sidewalks and storefronts crammed with enough *tourista* crap to power a smaller country's GDP.

The stores were mostly empty right now, but the restaurants looked too full.

I sighed. If I had to wait anyway, I might as well wander up the street a ways and see if I could find one that looked like locals patronized it, instead of just the tourists.

Not twenty paces along the sidewalk—beach side, so I didn't have to deal with eager salespeople—and already the old game kicked in.

Spot the Dealer.

One of the things I learned in the DEA is that pretty much anytime you get enough people together, there'll be at least one drug dealer present. Became a game with my class of trainees. We'd go to malls, shopping centers, sporting events, nightclubs, and so on. We'd watch the crowd, place our bets, then one of us would "try to cop."

Not actually trying to buy. Just asking the right question to establish it was possible. "Are you holding?" or whatever the local variant was. And every locale had its own variant. In this particular beach town, the question was either "*Fumar?*" or "*Oler?*" depending on whether you wanted pot or coke. Either worked for meth, apparently. And I forgot to ask about the opiates. Reminded myself to do that before heading back home.

I spotted three potentials as I strolled along. Two guys, one girl. All dressed nondescript. Baggy jeans and plain Ts. Hair slicked down, could be any color from dark blond to black, in this lighting.

All three lingered on the street, paying the right kind of attention. Noting who was passing them. Assessing, but assessing like salesmen, not robbers. Is this my target audience? Does this person seek what I'm selling?

Except, of course, they didn't have any visible product to sell.

Wrong game to play right then. Spoiled my mood. After a long, fun day, I was tensing up again. My jaw clenched, shoulders tightening. I didn't have time for this. I wasn't down here for street rips. I was down here on the exchange program, sharing information and training with the Federal Police.

Took a deep breath and rolled my shoulders. Tried to recapture that languorous feeling, but the sun was nearly gone. I was seeing as much by yellow streetlights as by what remained of the day. And I couldn't smell my coconut lotion for the gas and oil smells of the street. My stomach continued to complain that it wanted one more round of fish tacos.

I had to look away from the crowds. Try to reset myself.

That was when I spotted him.

I'd have noticed him even if he weren't gorgeous. No way to miss a guy who sits on a bench that way. With his butt on the back of the bench, and his feet on the seat. Arms resting on his thighs like his shoulders wanted to slump and he wouldn't let them.

And those thighs were as lean and tight as the rest of him.

Growing up around the beaches of Malibu, I've always had a thing for surfers. This guy, he wasn't a surfer. Too pale for that, and his blond hair didn't get enough sun to get the right shade.

But Lord, he had the body. Slender and *tight*.

He even dressed right. Checkerboard Jams instead of something too tight and showy, and brown boat shoes over bare feet.

Normally I'd've just enjoyed the sight in passing, and gone on about my way. Especially since I had an op tonight. But it was my last night in Mexico, and I hadn't had any time to flirt all week. Even after an afternoon alone on the beach, in my best bikini. Must have gotten too good at the casual keep-away vibe.

If I came back without a story about the boy I met in Mexico, my team would never let me hear the end of it.

So I slowed up as I approached.

"You look like you just lost your best friend."

He looked over at me, his gray eyes distant. Didn't even give me the subtle check-out, which meant one of three things: 1) he was a gentleman, 2) he was wrestling with something serious, or 3) he liked his women chesty, which I was not.

"Might've," he said with a shrug. "Not sure yet."

I ruled out option one right away. This was a bad boy. Now I could claim I just had the right kind of eye to spot bad boys a million miles away, but really, the kind of scar he had along the left side of his ribs only comes from a knife.

Option three, well, if that was the case he'd shoot me down soon enough. And so what? Wasn't like I wanted to sleep with the guy, or like I'd lose any Zs over a hottie who couldn't appreciate my trim build.

So I decided to assume option two. I joined him on the bench, sitting just the way he did.

"Tell Juanita all about it," I said. Wasn't supposed to use my real name on the street down here. Just in case.

"Believe me," he said. "You don't want to hear this."

"Long story?"

"Very."

"So tell me over fish tacos." I tugged on his elbow. "I'll even buy, if you tell me your name."

"Jon," he said, blinking and frowning like the answer came out before he thought about it.

"Well, Jon," I said with a smile. "I'll buy, you talk."

Maybe it was my smile. Maybe it was the teasing tone. Maybe it was the offer to buy. Whatever it was, it was like someone got home and turned on the lights. His eyes really looked at me now—staying to my face, but in that way that I knew meant he'd checked me out with peripheral vision—and his smile was worth seeing.

We found a little place, tucked back in from the street. Ordered fish tacos, and a Dos Equis for him and a bottled water for me. *Almost* changed my mind on the possible gentleman front, because he ordered the beer without thinking and apologized. Didn't want to order beer on my dime, if I was drinking water.

But decent manners alone do not a gentleman make. He scanned the little restaurant, eyes lingering on the same things mine did.

The big guy in the corner, eating alone. A local. Nose broken at least twice. Ears boxed. Definitely the kind who liked to fight. Like maybe if anyone joked about such a big guy at such a little round table.

The fact that the tables near him were empty seemed to confirm that he was trouble. Locals were eating here, and knew not to crowd him.

Two exits, and the front door was the only good one, if there was trouble. Back exit was through the kitchen. Tight hallway. Even one person in the kitchen coming out at the wrong time could close it off.

Two plainclothes police at a table by the counter. Keeping an eye on the guy in the corner.

Jon frowned when he spotted the cops. Covered it quickly, but still. Bad boy confirmation.

Other than that, the place was nice enough. Well swept floor, not too many flies. Three kinds of hot sauce on the table. Decent paper napkins, not like those kind you need six of just to get grease off your fingers.

Brown stucco walls, decorated in broken piñatas. Colorful, but sad, in a way.

No music in here. Fútbol on a decent flat-screen television, set high on the side wall. Broadcasters so excited, it must have been the playoffs or something.

We were the only ones not watching the game. Even the cops took turns watching the game and the big guy.

"So, why might you have lost your best friend?" I asked after we had our drinks.

A flash of pain in those storm gray eyes, but then he assessed me again. Odd. His eyes frowned like he spotted me for an officer of some kind. He sipped his beer, and it looked like he was buying time.

He looked away and shrugged. Took a deep breath.

When he looked back, I only saw the pain. Figured maybe playing the old game again had made me paranoid.

"Work," he said. "Without going into the gory details, we're freelancers. And he's started taking work that's outside our focused area of expertise. Work I don't want to do. He says it's a one-time thing, but I don't buy it."

"Well," I said with a lopsided smile. "That was vague. If I'm buying you dinner, I want a *story*."

He furrowed his brow in the cutest way. Then I caught him glancing at my shoulders and throat before he spoke again.

"This story's too long for fish tacos."

"Then tell me how you got that scar?"

"This?" he said with a smile. Familiar territory. A story he's told a thousand times, and he's ready to tell it again. Might even perk him up, if that first smile was any indication.

"That," I said with a nod. And I reached out and ran my finger across all six inches of scar, which made him smile even wider.

"Well," he said, drawing the word out. "This was about five years ago. I—"

My phone chirped a text message. Didn't have to see it to know what it was. I threw enough pesos for dinner and a decent tip on the table as I stood.

"Wait," he said, and I memorized the way he reached for me. The raise of his eyebrows. The troubled look in his eyes at the thought of me getting away.

That moment alone was worth the cost of dinner. But it did make leaving harder.

"Sorry," I said with a sigh. "Work calls. Maybe we'll run into each other again sometime."

And I hustled out the door before I was tempted to kiss him goodbye.

3

JON

Even the night seemed to be saying this was a bad idea. Coyotes howling in the distance like they were laughing at us. Night sky flashing now and again with lighting from the storm out over the sea.

Got a bitter laugh out of me, the first time I noticed it. It was a clear sky above us. More stars out here, in the middle of nowhere, than I'd ever seen before in my city-boy life. And still it was a dark and stormy night.

We really were out in the middle of nowhere. Part of Baja is littered with, well, litter, but also abandoned, half-finished houses. Little structures of brick, lacking only the frames and glass for the windows, the doors for the doorways, and, oh, yes, the roofs for their houses and garages.

Derek said the exchange was due to take place in one of those abandoned places.

Our part of the plan was simple.

We drove our car out and parked about two miles away, just off the road. Little piece of paper on it swearing it was out of gas and we were going to be back as soon as we could get a gas can. Figured that would sound enough like a stupid tourist trick to fool anyone who bothered checking on it.

If they even spotted the car in the first place. Only a half moon above us, and a dark car a few hundred feet off the road was pretty easy to lose among all the big bushes of the desert around here.

From there we took a small cart with great big, off-roading wheels, and pushed it parallel to the road in the right direction.

Plan was simple. First crew arrives. Arranges the boxes. Retreats outside to smoke. Derek's "contact" assured us that this was standard procedure. They waited outside so they could see anyone approaching, but they'd been doing this so long they only watched the road side. They'd never see us approaching from the back.

The crew supposed to pick up the crates would show up about half an hour later. Enough time to make sure everything was ready, and maybe a little extra to make the first crew sweat.

Politics and power games were everywhere.

All we had to do was slip in during that half hour, find the right crate, get it onto the cart, and get gone.

Derek called it simple. Dared to smile as he said it.

I thought it sounded like a clusterfuck waiting to happen. Might even have been an excuse to give those drug boys a chance to play Shoot the American.

Didn't bother saying any of that. No point.

Thus, I picked my way across the rocky, dirty desert by night. Even a handful of miles from the sea, the ground was crusted with salt here and there. Especially by the roads, but even out here.

I made Derek push the stupid cart, but I had to help him here and there anyway. Get it over rocks and steer around the jutting bushes that were nothing but a collection of branches full of thorns. Didn't look like they ever had leaves, much less any kind of blossom. Wouldn't even want to call them a cactus.

The night was warm enough. We were dressed like what we were: thieves. Black cargo pants. Black, long-sleeved shirts of a thin brand of cotton to slick away sweat. Black gloves of the same material. Black sneakers and socks. Black caps pulled down tight. Black greasepaint on our faces and necks.

Each of us had a 9 mm on his belt. No more than a dozen bullets each, but that didn't matter. Not really. If we needed more than a dozen bullets, we were toast. These guys were likely to have AKs.

I hated the smell of greasepaint. Even the dry odors of the desert would have been preferable. But no way I was going with a full face mask. Not in this heat. Could get sweat in my eyes at the wrong time.

Death sentence.

But then, the whole gig was feeling like a death sentence.

Took us the better part of an hour to get into position, hiding behind a big rock, maybe a hundred yards behind the right house. Damn near got blinded when I spotted the first Jeeps' headlights. So bright they could have signaled ships in a storm.

I had to turn away to avoid spoiling my night vision. Derek did too. We flattened against the rock and waited until we heard the Jeeps running roughshod over the desert dirt and rocks. Waited until we heard engines cut.

Worked in our favor though. These guys would need time for their eyes to adjust, and while they did I took a count.

Six Jeeps.

"Six?" I hissed at Derek. "There were supposed to be three."

Derek sucked in his lips. Shook his head. "Something's wrong."

"Better believe it," I said. "Both crews are here now. Let's bug out."

"No," he said. "We need to do this."

"Like hell."

Derek put his hand on his pistol.

I blinked at him. Felt like I didn't even know the man in front of me.

"We're doing this, Jon. It won't be so bad. You'll see. Maybe the numbers are bigger, but they'll follow the same procedure. All we have to do is wait."

The sounds of Spanish. Rapid fire. Not like anyone was angry, far as I could tell. Just the normal speed they spoke. Maybe they were cokeheads or something. Couldn't follow any of it.

We crept up on top of the big rock for a better view.

"Derek," I said, pointing at the layout of the twenty men in fatigues, all with AKs. Even the ones moving crates had assault rifles strapped to their backs. "That's two crews. One off-loading, one watching. And counting."

"No," Derek said.

"We need to—"

Suddenly the area flooded with light. Voices through bullhorns. I recognized *armas* as weapons, so it had to be the call to throw down weapons and surrender.

Either the *Federales*, or the army. Coming in from two sides. Whichever they were, this was more than I signed on for.

"Now's our chance," I said. "We slip away into the night before they notice us."

"No," Derek said with his ready-for-action smile. "This is perfect. While the cartel and the *Federales* are busy with each other, we snag the crate and skip."

"Are you insane?"

"It's perfect," he said again. "We just need to get them shooting."

Derek raised his pistol. Aimed at one of the good guys. I smacked the top of his arm just before he fired. Bullet slammed into the back of the abandoned house.

Shot did its job anyway. Guns blazed on autofire. Shouts through a bullhorn.

And back here on the rock, Derek and me, facing off. Murder in Derek's eyes.

I threw my pistol away.

"Fuck this," I said. "I'm gone. Shoot me in cold blood, if that's who you are now. If we go after that crate I'm dead anyway."

For the first time in my life, I turned away from Derek.

And that's when I found out the good guys were coming in from *three* sides.

4

MARIA

Dawn was breaking by the time we'd gotten through most of the processing, after the Clusterfuck in the Desert. Not the official designation of the op, but it might as well have been.

Five dead on the cartel side, six more wounded. None dead on our side, yet, but only because the Federal Police had medical standing by. Just in case. Eight of ours in the infirmary. One might not wake up.

I was still supposed to go home today. As of right now, just after six in the morning. Carmelo, my handler, said the official word had to wait until all the interviews and paperwork were done, but as long as my superiors back home were willing to make me available, if necessary, chances were I'd make my flight.

I wanted to stay. Wanted to see this through to the end. Seemed like the least I could do. But it wasn't my call to make.

One call I could make, though, was whether or not I conducted any interviews. Part of the exchange program, after all, was to compare interview procedures. Plus, two of the guys we'd snagged were Americans. Might say different things to me than they would to the locals.

My paperwork was done, so I went to see about those interviews.

First guy didn't give me much. Said his name was Jason Gibson. Matched his passport, but I had my doubts. Career criminal type, from the way he sat on his hard plastic chair, to his immediate requests for specific types of junk food and soft drinks.

Had the balls to claim he was out in the middle of the night hunting for Mayan artifacts. Dressed in all black, down to the greasepaint, to avoid drawing attention, because he didn't want to have to turn anything in to the Mexican government. Carried a gun to "keep coyotes away."

Big nothing from that interview. The locals might get something if they sweated him for a few days, but not before.

The other American though . . .

An interview room is an interview room. They're all about the same, with a few minor variations in color and material. This place was no exception. Blank white walls, with a big one-way mirror. Camera up in the corner. Mics recording everything.

Steel table, painted brown, with a loop for cuffs. Hard plastic chairs. Red. One on one side, two on the other.

And always the smell of bleach and stale cigarette smoke.

I strolled in and plopped onto one of the two hard plastic chairs on my side. Dressed in my dark brown suit and tie, my hair tied back behind me.

My face deadpan as I stared across the table at the man I'd bought dinner for. Now cuffed to the table. Dressed all in black, even if his greasepaint had been washed away. His shoulders sagged when he saw me. His eyes looked sad as he realized who I was.

"So," I said, letting him hear the anger in my voice. Not fair, maybe. I'd known he was a bad boy. But still. "You're name's not Jon after all. It's Peter Stark."

"No," he said, voice as sad as his eyes, which were now studying the table. He shook his head slowly. "I told you the truth this afternoon. My name is Jon. Jon Rollins. My Washington driver's license number is WVVX66768212. Run it through the system. You'll see my face."

"You confirmed your other identity to agents earlier," I said.

"That was habit. A habit I need to break anyway. And besides." He looked up at me now. "I don't want to lie to you. Not to you."

Those words, or maybe the simple honesty of his tone, sent a shiver through me that I covered by shifting in my seat. Forced my brow down. My lips flat.

"Sure," I said. "Since you're in the mood to be all truthful, why not tell me what you were doing tonight?"

"My friend lost a good deal of money playing poker with Hector Cruz. More than we had with us. To cover his losses, my friend took a job for tonight, without asking me. We were supposed to steal a particular crate. Turn it in tonight. Get paid, and clear out."

I knew the name Hector Cruz. Major arms dealer, with connections all up and down the Americas. I also knew that one of the crates recovered tonight had a new, experimental variety of explosive rounds.

I further noticed that this story filled in some of the details of the vague version Jon told me over dinner. I wasn't sure how I felt about that.

"Is that what you and your friend do? Rob arms shipments?"

"No," he said. He drew a deep breath. Let it out slowly. "What we do, we've never been arrested for. Hell, no one has ever even informed the police about our jobs."

"Then there's no reason not to tell me."

His eyes flicked to the cameras, then the one-way mirror. Back to me.

"If word of this gets out, we'll be murdered. Both him and me." His voice was simple. Matter of fact.

"Have you committed any of these crimes in Mexico?"

"Nope. We weren't supposed to work down here at all. Just a vacation."

"One sec." I slipped back out of the room. Spoke softly to Carmelo, who was watching. "Any chance we can kill the recorders in there?"

"None." Then he shrugged. "But if he's not providing evidence to any crimes you or we care about, something could happen to the recordings . . ."

I nodded. It would have to do. Went back into the room. Took my seat.

"I think we can keep this quiet."

"Then I'll trust you," he said. And I didn't like the way his words gave me a warm feeling. But I let him keep talking. "We'd move into a city. We'd study the local rackets. Take six months, maybe a year or more if we needed. We'd figure out who was running things. From there, how the money moved. From there, what kind of cycles the big boys followed, when it came to hiding money overseas."

He shrugged. "From there, it was a simple matter of figuring out the weak spot in the chain. We'd hit the weak spot, clear five or six figures in cash, and split town. Hit a new town, and do the same thing. Always slow and careful. Never rushing."

I whistled. Jon, Peter, whatever his name was, was right. If word of this got out, they were dead within a week.

Also, assuming all this was true, arresting him wouldn't do any good. The victims would deny the crimes—they'd never want us figuring out how they moved their money . . .

I smiled. Saw a potential upside to all this. Maybe more than one.

"So," I said. "Where does this partnership of yours stand?"

"I'm done." He shook his head slowly. "My friend has changed. Maybe he's been changing for a while now, and I just didn't realize it. But I'm done." He sighed. "If I have a choice, I'll go back to business school, or maybe—"

He broke off. Looked at me. Saw the same upside I did.

"Look," he said. "My friend, he knows crime better than I ever will. But me, I know money. I was always the one who figured out how the money was moving and where it was going. If you guys can give us a pass for tonight, I would be more than happy to work with you guys in the DEA as a consultant about money laundering and hiding. Maybe even become an agent, if you'd have me."

I almost asked how he knew I was with the DEA, but I did have an ID tag hanging on my hip.

"Your friend discharged a firearm," I said, maybe a little louder than I had to, to cover the way my heart was beating faster right then. "Maybe at the police. Can't be sure. Not sure they'll let him walk for that."

They'd already decided to give Jason a slap on the wrist and send him back across the border. We'd already determined that Jon and his friend weren't part of the cartels. Just two Americans doing something stupid. And the way Carmelo put it, if they arrested every American who did something stupid, they'd lose ninety percent of their tourist trade.

I looked into Jon's eyes, and remembered what he said about not lying to me. And I realized I didn't want to lie to him either.

I shook my head. "They're going to let you both go anyway. Give you a slap on the wrist and send you back across the border."

Jon's eyes widened, and he nodded. Then he got this determined look.

"My offer still stands."

"Why?"

"Yesterday," he said through a sigh, "yesterday I thought I knew what my life was. Told myself I was performing a public service. Keeping American money out of foreign accounts and going into American businesses. Not a good guy, but not a bad guy either. Not really."

He hung his head forward. Started to say something, then stopped and started again.

"My friend, he showed me what we are. Just criminals, pulling jobs." He glanced up at me, and back down. "But maybe I could be more than that."

"Maybe you can," I said. I stood. Started for the door.

"Thank you, Juanita," he said.

I smiled at him. "My name is Maria."

I wrote "Gun Running on Vacation" for an anthology called Fiction River: Chances. *The idea for the anthology, as I recall it, was couples coming together against the whims of fate. Well, to me, that sounded like a federal officer and a career criminal. But the story itself didn't come together until I thought about the setting. I went down to the Sea of Cortez a few years back, on vacation with my oldest friend in the world. I was struck by the beauty of the chapparal and rocky hills, and by the way the warm water of the sea stayed so shallow for well over a hundred yards from the beach. But that wasn't all. On the drive down there from California, we passed by a number of places where the chapparal was littered with the sun-bleached bones of old houses. Their frames and walls remain, but their windows, roofs, doors, all gone. Possibly never installed in the first place. A mournful contrast to the beauty surrounding them. I could imagine all sorts of criminal exchanges and transfers taking advantage of all those house-skeletons. A great place to have my career criminal get caught doing something that would end his criminal career but might just open up a new path for him.*

Keith Lee Morris *is the author of five books of fiction, including the novels* The Dart League King *(Tin House Books) and* Travelers Rest *(Little, Brown). His stories and essays have been published in* Cincinnati Review, New England Review, Ninth Letter, A Public Space, The Daily Beast, Electric Literature, *and elsewhere. He teaches at Clemson University, where he serves as editor of* South Carolina Review.

SLEIGH BELLS FOR THE HAYRIDE

Keith Lee Morris

The woman who came to pick up the heroin was deaf. Later Glen realized he'd known that from the minute he saw her. There must have been some little clue, a certain darting of the eyes or clench-jawed expression, something he recognized from all the years with his brother, Donald. But there would never be a way to go back and determine.

The Palms was exactly how it sounded—a huge nondescript condo development with pink stucco walls and vaguely Spanish flourishes built around a weedy inner courtyard with too little shade. It was early December and hot, even for Florida, a depressing heat that made you think longingly of those old paintings of places in New England, people harvesting pumpkins and hunting turkeys with blunderbusses, wearing Pilgrim hats and whatnot, getting the sleigh bells out to put on the horses for the Christmas hayride. Here in Jacksonville it was sweaty and humid and eighty-two degrees, and a rank smell blew up into the courtyard from the Saint Johns River half a mile off.

He didn't know why he'd agreed to bring the stuff for Arturo in the first place, other than that he could use an extra hundred bucks for going five minutes out of his way, which was how Arturo had put it to him. Glen knew there were drugs going around the construction crew, but he generally stayed uninvolved other than smoking the occasional joint in the truck after work with one or two of the other guys. Arturo made himself out to be some big-shot dealer—heroin, morphine, meth, weed, X, any kind of pills, got your Xanax, your OxyContin, you name it. Maybe that's why he had agreed to do it—just to see to what degree Arturo was full of shit.

So here he was standing in the breezeway of this bullshit condo courtyard in Englewood with a half-ounce bag of brownish powder in his work pants, waiting by the Coke machine where Arturo had told him to. And then this deaf woman comes. When she walked up, he was holding the baggie in his hand, checking out the color and the texture. It seemed totally harmless—some stuff that looked like brown sugar in a plastic bag. How could that possibly lead to trouble? Maybe that was how he knew the woman was deaf—she came toward him frantically waving her hands for him to put the bag away, but she didn't make a sound.

He was amused a little. A quick scan of the area showed they were all alone there near the stairwell. Yeah, okay, it was a felony, technically, but only if you got caught, and there wasn't anyone around to catch them. Some old dude with a walker, maybe, scuffling through the crabgrass.

The woman pulled him farther back into the recess past the Coke machine. "Okay, okay," he said to her, and held up a hand to calm her down. "Where's the money? Just give it to me, and we'll get this over quick." Again he pulled the bag out of his pocket and again she was in quite a hurry to push his hand back. Still hadn't said anything.

The obvious thing—she was dark skinned, had dark hair, high cheekbones, most likely Latina, but he couldn't tell for certain—would have been to assume she didn't speak English, but when he talked to her more slowly now, it was to let her see his lips, like he'd always done with Donnie. "I need money," he said to her. "Arturo"—he waved his hand vaguely in the air to indicate someone far away—"said you'd have the money ready. I just need to get it from you. Or somebody." Then he did it automatically, began signing—*I need money*.

She looked surprised, but pleasantly so. Her hands started moving, but she was going way too fast. He hadn't seen Donnie face-to-face in years, so he was out of practice. "Slow down," he mouthed to her.

She swiped a strand of hair from her eyes and nodded. She looked as if she might be on the verge of crying. He really hoped she wouldn't. His intention had been to get rid of the baggie, collect the thousand dollars, peel off a hundred-dollar bill for himself as Arturo had said to, take the money to Arturo, and go get himself a nice steak dinner for a change, maybe at one of the touristy places down along the waterfront. He hadn't bargained on complications or anyone crying, much less this woman. She looked like a decent type, not a heroin addict. She was only a little over five feet tall, about a foot shorter than he was. Her dark hair was neatly tied back, and her skin was clear for a woman her age—he guessed she was in her forties—and she wore a modest knee-length dress with white shoes that looked like what you'd wear if you were a nurse or a housekeeper at a hotel. Her eyes were very dark and very large, and he could see how he might be tricked into feeling sorry for her.

For about the past minute she had been signing frantically. He moved his right hand along the back of his left hand, fingers to wrist, to say *Slow down*. He hadn't been paying attention to her. The only thing he'd picked up was the sign for *dead*. If someone was dead, he was out of here. "Slow down," he said to her out loud. She stood in front of him, breathing heavily. There was sweat on her upper lip and her collar was damp. He looked out across the courtyard again. No one there but a Latino kid riding slow on a bicycle, heading out toward the main street that ran by the complex. Rush of traffic out beyond the parking lot, loud whoosh of the industrial-size air conditioner near the stairwell, buzz of the Coke machine. It seemed like maybe a good idea to leave, but the woman needed someone who knew sign language. He had known it all his life. Donnie, his older brother, lived in some town full of wealthy people up in Connecticut and made his living doing animation for TV. He was fantastic at drawing, could always do anything with a pencil faster than anyone alive, as far back as Glen could remember.

He was about to leave. It wasn't like he owed that dumbass Arturo anything. He could just take Arturo's shit back to him and tell him to make sure next time he sent someone on an errand it wasn't all fucked up, with deaf women signing about dead people. Why was she doing that again?

"Look," he said, holding out the bag. "Do you want this?" he asked, moving his lips exaggeratedly, like he never used to do with Donnie. But then, when he was little, with Donnie as his most constant companion, signing had seemed almost more natural than speaking.

No, she signed, she didn't want it. Her husband did.

And where was he?

She motioned for him to follow her. He made the sign for *money*. Was the husband going to give him money? But the woman didn't see. She was headed up the stairs.

From the third floor you could look out past the courtyard and the parking lot to some tin-roofed warehouses and barbed-wire fences and a highway with trash floating in the drainage ditch. A few skimpy palm trees, their mop-like tops tossed around by the ocean breeze. And far off there, almost a mirage, the Saint Johns River, a low glitter in the evening sunlight, marked by the twisting shapes of birds.

The apartment was dark and stuffy and smelled like sweat and cigarettes and weed and something that had been cooking on the stove. All the lights were off, but the blinds were open on the window, so it was pretty easy to see the dead guy on the sofa. He lay on his stomach, his face turned in toward the cushions, one hand hanging limply down onto the rug. It had been awhile since Glen had seen a dead person.

The woman seemed unconcerned. She'd seated herself at a small table over by the window and was busy writing something on a legal pad. Clearly, somebody needed to call the police, and maybe the woman couldn't do it because she didn't speak. But of course she could text. Back when Glen used to have a cell phone, the flip kind where you had to press the buttons over and over to get the letters you wanted, Donnie would send him texts telling him to get a smartphone so they could communicate more regularly. But he didn't want a smartphone. The name alone suggested all sorts of judgments and obligations. And he didn't like to text in the first place because he wasn't a good speller. Was it possible to text 911? Somebody needed to call the police, and if it was going to be him, it wasn't going to happen while he was carrying around a baggie of heroin in his pocket. No, the heroin was going to have to go straight back to Arturo, and quickly.

The dead guy rolled over on the sofa. Something hot and dizzy happened in Glen's brain when he saw that, and he jumped a little. He would have yelled if the apartment hadn't been so quiet. He looked over at the woman, who was laughing behind one hand. It was the first time he'd seen her look anything other than frantic or exhausted, the two states she seemed to oscillate between. She wagged her finger at the man on the sofa as if to say, No, no, that's not the dead one, and pointed at the letter she was writing on the legal pad. The previously dead guy started snoring softly and the woman took a minute longer to finish scratching her note on the pad. The air conditioning kicked on. The sun came down lower and shone full through the blinds. The woman signed to ask him if he wanted a glass of water, and he signed back *no*, and she asked if he wanted a beer—and he did want a beer, actually, but he said out loud, "No," and the dead guy's face twitched.

The woman came over and turned on a table lamp and motioned him to sit in a chair and handed him the letter she'd written. She had fine, clear handwriting, and Glen sensed that it was a well-written letter in general, all the way down to the spelling and the commas. It looked like the kind of letter Donnie would write, and her handwriting might have been even more perfect than his . . . prettier, for sure, more feminine. It made him look at the woman again to see if there was anything about her to find attractive. She was staring at him expectantly, though, and she frowned a little, so he started reading.

The upshot of the letter was that her husband's uncle ran a funeral home, and she and her husband worked for him, picking up and transporting dead bodies. Today they had picked one up but had so far failed to deliver it. This meant they were in trouble. Could he help? She would pay him one hundred dollars to help her get the body to the funeral home. It was the second time today he'd been offered a hundred bucks. Maybe, somehow, there was a future in all of this.

There were several things he wanted to ask. First, he signed to her the best he could, he wanted to know if the man on the couch was supposed to be the dead person or her husband. At that she laughed quietly, once again putting a hand over her mouth, as if she were doing something impolite. When she laughed, her brown eyes glowed. There was something moderately attractive about her, he decided. He wondered what she would sound like if she spoke—would her voice be high or low? He could still remember Donnie's voice, how it sounded like some weird kind of imitation. You could understand him pretty well, or at least Glen could, who heard him speak most often. But eventually he had quit speaking altogether. When Glen asked him why, Donnie said that speaking was like walking along a strange trail without ever being able to look down at your feet.

She nodded at the man on the couch. *Husband*, she signed. *Not dead. Drunk.* She started to sign something more, but he wasn't following it, and she grabbed the pad from him and wrote for a minute and tore out a page and handed it to him. *We picked up the body and he was afraid if we went straight to the funeral home we would miss Arturo*, the note said. *But when we got here Arturo said no one could come until 5:00 and so he got drunk and passed out.* She nodded at the sofa as if to say, Lo and behold, there he is.

OK, he signed back. And then, *Where is the dead body?* And she told him that it was in the van. Why didn't she just drive it to the funeral home herself? Because she didn't have a license.

When they got down to the parking lot, he didn't ask to see the body, and he made a conscious effort not to turn and look as he got in the driver's seat and started the engine. The windows had been left rolled down, he noticed. Every time the van slowed you could feel the smell creep up, as if it had tentacles. *Four hours*, she signed to him, motioning with her head toward the body. *Too long.* She circled her closed hand over her heart—*sorry*, that meant.

He remembered most of the language pretty well. Pointing him along the sun-blanched streets and eventually onto I-95, she kept up a brisk conversation, asking questions and telling me about herself—How had he learned sign language? His brother was deaf. Where was his brother now? North. What kind of work did

Glen do? Building. Had he grown up here? Yes. She had grown up here too. She lost her hearing after a childhood illness. She could still remember sounds, wind in the trees and car engines and human voices. Glen watched her carefully, glancing back and forth between her eyes and her hands and the traffic. He took his hands off the wheel for a second. *Married*—he signed to her. *How long?* One year. Was her husband deaf? Only when he wanted to be. They both smiled at that. *Funny*, Glen signed.

This was something he also remembered, the easy familiarity of the language. It was more intimate than speech in a way. It was like being with another person in a foreign country, or at least it's what he imagined such a thing would be like. You understood each other but no one understood you, and even if it was in a van driving along I-95 with no one else around, the feeling was the same. In elementary school he and Donnie used to sit together during lunch hour, at the picnic table next to the monkey bars, and sign about the girls in Donnie's grade. They used to laugh at him for sitting with Donnie, a kid in the special-needs classes. Most of the kids didn't know Donnie was his brother. Sometimes Glen would try to ignore Donnie over at the table where he sat all alone watching the kids on the monkey bars, but he could never do it. It was as if he were seeing recess from Donnie's eyes, experiencing it in a silent whirl of sunlight.

They drove south down I-95 until it was almost fully dark, and then she motioned him to turn off east, onto Racetrack Road, which led toward the ocean. They drove along with only the hum of crickets out the window and the passing cars, and there was no music on the radio. It occurred to him that they hadn't spoken in a while. He fell into a habit he'd had as a kid, which was to look at the world as if it were a movie screen with the sound turned off, trying to understand it the way Donnie would understand it. The colors and the shapes and the sharp lines between things, depth and perception, height and distance, that would be everything, and for that reason the world would all be alive in the way that made Donnie so good at drawing pictures. He would try just to see, to cut off all the other senses, and to know, for instance, what a leaf looked like as it fell to the sidewalk during a storm, or how a train appeared when it passed, as noiseless and smooth as a fish. He tried to do this now, for the first time in a long time, and the woman sat silently next to him, her arm resting on the console between them.

He considered what it would be like if he and the woman were married, if they did this together every day, if it were his job to drive dead bodies to the funeral home. Would that be better or worse? He had given up on the idea of getting married and having children. There were too many times nowadays when he couldn't get construction work, and he had no education and he wasn't particularly responsible or resourceful or motivated. How had it gotten like that? When they were growing up, Glen had assumed that he would be the one to succeed. Now Donnie had a wife and a son and a nice house in a place where it wasn't so hot, where Glen imagined the air was crisper and cleaner and the visual lines were sharp and regular and strong.

You could smell the dead guy when you stopped at a light. The rest of the time the only reminder was the occasional vibration from the box when the van hit a bump in the road. The box was like a cheaper version of a coffin, clamps on the side, a dull metal finish, dents and scratches that made it look like it had been beaten around some. He tried not to think about the dead guy or how the dead guy might have died and tried to imagine that he and the woman were driving somewhere else on some different type of business. Most work he'd done in his life was like that—something you did while you tried to imagine doing something else.

He wondered if the woman was hungry. He was hungry himself. He signed to ask her if she wanted to stop and eat, and she smiled at him and nodded. It had been years since he'd been on this road in this part of Duval County, and it had changed. When he was a kid, they used to drive out this way to Ponte Vedra, and the road then had mostly been a two-lane strip between palm trees and longleaf pines, the occasional shanty serving cold beer and crab. Now there were strip malls and fast-food joints. The woman motioned him to the drive-through at Wendy's and signed that she didn't want to leave the body and go inside. He had foolishly imagined sitting down with her somewhere, realized now that he wanted to get a better look at her. He had started to like the way she looked, despite the dress and shoes that seemed like part of a uniform.

When they got to the window, the woman tried to hand him a ten, and Glen waved her off and handed a twenty over to the Black girl who gave him his Cokes and the bag of food. It seemed like he could go whole days now without seeing another white person. He didn't mind. It was the white people who generally looked down on him.

The girl counted out his change. Her features drew inward slightly, and she looked at him in a curious way, and he wondered if she could smell the body. It wasn't that noticeable to him anymore.

He turned back onto the road, and the woman handed him his cheeseburger and fries, and she jabbed a straw in his Coke and put it in the console for him and set two napkins next to the Coke where he could grab them easily while he was driving. It was just like they were two people who were together all the time, and they were going on a trip someplace exciting. He could see how he was getting attached to the idea of this woman even though he had been with her only for an hour or two, and it made him angry at himself, his stupidity and his desperation. So they knew the same language. Did that make him anybody in her life, somebody important? He had taken on this bullshit job for Arturo, and so far he had put himself through a couple additional hours of trouble, and he hadn't seen any money for it yet, and in fact he was out fifteen dollars for the Wendy's food, which wasn't what he'd imagined eating tonight anyway.

The woman waved her small hand slowly out the window, letting the breeze blow through her fingers. She held her chicken sandwich in her left hand and ate it in tiny bites while she stared out the windshield at the line of trees against the purple sky. He reached over and touched her arm to get her attention, and she smiled at him. That made him feel good. He wasn't such an unattractive person. There was nothing much notable about his appearance, he guessed, but he was in decent shape, and he was a little younger than he supposed she was, and he looked like someone who'd worked all day instead of gotten drunk and high and passed out on a couch.

"Does your husband sign?" he asked her. He could see how quickly her eyes moved to his lips. She shook her head vigorously and looked out the window. Even though it was mostly dark inside the van, she'd known what he was asking almost before he'd finished. His brother, he remembered, had an unsettling way of knowing things. One time he and Donnie had been walking on the railroad tracks, arguing about the new hockey team, the Florida Panthers, about whether you had to like them just because they were from Florida. It was stupid, Glen was saying, a winter sport where there wasn't any winter, and Donnie had tapped him on the arm, *Is there a train coming?* And there was—not close enough to be dangerous, just now coming into view, in fact, beyond the bend at Southside Park, but there behind them sure enough. How had Donnie known? Glen asked. Because he could tell, Donnie signed, that Glen was hearing something but not listening. Only then did he register the clanging of the bells at the railroad crossing far away, though it had been in his mind the whole time.

Now the woman directed him off on a narrower road to the right, and he drove the van slowly, enjoying the quiet night out the window and the dark line of pine trees eclipsing the moon. He wanted the drive to last as long as possible. When they got to wherever they were going, there would be unpleasant work to do.

The woman reached in a purse down at her feet, pulled out her cell phone, and started texting. He'd lost his own cell phone at a bar on purpose one night a few weeks ago after work, and he'd avoided replacing it. He didn't want a cell phone. He hated them. He hated Facebook, seeing his high-school friends and hearing about their dogs and babies and dying grandmothers. He disliked communicating with people in general, and he didn't want to talk with them any more than was necessary, even if this meant that people from work and his mother and Donnie were constantly frustrated with him for not being available. Arturo, in fact, was very likely freaking out right now. He thought about asking the woman to text Arturo, but he didn't know his number. It was strange how easy it was to forget you had a thousand dollars' worth of heroin in your pocket. It didn't worry him much. He wasn't particularly scared of Arturo. He couldn't remember the last time he'd been scared of anything.

He fumbled around on the panel and found the dome light and turned it on. She looked up from the phone, startled, and motioned for him to keep going straight, as if there were any other direction. The road was notable only for that one thing, its utter straightness and lack of available turnoffs, and maybe for the constant, unbroken line of trees. He had never been on this road in his entire life, he was sure of it.

Who are you calling? he signed. *Husband*, she said. He'd be awake now, she hoped. Glen checked the dark road in front of him and took his arms from the wheel for a moment and crossed them over his chest, the sign for *love*. He hadn't made that sign in a long, long time. He raised his eyebrows, formed his face into a question. *Do you love your husband?* he meant. He had no idea why he would ask her that.

It surprised him that she answered so quickly, her fingers opening and snapping shut. *No.* He looked back at the road and turned off the dome light. In a minute she tapped him on the arm, and he turned the light on again. *Life is hard*, she signed.

He nodded, although he wasn't sure he agreed. It wasn't a subject he considered much, the relative difficulty of existence compared to some presumably less difficult state. But maybe it was hard if you were a deaf woman married to someone you didn't love, just because that person was the only one who would marry you, possibly, despite your dark brown eyes and quite attractively smooth complexion, and your job was retrieving dead bodies, and your husband couldn't even manage to do that responsibly, deliver a dead guy in a crate, because he was a drunk and an addict and a fuckup and most likely an asshole too. Maybe then life was hard. But for Glen life wasn't hard. You got up in the morning, and you shaved or didn't shave, ate or didn't eat. Four or five days a week, depending on the weather, you were on the job by 8:00 A.M. and the other days you weren't, so you slept a little later and went to Waffle House and read the newspaper. Hard? Was that the right word? There wasn't much hard about it, except on days like today when, for some reason, stupidly, you had saddled yourself with a baggie of heroin and a dead body and someone who needed your help, and the road you were on seemed to stretch forever through the live oaks draped with Spanish moss and the pine trees. Then life got a little hard and it made you tired and you wondered why you were doing things.

He turned on the radio, found the classic rock station he usually listened to. He was watching the road in the headlights, so she had to tap him on the arm before she signed, *You like music?* He shrugged. He used to like it, but he didn't pay much attention to it anymore. The songs were the same songs he'd been listening to for twenty or thirty years, so he didn't really hear them, and when they played a new song he hadn't heard before, it annoyed him, and he turned off the radio.

You? he signed back. She smiled. Yes, on the one hand it was a dumb question. But he remembered that Donnie liked music, that he claimed he could hear it. It took him a second to remember the sign, but then it came to him. He frowned and put his index finger to his chin and twisted it. *I'm serious.*

She looked ahead at the road and edged forward on the seat like she was searching for a familiar landmark. *I remember it*, she signed. *Music.* And then she swayed back and forth for a moment. The moon rode smoothly along and the dark trees flashed in the purple light. What was she listening to? What did it sound like, a kind of music that only you could hear?

Soon she stopped, and she started texting. *Husband?* he signed, taking his hands off the wheel. He wasn't even sure she could see him. She signed back something he didn't understand. He shook his head and turned on the dome light. She spelled it out. *Uncle.* He turned off the light, and they drove along in silence under the retreating trees. She looked at the phone and didn't seem to be seeing anything. It began to bother him for the first time that he didn't know her name.

The trees on the driver's side gave way suddenly, and there was a road, then a flashing stoplight, a line of cars, an outlet mall that materialized out of nowhere, the names of the stores blazing garishly. She motioned for him to turn, and he was on an access road with traffic, and there was a sign saying two miles to Ponte Vedra, and then she was motioning him to turn into the funeral home, a place with low palm trees in even rows and clusters of brightly lit glass globes on tall posts.

She signaled him to pull behind the building where there were no trees and only a halogen lamp above the doorway, a few late-season moths flitting strobically in and out of the light. At her direction he backed the van up to a concrete ramp to the doorway. He shoved the gearshift into park. She looked around the parking lot like something was missing. She started texting again. The last of the sun was going down, and he watched car lights swing into the entrance of the outlet mall. A few minutes ago he had thought they were the only people left in the world.

The woman opened the door and got out of the van. He didn't know what she was doing. He got out himself. She hurried to the back door of the funeral home and pulled on it, but it wouldn't open and she squatted there on the concrete ramp and cupped both her hands over her mouth and started to cry.

That was the last thing he needed. Even a steak dinner wasn't worth it. He knelt down next to her, but her eyes were closed and he didn't want to startle her with his hands. She smelled, when you got this close, like bleach. It wasn't a bad smell. He hazarded a touch on her shoulder and was surprised to feel her shaking hard under his fingertips. She took one hand from her mouth and wiped tears from her eyes and looked at him with a grateful smile, her eyes big and watery. He took her hand in his. Her trembling fingers were tiny and thin. He hadn't looked at a woman's face, into her eyes that way, in longer than he could remember.

Some kind of bug swooped down from the light and buzzed against his forehead, and he swatted at it until it flew off. He thought this would make her laugh but it didn't. She kept staring at him as if gauging his capacity to save her from something.

Trouble, she signed. *Trouble.*

A wave of fatigue passed over him. There was a leaden feel to his hands and his feet, as if they were weighted and attached to pulleys. He had spent most of the day in a ditch clearing out rocks and debris for a new water line, and his head was still filled vaguely with the noise of the backhoe. This wasn't what he wanted to be doing. His apartment would be dark and quiet, and his cat, Rusty, would be waiting for him by the door. Every night when he finished watching TV and went to bed, Rusty curled up on his pillow.

"What's wrong?" he said to her out loud, making sure she watched him there under the light.

Then there came a long, confused explanation that included spelling things on her phone and signing to him and gesturing. The uncle felt sick and had gone home and wasn't coming back. He was teaching the nephew a lesson. But there were rules about handling bodies. This meant trouble.

Dull-colored moths batted at the halogen lamp. He questioned his capacity to fix anything. *What do I do*, he signed.

She stood and walked away a little distance and used the cell phone while he thought of his dark, quiet apartment. She walked back over to him. She signed, *Husband*, and held the phone out to him.

The text, presumably from the husband, said, *He won't come out there. He's being a dick. Just dump the fucker.*

What? her response said.

Dump the fucking body by the door, the husband said. *How'd you get out there? Who's with you?*

Nice man. He's helping me.

Tell him if he touches you I'll kill him.

That was the end of the texts. She made a circle over her heart. *Sorry*, she was telling him. She had called him a nice man. He could knock the husband out with a single punch, he knew it. He could strangle him easily with his bare hands. Dumb fucker passed out on a couch. He'd love to go back there right now.

Not smart, he signed.

What? she signed back.

What he wants.

She shrugged and looked down at the pavement. He reached out and lifted her chin with his fingers, feeling a pang at how she let her eyes be guided to his lips. "What's your name?" he said to her.

A-l-e-s-a. Alesa.

She stared into his eyes and he didn't move and she walked off again and started texting. In a minute she came back over to him and held out the screen for him to see.

I said dump the fucker there. Do what I say. Jerry will have to come out there unless he wants to get in trouble too. Tell that asshole to help you get the fucking guy out of the van. Do it. Now.

Circle over the heart again. Sorry again. She smiled at him sheepishly. Yeah.

Tell that fucker I'm coming over to kill him, Glen wanted to sign, but he was tired and it was too hard to figure out how. *What do you want?* he signed instead.

She motioned with her head to the rear of the van.

"Okay," he said out loud and went over and pulled up the door handle and swung the doors open wide. The sour smell wafted past him and then he didn't smell anything. She came and stood next to him and they looked at the cheap metal casket.

How, he signed.

She held one finger up to say wait a second, then she typed on her phone: *Jerry and my husband do this part.*

He shrugged, and she shook her head slowly to say yes, she understood, she was sorry things were so difficult. He jumped up into the van and held his breath and got to the far end of the box and slid it forward with a grunt. It was about as heavy as he figured it would be. He was trying not to breathe in, but he couldn't help it and his nostrils filled with the smell. He shoved the box halfway out the door and jumped down and motioned for her to come up next to him. He showed her how to get her arms underneath, and then he pulled a little so that the weight could settle onto both of their arms, but he could tell it was too heavy for her to hold on her own. He held it up by himself and nodded to her to get up in the van. It had cooled off a good deal since the sun went down, but it was still warm, and now that he had no hands, beads of sweat trickled down his forehead and stung his eyes. He shook his head vigorously and squinted to see what she was doing. She was hunched at the box and pushing as he would have told her. He pulled on his end and the box shook loose and started shifting bit by bit out the door.

He wanted to warn her not to push it too close to the edge, but there was no way to do that with his hands occupied, and he watched it happen helplessly, her on her knees and shoving as hard as she could to get the box out. He shouted, "Whoa, hey, whoa!" but it did no good. The box slid forward suddenly as if its path had been greased, and the far end slid with a scraping noise off the bed. He tried to catch it and ease it back, but he only stumbled, and the box twisted and turned sideways and fell on top of him there on the pavement. The box caught on his foot and he could feel his ankle turn and pop under the weight, and he shouted and struggled out from underneath to find the woman standing with her mouth open and her hands holding the sides of her head and the box tipped on its side with the clasp broken and the dead man's arm splayed on the ground.

He scrambled to his feet. The sight of the arm startled him at first, as if he needed to defend himself against it somehow, but then everything was still except for the moths tapping against the light. He had a vague impression of the woman and her strange moaning sounds, but he was taken for a moment with the idea of the body, with an awareness of its strange, inert integrity, how alone it was, how completely forgotten the person it used to be. He saw himself in his apartment, as immobile as the body in the casket, one arm hanging off the couch, Rusty licking his dead fingertips. No one would know or care.

Except maybe the woman, who came to his aid now, helping to steady him on his feet. *OK? OK? OK?* she signed to him feverishly. Her arm was around his waist and her shoulder was under his shoulder, supporting him. She looked up at him with her warm brown eyes.

"Okay," he said. Then she bent to the casket, trying to tip it back right side up.

He wondered later—for years—what might have happened had he not seen the cop car from the corner of his eye. Was there a threshold that could have been crossed, a connection that might have been more than temporary, a future that could have been other than imaginary, something he might not have betrayed. At the traffic light on the road to the outlet mall, the cop car hesitated, not moving forward as the other cars did. That was the first time he'd thought of the heroin in quite a while. He imagined what they looked like, the two of them and the dead body, there in the circle of the halogen light.

The woman, Alesa, was occupied with the business of the casket. The cop car shifted lanes and made the turn in their direction. He looked down at the part in Alesa's dark hair and her tiny hands fumbling at the clasp on the box. Already, he was trying to remember her face. He hobbled around the van to the passenger door, opened it, shoved the baggie of heroin in the glove box, and stumbled across the parking lot on his swollen ankle toward the road to the outlet mall. He moved out of reach of the halogen light and knew he was swallowed into darkness. This was what came of all your plans. Maybe not for some people, but for him. He saw the cop car turn into the funeral home and Alesa still bent over the casket, unaware. He watched until he saw her turn to where she thought he was standing.

Then he pushed ahead as fast as his leg would carry him. The ankle was badly sprained. He wouldn't be going back to work, anyway. He was glad Arturo didn't know where he lived. If he could get to the outlet mall, he could find a ride or take a bus home. He tried to think of something pleasant—how he would go visit Donnie and his family soon, up north where it was cold and snowy, where it was a real holiday. He didn't turn to look behind him. There was no need to. He could picture even in the midst of his reverie—the frosty wind, the flying snow, he and Donnie and the family under warm blankets in a sleigh, gliding smoothly over the countryside—the moment when she turned to find him gone.

I wrote the first version of "Sleigh Bells for the Hayride" way back in about 2014. It was an outlier for me, since I usually write about Idaho, where I'm from, or South Carolina, where I've lived for the past twenty-plus years. I really can't even say where the story came from, except that my parents once lived outside of Jacksonville and my wife and I once got lost on a lonely road there, and the mother of one of my son's friends told me that she and her husband worked their way through college delivering bodies to funeral homes and, when I started writing the story and Glen first met Alesa in the stairwell, I knew there had to be both a barrier to and a conduit for their communication. The story sat on the editor's desk at one of the big commercial magazines for close to a year before it was rejected. A few other places that seemed like good fits also passed on it, and I started to sense that this particular kind of story was falling out of favor. Since I'm lazy and lack focus, that was reason enough to let it sit idle for a few years. But after Trump was in office and busily going about destroying the whole world's morale and our general sense of decency, I reread the story. The isolation and hopelessness and alienation that I felt had become so pervasive, and that had prompted me to write the story in the first place, seemed even more *pervasive and more relevant, not less. So I sent the story to* Cincinnati Review, *and I thank them for accepting it. I wanted Glen's decision to abandon Alesa in the end to represent what I would call a failure of moral imagination, in which we're unable or unwilling to appreciate or envision other people's experience sufficiently to make it part of our own, and lack the conviction and the stamina to try to make things better, even for ourselves.*

Gwen Mullins *worked in corporate America for nineteen years before coming to her senses and running away to write. Her stories and essays have been featured in* New Ohio Review, African American Review, The Bitter Southerner, The New Guard, PANK, *and* Green Mountains Review, *among others. Her first novel, with a working title of* They Say You Always Have a Choice, *is currently pending publication, and she is working on a second novel as well as a short story collection filled with errant preachers, straying spouses, and decisions that made sense at the time. In the winter of 2020–21, she served as the Writer in Residence for the Kerouac Project in Orlando, and she currently works at the University of Tennessee at Chattanooga in the Writing & Communication Center.*

VIOLENT DEVOTION

Gwen Mullins

Two weeks ago over a dinner of fried chicken, purple-hull peas, and buttered corn, Red McClendon's family talked about the girl, Vera Martin, who disappeared one night after she left the ShopRite on Sand Mountain. Red's son Jackson worked part-time as a bag boy at that same store, but he claimed he couldn't remember if he'd been at work the night the girl went missing.

Red saw the girl's picture on the news, a curvy young woman with thick, dark hair that hung in braided ropes down her back, her skin smooth and tan as river stone. Something about the way she tilted her head in the news photograph reminded him of Rosie, his own daughter. Red did not think too much about Vera Martin's disappearance at first. He, like most of the folks he knew, assumed she would turn up in one of the trailers pocked with scattershot at the foot of the mountain, strung out on meth, or maybe in a Marietta hotel room with a man old enough to be her father, or her teacher. Red's own sister ran off with three different boys before she even finished high school.

"Jean Anne always came back, after her money ran out or when she got tired of eating frozen burritos from the Chevron," Red said.

Red's wife Loretta pursed her lips, busied herself with grinding pepper over her dinner. She always got quiet when Red brought up the less savory aspects of his past.

"But Vera Martin was a nice girl, from a good family," Rosie said.

Red blinked as he absorbed the implied insult to his sister, his parents. True, Red's father was a casual drunk, dead now ten years, his mother a fallen debutante who sucked fentanyl lollipops to ease her supposed migraines. His sister Jean Anne still meandered around the edges of Red's life, calling only when she needed money.

"I'm sorry, Daddy. I didn't mean, you know." Rosie picked crust from her chicken and piled it on the side of her plate. She liked to eat the chicken meat first, the breading after.

Red's boy Jackson chewed steadily, his meal half-finished even though the rest of the family had barely started eating. Jackson made a snorting noise. "Everybody knows Vera Martin's a whore."

"She is not. She's a cheerleader," Rosie said.

"Exactly." Butter and corn milk dripped down Jackson's chin. "Besides, it sounds like she doesn't want to be found. Bitch like that, she could be halfway to the border with her Mexican boyfriend by now, riding in the back of one of those spic trucks."

"That's enough of that, Jackson McClendon," Red said.

Jackson shrugged, wiped his mouth on a paper towel, and bit into a chicken leg, the salted crust shattering against his strong white teeth.

The kitchen light flickered as the air conditioner clicked on, and Loretta made the old joke, "We know you're there, Papaw Duncan," that she always made when the lights dimmed in the house that once belonged to her grandfather. They spoke of other things, and Red felt safe and proud, with his family all around the sturdy kitchen table, the linoleum floor gleaming and the smell of the good food in the air.

Red told himself it began only a couple years ago, when Jackson was sixteen and Rosie had just turned fourteen, and their brindle mutt Butterscotch went missing. Butterscotch was a loyal dog, one who yelped and ran in circles each afternoon when Rosie stepped off the school bus. When Loretta cooked, Butterscotch curled behind her the kitchen, waiting for a scrap of biscuit dough or one of the liver-flavored dog treats Loretta kept in a green ceramic canister next to the flour and the corn meal.

In the evenings, Butterscotch tagged along with Red during his after-dinner walks. Sometimes, Red and Butterscotch ambled along the lonely county road until they reached the old Stooksbury farm a mile up the way. Other times, Red preferred to stroll among the trees and meadows of his own property, looking for signs of groundhogs and coyotes while the whip-poor-wills called to each other in the twilight. Everyone loved Butterscotch's easy company except Jackson, who claimed the dog's hide made him sneeze. If she came too near Jackson, he would stomp his foot on the ground and she would skitter away, her stub of a tail clamped tight against her backside.

"What if the coyotes got Butterscotch?" Loretta asked.

Rosie stood on the front porch, calling Butterscotch's name and shaking the canister of treats.

Loretta continued, "Or she got into some poison? Lydia's dog almost died after he lapped up spilled antifreeze in their driveway."

"She's probably just chasing squirrels in the woods," Red said.

But the next day, when Butterscotch still had not returned, Red knew something more serious was keeping her away. Butterscotch never disappeared for more than an hour, and she never failed to show up for her nightly bowl of kibble. While Jackson slept in and Loretta fretted over her coffee, Red and Rosie set off to find the dog, tramping through the acreage behind the house, calling her name. Red carried his shotgun broken open in his arms as he always did when walking through the woods, ever since one of his cousins was mauled by a bear up near Fontana Dam. The shells in his pocket clanged next to a plastic baggie of dog treats.

A sound like a baby whimpering filtered through the trees.

Red said, "You wait here."

"But, Daddy . . ."

Red swallowed, made sure his voice would come out steady before he turned to his daughter. "It could be nothing. But wounded animals are unpredictable, and I don't want you getting hurt." In truth, Red was afraid of what he would find. He wanted to protect Rosie from seeing her dog with its flesh shredded from tangling with a raccoon or its leg broken in a trap set by a hunter who had no respect for property lines. Rosie pleaded with her big dark eyes, but she stayed behind while Red forged ahead through the underbrush.

When Red saw Butterscotch tied to a pine tree, he wished he had not allowed Rosie to come with him at all. Butterscotch's gums were caked with blood from chewing at the rope. Her hindquarters drooped away from her body and rested in her own excrement. My poor Butterscotch, he thought. Who would do this to my sweet dog? Red flipped open his pocketknife and sawed at the rope that bound her to the tree. Up close, he could smell Butterscotch's damp fur, could see the unnatural dip in the middle of her spine. Her tail and back legs lay against the ground as if they had no relation to the rest of her body.

"Daddy, is it her? Is it Butterscotch?" Rosie called.

Red considered lying, telling her it was a rabbit with a chewed-up back leg that had not quite escaped a fox, but before he could make up his mind the dog tried to pull herself up with her front paws, yelped, and fell back to the ground. Rosie came running, calling out for Butterscotch.

She fell to her knees beside Red, her hands held toward the dog, her voice shaking. "Who did this? Who could have done such an awful thing?"

The dog shuddered, whimpered again. Red had no words of comfort for his daughter, no way to explain such cruelty. He had seen something like this a few months prior, when he came across a maimed kitten behind his utility shed. A few months before that, he found the bloodied wings of a sparrow under the bushes along the driveway. His heart clutched and stuttered around the possibilities of who, when, why, just as it had then. Both times, he had written the wounded animals off as the work of coyotes or owls, though he knew such predators were unlikely to abandon their fallen prey quite so readily.

He pushed other possibilities as far from his mind as he could.

"I don't know, honey. I can't understand a person who would do something like this." Red stood, reached into his pocket for shells, loaded the gun.

"Daddy, no! She'll be okay. We just need to get her to Dr. Murrah. She'll fix Butterscotch right up. Please don't hurt her." Rosie pulled at his arm until Red dropped one of the shells among the pine needles at his feet.

"Rosie, stop it. Listen to me. Butterscotch is hurting. This is the kind of thing she won't get better from. We have to do the right thing, the merciful thing."

"Daddy, please," she whispered through the fist she pressed against her lips.

Red hesitated, his eyes sweeping over his sobbing daughter and his wounded dog. "Rosie, honey, you need to move back a ways. You need to be strong, for Butterscotch's sake."

Rosie stumbled back toward the wooded path, her shoulders heaving. Red knelt beside Butterscotch. She opened her eyes, licked his hand. "I'm sorry, girl. You were a good dog."

He wondered if Loretta and Jackson heard the report of the shotgun from the house.

Red pushed back through the underbrush to his daughter, prepared to comfort her, to still her sobs even while his own heart quaked with grief and loss. His family never allowed pets when he was growing up, and he was surprised how much he had come to rely on Butterscotch's unconditional affection. Rosie stood straight by a gnarled hemlock, her eyes rimmed red but clear, her hands balled into fists by her side.

"He did this," she said.

Now, two long years later, Red remembered the dread he felt when he said, "Who?"

"You know," she said. "I know you can see it, even if Mom doesn't."

"Who, Rosie?" Red did not want to speak the words.

"You know." Rosie lifted her trembling chin.

Red handed her the shotgun, slipped off his canvas work coat, and walked back to drape the jacket over the dog.

Later that day, Red and Rosie returned with a tarp and a shovel to bury Butterscotch in a shady spot not far away from the tree where they had found her. They marked her grave with a heart-shaped stone, planted iris bulbs in the loose dirt so that they would bloom in the spring. Red told Loretta the coyotes got the dog real bad, so he was forced to end her suffering. Butterscotch's canister of dog treats still sat on the kitchen counter, but they never got another dog, not even when Loretta's friend Heather offered them first pick from her coonhound's litter the following spring.

Even when Jackson was a little boy, Red and Loretta argued over how to raise him, when to discipline, what was normal, what was not. The day ten-year-old Jackson slammed a length of firewood against his little sister's head because she misplaced one of his Matchbox cars, Red grabbed Jackson by the arm and dragged him to his room. Jackson howled and kicked the bedroom door while blood dripped into little Rosie's eyes and onto the carpet. If Loretta had not been a quick-thinking nurse with a supply of butterfly closures and medical-grade superglue, Rosie might have needed stitches.

After Rosie was patched up and Jackson was permitted to leave his room, the boy made a show of bringing cups of milk to his sister while she lay on the couch watching cartoons. When Jackson leaned over Rosie to adjust her pillow, he whispered something that made her shake her head and push away from him. Red could convince neither Jackson nor Rosie to tell him what he said.

What did Red know about raising a good boy, a good man? It was a miracle he himself had not turned out like his own father. As the children grew, Red doted on Rosie, the baby, while Loretta ran point on raising their son. The coldness in Jackson's eyes always chilled Red, but he blamed himself for not being able to love his son as much as he should have.

When he was a boy, Red's uncles took him on hunting trips, picking up some of the slack left by his own father. Red remembered these hunts for the closeness they forged between men and boys in the woods, a closeness that tied him to his family and the land but that no one ever spoke of in living rooms or around kitchen tables. When Jackson was twelve, Red took him on a hunting trip with his old Uncle Frank and some of his McClendon cousins.

"It's okay if you don't want to pull the trigger," Red told Jackson. "It's hard, especially the first time."

Red explained that deer were overpopulating the area, and as long as they processed the meat they were doing right by them, helping the remaining deer to survive. This rationale was the same provided to Red by his Uncle Frank when Red was a boy, and it helped him get through his first hunt. Even though tears had filled Red's eyes when he looked through the scope into the liquid-black eyes of a young buck for the first time, he aimed true, squeezed the trigger. Jackson nodded grimly as Red talked, stayed silent as they waited in the blind in the woods during the last days of the season. But Jackson did not hesitate or cry when the doe was in his sights, had actually smiled just before he squeezed the trigger. When Red showed Jackson how to field dress the deer, blood streaking his face and arms, Jackson laughed at the sucking, ripping sound of the hide pulling away from sinew and muscle, whistled with unsolemn delight when the steaming, glistening slop of intestines spilled from the deer's warm carcass. Uncle Frank and the cousins looked sidelong at Jackson, their lips tight, the lonesome cold closeness of men in the woods fractured by Jackson's mirth.

Red and Loretta hoped Jackson would outgrow his fits of rage, the way he barked and snarled when he did not get his way, like the time he hurled his pet hamster Lolly against the wall after Loretta insisted he clean out the animal's stinking cage. When Rosie received too much attention, Jackson would slip behind her, whisper something only she could hear until she shook her head and her eyes grew wide with terror. Once, Red thought he heard Jackson whisper, "You smell like a dog's cunt," but both kids refused to divulge what Jackson said. Red found that he could not repeat what he thought he heard, so again he let the matter drop.

By the time Jackson was a teenager, it seemed he had matured, calmed down. He projected a steady, unnerving calm that even his teachers commented on. "Such a serious young man," Ms. Fitzsimmons said, rubbing her hands together and avoiding Red and Loretta's eyes during the annual parent-teacher conference. "Always so . . . watchful."

Red hoped that his boy was good, but he did not believe it in his heart. Something tingled at the back of his throat when he observed his handsome blond son, like a nagging sickness he could never quite shake.

The Wednesday before Loretta was scheduled to go out of town for a ladies' weekend in Gatlinburg, Red came home to a house redolent with braised meat and pine-scented cleaner. Loretta had put a chuck roast in the Crock-Pot that morning, then she spent her day off from the hospital reorganizing the pantry and cleaning the bathrooms. Growing up, Red rarely came home to the smells of cooking, the sparkle of a freshly mopped floor, and he loved Loretta for being, among other things, so different from his own mother, for helping create a home that did not resemble the McClendon house of his youth.

As Red hung his jacket on a peg behind the front door, Loretta announced that hikers had found Vera Martin in a lonely stretch of woods forty miles from the grocery store parking lot where she went missing. One of Loretta's friends was dating one of the hikers, and she had poured out the lurid details during book club the night before.

"They won't report everything on the news, especially since Vera is a minor, but what Tracie told us, well, it's just horrible." Loretta placed the roast surrounded by carrots and potatoes in the center of the table.

Red frowned at the note of casual glee in his wife's voice at having the inside scoop on such a public occurrence. Loretta was a good woman, but he never cared for the way she relished gossip. That part of her reminded him of the way people whispered about his own family, their eyes bright with information about his father's stumbling fistfight at the local bar, his sister's spiral downward from drill team captain to oily-haired delinquent.

Rosie tapped at her phone. Jackson wandered in from his bedroom, his hair tousled from a late afternoon nap. Neither appeared to have heard the news about Vera Martin.

"Rosie, grab that bowl of gravy from the stovetop, will you?" Loretta asked.

Red took stock of his family, his home. The meat steamed on the table and Loretta was wearing that blue top he liked. Rosie had just gotten her driver's license but still made sure she was home for dinner every night, and with any luck Jackson would be going away to college or perhaps the police academy in the fall. Red thought of his own family suppers, sad affairs that involved heating frozen dinners and eating in front of the TV. Sometimes he made fried bologna sandwiches for himself and Jean Anne while his mother rested and his father poured himself glass after glass of Jim Beam.

He wondered how Vera Martin's parents were managing after finding their daughter. So many lost days of hoping, of searching. "Could they tell how she died?" he asked.

At this, Rosie looked up from her phone and Jackson swiveled his head toward his father. "Who died?" Uncharacteristic interest piqued Jackson's voice.

"Oh, that's just it." Loretta's voice dropped an octave, grew breathy. "Vera Martin's alive, but only barely."

A creeping dread filled Red's belly, and the smell of the roast which made his mouth water when he opened the door now made him feel like gagging. That girl, alive, but in the middle of the woods too far from where other people might be? He drank from his glass of tea, swished the liquid around in his mouth. Rosie must have made the tea, because it was too heavily sugared for his liking.

"Was she—" Red paused, picked up his fork, put it back down. "What I mean is, did anyone do anything to her?" Red pushed the image of his whimpering dog and the squashed kitten out of his mind. He avoided his daughter's gaze. Everyone at the table except Loretta had gone still, as if they were all holding their breath. No, Red thought. Nothing like that would have happened to Vera Martin, a good girl from a nice family.

When Loretta responded, her voice was normal again, somber. "Nobody raped her or cut her up, if that's what you mean. She was tied to a tree, out where the Park Service marked off the area for plant regeneration or invasive beetles or something. It's only luck the hikers found her, since no one is supposed to go out that way."

"Bats," Rosie said. Red could feel his daughter's eyes on him as he jiggled his fork.

"Bats?" Loretta asked.

"We talked about them in Ecology Club. There are bat caves up near Nickajack, and they're trying to stop the spread of some sort of white fungus. Once one bat gets infected, they can spread their sickness to the whole colony." Red stopped playing with his silverware. The curling, dark hair that always slipped out of Rosie's ponytail framed her face, and her neck grew splotched the way it did when she was upset. Or scared. "Remember?" she said. "I told you guys about it last month."

"Okay, well, bats then," Loretta said. Red could tell she wanted to get on with her story, tell them the parts that would not be released to the news stations.

Jackson helped himself to the roast, and they all followed suit. Red forced his hands to work, pick up the bowl of green beans, scoop some onto a plate rimmed with goldenrod flowers that Loretta's grandmother had passed on to them when they married. Rosie drummed her heel against the floor until the table shook and Loretta said, "Goodness, Rosie, sit still."

Red spooned gravy over his meat, drank more of the saccharine tea. He risked a glance at Jackson, but the boy simply ate, forking roast into his mouth, sopping gravy with a slice of white bread. Red recalled the story of Old Green Eyes, the urban legend about a Union soldier's ghost who crept up and carried off kids who went parking near the tower in Battlefield Park. It could be anyone, he thought. Some loony from the back side of the mountain who roamed the woods, even the woods behind Red's house, hurting living things and tying up that girl.

"Could be anyone," he said, before he realized he was speaking out loud.

"Exactly." Loretta poured more tea into Red's glass. "Tracie said when they found her someone had cut off her hair—she had these two long braids—and nailed them to the tree where she was tied."

"Jesus, that poor girl." Rosie held her body still, but her voice shook.

"There was another thing, something they definitely won't talk about on the news," Loretta said. "She was wearing all her clothes, but her sweater was sticky and covered in leaves and pine needles."

"Was it pine sap or something?" Rosie asked.

Red's heart ached for his daughter's innocence, and he wanted to tell Loretta to shut up, stop talking, that discussing Vera Martin's barely alive state was hardly appropriate dinner table conversation. Gravy coagulated around the beef and carrots on his plate.

"No, honey, it was—" Loretta caught herself, flushed a deep plum. "It was, you know, stuff that comes from a man."

Rosie tilted her head to one side before understanding bloomed in her eyes. She dropped her hands to her lap. "I thought you said nobody raped her?"

"No, it looks like, they just, you know . . ."

"Loretta, I think that's enough. There's a reason they wouldn't talk about that on the news. It's not—" Red paused, struggling to find the right word. "It's not decent."

"I told you she was a whore," Jackson said.

His son's quiet calm, the casual way he spoke about the girl while he chewed his beef, turned Red's blood cold. The sweetness of the tea coated his teeth, clogged his throat. Loretta stared at her son. Rosie pressed a fist to her lips.

"Son, no," Red said. His voice cracked.

Rosie slid her plate away, snatched up her phone, stomped away from the table. Jackson mopped the last of the food from his dish with a slice of bread, stacked his plate and utensils in the dishwasher.

"Thanks for dinner, Mom. I was starving." Jackson grinned, looked sidelong at his parents. "I've had such an appetite lately."

Whatever other news Loretta possessed about Vera Martin she kept to herself for the remainder of the evening. Red poured himself a tumbler of whiskey to wash the taste of sugar and gravy from his mouth. He drained the glass, poured himself another. He rarely drank, and the whiskey gave him a pleasantly detached feeling that allowed him to get through the hours until bedtime.

The whiskey wore off around three in the morning. Red tossed and turned in half dreams, his stomach roiling. Disfigured birds, maimed animals, the way the color drained from Rosie's face when Jackson whispered something only she could hear, that girl tied up in the woods. He willed himself fully awake, sat up in bed. Moonlight streamed in through a gap in the curtains and streaked across the bedspread.

Loretta stirred, murmured, "Can't sleep?"

"I should know better than to drink. It never did sit right with me."

"There's more."

Red rubbed his face, his temples. He stood to look out the window, his back to his wife. The floor was cold against his bare feet. "More what?"

"About that girl, Vera. More that I didn't say at the table."

The woods lay still and quiet behind the house. Red loved this land, the way the colors changed in the trees, the smell of earth and pine. After he and Loretta married, he bought the house, along with twenty acres of wooded hills and dormant fields, from her father for an honest price. Ezra, a tough old brimstone preacher with eyes like flint, extracted a promise that if anything ever happened, a divorce or a parting of ways, Red would return the land to Loretta, to the Duncan family. Dirt was like blood, the old man said. It binds you, from one generation to the next.

"Tell me the rest," Red said.

Loretta took a deep breath. "She stayed alive because whoever took her left the gallon of milk she'd bought at the ShopRite in her lap. It was going sour but it was half-drunk. And there were dog biscuits, a pile of them, next to her, like she was some kind of animal. Tracie's boyfriend Gene thinks that's why his dog ran over to her."

Red barely made it to the bathroom before he threw up. Whisky and tea, half-digested meat, flecks of carrot and potato. He retched until nothing more came out, then spit, rinsed his mouth with water. When he returned to bed, Loretta was sitting up, her arms wrapped around her knees.

"You okay?"

"Yeah. Probably just my ulcer. It acts up sometimes." Red felt drained, washed out.

"What if the man who did that to Vera Martin is still out there?" Loretta's hand moved to her throat. "What if something like that happened to Rosie? Gene told Tracie that the girl could hardly talk, that her eyes were all crazy and empty and she curled up in a ball when they cut her loose. He said she couldn't even tell them who did those things to her."

Red knew then what must be done. He had known, deep in his marrow, the way things could end, though he fought against the knowledge of what his boy was, what the boy might become, ever since he came upon his son giggling in the woods at a vixen, her vulpine nose sleek and bloody, screaming as she tried to gnaw her mangled leg free from the jagged steel trap that Red had relegated to the back of the shed but neglected to throw away.

"Nothing's going to happen to Rosie. She's a good girl. We're a nice family."

Loretta lay down, and Red nestled beside her. He rubbed her back until she fell asleep. He prayed for himself, for Vera Martin, for his boy. Prayers for healing, understanding, forgiveness. I'll wait until Loretta's in Gatlinburg, he thought. He would get Jackson into some kind of treatment, a program to help boys work through the darkness in their hearts. Surely there was some sort of medicine that could help, some kind of therapy. He would get better. Everyone could heal, could beat back whatever demons lurked inside, with proper treatment.

In the cold light of the morning, Red questioned his own pre-dawn revelations. Whoever hurt Vera Martin really could have been anyone—a hitchhiking vagrant, a passing trucker, an angry ex-boyfriend. Some years prior, the whole town was on high alert after two men pried open a window in Moccasin Bend's psych ward and disappeared into the surrounding forest. The men were only found when one of them tried to choke a female clerk who refused to sell them a case of Miller High Life unless they presented identification. The police found ropes, two bags of beef jerky, and a video camera in the cave where the men had been hiding.

Thursday passed in a dream, even when Red watched the news reporter standing in front of the site where Vera Martin had been found. No evidence, no clues, but police were investigating. The Martin family requested privacy while their silent daughter recovered. Loretta did not mention the girl's name again.

Friday morning after Jackson and Rosie left for school, Loretta insisted she would stay behind, that she did not need to go to out of town given all that was going on.

"You've been planning this trip for weeks. I'll take care of things here," Red said.

"Make sure Rosie doesn't go out alone, not until they catch whoever took that Martin girl," Loretta said.

Red clenched his jaw, nodded. "I'll keep an eye on her. You don't have to worry about us."

Red helped Loretta carry her things to her car—a heavy suitcase, a casserole, a pan of brownies, and three bottles of wine for a single weekend trip. Red called in to work, told them he was sick, which was true enough. He certainly felt ill while he searched his son's bedroom. He checked closet shelves, under the bed, between the mattress and box springs. Red watched enough crime shows to know he should check other places too—in air vents, the back of Jackson's dresser, the undersides of drawers, between pages of books, in jacket pockets. He found only crumbled tissues in Jackson's trash can and a long dark hair stuck to one of Jackson's plaid flannels. The hair could be Rosie's, Red thought, caught on the rough material when Loretta tumbled their clothes all together in the wash. He returned to the kitchen, heated his tepid coffee in the microwave. On impulse, he opened the dusty green canister that held Butterscotch's dog treats.

The canister was empty.

I'm being paranoid, Red told himself. Worried over nothing. Loretta probably threw those dog biscuits out months ago. But there was still that itch at the back of his throat, that dull acid in his belly. I'll just talk to him, see what he was doing the night the girl went missing. Maybe he didn't even work at the ShopRite that night. Maybe he was out with friends, at a basketball game or a movie. Maybe he was on a date. Red tried to recall who Jackson's friends were, but it had been years since another kid had come to the house. Jackson talked about girls like he knew them, but he never brought one home. Red realized how little attention he paid to his son's life, even though he knew all of his daughter's best friends, suspected which boys she had crushes on.

Red walked his land, his hands shoved in his pockets against the cold and his shotgun slung across his back, thinking about how to approach his son, what to do if Jackson laughed in his cool way and stared back at him with his flat eyes. When Red reached Butterscotch's grave, the iris blossoms were long gone, the leaves brown and folded over. Could he go to the police with a clipping of his son's hair, ask them to match it against the stickiness on the girl's shirt? Red imagined collecting Jackson's hair in a plastic bag, tucking it in his jacket, standing with his hat in his hands at the front desk of the small police station that covered Sand Mountain, and saying . . . what, exactly? Maybe he could call Eliza, the first female sheriff in the tri-county, and explain the situation. He took Eliza to a homecoming dance one year, kissed her once or twice before he met Loretta. He remembered Eliza as a patient girl with coal-dark eyes who missed nothing, but she had long since married and divorced, raised a daughter of her own, a girl about the age of Vera Martin. No, that was no good. What if there were no match? Everyone at the station would know what Red suspected of his own son, blood of his blood. Eliza and the others would whisper about his family just like they had when Red was young. Worse, what if there were a match and Eliza arrested Jackson, put him in cuffs and drove him away? Jackson was eighteen, an adult. Red knew what happened to good-looking young men, especially sex offenders, in prison. The whole thing would break Loretta's heart. She would never forgive him for turning their son in, for trusting Eliza with information he could not share with his own wife.

No, he thought. There has to be another way. He'd worked so hard to have a good family, a respectable wife and a responsible daughter. As for Jackson, well, all he had was suspicion and doubt and that feeling at the back of his throat.

When the kids came home from school, Red suggested they go out for dinner to the Italian-Greek diner on the ridge. Maybe he could work the conversation around to where they'd all been the night Vera Martin left the ShopRite with a gallon of milk.

"I'm sorry, Daddy. I told Brandy I'd come over and watch movies with her," Rosie said. "Okay if I take your truck?"

Red nodded. "Call me when you get there, and before you leave to come home."

"Your little friend Brandy's really filling out," Jackson said.

Rosie glared at her brother, balled her hands at her sides. "You stay away from us."

Jackson slunk toward his room. He did not respond to Red's offer of dinner, and Red was relieved he would not have to sit in a booth at a restaurant, trying to make small talk with his taciturn son while his heart raged against all he needed to understand, would never understand, about his boy's life. Within minutes, the sound of a video game, some sort of war game played online with a headset, blared from Jackson's room.

Red made himself a cheese and mayonnaise sandwich, pulled three baby dills from a jar, ate alone at the table. He always forgot how much Loretta filled out a room with her chatter and bustling, how empty the house felt when she was gone, even if the kids were around. When she called to tell him that they were settling in and the cabin boasted a wonderful view of the mountains, he forced cheer into his voice.

"Rosie's at Brandy's house, Jackson's playing that game in his room, so I'm just having a sandwich. I may work on that cedar chest I've been meaning to finish this weekend," he said. Women laughed in the background. Loretta giggled and said she had to go, that she'd call back sometime later, but her cell service was spotty.

Red carried the second half of the sandwich to his shed, stared at the two-by-fours and his miter saw, shuffled his feet in the sawdust. He picked up the plans for the chest, put them back down. Tomorrow, he thought. I'll work it all out tomorrow. He finished his sandwich in the shed and sat awhile in the cool dusk before he went back to the house. The video game still sounded from Jackson's room. Red stayed up until Rosie returned home, then he turned out the lights, locked the door. Jackson's war game droned on.

Red woke before dawn to the sound of irregular thumping. He thought perhaps they were in the midst of a hailstorm before he realized the sounds were coming from inside his own house. It was as if he felt rather than heard the reverberations that jerked him upright in his empty bed after a night of fitful sleep. He was not accustomed to sleeping in the big bed without Loretta's solid warmth at his side.

When Red bolted from his bedroom in the thinning darkness, his pulse buzzing in his ears, both Rosie and Jackson's doors were open. He got Rosie, he got my baby girl, Red thought. He ran to his daughter's room—empty, the covers thrown back, clothes piled in the floor. A clattering noise from across the hall, and then he was embracing Rosie, her hair wild, her face damp.

"Did he hurt you? What was that noise?"

Rosie leaned against him, and Red held tight to her. She felt like she was melting, collapsing. "Rosie?"

"I can't live with him, Daddy. I've got to get out of here."

Rosie was folding, slipping. He lowered her to the ground, knelt next to her.

"What happened?"

"He said that he'd like to do things to Brandy. He seemed so serious, like he really would. He said such terrible things, about what he'd do, and he held me down and I couldn't get up and, Daddy, I thought he was going to do things to me, too, so I kicked him and chased him out of my room, and, I just can't, Daddy, not anymore, I can't stand him." She sobbed, her head against her knees.

Something like grief, but cleaner, washed through Red when he straightened. "Why don't you get out of here for the day? Go into town with your girlfriends or something to get your mind off things? I'll handle your brother."

In Jackson's room, books were strewn across the floor. One of the thrown books had left a hole in the drywall. Jackson, leaning against his headboard, looked up through his eyelashes and grinned at his father.

"She's lying," Jackson said.

The cool quiet of early morning reminded Red of the times he went hunting with his uncles and cousins, of the solidarity of quiet, serious men in the forest. He wished he had been able to share that sense of wonder with his own son, with his own father.

Late Saturday evening, Red smoothed his hand over the woodgrain of the finished chest, shut the hinged lid, and left his shed. The sun dropped behind the mountains and the sky turned the color of placenta, of port wine left in a glass overnight, of a swollen hematoma. The color of blood, that's what it was. Blood in the skies, blood thrumming hot through his veins.

Red felt like he had been awake for days. His shoulders ached from woodworking, his back threatened to seize up, and the sawdust that clung to his unshaven jaw was streaked with dried sweat. If I were a better man, Red told himself, I could've yanked my son free, could've found some merciful way to set him on the right path before he infected us all. Could've put an end to things sooner, at least.

He found his son in his bedroom, his headset on and scenes of war splayed across the screen. "Son, let's take a walk," he said. Red rubbed his hand across his jaw. Jackson grumbled, but he dropped the controller and tossed his headset on the bed. On their way out, Red grabbed his shotgun, as was his habit.

This story was inspired, if you want to call it that, by news stories like the one from The Washington Post *on September 22, 2018, in which a man goes free after kidnapping and sexually assaulting a woman in a manner similar to what happened to the young woman in "Violent Devotion." I was fascinated and repelled by the idea of a legal system that let that man go back home with his wife and two kids with little more than a reprimand, and that minor obsession led me down a path lined with all the people who interact with predators—parents, siblings, coworkers, teachers—and all the people who say they had no idea that the person they knew was a bad human. From there I began to wonder what I would do if I suspected my own child, blood of my blood, was a danger to others, and late one night I woke with the bones of this story fully formed in my head. For once, I had the sense to get up and write it all out while the story-dream still flickered. "Violent Devotion" does not focus on the perpetrator or even the victim, but rather on the reactions, inherent sense of culpability, and subsequent responsibilities of the ones who recognize the devil in their midst for what he is. I am sorry, though, about what happened to the dog.*

Jo Nesbø *is a musician, songwriter, and economist, as well as one of the leading crime writers in the world. He is recognized for having widened the scope of the thriller with his unusual literary qualities and ambitions, his psychological insights, and his in-depth knowledge of life in a modern, globalized world. His books have garnered countless international awards, sold fifty million copies, and been translated into fifty languages. In addition to the Harry Hole series, he is the author of stand-alone novels* Headhunters, The Son, Blood on Snow, Midnight Sun, Macbeth, *and* The Kingdom, *as well as several children's books in the Doctor Proctor's Fart Powder series.*

BLACK KNIGHT

Jo Nesbø

TRANSLATED BY ROBERT FERGUSON

PART ONE: THE OPENING

"You can feel your eyelids getting heavy," I said.

The pocket-watch—maker unknown but weighted by sufficient gold to keep it swaying steadily for some time—had been in the family's possession since 1870.

"You are feeling tired. Close your eyes."

The silence was complete. The street-facing windows were triple-glazed, so that not even the chiming from the mighty bells of the Duomo di Milano penetrated. It was so quiet that the absence of ticking was noticeable. The hands were splayed out on each side from the moment the watch breathed its last. Now the mute object was minus the function a watch is meant for.

"When you wake up you will not remember that you were gravid or that you've had an abortion. The child never existed."

I felt suddenly on the verge of tears. When I lost my own child I also lost what we psychologists call my affective control, meaning that I could whimper and blubber over the slightest thing that reminded me of it. I pulled myself together and continued:

"It will seem to you as though you came here to be cured of a nicotine addiction."

Ten minutes later I carefully woke Fru Karlsson from her trance.

"I don't feel any craving at all," she said as she buttoned her mink coat and looked at me.

I was sitting behind my desk and taking notes with the Montegrappa pen I had come across many years ago in an antiques shop. Patients like to see you making notes, it makes them feel a little less like something on a conveyor belt.

"Tell me, Dr. Meyer, is hypnosis difficult?"

"It depends what you're hypnotizing," I said. "As film directors say, the hardest to work with are children and animals. And it's easiest with a receptive and creative spirit like yours, signora."

She laughed.

"There are rumours that you once managed to hypnotize a dog, Dr. Meyer. Is that true?"

"Just rumours," I smiled. "And even if I had, I have a vow of confidentiality as regards all my patients."

She laughed again. "But what power it gives you!"

"I'm afraid I'm as powerless as anyone else," I said, searching through the desk drawer for an ink cartridge to replace the one in the pen, now empty. The leader of a local chess club I used to belong to once said to me that the reason I always lost was not that I didn't know what I was doing, but that I sabotaged my own chances of winning through my bewildering weakness for the weak. He suspected that I would prefer to sacrifice a castle rather than a knight because I *liked* the knight better: Or because I thought of myself as a knight.

"They're pieces, Lukas," he said. "Pieces! The knight is the least valuable, and that is a fact, not preferences."

"Not in every position. The knight can get himself out of some pretty tight situations."

"Knights are slow and always arrive too late to save anyone, Lukas."

I found the ink cartridge, a narrow metal sleeve the same length as the pen, and with a thin steel tip like a hypodermic syringe. I realized it would be my last one, that Montegrappa pens and cartridges were no longer produced. Like so many other uselessly beautiful quality products it had vanished beneath the merciless pressure of global competition.

I wrote slowly, reverently, careful not to waste my words. Fru Karlsson would start smoking again. And she'd tell all her friends that Dr. Meyer was no good so I'd spared a rush from that quarter. She wouldn't remember she'd had an abortion. If she ever did it would be because something had overridden the hypnosis. A special word, a mood, a dream, it could be anything. As in my case. At times I've thought I might like to obliterate Benjamin and Maria from my memory. At other times not. Anyway, it's been a long time now since I had the ability to hypnotize myself. One learns too much about it. Like the conjuror no longer able to enjoy being fooled, even when one wants to be.

Once Fru Karlsson had gone I packed my beautiful black leather Calvino bag. I'd bought it because it had the same name as the anti-Fascist rebel Italo Calvino. And, of course, because I could afford it.

I knotted my Burberry scarf and walked into the reception area. Linda, who was the receptionist for me and the two other psychologists in our joint practice, looked up.

"Have a nice day, Lukas," she said with an almost inaudible sigh and a scarcely noticeable glance at her watch, which showed, as usual, that it was still only three. She used this Americanism not, primarily, to bless the remaining hours of daylight, or until I went to bed, but to point out the injustice in the fact that my working day was so much shorter than that of my two colleagues, and therefore hers. I think she believed—or thought she believed—that my not taking on more patients showed a lack of solidarity, but there was no way she could know that in recent years the psychology practice had become secondary and functioned more or less as a cover for my other, real job. Which was to kill people.

"Have a nice day, Linda," I said as I strolled out into the lovely December sunshine.

I've never quite been able to make up my mind whether or not Milan is a beautiful city. It has been in the past, you only need to look at the pictures from back then, when Milan was a city in Italy, and not in Capitalia, as I call the stateless condition the world is in today. Of course, before the last of the physical world wars it had been almost supernaturally beautiful, but even after the bombs the city has preserved a discreet but distinct elegance in which the fashion houses in particular had influenced the style and taste, and vice versa. In the days before the sixteen giant business cartels assumed control of Europe, North America, and Asia, factory emissions were subject to central authority regulations, which meant that even in Milan, with one of the worse air-pollution problems in Europe, one could still on a good day see all the way to the white peaks of the Dolomites. Now it lay over the city in a constant veil, and those who could not afford the overpriced air conditioners now in the hands of a monopoly lived lives that were short and sickly.

The cartel-run media tell us that people are richer than ever before and prove it by presenting us with statistics showing the real income per inhabitant. The reality is of course that the creators and directors of the cartels earn a thousand times more than the average worker. Eighty percent of them are on temporary contracts with no chance to plan for the long term. They have to live in the ever-expanding slum that surrounds the city on all sides save in the north.

After Milan became the center of European finance, with the Borsa Milano and the headquarters of seven of the cartels, the population exploded. The city was now not only the largest in Europe but also harbored the world's third-largest slum. I'm no socialist, but you don't need to be one to feel a longing for a time when incomes were lower but distributed more evenly, and there was a functioning state that did its best to help those who were struggling.

I passed the Duomo di Milano. In front of the imposing cathedral, queues of the tourists and the faithful extended into the large square of the Piazza Duomo. At the other end of the square I passed the tables of what those of us working in the business call

Café Morte, Café Dead. The men sitting there—and they were exclusively men—had newspapers and phones in front of them while their eyes swept the square in search of possible employment. The market for contract killing had grown exponentially once the cartels and an unregulated open market took over, and those offering the service could principally be divided into two classes, a bit like prostitution. Café Morte was the outdoor market, for the street-walkers. Customers using the place could get a job done for a fee in the region of 10,000 euros. The quality was variable, as was the discretion offered; but in a society in which both the police and the authorities were drastically reduced and institutionally corrupt the risk of being caught was acceptably low. So the response of the family members or the employers of a target was quite commonly to arrange a contract killing. It meant that the business—like gun running or drug smuggling—was expanding.

The first cartel killings, in which personnel from rival cartels were killed in order to weaken their competitors, were carried out by taxi drivers, and it's generally believed that that's why we're referred to as "drivers." But you've got those who wait for their fares at a taxi rank like the Café Morte, and then you've got the limo drivers, the ones who work the indoor market, the luxury prostitutes, the ones you need to approach through a middleman called a "fixer." Drivers like that have reputations and can cost as much as ten times what they charge at the Café Morte, but if you want to take out some well-protected employee from one of the cartels then these are the ones you need to hire. People like me.

I had no idea I had a talent for work of this kind, would even have thought the opposite. But a high degree of empathy can also help in understanding how an opponent thinks. In the two years I'd been in the killing business I'd become one of the most in-demand names. Income from my psychology had been sinking from the day my son turned eight years old and died, and after Maria committed suicide it dried up completely. But money wasn't the reason I became a driver. As a psychologist I'm used to deducing people's simple and often banal motivations, and that includes my own. And my motive was revenge. I was able to live with the fact that my child had been born dumb. That was just mere chance, no one's fault, and it didn't spoil anyone's happiness. But I couldn't live with what had taken Benjamin's life: human greed, businessmen who had worked out that if they took a few discreet shortcuts around the expensive fire regulations required for their electrical products they could sell them cheaper than their competitors and still increase the profit margin. I realize it might seem a bit strange to claim that a defective bedside lamp could be the cause of a man abandoning his humanity and embarking on a career as a spreader of death. And I use the word "spread" advisedly; because I didn't have one name to focus my anger on I had to take revenge on all those who ran the cartels and took those kinds of decisions, those whose unscrupulous worship of Mammon had taken Benjamin and Maria from me. The way a terrorist whose family has been killed by a bomb will fly a plane into a skyscraper full of people he knows aren't personally responsible for his loss but who are still complicit in their death. Yes, I knew exactly why I had become a man who murdered prominent members of the cartels. But such knowledge doesn't change anything; insight like that doesn't necessarily lead to a change in behavior. Spreading death did nothing to slake my thirst for revenge—I had to keep going. I could of course have ended my own life, but the sudden realization that life is meaningless doesn't necessarily mean that people want to stop living. People like Maria are, after all, the exception.

I carried out a test which I did at regular intervals, letting my gaze sweep across the pavement tables outside the café. Noted that I still did not register any flicker of recognition in the gazes that met mine. They simply recorded the fact that I was not a customer and moved on. Good.

To carry on making a living in the limousine trade it was imperative that no one—not even the customer—should know your face. The fixers took twenty-five per cent of the fee and they were worth it, if for no other reason than that we could hide ourselves behind them. Among those who got taken in the limo branch—and by "taken" I don't mean by the police—there were more fixers than drivers. You only had to look at the gravestones in the Cimitero Maggiore to know that.

In addition to my unquenchable thirst for revenge I had certain other advantages as a driver. One of them was Judith Szabó, known simply in the business as the Queen. She was one of the three or four best fixers and her abilities were legendary. People said the Queen never left a boardroom meeting without a deal, and at this moment in time I was her only regular client. And only lover. I think. Of course, I can't be certain—her previous steady client also believed he was her only lover. Another advantage was that unlike many of the other drivers I had a credible cover, at least I did as long as I had enough patients not to make it seem odd that I should keep on turning up at the office. My third and most important advantage was that I had a murder weapon the others didn't. Hypnosis.

I stopped at a pedestrian crossing and waited for the light to change from red to green, all senses on the alert. I no longer like standing still in a public setting without knowing who the people around me are. A rifle with a telescopic sight and silencer behind one of those French balconies, a knife in the back as the lights change to green, the blade up into the kidneys so the initial pain is so great the victim is unable to make a sound but is left lying there as the crowds move on.

There was a time when drivers were at the top of the food chain, or at least had no need to walk in fear of their lives. This was before the cartels began employing the best of them on a permanent basis, so that the drivers themselves became key employees and, as such, legitimate targets. The cartels had organized their own militia, which were in practice above the law, and competition for the markets—meaning principally technology, entertainment, and medicine—was becoming more and more reminiscent of old-fashioned wars than old-fashioned capitalism. I had recently read an article that compared the situation with that of the Opium War of 1839, when the British East India Company, with the support of the British government, went to war against China to defend their right to export opium to the Chinese, on the basis of the mercantile principle of free trade. Today it was no longer about opium but technology, entertainment, a kind of mild stimulant known as *artstimuli*, and medicines that extended one's lifespan.

The strange thing was that while the markets were deregulated and the competition in every way tougher, the number of actors had fallen, not risen, and the incidents of mono- and oligopoly more frequent as a result of the acquisitions. Because as they say in the world of the sharks: size is everything. Or rather, size won't help if you've got no teeth. The teeth were the best brains, the best inventors, the best chemists, the best business strategists, and in due course these rose to the same status and wage levels as the top footballers. But after a while those companies that were unable to afford these wages—and were unscrupulous enough—began to kill the best brains of the others as a way of lowering the standards and enabling themselves to compete. The best companies had to respond in kind in order to remain market leaders, and the best chemists, inventors, and leaders were replaced by a new aristocracy: the best contract killers. It looked as though the company with the best killers would, in the long run, turn out winners. And that's what started the cannibalizing process we're in the middle of now. Companies hired killers to kill their competitors' best contract killers.

And that's why I froze when I heard the voice behind me, and a little to my left, in what is so aptly called the driver's *blind spot*. It wasn't because I recognized the voice—I didn't—and yet I knew it had to be him. Partly because he spoke the Neapolitan variant of the Calabria dialect, which was why they called him "il Calabrese" (Broccoli). Partly because I had been halfway expecting him to appear sooner or later. Partly because no other driver but Gio "il Calabrese" Greco could have sneaked up on me like that. And partly because I could see, reflected in the windscreens of the passing cars, that the man behind me was wearing a white suit, and Greco always wore a white suit when out on a killing.

"Now that's quite an achievement," said the voice into my ear.

I had to steel myself not to turn. I told myself there would be no point, that if he was going to kill me he would already have done so or would do before I could do anything about it. Because what we are talking about here is the best driver in Europe. This is not a matter of opinion. For several years Greco had been the highest paid driver in Europe, and we live in an age in which it is generally accepted that the market is always right. According to Judith, when she was Greco's fixer she could get double what Thal, Fischer, or Alekhin were paid.

"Think you're better than me, Lukas?"

I stepped back half a pace as a trailer whizzed by in front of my face and made the ground shake.

"To the best of my knowledge they pay you three times what they pay me. So no."

"What makes you think I'm talking shop, Lukas? I'm wondering if you think you fuck her better than me?"

I swallowed. He laughed. A hissing laughter that began in a T and then turned into a long, jerking S.

"I'm joking," he said. "I am talking shop. The killing of Signor Chadaux. The board of his company couldn't decide whether it was a traffic accident or a suicide. So they called in an expert on death. Me. Because on the footage from the traffic-monitoring camera—" he pointed up toward the facade on the other side of the road where I knew the cameras were mounted—"you see Signor Chadaux standing with the other pedestrians waiting for the red light right where we're standing. But when the lights changed to green and everyone began to cross, Signor Chadaux was left standing here alone. He looks like he's asleep on his feet as another crowd of pedestrians comes up alongside him. But then the lights change to red, he closes his eyes and moves his lips, as though he's counting inwardly. Have you seen the recording?"

I shook my head.

"Then perhaps you saw it when it actually happened?"

Again I shook my head.

"Really? Then let me describe it for you. He steps straight out onto the pedestrian crossing. Know how many cars ran over him before they managed to stop the traffic? No, then you probably don't know that either. Let me tell you something they didn't put in the newspaper, and that is that Signor Chadaux had to be scraped off the asphalt like chewing gum."

"Did they find out whether it was an accident or a suicide?"

Greco laughed that thin, hissing laughter of his. Softly, but so close to my ear I could still hear it above the traffic.

"Chadaux's company is a competitor of one of the companies you're working for. You believe in coincidence, Lukas?"

"Sure. They happen all the time."

"No, you don't." Greco wasn't laughing anymore. "I studied the video a few times, then I came down here to take a closer look. In particular I checked that traffic light that you can see in the video Signor Chadaux has his eyes fixed on."

Gio Greco pointed to the set of lights directly opposite us. "It has screwdriver markings on it. And when I checked the security camera it turns out it was down for about an hour the previous night, not that anyone could explain why. How did you do it, Lukas? Did you install a screen in the traffic light which you could use your phone to communicate with to hypnotize Signor Chadaux? Did you tell him when to step out into the road, or was there a trigger? The red light, for example?"

Through the winter cold I could feel the sweat breaking out over my whole body. I had only ever spoken to Greco twice before, and I was afraid both times. Not because there was anything to be afraid of—this was before drivers were used to liquidate each other out. It was just his aura. Or rather, the absence of an aura, the way cold is just the absence of warmth. The way pure evil is just the absence of mercy. As I see it, a psychopath is not a person possessing a special quality, but someone just lacking something.

"Have they put you on to me?" I asked. "Chadaux's company?"

On the traffic lights in front of us the red figure gave way to the green, and on either side of us people streamed across. If I moved, would I get a bullet in the back?

"Who knows? Whatever, you don't sound as if you're all that afraid to die, Lukas?"

"There's worse fates than leaving this vale of tears," I said as I watched the retreating backs of the pedestrians who had left us alone on the pavement.

"Better than being left—I think we can agree on that, Lukas."

The first thing that occurred to me was, naturally, that he was talking about how Judith had left him. It would have been naive to suppose that he wouldn't find out somehow or other that I had taken his place as both her client and her lover. But something in the way he said it made me think he might have been referring to me. That it was me who had been left by my son Benjamin and by my wife. I had no idea how he might have come by such information.

"Hello, I'm . . ." he said in English. The words came slowly, rhythmically.

I stiffened.

"Relax," he said with a soft laugh. "I'm not going to shoot you here right in front of the security cameras."

I forced one foot forward, then the other. I walked on without looking back.

The most obvious reason Milan has become the capital for Europe's drivers is, of course, that it has become a center for technology and innovation. The best brains are here, the richest companies. The city is a watering hole on the savannah where animals of every kind congregate; apart from the handful of herbivores so large they've got no need to worry, most of us are hunters, prey, or scavengers. We live in a symbiotic relationship of fear from which none of us can escape.

I walked along one of those narrow cobbled pedestrian lanes that twist slightly so you can't see far ahead. Maybe that's why I always choose this route to my office: I don't have to see everything that lies ahead.

I passed the small, exclusive fashion shops, some of the less exclusive, and the workshops housing the craftsmen who experienced a renaissance after the mass production of so many goods came to a standstill as a result of the shortage of raw materials.

My chessboard was waiting at home for me, set up for my favorite game, Murakami versus Carlsen. It was a game from the years after Carlsen peaked, but well known because in the very early stages Carlsen wandered into a trap so obvious and yet so cunning that it was afterward called the Murakami Trap and became as famous as the Lasker Trap. Murakami would later use a brutal variation of the trap in an even more celebrated game of lightning chess, against the young Italian comet Olsen, from right here in Milan.

My heart was still pounding after the encounter with Gio Greco. I knew, of course, that murder in the street wasn't his style; he left that kind of thing to the drivers. But when he had said "Hello, I'm . . . ," I had felt certain my time was up, and I would soon be meeting Benjamin and Maria again. I don't know whether it's because Greco is a fan of Johnny Cash, but his calling card, his farewell to his victims is, according to legend, "Hello, I'm Greco." I know some people say he only began saying that *after* the legend arose. If he wasn't actually present, that is. Because he was capable of remote killing too, as the case of the spectacular attack on the Giualli family in the Sforzesco Castle the previous year showed.

I knew no one was following me, but naturally I couldn't help wondering why he had suddenly appeared like that and given me just half of his famous line. Because Greco had been right; I didn't believe in coincidences. Was it a threat? But why should I take the threat seriously when both he and I knew he could have done the job there and then; it would have been a perfect opportunity. What was he planning? Maybe he just wanted me to believe he was planning something, maybe that was just an old lover wanting to make sure the new one didn't sleep too well at night.

My thoughts were interrupted by loud voices and shouts ahead of me. A crowd of people were gathered in the narrow street, standing with their heads looking upward. I looked up too. Black smoke was belching out from a French balcony on the floor below the top. Behind the balcony bars I saw something, a pale face. A boy. Eight maybe? Ten? It was hard to tell from below.

"Jump," shouted one of the onlookers.

"Why doesn't someone run up and get the boy?" I asked the man who had shouted.

"The gate's locked."

Others came running. The crowd doubled, trebled in size and I realized I must have arrived just after the fire had been discovered. The boy opened his mouth, but no sound came out. I should have realized at once, and maybe I did. It probably wouldn't have changed anything; I could feel the tears welling up inside.

I ran to the gate and hammered on it. A small aperture opened and I was looking into a bearded face.

"Fire on the sixth!" I said.

"We're waiting for the fire brigade," the man answered, his voice suggesting a line already learned and rehearsed.

"That's going to be too late—someone has to rescue that boy."

"The place is on fire."

"Let me in," I said quietly, though everything in me wanted to scream.

The gate opened slightly. The man was tall and broad, with a head that looked as if it had been beaten down between his shoulders with a sledgehammer. He was wearing an ordinary driver's uniform, a nondescript black suit. So when I pushed my way in and past him, it was because he allowed me to do so.

I sprinted up the stairs, the toxic air scorching my lungs as I ran, counting each floor. When I stopped on the sixth there were two doors. I grabbed the handle of the one on the left. It was locked, and I heard the furious barking of a dog within. Then I realized the balcony was on the right side of the front of the building and tried the handle of the second door.

To my surprise it opened and smoke came billowing out. Behind the black wall I glimpsed flames. I pulled a piece of my woollen coat up over my face and went in. I couldn't see much, but it seemed to be a small apartment. I headed in the direction the balcony had to be and banged into a sofa. I shouted, but there was no reply. Coughed and headed on. Flames licked from an open fridge door and on the floor in front of it lay the twisted and charred remains of something. A bedside lamp?

As I say, I don't believe in coincidences, and this was an orchestrated replay, arranged for my benefit alone. Yet I still had to do what I knew I was expected to do—I could see no alternative.

A sudden gust of wind briefly wafted the smoke away from the balcony door and I saw the boy. He was wearing a dirty blazer with a badge on it, a stained, threadbare T-shirt and trousers to match. He stared at me with wide-open eyes. His hair was fair, just like Benjamin's, but not as thick.

I took two quick steps forward and wrapped my arms around the boy, lifted him up and felt the small, warm fingers grab the skin at the back of my neck. I raced toward the front door, coughing smoke. Found it after feeling my way along the wall, tried to locate the handle. Couldn't find it. I kicked at the door, put my shoulder to it, but it wouldn't budge. Where the hell was the door handle?

I got my answer when I heard the hissing from the fridge, like the sound of air escaping from a punctured hosepipe. Gas streamed out, igniting the flames and illuminating the whole apartment.

The door had no handle. No keyhole, nothing. Directed by: Gio Greco.

Without letting go of the boy I ran back to the open balcony door. I leaned over the wrought-iron railings on the shallow balcony.

"Breathe," I said to the boy, who was still staring at me with his wide-open brown eyes. He did as I instructed, but I knew that no matter how far out I held him, we would both soon die from carbon monoxide poisoning.

I looked down at the crowd in the street below, the faces staring up open-mouthed. Some were shouting, but I heard nothing, their words were drowned by the raging of the flames behind us. Just as I didn't hear the sirens of the approaching fire engines. Because there were none.

The man who had opened the gate for me, he wasn't just wearing the same suit as the others at the Café Morte; his face also had the same cold, closed expression, as dead as his victims.

I looked to my right. There was an ordinary balcony there, but it was too far away, there was no chance of reaching it. No balconies to the left, but there was a small ledge leading to the nearest window in the neighboring apartment.

There was no time to lose. I held the boy a little bit away from me and looked into his brown eyes.

"We're going there, so you're going to have to sit on my back and hold on tight. Understand?"

The boy didn't answer, just nodded.

I swung him over onto my back and he held around my neck and wrapped his legs around my stomach. I stepped over the railing, holding fast to the rail as I placed one foot on the ledge.

It was so narrow there was room for only a small part of one shoe, but fortunately they were my thick winter shoes, stiff enough to provide some support. I let go of the railing with one hand and pressed it against the wall.

People down below were screaming up at us, but I was hardly aware of them, or of the height. Not that I'm not afraid of heights, because I am. If we fell we would die, no question. But since the brain knew that the alternative to balancing on the ledge was burning alive it did not hesitate. And because balancing requires more concentration than the summoning of desperate powers, the brain temporarily closed down the fear side since that served no useful function in the current situation. In my experience, both as a psychologist and as a professional killer, we human beings are surprisingly rational in that respect.

With infinite care I let go of the railing. I was standing with my chest and cheek pressed in against the rough plaster and felt myself in balance. It was as though the boy realized he had to remain quite still on my back.

There was no longer any shouting from the street below; the only sound was that of the flames that were now outside on the balcony. In a sort of slow shuffle I started to move carefully to my right along the small but hopefully solid ledge. Solid it wasn't. To my alarm I saw it disintegrating in gel-like pieces beneath my feet. It was as though the pressure from the shoes created a chemical reaction in the ledge, and I could see now that it was a slightly different colour to the rest of the facade. Since I was unable to stand in the same place for more than a few seconds before the ledge began disintegrating I kept moving. We were already so far from the French balcony that retreat had become impossible.

When I was close enough to the window in the neighboring apartment I carefully loosened my Burberry scarf with my left hand while holding on with my right to the protruding windowsill. I had been given the scarf by Judith as a fortieth birthday present, along with a card on which she had written that she liked me a lot, a joke referring to the strongest word I ever used to express devotion to her. If I could manage to wrap the scarf around my hand I could break the windowpane, but one end of it was trapped between the boy's arm and my neck.

The boy gave a start and moved as I jerked the scarf free, and I lost my balance. With my right hand gripping round the windowsill and only my right foot on the ledge I swung out helplessly from the facade like a barn door on hinges, almost fell, and then at the last moment managed to grab hold of the window ledge with my other hand.

I looked down and saw the Burberry scarf gently drifting down toward the ground. The height. The hollow feeling in my stomach. Got to keep it out. I raised my bare right fist and punched the windowpane with all my might, trying to tell myself that by hitting so hard I was reducing the risk of cuts. The glass shattered in a shower of shards and I felt the pain race up my arm. It wasn't from the cut but because my fist had hit something hard. I grabbed hold of whatever this hard thing was, leaned to one side, and saw that my punch had landed on a metal grid. It was hinged on both sides and locked in the center with a large padlock. Who puts wrought-iron bars on a sixth-floor window?

The answer was obvious.

Through the bars I looked into a small, bare, dimly lit apartment. No furniture, only a large fire-axe hanging on the wall directly facing me, as though on exhibition. Or to put it another way, as though Greco wanted me to see it immediately.

Scrabbling, scraping sounds. A dark figure ran over the floor snarling and jumping. I felt the wet jaws and the teeth across my fingers holding round the bars. Then it dropped down to the floor and began howling furiously.

Instinctively I leaned backward as the dog jumped up at me, and now I could feel the boy's small hands slipping down my neck. He wouldn't be able to hold on much longer. We had to get in there, quickly.

The dog—a Rottweiler—sat on the floor directly below the window, slathering from its open jaws with white, glistening teeth. It stood up on its hind legs and leaned them against the wall, but its snout kept butting up against the bars and it was unable to reach my fingers. As it stared at me with a cold, expressionless hatred I noticed something dangling from the collar around its thick neck. A key.

The dog gave up. Its forepaws slid down and it sat on the floor, barking up at me.

The boy tensed his legs and tried to ride higher up my back. He was whimpering softly. I stared at the key. At the fire-axe. And at the padlock.

Greco was willing to sacrifice a piece.

That's what the great chess players do. Not to give the opponent an advantage but to improve their own position on the board. At that exact moment I couldn't see what his plan was, but I knew he had to have one. During a chess tournament in Nottingham in 1936 Emanuel Lasker, the German world chess champion, watched his opponent think for half an hour before finally offering him a major capture. The German declined the offer but went on to win the game. When he was asked afterward why he hadn't taken the piece he replied that when an opponent as good as his thinks about a move for half an hour before deciding that the sacrifice is worth the reward, then he certainly wasn't going to respond by making the exact move his opponent had been expecting of him.

I thought about it. Ran through it. And made the move my opponent had been counting on.

I squeezed my left arm between the bars. It was so tight the sleeves of my jacket and shirt were pulled up exposing the naked, bloodied skin. My offer to the dog. Which responded silently and at lightning speed.

It twisted its lips and I could see the teeth sink into my underarm. The pain didn't come until it clamped its jaws. I pushed my right arm through, but as my hand stretched for the key around its collar the dog pulled my left arm down toward the floor in an attempt to get away from my free hand.

It isn't true that certain breeds are able to lock their jaws, but some bite harder than others. And some are more intelligent than others. Rottweilers bite harder and have a higher IQ than most. So high in fact that I chose a Rottweiler when I made a bet with two other psychology students that I could make an animal perform simple tasks—such as nodding several times, for example—under hypnosis. But the only thing I managed was to get it to sit quite still, and there was nothing new in the fact that a few simple techniques can get animals—everything from dogs and chickens to pigs and crocodiles—to lie motionless and apparently under deep trance. The hypnotist can only take partial credit for this catatonic state, which is due as much to the instinct to "play dead" in situations in which flight is impossible. The aim is to arouse the predator's reluctance to eat something that is already dead and possibly diseased. But it was obviously new enough for my two friends, who handed the money over and earned me an undeserved reputation as the great animal hypnotist. And at that stage of my life I couldn't afford to turn down either one.

I forced my right hand in between the bars until I could reach down to the dog and let my hand rest lightly on the animal's forehead. Moved it slowly and rhythmically back and forth while keeping up a stream of low talk. The dog looked up at me without releasing its jaws. I don't know what it was feeling. A hypnotist is not, in virtue of his trade, any kind of sage. He's just someone who's learned certain techniques, an average chess player lacking in any particular insight who makes the opening gambits he has seen praised in some book. But obviously there are both good and bad hypnotists, and I was, after all, one of the good ones, perhaps even one of the best.

Even in humans, what hypnosis does is leapfrog over the slow cognitive processes, which is why it works so surprisingly quickly, quickly enough for a man waiting at a pedestrian crossing to be manipulated by simply looking into a traffic light for a few seconds and seeing there some previously implanted trigger.

I saw the dog's eyelids half close and felt the jaws relax. Continuing to speak slowly and calmly I moved my right hand to the chain-collar, released the key, and pulled it toward me. At that same moment I felt the boy's grip loosen and his body start to slide down my back. I reached out behind me, grabbing across the little body and caught him by the lining of his trousers before he fell off. I held on to him but knew I wouldn't be able to do so for long.

I had managed to hold on to the key by pressing my thumb inside the key ring; now I had to work it out and get it in the padlock in the middle of the bars. It couldn't be done with one hand. The bite was almost completely relaxed now and carefully I pulled my arm away, feeling at the same time how I was also pulling at the dog's head. The teeth of a predator incline backward, I reflected. It's logical, so that they can hold on to their prey. So very carefully I pushed my arm a little further inward before lifting it; and this time my hand came free. The blood ran down my forearm and into my palm so that I almost slipped off as I gripped round one of the bars with my little finger and ring finger.

"Hold on tight for ten seconds," I said loudly. "Count out loud."

The boy didn't answer but renewed his grip around my neck.

I let go of him and using the other three fingers and my right hand I managed to get the key in the padlock and turn it. The hasp sprang up. I pushed one side of the grid open and turned so that that the boy could climb off me and get in through the window.

From the street below came the sounds of applause and bravos. I entered the apartment. The dog sat quite still, staring off into space, or perhaps deep into itself, who knows? I don't read the professional journals anymore, but I do recall a listing once of animals believed by researchers to experience an "I," and that list didn't include dogs.

The door was lined with a blank metal plate and like the door in the neighboring apartment it had no handle. To make sure it was actually locked I gave it a little shove with my foot before lifting the fire-axe down from its two hooks on the wall. I tested its weight and studied the door.

Blood from my arm dripped onto the wooden floor below me with a deep, sighing sound. I heard another sound and turned to the window.

The boy was standing directly in front of the dog. He was stroking it!

I saw the muscles tense beneath the dog's smooth dark fur, saw its ears prick up. The trance was over. I heard a low growling.

"Get away!" I shouted, but I knew it was too late. The boy managed a half-pace back before his face was splattered with blood. He sank to his knees, a look of shock in his eyes. The blade of the axe was wedged into the wooden floor directly in front of him, and between the blade and the boy lay the decapitated dog's head with its twisted lips. The heart pumped two final spurts of blood from the mutilated body.

For a second or two I simply stood there. And only now did I realize that so far not a sound had come from the boy's lips. I dropped to my knees, right in front of him. Took off my coat and wiped the blood from his face with it before placing a hand on his shoulder and making eye contact with him, then shaping my words with my hands:

You're a mute, is that right?

He didn't respond.

"Are you a mute?" I asked in a loud, clear voice.

The boy nodded.

"I had a son who was a mute too," I said. "He used sign language, so I can understand that. Do you know sign language?"

The boy shook his head. Opened his mouth and pointed in toward the gap. Then he pointed to the axe blade.

"Oh Jesus," I said.

The phone rang.

I took it from my jacket pocket. It was a FaceTime call, unknown number but I had a hunch who it was. I pressed the answer button and a face appeared on the screen. It looked like a Guy Fawkes mask, the mask once used by idealist revolutionaries the world over to protest against the powers that be, the nation state. With the thin moustache, the goatee beard, and the unfailingly ironic smirk that contracted the eyes, Gio Greco looked a bit like a pig.

"Congratulations," said Greco. "I see that the two of you have made it to the torture chamber."

"At least there's no fire in here," I said.

"Oh, when you see what I've got lined up for you'll be wishing you'd died in the fire."

"Why are you doing this, Greco?"

"Because the Abu Dhabi cartel are paying me two million. You should feel honored, it's a record price for a driver."

I swallowed. Acquiring a reputation as a top driver carries its own risks, greater and smaller. Greater, because the price on your own head goes up; smaller, because other drivers won't take a job where they know there's a good chance they'll be the ones that end up in a grave. I'd been relying on that smaller risk to give me some protection.

"I could actually have pushed the price even higher," said Greco. "If they'd been the ones who approached me."

"So you were the one who went to them?"

"The job was my suggestion, yes. And I knew I could offer them a price they couldn't refuse."

The sweat was prickling all over my body, as though it thought that getting rid of liquid like this would improve my chances of survival.

"But why . . . all this? You could have just shot me at the pedestrian crossing."

"Because we had the budget for something a little more extravagant than a bullet, something that would get us talked about in the business. Creating a reputation is, after all—"

"Why?" I had shouted, and saw the boy looking at me with frightened eyes. There was silence at the other end, but I could almost hear his contented smiling.

"Why?" I said again, struggling to keep my voice calm.

"Surely you must know that. You're a psychologist, and you're fucking the Queen."

"Is it jealousy? Is it as simple as that?"

"Oh, but jealousy isn't simple, Lukas. See, after Judith left me I sank into a pretty deep depression. I ended up seeing a psychologist, and he told me that in addition to depression I was suffering from narcissism. I don't know whether it makes sense to say someone *suffers* from having a well-founded self-image, but I told him anyway I'd come for some happiness pills, not to get a fucking diagnosis about completely different things."

I said nothing, but what Greco told me was classic narcissism, where the narcissist refused to recognize the personality disorder or seek treatment for it, and that it was typically through depression that those of us in the health service got to meet the half percent of the population the diagnosis applied to.

"But he wouldn't stop, the idiot," Greco sighed. "Before I shot him he managed to tell me that a characteristic of narcissists is they have a highly developed sense of envy. Like the first narcissist in literature, Cain. You know, the guy in the Bible who killed his own brother out of jealousy. Well, I guess that just about sums me up in a nutshell."

I didn't know whether this shooting his psychologist was a joke, and I had no intention of asking. Nor did I propose to point out the futility of taking revenge for something you know you can never get back. Maybe because that was exactly what I was doing with my own life.

"Now do you see, Lukas? I am the victim of a personality disorder that makes me want to see you suffer. I'm sorry. There's nothing I can do about it."

"I suffer every day, Greco. For God's sake, kill me and let the boy go."

He smacked his lips three times, the way a teacher responds when a pupil gets the addition wrong on the blackboard.

"Dying is easy, Lukas. And your suffering is less now, because the Queen is good medicine, don't you think? OK, I want to open that wound up again. I want to see you squirming on my fork. I want to see you trying to save the boy. And failing again. I hear that when your son had smoke poisoning you drove him to the hospital but you got there too late."

I didn't answer. When we smelled the smoke in the middle of the night and ran into Benjamin's room where he was lying next to that smoldering bedside lamp, he'd already stopped breathing. I drove as fast as I could, but I'm no racing driver and the hospital was too far away and as usual I was a knight on the wrong side of a chessboard.

"The boy's vocal cords," I said. I had to swallow. "Was it you who cut them?"

"To make him more like your son. So blame God for the fact that your wife gave birth to a mute."

I looked at the boy.

Where had Greco found him? Probably in a slum on the outskirts of the city, a place where the sudden disappearance of a small child wouldn't excite much attention.

"I can just jump out the window," I said. "And put an end to the whole game."

"If you do the boy's guts will be destroyed by gas."

"Gas?"

"Just one touch on the keypad." Greco held a small remote control up to the camera. "It's a new invention by one of the cartel's chemists. A type of mustard gas that slowly corrodes the mucous membranes. It is extremely painful and can take several hours. You puke up your own guts before you bleed to death internally."

I looked around the apartment.

"Forget it, Lukas, it'll come through the ceiling and the walls, you won't be able to stop it. In one hour exactly I'll press the start button. Sixty minutes, Lukas. Tick-tock."

"Fire engines are on the way—the firefighters will hear us shouting."

"The fire's already out, Lukas. It was only a thin coating of spirits across a fire-retardant plus a burning fridge. No one's coming. Believe me, the two of you are alone."

I believed him. I looked at my watch and coughed. "We are all alone, Greco."

"You and I are alone at least, now that she's been taken from us both."

I looked up at that Guy Fawkes face of his again. *Taken from us.* What did he mean?

"So long, Lukas."

The connection was broken and I was staring at a blank screen. Things freeze from the outside, but the cold I felt came from inside and was spreading outward. He couldn't have . . . ?

No. It had to be something he wanted to trick me into believing. But why?

So I'd get on the line to Judith at once to check that she was safe, so that he could trace the signal to her hiding place? No, he knew enough about things to know that, like him and like Judith, I had a phone that could switch arbitrarily between such a large network of the cartels' satellites and private base stations that it would make the signal impossible to track.

I stared at the ceiling and the walls. Looked at my watch, at the second hand that jerked remorselessly onward.

Tried to think clearly, to work out my next move, but it was impossible to know if my brain was functioning rationally, like the climber on Everest, knowing that the lack of oxygen at altitude enfeebles his powers of judgment and yet not being helped by that knowledge, confusion is confusion.

Sixty minutes. No. Fifty-nine.

I had to know.

I called her number, my heart pounding furiously as I waited.

One ring. Two.

Pick up. Pick up!

Three rings.

PART TWO: THE MIDDLEGAME

In another of Murakami's games his opponent lost it all in the middlegame. Not because Olsen played badly, but because he was under pressure after falling into the Murakami Trap in the opening. The pleasant-mannered but always silent Olsen had used up valuable time in trying to work out his response and it left him struggling against the clock as well as Murakami's strongly positioned and numerically superior major pieces. A frequently rehearsed argument revolves around the issue of whether Olsen sacrificed his queen, or Murakami took it. Most people, myself included, think it obvious that Olsen would not voluntarily have sacrificed her, and that all he achieved when Murakami took the piece was a postponement of the inevitable. In an ordinary game Olsen would have resigned and handed the victory to Murakami, but in lightning chess there's always the chance your opponent will be stressed into making a catastrophic mistake. So Olsen chose to suffer on and allow himself to be cut up, piece by piece; all the while his one remaining black knight hopped about like a headless chicken. Playing that game over again, move by painful move, was like enduring a Greek tragedy. You know how it's going to end; the object is only to find the most beautiful way of getting there, what the drivers call *the scenic route*.

I met Judith Szabó while she was still Gio Greco's fixer and girl-friend. It was at a ball at the Sforzesco Palace that Luca Giualli, head of the Lombardy cartel, had purchased from the commune and turned into his own private fortress. In addition to hiring a small army to take care of the family's security he had employed me to look for holes in the security routines and pick up signs of any imminent planned attacks.

I was standing by the piano in the atrium looking out across the crowds of the rich and the powerful in their tuxedos and ball-gowns. I noticed her, even though she tried to carry herself just like any other guest. Not only because she was so strikingly beautiful in her bright red gown and long, raven-dark hair, but because she had been unable to resist approaching me like a professional.

"You're not doing your job especially well," was the first thing she said to me.

She was a couple centimeters taller than my 175.

"You must be Judith Szabó," I said.

"See, that's better. How did you work that out?"

"I hear things. And you walk around like a queen and look around like a driver. Your name isn't on the guest list, so how did you get in?"

"I am on the guest list. As Anna Fogel, from the Tokyo cartel. There's an invitation in the same name. It was just too easy to hack the system, and the check on my fake ID was embarrassingly feeble." She flashed a bank card at me.

I nodded. "And why wouldn't I just sound the alarm now and have you cuffed?"

She smiled briefly before nodding in the direction of Luca Giualli, who stood conversing with the mayor of Milan, a man who had spoken enthusiastically of returning to the city-state model of Italy.

"Because—" said Judith Szabó, and I knew more or less what she was about to say—"to do so would reveal that you had allowed a potential assassin to get so near your employer that she—had she so wished—could have killed him."

"Then why are you here?"

"To deliver a message. From you know who."

"The Greek. Broccoli head."

She smiled thinly. "He just wants to find out whether you're as good as they say you are."

"Better than him, you mean?"

Her smiled broadened. Her eyes were so lovely. Cold and blue. And I thought at the time, she has a psychopath's pulse, her heart would beat slowly in a life-or-death situation. Later I would discover I was mistaken, that she was simply a consummate actress. And that the reason she was able to act the psychopath so well was that she was living with one.

"And now at least we know you aren't the best, Herr Meyer." She looked into my eyes as she brushed something from the lapel of my Brioni tuxedo, though I knew there was nothing there.

"Excuse me, Herr Meyer, I've got someone waiting for me."

She must have seen how I lifted my gaze above her shoulder and slowly shook my head, because she tensed, turned, and looked up at one of the interior balconies in the atrium. It was too dark for her to see whether there was anyone in the darkness behind the open balcony door, but when she lowered her gaze she saw the red dot of a laser beam dancing across her gown.

"How long has that been there?" she asked.

"Red on red," I said. "I doubt whether any of the guests have noticed it yet."

"And how long have you known that Anna Vogel doesn't exist?"

"Three days. I asked for every name on the list to be double-checked, and when Anna Vogel cropped up and there's no one of that name in the Tokyo cartel it naturally made me curious about who you might be. And it looks as if my guess was right."

That smile of hers was no longer quite so steady.

"What happens now?"

"Now you go back to the person waiting for you and tell him that he's the one who's been sent a message."

Judith Szabó stood there, studying me. I knew what she was wondering about. Whether I had planned to let her go or had made my mind up on the spot.

Whatever, two weeks later I would have reason to regret that decision.

Fourth ring.

She always has a phone close by, always. Please, Judith.

Fifth ring.

Don't be dead.

I called her two weeks after that meeting at the Sforzesco Palace.

"Hello," was all she said.

I recognized her voice at once. Probably because I'd been thinking about her.

"Hi," I said. "I'm calling because you rang this number. Can I ask how you got it?"

"No," she said. "But you can ask if I'm free for dinner this evening."

"Are you?"

"Yes. The table's booked. Seven o'clock at Seta."

"That's early. Will I survive?"

"If you're punctual."

I smiled at what I took to be a joke.

But I was on time. And she was already seated at the table when I arrived. As before, I was struck by the austerity of her beauty. No sweetness, just healthy, symmetrical, and properly proportioned. But then those eyes of hers. Those eyes . . .

"You're a widower," she said, once we had got a little shop talk out of the way without revealing any secrets.

"What makes you think that?"

She nodded in the direction of my hand. "No driver wears a wedding ring. It tells you something about them. It makes them potentially vulnerable, knowing that there's someone they love."

"Maybe I wear it as a distraction. Or maybe I'm divorced."

"Maybe. The pain in your eyes tells me something different."

"Maybe that's from all the victims I have on my conscience."

"Is it?"

"No."

"Well then?"

"Tell me something about yourself first."

"What do you want to know?"

"There's probably quite a difference between what I want to know and what I'm permitted to know. Start anywhere you like."

She smiled, tasted the wine, and nodded to the wine waiter who, without asking, had known who would be doing the tasting.

"I'm from a well-to-do family. My every material need was met, but none of my emotional needs. The closest to that was my father, who abused me regularly from the age of eleven. What d'you think a psychologist would make of that and my ending up in this business?"

"You tell me."

"I've got three university degrees, no children, I've lived in six countries and always earned more than my lovers and my ex-husband, and I was permanently bored. Until I started in this business. First as a client. Then as . . . a little more. Right now I'm Gio Greco's girlfriend."

"Why not the other way round?"

"What d'you mean?"

"Why don't you say Gio Greco is your boyfriend? You use the passive form."

"Isn't that what strong men's women usually do?"

"You don't strike me as someone who's easy to dominate. *Right now*, you say: that makes it sound like a purely temporary arrangement."

"And you sound like a person preoccupied with semantics."

"The mouth overflows with what the heart is full of—isn't that what they say?"

She raised her glass and we drank a toast.

"Am I mistaken?" I asked.

She shrugged. "Aren't all relationships temporary arrangements? Some end when the love is gone, or the money, or the entertainment value. Others when there's no life left. What happened in your case?"

I twirled the thick-bellied wine glass between my fingers. "The latter."

"Competitors' drivers?"

I shook my head. "It was before I entered the business. She took her own life. Our son died in a fire the year before."

"Grief?"

"And guilt."

"And was she? Guilty?"

I shook my head. "The guilty one was the maker of the Mickey Mouse lamp in the bedroom. It was made of a cheap and highly inflammable material in order to undercut the competition. The maker denied any guilt. He was one of the richest men in France."

"Was?"

"He died in a fire."

"We aren't by any chance talking about François Augvieux who burned to death on board his yacht in the harbor at Cannes?"

I didn't answer.

"So that was you. We always wondered who it was. There was no very obvious client. An impressive debut. Because it was your debut, wasn't it?"

"The world doesn't need people who refuse to use their power to do something good."

Again she put her head on one side, as though to study me from another angle. "Is that the reason you're in this business? To kill unscrupulous profiteers and revenge your son and wife?"

It was my turn to shrug. "You'd have to ask a psychologist about that. But tell me, what would the Greek make of you and me sitting here and dining together this evening?"

"What *would*? What makes you think he doesn't know?"

"Does he?"

She smiled quickly. "He's out on a job. And I'm on a job too. I'd like to have you in my stable."

"You make me sound like a racehorse."

"You got anything against that?"

"Not the analogy. But I don't need a fixer."

"Oh, but you do. You're too easily outmaneuvered without one. You need someone who's got your back."

"The way I recall it, you were the one who got outmaneuvered."

"I hope you don't take this personally, Lukas, but you shouldn't be here right now, you should be with your client."

I could feel my pulse quicken.

"Thanks, Judith, but Giualli's safe enough in his fortress; and there are no traitors in our crew, I've made sure of that personally."

Judith Szabó took something out of her Gucci bag and placed it on the tablecloth in front of me. It was a drawing or a print. It showed a cat running with something that looked like a lit explosive charge fastened to its body. In the background was a castle.

"This is a five-hundred-year-old illustration of an offensive tactic used by the Germans back in the sixteenth century. They would capture a cat or a dog that had found its way out through one of those little escape routes animals always find as a way out of the fortress or village they come from, then tie an explosive charge to it and drive it home. And hope the animal would get back up through its tunnel before the fuse burned down."

I felt a prickling between my shoulder blades. I already had a pretty good idea of what was coming next. It was something I hadn't—and should have—thought of.

"Gio is . . ." She seemed to be looking for the words. And as well as not being weak, Judith Szabó didn't strike me as a person who had trouble finding her words. When finally she did, she spoke quietly, and I had to lean forward to hear.

"I've got no problem with the method as such—it's our job, after all, and we do what we have to do. But there are limits. At least, there are for some of us. Like when that boy who lives with his mother at Sforzesco, Anton . . ."

The name made me jump. Paolo Giualli and his wife, twenty years younger than him, were good people. Good, at least, considering how rich and powerful they were. They had three well-brought-up children who treated me with a distant courtesy, which I reciprocated. Things were a little different with Anton, the five-year-old son of the cook, who lived in one of the service flats below stairs and was so like Benjamin I had to make a conscious effort to control my feelings for him. Judith Szabó stopped, maybe noticing that the name had a particular resonance for me. She coughed before continuing: "So Anton is going to be the cat," she said.

I was already halfway out of my seat.

"It's too late, Lukas. Sit down."

I looked at her. Her voice was steady but I thought I could see tears in those blue eyes of hers. I knew nothing. Only that I was, once again, the knight.

Several days would pass before the testimony of witnesses and forensic examinations revealed what had happened. The Giualli children were accompanied by bodyguards wherever they went—at home, at school, at ballet, at karate, visiting friends—but the same thing didn't apply to children of the staff. All employees were searched on arrival and departure—for treachery is, after all, a part of human nature. But the chances of their being kidnapped were regarded as remote, especially since all employees had signed a contract which clearly stated that, in any such eventuality, their employer was absolved of any responsibility.

When Anton returned home from school that afternoon, an hour later than usual, he was in a state of exhaustion and told his mother how he'd been stopped by a man on his way through the Sempione Park. The man had held a cloth against the boy's face, everything went black and Anton said he had no idea how long he'd been out before waking up beneath one of the bushes in the park. His neck and throat were hurting, but apart from that he was feeling as well as could be expected. When asked to describe the man all Anton could remember was that, in spite of the heat of the day, he had been wearing an overcoat.

His mother had straight away spoken to Luca Giualli who at once rang the police and the doctor. The doctor had said the pains and the swelling around the neck could indicate that something—he declined to speculate on what it might be—had been forced down the boy's throat. But he couldn't say anymore until he had taken a closer look.

According to the police report, four officers had been approaching the entrance to the fortress when the explosion occurred. The charge contained in the gelatine bag in the boy's stomach would not have been powerful enough to kill Luca Giualli and his wife had they been in their part of the fortress and Anton in the service flat. But they were—as we said—good people, and they were not merely close by but actually in the same room, so that there was little left of any of them once the police and the fire brigade had made their way through the ruins.

These details were still unknown to me as I sat that evening in one of Milan's best restaurants looking into Judith Szabó's blue eyes. What I knew for sure was that Anton was dead, and probably Luca Giualli too. That I had failed to do my job, and that it was now too late. I realized too that Judith Szabó had not been joking when she said I might be dead if I turned up late.

"At that ball," I said, "I should never have let you go."

"No, you shouldn't have. But you wanted to send a message to Greco, didn't you?"

I ignored that. "You invited me here so I wouldn't be at the castle when the boy came home. Why?"

"At the ball I realized you were good. You would have smelled the fuse and possibly saved Luca Giualli."

"Was it Greco's decision to get me out here tonight for this meal?"

"Greco takes all the operational decisions."

"But?"

"But this was my suggestion."

"Why? As you see, you've overestimated my ability to sniff out anything at all. When you invited me here, I thought—" I stopped and pressed my thumb and index finger into my eyes.

"Thought what?" she said quietly.

I breathed out heavily. "That you were interested in me."

"I understand," she said, and laid her hand over mine. "But you aren't mistaken. I am interested in you."

I looked down at her hand. "Oh?"

"The main reason I got you out of the way is because I didn't want you to die too. You let me go the last time we met. You didn't need to—I don't even think it was something you planned. So it was my turn to show a little mercy."

"Showing mercy is not the same as being interested."

"But I'm telling you I am. I need a new client. I think I've just lost the one I had."

She looked down without moving her hand from mine. With her other hand she lifted the serviette from her lap and held it out to me.

"You're crying," she explained.

That was how things started between me and Judith. With tears. Was that the way it was going to end too?

Six rings.

Seven.

Eight.

I was about to hang up.

"Hey, lover boy. I was in the shower."

As I breathed in hard I realized I had been holding my breath.

"What's up?" she asked, worried, as though she'd read my silence.

"I'm in a locked apartment with a mute boy—"

"Gio." She said it before I'd finished my sentence.

"Yes," I said. "I was afraid he'd traced you too."

"He can't find me here, I've already told you that."

"Everybody can be found, Judith."

"Where are you?"

"That's not important, you can't help me. I just wanted to hear that you're OK."

"Lukas, tell me where—"

"Now you know he's trying to reach you by using me. Stay hidden. I . . ."

Not even now, in this situation, could I make myself say it.

Love.

That was a word reserved for Maria and Benjamin. Over the course of the year in which Judith and I had been together it had occurred to me that maybe one day I would be able to say it and mean it. But no matter how much Judith fascinated and interested me and in all sorts of ways made me happy, that was one door that seemed locked shut.

". . . am so fond of you, my darling."

"Lukas!"

I hung up.

Leaned against the wall.

Looked at my watch. It was working against me, that much I realized. But why had he given me all this time? Why run the risk of my calling up my allies and summoning them to come to my assistance, rescue me? Or perhaps even the police?

Because he knew I had no allies, or none willing to go up against someone like Gio Greco. As for the police, when was the last time they got involved in a stand-off between drivers, with or without an innocent boy as bait?

I beat the wall with the palm of my hand and the boy looked startled.

"It's all right," I said. "I'm just trying to think."

I put my hand to my forehead. Greco wasn't crazy, not in the sense that he acted irrationally. It was just that with his particular personality disorders—a more precise diagnosis would probably be *malign* narcissism, which isn't far away from psychopath—he operated with a rationale that was completely different from that of so-called normal people. If I was to predict his next move then I needed to understand him. We were revengers, both of us, but that was where the similarity ended. My crusade against the cartels was not just a form of spiritual cleansing, a way of muting my own pain; it was also principled: I wanted to tear down a world order in which the greediest and most unscrupulous profiteers had all the power. Greco didn't want to torture me as a matter of principle, but for the brief, passing, and sadistic pleasure it gave him. And in pursuit of that pleasure he was prepared to sacrifice the lives of innocent people. That was it. That had to be the reason why he didn't just start the torture or the killing straight away; the pleasure would have been *too* brief. He wanted first to enjoy the knowledge that I knew what lay in store for me. This—my fear—was just his starter.

I went over my reasoning again.

There was something there that didn't quite add up.

The direction in which I was thinking, that he just wanted to see me suffer—that was something he'd planted, it was exactly what he *wanted* me to think. It was too simple. He wanted something more. What does a narcissist want? He wants affirmation. He wants to know he's best. Or, even more important, he wants everyone else to know he's best. Naturally. He wants to show the whole business, the whole cartel world, that he's better than me.

So far he'd managed to make me go along with everything he'd planned. I had run up the stairs to rescue the boy. I had managed to get us over to the other apartment. I had used the axe the way I was supposed to use it. I had . . .

I froze.

I had called Judith. He'd arranged it that way. He wanted me to call her. Why? Phone calls couldn't be tracked and phones located the way people once could be. Silence.

I took the phone out again, tapped in her name. Pressed the phone to my ear. Silence.

The phone wasn't ringing. I looked at the screen. The symbol showed not just a bad connection, it showed no connection at all. I crossed to the window, held the phone. Still no connection. We were in the middle of Milan, it wasn't possible. Or, of course, it was possible. If someone installed a jamming apparatus in a room they could turn the jamming signal on and off at will.

I stared at the walls, trying to see where Greco might have hidden the box. On the ceiling, maybe? Was the box there to ensure I couldn't call anyone once I had—predictably enough—called Judith? Greco probably thought that after all there just *might* be someone I could call who could possibly do something to upset his plans.

Accept. I had to accept that that possibility no longer existed. And I had to stop thinking about why it was he might possibly have wanted me to ring Judith, because there was nothing at all I could do about it. At least now she knew he was on the warpath, and I had to believe her when she said that she couldn't be traced through the phone, and that he didn't know where her apartment was, because not even I knew that.

I looked at my watch. And at the boy.

I had no doubt at all that Greco would use gas; he'd done so before. When the most brilliant inventor in the largest of the three electro-cartels took his vehicle in for repairs Greco had bribed a mechanic, entered the place by night and simply installed a gas pellet in the gearbox that would break open when the inventor put the gear lever into overdrive. The cartel's security people had come for the car the following day, checked it for any explosive devices and then driven it through the heavily trafficked city streets to the house where he lived. It wasn't until a few days later, when the inventor drove to his country home by Lake Como, that the car was out on a motorway and in due course he moved up into overdrive. The car went off the road close to one of the large bridges, rolled over, and was crushed against the cobbles of a village square directly below. The death was recorded as a road accident. Not that insiders didn't know gas was involved, for the death of everyone who is important for a company's competitive success is always regarded as suspicious and involves an autopsy. But according to Judith the electro-cartel was anxious to play down the vulnerability of its security system as being bad for its reputation. The irony of it all was that within the drivers' world I was the one given the credit for the attack, merely because on one occasion I had answered a query from another limo driver about how to eliminate this chemist who had an army to guard him and who rarely left his fortress home, and then only in a bulletproof car with his own personal driver and bodyguards for a skiing trip to the mountains at Bergamo. I suggested that one should track down the personal driver and hypnotize him without his knowing it, simply prime him with a trigger word which—when he heard or read it—would immediately put him into a trance. This type of hidden hypnosis leaves the person apparently exactly the same, and he feels exactly the same too. I suggested the trigger word should be a place name he would be bound to see along one of the fastest and most dangerous stretches of road between Milan and Bergamo.

I don't know whether Greco was ever told of my suggestion and that was what inspired him, or what he thought about me being given the credit for the attack. The point is, I would never have carried out such a mission; I never do jobs in which innocent people can die.

Again I looked at my watch. The problem wasn't that time was moving too fast. It moved slowly, but I was thinking even slower.

I had to get the boy out of the apartment before the gas was released.

If I could get the people down in the street to tear down one of the shop blinds, might they possibly be able to use it as a jumping sheet?

I crossed to the window and looked down.

A man in police uniform stood down there. Apart from him the street was empty.

"Hey!" I suddenly shouted. "I need help!"

The uniformed man looked up. He neither responded nor moved. And although he was too far away for me to see his face clearly, I noticed that the big man's head seemed to have been beaten down between his shoulders. The pedestrian precinct was closed at both ends of the block by security tape, presumably fake too, like the uniform. I closed my eyes and cursed inwardly. Big as he was, and wearing that uniform, he probably had little trouble telling people to move on. The drama moreover was at an end; the fire had been put out and the boy and I presumably rescued. I looked across to the other side of the street. Tried to estimate the distance in meters. The fake policeman crossed the street and disappeared through the gate directly below me.

I stepped back inside and studied the apartment again. With the same result. There was just us in here, the four walls, a fire-axe and the decapitated body of the dog. I walked round the walls, hitting them with my fist. Brick.

"You know how to write?" I asked.

The boy nodded.

I took the Montegrappa pen from my inside pocket and handed it to him.

"What's your name?" I asked, pulling up the sleeve of my coat so that he could write on the cuff of my white shirt. But it was saturated with blood from the bite wound, and before I could pull up the other sleeve he had turned to the wall and was writing on the pale blue wallpaper.

"'Oscar, eight years old,'" I read aloud. Then I said: "Hi, Oscar, my name is Lukas. And you know what, we're going to have to get out of here."

I'd worked it out already. It was about eighteen meters down to the street. Tying together the coat, the shirt, and my trousers I would be able to lower Oscar four meters down. Using his own clothes would make that six meters. I could probably let Oscar go from a height of four meters without him getting seriously injured. But even for that I would need another eight meters. And where was I going to find that in an apartment that had been completely stripped?

I stared at the dog. We had not had much anatomy during our psychology studies, but one of the things I did notice—apart from the paper-thin bone between the eye socket and the brain—was that the human body contained eight meters of intestines. Or intestine. Because from the anal aperture to the throat is one long tube. How much weight could an intestine bear? I thought of my uncle in Munich who served sausages linked in their skins and how as a kid I used to try to pull them apart. In the end I always had to use a knife.

I picked up the axe.

"Think you can help me, Oscar?"

The boy looked wide-eyed at me but nodded. I showed him how I wanted him to hold the dog's body between his knees and hold the front paws out to the sides and back, so that the dog's stomach lay open and distended in front of me.

"Close your eyes," I said.

It's remarkable how delicate we mammals are. All I had to do was draw the sharp edge of the axe up through the fur and the belly opened, and the guts tumbled out. So did the stench. I immediately began to pull the intestine out, concentrating on breathing through my mouth.

It was hard to see in all the blood and slime, but I located what looked to me like two ends and cut them off. Tied a knot in each end to seal off the openings. It didn't look like eight metres, hardly even five. But the material seemed flexible, so maybe with a little weight on one end it would stretch to eight?

I took off my clothes and tied them together using a reef knot. It took a while, since it was a long time since I had practiced the knots I learned from my father, in the days when I thought I was going to go in for competitive sailing, as he had done.

After several failed attempts I finally got it right, but when I tried to secure the intestine to the sleeve of the coat the two wouldn't connect; the sleeve simply slipped out through the knot. I tried to think hard as I sat there on the floor in only my underwear, shivering in the cold draft coming from the window. It just didn't work. I swore out loud and looked at my watch. It was now more than half an hour since Greco had begun his countdown.

I had another go, this time using a longer section of sleeve; but again the slippery, slimy gut just glided out through the knot. I threw the gut and the coat aside, lay back on the floor, pressed my stinking bloody hands to my face and felt the tears welling up.

He had me exactly where he wanted me.

A small hand lifted my own from my face.

I looked up and there was Oscar holding something up in the air. The gut and the coat sleeve. Knotted together. I took hold of it and pulled at the two ends, but they held fast. I stared in disbelief at the knot. And then I recognized it. It was a sheet bend. And I remembered what my father had said when I told him that Maria and I were going to get married. That with certain women the knot to use was a bowline, easy to tie and easy to untie. But getting married, the knot to use then was a sheet bend; the harder you pulled, the tighter it got.

"Where did you learn . . . ?"

Oscar saluted with two fingers held to his forehead.

"Cubs?"

He nodded.

Just then the phone—which I had placed on the floor, along with my keys and wallet—began to vibrate. I picked it up. FaceTime again, and once again I had a full-strength signal.

I pressed Take Call and again Greco's face filled the screen.

"Hi, Lukas. She's on her way. Look, she's just parked outside."

He held the phone up to a computer screen. I saw a street, obviously in a fashionable residential area, and the door of an Alfa Romeo opening. I felt as though someone had injected iced water into my chest. The woman who got out and crossed the road moved like a pro. And like a queen.

Greco spoke from behind the phone: "When you can't find them, the thing you have to do is make them come to you."

Judith was wearing the red coat she always wore when attending business meetings. When she was going to war, as she used to say. She removed it before the meeting started and wore beneath it a snowy white blouse. That symbolized a blank sheet of paper, she said. A willingness to compromise. And before she put her coat back on again she had always got a deal for her client. *Always.* It was so obvious when I thought about it now, the way you understand every genius chess move once it's been shown to you.

Gio Greco had been Judith's lover longer than me, he knew her better. He was also a better chess player than me. He knew I would call her when he said those words: *"You and I are alone at least, now that she's been taken from us both."* And he knew what she'd do once she realized Greco had me in his power; go and see him and do what she was best at doing: negotiate a deal.

Greco's grinning face filled the screen again: "You look like you realize what's happening here, Lukas. The Queen is going to die. All is lost. Or is it?" He lowered his voice dramatically, like a game-show host on one of those franchises spewed out by the Tokyo cartel. "Maybe you can save her after all. Yes, you know what: I'm going to give you one last chance to stop me. You can use your weapon. The great Lukas Meyer will hypnotize the terrible Gio Greco and save the day. Come on. You've got about fifteen seconds before she gets here." Greco opened his eyes wide as though to show how ready and responsive he was.

I swallowed.

Greco raised a slender, shaven eyebrow. "Something wrong?"

"Listen—" I began.

"Can't do it, Lukas? Performance anxiety? Do you get that too when she needs fucking?"

I didn't answer.

"OK, that wasn't really fair," said Greco. "See, that psychologist I was telling you about, he suggested hypnosis as a cure for depression, but when we tried it, it turned out I'm not a good subject. He said it was because of my so-called personality disorders. I'm immune to it. I mean, there must be some advantages to being insane."

Laughter. The T and the long S again, like the hiss of a punctured bicycle tire. Then he was gone from the screen. The phone appeared to be placed on a shelf or suchlike, and I saw something that looked like a hallway and an oak door with an entry phone. There was a jarring, ringing sound. Greco appeared on the screen again, his back to me, his white suit gleaming. He seemed to be holding something up in his hand so that I couldn't see. He picked up the entry phone with his free hand.

"Yes?" Pause. Then, in a surprised voice: "No, is that you, darling? How lovely, it's been such a long time. Well, well. So at least you still remember where you used to live."

He pressed the button on the entry phone. I heard a distant buzz and then the sound of a door opening. I was clutching my own phone so hard I thought I might crush it. How could Judith, who was so intelligent, who knew Greco so well, fail to see that he had smoked her out from her hiding place by using me? The answer came back as quick as the question. Of course she knew. And still she'd come. Because there was no alternative—this was her only chance to save me.

I wept. No tears came, but my whole body was sobbing. I wished I'd lied to her. Told her I loved her. Given her that at least. Because she was going to die. And I was going to watch.

Greco turned his piggy face in triumph toward me. And now I was able to see what he was holding in his hand. A karambit. Curved handle and a short blade bent like a tooth. A knife with which to slash, chop, or stab. And which, once it's in, does not let go.

I wanted to break the connection but couldn't bring myself to do it.

Greco turned toward the door and opened it, holding the knife in the hand behind his back so only I could see it. And then she came in. Face pale, her cheeks a feverish pink. She embraced him, and Greco let her do it without taking his hand from behind his back. Now I could see them both in profile.

"Run!" I shouted into the phone. "Judith, he's going to kill you!"

No response. Greco had probably put his phone on mute.

"How nice," said Greco in a voice that sent a short, hard echo round the hallway. "To what do I owe this visit?"

"I regret it," said Judith, out of breath.

"Regret?"

"Regret leaving. I've thought about it for a long time. Will you have me back?"

"Wow," he said. "Even before you've taken off your coat?"

"Will you?"

Greco bobbed up and down on his heels.

"I—" he said, and sucked on his upper lip "—will take Judith Szabó back."

She breathed quickly and put a hand against his chest. "Oh, I'm so happy now. Because I want you, Greco. I know that now. It's just that it's taken me some time. And I'm sorry about that. I hope you can forgive me."

"I forgive you."

"Well. Here I am." She took a step toward him, her arms wide. Greco stepped back. She stopped and looked at him in confusion.

"Show me your tongue," he said quietly.

For an instant Judith looked as though someone had just slapped her. But she recovered quickly and smiled.

"But, Greco, what—"

"Your tongue!"

It looked as though she had to concentrate, as though this involved a highly complicated locomotor operation. She half opened her mouth, and then out came her pale red tongue.

Greco smiled. He looked almost mournfully at the exposed tongue. "You know very well I would have taken her back, Judith. Her. The one you were. Before you turned into someone else and betrayed me."

The tongue disappeared.

"Greco, darling . . ." She reached out to him, and he took another step back.

"What's the matter?" she asked. "Are you afraid of me? Your people searched me at the door."

"I'm not afraid. But if there was anyone I was afraid of, it would be you. All I can do is admire your courage. But then, you have always defended the one you love. That's why I was certain you would come. That's your method, after all: *go directly to the root.*"

"What do you mean?"

"Come on, Judith. You're a better actress than that."

"I've no idea what you're talking about, Greco."

But I did. That was her mantra as a fixer. *Go directly to the root.* When she was contacted with a commission, something which, for obvious reasons, almost always happened via a middleman, she always made it her business to find out who the real customer was and pay a visit to that person. It was always a risky business. She might lose the commission, or expose herself to danger, but she insisted on going *directly to the root* in order to fix a price and agree on the conditions. She always got a better price, she maintained, because she could do without all the middlemen taking their cut, and there were no misunderstandings about what was included in the service and what was not. And I supported her tactic of going *directly to the root* because I wanted to know the reason for the commission, what the intended result of it was. My road to heaven was paved with the evil intentions of others, and I just wanted to make sure that the greater evil didn't win out.

"Maybe, *maybe* I want this, Judith Szabó. I like your tongue. You've come to negotiate. So make a start. What are you offering to spare his life, your psychologist?"

She shook her head. "He's been out of my life a long time, Greco. But yes, of course, I expect you not to harm him."

Greco put his head back and laughed his T and S laugh until his piggy eyes disappeared behind his round cheeks. "Come on, Judith, a negotiator has to lie better than that. You know what I wish?"

I shuddered as he reached out a hand to stroke her cheek.

"I wish you'd have loved me enough to do what you're doing for him."

Judith stared at him, her mouth open. One hand continued toward her cheek. The other tightened its grip on the handle of the knife behind his back. I could see the tears welling up in her eyes, the way her body seemed to collapse inside; she was already moving her hands up to protect herself. She knew pretty well what was about to happen. That this had always been the likely outcome. And that now it was too late for regrets.

"Hello . . ." he said.

"No!" she shouted.

"No!" I shouted.

". . . I'm Greco," he said.

He swung the knife in a tight arc so swiftly it seemed to leave a trail of silver through the air.

Judith stared at him and at the knife. The blade was clean. But her throat had opened. Then came the blood. It splashed out, and she raised her hands as though to prevent it falling onto her coat, her present. But as she pressed her hands to her neck the pressure increased and blood sprayed from between her fingers in thin jets. Greco backed away but not quickly enough; blood splashed on the sleeve of his white suit jacket. Judith's legs gave way and she fell to her knees. Already her eyes were glazed; oxygen was no longer reaching the brain. The hands fell lifelessly from the neck, already the volume of blood had diminished. For a second or two her body balanced on the knees, and then she collapsed forward, her forehead hitting the stone floor with a soft thud.

I screamed into the phone.

Greco looked down. Not at Judith, but at the sleeve of his jacket as he tried to wipe away the blood. Then he walked over toward the phone, and I didn't stop screaming until his Guy Fawkes face filled the whole screen. He looked at me without saying anything, with a sort of mild solemnity, like a mourner. Was that what he was? Or was he acting the sympathy in a parody of the undertaker's professional solemnity?

"Tick-tock," said Greco. "Tick-tock." Then he broke the connection.

I tapped in the police emergency number and pressed Call. But of course I was too late, I no longer had a signal.

I collapsed onto the floor.

After a while I felt a hand on my head.

It was stroking me.

I looked up at Oscar.

He pointed to the wall, to the words he had written there.

It wil soon be beter.

Then he put his arms around me. It was so unexpected I didn't have time to push him away. So I simply closed my eyes and held the boy. The tears came again, but I managed not to sob.

After a few moments I held him a little away from me.

"I had a boy like you, Oscar. He died. That's why I'm so sad. I don't want you to die as well."

Oscar nodded, as though to convey that he agreed with me, or understood me. I looked at him. At the dirty but fine blazer.

And then, as we carefully made our knotted rope of clothes and guts, I told him about Benjamin. The things he had liked (old things like big picture books, gramophone records with funny covers, Grandad's toys, especially marbles; swimming; Daddy's jokes), the things he didn't like (fried fish, going to bed, having his hair cut, trousers that made him itch). Oscar nodded and shook his head as I went through the list. Mostly he nodded. I told him one of Benjamin's favorite jokes and that made him laugh. Partly because it's stupid not to laugh when there are only two of you, but mostly, I think, because he thought the joke was pretty funny. I told him how much I missed my boy and my Maria. How angry it made me. The boy just listened, responding now and then with facial expressions, and it occurred to me that now he had taken over my job as the mutely listening psychologist.

I asked him to write something about himself on the wall while I tightened all the knots and got our rope ready. He wrote in keywords.

Brescia. Grandad blazer factory. Nice house, swimming pool. Men with guns. Daddy Mummy dead. Run. Alone. Doghouse. Dog food. Football. Black car, man in white clothes.

I asked questions. Joined up the dots. He nodded. Large, shiny child's eyes. I gave him a hug. That warm little chin nestling in the pit of my neck.

Looked at the dog's head lying on the floor behind him. Dog's eyes. Child's eyes. Pig's eyes. Tick-tock, tick-tock. I closed my eyes.

Opened them again.

"Oscar," I said. "Get out the pen. We're going to try something a bit weird."

He took out the Montegrappa pen. The kind of beautiful thing they don't make anymore.

PART THREE: ENDGAME

Once Olsen's queen was off the board and the decision had been taken it was as though Murakami gave his opponent a short breathing space. He could afford it—Olsen was the one running out of time—and it looked as though Murakami, instead of bringing matters to a quick conclusion with a coup de grâce, preferred instead to take the opportunity to show off to his audience, the cat's last sadistic moments of play with the mouse. The even-tempered and silent Olsen had completely abandoned his bloodied defense of the king and instead moved his black knight to the other end of the board, as though in denial of the grim reality of his situation, a general playing a round of golf as the bombs rain down around him.

"Don't be afraid, Oscar. You won't fall."

I spoke calmly. Established eye contact. My heart was beating hard, probably as hard as his was. The gut was fastened around his chest in a bowline knot. He'd taken off his outer clothes and we had attached them to the end of the line, and now the half-naked child's body, still wearing his shoes, was dangling above the cobblestoned street below, his hands holding tight around the balcony railings.

"Now I'm going to count to three," I said, struggling to keep my voice calm. "And you let go on three? OK."

Oscar stared at me, panic in his eyes. He nodded.

"One, two . . . three."

He let go. Brave boy. I stood with one foot braced against the wall by the window and felt his body weight stretching the intestine downward. It held. We'd tested it inside the apartment and I knew there was no reason it wouldn't hold now, just because it was eighteen meters above ground. I'd wrapped the gut around my wrist twice in order to brake, but still I could feel it begin to slip.

That was all right—the idea was to lower him down, only it mustn't happen too fast. I would have to brake when I reached the join with the coat, and if that was too abrupt then the whole gut might snap.

Oscar slipped down and away from me. All the time we kept our eyes on each other.

At the junction with the coat I had to brake and saw how the gut stretched like an elastic band. I was certain it wouldn't have held my eighty kilos, but the boy can't have weighed more than twenty-five. I held my breath. The gut swayed and stretched. But it held. I continued paying out the rope, quickly, before it could change its mind. On reaching the last item of clothing, the boy's blazer, I leaned out as far as I could to make the drop to the street as short as possible for Oscar, holding on to the sleeve with one hand and with the other around a railing.

"One," I said loudly. "Two, three."

I let go.

Oscar landed feet first, I heard his shoes hit the cobblestones. He fell over. Lay there a moment or two, as we had agreed on beforehand, to check that he was uninjured. And then he stood up and waved up at me.

I hauled up the rope and untied his clothes. Dropped them down to him, and he quickly put them on. I saw him checking the blazer pockets to see if everything was there; the pen, the money I had given him, and the key to my apartment. I knew it was a vain hope, but at least that was what it was: a hope.

It didn't last long.

Two men in black drivers' suits emerged from the gateway, one of them the big man with no neck. They started chasing Oscar and caught up with him before he reached the security tape. They carried him, jerking and struggling, over to an SUV that stood illegally parked in the pedestrian street.

I didn't shout. Just watched in silence as the car disappeared.

I had done what I could. At least the boy wouldn't die breathing in Greco's hellish gas. He might even let Oscar go. Why not? Once the king has been checkmated, the other pieces can stay there untouched. And drivers—most of them at least—don't kill just for the sake of it.

I went back inside the apartment, untied my own clothes from the gut and started to dress. The dog's head looked up at me, one eye gouged, the other one whole.

Did I believe that? That Greco would take pity on Oscar?

No.

I looked at my watch. Twelve minutes to go before the gas came billowing out into the apartment. I sat on the floor and waited for the phone call.

Outside, it was growing dark.

Greco rang two minutes before time was up.

The phone was probably mounted on a tripod and the screen showed what appeared to be his room. Bricks, wood. Large white surfaces. Outside, on a large terrace, a Christmas tree with its lights lit in the evening dark. At the veranda door two armed guards, muscles bulging beneath tight-fitting black drivers' suits. Greco sat on a white leather sofa, and beside him, legs dangling, was Oscar. His blazer was buttoned up wrong, the Montegrappa pen visible, clipped to the breast pocket. He looked frightened and exhausted from crying. On the coffee table in front of them was a chessboard that looked, from the position, as though it was nearing the endgame. Next to it lay the karambit and the remote control for the release of the mustard gas.

"Hello again, Lukas. An eventful day, don't you think? And that's probably a good thing, since it's your last."

Greco rubbed the sleeve of his jacket with a cloth. That bloodstain. He couldn't seem to get rid of it.

"I just hope it's over soon," I said.

"Actually, I had thought of putting our boy here in a bedroom with a bedside lamp and pressing the button. But it was too much . . . bother. And I like this knife." He reached out for the karambit.

"Don't you understand how sick you are, Greco?" My voice was tight and hoarse now. "This is a child. An innocent child."

"Precisely. That's why it surprises me you didn't take your own life while you had the chance. All this—" he gestured broadly with his hands—"would have been completely unnecessary if you'd had the brains and the balls to jump out the window."

"But you would have killed the boy anyway."

He grinned broadly. "Why on earth should I do that?"

"Because you are who you are. You have to win. If by taking my own life I had saved the boy the victory wouldn't have been yours alone, it would have been a draw."

"Now *that*," laughed Greco, "is sick. And you are, of course, absolutely right."

He picked up the knife and turned toward Oscar, who sat with eyes closed, as though the light were too bright, or to shut out the world. Greco put his other hand on the boy's head. Long S-sound. Then he coughed and began:

"Hello . . ." he said, in that familiar, slow, clear, singsong voice.

I forced myself to keep my eyes open and watch the screen.

A spasm passed through Oscar and his hand went up to his breast pocket, took out the Montegrappa pen clipped there, and opened it in a single, fluid practiced movement. Greco observed him with an amused smile.

". . . I'm Greco," he concluded, stressing each syllable.

Oscar had taken out the needle-shaped cartridge and was holding it upside down in his little hand. The whole thing had taken less than three seconds, same as the last few times we'd rehearsed the sequence of moves. And now he swung his hand. He was a bright boy and by the time we'd finished he was hitting the eye in the dog's head every time, even when I held it high above him and moved it about. Hit it again and again, as calm and collected as a robot, the way hypnotized people are. Until we were down to two and a half seconds from when I gave him the trigger words, "Hello, I'm Greco," to him taking the pen out of his breast pocket, removing the cartridge, and stabbing.

I saw the point of the cartridge penetrate Greco's eye, and could sense how it slipped through the paper-thin bone at the rear of the socket and on into the brain. Oscar's small, balled hand against Greco's face like a growth, like broccoli. Greco was staring with the other eye, not at Oscar but at me. I don't know what I saw there. Astonishment? Respect? Fear? Pain? Or perhaps nothing. Perhaps those muscular spasms passing across his face were the result of whichever center of the brain the cartridge point penetrated, as I recalled from my student days how we could get dead frogs to move their legs by stimulating the nervous system.

Then Greco's body suddenly relaxed, and he exhaled in a long gasp, his last S, and the light in the remaining good eye went out, like the red light on a piece of sloppily produced electronic equipment. Because in the final analysis perhaps that's all we are. Frogs with conduits that transmit impulses. Complex robots. So advanced we even possess the power to love.

I looked at Oscar.

"Hi, I'm Lukas," I said.

He emerged immediately from his trance, dropped the cartridge and looked at me. Next to him, his head lolling on the back of the sofa, lay Greco, the cartridge sticking out of his eye as he stared up at the ceiling.

"Keep looking at me," I said.

I saw the men behind Oscar who had raised their machine guns but who now stood as though frozen to the spot. No shots had been fired. For there was no longer any danger to be averted. No longer a boss to be protected. And, their brains were telling them, though they could not have formulated the thoughts themselves: no one left to pay them for killing this boy, this child whose body would haunt them for the rest of their nights were they to kill him.

"Stand up slowly and walk outside," I said.

Oscar slid down from the sofa. Picked up the two parts of the Montegrappa pen from the floor and put them in his pocket.

One of the men had approached the rear of the sofa. He lay two fingers against the corpse's carotid artery.

Oscar headed for the hallway and the front door.

The men exchanged quizzical looks.

One of them shrugged. The other nodded and spoke into the microphone on his lapel.

"Let the kid go."

A short pause as he adjusted his earpiece.

"The boss is dead. What? As in finished, yes."

Greco lay staring up at the heaven he'd never get to. A solitary red tear ran down his cheek.

It took me almost three hours to cut my way through the metal-reinforced door, by which time the blade of the axe was so dull it functioned more as a sledgehammer.

I saw no one either in the entrance or outside as I walked into the street. They had probably been informed the operation was canceled. Were probably already on their way to other jobs for other bosses, other cartels.

I made my way through the dark streets without looking over my shoulder. I thought of the chessboard on my table back home, where Carlsen had just stepped into the Murakami Trap and in eighteen more moves would resign. As I walked along there I couldn't know that in twelve years' time I would be watching that famous game in which Olsen, who has likewise fallen into the Murakami Trap, moves his black knight to F2 and looks over in silence at the disbelieving and despairing Murakami.

Reaching the block where my apartment was I rang the bell. There was a click from the entry phone, but no voice.

"It's me, Lukas," I said.

A buzz. I pushed the door open. Going up the stairs I thought of all the days after Benjamin and Maria were gone, when I had dragged my feet up these steps and dreamed they would be standing in the open doorway waiting for me. As I stopped on the final landing, suddenly so tired it was like a pain in my chest that almost dropped me to my knees, I looked up. There, in backlit silhouette in the doorway, I saw that little figure, I saw my son.

He pointed to his eyes and looked at me. I smiled and felt those lovely warm, wet tears rolling down my neck and in beneath my shirt collar.

Oscar and I walked through the ruins of Brescia, hand in hand. It had been a poor city, actually one of the poorest in Italy, although being in a rich part of the country it wasn't easy to tell from the outside. But Brescia failed to survive the collapse of the nation state and in time had become a slum.

We stood in the street and looked through the fence at the old clothing factory, which was now just an abandoned site, a burned-out shell that appeared to be home to a pack of wild dogs. I had had to fire a warning shot toward them to keep them away.

We walked through the gateway of a house that had clearly once been beautiful. Not ostentatiously large, and built in a tasteful art deco style. The white walls had brown damp stains on the outside, the windows were broken, and a sofa dragged halfway out through one of them. From within came the echo of a dripping sound, as though from a grotto. We walked round the back, where snow still lay in patches on the grass, faded brown after the long winter.

Oscar stood at the edge of the empty swimming pool full of snow and rubbish. The tiles were cracked and the rim of the pool a dirty brown.

I saw Oscar's eyes fill with tears. I pulled him toward me. Heard the quick, short snuffles. As we stood there the sun broke through the mingled clouds and smoke and warmed my face. Spring was on its way. I waited until he'd finished snuffling, then held him away from me and told him in the sign language we'd been practicing that the summer wasn't far away, and then we'd go to the coast and swim in the sea.

He nodded.

We didn't go into the house but I saw the name plate on the door. Olsen. Despite the adoption we'd decided that Oscar would keep the name. In the car driving back to Milan we ate the panzerotti I had bought in Luini, and I turned on the radio. They were playing an old Italian pop song. Oscar drummed away energetically on the dashboard, miming the words to the song as he did so. The news came on afterward. Among other things there was an item about how the now forty-year-old Murakami had once again defended his world title. We could see the outlines of Milan as Oscar turned toward me. I had to slow down to read all the signs he was making, concentrated and careful:

"Can you teach me to play chess?"

First of all, in spite of its dark content, I had great fun writing "Black Knight." Maybe because at the time I was following world champion Magnus Carlsen playing in a chess tournament. In that context, this story describes the endgame. It is set in a not too distant and bleak future where democracy has been abandoned and replaced by global corporations and big city-states. The company competition has escalated into warfare and murder has become a lucrative business. The targets are the competitor's key personnel, including their best assassins. "Black Knight" is a deadly chess game between two top hit men, set in one of the city-states from the Renaissance: Milan. The two hit men are professionals, but everyone, even human killing machines, has a past, regrets, losses, and hopes. And with their pasts intertwined, perhaps this time their motives are more than just business as usual.

Joyce Carol Oates, *a resident of Princeton, New Jersey, is the author most recently of* Extenuating Circumstances: Tales of Crime and Suspense *and the novel* Breathe. *She is a recipient of the 2019 Jerusalem Prize and the 2020 Cino del Duca World Prize as well as the Bram Stoker Award, the National Book Award, the National Book Critics' Circle Lifetime Achievement Award, and the President's Humanities Medal. She is currently Visiting Distinguished Professor in the School of Arts at Rutgers University (New Brunswick).*

DETOUR

Joyce Carol Oates

Too early for spring, you couldn't trust such blinding-white sunshine in mid-March. And the smell of damp earth thawing, reviving—too soon.

The result was, Abigail was feeling light-headed. Unreal.

A seismic sensation, as if the very earth were shifting beneath the wheels of her car on the familiar drive home.

Staring ahead, dismayed—blocking the road was a barrier with a jarring yellow sign: DETOUR.

"Damn."

Rarely elsewhere than in her car did Abigail address herself and usually in an exclamatory/exasperated tone. If anyone had overheard, she'd have been mortified.

"God *damn*."

Three-quarters of the way home, and now she'd be forced miles out of her way. For these were country roads that intersected infrequently, unlike urban streets laid in a sensible grid. She would return home later than she'd planned and have less time to herself before her husband returned from work.

That dreamy interlude, preparing a meal with care, for just herself and her husband. A fireside dinner, with lighted candles.

And she had good news to share with Allan, which she would keep for just the right moment.

Darling, guess what!
The lab report—?
Yes! Negative.

Not totally unexpected news. Not after months of treatment. But exhilarating nonetheless, for in a year of medical news not invariably *good*, even *mildly good news* is welcome.

One by one, with robotic precision, drivers in vehicles ahead of Abigail were turning onto a smaller road. She wondered at their docility—*she* was tempted to drive around the damned barricade.

Her house was less than a mile away. Should she take a chance and try to drive directly to it? No impediments or construction were visible in the road.

You had to resent the nonnegotiable nature of DETOUR: ask no questions, no one to ask, simply follow the "detour" on trust that it will lead you to your destination.

Was ignoring a detour illegal? Was it dangerous?

What a strange thing for Mom to do! Getting a traffic ticket, a summons, the first in her lifetime . . .

She was not an impulsive person. No.

Thirty years she'd lived in the same house in the suburban countryside, five miles west of Stone Ridge, New Jersey, with her husband and, while they'd been young, their several children; thirty years, the unvarying route on North Ridge Road. In all those years she'd driven into the surrounding countryside only rarely and had little knowledge of the network of rural roads. She could not recall encountering a detour, or if she had, how inconvenient the detour had been.

She'd hoped to have more time to herself in the house, in the kitchen, her favorite room in the house, before her husband returned from work. Though possibly, Allan was already home, for he'd become semiretired the previous year, his schedule varying from week to week as his (legal) services were required at his firm.

Her husband's custom was to recount his day to her in detail: what he'd done at the office, how much (or how little) he'd accomplished, with whom he'd had meetings or met for lunch or spoken on the phone. There were ongoing narratives—names that had become familiar to her over the years, though she'd met only a few of her husband's colleagues; ongoing themes of rivalry, alliances, sudden rifts, feuds, tragic developments, startling consequences. In these accounts, Allan was invariably the protagonist: the center of the narrative.

Though Abigail did not always listen closely to these accounts, she took comfort in hearing them. Impossible not to feel a wave of tenderness for the man who, through the years, from the very start of their marriage, solemnly recited to his wife the banalities of his life, as a child might recite the events of his life to his mother, secure in the knowledge that anything he did, anything he said, because it was *his*, would be prized by his mother if not by others.

In exchange, Abigail told her husband of her day, more briefly. For she was the wife, she had a dread of boring *him*.

As a young woman, indeed as a girl, Abigail had learned to shape herself to fit the expectations of others. If there was a singular narrative of her life, it had the contour of a supple, sinuous snake, ever delighting in its contortions and in the shimmering iridescent camouflage-skin that contained it.

Even as a mother! Perhaps as a mother most of all.

Crucial not to let them know. How frightened you are, how little you know. How astonished you are that they have survived.

For nothing is so flimsy-seeming as a human infant. Soft-skulled, soft-eyed, with such tiny lungs, you fear they might collapse with wailing.

"Damn!"—her car was bumping, jolting. A fierce winter had left the narrow country road in poor condition, potholed and rutted. Following a line of other vehicles, Abigail was forced to drive unnaturally slowly, gripping the steering wheel in both hands. A throbbing pain had begun at her temples, the sensation of unreality deepened.

Surely the detour would double back soon. You had to surmise that a detour describes a half rectangle around an impassable road, the object of which is to lead back to that road on the other side of the blockage. But Cold Soil Road seemed to be leading in the opposite direction from North Ridge.

Oh, where was her cell phone?—she should call Allan to tell him that she'd probably be late. But her handbag was out of reach in the back seat, where she'd carelessly tossed it.

In late afternoon the sun was unnaturally bright. The sky resembled a watercolor wash of pale oranges, reds—too "pretty" to be real—and of a particularly banal prettiness, like calendar art. Deciduous trees that only the previous week had been skeletal and leafless were now luminous with tight little greeny buds.

Too soon!—Abigail felt a frisson of alarm, dread.

Cruel to awaken the dead, in spring. More merciful to let us sleep.

From Cold Soil Road her car was shunted onto a narrower country road that seemed to have no name, or at least she could not discover any name. No choice but to follow the DETOUR signs, with resentment and mounting unease, though a left turn should have been followed by a right turn to begin to complete the (rectangular) figure of the detour and not this slow curve leftward into the countryside . . .

Where am I being taken? This is wrong.

Traffic was sparse on this unnamed road. No one seemed to be coming in Abigail's direction, all traffic in the other direction, strung out along the detour like dispirited Bedouins. Worse, after so much jolting, the steering wheel of Abigail's car seemed to be loosening; each time she turned it, the car responded less immediately, as if she were driving on ice.

At last, at a curve, she turned the wheel with no effect at all—the car continued forward, off the road and in the direction of a shallow ditch. Panicked, she pumped the brake pedal, but this, too, had little effect.

Something struck her forehead, as if in rebuke. She heard a murmur of startled voices at a distance, witnesses to her folly.

She cried in protest. *No!* It was not her fault, something had happened to the steering wheel.

The front wheels of her car were in the ditch, the rear of the car remained on the roadway. The windshield had seemed to fly back toward her, striking her forehead. She was sobbing with frustration, dismay. What had happened to the steering wheel? And the brakes—useless.

Much effort was required for Abigail to extricate herself from the tilting car. Pushing the driver's door open, climbing out into the road, panting. Her heartbeat was erratic, like her breath. She'd been so taken by surprise! Her balance had been affected, she walked as if on the listing deck of a boat.

A vehicle approached, she waved frantically for it to stop, but the driver seemed not to see her, continuing past without slackening his speed. The vehicle's windshield shone with reflected sunshine, she could not see the driver's face.

Calling after in a pleading voice—"No, wait! Please don't leave me . . ."

Her handbag, containing her cell phone, had been left in the car. She could not bring herself to climb back into the car. Fortunately, the ditch was fairly shallow, the car's front wheels submerged in less than a foot of water, but the water smelled brackish, foul; she did not want to wade in it, still less did she want to grope around in it, where water had begun to seep inside the car with a hoarse, gurgling sound, as of occluded breathing.

Peering through the side windows, she couldn't see her handbag, guessing that it had been flung down onto the floor. No, she couldn't retrieve it, not her cell phone, not her wallet . . . The car key was still in the ignition, she couldn't bring herself to retrieve that either.

In the interim, another vehicle had passed in the roadway. If the driver had seen her, and her car partway in the ditch, the driver gave no sign, but drove imperturbably on.

She climbed back onto the roadway, trying to hold herself erect, unswaying. She understood: it was crucial not to give an impression of drunkenness or injury. (Was her face bleeding? A stranger would not wish to bloody the interior of his car.)

Her fingers, gingerly touching her throbbing forehead, came away unbloodied, but her nostrils felt loose and runny—was her nose bleeding? She hoped it wasn't broken, she dared not touch it for fear of injuring herself further.

But what had happened to her left shoe? She was standing in just one shoe; on her left foot was a light woolen sock, soaked from the ditch.

Miserably she looked around on the roadway to see if the shoe was there—but no, of course the shoe was inside the car, no doubt on the floor in the front, where brackish water was seeping in.

No choice but to make her way, limping, half sobbing, along the road in the direction of a house nearby; she would ask to use a telephone. This was not an unreasonable request, though she was looking disheveled and her damned nose was leaking blood.

Now! You must prove yourself.

A curious sort of anticipation overcame her. Almost euphoria.

Most of her life she'd been *waiting*—for what, she hadn't known.

As a bright and curious girl-child, waiting for her true life to begin. As a restless but shy adolescent, waiting for her true life to begin. Before she'd met the man she would marry, waiting for her true life to begin. And then, in the months before she'd married this man, waiting for her true life to begin.

Before she'd had her first pregnancy and her first baby—waiting for her true life to begin.

And since the children had grown and gone away—waiting for her true life to begin.

Something meant for me alone. Just—for me.

That has been waiting for me to arrive.

Because I have not been in the right place until now.

But now—am I in the right place?

It was comforting to see that the house she approached wasn't a derelict farmhouse like others in the area, but a house that resembled her own: a dignified Colonial of wood, brick, and fieldstone; not new, in fact probably at least one hundred years old, but beautifully restored and renovated: roof, shutters, and windows replaced and the clapboards freshly painted creamy white, which suggested that the property owners were affluent, like Abigail and her husband, who lived, Abigail calculated, about three miles away—if you took not the circuitous detour but a straight line.

Gravel horseshoe driveway, spacious front lawn with evergreen shrubs, several acres bordered by tall oaks, at the rear a barn converted into a three-car garage.

Abigail's heart lifted! Whoever lived in this house would not be suspicious of her but would recognize her as a neighbor.

Possibly, whoever lived in this house knew her and, yet more possibly, knew her husband.

Possibly, these homeowners had been guests in the R——'s house and would be grateful to return their hospitality.

Before ringing the bell beside the front door, Abigail dabbed at her face with a tissue, which came away stained with blood; she used another tissue to wipe her damp eyes and to blow her nose, cautiously. (Yes, her nose was bleeding.) With a stab of guilt she recalled having heard the front doorbell in her house ring not long ago, and standing very still, waiting for the ringing to cease and whoever it was to go away from the door; for no one of her or Allan's acquaintance would have rung the doorbell without first notifying her that they were coming, and no one who rang the doorbell without first notifying her was anyone she'd have wished to see.

A second time she pressed the bell buzzer, politely. She would not press insistently on the buzzer, for such an act would signal aggression, a kind of threat. Nor would she knock loudly on the door and frighten or antagonize whoever might be inside, listening somewhere in the interior of the house.

Rehearsing what she might say, with an apologetic smile—*Excuse me! I am so, so sorry to bother you, but I was following the detour and I've had a little accident, my car is in a ditch! If I could use your phone to call my husband . . .*

Though she might have said *call AAA* or *call a garage*, she preferred *call my husband*, as this phrase indicated not only the likelihood of a nearby household but the stability of a lengthy marriage.

And she would give her address, to establish her identity as a fellow property owner, with all that that entailed of prohibitively high property taxes in Bergen County, which was, of all counties in the state, one of the most affluent, thus one in which the subject of taxes provided homeowners with an immediate subject with which to bond in sympathy—*We live over on . . .*

For a confused moment, not remembering: Was it *Ridge Road? North Ridge?*

Ringing the doorbell again, listening for a response. None.

Her forehead throbbed, her nose was leaking blood. If only she'd remembered to bring that damned cell phone with her!

Despite the prematurely balmy air, she was shivering. The sole of her left foot ached; she'd stepped on sharp stones.

Then recalling: there was surely a side entrance to the staid old Colonial, a door that led into a small vestibule and then into the kitchen.

Limping, favoring her shoeless foot, she followed a flagstone path around the side of the house, and there indeed was an entrance, as in her house. And here too was a doorbell, which she pressed with more confidence—in her own home she understood that whoever pressed the buzzer beside the kitchen door was likely to be someone familiar with her household, the FedEx deliveryman or the gas meter man or a friend; those who rang the front door were likely to be strangers, about whom a homeowner would naturally feel wary.

Are you hiding in there? Please—if you are hiding—I only need to make a phone call, you are under no obligation to help me further . . .

I am not injured. I am not bleeding! I promise.

I am your neighbor.

But no one came to answer this door either. Abigail shaded her eyes to peer through the window: there was the vestibule, with coats, jackets, and sweaters on hooks, boots on the floor, exactly as in her house, and a doorway opening into a kitchen. Bars of sunshine fell slantwise on a tile floor not unlike her own, a deep russet brown. And hanging on an overhead rack, shining copper utensils.

"Hello? Hello? I—I'm in need of—help . . ."

It seemed to her that she was being observed. A surveillance camera eye, somewhere overhead. On the doorframe, a discreet notice, like one beside the kitchen door of her house: THESE PREM-ISES PROTECTED BY ACHILLES HOME SECURITY, INC.

Then she realized: whoever lived here surely kept a spare key outside somewhere, beneath the welcome mat or beneath a flowerpot or urn, as she did.

The key to this house wasn't beneath the welcome mat, Abigail discovered, which was reasonable: keeping an outdoor key in such an obvious place was an invitation to a break-in, as her husband had warned. Better beneath a flowerpot, an urn, or a wrought iron chair or table in a nearby courtyard, which was a little distance from the door and not so likely to be discovered by an intruder, though in this case Abigail was thrilled to discover the key within minutes, beneath an ornamental urn a few feet from the door.

Managing then to unlock the kitchen door and stepping inside into a warm, yeasty-smelling interior that felt welcoming to her, she had no fear that an alarm would ring, as indeed no alarm rang. Though certainly she was ill at ease, and would stay in the house only long enough to make a telephone call; she would then return to her incapacitated car and wait for help from AAA, and would not inconvenience anyone if she could avoid it.

"Excuse me? Hello? Is anyone here? I—I only just need to make a phone call . . ."

Her voice trailed off, uncertainly. She stood very still, listening. (Was the floor creaking overhead? Was someone upstairs, also very still, listening?) After a moment she decided no, just a distant sound of wind in trees, an airplane passing overhead.

Her mouth had gone dry with anticipation, excitement. Her heartbeat, triggered by the accident with the car, continued rapidly, with a kind of exhilaration.

So long *waiting*—for what?

But where was the telephone? Abigail expected to see a wall phone in the kitchen, in the approximate place where there was a wall phone in her kitchen, but the design of this kitchen did not precisely resemble hers. And the counters were olive, while her counters were, less practicably, white; the deep-sunken aluminum sink was in a different location from where hers was, as was the Sub-Zero refrigerator and the ovens set in a wall—(as in her kitchen, there were two ovens, one above the other). Close up, the tile floor did not so closely resemble the tile floor in her house but was of a darker hue.

Looking so intently for a telephone had caused the light-headedness to return, as well as a curious fatigue mixed with anxiety, as if, even as Abigail understood (of course!) that she was trespassing in a private household, and had no right to be here, and

was behaving very strangely for a person who valued privacy as she
did, nonetheless she felt a strong impulse to lie down somewhere,
in some quiet place where she would trouble no one and no one
would trouble her, and when she was rested and thinking clearly
again, she would complete the task for which she'd entered the
house of strangers . . . Though for the moment the very concepts
phone, call, husband had passed out of her consciousness.

She knew her name, though: *Abigail R*_____. And the address
of the house in which she'd lived for thirty years—she was sure
she could recall it, if required.

However, as long as she was in this (unfamiliar) house and no
one seemed to be home and she was certainly disturbing no one,
she reasoned that she might as well use a bathroom, for she'd been
needing to use a bathroom since the accident, she winced at the
loud sound of the toilet flushing and the groan of old pipes, an
echo of the pipes in her own house that needed replacing. And
afterward, taking time to wash her face with cool water, dabbing
at her bruised forehead and blood-stippled nose with wetted tissues. A strong smell of lavender soap lifted to her nostrils, a scent
that brought comfort.

The children in this household too had grown and gone away,
she thought. For you could not have such luxury soap in a downstairs bathroom if there were children in the house; you could
have only utilitarian soap, and even this they'd leave filmy with
the grime of their hands. Impossible, too, to have such delicate
linen guest towels!

And so, there was something sad, bittersweet in the soap scent.

Wincing, too, to see her face close-up in the bathroom
mirror—often she was mystified that she looked so unlike herself,
more resembling one of her older female relatives than herself; though
in the eyes of the world, she supposed, she was—still—considered an
attractive woman, well-groomed, poised, cultured. Her skin was still
relatively unlined, her hair thick and glossy. She had not the courage,
for instance, to dress other than expensively, as she would never have
dared to appear in public without judicious makeup; her daughters,
who'd scorned makeup when young, would have been appalled to see
their mother without it, even in the privacy of her home.

Wiping her hands on a linen hand towel as discreetly as she could and returning the towel to its proper place as neatly as she'd found it.

Thank you! I am so grateful. I will not stay long, I promise.

Continuing now through the downstairs of the house, looking for—exactly what, she couldn't recall, but she would recognize it when she saw it. A small item. A small item placed on a table . . . Unsteady on her feet and indeed the floorboards of the house were uneven, a characteristic of older houses, like basements— "cellars"—with oppressively low ceilings that could never be raised.

Giddiness increased, unless it was faintness. The sensation of unreality grew like waves lapping about her legs. She was hesitant to lean forward and lower her forehead to her knees to increase the blood flow into her brain, for she feared the action might make things worse and she would fall in a dead faint and be discovered by strangers and reported to authorities.

Had to lean against walls. Against the backs of chairs. She seemed to know the way—somewhere. Feeling the need to go upstairs, surrender her pride, and crawl on hands and knees up the (carpeted) staircase, out of breath and wincing with pain.

At the top of the stairs, resting for several minutes before heaving herself to her feet. Almost there, she consoled herself. Wherever it was she needed to go. She'd have to conserve her strength, dared not squander it heedlessly; once she'd slept for an hour, she was certain to feel much better and to know what to do next.

Someone she'd meant to contact—a husband? *Her* husband?

His name had fallen away, his face was a blur. His name—well, she would know his name, to which her own name was attached . . .

With the instinct of a blind creature she staggered into a room containing a bed. At the top of the stairs, first right. It was a large room—it was a large bed. Her trembling hands managed to pull back a satin comforter so that she could fall into the bed with a shuddering sigh—every bone in her body dissolving, disappearing into the most exquisite sleep; and when she opened her eyes, she found herself staring at a ceiling less than eight feet above her head, unless it was a low-hanging cumulus cloud. She smiled at the sight! Her brain was well rested, a kind of balm had washed over it.

The bed was so large she felt dwarfed within it. The sheets were of exceptionally good quality but dampened by her sweaty sleep, for which she felt chagrin; she reasoned that if she had time, she would change the sheets, and no one would be the wiser.

She lifted herself onto her elbows, staring. Where *was* she? This was not a bedroom familiar to her, yet it "felt" familiar—spacious, with pale rose (silk?) wallpaper and attractive furnishings that looked like family heirlooms. One of them was a massive mahogany bureau, atop of which a row of framed photographs had been placed with loving attention.

For you are securely *in the world* only if there are such photographs of loved ones to testify to your existence, and your worth.

From the bed, however, Abigail could not make out the faces in the photographs. Some were very likely older relatives, others were children. But all were hazy with light reflected from the windows, unnaturally bright for a late afternoon in March.

Here was a rude surprise: Abigail's clothes had been removed from her body!

So strangely, she appeared to be wearing a nightgown. Neither familiar to her nor unfamiliar: a nightgown of soft flannel in a pink floral pattern, that fitted her naked body loosely.

She blushed hotly to think that someone had dared to undress her while she'd been asleep and had put a nightgown on her, as one might prepare a child for bed or undress a hospital patient; she'd given no consent to anyone to touch her, still less to remove her clothing . . . That she'd been undressed—and dressed—without having awakened suggested that she'd been sleeping very deeply, perhaps for a longer period of time than she'd imagined.

"Hello? Is someone here?"—her voice seemed to reverberate in the air close about her.

On her feet, shakily. Bare feet on a carpeted floor. Even the light woolen socks had been removed by whoever had dared to undress her.

While she'd slept, her heartbeat had slowed. Now it was rapid again, painful. All her senses were alert.

She must escape! Must find her clothes and dress and slip from the house. Whoever had dared touch her might return at any moment.

Shuddering to think it might have been a *he*. A stranger, daring to strip her naked even as she lay oblivious in sleep as profound as death.

She searched for her clothing in the room and could not find it, though her single shoe lay on the carpet beside the bed as if it had been tossed down. She thought—*But just one damned shoe is useless!*

In fact, this was not true. Had she not climbed out of her car and walked along the roadway and entered this house wearing but the single shoe?—she could do this again if necessary.

Another surprise: when she tried the bedroom door, the doorknob was loose in her fingers.

So, though the doorknob *turned* and *turned*, it did not open the door.

She pulled at the doorknob. Yanked, tugged.

Panicked, she called out, "Hello? *Hello?*"

Rapping on the door with her fist. "Hello? Is somebody there? I—I'm in here . . . I'm upstairs, I'm *here*."

She pressed her ear against the door. Beyond the rapid beating of blood in her ears she could hear—something . . .

Voices? Footsteps? A door opening, closing? The ordinary sounds of a household, at a little distance.

Desperately she struck her fists on the door. Calling out, crying—*"Hello hello hello! Let me out!"*—until her throat ached, her voice was cracked and hoarse.

Was she being kept *captive*? Was she a—*captive*?

Of course it was likely a mistake of some kind. A misunderstanding.

Mistaken identity, was it? She, Abigail R———, closely resembled another woman, perhaps . . . This other woman was the one intended to be *captive*.

Standing now close by the mahogany bureau, still she couldn't make out faces in the photographs. No matter how she squinted, the faces inside the frames—adults, children—remained out of focus, hazy with light.

And the view from the second-floor windows: tall trees, mostly leafless, a landscape that was still sere and bleached from winter, though beginning now to revive; since trees surrounded the house, there was no visible horizon, all was foreshortened.

Yet when she looked more closely, she saw that the scene was flat and unconvincing, like a stage set; trees, grasses, sky, overly bright sun seemed all at the same approximate distance from her, lacking depth.

The wave of dizziness intensified. Was *she* flat as well, in this landscape?

When had "perspective" come into human consciousness?—she tried to recall.

Medieval art was strangely flat; there was no illusion of depth. Human faces lacked expression, as if the artists of the time did not "see" the plasticity of the normal face. Children did not resemble children, but rather stunted adults.

She pressed her heated face against the windowpane, trying to see at a slant—a corner of the barn that had been converted into a garage, a glimpse of the country road where her car was stranded a quarter mile away, front wheels in a ditch.

Oh, why had she abandoned her car so quickly! She should have tried to free it from the ditch. If she'd rocked the car forward and back, forward and back, gaining momentum by degrees, as a more confident and skilled driver might have done, she might be home now. Instead she'd given up at once, defeated.

Instead she was trapped in a stranger's house. Only a few miles from her own house, *captive.*

Her bladder ached sharply, as a child's bladder might, in animal panic.

A bathroom adjoined the bedroom, Abigail went to use it, hurriedly.

Here was a spacious, white-tiled bathroom that was clearly in frequent use. Thick towels hung on racks, slightly askew. There were two sinks, neither entirely clean. A mirror just perceptibly spotted. Electric toothbrushes (two), a twisted tube of toothpaste, hand lotion, hand mirror, hairbrush, combs (two), cuticle scissors, tweezers . . . At least two people used this bathroom. Abigail lifted the hand mirror and saw, yes—it was a silver mirror, heavy in the hand, ornately engraved but in need of silver polish.

Mirrors ran the length of the bathroom in panels. In each mirror a wraithlike figure in a shapeless gown, like a shroud, stared at Abigail, aghast.

Then she saw the bathroom had a second door that might lead into another bedroom or into a hallway, but when she seized the doorknob to turn it, she discovered that the door was locked.

She could have sobbed. The doorknob had turned in a normal way but to no avail, the door was *locked.*

Stumbling back into the bedroom, Abigail saw to her astonishment that a stranger had entered the room in her absence. At first she could not see his face clearly—it was blurred, like a smudged thumb. He must have unlocked the door—the door with the broken doorknob—for there appeared to be no other way into the room. And what was he carrying?—a heavy cut-glass vase of dazzling white flowers that exuded a pungent fragrance. Gardenias.

Flowers for the invalid!—for *her.*

"Why, darling! What are you doing out of bed?"

He was startled, alarmed. Genuine concern for her, an undercurrent of dismay and exasperation.

"And your feet—*bare.*"

Abigail was sure she'd never seen this man before. He had thick white gnarled-looking hair, a low forehead, and a broad, flushed face; he wore a dark pin-striped suit that fitted his stocky figure somewhat tightly, a white shirt and necktie, polished dress shoes. Indeed, he'd brought the bouquet of white flowers for Abigail, setting the vase on a bedside table.

How powerful, the sickly sweet smell of gardenias! Abigail felt dizzy, dazed, as if ether had been released into the airless room.

Stunned speechless as the stranger addressed her worriedly: "Please go back to bed, darling. D'you want to catch pneumonia again? Next time might be fatal. And what if you'd fallen when no one was here!"

"But I—I—I don't belong here . . ."

"Bare feet! For God's *sake.*"

He would have led Abigail forcibly back to the bed, but she shrank from him, rebuffing his hands, preparing to scream if he touched her—but he did not touch her; instead, unexpectedly, he shrugged and turned aside, as if Abigail's behavior had offended him.

"Ah, well. It's just good that I've come home. I never know what—what in bloody hell—I will discover."

He laughed, harshly. Clearly he was disgusted. But he was dismayed. Yanking off his necktie and hanging it in a closet on a rack of other ties. Abigail could see that these were expensive designer ties. His back to her, oblivious of her, matter-of-factly he removed his suit coat and hung it carefully in the closet; removed his white dress shirt, his trousers, and his shoes to change into more comfortable attire—red plaid woolen shirt, khaki trousers, moccasins.

A heavy sigh—"Jesus Christ. I *never know.*"

Abigail stood staring, astonished. This stranger was changing his clothes before her eyes with the casual disdain of a husband. Almost, she was moved to apologize, for clearly there was a profound misunderstanding between them.

To Abigail's greater astonishment, the white-haired man proceeded to recite to Abigail, in grim detail, his day: an early morning conference call with clients in Tampa and Dallas; a luncheon meeting at the club with _____, _____, and _____; much of the afternoon spent at his desk, going over accounts with _____; then, on the phone with _____; then, another conference call with clients in San Diego and Houston—

Abigail interrupted: "Excuse me!—but I want to go home . . ."

The white-haired man ceased speaking. A coarse red blush deepened at the nape of his neck. All this while he'd been standing with his back to Abigail, stiff and unyielding, refusing to face her. She sensed that he was very angry; he had not liked being interrupted in the midst of his report, which had seemed to him important and should have impressed his listener.

"I—I said—I want to go home . . . You've locked me in here, I don't belong here, *I want to go home.*"

Abigail was shivering violently. The sensation of faintness deepened. She said, stammering, "You—you have no right to keep me here! It's against the law—to keep me against my will! I never consented. I don't know you. I had an accident on the road, but

I'm not injured—I don't need any medical care—I've been able to rest, and I'm ready now to leave—*I want to go home.*"

"Darling, you are home. Please just get into bed."

Gently, grimly, the man reasoned with Abigail. He was several inches taller than she and at least thirty pounds heavier, his breathing audible. He might have been appealing to a neutral observer—he was being the most reasonable of men.

Abigail protested: "I—I am not home. I don't know who you are. This is wrong—this is not my home . . ."

"Of course this is your home! You're just very tired, dear. It's time for your medication."

"No! No medication!"

Abigail's voice rose in alarm. The white-haired man dared not press the issue.

"It's a mistake. I don't belong here. There was a detour. At North Ridge Road . . ."

Buoyantly these words came to Abigail, as precious as a life jacket to one drowning in treacherous waters—*North Ridge Road.*

Other words she'd lost, could not retrieve, but somehow these crucial words had returned to her, which she was sure would impress her captor.

"Detour?—I didn't notice any detour, darling. You haven't been out—what would you know of detours and road conditions? *I've* been out. I've never heard of any North Ridge Road—I think you must mean Northanger Road. But that's nowhere near here, that's over in Hunterdon County." The man spoke patiently, and with an air of sorrow. Though white-haired, he wasn't elderly; probably in his early sixties. You could see how disconsolate he was. How close to despair. How bitterly he blamed *her.*

And how awkward Abigail was in the flannel nightgown that fell billowing to her ankles and would have tripped her if she'd dared to push past her captor and escape out the door . . .

But no: she seemed to recall that there was no escape through that door, at least for her.

No escape!—as her captor insisted that she return to bed, as if she were ill. As if the fault were somehow hers, that she was in this predicament and he was obliged to be with her, overseeing her. For of course she could not be trusted to be alone. For of course she had proved that by her behavior. Insisting that of course she *was* home, this was her *home*, it was upsetting to him, as it was to their children, when she demanded to be allowed to go home when this *was* her home, for she was only just tired, and she was only just confused and had not taken her afternoon medication; but she should be comforted to know—*she was home, this had been her home for thirty-two years.*

Abigail protested: "But—you are not my husband! This is ridiculous."

"It *is* ridiculous. *Of course* I am your husband, and you are my wife."

For a long, painful moment they stared at each other. Each was trembling, furious.

The thought came to Abigail—*You have hurt this man's feelings terribly. What if he is your husband—what if you are mistaken?*

The sensation of faintness deepened. Vertigo, in the brain.

A mistake, some sort of mistake, but whose fault?—Abigail could not comprehend.

More likely, Abigail thought, the man with the gnarled-looking white hair and wounded, peevish face was intended to be her husband but had been poorly chosen for the role; as she, Abigail, the wife of another man, had been cast as his wife just as poorly.

As the house in which she found herself, this very bedroom, was intended to replicate or to actually be her bedroom, and her house—yet was not.

Abigail recalled that dreams are inaccurate in small, baffling ways. Why?—to understand, one would have to understand the human brain, which is beyond comprehension.

A small mistake can be a cataclysmic mistake. Once such a mistake has been made, who can unmake it?

Why didn't they send better actors!—Abigail had to laugh.

And then: if they'd sent better actors, she would never have realized. A captive, and the "husband" the captor, the keeper of the key, and she, the "wife," would never have realized.

"You are very tired, dear. And you know, darling—you are not well . . ."

Silently she demurred. Yes. No. But yes—she was very tired.

The man had the advantage, obviously. He must have a key to the door, for he had dominion over the house. As the roles had been cast, to the male has gone the dominant role, and it would be futile for Abigail to protest so late in her life. If the stranger confronting her would not acknowledge the imposture, if he continued to behave belligerently as if Abigail were, indeed, his *wife of thirty-two years*, there was little that Abigail, his captive, could do about it.

A weariness had settled over her like a fine-meshed net.

With a forced affability, as a husband might do, moved to magnanimity in the face of a sullen and unreasonable wife, the man reverted to the (familiar, comforting) subject of *his day at work*: conference calls, meetings, luncheon. He spoke of his plans for the next day and the next, reciting more names, a litany of names, ———, ———, and ———. For if you are a man among men, you are securely *in the world* only if there are such witnesses to testify to your existence, and your worth.

In this way, beating Abigail down as one might beat down a defenseless creature with a broom, not injuring the creature but (merely) beating it down, down, wearing it down; the captive swayed on her (bare) feet, very tired now, faint-headed, weakened as the fine-meshed net tightened about her. When had she eaten last, she could not recall. When had she slept last, she could not recall. When had she drawn a deep breath of fresh air, the kind that fills the lungs to capacity and thrills the soul, she could not recall. When had she heard her own name enunciated, what name was hers, she could not clearly recall. Perhaps she was anemic, her blood would require an infusion. Perhaps her brain had begun to dry, crumble like clay. Perhaps she could no longer chew and swallow solid food; soft-blended food would have to be provided by her captor or captors, or she would perish.

The exasperating certitude with which the white-haired man spoke made Abigail realize that she'd lost such certitude. In the accident perhaps—her forehead slammed against the windshield.

That was it: the beginning. Her fingertips touched the swollen bruise, sensitive between her eyebrows, as a third eye, yet unopened.

She'd misplaced crucial words. She'd left her handbag behind, and the small electronic device with which (she knew! she felt this so strongly) she could have summoned her true husband, who would have annihilated this imposter. She'd lost the key to—something. What, she wasn't sure. In a shadowy region of her brain, these crucial words resided, but she could not locate the region, and if she did, she could not have opened the door, which was locked, or its doorknob sabotaged so that it turned uselessly in the hand. Now she recalled that she'd been seeing signs in recent days, weeks: the faces that mirror your own face, familiar faces that behave in unfamiliar ways, faces whose expressions you must decipher in order to decipher your own condition—those faces that have been smiling, alert, admiring through your lifetime but have now (inexplicably) ceased to smile. When these faces betray alarm, dread, pity, you shrink from being seen by them and you no longer wish to see *them*.

She cried how she hated him!—why didn't he let her *die*?

Pushed his hands away, screamed at him not to touch her even as he protested: "But I love you! My darling wife, please . . ."

Now he did advance upon her. Clumsy, weeping. As an older man might weep, unpracticed in tears. His arms in the woolen shirt around her, Abigail in the flannel nightgown smelling of her body. She was not without shame—*shame* would cling to her to the last.

Holding her tight. Holding her as a drowning man might hold another person, desperate that she not escape. Abigail could not breathe, this person was squeezing the breath from her. Arms against her sides, bound tight. As together they staggered toward the bed, fell heavily onto the bed. The physical reality of another's body is always a shock—*size, density, heat*. His tears wetted her face. She had not the strength to break free. Until at last, too exhausted to resist, she lay beside her captor, weeping with him, in deference to him, her brain blank, annihilated. Her eyelids were too heavy to keep open and so what bliss to surrender to sleep; what bliss, the sweet, sickly, dazzling white smell of gardenias that pervaded the room entering her nostrils, flowing up into her brain like ether, precipitating the most delicious sleep in the arms of the stranger.

His arm over her, heavy, comforting.

"My darling wife! I will never abandon you."

Something was pressing on her chest. An opened hand, a sweaty palm. Terror of suffocation.

Waking abruptly to glaring light. Was it another day, a morning, or was it the same day, interminable?—had she endured a *night*?

But sleep had bathed her raw, aching brain. She could think more clearly now.

Here was the shock: beside her in the rumpled bed lay the man—the man with the gnarled-looking white hair, the stranger intended to be *her husband*, on his back, open-mouthed, asleep, breathing deeply, as a drowning man might suck at air.

Stunning to Abigail to realize that she'd slept beside her captor. Hours of oblivion, shame.

In her sleep she had not known. Yet she must have known. Could not have *not* known.

Again it came to her: how large, how solid, how purposeful, how *real*, a (masculine) body beside a (female) body, horizontal in a bed.

In the night the man must have pulled off the red plaid shirt—his fatty chest was exposed in a thin, stained undershirt. Beneath the satin comforter his lower body might have been naked. (She could not bear to look. *Would not.*) On the carpet beside the bed lay the man's red plaid shirt, trousers that looked as if they had been flung down.

The white hair was disheveled. The face showed strain, fatigue. Coarse hairs had begun to sprout on the jaws. The eyelids quivered. A whistling sound in the nose. Oh, she'd been hearing that whistling in her sleep, it had insinuated itself into her sleep, in her dreams, a bright red thread of mercury, a poison seeping into her brain. Abigail shrank from the man, in revulsion for his damp, perspiring body and in dread of waking him. A despairing thought came to her like a reversed prayer—*Will I have to kill him to be free?*

An unnatural light shone through windows overlooking a flattened landscape, a bright-blue papier-mâché sky. Piercing laser-white of spring sunshine, from which there is no escape.

And the sweet-poisonous smell of gardenias—this too clung to bedsheets, pillow, her hair, which was matted and wild about her head, as if she'd been a captive not for less than twenty-four hours but for many days.

On her (bare, tender) feet!—carefully easing out of the bed. Scarcely daring to breathe for fear that the imposter-husband would awaken suddenly.

She must escape her captor.

She must act quickly, immediately.

She must not allow her captor to take the advantage again. To wake, to overcome her.

Rapidly her thoughts careened along a roadway to an unavoidable destination: she would break the vase over the man's head as he slept, cracking his skull and rendering him helpless; the blow might not kill him, for Abigail had no experience committing so desperate an act, no sense of how much strength might be required to execute it; nor did she want to hurt another person, even an adversary. Even a poorly cast actor meant to be her husband.

And if she rendered her captor unconscious and helpless, where would she find the key? In a pocket of his trousers? In a drawer somewhere in the room? She had no idea.

Absurd, she could never hurt another person. Not Abigail R___! She had neither the will nor the strength.

He was not to be blamed, perhaps. As blameless as she. As confined.

But she was trembling with excitement, adrenaline flooded her veins like liquid flame. So long as the man slept, she had a chance to escape. So long as he possessed no consciousness of her, she was free of him. In a closet she discovered women's clothing, she snatched at a jacket, at slacks, a soft jersey fabric that would be warm against her bare legs, a pair of shoes sturdy for running.

On the bed, amid rumpled sheets, the white-haired man continued to sleep heavily. His breathing was irregular and hoarse, painful to hear. In his nose, the thin whistling sound that grated against Abigail's nerves.

For some minutes, as in a curious trance of lethargy, Abigail regarded the *imposter-husband* with mounting rage. Obviously he was the one who'd undressed her. Apart from Abigail, he was the sole actor in this preposterous, haphazard drama in which she'd been confined. He had gazed upon her naked body, he had dared to touch her, commandeer her. He had dared to lock her in this room, and he had dared to overwhelm her with his superior weight, his very anguish, he'd dared to force her to lie docile in his arms, too weak to resist. All that he'd done he had done to *her*.

Waking from her trance as if someone had snapped their fingers to rouse her, Abigail stealthily lifted the heavy cut-glass vase and carried it into the bathroom, removed the flowers, and, as quietly as she could manage, poured out the water; breathing calmly, thinking calmly, silent on bare feet, she returned swiftly to the bed where her captor lay sleeping, and not giving herself time to think, she raised the vase high over her head and brought it down hard on the skull of the slumbering man, who wakened instantaneously, gave a high, shrieking cry, thrashing, bleeding profusely as with fearless hands Abigail again lifted the vase as high as she could and brought it down a second time against his skull . . .

Wanting to cry in triumph—*It isn't my fault. You took me captive. I didn't choose this. You will survive.*

Quickly then, Abigail dragged up the comforter to hide the ruined, blood-glistening face. The body had convulsed and had ceased twitching.

She knelt beside the man's discarded clothing. Searching pockets, frantic to find a key.

Hastily she pulled off the bloodstained nightgown. Hastily she washed her hands in the bathroom, taking care that no faint blood residue was left on the towel. She threw on clothes she'd pulled from the closet, scarcely troubling to note whether they fitted her. No time to spare, shoving her (bare, tender) feet into shoes that fit, or nearly. In the other closet she discovered, in a pocket of the dark pin-striped suit coat, a key chain—keys; to her sobbing relief, one of them fitted the bedroom door and allowed her to open the door with a single assertive twist of the knob.

"Yes! Like this."

Now she had only to retrace her steps. Hurriedly, down the stairs, through the kitchen, and out the rear door into fresh, cold, bright air, no one to observe, no one to call after her, now frankly running in the awkward shoes of a stranger, panting, out to the road and along the road a quarter mile or so to her car, which was exactly as she'd left it the previous day—front wheels in a shallow ditch, rear wheels on the road.

In a haze of exhilaration, running in bright, cold air. How rarely she ran now, in this phase of her life! After the confinement of the bedroom, after the stultifying embrace of the captor-husband, what joy to draw air deep into her lungs.

So relieved to see her car, Abigail laughed aloud. Though the car was shamefully mud-splattered. Her husband would be astonished, disapproving. *What have you done, Abby! I just had that car washed.* A white car, impractical. After a little difficulty she managed to open the door to the driver's seat, managed to climb inside. There, the key in the ignition!—just where she'd left it.

"Yes. Like *this*."

And now, would the engine start?—Abigail shut her eyes, turned the key. After a little hesitation the familiar sound of an engine starting. Her luck had held.

Now the task of rocking the car forward and back, forward and back, determined to get the front wheels free, until at last the wheels began to gain traction, borne by momentum. White exhaust billowed up behind. The wheels strained, but took hold. Abigail laughed aloud in sheer relief.

With a final jolt, the car was up on the road. Four wheels, solidly on the road. She could breathe now. Her eyesight had become sharper, she was breathing more deeply. Since taking up the vase of flowers in her hands—making her way silently into the bathroom—she'd been electrified by a rush of adrenaline that had not yet subsided. If only she'd had more faith in herself the previous day—if only she'd been guided by instinct—she would be at home now, and safe.

Driving back in the direction of North Ridge Road. At least she believed that she was driving in the direction of North Ridge Road.

Several miles, passing few vehicles. She wasn't seeing detour signs. Yet the landscape seemed familiar. And there, abruptly, was North Ridge Road.

And there, again—the barricade and the jarring yellow sign: DETOUR.

Again, no one in sight. No road crew repairing the road, no impediment that she could see, beyond the barricade itself.

This time Abigail drove around the barricade, boldly, with no difficulty, onto the grassy roadside and back up again onto the pavement, and continued on North Ridge toward her home, which she calculated was less than two miles away.

The sun was still unnaturally bright, luminous. Budding leaves were just perceptibly greener than the previous day. Her heart was suffused with hope, within minutes she would be home.

It is always melancholy to drive home alone, to an empty house, and all the more melancholy to be driving at dusk as I was on an evening in February 2020, when I encountered an unexpected detour sign on the (semirural) road in Hopewell Township, NJ, several miles outside Princeton.

This sign, which should have been innocuous, was jarring to me, and alarming, as I was routed off the familiar main road and onto a succession of smaller side roads; within just a few minutes, I found myself on a totally unfamiliar country road that I was sure I'd never seen before. The experience set me thinking about the unexpected detours in our lives . . . akin to those blows "out of nowhere" that knock boxers out since they don't see them coming, can't anticipate them, and consequently can't defend themselves against them.

When we veer out of our normal routes, we may be the identical person we'd have been in the "normal" setting, yet things may happen to us that evoke in us unexpected reactions, as if a part of our personalities has been jolted into life sheerly by accident. So, too, in this story a woman is rerouted from her "normal" conventional life onto unfamiliar country roads, taken ever farther from her home until at last she has a small accident and has to walk to a nearby house for help: a house very like her own house, though crucially different.

In this new setting, she is identified by a stranger who seems to know her intimately; she finds herself his captive, though (perhaps) she is only his wife, and the "captivity" is just marriage. But in this new setting, she is struck by the arbitrary nature of the captivity, and by the fact that she doesn't have to be defined in this way. (Or does she?)

Rare in my fiction, a radiantly happy ending—for the woman who defies the detour.

Annie Reed *is the award-winning author of well over three hundred short stories in a wide variety of genres. Her stories appear regularly in* Pulphouse Fiction Magazine *and* Mystery, Crime, and Mayhem, *and her acclaimed story "The Color of Guilt" appeared in a previous year's best mystery volume. Her short fiction has also been selected for inclusion in study materials for Japanese college entrance exams. Her* Unexpected *series of short story collections showcase the best of her work. Her mystery novels include* Pretty Little Horses *and* A Death in Cumberland. *She lives in Northern Nevada.*

LITTLE CITY BLUES

Annie Reed

"I think my wife's having an affair," Bill Claymore said.

In the couple years I've been in business, I could count on the fingers of one hand the number of times I'd been hired to tail an unfaithful spouse. Nevada's a no-fault divorce state. All a guy had to do was tell the judge he and his wife didn't get along. Nobody had to prove infidelity, not unless there was money involved, and Claymore didn't look the type.

The guy who sat in my client chair was midforties, slender, dark hair going thin at the top. He wore wire-rim glasses, and the threadbare jacket that hung loose on his frame told me his suit dated back a good ten years before Mr. Johnson had sent me and a hundred thousand of my closest friends to fight in Vietnam. That had been in 1964—a lifetime ago from my perspective.

"Prenup?" I asked him.

"What?"

"Prenuptial agreement," I said.

In a town like Reno you could never really tell who had money and who didn't. Claymore had told me he was an accountant. For all I knew, he could be hiding the fact that he'd won big at one of the local casinos and netted himself a trophy wife to boot.

"Oh." He said it like the thought had startled him. "No."

"Kids?"

If Claymore was gearing up for a custody battle, I wanted to know that going in. Custody battles could get nasty.

"It's nothing like that," he said. "Really. I just need to know. I mean, wouldn't you?"

Would I? The last serious relationship I'd had was before Vietnam. And after? Well, let's just say after Vietnam everything changed.

"It's going to cost you," I said. "I don't work for free."

"I have money."

He reached down for the battered briefcase he'd brought with him to my office. I held up my hand to stop him.

The instincts that got me through Vietnam not quite in one piece didn't translate well to civilian life. When he sat down in my client chair, he'd put the briefcase on the floor by his feet. Most people would do the same thing, but that meant I couldn't see the briefcase from my side of the desk. If he triggered spring-loaded latches to open the thing, I wouldn't be able to see those latches pop open. Sudden, sharp metallic sounds like that put me right back in the jungle, and that might not end up well for Claymore.

I didn't have that many paying clients that I could afford to have this one think I was crazy.

"Let me tell you my rates first," I said, trying to make things seem normal and natural. I quoted him a fee I thought matched his circumstances.

I'm not a high-rent detective. I'm too young for any of the big law firms to put me on retainer, even if they could put up with my brand of crazy. If the building manager could find another tenant willing to pay actual money for my closet-sized office, he'd kick me out in a heartbeat. That's how often I'm late on the rent.

My office is on the third floor of a forty-year-old building on the seedy side of downtown. A liquor store and a pawn shop take up the first floor, a legal aid office occupies the second. Most of the third floor is vacant. A sign on a door down the hall is for a dental office, but I've never heard a drill or smelled any of that goop dentists spread over your gums to deaden the pain.

I like being the only tenant on this floor. I don't have to worry about someone coming up behind me. Bad things happen when someone touches my back, even by accident.

Winos camp out at night in the ground floor lobby, and some of the legal aid clients haven't bathed in weeks. That kind of stink seeps into the woodwork. I don't mind. Compared to the places I've been overseas, the smell's not so bad.

The fact that Claymore actually kept his appointment when he got an eyeful—not to mention a snootful—of my office told me two things: he was serious about needing my services, and he couldn't afford the guys the big law firms have on retainer.

He didn't even blanch when he caught sight of me.

I'm six foot five, all muscle, no fat, thanks to boot camp and all the time I spent slogging through the jungle with a radio pack on my back. As a parting gift for my military service, I got a purple heart and a set of scars no amount of plastic surgery will ever fix. Only some of them are on my face. Most days when I get up, I feel like an old man at twenty-three. Old and jaded and apparently menacing as hell, from what I've been told.

Claymore agreed to the fee I quoted, including the amount I wanted up front. I had him sign one of the blank contracts I keep in my desk, and I wrote down his wife's name, their home address, and jotted a few notes down about her routine.

"I brought a picture of my wife in case you wanted one." Claymore hesitated, giving me a wary look. "It's in my briefcase along with the money."

So I had spooked him. "Just open it up where I can see it," I told him.

He put his briefcase on top of my desk, opened it, and turned it around so I could see the contents.

The inside of Claymore's briefcase was a mess. Odd for a guy who made a living dealing with neat rows of precise numbers, but like a lot of messy people, he knew exactly where to find what he wanted.

"Carolyn," he said as he handed over a color snapshot. "Jennings." A look of discomfort flitted over his features. "She kept her maiden name."

Of course she had. The trim, pretty brunette in the picture had a stubborn set to her chin. She'd probably burned her bra and protested the war, to boot.

The picture was a candid shot of Claymore's wife talking to a guy a couple decades older than she was. She was paying attention to whatever the guy was saying, but she was no vapid ingenue.

"This the guy you're worried about?" I asked Claymore.

"Him?" Claymore seemed genuinely surprised. "Good Lord, no. He was just some guy we met at a company party. Carolyn said she was trying to be nice, but I don't think she liked him very much."

I said nothing, waiting for Claymore to elaborate.

He fidgeted, uncomfortable with the silence. Most people were, especially when I got quiet. I guess that's part of what makes me so menacing.

"She said he wasn't very liberated." He glanced down at his hands. He wore a plain gold band on his ring finger. "I'm not either, to be honest. Carolyn quit wearing her wedding ring a couple years ago. I can't quite get rid of mine."

When a guy stopped wearing a ring, it was a good bet he was on the prowl. Liberated or not, I figured a woman would want to keep wearing hers unless she was out doing the same thing.

Claymore pulled out a plain white envelope from the briefcase. "She has a job at Biggie's Little City. I don't know doing what. Whenever I ask, she tells me it's none of my business."

I suppressed an urge to snort. I know a few liberated women, but there's a difference between liberated and just plain bitchy. Claymore might not want to admit it, but it sounded like his wife had already checked out of the marriage and was just biding her time until something better came along, whatever that something might be.

"She says she's been putting in a lot of overtime getting ready for the grand opening," Claymore said. "I don't know what else she does with her days."

Or her nights. He didn't have to say it for me to hear it.

"What was she doing when you got married?" If she'd had a profession then, chances were good she'd just slid over into doing the same thing at Biggie's.

He sighed. "Student at UNLV, in the Masters program. Something to do with feminist literature, I think, but she didn't finish."

I didn't think that would give her a leg up in the casino industry, but what did I know?

Claymore wrote a phone number on the front of the envelope. "That's my direct line," he said, handing the envelope over. Inside were three one-hundred-dollar bills.

I'd told him I only wanted two hundred up front. I didn't give him back the extra hundred.

I put the envelope with the cash in my center desk drawer and leaned back in my chair. The springs squeaked under my weight. On the street below, an ambulance wailed by, lights flashing. The downtown hospital's less than a mile from my office. I was used to ambulances. Claymore wasn't. He twitched at the sound, glancing nervously out the window as if he just realized what part of town he was in.

I gave him an out. "I don't need anything else," I said.

He closed his briefcase and stood up. "I'll want pictures," he said, almost like an afterthought. "Every day. Will that be a problem?"

A guy I knew at Fotomat owed me a favor. I could get prints in an hour if I had to.

"Nope," I said.

I told Claymore I'd start tailing his wife in the morning. He started to argue with me, but I shut him down.

I had my reasons for wanting to start in the morning. It was near the end of the workday. Even if Carolyn was a workaholic, I'd have a better chance of establishing her routine if I started fresh in the morning.

Not that I intended to outline my plans for my new client. Claymore had gone from a somewhat naive, befuddled husband of a liberated wife to a potentially meddlesome, controlling son-ofabitch now that he'd paid me. If he thought he could dictate how I did my job just because he had twenty years on me, he'd be in for a rude awakening. I'd had enough of that crap in the military.

After he left, I swiveled my chair around so I could look out the window. The neon lights of the Club Cal-Neva lit up the other side of the street.

One of the hostesses who worked in the Cal-Neva's second-floor coffee shop liked me. Not a lot of women could deal with my scarred face, but she didn't seem to mind. I made a point to eat there whenever I was flush.

Tonight I was definitely flush. Thanks to Claymore, I had enough to pay this month's rent. I could even splurge for a blue-plate special. Ham and eggs for a buck ninety-nine.

I'd just made three hundred dollars cash, and all I had to do was tail a liberated, cheating wife.

I started following Carolyn Jennings the next morning.

The address Claymore had given me was for a neat little suburban duplex not far from the university. Two driveways, two yards, one shared center wall. The American Dream on a budget.

Claymore's wife left the duplex by herself at seven-thirty-five. She got in a pale blue Volkswagen bug and only gave the street a cursory glance before she backed out of the driveway. I watched her in the rearview mirror of my old Ford Falcon. She didn't look at me as she drove past where I'd parked on the street in front of the other side of the duplex.

Tailing someone in traffic isn't all that easy. Just try trailing after someone who says "just follow me" to a place you've never been when they don't give you any actual directions. Stop lights make the job harder, and downtown Reno's lousy with stoplights.

The only saving grace I had was that blue Volkswagen. Her car was distinctive enough I could keep an eye on it even in morning traffic. I even let a couple cars get between us, especially once I figured out she was going directly to Biggie's Little City.

Biggie's was a bastardization of Reno's nickname—the Biggest Little City in the World. Biggie's was advertising itself as the biggest little casino in the world. My seventh grade English teacher was probably rolling over in her grave at the oxymoron.

I had to give Biggie's credit for trying. The casino complex out by the airport eventually planned to have its own nine-hole golf course, outdoor and indoor tennis courts, an outdoor pool, a camper lot for gamblers who took their home-away-from-home with them whenever they traveled, a shopping mall on the lower level of the hotel, and an outdoor go-cart track for the kiddies. All that along with the tallest hotel tower in town. I'd also heard they had plans to build a man-made marina for speedboat races, but I'd believe that when I saw it.

The whole idea behind Biggie's was to compete with the big boys down in Vegas—the hotel-casinos that had started to bill themselves as destination resorts. Some of the casinos in downtown Reno had already given themselves a facelift, but there was only so much they could do since they'd been built practically on top of one another. There was a lot of vacant land out by the airport. Biggie's had a lot of room to expand, and the money men behind the project had to be betting not everyone wanted to stay downtown.

So far only the casino and the hotel were open for business. The rest of the project was scheduled to open in phases. Heavy equipment and men in hard hats swarmed over the back side of the property, not quite out of sight of the shiny, brand-new facade out front.

When I pulled into Biggie's front parking lot at seven-fifty, the place was already a hive of activity. The marquee out front advertised Biggie's official grand opening the next night. The headliners for the grand opening party in the showroom would have drawn standing-room-only crowds in Vegas. Pretty impressive for the newest kid on the block. The money men had sunk some serious cash on a bet that wasn't a sure thing. Even in Nevada, casinos could fail.

An illuminated map on a free-standing column just inside the casino's front doors told me where to go if I wanted the elevators to the hotel towers or if I wanted to take the escalator down to the lower-level retail shops. The hotel registration desk, a long counter with six stations, was on my left, and the casino floor was dead ahead, already swarming with early morning gamblers busy shoving coins into row upon offset row of slot machines.

Casino floors were always arranged in a maze. You could never walk through a gaming floor in a straight line, the better to entice visitors to stop and drop a few coins in one of the brightly colored slot machines along the way. It made trying to tail someone a pain in the ass, but I'm tall enough I could see over most of the slots.

Biggie's had been open a little more than a week. I'd seen a story in a newspaper someone had left behind at the Cal-Neva's coffee shop. Soft openings like this were standard stuff. It let the staff work out the kinks before the high rollers showed up for the official grand opening.

Tomorrow's official grand opening was for show. Get the mayor or some other local celebrity to cut a ribbon with a pair of oversized scissors, then they'd throw the doors open for the cameras. The real business happened when the high rollers showed up.

High rollers would get their rooms comped and be treated like royalty. The idea was to get them used to taking a quick limo from the airport instead of a longer trip to downtown and then putting them up in luxury accommodations in a casino resort that really appreciated their business.

The kind of money the high rollers would drop at the baccarat tables or in the poker room would set me up for an entire year or more. Hell, just the cost of a single-night's stay in a high roller suite would pay my rent for a couple months and leave me enough money to order off the menu at the Cal-Neva.

You'd think the constant noise inside a casino would bother someone like me. All those coins dropping into trays, the electronic beeps and jarring tunes from the slots, not to mention all the flashing lights, had to trigger me, right? Not so much. I grew up in Reno. Casino food was relatively cheap. My parents used to drag me and my sisters along to eat at the casino buffets at least once a month, especially after I hit my growth spurt and became a bottomless pit, according to my dad. We always had to walk around the casino floor to get to the buffet line.

I'd never gotten used to the sound of an enemy sneaking up behind me, or the rapid-fire whine of bullets whizzing past my head. Or the screams of the wounded. But I could put up with casino noise just fine.

I pretended to study the illuminated map while I scanned the casino floor for Claymore's wife. I'd spotted her blue Volkswagen in a side section of the parking lot, probably employee parking only.

Claymore'd told me he didn't know what his wife did at Biggie's. I didn't see her out on the casino floor, and she wasn't manning any of the stations at the registration desk. A couple cocktail waitresses in skimpy outfits were circulating among the early-morning gamblers, Bloody Mary cocktails, complete with celery stalks, on their trays. I spotted a conservatively dressed Keno runner making her way through the slots. None of those women were Claymore's wife.

So what kind of work would a liberated woman consider doing in such a male-oriented adult playland? She was pretty young for middle-management, at least according to the picture Claymore had shown me, but that didn't mean anything. She was attractive enough and she didn't wear a wedding ring. She might think she was on a management track when in reality the money men were just keeping her around for eye candy to impress the high rollers. Sort of a high-level version of my hostess friend at the Cal-Neva. According to Claymore, Carolyn had gone to college at UNLV. She might have made the right kind of connections in Vegas to get a halfway decent job in the casino industry.

Biggie's business offices would be buried somewhere out of sight. According to the illuminated map, meeting rooms were downstairs next to the retail shops. Administrative staff probably worked down there as well. If Carolyn Jennings worked in the business office, I'd have a harder time getting eyeballs on her during the day, but it wouldn't be impossible.

Time for me to start earning Claymore's money.

I don't like crowds, sudden movement, or unexpected noise, like the snap of the latches on Claymore's briefcase. I can deal with the cacophony of sounds in a casino as long as I don't have to walk through a mass of people.

I haven't decked anyone who bumped into me from behind in months. Most days I feel like somebody should give me an award for that, like they do at AA meetings for drunks who've managed to stay sober.

My name is Mike Templar, and I'm a recovering soldier.
"Hello, Mike."
It's been six weeks since I punched somebody in the face.

I still felt bad about that last time. An old guy had come up behind
me on the street, just a random homeless guy looking for a handout.
He'd made the mistake of touching me on the shoulder. Without
even thinking about it, I'd whirled around and decked him.

He'd looked at me like I was the devil incarnate, shrinking
away from my scars and my outstretched hand when I bent over
to help him to his feet.

I'd given him the last five I had in my wallet. Instead of going
into the Cal-Neva for a blue-plate special like I'd planned, I'd gone
home to a can of Campbell's chicken noodle soup.

At least I hadn't dropped to the sidewalk and gone for my gun.
There's a reason I don't carry the thing when I'm out in public.

Biggie's wasn't all that busy this early in the day, so crowds
weren't going to be a problem. Tomorrow night this place would be
a zoo. I didn't plan to be around for the grand opening. Claymore
hadn't paid me enough to let me post bail.

I wandered through the maze of slot machines, keeping an eye
out for Claymore's wife. To keep from drawing any unwanted attention from casino security—I didn't want to look like I was casing the
joint—I dropped a few nickels into slot machines here and there. I
wanted it to look like I was on the prowl for the perfect machine.

The cashier's window was near the back of the casino next to the
showroom entrance. The lone cashier was a man in his midfifties.
No Carolyn Jennings in evidence. The showroom entrance was
closed off. So was the nightclub next to the showroom.

Biggie's had a total of nineteen bars scattered throughout the
casino floor. Nineteen. I counted them twice. Most of them were
closed at this time of day. The few that were open had small seating
areas that couldn't quite be called a lounge. A few gamblers, mostly
older guys, sat by themselves next to the open bars, a half-empty
drink in hand, reading the sports section of the newspaper. Biggie's had a sports book at the far end of the casino floor, but the
bank of televisions on the wall were all dark. After the grand
opening, the sports book would probably be open 24/7.

The poker room and baccarat tables were dark too, as were most
of the blackjack tables and the roulette wheel. Biggie's had three
restaurants and a buffet, but only the coffee shop and the buffet

were open. Carolyn Jennings wasn't visible in either one, nor was she working any of the open bars.

Satisfied she wasn't anywhere on the casino floor, I took the escalator downstairs and spent some time strolling through the shops on the lower level. Mostly high-end fashion stores with a collectibles shop, a jewelry store, and a movie theater thrown in the mix, along with a sandwich shop that was part of a national chain. The marquee on the movie theater read *Coming Soon*, although the smell of buttered popcorn from a candy store across the wide corridor from the theater made me wonder when the last time was that I'd gone to see a movie, or even what I'd seen. Probably something really thrilling since I couldn't remember.

All the stores in the lower level had plate glass windows. I couldn't see Carolyn Jennings in any of them.

It was starting to look more and more like she worked in the casino's business office. I'd walked past the closed doors for the meeting rooms at the far end of the retail level. Next to the meeting rooms, an unobtrusive door, solid with no windows, bore the name "BLC Incorporated."

I could get inside if I really wanted to, claim I had an appointment with the marketing manager but forgot what day it was for, but tailing a cheating spouse is all about surveillance, not confrontation. Claymore's wife wasn't supposed to spot me. My job was to follow her, and if I caught her doing something with someone she shouldn't, get the proof. Claymore didn't seem to give a shit about what job she had, and where she worked in the casino only mattered to me if her job made it hard for me to tail her.

I knew she was on-site somewhere, and I'd narrowed it down to the business office. I had a Pocket Instamatic with me in my jacket. If I had to take pictures on the casino floor, the lighting would make it iffy to shoot without a flash. Light down by the shops was better. People needed to see what they were buying. My 35 mm with the telephoto lens would do a better job no matter where I was, but casinos frowned on people taking pictures on the gaming floor, so my smaller Instamatic would have to do. If dark, grainy photos were all I could get, Claymore would have to settle. I wasn't a spy, and I wasn't on retainer to one of the big law firms. I didn't have the kind of covert equipment those guys did.

I caught a break around two in the afternoon. I was sitting at a bar near the back of the casino floor, only one row of slot machines between my back and a nice, solid little half-sized wall that divided the waiting area for the buffet from the casino. I was nursing a gin and tonic and resting my tired feet. I could see the glass-walled baccarat room from where I sat since it was raised a few steps above the main casino floor.

I'd managed to strike up a conversation with the bartender by pretending I didn't know anything about baccarat. He'd just launched into a diatribe about how poker was better than baccarat any day of the week when I saw Carolyn Jennings on the casino floor.

Claymore's wife had on more makeup now than she did in the picture Claymore had given me, and her long brown hair was pulled back in a sensible bun at the nape of her neck. She wore a loose-fitting black dress that draped over her shoulders, pulled in at her narrow waist, and flowed down to midcalf, accentuating her trim frame. She was with two men in flashy suits. The three of them walked up the short flight of stairs to the glass-walled baccarat room and went inside.

I took my drink over to the bar. "Who's that?" I asked the bartender, pretending the kind of interest in Claymore's wife that I didn't have.

He followed my gaze. "You mean the woman?"

"Yeah."

"One of the assistant managers. Don't know her name, but I've seen her around." He shrugged. "Too many people here, and we're all new to each other. She's not my boss, that's all I care about."

I didn't have to ask the bartender who the two men with Claymore's wife were. They had the kind of tans people in Vegas sported year round. The suits combined with their pinkie rings and entitled expressions pegged them as bigwigs intent on seeing how the grand opening of their shiny new asset was shaking out.

I kept my eye on the trio. I'm not a lip reader. I couldn't understand what they said behind the glass walls of the high roller room, but it was pretty easy to tell when Carolyn pointed out the security cameras in the ceiling over the baccarat tables. Casinos were big on surveillance. I had no doubt eyes had been on me since the moment I set foot on the casino floor.

"Big-time stuff coming up tomorrow," I said to the bartender. "Gonna make your month in tips, I bet."

His mouth turned down. "Not me. I'm not working tomorrow night." He spared another glance at the high roller room. "Too many high-profile customers. They don't want us new hires screwing up."

"Afraid you won't shake the martini right?"

"Cute," he said, catching my Bond reference. "All I know is everybody who works the bars gets the night off. Special crew coming in from Vegas to work the bars, just like special dealers coming in to work the high roller room. I hear they all have nice big tits."

Window dressing. That didn't seem to be the sort of thing a liberated woman would be comfortable with. Then again, she was only an assistant manager, which likely meant her opinion counted for diddly-squat with the guys who were really in charge.

If I hadn't figured it out before, I knew now, thanks to my chatty bartender, that the money behind Biggie's operation came from Vegas. And why not? If the casinos in Reno wanted to give Vegas a run for its money in the destination resort business, what better way for the guys down south to assure themselves they wouldn't be losing any money to their smaller cousins up north than by actually owning Reno's first destination resort hotel-casino.

I finished my drink, left a good tip for the bartender, and wandered around the rows of slot machines, plugging in a nickel here and there, until I found a good angle where I could see the high roller room and still look like I was interested in the slots. I slipped the Instamatic out of my jacket pocket.

My hands were big enough I could hold the little camera in one hand and take a picture without anyone catching on. Can't look through the viewfinder that way, but I've practiced long enough I can usually get a decent enough picture.

I snapped a couple shots of Claymore's wife and the two Vegas guys.

The older guy turned his head in my direction. Not all of a sudden, like he'd seen what I was doing, but more like something got under his skin and he had to look. Guys who'd been in country got that way. Hyperacuity, the VA shrinks who'd come to see me in the hospital had called it. I called it survival instinct.

I slipped the camera back in my pocket, making the move look like I was fishing for more change for the slots. I fed a few more nickels into the nearest machine just to make it look good.

The Vegas guy turned toward Carolyn and said something. She glanced in my direction and then looked quickly away.

Facial scars got that kind of reaction from people. The doctors at the VA told me I was lucky I didn't lose an eye. The guy on patrol with me had lost his life. His body had shielded me from most of the blast, but I was half a head taller than he was. I've got more scars in places that don't show in polite company.

I turned around and walked away like the attention had upset me. If I had lost an eye, an eyepatch would have made me look mysterious. The scars on my face just made me look wrong.

I stiffened involuntarily when I heard footsteps coming up behind me. Even with brand new carpeting on the casino floor, I could still tell when someone was following me.

I forced myself to turn around slow and keep my hands at my sides. It wouldn't do to punch somebody at Biggie's when I was supposed to be as inconspicuous as a guy my size could be.

Carolyn must have recognized the coiled tension in my body. Her face paled, but she stood her ground.

"I didn't mean to stare," she said. "It was rude of me. I'd like to offer you a drink on the house."

Her voice was soft and melodious, not at all the strident, empowered tone I'd come to expect from the liberated women I'd met since I'd come back from Vietnam. She didn't have an accent, at least not one I was able to pick up, but her manner reminded me of a genteel Southern woman. Her eyes were soft brown close up. The intelligence I'd seen in her expression in the photograph Claymore had shown me was intensified in person. This was one very smart lady. There was a lot going on behind those soft brown eyes.

"Thanks," I said. "But it's not necessary. I wasn't insulted."

She nodded her head, a slight gesture more to acknowledge what I'd said than to agree with it. "Still, I should know better. If you don't want the drink right now, I can give you a coupon for one. Come back whenever you want to claim it. Would that be all right with you?"

I couldn't very well say no to that, so I just nodded.

She led me to a different bar than the one I'd been cooling my heels at. The bartender was a pretty blond. The plain white blouse she wore didn't hide her ample cleavage. She'd probably be working the grand opening, and I'd be willing to bet the buttons on her blouse would be open just enough to reveal a good portion of her assets.

"I need a coupon," Carolyn said to the bartender.

The bartender clearly recognized Carolyn. She handed a slip of paper over, and Carolyn initialed it.

"There's no expiration," she said as she handed the coupon to me. "You can use it anytime, but I hope I'll see you back here soon."

I'd be back soon, but I hoped she wouldn't see me.

Tailing her was going to be a pain in the ass after this.

I killed a little more time in the lower level of Biggie's.

I bought a San Francisco Giants baseball hat in a store filled with football and baseball clothing and memorabilia. I had the clerk take the tag off, and I wore it out of the store. In a souvenir shop I bought an overpriced T-shirt with Biggie's logo on the front—a grinning, cartoonish cowboy lassoing a slot machine floating over an outdoor pool—and a black fanny pack. I changed into the shirt in a men's room and shoved my old shirt and jacket in the bag from the T-shirt place. I put my Instamatic in the fanny pack and cinched the thing around my waist.

It wasn't much in the way of disguises, but it was the best I could do on short notice. I kept the receipts in the fanny pack in case Claymore wanted an accounting of my expenses. I wasn't about to pay for the clothes and the fanny pack—a damn fanny pack—on my dime.

I bought a sandwich filled with slices of spicy cured meat at the sub shop and sat at a table that had a good view of the front door for the business office down the long corridor. There weren't a lot of people wandering around the shops, so I didn't have to get too close. I pretended to read through the ads in *The Big Nickel*, a freebie sales rag put out once a week by one of the local newspapers, while I waited to see if I could spot Carolyn again.

Sure enough, I'd almost polished off the sandwich when she walked past me, headed toward the business office. The two guys from Vegas were still with her, along with another guy I hadn't seen before.

The new guy was maybe ten years older than me, and he had the look of someone who never went out in the sun if he could help it. He wore thick-lensed glasses with black plastic frames, and his dark hair was cut short enough to show he was going bald on top. His charcoal gray suit was rumpled, but it looked like it had been well-pressed at one time. Maybe he'd just gotten off a plane. He held a black briefcase in one hand and a drink in the other. There wasn't much gone from the drink.

The trio stopped in front of the door to the business office. One of the Vegas guys was doing most of the talking, and it looked like he was working hard to impress the guy in the suit even though both the Vegas guys had a good fifteen years on him.

Carolyn stood slightly behind the two men, but it was clear, even from where I was sitting in the sandwich shop, that her attention was on the guy with the briefcase.

Was this the man Claymore was worried about?

I held *The Big Nickel* with one hand and fished the Instamatic out of the fanny pack with the other. I snapped a couple of pictures of the four of them. The Instamatic didn't have a zoom feature, but at least it would show all three men with Claymore's wife.

A few minutes later, the group broke up. The Vegas guy clapped the guy with the briefcase on the back, pointed toward the bank of elevators that led to the guest rooms, and then headed off down the corridor toward the casino floor.

The new guy handed his briefcase to Carolyn, and she took it with her when she went inside the business office.

Was she putting it in the casino's safe? Did that make the new guy a courier or a high roller? The Vegas guy had sure acted like the new guy was important. Vegas bigwigs didn't give a shit about couriers, just like generals hadn't given a shit about us grunts on the ground. We were all just pawns on the board.

I got a better picture of the guy in the rumpled suit when he walked past me on his way to the hotel elevators. He never looked my way. Instead, he stopped by a trashcan and dropped his barely touched drink inside. He fished a hotel key out of his pocket and peered at it through the thick lenses of his glasses, then with a disgusted expression, took the glasses off and shoved them in the inside pocket of his suit jacket.

His eyes were a brilliant blue and sharp as a tack. I thought about snapping another picture, but I got the feeling that if I did, he'd know it.

I wasn't the only one in disguise down here. The rumpled suit was misdirection, just like the thick-lensed glasses. His face was pale, sure, but I caught a hint of a tan line around the sides of his neck. He'd had a haircut in the recent past.

Something was going on here.

Something involving the Vegas guys? Could be, but it wasn't any of my business.

I'd been hired to tail a cheating wife. That was it.

Only I hadn't gotten those kind of vibes from Carolyn Jennings. I liked her. She'd been nice to me when she didn't have to be, but she hadn't hit on me. That didn't mean anything. I wasn't the kind of guy most women would hit on. The hostess at the Cal-Neva was a rare exception.

I looked at my watch. It was nearly four. Time to head out to my car. I knew where Carolyn had parked her blue Volkswagen. I could pick up the tail again there and see if she led me anywhere interesting.

So far this day had been a bust, but it didn't matter. Claymore only thought his wife was cheating. I didn't much like the guy, but I'd be happy to take his money no matter how things turned out.

My client wanted to see the pictures that night, even after I told him I didn't catch his wife doing anything incriminating.

"I told you I'd want pictures every day," he said after I'd given him a quick verbal rundown.

I'd pulled into a gas station two blocks from Claymore's house to call him at the number he'd given me. I'd followed Carolyn from Biggie's to a local grocery store where I'd pushed a cart around while I watched her pick up a chicken, a few vegetables, and a quart of milk. She'd gone home directly afterward.

She'd parked her Volkswagen in the driveway again. If she left, she'd be easy to spot. But if I took the film to my guy at Fotomat, she could leave and come back, and I'd have no way of knowing it. I figured I was safe making the phone call. Cooking that chicken was going to keep her busy for at least an hour or so.

"I thought you wanted me to watch her," I told Claymore.

"She's in for the night. Once she's home, she stays home."

For all he knew. The number he'd given me was for his inside line at work. It was after seven. Just how late did the guy work, anyway?

I told him to give me an hour, and he told me to meet him at a bar on Commercial Row.

I knew the place. It was a dive. He didn't strike me as a guy who'd frequent that part of town, but I was beginning to have serious doubts about my client now that I'd met his "cheating" wife.

Before he hung up, he told me to bring the negatives along with the prints. Most people were content with the pictures, but I didn't need the negatives.

I had to bribe my guy with an extra ten to keep the Fotomat open long enough to process the pictures. I told him to make a second set of prints for me, then I went to the ice cream shop next door for a chocolate cone while I waited.

I separated out the prints before I went to meet Claymore. The pictures were good enough I could make out Carolyn and the men she was talking to. Claymore should be happy. I put my set in the glovebox of my car and gave the other prints and negatives to my client when he showed up at the bar.

He didn't look through the photographs. He just slipped the Fotomat envelope into his jacket pocket.

"She's working the grand opening," he said after he'd polished off half his gin and tonic. "Or at least that's what she says she's doing."

I had a whiskey neat. The booze was watered down, the music in the bar was loud, and the cigarette smoke was thick enough to cut with a knife. I felt like I was back in a bar in Vietnam.

Claymore threw back the rest of his drink. "I have to get home," he said, standing up. "Check in with me tomorrow."

He left the bar without waiting for me to finish my drink. Fine by me. He'd paid for it, and far be it from me to turn down free booze. In fact, I had a second round on him.

When I left the bar, it was a little after ten. The night was cooling off. Give the town another month, and it would be hot and muggy at this time of night. I was still wearing the Biggie's T-shirt. My jacket, along with the fanny pack and my set of the photographs, were still in my car.

I looked up at the night sky. Too much neon and too many bright lights for me to make out anything except the brightest stars. In the jungle you could look up at night and see a canopy of stars through the overgrowth of trees. That was the only thing I missed about Vietnam.

Something made me drive by Claymore's duplex before I went home.

There wasn't a second car parked out front. Carolyn's blue Volkswagen was still parked in the same spot in the driveway. The lights were off inside the house. She'd packed it in for the night.

Claymore didn't live here, at least not now. Whether she'd kicked him out or he'd left in a jealous snit, she lived here by herself.

He hadn't come right out and said they were living together, but he'd sure implied it.

My client was lying to me about his marriage.

And if he'd lied about that, what else was he lying about?

Claymore jumped me when I opened the door to my apartment.

I live in one of those studio things built at the back of a free-standing garage. A mother-in-law apartment, I believe is the proper phrase. Mine was behind an old brick house off California Avenue in a part of Reno where the narrow streets are a warren of one-way avenues clogged with parked cars on both sides. My landlord's an old fart who gives me a break on the rent because I mow his lawn, take out the trash, and wash his Cadillac once a week whether it needs it or not.

The lock on my apartment door's a flimsy thing, the kind you can jimmy with a credit card. That had never bothered me. It's not like I have much to steal. I keep my 35 mm camera locked in the bottom drawer of my desk at the office. If someone wants my old records and the turntable I had before I got shipped overseas, more power to them.

The instincts I'd developed during the war made me tense up right before Claymore swung a tire iron at my back. The guy was fast. I dropped to the floor just a split second too slow. The blow struck me in the left shoulder, and I felt something inside my shoulder give way.

If I stayed on the floor, he'd crack open my skull. He must have anticipated that I'd drop to the floor. That was the only way he could hit my head.

He was a lot stronger than I'd initially pegged him for. His mild-mannered accountant persona had been a disguise, just like the too-big jacket he'd worn to my office had hidden his muscles. The Claymore I was seeing now was a killer, just like I'd been back in Vietnam.

I'd worked hard since I'd been back home to tamp those instincts down, but military training ran deep. I rolled to my feet, ignoring the fire in my shoulder. I'd survived worse.

I had height and muscle mass on Claymore, and I was mad. He'd lied to me all along. He'd used me, just like the military had used me. Whatever Claymore had wanted from me, he'd clearly gotten it, and he'd decided to take me out. To wrap up loose ends.

Well, the hell with that.

People tell me I look menacing, and that's when I'm not mad. You don't want to know me when I'm angry enough to see red.

The next time Claymore swung the tire iron at me, I stopped it with my right hand. To him it probably felt like he'd hit a brick wall.

The blow might have cracked a bone in my hand, but I didn't care. I ripped the tire iron out of his hand and threw it to the floor.

Then I punched him. A solid right to his jaw.

Claymore hit the floor, and I went after him. A body blow to steal his breath, then two more quick punches to the face. I felt his nose break. A third punch and he was out cold.

I made myself stop. If I kept going, I might have killed him, but my killing days were over.

I don't have a phone in my apartment. I knocked on my landlord's door until a light went on in the living room. He took one look at me and blanched. When I asked to use the phone to call the cops, he stepped aside without a word and let me in.

He'd never seen me like this before. I had Claymore's blood on my right hand and my left arm hung useless at my side.

While I stayed on the phone with the cops, my landlord kept giving me sidelong looks, like I was a stranger. It made me wonder if I'd have a place to live after all this was over.

A week later the door to my office opened and the guy I'd seen in the rumpled suit and the thick-lensed glasses give a briefcase to Carolyn Jennings came into my office.

"Ben Burdett," he said, extending his hand over my desk.

I stood up and shook hands briefly with my right. I hadn't cracked a bone when I'd stopped Claymore's blow, but my knuckles were still sore. My left arm was in a sling thanks to a separated shoulder and broken collarbone. I wouldn't be up to tailing anybody for a few weeks, but I'd kept what was left of Claymore's three hundred dollars. I'd be okay until I healed.

At least my landlord hadn't kicked me out. In fact, after he'd gotten over the shock of what had happened in my apartment, I think he liked the idea of having a hard-ass like me around. He said it made an old fart like him feel safer.

I lowered my bulk into my chair. My shoulder ached, but as pain went, I'd been through much worse. What they'd done to me in the VA hospital while my burns healed still gave me nightmares.

"What can I do for you, Mr. Burdett?" I asked.

He sat down in one of my client chairs. His blue-eyed gaze was just as direct up close as I'd suspected. This guy missed nothing.

"I thought you deserved an explanation," he said. "All things considered." He paused, giving me a hard look. My scars didn't seem to bother him one bit. "I trust you'll keep what I tell you confidential?"

If I hadn't been nursing broken bones, I might have shrugged. "You haven't told me anything yet, but sure."

He slid a business card across my desk. I recognized the FBI logo. Good old J. Edgar's personal law enforcement agency, or so people said.

"I'm afraid you stumbled into an ongoing investigation," Burdett said.

And why would the FBI be investigating Reno's newest, flashiest casino? Mob connections. That had to be it. The money men behind Biggie's had poured serious money into the project. The Gaming Control Board wouldn't have approved the casino's gaming license if any of the principals had mob connections, but that didn't mean mob money still wasn't involved. It would just be harder to prove.

Burdett had been undercover. Doing what, I didn't know, and I doubted he would tell me. He was just sitting back in my client chair, giving me time to work all this through on my own.

"How was Claymore involved?" I figured it wouldn't hurt to ask. Claymore was the whole reason I'd been involved.

"We think he was hired by the people we're investigating to see if the FBI was snooping around."

"And I gave him your picture," I said.

No wonder Claymore wanted pictures every day. When he looked through the pictures in the Fotomat envelope, he must have recognized Burdett even with the thick glasses. Once he got what he needed from me, I was a disposable loose end.

"What about the Vegas guys?" I asked. "They didn't recognize you?"

Burdett blinked at me, then he smiled. "The two guys in the flashy suits? They're from LA. Hollywood producers. A couple of the legit backers."

Hollywood. That explained the tans.

"Claymore's the only mob guy who's gone anywhere near the place," Burdett said. "He got his ass thrown out when security recognized him."

So Claymore had been blackballed, which meant he needed a convenient patsy to do his work for him. That's why he came to see me. He figured I needed the money bad enough I wouldn't ask him any questions.

I still had a lot to learn about this business. Number one on my list from now out would be to not take everything a client told me at face value.

Burdett stood up. He'd told me what he could, but there was one more thing I needed to know.

"What about Carolyn?" I asked. "They weren't married, were they."

Burdett hesitated, which made me think he wasn't going to say anything. Then he surprised me.

"She's a sweet woman, if a little on the liberated side. She met Claymore at a function when she was in grad school. Told my partner he gave her the creeps. As far as we can tell, she's exactly what she says she is—one of the assistant managers in accommodations, although I get the feeling she'll be escorting some of the high rollers around." His professional demeanor softened a little. "When she figures out she was hired as eye candy, I expect she'll be moving on."

He left without another word.

I still had the drink coupon Carolyn had given me in my wallet. I could go back and look her up. Her eyes had been kind and she hadn't flinched away from my face, but I had a feeling she'd forever be out of my league. Besides, there'd always be Claymore's big lie between us, even if she never found out I'd been hired to follow her.

I took the second set of photographs I'd taken for Claymore out of my desk drawer. Burdett hadn't asked for them, and I hadn't volunteered they existed. Before I tossed them in the trash, I took out the best photo of Carolyn and put it back in my desk.

Time to lock up for the day. The hostess who liked me was on shift tonight at the Cal-Neva. I could afford to splurge on a blue-plate special. Ham and eggs for a buck ninety-nine.

I'd given the fanny pack I'd bought with Claymore's money to my landlord. He'd actually been happy with the thing. "It'll give me a spare," he'd said.

I wondered if the hostess was a Giants' fan. A lot of people in Reno rooted for the San Francisco sports teams.

If she was, I wondered if she'd want a practically brand-new Giants hat.

I liked the Oakland A's better myself.

---

*I grew up in a gambling town and for years worked in a low-rent office building on the wrong side of casino row much like Mike Templar does in "Little City Blues." Many of my experiences as a newly minted adult working within a stone's throw of my hometown's major casinos found their way into this story. The fact that this story was a period piece written specifically for the Long Ago themed issue of Mystery, Crime, and Mayhem also gave me an opportunity to explore other issues relevant to the late 1960s, like the experiences of Vietnam veterans upon their return to the States. Although I have to say, realizing that the late sixties is now considered "long ago" came as a bit of a shocker.

International bestseller **Kristine Kathryn Rusch** *writes in a variety of genres, depending on her mood. She's been a bestseller in mystery, science fiction, fantasy, and romance. Her work has sold millions of copies. Her credentials are too long to list here, but here are some of the highlights of her mystery career.*

She's won the Ellery Queen Reader's Choice Award and has been nominated for the Edgar and the Shamus awards under her own name and under her Kris Nelscott pen name. She's also been nominated for the Anthony award, as well as several other mystery awards. Her hard-boiled Kris Nelscott novels often get picked as top ten books of the year, both here and overseas. Her Smokey Dalton series is in development for a limited television series.

She occasionally writes mystery novels under her Rusch name. The most recent novel is a genre mashup called Ten Little Fen, *which expands her popular Spade/Paladin short story series into the longer length. Find out more about her work at kriswrites.com.*

GRIEF SPAM

Kristine Kathryn Rusch

Day sixteen since Rob's death, not that Lucca was counting—oh, hell, of course she was counting. The days, the hours, the minutes. She was counting everything because that was the only way to keep her brain focused.

But not focused well enough apparently, because she woke up that morning, like she had for the past fifteen mornings, reaching for Rob on his side of the bed, wondering why he had gotten up so early, wondering what day it was, wondering if she had forgotten to drive him to work, wondering—

And then she remembered. Sledgehammer, nightmare, emotionally devastating.

Those words didn't even describe it.

More like existing between being and nothingness. She rested on the soft king bed, pillow scrunched beneath her head, covers wrapped around her like a hug, the cats pressed against her as if they were afraid she would leave too, and let the reality sink in.

She used a trick, one she had developed ten days ago. She reviewed everything in her head.

She started with the obit, because she had had to write it, and she had the damn thing memorized:

> *Robert Zedder, 48, loving father and husband, died in a single car collision on Route 73, just outside Watersville. Beloved assistant principal of Anderson High School, Zedder had worked for the Watersville School District for twenty-five years. Recipient of Teacher of the Year for five years running, Zedder maintained his teaching career while working in the high school administration. He leaves behind his wife, Lucca Kwindale, his daughters Annette, Sybil Washington, and Marla Zedder-James, and three granddaughters . . .*

At which point, Lucca's throat ached—every single time. He would never see Annette graduate from college, never see the grandbabies grow, never see their babies, never see—

Lucca made herself sit up. The cats lifted their heads, startled, bits of their fur floating in the semilight of the early morning filtering in the bedroom window. A bedroom on the east side of the house had been Rob's idea, since he had to get up early for school. Too early, she had always complained, and he would laugh.

Self-employed people don't understand schedules, he would say, and by that he would mean *she* didn't understand schedules, never realizing that self-employed people had to schedule better than anybody else, or no one would think they were working.

Old arguments, now irrelevant. Lucca ran a hand over her face. Day sixteen. He had died on a Tuesday (a Tuesday in April, four days before taxes were due, at four in the goddamn morning—what had he been doing driving at four in the goddamn morning?), which meant that this was Thursday, some mucky-muck day at the end of April, nearly May, which he used to say was his favorite month.

Mucky-muck day. She'd learned that phrase from him too. She had lived half her life with him—married at twenty-four—and she was having trouble separating herself from that. Having trouble figuring out how to move forward, how to think, even. Strangely, it had been easier in the first few days after his death because there had been—ironically enough—a schedule.

So, last night, she realized she needed a new schedule. The nonexistent schedule, she would have said to him, had he still been alive, and she would have said it with a smile, and just enough sarcasm and bite to let him know she kinda resented the way he had minimized her work each and every day.

He would have heard the bite, and it would have made him defensive.

He was helping people, he would have said, teaching kids how to be good citizens, making sure the school ran well, working toward the future.

He hated her work. She didn't hate his, but she thought it was dreary.

She didn't see her work as noble—only private detectives in novels were noble—but she saw it as useful and interesting, and a whole hell of a lot less dangerous now that she did 90 percent of it online.

She and her crew. Her crew, who were taking point at the moment. Her crew, who probably needed some kind of pep-talk acknowledgment from her.

Later today, she would head to the office where the crew worked. She would give them an hour. She figured she could handle an hour without tears. Maybe an hour would give her enough focus to put her pesky emotions in their place.

She'd read about grief. Hell, she'd combed the web to find out everything she could about grief.

It's a process, the websites told her.

It's harder when things are left unsaid, the websites warned.

Be aware, they counseled. *The emotions come in waves.*

Emotion*s*, not emotion. Not sadness, not mind-numbing despair. But sadness *and* mind-numbing despair. Anger *and* denial. Shock *and* acceptance. Depression *and* bargaining—wait. Bargaining with whom? With the idiot who was out driving at four in the morning on a school night? Who probably fell asleep behind the goddamn wheel, missed a turn, and slammed into a concrete abutment that was slated to be repaired by the Department of Transportation next summer, because the damn abutment was an accident magnet?

Whew. She let out a small breath. Anger. It billowed when she least expected it. She didn't think of herself as an angry person, but she certainly wasn't a calm one either.

Never had been, never would be.

She had made a list the night before, so she wouldn't have to think about her day. Thinking about the day, she believed, was what had paralyzed her this past week. Now that the funeral was over. Now that the girls had gone home to their separate cities, their separate lives, and their separate grief. Now that the planning was done.

Yeah, right. The lack of schedule had paralyzed her. Not the loss of Rob. Not that at all.

Lucca grabbed her robe from the chair beside the bed, slipped her feet into the worn slippers she'd meant to replace at Christmas, made a brief stop in the bathroom, avoided the kitchen where the cats were already gathering for their breakfast treats, and proceeded down the side hall to her home office.

A second master the builders had called it when they slapped this place together from custom pieces. She didn't care about what they called this part of the house. When she and Rob had looked for the perfect home to raise their family in, she had insisted on the home office, as far from the main living quarters as possible.

She just wanted—and got—two rooms and a bathroom to herself so she could have an outer office and an inner sanctuary. She even had her own entrance—very important in the early days, when (stupidly) she let the clients come here.

She had never told Rob about the guy who had threatened her at knife point, or the cheating wife who had shown up with a shaking gun in her right hand. Rob couldn't have done anything about it except worry. In his later years, he had put on weight around the middle, always intending to exercise, and never exercising at all.

If he had been alone with someone who had become violent because of her work, he wouldn't have been able to defend himself.

He would have died, because of her. (Of course, this year, he had died because of him. Or the damn abutment. Or the stupid car.)

It had taken a knife and a gun, and a couple threats left on her voice mail to wake her up. Fortunately, before anything had happened.

Before someone had gone after her family with evil intent.

That year—ten years ago now—Lucca had decided on an outside office, the farther away the better. Rob had complained bitterly, about the distance, the expense, the location—everything. Initially she thought he was being controlling—he didn't want her away from the house. Later, she thought maybe the outside office made her work even more embarrassing to him.

He thought of private detectives as blue collar. He'd once said, *What a waste of an education, Lucca. You were Phi Beta Kappa, second in a class of five hundred at one of the most prestigious universities in the nation. I tell my kids they want to achieve all those goals so they'll get the best jobs ever, not dig through someone else's underwear to see if it has holes.*

She'd walked away from him that day. Hadn't even fought back. They'd said a lot of ugly things to each other in their fights, but neither of them had ever walked away before.

And he knew—because he wasn't dumb (wasn't Phi Beta Kappa either, but wasn't dumb)—that if he kept pushing her like that, she would walk away for good.

So she'd got her outside office. Smartest decision she'd ever made, besides going back to school to learn the ins and outs of computer research. As the business grew, the offices grew, the staff grew, and she out-earned Rob by more than double.

Although, since she handled the family finances, he never knew that. He hadn't known a lot of things, because she'd stopped telling him.

There had been no point.

And now, he would never know. Her legs buckled at the thought. She put a hand on the wall, wondered if, now that he was dead, he actually did know. Maybe he knew everything now. Some cultures believed that consciousness spread all over time, learning life's lessons.

She made herself stand up, let go of the wall, keep moving. She wasn't a weak person, no matter how she felt. She wasn't superhero strong, either, but she could move forward in the face of all difficulties.

Rob'd said once, after Annette was born, that he thought Lucca could give birth, then take a five-mile hike, and cook a six-course meal, all in the same day.

She didn't have that kind of stamina now—in fact, she couldn't remember the last time he had said something like that—but she was usually stronger than she had been these past sixteen days. Not the kind of woman who sobbed alone in her bedroom, with only her cats for company.

Lucca opened the hallway door into her office. The door led into the outer sanctum, once the reception, now a dump spot for old paper files, boxes, and photographs that should probably never see the light of day.

The inner office remained her home office, six different kinds of computers and two laptops, three routers, all hard-wired in, plus two different Internet hot spots through two different companies. She did searches here that she didn't want on her office network, and she routinely cleaned off and dumped computers when she had stumbled on some truly perverted stuff in the course of an investigation.

Usually she used the client's computer for that, going through whatever they let her investigate, sometimes in her office, sometimes in their home. But she'd been doing this long enough that she got a sense of people, and she could tell if they were the kind who might make her life a living hell.

In the middle of the computer jungle was her personal laptop, the one she used for family emails and her private social media accounts—the ones only shared with her daughters, her extended family, and a handful of close friends. She made sure she bought a new laptop every year, something cheap and not very sophisticated, and carried it with her on vacations and in the car.

She liked to think of that computer as an extension of the woman who lived in this house, the woman who had married Rob, bore three children, and raised them in as old-fashioned a way possible. Sometimes she thought of that woman as the fictional version of herself, the one she presented to the family and to the neighborhood, not the hard-assed broad who knew when a client was lying to her, or who had talked down that guy with a knife.

She grabbed the computer out of her old leather recliner, the one piece of furniture in the entire house that predated every-thing, from her relationship with Rob to the move to this city. An old boyfriend had bought the chair for her, the only piece of furniture in her entire one-bedroom apartment. She'd slept in the damn chair for nearly three months, long after he had broken up with her.

Rob hadn't known where the chair came from, only that she wouldn't part with it because it had been in her first apartment. He hadn't asked more.

She sank into it, robe parting along her knees. She cradled the laptop to her chest, thinking about her future while all wrapped up in her past.

Well-made furniture often outlived the people who first owned it. Well-built houses did too. Stuff lived longer than people, than husbands, than true love.

Sometimes stuff held its secrets—like this chair—secrets that would die with her. And sometimes stuff broadcast the secrets far and wide, once the stuff had been found in a hidden compartment or in the back of a closet or tucked (forgotten) in the pocket of an old coat.

She used to love ironies like that.

She used to love a lot of things.

She shook off the thought, opened her laptop, and typed in her password. The screen bounced into life, informing her that she hadn't opened the laptop in seventeen days—a notification she set up for herself so that she would know when she'd neglected her personal life for much too long.

Seventeen days.

He'd been dead for sixteen.

She couldn't remember why she had been on the computer the day before his death. Probably checking Facebook, seeing what the girls were doing, looking at the pictures of her grandbabies, or maybe even downloading music for her marathon exercise sessions.

It all blurred.

She took a deep breath before opening her email program. She knew what she would find. Dozens (maybe hundreds) of condolences. Lots of offers of help—whatever that meant. Grief spam (a widowed friend had warned her about that). And way back, normal emails, the kind that had been sent Before, the kind that had assumed normal would continue, not just for hours, but for days, months, and years.

She clicked on the computer's built-in timer, set it for an hour, then opened the email program. One hour. If she didn't want to read the condolence letters she didn't have to. She could just spend that hour deleting the grief spam.

The email downloaded faster than she expected. Three hundred emails, according to the little bar, most of them from familiar names. She watched the subject lines change from mundane things to topics like *Thinking of You* and *Call Us If You Need Anything*.

And then, in the middle of it, emails from people she didn't recognize, with the subject lines in all caps.

THE TRUTH ABOUT ROBERT ZEDDER; SEE WHAT ROBERT ZEDDER HAD DONE IN THE DAYS LEADING UP TO HIS DEATH; DISCOVER WHO ROBERT ZEDDER REALLY WAS.

On and on and on. That wasn't the grief spam she had been expecting. She had expected (and gotten) *Meditation for Widows* (Jesus, she was a widow now), *Join Our Grief Community*, and *Avoid Scams Targeted at the Grieving* (she thought that particularly pernicious).

But the ones with Robert's name, those disturbed her.

She looked at the dates of the emails, saw they had come to her after the obituary was published (every-damn-where), and slammed the laptop closed.

Fucking predators. That was a particular kind of nasty that she would delete when she was calm enough. When she wasn't feeling like isolating and opening each email before sending malware directly to the sender. When she wasn't feeling like tracking down the IP and finding the person's exact address, and going there and—

She made herself breathe, again.

She set the laptop aside and stood. The timer would go off, but it wouldn't repeat, so she could just leave it.

She needed breakfast anyway.

After that, the kitchen felt like a haven, rather than a reminder of Rob's absence. Even though his favorite shoes sat haphazardly under the table in the breakfast nook, where he had taken them off the night before. Even though his nasty protein powders still cluttered up her granite countertop. Even though the mail was piled a bit too high on the island.

Light poured into the windows that surrounded the nook, and outside, leaves had sprouted on the trees that gave this part of the lawn so much privacy.

The three cats twirled and meowed on the tile floor, waiting for her to take care of them, which she did—the standard morning routine, the same as it had been a month ago—filling bowls, filling water, giving them a bit of soft food.

She followed the routine, because she had promised herself routine, poured some shredded wheat, dressed it up with fresh strawberries someone had left, added a side of peanut butter toast for protein, took her damn vitamins, and made coffee.

Routine.

Except she couldn't turn on the TV under the counter, couldn't open her tablet to see the news of the day, couldn't bear to do more than stare and eat. Finally, she picked up her phone, tapped it open—and found nearly a dozen texts and messages from her daughters.

The most recent came from Antoinette.

Mom! Where Are You?

Followed by one from Marla.

Mom, we're getting concerned.

And from Sybil.

Mother, you need to pick up the phone.

Lucca scrolled through before she did, not willing to be blind-sided by anything, but afraid she might be.

Her phone vibrated in her hand. She had shut off the ringer days ago. The screen lit up: the call was from Antoinette.

Lucca leaned against the kitchen island, bracing herself, gaze on the empty cat dishes still littering the floor, and answered the phone.

"Hey, baby girl," she said, as she always did when greeting her youngest.

"Mom. Where *were* you?" Antoinette's voice hadn't shaken like that since she was six, and broke her leg after falling out of a tree.

"I—um—." Lucca glanced at the clock on the microwave. It was eleven-thirty, much later than she usually got up. "I have been keeping the phone in the kitchen."

She had expected Antoinette to say something about that, but she didn't. Instead, Antoinette took an audibly shaky breath, and said, "They're not true, are they? Those screenshots? They're made up, right?"

Screenshots? Lucca felt dizzy. Outside of the house, Rob was alive, handling the kids at school with his usual mixture of aplomb, severity, and humor, taking the small emergencies. He would have handled this, this call, the girls upset. He would have dealt with it, because he handled kids. All the kids.

"What screenshots?" Lucca asked, wishing she didn't have to.

"You haven't *seen* them? Mom, aren't you getting your email?"

Lucca's breakfast rolled in her stomach. Those emails—they had gone to her daughters.

"I downloaded it," Lucca said, "but didn't look at it."

Not really. Just enough to see those subject lines—*The Truth About Robert Zedder.*

The truth.

"You have to look, Mom." Antoinette's voice wobbled. "You have to do *something*. It can't be about Dad. It can't."

"It probably isn't," Lucca said as calmly as she could manage—more calmly than she expected, in fact. She was talking to her daughter now as if Antoinette were an unruly client. "A widowed friend of mine warned me about the email. She called it grief spam."

"And you didn't warn us?" Antoinette asked. "You should have warned us."

"I didn't think you'd get any," Lucca said. *I didn't think it would be personal either,* she wanted to add. *With Rob's name and everything.* "I'll text your sisters and then take a look."

"It's awful, Mom," Antoinette said.

"I'll keep that in mind," Lucca said, and hung up.

She texted her other two daughters and told them to hold tight; she was investigating. They knew that investigating was one of Lucca's most serious words.

Then she headed back down the hall, clutching the phone, and bracing herself. Antoinette said the spam was awful, but it couldn't be worse than identifying Rob's body through that stupid camera at the morgue, or looking at his embalmed but broken face, and calmly agreeing with the mortician that the casket should remain closed.

Lucca was braced—and weirdly, a little relieved. Something to do. Not make-work. Not work for the sake of work.

Something that mattered. For her girls.

Lucca set the phone on the side of her big desk, then grabbed the laptop off her leather chair. She pulled back her desk chair, and sat down, placing the laptop in the center of all the equipment.

She'd done this kind of work a million times before. She knew how to look at sensitive information on someone's personal laptop. She was just going to pretend this laptop wasn't hers.

Lucca isolated the laptop. For the moment, it didn't have to be attached to any Internet connection; she had already downloaded the email.

Then she tugged her robe tightly closed, leaned forward, and opened her email program.

There were more of those grief spam emails than she had thought. Before she even opened them, she glanced at who had sent them. She didn't recognize the name on the account, but the actual address used to send the email had a dodgy URL. She didn't go there. She had another system she would use for that, or maybe, if things weren't as bad as she feared, she would report the URL to the office, and let her staff work on this.

She paused over the Rob-specific emails. There were at least a dozen of them, maybe more if she checked her spam filter, which she wasn't ready to do yet. Whoever had set up the subject line had done so with care, so that the emails *wouldn't* get caught in the spam filter.

Her hesitation was not unusual. She needed to figure out how best to deal with these emails.

But if she had been opening the emails in real time, rather than ignoring her personal laptop altogether, she would have opened a few one day, and more the next.

So the best thing she could do was open these emails in chronological order.

She let out a small breath. Whoever had sent these emails had waited more than a week for her to open them, and then, when she hadn't, had sent email to her daughters.

Had she not been an investigator, she would have immediately thought that all of this was personal. But her daughters were listed in the obituary, and anyone with a computer and the sense of a half-wit could find them.

Lucca's mouth was dry, and she wished she had grabbed her coffee. But she hadn't. Then she clicked on the first email—received a day or so (maybe hours) after the obituary was published.

The Truth About Robert Zedder! The interior screamed, just like a headline.

Then it quoted the obituary—loving father and husband—with several attached pictures underneath the words.

The pictures were what she expected. Blurry images of a man who might or might not be Rob, kissing a woman who was definitely not Lucca.

Lucca could fake up this sort of thing in less than fifteen minutes. She could search for the images on the Internet and see where they were pulled from, and maybe even identify the couple.

But she didn't.

Instead, she opened the next email.

It had a subject line similar to the one she had just looked at, and the format was the same. Only this one was focused on "loving father." Again, blurry photos, clearly obscene and awful, with a man and a girl who couldn't have been more than eight.

The man might've been Rob. But he might've been any other dark-haired middle-aged tubby white guy.

This stuff was generic, disgusting and hideous, designed to upset the recipient. But Lucca had seen worse, much worse, from people she had thought she had known. Those upset her.

This was a poor attempt at—what, exactly?

She couldn't find anything that stated a purpose in the email. Not a link, not a request for money, not a claim of blackmail, nothing.

It looked like someone was trying to destroy Rob's reputation, but surely anyone who would want to do that would know that Rob's wife was a private investigator and would be able to figure out who had sent the emails.

Or maybe it was some kid at the high school who had hated Rob, and decided to get revenge on his family.

Lucca let out a small breath. That thought made her feel a little unclean. It would take a special kind of budding young sociopath to come up with something like this.

But this could be an entire blackmail campaign, with the ask at the end. The fact that there were a dozen or more of these things led her to believe that inside these emails would be some kind of escalation—she just wasn't sure what it would be.

She backed up her email program and all of the emails on two different thumb drives, just in case opening one of the other emails would destroy her entire computer. Such things happened a lot to her clients, and her team was usually called in too late to deal with the mess.

While the program was copying onto the thumb drives, Lucca used time to take a quick shower (first time in two days!), put on the jeans and denim shirt she had laid out the night before, heat up some coffee, and grab one of the chocolate banana muffins someone had given her.

The orgy of food had been amazing right after Rob's death, and Lucca had expected it to slow down, but since she wasn't communicating (much) with her friends, they had taken to leaving food baskets on her doorstep.

People were worried about her, and she found that both touching and irritating and, at the moment, highly convenient.

She walked back into the inner sanctum just as the laptop bonged its little *I'm done!* sound. She pulled the thumb drives and labeled them, setting them near her phone as something to deal with later.

Her phone's screen flared on, showing four more texts from her daughters, getting more and more insistent.

Lucca couldn't ignore them, not with the girls so very upset. So she sent a group text to all three of them, telling them to calm down—she had this—and then went back to work.

The next two emails were just as generic as the first two. Then the tone of the emails changed.

See What Rob Zedder Did In The Days Before His Death! emails actually had photographs of Rob, taken primarily off security cameras from convenience stores, traffic cameras, and bank systems.

She felt a flash of irritated responsibility—she was going to have to let all those organizations know they had been compromised.

Then she sipped her coffee, which was already tepid, crammed part of the banana muffin into her mouth (more chocolate than banana, and good), and looked at the first *What Rob Did* email more closely, to see why the anonymous emailer thought these would be upsetting.

She couldn't see anything upsetting, even when she made the emails larger. She didn't click on the photographs, though. She would click links and photographs after she had finished the initial glance at the emails.

She was about to give up on that particular series of emails when she figured out what was wrong: the time stamps on each photo—and they all had time stamps, because they were from security cameras—were in the middle of the day, when Rob was supposed to be at the high school.

Her first inclination—her investigator's inclination—was to call the school to see if Rob had actually been at work at those times on those days. But that could wait. Because she still didn't know the purpose of these emails, and she didn't want to be manipulated into any kind of unusual behavior.

The next three emails were simple threats with varying degrees of menace. The upshot of each? *We have more information on Robert Zedder* and the implication was that they would release that information, ruin Rob's reputation, and destroy everyone's belief in him.

But for what gain? She couldn't find that, not yet.

That was beginning to bother her.

Finally, she got to the last three emails. They all had the subject header *Discover Who Robert Zedder Really Was*, but the headline in each email was different.

The first said, *You Think You Knew Robert Zedder. You Were Wrong.*

Buried into the body of the email were more pictures. Only these were screenshots. The first series appeared to be screenshots from Snapchat on someone's phone. The snippet of conversation, from almost a month ago, would have disappeared by now—stuff remained on Snapchat for only twenty-four hours or so—but someone had thought to preserve it.

And augment it.

One of the handles—midfindotdlegercom—had a computer-drawn fake-handwritten scrawl next to it, identifying it as Rob's. The posts were nasty, vicious, hate-filled, calling out someone for being transgender. Lucca wouldn't have believed it was Rob at all, except that she recognized the handle.

Rob loved using parts of words in a patterned repeat. He had taught her that trick back in the days when passwords didn't need numbers and punctuation. This particular handle came from the words *Middle Finger Dot Com.* (*Mid-Fin-Dot-Dle-Ger-Com*).

Her phone vibrated across the desk. She glanced at the laptop's clock, realized she'd been working for nearly two hours. That call had to be from one of her daughters.

Lucca picked up the phone, glanced at the screen, but didn't answer. The caller had been Marla this time.

I'm still working on it, Lucca texted all three of them. She didn't tell them she had only just gotten to the screenshots.

Given Antoinette's text earlier that morning, the three girls suspected these messages were from Rob as well. He had probably taught them the same trick that he had taught Lucca.

She made herself focus, rather than think about how her daughters were feeling. Right now, they were just clients, and she was going to treat them that way.

Treating them that way enabled her to keep her distance from this, so that she didn't think about her husband, Rob. Instead, she was focusing on some guy named Rob, who might or might not have been a pig on Snapchat.

Although the screenshots weren't just from Snapchat, but from other apps that provided "privacy," deleting messages some time after they were posted. There were even a few screenshots from

Facebook's Messenger app, the special feature that also made messages disappear.

And none of the posts were nice. All of them were nasty, trollish, horrid pieces—taking apart gays, African Americans, and women. Vicious, hideous stuff, the kind of things that Rob The Saintly would have told her that he didn't want "his kids" saying in school.

With some trepidation, Lucca opened the last email.

She had expected some kind of ask or a request to go to a website or a demand for money so none of this would go out.

And there was none.

Just two sentences:

Aren't you happy to be rid of that asshole now? You really should thank me.

And then, nothing.

Nothing at all.

She had to stand up after reading those two lines. She grabbed the last part of the muffin, ate it without really thinking about it, and chased it with the remains of the coffee.

Then she went into the kitchen to get more.

She was fully aware that she was dealing with her sudden stress by shoving it down with food. Which was better than what she had been doing all week, which had been avoiding food, except when her body reminded her.

She grabbed another chocolate-banana muffin, poured more coffee, thought for a brief minute about actually putting something healthy in her body, and then decided against it.

She was working. It shouldn't matter that she was working on something about Rob. She needed to act as if she hadn't met him at all.

Although if she hadn't met him, she would think he had written all that crap in the screenshots. She might even consider that he had done the stuff in the blurry photos.

She shuddered. If she had spent years sharing her bed—her life—with a creature like the one in "loving father" then she should be indicted herself.

She didn't even remember sitting down in her leather chair. One moment she was in the kitchen, the next she was checking her spam filter. There had to be an ask, somewhere. Or a demand. Something to make this effort worthwhile to the sender.

She didn't find it in the spam filter or in the junk folder. She checked through the email again to see if she had missed something.

She hadn't.

Could it be that the person who had sent these emails hadn't wanted a response from her? Had they sent emails to her daughters because the barrage that came to Lucca was done? Were they trying to convince the family that Rob wasn't the person they had thought he was?

Lucca stood, remembering Antoinette's voice, shaking like it had when she was six. Seeing the texts from all three of her daughters: *Mom, those screenshots aren't real. Are they?*

Already the doubt. Already the worry.

Some poison had wormed its way into Lucca's family—and she wasn't sure how to get it out.

First things first, though. She had to find out what her daughters had received. She texted them, telling them to forward the emails to her personal laptop account rather than any business account, like she would have if they were clients.

She figured the laptop account was already compromised—hell the laptop itself might've been compromised—so she was just trying to contain the problem into one space.

Besides, she was trying to act like a client would. If someone was monitoring the online communications—as Rob's wife, not as Lucca Kwindale, private investigator—they would expect the daughters to forward their emails. A healthy family would work together, and Lucca's family had been healthy.

Hadn't it?

She rubbed a hand over her face. It would be so easy to blame the grief or the exhaustion on her emotional roller coaster, but that wasn't entirely why she was having doubts.

There had always been parts of Rob she hadn't understood, and as he had gotten older, parts she hadn't liked. They were a true mismatch, the kind that happened when people got married too young.

She hadn't left because of the girls, although she had been toying with it now that Antoinette was nearly out of college. The household hadn't had to remain stable, she had been thinking, and she had seen no reason to live in the big house with a man she wasn't really sure she would have talked to if they had met now.

Lucca gathered the crumbs of the second muffin, not remembering consuming all of it. She dribbled them into her mouth like a teenager.

She had been dealing with those thoughts—the thoughts of divorce, of leaving—ever since Rob had died. She hadn't told anyone about that, not because she felt guilty, but because she didn't.

Maybe that was why the doubts had come so fast. She hadn't liked him, not the man he had become.

But it was a stretch to think he had skipped out of work and even more of a stretch to think he had written all those nasty things on all of those social media sites.

She wiped off her fingers, sipped even more coffee, and went back to work. She had a moment of trepidation as she attached the laptop to her dedicated Internet line. She half expected the laptop to freeze up, or ransom ware to appear, but nothing like that happened.

She downloaded the email, then immediately went offline. She would do the other work—going to the websites and links—later, depending on what she found.

She isolated her daughters' emails by daughter, wondering if they got different emails. Lucca started with Marla's because she was the eldest. She was also the most visible of the children, and ostensibly, the one with the most money. If Lucca were doing this horrid thing, she would have gone to the wife first, and then getting no response, to the eldest child, and worked her way down.

But if Lucca had been doing this horrid thing, she would have asked for money to keep the damn information off the streets, rather than sending that pointed final email.

The emails weren't quite the same. First, Marla hadn't received all twelve. She had only received seven—although Lucca would ask her to double-check her spam filters.

The first three were exactly the same, including the hideous "loving father" email. There was only one in the middle, with photos showing Rob coming out of a hotel, photos taken by the security camera of a bank. Lucca had received those photos as well.

The last three were different, though. They were screenshots, yes, but they were from private chat boards. The handle was the same as on the ones she received—midfindotdlegercom—and Rob's name had been "written" in the same red lettering as on her screenshots.

But these were worse than Lucca's. Not in political content, but in personal content. They would dig directly into Marla's self-esteem.

I got "blessed" with three daughters, one of the posts read, *and all of them take after my wife, who is no prize, let me tell you. I was happy to have married the oldest daughter off, because she made bitchiness her life's work. Couldn't wait for her to move out.*

And another:

Don't get your girlfriend pregnant, no matter what you do. If I'd used a condom, I wouldn't have been "blessed" with the Bitch Queen of the Universe as a daughter.

Lucca took her hands off the keyboard. She stepped away from the laptop, because if she didn't, she would put her fist through the screen.

Those posts were Rob's. She knew it as clearly as if she had heard him say those things.

One of his favorite sayings was "Bitch Queen of the Universe," only he'd used it to describe a woman he worked with, as well as the Watersville's mayor. Lucca had never heard him use it to describe his daughters, though. Although he hadn't really liked Marla.

He'd said that to Lucca many times over the years, always in a perplexed way. *Isn't a father supposed to fall in love with his child?* he'd ask.

The question was plaintive in the beginning, then biting later. He'd actually talked about getting a DNA test when Marla was thirteen and difficult. The subtext was—always had been with her—that she was Lucca's fault.

Lucca, for not being on the pill. Lucca, for refusing to terminate the pregnancy. Lucca, for trapping him into marriage—even though he had been the one to ask her. She had told him, more than once, that she was perfectly willing to raise the baby alone.

And that was the thing that bothered her the most. Only two people knew that Lucca had been pregnant when she got married. They hadn't lived near family at the time, so they had "eloped," going to Vegas for a quickie wedding.

She had been four months pregnant, but not showing from the angles of the photographs they had taken. That had been July. Marla had been born in December. And with her birth announcement, they had included the announcement of their marriage, changing the date so that it seemed like they had gotten married in March instead.

Her parents had been wounded that Lucca hadn't had a traditional wedding, but they had known that their middle child had never been a traditional person. His parents were crushed, and that was when the blaming had started.

If only I had worn a condom he would say until finally Lucca had shushed him.

You keep saying that and when the baby gets older, she'll have a complex Lucca said.

She had been a young twenty-four when she married him, still naive enough to believe that two parents were better than one, idealistic enough to think that love (even pallid love, like theirs) would survive anything, hopeful enough to believe that a second child would make things better, and tired enough to figure out that a third child wouldn't make that much difference—especially when she, like her oldest sister, hadn't been planned.

Lucca glanced at her phone. No texts now, except one from her office.

Call when you're feeling up to it, her office manager wrote.

Lucca certainly wasn't feeling up to it at the moment. If she talked to anyone, she'd bite their head off.

She sat back down.

Time to find out if her other daughters had gotten similar emails.

Time to find out exactly what the hell was going on here.

Both Sybil and Antoinette had received seven emails, and four of them were exactly the same as the ones Marla and Lucca had received. But the last three were different in each case, personal, and nasty.

And clearly written by Rob.

The things he had written about Sybil and the fact that she had embraced the traditional values of her husband were breathtakingly vicious. Compound that with the slurs Rob wrote about Sybil's conversion to Catholicism, and the devastation was complete.

Lucca's heart ached for her daughter, who didn't deserve any of that, no matter how holier-than-thou she had gotten when Rob confronted her years ago.

He hadn't liked any religion, not deep down.

Maybe Lucca should have had that religious funeral after all, not as a sop to Sybil, but as a fuck-you to Rob.

If only Lucca could do it all over again.

She hesitated before opening Antoinette's emails. Sybil and Marla were women full-grown, and they had their own families who loved them, and could help them through this.

But Antoinette had just broken up with her girlfriend, and had had to move out just the week before Rob died. Antoinette had been fragile then, losing a love she had thought would be permanent.

Lucca couldn't quite imagine how her daughter felt now.

Particularly since half the stuff Rob had said about her had been ugly too. The homophobic slurs that Lucca had received in her three emails appeared in Antoinette's emails, and they seemed worse, because they were actually combined with some kind of weird empathy.

I got a butch daughter, one of the comments read. *She's perfect except for her predilections. I'd thought she was the daughter of my dreams until I realized she had this flaw. I know without asking that the bitch-wife won't tolerate any kind of conversion therapy, so we gotta live with a near-perfect child who is going to destroy her entire future by either being too butch to ever get a high-end job or being too focused on politics to do good work at whatever job she does get.*

Lucca's lower lip trembled. A tear ran down her cheek, but she wasn't mourning anymore. She wasn't grief-angry anymore either. She was sad for her daughters.

Who would do this to them? They didn't need to know how their father had actually felt.

Lucca had known about some of his feelings, but not all of them. And she had never put them together into such a vile package.

She had no idea what she would say to her girls.

Aren't you happy to be rid of that asshole now? the emails asked.

If it had just been her, yes, she would have been.

But what he had done to their daughters . . .

Had his attitudes shown up in the way he treated them? Had they already known how he felt?

Probably. Kids weren't stupid.

Adults were.

The office was a buzz of activity.

Set in the back corner of a two-story strip mall from the 1960s, Kwindale Investigations took up two-thirds of the lower L. The entry was behind some badly placed stairs. She could have moved the entry to another part of the L, but she didn't. She liked to make the clients work a bit before they hired her.

Three cars were in the parking lot when she pulled in, and all three belonged to her employees. She walked through the front, laptop under her arm. She had spent an inordinate amount of time cleaning herself up—changing out of the jeans and denim shirt, and opting for khakis and a white summer sweater instead.

She wasn't going to look like death warmed over anymore, not for the asshole she had married.

She was aware that the bitterness she felt was, in part, from the emails. The sender had achieved his goal in that, at least. But not all of it. If she hadn't already been toying with leaving Rob, she would have been a lot more confused, maybe even spiraling deeper into some kind of depression.

Right at the moment, though, depression seemed very far away. What she wanted was to mutilate her husband's corpse and castrate the person who had sent the grief spam to her daughters.

Why she thought the perpetrator was male, she had no idea, but she was convinced of it. And her hunches were almost never wrong.

The office seemed blessedly normal. The windows to the street were shaded, but the reception area was brightly lit thanks to the three sunlamps that her receptionist kept around the desk.

Smaller offices opened off this bigger room, and directly behind the reception area was a conference room with a long Formica table. Usually the table was filled with employees working off company laptops, but occasionally Lucca cleared it for a gigantic meeting with clients.

The office smelled of fresh oranges, which meant it was around two in the afternoon—exactly when Cornelius, her very first hire and now her right hand, had his midafternoon snack.

Lucca waved at the receptionist who started to ask how she was. Lucca pretended she didn't hear, opened the door to Cornelius's office without asking, and stepped inside.

He was a big man with a close-cropped afro. He favored loose clothing—today's shirt was a white-and-tan weave that looked like expensive "local" sourced material, just the kind of politically correct clothing he preferred. His gym bag was half open against the far wall, some sweat-stained clothes hanging out of it.

He stood as she came in.

"Lucca," he said in his deep Georgia-accented voice. "I didn't expect you."

"Said I might be in today." She set the laptop on his desk.

"Yeah, but when you didn't return my call earlier, I figured you weren't coming." He frowned down at the laptop.

"I didn't even listen to the message," she said. "I need you on a case."

His eyes narrowed. She never said things like that—not anymore. Now, he brought in his own cases, just like she did.

"That's your computer," he said.

She nodded. It hadn't taken much for him to deduce that. She had stickers across the top of the laptop marking it as *Property of Lucca*. She had learned that the hard way, when she had accidentally opened a client's laptop thinking it was hers.

"The girls and I are being targeted by a spammer," she said. "I need you to find out who it is. I also need you to look at the photos in the early emails and see if they're just generic Internet images, blurred, or if they're actually what they purport to be."

Cornelius slid the laptop to his side of the desk, then rested his fingertips on top of it.

"About that, Lucca," he said.

She frowned. "About what, exactly? I need you on the job. I don't want anyone else to see this—"

"No," he said. "About the spammer."

His expression was serious. He paused just long enough for her breath to catch.

"You got some spam too," she said.

"No," he said, "actually, we didn't. But the school district called. They got quite a bit, and they wanted us—they wanted me, specifically—to see if it was legit."

Lucca's cheeks heated. "Spam about Rob?"

Cornelius nodded.

"In email?" she asked.

He nodded again.

"When did it start showing up?" she asked.

"Right after he died," Cornelius said. "That morning, in fact."

She frowned. She hadn't expected that. The school district had gotten email before she had, which changed the focus of everything.

"What kind of email?" she asked.

"To tell the truth about Rob," Cornelius said.

"Pictures of affairs, and child abuse, and screenshots from chat rooms?"

Cornelius actually leaned back just a little. His face didn't register surprise, but his body did.

"No," he said. "Financial records."

She blinked, unprepared for that. "What kind of financial records?"

"The hacked kind," Cornelius said. "Rob's financial records."

"And mine?" she asked.

Cornelius shook his head. "Just his, from one local bank and two online banks."

"Online banks?" she asked. "We don't bank at online banks."

"I know," Cornelius said quietly. Everyone who worked at Kwindale Investigations knew what she thought of online bank security for some of those new start-up banks.

Rob had known that too.

"Rob had accounts of his own?" she asked.

Cornelius nodded again. It was almost as if he wanted her to make some kind of leap on her own.

"With what money?" she asked. "His paycheck was direct deposited into our joint account."

"He started the accounts with the school district's money," Cornelius said softly.

It took her a moment to connect the dots. Five years ago, Rob had been temporary treasurer for the school district when the original treasurer had been fired for cause. Rob had repaired the books, and had gotten them ready for a forensic accountant. Or so he said.

"Rob was the one embezzling?" Lucca asked. "Not that woman who got fired?"

"Oh, they both were, just at different times." Cornelius's fingers tapped Lucca's laptop. "He just took her ideas and improved on them."

For the second time that day, Lucca's knees gave out. She sat in the closest chair, a wooden thing without a cushion at all.

"And no one noticed money was still disappearing?" she asked.

"A lot of money went missing the first time," Cornelius said. "Or rather, Rob's reports said a lot of money went missing. He postulated there was one account that still had school district funds draining into it, but no one could find the fund."

"Because it was his," she said.

Cornelius didn't even bother to nod this time. He just watched her as if he expected her to burst into tears.

She was long past tears. She was long past anger. She had moved into an emotional space she had never occupied before. It was a kind of calm that felt powerful, as if it had a lot of energy behind it.

"How long have you been working on this?" she asked.

"Long enough to know I needed to notify you before you met with an attorney to help you with Rob's estate," Cornelius said.

She hadn't yet found an attorney. There had been no hurry because, under state law, everything passed directly to her. She had wanted to use Rob's death to put her own finances in order, to make sure the girls were cared for in a way that *she* wanted, not the ways that Rob had suggested.

The bastard.

Lucca let out a breath. When she had gone to an attorney and done a search of everything, she would have found these accounts. If she had waited a long time, it might have been hard to prove she hadn't known about them.

Embezzling. She hadn't expected it. But then, she hadn't expected any of this.

"How much are we talking?" Lucca asked, surprised her voice sounded as calm as it did.

"Enough that it puts him into the WTF category," Cornelius said.

It worried her that he didn't give her an amount. Although she had an idea from what he said. The WTF category was one they used in the office for the truly stupid, usually spouses who cheated on their partners and were blatant about it.

But with financial crimes, the WTF category was even more what-the-fuck. Kwindale Investigations (particularly Lucca and Cornelius) saved WTF on financial crimes for the person who had stolen or embezzled a boatload of money, and should have shipped the funds to one of those banks that kept no records, and then the person should have run off to a country with no extradition.

Doing it this way was just a guarantee that the person would eventually be caught.

Lucca rubbed a hand over her face, thinking about it all, thinking about Rob, wondering why he had become that man.

She had no answers.

"You're sure he did this," she said.

Cornelius nodded. "Our lovely hacker sent hundreds of emails of your husband in the one bank, and we could focus down on some of the forms he was filling out. He had the right account numbers."

Hundreds of emails. Lucca and the girls only had a few.

Lucca didn't say anything. She was trying to get her brain to function faster, but it was still stuck in grief mode.

"We've had two weeks to investigate this, Lucca," Cornelius said gently. "We're sure it was him."

She nodded. She had only had hours to investigate the grief spam she had received, and she was certain that the most harmful posts had been his as well.

"Do you know who is doing this?" she asked.

Cornelius sat down at his desk, putting it between him and her. He used to put furniture between them when he was a new hire, afraid she would get angry at him.

She never got that kind of angry, although she often made him redo a lot of his work, back in those days.

He was so far past redoing anything, so far past needing supervision, that she trusted every word he had said.

Of course, she had trusted Rob too—or had she? She had handled the family finances for years. Rob had been on a budget that they both set. She had kept to her budget too, except for her business. And all of the money she had earned at her business had gone back into her accounts.

He couldn't touch it.

Her famous hunches—she hadn't been paying attention to them when it came to her husband.

But to be fair to herself, he had been grandfathered in. He had been around before her hunches were something she trusted.

What had she said once about a client? That the woman had been a frog in a pan of cold water. The frog hadn't noticed that the water was heating up, until it was too late.

She had been that goddamn frog. How had she become that goddamn frog?

"Lucca?" Cornelius said.

She blinked, realizing he had been talking and she hadn't heard him.

"I'm sorry," she said. "Tell me again."

He bit his lower lip. "We've been focused on the embezzlement."

He didn't say anything more. He had been saying more when he had spoken the first time.

But he didn't need to say more. The client was the school district, and the school district had just discovered a major crime. Who had alerted them to that crime mattered less than the crime itself.

Lucca reached for the laptop. "You've got your hands full," she said. "I'll take care of this."

Cornelius's fingertips still rested on the silver surface, near Lucca's name.

"No," he said. "We have the resources here. We'll take care of it."

"I'm not sitting at home anymore," she said.

He frowned at her, then sighed. "Take care of the girls," he said.

"I will," she said. "And one way I will is to shut this asshole down."

Cornelius nodded. "I agree. That's important," he said. "But you can't be involved in this."

"I'm not a victim," Lucca said. "I can do this."

"But, Lucca," Cornelius said gently. "You are."

That rage she had been sitting on engulfed her. It took all of her strength to block the next words out of her mouth.

I am not, she would have said to him. *I am clearheaded and ready to work. I* need *to work. I* need *to catch this guy. I need to feel . . .*

Useful.

The word caught her, defused the rage, and made her tear up.

Cornelius didn't see the fight she was having internally. He was saying, "We're going to have to go to court and give testimony on this case, since we found the embezzlement thanks to this guy. We can't have you in the middle of all that, Lucca. You're going to have to deal with the legal ramifications. These crimes have had an impact on you, whether you want to acknowledge that or not."

The crimes have had an impact on you. The words she had designed to convince victims who hated the word to accept that someone had hurt them.

"What can I do?" she asked.

"Let us track him down," Cornelius said. "And then we'll figure that out."

After Lucca left Cornelius, she went to her private office. It was neater than her home office. The desk was empty except for her computer, and the files she'd been working on—the paper files—were nowhere to be seen.

She had abandoned a dozen investigations in progress when Rob died, and she hadn't given them a second thought until now. Cornelius had clearly stepped in and taken over. She opened the computer, saw that he had assigned the cases that were nearly finished to the newest investigators, and gave the rest to the more experienced investigators.

Normally, he probably would have kept one or two for himself, but he hadn't, which told her how all-encompassing this investigation for the school district had been.

She sat down, and rubbed a hand over her face. She was tired. Not physically tired. Emotionally tired. She'd probably experienced every negative emotion possible so far today, and she would probably experience a few more before the day was out.

Starting with the emotions that were coming in the next few minutes.

She texted her daughters jointly and asked if she could set up a video conference. She would rather be discussing all this with them in person, but everyone lived in different cities.

She had already toyed with the idea of telling the girls what she had learned later, when the investigations were done, but that would leave them with the uncertainty and the pain of those posts Rob had completed.

Better to rip off the Band-Aid quickly, as she had learned in her first few years of mothering. Sparing a child pain by not telling her something, or by telling it slowly, usually compounded the pain.

And this pain—thank you, Rob, you asshole—was impossible to ignore.

The girls were all available now for a video conference, and she braced herself. The last thing she wanted to do was tell her daughters that everything was true, and that there were even worse accusations.

But she was going to.

The call went through, and one by one, her daughters appeared on her computer screen. Marla had her curly hair pulled back, her face gray, and the shadows under her eyes deep. She looked like she hadn't slept in days.

Sybil wore a black blazer that accented her broad shoulders. A gold cross glinted on the Peter Pan collar of her black blouse. The color suited her, and gave her cheeks color, but her eyes resembled Marla's—sunken and haunted.

Antoinette's short black hair hadn't even been combed that day, or if her hair had been, she had run her fingers through it so many times it stuck out haphazardly around her face. Surprisingly, though, her eyes were dry. In them, Lucca saw a reflection of her own. Antoinette's voice hadn't shaken with unshed tears this morning; it had shaken with complete fury.

Lucca had forgotten that side of her youngest: when Antoinette got hurt, she rose up in righteous wrath, ready to do battle. She had even done so that day long ago when she'd broken her leg. Lucca had had to stop Antoinette from hitting the tree with her tiny little fists.

"It's true," Antoinette said tightly before anyone else could even say hello. "All of it. It's true."

"I don't know about all of it," Lucca said. She fell into a tone that she hadn't used in years—Reasonable Mom Voice. It said *This is awful, but I'm going to be calm, so you be calm too.* "But the screenshots, from what I can tell, they were written by your dad."

The girls all started talking at once. Angry, vengeful, tear-filled, horrified. And then Sybil burst into shaking gulping sobs, and all three of the others tried to comfort her from far away.

It was at that point that Lucca realized this wasn't a one phone call kinda thing. She was going to have to work with her girls on this horrid mess Rob had left them with every single day, maybe more than once.

Cornelius had been right: she was too close emotionally to do any of the fine computer work. Her computer work was going to have to be with her daughters, her friends, her colleagues—everyone who had known Rob, or thought they had.

Aren't you happy to be rid of that asshole now? The final email—all of the final emails—had read. *You really should thank me.*

Thank me.

As she talked to her daughters, as she listened to their pain, those last two words rolled around in her mind.

She wasn't going to thank whoever did this when she found out who it was. She really was going to eviscerate that person. Because her daughters hadn't needed to know any of this about their father. They could have blithely continued with their lives, feeling ambivalent about him, as Antoinette was saying right now ("I kinda knew he didn't like my choices, but I didn't realize . . .").

The jerk who had done this had taken any delusions her daughters had had away from them. And he wanted *credit*.

Which meant he wanted to be caught.

Something niggled in her mind at that.

"Mom?" Marla said. "You okay? Mom?"

Lucca blinked, focused, saw all her daughters looking at their cameras, trying to see through their screens into hers. She wondered what she looked like. Probably as discombobulated as they did.

"No," she said. "I'm not okay. But I'm better than I was yesterday. I have a mission now. I'm going to figure this out for all of us."

When she was done with this call, though, she'd call each of her daughters individually, see if they needed her to come visit. Because she had broad shoulders, just like Sybil. Besides, part of her had divorced Rob emotionally years ago.

The girls were dealing with the loss of their father in two ways: they were dealing with his physical loss, and the loss of the man they had thought they knew.

Aren't you happy to be rid of that asshole now? You really should thank me.

Those words . . .

Lucca's brain caught the thought that had been niggling, held it, and let her examine it.

This guy, he was bragging. Not about the revelation.

About getting rid of Rob.

"Mom?" Sybil asked, her question sharp. "What are you thinking?"

Lucca made herself smile, knowing the smile was bitter and ironic, and not entirely caring.

"Oh, honey," she said in that Mom voice. "You really don't want to know."

When the most painful call of her life was finally over, Lucca stood. She was shaking. She had been emotionally drained before the call, and the conversation hadn't helped that—or the guilt. She should have seen what her husband had become.

Or maybe she should have seen what he was.

She could make all the excuses she wanted, but she was a woman who had prided herself on her ability to read people, and the one person in her life that she was (in theory) closest to was the one she had misread completely.

Which made her question whether or not she had misread others along the way.

She made herself take a deep breath. Now was not the time to doubt herself. She needed to be strong, for the girls—and for herself. She needed to figure out what happened.

She shut down the computer, then paced the small space between the desk and the door.

The police had assumed that Rob had been in a single-car crash. He was a respected high school principal, slightly tubby, middle-aged, a perfect candidate for a heart attack while driving, or for a stroke. He might have fallen asleep at the wheel, the police officer who had called her had said, or maybe he had simply missed the corner in the dark.

Nothing unusual in their line of work, or so the police thought.

Because they hadn't known about the double life, about the embezzlement. About the person who had been watching and photographing Rob. Or who had been stealing photographs from security cameras.

The police hadn't known any of that, so they had no reason to investigate the matter further.

You really should thank me.

She owned the car now, or what was left of it. The impound had left a message on her phone a few days ago, asking if she wanted to claim the car. She only had a week or so, they said, to remove any belongings from the trunk or the back seat of the car. If the impound yard had left her that message, that meant there had been items left in the car.

Items that might give her a clue to Rob.

Or to the hacker, the stalker, or whoever he was.

She grabbed her purse, and let herself out of her office, waggling her fingers at Cornelius as she passed his office on the way to the main door.

He frowned at her, mouthed *Are you okay?* She nodded her answer, then let herself outside, stopping for a moment in the bright sunshine.

It seemed incongruous, that sunshine—the opposite of the way she felt. It was a mocking sunshine, rather like the sunshine on 9/11 in New York. The kind of day that should have been perfect, if not for the plume of smoke trailing into the blue, blue sky.

Then Lucca shook her head. Rob had been dead sixteen days. The 9/11 analogy belonged to Day One, not Day Sixteen. By Day Sixteen, she should have been firmly inside the new reality of life without Rob.

Only Day Sixteen had turned into a brand-new Day One, the day in which she discovered that she had spent decades living a lie.

You really should thank me.

She got into her van, backed out of the small parking area, and drove as carefully as she could to the police impound yard at the north end of Watersville.

She had been to the impound yard dozens, if not hundreds, of times before, always on a case, always looking for whatever it was that someone had left behind.

Like she had almost left things behind. She would have, if she hadn't discovered Rob's perfidy. If the grief spam hadn't tilted her in the right direction.

Although it really wasn't fair to call what she had received grief spam. That had been the casket offers, the avoid-estate-tax directives, and the invest-your-inheritance scams. What she had gotten—what everyone who had been close to Rob had received—had been wake-up emails of a kind that was, in many ways, much worse than the grief spam. Grief spam was impersonal, at least.

This stuff . . .

She shook it off, trying not to think about her daughters' faces as she had seen them that afternoon. Lucca would look over Rob's car, get her belongings, and if she found nothing, go home.

The impound yard was in the bottom of a hollow about one hundred yards from the entrance to the dump. During the wettest springs, the impound yard flooded thanks to the intersection of crisscrossing rivers that had given Watersville its name.

Behind the impound yard's chain-link fence, twenty or so cars had been stored as closely together as possible. They were the cars that had been towed here because they were parked illegally or because they had been booted and then abandoned. About half of those cars would get claimed every day, and the rest would eventually get resold at the police department auction.

Behind them, a squat brown building stood. It had enough room for two city employees, one tougher than the other because people sometimes got violent over their cars.

The damaged and destroyed cars, the cars that might be evidence in an actual crime, and the cars that had been stolen (and unclaimed) covered the vast brown dirt between the impound yard and the city dump. She knew from personal experience that some of those cars had sat on the dirt for years, waiting for someone to make a decision about their disposal.

She couldn't see Rob's pride and joy, the stupid red Camaro he had bought without telling her, so soon after Antoinette left for college. They had fought over that stupid car, because Lucca had believed they couldn't afford it. He said he would handle the payment himself, using the money he had out of the family budget for his own discretionary spending.

Since he had done that, she hadn't thought about the damn car again. But now that she knew about Rob's extra accounts, she figured that was what he had been using to pay for the stupid Camaro.

Lucca pulled open the door to the brown building, saw one of the employees—Stu—sitting behind the ancient desk. He stood when he saw her. He was wearing a white T-shirt with a band logo on it, the ridiculous green shirt the city made him wear draped over a chair.

"Hey, Lucca," he said gently. "Sorry about Rob."

She nodded, unwilling to acknowledge that sentence given the mood she was in.

"I hope you're here on a case," Stu said in that same tone.

"You guys called, said there were personal items in the Camaro." She sounded normal—at least, she thought she sounded normal.

"Yeah," Stu said. "I can get them for you. You don't need to see that car."

"Actually," she said, "I do need to see the car."

"Honey," Stu said, "you really don't."

He had never called her "honey" before. The "honey" this time wasn't condescending, just affectionate. His lower lip was turned down a bit, and a frown creased his forehead.

Lucca wasn't going to tell him about the emails or the embezzlement or her suspicions. But she did need to ask him a few questions.

"You ever lose somebody close to you, Stu?" she asked.

"My mom." His frown grew deeper. "Two years ago."

"Then you know how it is," Lucca said. "Sometimes you get an idea in your head and you have to do what you can to get it out of your head."

He took a deep breath, clearly not sure what she was referring to. But she had united them in grief, and that had somehow made him willing to listen.

"The car look unusual to you?" she asked.

His lips got even thinner, as if he were holding back his words. After a pause that was seconds too long, he said, "It was totaled, Lucca, and the interior . . ."

"I know," she said, although she didn't, exactly. But she had dug through cars whose owners had died inside, sometimes in accidents, and in two instances by gunshot, and she knew that interiors were often filled with blood and brains.

"It's been in the sun," he said.

"I figured," she said.

"You don't need to—"

"Please, Stu," she said. "Answer me. Does the car look unusual to you?"

He closed his eyes as if willing her to go away. But she wasn't going to.

"The dents are wrong," he said, as if she had tortured the phrase out of him. "The back dents. They're all wrong."

He led her to the car—he insisted, and she wasn't going to argue.

The Camaro had been dumped in front of a group of cars that were almost unrecognizable as vehicles. They were twisted hunks of black and silver metal, accented by flat tires, popped hoods, and dented car doors. At least the Camaro looked like a car. A ruined car, but a car all the same.

The front end of the Camaro formed an uneven U. The bottom of the U still held the shape of that concrete barrier. She recognized it, had driven by it a million times before Rob's accident, and had always thought of the barrier as a hazard. She hadn't driven by the barrier since, because she knew the Camaro's silver paint would still be scraped along the edges.

She really hadn't expected to see that the Camaro had hugged the barrier. They probably had to use some special equipment to peel it away.

"Did they use the Jaws of Life?" she asked Stu.

He was staring at the vehicle as if it had harmed him personally. "No," he said. "The car wasn't hard to remove. The tires remained intact, so they could just pull it backward. There've been so many accidents, the tow-truck drivers know how to get vehicles away from that barrier now."

Then he glanced at her to see if that sentence had offended her. It hadn't. Truth rarely offended. It was the lies that hurt.

That thought made her think of her daughters' faces, and tears threatened.

Stu put a hand on her arm. "I told you, this isn't a good idea."

Lucca willed the tears back. "Show me the dents."

As if there weren't enough dents. As if the car wasn't completely destroyed.

He gestured, but her eyes didn't follow quickly enough. They were still riveted to the front of the Camaro, to the windshield, which had bent with the frame, but hadn't shattered. It had spider-webbed instead, and Rob's blood decorated the cracks—black now with two weeks' worth of sunshine and decay.

That thought calmed her. He was gone. He was really and truly gone. Yes, he was still hurting them, but his actions were in the past. They were finite. Once she found out everything he did, she would be able to deal with it.

And, more importantly, she would be able to figure out how to help her daughters deal with it.

Stu looked at Lucca, clearly giving her a moment. "You still want to see it?"

"Sorry," she said.

He gestured again, and this time she watched. She still didn't see what he was gesturing at.

"Just take me over there," she said, and hoped she didn't sound exasperated.

He walked cautiously across the dirt, then crouched beside the Camaro.

"Here," he said, his hand above several deep scrapes on the rear driver's side. "And here." He moved a little closer to the rear bumper.

Rob had bought a black bumper cover for both bumpers, so they "added to the classiness of the vehicle" or so he said. She thought they made little difference.

The bumper cover was torn in three places now because the bumper itself was dented, with small V-shaped dents, spaced oddly along its length.

Rob had been protective of this car. He had come home one afternoon bitching that someone had opened a door and made a dime-sized groove near the gas tank.

He would never have allowed something like these dents.

"You think this happened at the same time?" she asked.

Stu shrugged. "I don't know about the timing of these, or the one on the driver's side," he said. "But look at this."

He moved to the passenger side of the car, and pointed to the rear bumper there.

It took her a moment to realize that the cover remained, hanging by its edges, but the bumper itself was so crumpled that it almost looked flat. It was also silver and blue, which struck her as odd.

She looked over at Stu. He was frowning.

"Think about this." He pointed at the damage in the back. "Here." Then he pointed at the gigantic U in the front of the vehicle. "And there."

She stepped back so she could see both together.

"The bumper stuff wasn't tow-truck damage?" she asked.

"They didn't attach to the bumper," he said. "They put the car on a flatbed."

"Oh." She swallowed. If she had hit the Camaro in that exact spot with a lot of force on the road not too far from the concrete barrier, she could have sent the Camaro into the barrier, in just that way. Rob wouldn't have had time to correct.

She had thought of that scenario often on that bit of road, especially when someone had been tailgating her. She had known just how easy it would have been to get accidentally shoved into that barrier, which was why so many people had been injured there.

"You're saying this was deliberate?" she asked.

"If I were the investigating officer, I'd take a look," Stu said. "The same paint is on both sides and the back end of the car. Had your husband been in an accident with the vehicle before this?"

"No," she said. She had seen the car the morning before the accident. The Camaro's red paint had glistened in the early morning sunlight as Rob had driven off to school—or at least, that was where she had thought he was going. Now, she wasn't sure. Then, she had thought, like she had every morning, that Rob was stupid to take his expensive midlife crisis and park it in a spot marked Principal, putting a gigantic target on his toy.

"So this was all new," Stu said.

"Yeah," she said.

"Then someone kept hitting him," Stu said.

"You think they forced him into the barrier?" she asked.

"Dunno that. It would take a crash scene investigator to know for sure and it might be too late to do a great examination. But if your husband was speeding to get away from someone, then looked over his shoulder, and didn't realize quite where he was, he could have driven into that barrier. And honestly, given the way the Camaro's built, he would have had to have been going really fast—way over the speed limit—to do that kind of damage to the vehicle."

She walked around the Camaro. She couldn't quite get to the front, which was fine. The windows on both the passenger and driver's side had cracked from the impact, but not as badly. The rear window was just fine.

But the sides were scraped, and the back was badly damaged. Stu was right; someone had definitely hit this car more than once. And the car wasn't rear-ended the way a car would have been had someone hit it after the accident with the barrier. Then the car would have accordioned. It hadn't.

"Did you tell the police?" Lucca had a hunch she knew the answer, but she asked anyway.

"They had already closed the investigation when they brought the car here," Stu said.

Which was why he could call her and tell her to pick up Rob's things.

"But you could have called them when you saw the damage," she said.

He opened his hands, as if to say *What can I do?* "I had no idea if the damage predated the final accident. I see a lot of stuff, Lucca."

She knew that. Which was why she had trusted him in numerous investigations. He saw things, but he was cautious.

She opened her purse, and rummaged around until she found one of her evidence bags. She pulled it out, along with a small scraper she had bought just for this kind of thing.

Then she walked over to one of the dents, crouched, and scraped some of the blue paint into the bag.

"Lucca," Stu said in a chiding tone. "Tampering with evidence."

"Evidence of what?" she asked. "At this moment, there's no case. And besides, the car's been sitting in the lot for more than two weeks. Anyone could have done this."

"You shouldn't be investigating," Stu said. "He was your husband."

The second person that day to warn her off an investigation. She would have paid attention too, if she had planned to bring charges. But she was just trying to figure out what had happened.

"Call the police when I leave," she said. "Please tell them I had said the car was undamaged the moment of the accident and—"

"And I got a twinge of conscience and felt they should reopen the investigation." He nodded. They had done this dance a few times before, but never on something so personal. "Sure thing, Lucca. As long as you're sure you want this."

Her gaze met his. His blue eyes were clear, but that frown remained.

Did he know something about Rob that she didn't? Oh, hell. Everyone probably knew something about Rob that she didn't.

"Yes," she said. "I want this. I want this very much."

And within the hour, she was back in the inner sanctum. Back when she started as a private detective, she did a lot of work for insurance companies. Often that involved identifying cars from hit-and-run accidents. She had learned a lot of short cuts to identifying paint chips, shortcuts that didn't involve a mass spectrometer or a chromograph.

She had learned long ago that the big forensic science stuff wasn't always necessary. Sometimes she just needed common sense—and the ability to hack into the police department records.

First thing she did was look at stolen car reports for that week in April, isolating blue cars only. She found six cars stolen, and only two had a shade of blue even close to the one she was looking at.

One of those cars had been found. It had been totaled. The police figured someone had taken it on a joyride.

She figured someone had used it to repeatedly slam into Rob's car.

Then she leaned back and stared at the car itself. It was a 2017 sports car with enough horsepower to go after a Camaro, and enough weight to do some damage.

The police report said the interior of the sports car had been wiped clean, which was unusual in a joyride. Usually the joyrider figured that the car was so damaged no one would dust for prints. And usually, the joyrider would be right.

Then she went back to the police report. The car was reported stolen at seven the morning Rob was killed. Four hours after he died.

Police discovered the car two days later at the bottom of an empty culvert about fifteen blocks from where the sports car had supposedly been stolen.

The car's owner lived nowhere near either place. He lived on the south side of Watersville, in one of the many apartment complexes that littered the freeway.

Yet he had called, saying he had come out in the morning to find the car missing. How could he have come out in the morning from his apartment to find the car missing from a completely different address?

The details didn't entirely add up.

She looked at the owner's name. The car was registered in the name of Thomas G. Hedges. Hedges. That name rang a bell.

Thomas Hedges. Tom Hedges. Tommy Hedges.

Yes, indeed. Tommy Hedges. He had gone to Anderson High School. His family had moved to Watersville the year before—something about a high-end divorce. His mother had moved the children to a small town to give them "real life." But Tommy had acted out, and Rob had finally expelled him.

Rob had been obsessed with the entire thing, because the mother had called the school board. It had all escalated and someone—Lucca couldn't remember who—finally took the mother aside and told her to send the boy to some rich kid's boarding school.

Lucca had gone to one of the school board meetings during all that, and she remembered the mother—too thin and dressed to the nines, an aging trophy wife who had been replaced by another trophy—sobbing, begging the school board to let her boy back in, saying he needed to learn how everyone else lived more than he needed to have a high-end education, despite his computer skills.

That had caught Lucca's attention, because she'd sat through a number of those meetings before, usually as Rob's support, sometimes for clients, and no one had said the quality of the education didn't matter. They had always been urging the Watersville School District to up its game, not implying that its sheer ordinariness was a plus.

But did Lucca remember this right? Had the mother actually said *Despite his computer skills*? Or had Lucca heard that elsewhere?

She moved to a different laptop to search for everything she could find on Tommy Hedges. She felt she had to move to a clean laptop just in case he did have mad computer skills.

Just in case he was the person she was looking for.

He had an online presence—everyone did, so that was no surprise. His Facebook page had been active years ago, but he rarely posted now. He did post images of his apartment a few months ago—a one-bedroom cookie cutter, remodeled a little, but its 1970s roots still showed.

Such a comedown, he wrote. *See what happens when you have to pay for shit yourself?*

His other social media accounts were just as sketchy until she stumbled on his second Twitter handle. It was Former-RichBoy1994, and the invective in it was startling. He wasn't nasty like Rob had been. Tommy Hedges didn't write nasty things about people of color or women or engage in any of those online hatred memes.

Instead, he called out hypocrisy, and blamed the system for robbing him of his life. He hadn't Tweeted much recently, but the day after Rob died, he Tweeted: *No one gets it. They think he's a goddamn saint.*

And then a day later: *I think I did this all wrong. I think if I don't get recognition, it will destroy me.*

She wondered if it was a confession, or if it had nothing to do with Rob at all, if she was making it all up.

She took her hands off the keys and shut the laptop. Stu's and Cornelius's caution had been right: she wanted someone to be guilty—not of killing Rob, but of hurting her daughters.

Lucca wanted to go after whoever it was so badly she had felt something new within herself: she had felt the willingness to blame someone else, based on almost no evidence at all.

She stood up, took the laptop, and placed it in the closet. Then she walked out of the inner sanctum into the messy outer sanctum.

Once there, she pulled her cell phone out of her pocket and called Cornelius.

"I think I have something for you to look into," she said. "And I think you'd better do it now."

After that, things moved both faster and slower than she expected.

Faster: the speed of the investigation into the car. Stu's phone call got the police involved, and since Rob had been well liked, the police decided to take another look.

They found all the discrepancies she found. The physical evidence was nearly overwhelming—all of it, scrapes and paint chips and a direct line from Tommy Hedges to Rob.

Tommy Hedges blamed Rob for everything bad that had happened to him after getting expelled from school. The police found other fake identities, other postings, and could link the young man to Rob's murder with startling ease. There was even traffic camera footage that showed the blue car trailing the Camaro. No footage of the actual hits with the car—clearly Hedges had been too smart for that—but there was enough to make a case against him.

Slower than expected: the embezzlement case against Rob. It looked like the school district would just take the money back, without getting too deep into the mess. Lucca wouldn't face charges, because it was pretty clear she knew nothing about any of it.

And while she found that embarrassing, it was also a relief.

Everything else seemed out of time. Her reactions were slower or swifter, depending. Her conversations with her daughters were awkward and sad.

She tried to book a trip to see Antoinette, but Antoinette claimed she was doing all right—that she had help—and recommended that she see Sybil.

Sybil said her church was helping, and Lucca's presence would just remind her of everything she didn't want to think about.

Marla said she had a therapist, and they were working on it one day at a time. But if Lucca felt like she needed comfort, then she was welcome to come visit.

Lucca wasn't sure she did need comfort. She wasn't sure what she needed.

She still cried too much, but she was no longer certain what she was crying about.

She had to break out of this funk. She was beginning to think the tears were coming from unexpressed anger—anger at Rob for leaving her with such a mess, for lying, for being a true bastard. And anger at Tommy Hedges for shattering her family with his horrid grief spam.

She couldn't do anything about her anger at Rob, but she could do something about her anger at Tommy.

It would just take a little time to arrange.

He was in county jail, because he didn't have enough money for bail and his mother refused to bail him out. But she had provided an expensive lawyer, and they had a strategy, which meant Tommy was not talking to the police.

But Lucca thought he might talk to her.

She didn't ask permission from anyone. She knew it would be denied. The police would worry that she was going to screw up the case; the lawyer probably thought she would be acting on the police's behalf.

She was prepared for this meeting, emotionally and physically. She knew what she could and couldn't get away with. She knew how to handle everything—even if Hedges tried to hurt her.

She had gone in and out of that jail more times than she could count, and the guards there gave her a lot of leeway. She had put away some of the worst criminals in Watersville. She had also gotten a few people out.

And she had always treated everyone who worked in the jail with respect, because she knew they had one of the harder jobs in the county.

The building was a squat 1970s cinderblock. She entered the way she always did, asked to see Hedges, and was told to wait. No one questioned her being there, no one asked her why she needed to see him. Just noted he hadn't gotten a lot of visitors.

Then she was cleared. She had to meet him in the main visitor's area. A family congregated near one of the bolted down tables on the far side of the room, the three children old enough to know where they were. They were looking around nervously, their parents talking quietly, the woman with her hand on the arm of the youngest as if afraid to let go.

Lucca took a table as far from them as she could get. She nodded at the two guards positioned nearest the doors, then waited.

It didn't take long for them to bring Hedges to her. He looked sallow in the orange short-sleeve jumpsuit, his hair cropped short, his skin blotchy. His gaze focused on her, and his eyes narrowed.

"You think I don't know who you are," he said as he sat down. "You're his wife. Lucca Kwindale."

No guard was close enough to overhear the conversation.

"You want to know why I killed him," Hedges said. "That's what everyone wants to know. Not *if* I killed him. *Why* I killed him."

His arms were flabby and, surprisingly for someone his age, without tattoos. She hadn't said a word so far, just watched him, and he seemed content with that.

"I'm not going to tell you anything about that night," he said. "My lawyer said I shouldn't talk to anyone."

He wanted her to ask why he was talking to her. He wanted her to feel special—look! I'm talking with you when I'm not supposed to—but she wasn't going to play that game.

"I don't care why you killed him," she said, her voice soft and low. "Believe me, I get it."

He raised his thin eyebrows. "You get it. You didn't get anything before. You're one of the dumbest bitches who ever walked. Or you're complicit in everything he did."

She thought she had been prepared for those sentiments, but she hadn't been. They stabbed, hard, because both statements were true.

But she had sat across from prisoners before—she had sat across from guilty people before—and she knew how to keep up the appearance of calm even when she wasn't.

"All I want to know," she said, "is why you sent the emails."

A tiny smile played at the corners of his mouth before he could get control of his face. "Some lawyer send you?"

She shook her head.

"Some prosecutor, to see if I'll talk?"

"If that were the case," she said, "we'd be in a different room, with more privacy, so that they could record everything."

"You probably have one of those tiny cameras on you," he said, arms crossed.

"I can't," she said. "I'm not authorized."

He made a face. She wasn't sure he believed her. He clearly weighed his choices for a moment: did he talk to her, risking a camera recording everything? Or did he walk away, and never find out why she was here?

She let him work it out. He had been obsessed with Rob. Rob was gone and she was all that was left. She was gambling that Hedges would choose to stay for that reason.

"So," Hedges said after a moment, and her heart did a little victory dance. "*You* want to know something."

"Why did you send those emails?" she asked.

"Bothered you, did they?" he asked.

"Yes," she said. "It makes no sense to me. You could have gotten away with everything if you hadn't sent the emails."

His crossed arms tightened, pulling on the jumpsuit. "Criminals are dumb," he said sullenly.

She quietly admired how he said that. He hadn't admitted any guilt at all.

"But you're not," she said. "What was the point? Rob was dead."

Hedges's eyes glittered. She recognized the rage in them; she'd seen it in her own eyes of late.

"He ruined my life," Hedges said so softly she could barely hear him over the echoey conversation across the room.

"I know," she said. "He expelled you from school and that started a spiral."

Hedges slammed his hands on the tabletop, making her jump. "It did *not!*" he shouted.

One of the guards came toward her, but she waved him off. The little family watched, the woman holding the youngest tightly against her as if Lucca had shouted at the little girl.

"That's what ruined you, right?" Lucca asked.

"*God!*" Hedges said. "Don't you *fucking* pay attention? Do I have to send more goddamn emails?"

His anger was a physical force. She could feel each word as if it were a punch.

"He didn't embezzle from you," she said.

"No," Hedges said. "He just fucked me."

"He fucked over everyone," she said.

"No," Hedges said again. "He *fucked* me."

His words rang in the concrete room. One of the children was crying. Now Lucca wished they had taken the conversation elsewhere.

And, she realized at that moment, she had deflected what Hedges was saying, tried not to hear it, would have set it somewhere else if she could.

"That second email," she said. "The images were generic."

"Because your goddamn husband was smart," Hedges said. "No contact in person, no pictures, no kiddie porn on his computer. Believe me, I looked."

Her heart started pounding.

"I had some pictures of my own, though," Hedges said. "Small camera, set up just right. But I kept looking at it. I. Kept. Looking at it. And he saw that, he found it, and *that's* when he expelled me. My mom thought I was acting out."

"You accused him?" Lucca said.

"Yeah," Hedges said. "No one listened. He was so fucking respected in this town."

Lucca's breath caught. That was why the police investigation into the accident moved so fast. They already had a police report from years ago linking Rob and Hedges, but it had been buried, possibly because Hedges was a juvenile, probably because Rob was the principal and above reproach.

Lucca swallowed, astounded at her own unwillingness to see her husband for who he was.

"No one told me," she said quietly.

And no one had even tried. She would have remembered.

"I know," Hedges said. "I found out later. The Old Boy Network buried the thing good and fast. They even convinced my mom I was a problem."

"She defended you," Lucca said, remembering the tearful school board meeting. "She tried to keep you here."

"Yeah, she thought that would be good for me. She thought I was making shit up because I was mad. *She* was the one who did that. She accused my dad of all kinds of crap he had never done." Hedges paused, took a deep breath, then narrowed his eyes. "Got your answers now?"

"No," Lucca said. She folded her arms and rested them on the tabletop. "I understand sending emails to the school board. I understand sending them to me. But to my daughters?"

That last word wobbled. She hadn't been able to hide her anger there.

"They're adults," he said.

"They loved him," Lucca said.

"Really?" he asked. "That asshole? Surely they knew what a jerk he was."

Maybe they had. And maybe they had been pretending, like Lucca had, that Rob was better than he was.

Sometimes losing the delusion was harder than losing the person.

"See?" Hedges said. "You should thank me."

"For what, exactly?" she asked.

His smile grew. "For all of it. For waking you up. For freeing you of him. For making sure he'll never hurt anyone again."

Hedges had just admitted to the murder. Her heart started pounding, hard, but she worked on keeping her expression neutral.

"Did he know it was you in the car?" she asked.

"He knew it was me for months," Hedges said. "Those emails didn't just come together after the fucker died, you know. He'd been getting them forever."

Rob had been getting more and more nervous. She hadn't really paid a lot of attention.

"What changed?" she asked.

Hedges eyes narrowed. "What do you mean?"

"Emails for months," she said. "And then, one night, you get in your car . . ."

Hedges laughed. "You don't know, do you? You really don't know."

Her cheeks warmed.

He touched one of his fingers to his own cheek, acknowledging her blush. "You don't know," he said with satisfaction. "He had just bought a condo in Perast."

"Where?" she asked before she could think the question through.

"Montenegro." Hedges's smile was wide. He was enjoying her ignorance. "No extradition."

She frowned. "But I didn't find any plane tickets."

"Because he was looking at charters," Hedges said. "That's how I caught him. Looking at charters. He had such a vast digital footprint. He had no idea I was onto that."

"You found it that night?" she asked, letting her own confusion into her voice. Her sorrow seemed to make him talkative.

"Just before I saw him at the restaurant. With one of the boys from the basketball team. The look on that kid's face—I sent the waiter over, told the kid there was an emergency at home, and then I watched while your husband left. He didn't see me until the first time I hit his car. I turned on the dome light, so he could see my face. And he looked scared."

Funny, she didn't care that Rob had been scared. She didn't care that he had died that night. She didn't care about him at all.

But their daughters—what this man had done—she wasn't going to let them come to a trial. And there would be a trial. Because Lucca had caught him.

He had asked about a camera, and she had lied. She hadn't told him she'd been wearing a small audio recorder disguised as one of the buttons on her collar.

She didn't tell him that. She didn't have to.

Prisoners in the county jail were not accorded the right to privacy unless they were meeting with their attorney, which he most decidedly was not.

She had thought she would feel more elated if she got him to confess.

Instead, she just felt dirty and sad.

"He hurt you," she said.

"Oh, yeah, that son of a bitch," Hedges said.

"But you're the one who has chosen to let that destroy you," she said.

His hands curled into fists. "I thought you might say something like that. I thought about that long and hard. Then I figured I could show you holier-than-thou assholes what it's like to have everything taken from you. I'd show you just how easy it is to get over events that totally destroy everything you've ever known."

She studied him for a minute. Then nodded. He was really smart. He could have chosen another way, no matter how difficult.

He hadn't.

And she saw no point in telling him that.

She stood, signaled the guard to let her out, and watched as the door swung back. She could leave. Hedges couldn't.

By his choice.

She had her answers. She also had a lot of soul searching to do. And daughters to help, in her own way.

She had some changes to make. She wasn't as good a detective as she had thought she was. She wasn't even as good a person as she had thought she was.

She needed to change all that. And the first step was selling the business to Cornelius. Then she needed to do some work, some investigation—not of bad guys—but of the way people survived trauma like her daughters were going through. Like Hedges had gone through.

"You're just going to bury this, aren't you?" Hedges shouted after her. "Do you know how many lives he ruined?"

She stopped before stepping all the way out. She turned her head so she could just see him over her shoulder, still sitting at that table.

"Not yet," she said. "But I mean to find out."

And she would.

Rob wouldn't have been the kind of man who could handle reparations. But she could.

And she would do it.

She owed the community that much.

She owed her daughters even more.

Maybe she *should* thank Hedges. Because without the grief spam, she would never have known. And her daughters would have had to work out their daddy issues on their own.

Then Hedges smiled at her—a mean and feral smile. No. She wasn't going to thank him.

She wasn't in the mood to thank anyone.

She'd been angry for nearly three weeks now. She'd probably be angry for many, many more.

She would use that anger. Because now she had a focus.

All she needed now was a schedule.

Because schedules had value, Rob. Schedules defeated bad guys.

Even when they were already dead.

Ironically, I wrote "Grief Spam" before the horror that started in 2020 and continues as I write this. I lost a lot of friends during that period (not as many as I would in the next two years) and, as grieving people often do, I got angry. Around that time, I found out that scam artists prey on the grieving. The scam artists read online obituaries and then attempt to pull money out of the survivors. I planned to write an angry, revealing story about grief spam. Instead, I wrote this.

Anna Scotti *writes in several genres; her work includes both stand-alone stories and an ongoing series for* Ellery Queen Mystery Magazine, *as well as a young adult novel,* Big and Bad, *that was awarded the 2021 Paterson Prize for Books for Young People. She also contributes poems to* The New Yorker, *and is the author of* Bewildered by All This Broken Sky *(2021), a collection that has received critical acclaim. Scotti leads grammar and creativity workshops for corporate clients in Los Angeles, and teaches seventh grade English, which takes far more courage than writing about murder in a shadowed room just past midnight by the light of a waning moon.*

A HEAVEN OR A HELL

Anna Scotti

It was all pretty straightforward until the dead kid climbed back up the cliff.

He wasn't actually dead, of course, but he'd been missing for four days, was presumed dead, and on top of all that, he was pretty banged up. A concussion, a broken arm, and two broken fingers on his good hand. At least three broken ribs, a collapsed lung, a fractured kneecap on one leg and a broken ankle on the other. Bruises and abrasions everywhere, even beneath his clothes, long shallow patches of raw, weeping skin where he'd banged against the rocks going down, or scraped against them climbing up again. I learned all this later, of course, when he'd been transferred back home to Cedars-Sinai Medical Center, in the affluent Beverly Grove neighborhood just east of Beverly Hills.

When I'd seen him on the news, he'd been just a skinny bundled body on a foldable stretcher being lifted up the last twenty feet of sheer cliff by a line suspended from a helicopter. He'd gotten pretty far on his own, but he wouldn't have made it up that last bit; a promontory of rock jutted out over the little ledge he'd tucked himself into. If a couple of hikers hadn't followed their nosy dog off the main trail, he'd have died there.

There were cop cars and ambulances, a couple news vans, and even a fire truck parked on the road, but the helicopter didn't stop; they hoisted him in and spun away, leaving the ground crew busy taking pictures and wrapping caution tape and, in the case of the news teams, opining importantly into their mics with all kinds of theories. I had a suspicion I already knew who it was, though the oceanside cliff he'd climbed up was a good five miles from where he'd fallen down. Tristan Gates, age fourteen. Blond, skinny, serious disposition, startlingly beautiful sky-blue eyes. A seventh-grader at the school where I worked as a teacher's aide, Kennerly Prep, located in the mountains above the city of Los Angeles.

Tristan and his brother Paul had been hiking with their father, Kevin Delman, along the breathtaking Lost Coast trails in Humbolt County, north of San Francisco. The boys probably weren't experienced enough for the trip their dad had planned, but he was a nut about the outdoors—camping, fishing, even hunting, though he was careful to let people know he never killed anything he didn't plan to eat. Kevin was single, and yeah, I'd noticed. Fit, nice-looking fortyish guys who earn a decent living and can hold up their end of a conversation aren't exactly in big supply in LA. Or, if they are, they're after twenty-something models, not thirty-something librarians.

I don't technically have the right to call myself a librarian anymore. I was one, once, and proud of it—mousy hairstyle, tortoiseshell glasses and all. I'd landed my dream job at the fabled Harold Washington Library in Chicago, and I'd been working on a PhD in library science, happy in my insular, literate little world, until the night my life caved in. It hurts to remember, and I don't think about it a lot. Reflecting on the betrayal that sent me spiraling into the bizarre universe of witness protection has more than once led me into that "gray drizzle of horror" named so aptly by William Styron. Let's just say, imagine your man, your guy, your inamorato, if you will, sleeps with your best friend. Oldest story ever told. Except then he kills her. And when you catch him in the act, he tries to kill you too, and laughs about it. Ouch. Ernest Hemingway said that the best way to find out if you can trust someone is to trust them. Gotta hand it to Papa, he was right on that time, because I did find out.

And I'll give my homicidal ex this much. It was a rueful laugh.

Tristan and Paul had transferred to Kennerly the year before I arrived, when they were ten and twelve, respectively. Paul had since graduated and gone on to public high school, but Tristan had been held back to repeat seventh grade, and was on track to graduate in the spring, just a little behind schedule.

Kevin wasn't actually their dad; he was a foster parent, but it was rumored he'd put through the paperwork to adopt, and it certainly seemed he was committed, given that he was picking up the fifty-grand tab for Kennerly, times two, without financial aid. He was a lawyer, and apparently a good one, but that wasn't his claim to fame. Kevin was in the running for sainthood. Five years earlier, a white-trash baby gang had masterminded a couple stickups in the alley behind a run-down apartment building in Venice. The bandits had ranged in age from ten to fourteen, and they were apprehended a few hours later at the Third Street Promenade, filling up on Wetzel's Pretzels and iced Cinnabons. The whole thing would've been almost cute except that the thirteen-year-old, egged on by his besties, had shot their second victim, a guy in his midthirties. Where they'd obtained a Davis P-380 semiautomatic, a firearm more prone to exploding in the hands of the shooter than actually killing anyone else, was a mystery. But they'd gotten hold of it somehow, and it had done the job nicely. The vic, a family man with two kids of his own, had managed to crawl to a neighbor's back door where he'd expired, awaiting an ambulance.

The irony was that Mike Delman had been a passionate gun-control activist. He and his wife had cobbled together a living with her earnings as a preschool teacher and whatever his non-profit had managed to offer. It hadn't been much, judging from their address and the banged-up CR-V Mike had been getting out of when swarmed by the kids. Not a traditional success like his brother, Mike had apparently been very well liked by nearly everyone who knew him. His colleagues, his kids' teachers, his wife's family—there'd been a never-ending testimony to his good-ness on the evening news for over a week.

But it was Kevin who'd emerged from the horror story with some dignity and purpose intact. He blamed the gun, and the morons who'd let it fall into the hands of children, more than he'd blamed the children themselves. The triggerman and his older brother were shut away in juvie for a few years, where they were no doubt hard at work building a network of associates and perfecting their trade. The eleven-year-old had family in Canada that was willing to take him. But the ten- and twelve-year-old brothers, Tristan and Paul Gates, were up for grabs. They'd been in foster care for most of their lives, and the people who'd been housing them at the time of the crime didn't want them back. So Kevin had stepped up, publicly forgiving the Gates brothers, and had started pushing through the paperwork necessary to give them a home.

The tabs had loved it. The grieving widow, Lois, had given a couple interviews expressing her dismay that her brother-in-law was bringing her husband's killers into the family fold. There had been some heartbreaking pictures of her two girls, the eight-year-old's eyes ringed with grief, the two-year-old's simply baffled. And then all three had vanished into a lawsuit involving the gun company, a pawn shop, and the Department of Children's Protective Services. Kevin had expressed his respect for his brother's widow, and his understanding of her point of view. "But," he'd noted in an interview with the *Los Angeles Times*, "there's no point to hating children. I hate what they did. But it's *our* failure as a society that let that happen. My brother would be the first to forgive these children and more than that, to beg *their* forgiveness for what we as a society let them become."

Powerful words. But now Paul Gates was almost surely dead, Tristan was in the hospital looking like last week's meatloaf, and Kevin Delman's halo might be in serious need of polish. It was entirely possible that Kevin had pushed his wards off a cliff, then followed them down. Had there been a struggle in which he was hauled overboard by a frantic kid half his weight? Or had he simply fallen in the confusion, or had he perhaps intended to make it a murder-suicide, then somehow lost his nerve?

I hoped it was none of the above. Kevin had impressed me as a thoroughly likable guy, and I wanted to believe the best of him.

I wanted to live in a world where a man could forgive the little thugs who'd murdered his brother, and then offer them a life as rich as the one they'd taken. I'd been as moved by Kevin's generosity of spirit, his essential goodness, as anyone, and I wasn't going to let go of it so easily. There were a thousand ways the accident could have happened, starting with the story Kevin himself had told the police: The boys had been taking a selfie at the edge of a treacherous cliff, Kevin had rounded a curve in the trail and hollered, in a panic, and at that moment, the boys had both gone over. Kevin had leapt to try to catch Tristan's T-shirt, missed, lost his balance, and followed them partway down, where he'd landed on a rough outcropping of rock. Both boys had missed the ledge and gone straight into the ocean. Kevin had watched them hit the water. He'd watched them float there for a moment, both his boys, facedown in the rough surf. Then they'd been pulled under and he'd crawled up the rocky cliff, dragged himself down the trail to his car, and, no longer in possession of his cell phone, had driven for help. But neither boy's body had been found. Neither had washed up on any patrolled part of the coast, though it was assumed someday they might. Both had been presumed dead, until Tristan was found shivering on that ledge, four days after the fall.

The year before, I'd briefly crushed on a dashing LAPD detective with leaf-green eyes, a movie-star smile . . . and a loyal wife. Because life delights in being just as weird as possible, Marta and I had become friends, and I served as a sort of aunt-in-training to their two boys, Diego and Tony Jr. I stayed away from Antonio Sr. for the most part because, as Ralph Waldo Emerson explained, "we are a puny and fickle folk."

But that night I gave Tony a call to ask about the Delman situation. Apparently Kevin and Tristan were in the same hospital, but on different floors, because Kevin was close to release, while Tristan was in the ICU. The brave boys and girls of the LAPD not being idiots—despite occasional evidence to the contrary—a uniform had been posted in the hall by Tristan's room. Children's Services had suspended Kevin's parental rights, including visitation, until the situation was resolved. But that didn't seem imminent. Tristan was unconscious.

"Not exactly in a coma," Tony explained. "Not exactly *not* in a coma either. Just—sort of reluctant to wake up, is the way the doc explained it to us." He sighed and I could almost see that feral grin. "Kind of like when you're sleeping late, you know . . . after a nice night, all sleepy and warm, and—"

"Love to Marta and the kids," I said hastily, and hung up. Tony loved to tease me, but what he no doubt saw as gentle fun rubbed a sore place in my heart.

There was no real reason for me to visit Tristan, except that he seemed particularly friendless at the moment, and I'd read that unconscious patients can often hear and remember what's said to them while they're out. I took the morning off work and gave the dogs an extra hour at the dog park, where they disappointed all spectators by exploring somewhat diffidently, as opposed to stretching those long limbs with a run. The truth is, greyhounds don't run much. They're fast, yeah. For a minute. Then they like to curl up and sleep.

When I'd fed and watered Vindi and Meme, I hopped in my little Versa and cut south to Venice Boulevard. Traffic is horrific between Santa Monica and midtown, but locals know surface routes that can sometimes beat the freeways. I parked six blocks from the hospital center and walked. I'm not exactly a penny pincher, but that walk saved me a twenty-dollar parking tab.

The cop on duty scanned my driver's license and let me in, but she watched from the doorway, unsmiling. Tristan was still asleep. His face was as white as salt, and part of his head had been shaved, exposing livid purplish bruises that made him look particularly vulnerable. One arm and both legs were in casts, the right leg suspended in traction. There were no flowers, cards, or teddy bears. The fingers of his good hand were splinted, so I laid my hand against his neck, the only unscathed part of his slight form that was available. "Tristan? Hey, buddy. It's Ms. Baker from school. Cam. Remember? I just stopped by to see how you're doing. The docs say you're about ready to wake up now."

I glanced at the cop. She was small, with severe posture and a lifted chin, cornrows tight and straight along her brown scalp. She met my eyes and shrugged.

"Tristan? If you could open your eyes, we could talk about what happened. The accident. You were very brave, climbing up that cliff to get help." Tristan's mouth moved very slightly. I wondered if he might be playing possum. "Do you remember that? You got pretty banged up, buddy. That's why you're here in the hospital. Your dad's here too."

Tristan swallowed. He didn't have much of an Adam's apple yet, but his jaw was clearly defined and I thought I caught a glimpse of the man he'd be someday. Intense. Focused. I'd seen that in the classroom too, as he struggled to grasp ideas that the other kids had nailed years earlier—complex sentences, subject-verb agreement, alliteration. Yet he was clearly bright. He had a precocious ability to read people and to forge quick connections. Teachers loved him and gave him every break conceivable, although everyone was aware of what he'd done; had he been an adult, he'd have been found guilty of felony murder.

Kids liked him too. Tristan was quiet, but he hovered on the fringes of the cool group of kids, and had been the object of more than a couple of first crushes. My own feelings about the Gates boys were a bit conflicted. I'd assisted in both of their classrooms, and I found them both likable and appealing, and more than that, vulnerable. Sensitive, and in Tristan's case especially, quite charming. But I'd been close to murder too many times to discount their involvement lightly. I couldn't look at Tristan, even now, pathetically injured and profoundly alone, without thinking of Mike Delman, his agonized widow, his bewildered daughters.

Tristan sighed. The cop shot me a glance and jerked her head toward the door. She hit a button and a couple nurses bustled in as I moved, reluctantly, into the hall.

Sure enough, a moment later, with nurses and techs gathered around his bed and CPS on the way, Tristan opened his eyes. Even from the open doorway, I noted their intense, limpid blue. He blinked. Looked around as if searching for something. When Tristan spoke, his voice was throaty and harsh, from disuse or from the tube they'd initially used to assist his breathing. But it wasn't his guttural tone that was shocking; it was his words, the first he'd spoken, presumably, in nearly a week. "I want a lawyer," Tristan said. And then he went back to sleep.

Kevin looked older than when I'd last seen him, but he was still a very good-looking man. Square jaw bristled with at least a day's worth of beard, golden-brown eyes, hair that had clearly once been the same color, but was now streaked with silver. It was a nice effect, just intensifying the blond. He looked like an aging surfer, the kind that takes care of himself. His eyebrows lifted with pleasure when he saw me. "Miss, uh—my favorite teacher's aide. It's nice of you to come."

"Cam," I told him. Cam Baker had been my name for nearly two years, and it sounded right.

He grinned. "Yes, sorry. I'm still a little out of it. Painkillers. I'm going home tomorrow, though. I see the doc at two-thirty and then I'm outta here." He gestured toward his knee, bandaged but not in a cast. "Torn meniscus. Hurts like a son of a bitch. But they're gonna let me try physical therapy instead of surgery." He stopped speaking suddenly. "Have you seen Tristan? They won't let me—"

I nodded. "I did see him. He was still sleeping, but as I was leaving, he woke up."

"Thank God." Kevin's eyes slid away from mine. "What did he say?"

I shrugged, studying Kevin's handsome face closely. "Not much. Just asked for a lawyer."

His pupils dilated. A sure sign of surprise, and sometimes one of fear. "A—why?"

I didn't reply. "Do you have a ride home tomorrow? I don't get off until three, but if you don't mind killing an hour, I could swing by around four."

He nodded. Caught my hand and squeezed it. "I—thank you, Cam. That would be ideal."

Kevin lived in a Tudor-style cottage in Encino with a rolling front lawn, xeriscaped with cactus, succulents, and birdbaths.

Apricot mallow tumbled over a cluster of boulders, messy and gorgeous, and the tiny, rose-pink flowers of a lemonade berry tree adorned a lattice frame along the wall that fronted the street. If you're not from LA, you might get the wrong idea from "cottage." Kevin's house was a two-story and had to have comprised at least four bedrooms and four or five baths. I knew there'd be a pool in the back, and probably a trampoline. A couple bikes rested against the three-car garage, and a longboard waited on the front porch. It was a massive skateboard, bright green. Kevin touched it as he fumbled for his keys. "This is Paul's," he told me. "He only got to ride it two, three times. I made him wait for it—he earned the money with grades. He was so excited—had to have a bamboo drop-down deck, and these wheels that—"

He broke off suddenly and for the first time I saw grief in his face. "I guess Tris will want it, if he, if they let him—"

His shoulders slumped and I took the keys from him. Worked the lock and waited while he limped inside and hit the keypad to turn off the alarm.

The furnishings were pure bachelor pad. I figured he'd bought the house when he took the boys in, and just used the furnishings from wherever he'd lived before. The sofa was low-slung and expensive, a big L-shape upholstered in a flat-woven beige fabric, a Viesso or something like it. There were chrome-and-glass coffee tables, a sleek leather armchair, and an enormous flat-screen TV that dominated a thirty-foot wall.

"If you've got time, we'll have a cup of tea," Kevin offered. "Or a drink, but I've got to abstain till the painkillers wear off. There's a decent cab franc, and some—"

"Tea's great," I interrupted. The kitchen was clean and modern, state-of-the-art circa 2010 or so, all stainless built-ins and granite countertops. Personally, I like the colored appliances that are coming back into style—rich browns and creams, or retro oranges and greens, but compared with the little breakfast bar at my pool-house rental, Kevin's kitchen was a dream. The big sub-zero fridge was decorated with sports schedules and school pictures and a tattered report card with the trademark blue Kennerly crest. I motioned for Kevin to sit while I filled the kettle and found mugs and tea bags. He had a big supply of plain old Twinings Earl Grey, and I liked him for that. Unpretentious, despite the zip code. I served him his tea in an LA Zoo mug and realized too late my own was emblazoned "World's Best Dad."

"I'm glad you're here," Kevin said softly. "Right now, Cam, it's good to have a friend."

Was I his friend? I barely knew him, but his plight, his posture, his heartbroken smile, moved me to pity.

Kevin looked exhausted and I knew I ought to go. But I've got a cat's curiosity and a librarian's memory and something was bugging me. "Kevin, why did Tristan appear so far from where you and the boys went over the cliff?"

He shrugged. "I guess the ocean carried him. Or he could have crawled along the beach until he found a way up . . ." He sipped his tea. "It's hard to think about."

"Well, you have to think about it," I said reasonably. "Because Tristan asked for a lawyer. You're a lawyer, but he didn't ask for you. Why? You'd think he'd want nothing more than to come home, to be with you, to—"

"You don't know a damned thing about it," Kevin said flatly. "I'm going to assume you don't have any kids, let alone one as troubled, as *damaged*, as Tristan. In his entire life, he's had no one to rely on but his brother. CPS let him down a dozen times, with crappy foster parents and group homes that were worse. Someone like you—educated, privileged, beautiful—you don't have any way to know what it's like to be a resident of crapville from the first day of your life. And now—he was unconscious for at least twenty-four hours, for God's sake. We don't know what he remembers. Does he even know who I am? Does he know Paul is dead? My nightmare is that he might think he's still back in that time—" Kevin faltered. "When my brother died."

He continued, but I was stuck on his description of me. I'm educated, yes, but he'd hardly know that from my job title. Privileged? That had once been true, I supposed. I wished I could tell him how it had felt to turn my back on my parents, my friends, my job, my life, and start over with nothing but a new name, a new hair color, and a minimum-wage job in a hair salon. And the "beautiful" part was a joke. I believe men when they tell me I'm sexy as hell. Pretty sure that's accurate, because I like men, I like sex, and while I enjoy solitude, occasionally I do get lonely. But I'm no classic beauty. I'm too wiry for that. My eyes are a little sad, and my mouth turns down naturally into a thin, slight frown. Or at least it has for the past eight years. Before that, I was a different person, and the truth is, sometimes I barely remember her. I think of her the way you'd remember your sweet, dumb kid sister who died.

Kevin touched my wrist. I didn't pull away, and he closed his hand around mine. The sorrow in his eyes moved me almost to tears. But I thought of Willa Cather's wry observation, "It is easy to pity when once one's vanity has been tickled." It wasn't exactly my vanity he was tickling now, though. His broad finger stroked my palm absently, almost as if he were unaware of it, as he looked into my eyes. A bleak smiled played around his lips. He touched my cheek with one finger, then traced a line down my jaw to my throat. "Will you stay, Cam?"

It's hard for me to get close to anyone. Part of it, I suppose, is fear. I was burned badly and I'm not eager to have it happen again. But it's also just a matter of effort. I can't really let my guard down; getting close to another person necessitates deceiving him or her. I'm forced to tell lie upon lie as the natural wish to know a new friend or lover inevitably leads to questions. *Where did you grow up? Did you go to college? Were you a nerd in high school, or a pop, or a loner?* Companionship from my dogs, and romance in the form of cheap one-offs, seem easier than navigating the treacherous path of real relationships. But Kevin was handsome and vulnerable, a combination I've been known to find irresistible. I was tempted.

Before I could answer, he took his hand away. Sat up straight and shivered, as if shaking off a chill. "Sorry. I'm out of line. You were really kind to drive me home and I feel like a boor."

I rinsed the tea mugs and put them in the drain. Kevin hobbled to the door ahead of me, opened it, then hesitated. Took my chin in his hand and leaned in slowly, giving me time to pull away. I didn't.

The kiss was slow and deep. He tasted clean, like tea and toothpaste, and his clothes smelled new. No doubt they'd been ordered online and delivered to the hospital. I hoped I was as fresh, although after a day of wrangling seventh-graders at Kennerly, I rather doubted it.

"Cam," Kevin said. "I'm going to hold the memorial for Paul as soon as Tristan is well enough to attend. If they—if I'm not allowed to stand with him—could you possibly step in? He'll have an escort from CPS, but it could be a stranger. He'll need a friendly face, and—"

His voice cracked. I put my hand flat on his cheek. Got on my toes and pressed my lips to his. This kiss was dry and chaste. "I'll be there for him," I promised. "If you can't be there for him yourself."

"You're right," Tony mused later, over coffee. "The key is, why did the kid come up so far from where he went over?"

Marta pushed a dish of cherries across the table toward me. I nipped the pit out of one, tore it open, and popped it into Diego's mouth. He drooled contentedly, leaning back against my meager chest as if it were a plush sofa. "The way I see it," I said, "the tide could have washed him up somewhere different from where he went over, but the current was going the other way. He'd be more likely to have drifted north than south."

Marta shook her head. "How do you *know* that, Cam?"

"Librarians—" I began, then broke off. I'd almost slipped. "Librarians can tell you almost anything," I continued weakly. "Or you can look it up on the Internet, I guess."

Tony shot me an appraising look. Cops can smell subterfuge. It's one reason I ought to stay away from them, instead of inviting myself to their homes to drink their coffee and hold their babies and hang out with their wives.

"So Tristan might have drifted," I went on. "Or he might have crawled along the beach looking for a good spot to climb up, but . . . not for five miles. Not with those injuries. The most likely scenario is that Kevin—the dad—is lying about where he went over."

Tony grunted. "Yeah. And the only reason I can think of for that is to misdirect us into looking for the kids in the wrong place."

Marta got up and took Diego from me, but not before I'd kissed the top of his sweaty, sweet-smelling head.

I nodded. "To be sure they were dead before the bodies were found. Or to keep them from being found altogether. So you're picturing the father pushing them over, then jumping too. But maybe finding himself on an outcropping and changing his mind . . ."

Tony shook his head. "More likely he staged it from the get-go. Pushed them over close to where Tristan was found. Then hiked five miles back, closer to the car, threw himself over where he knew there was a spot to land on. Somebody for sure went over there—there's broken shrubbery, a slide mark down the cliff, displaced rocks . . . and he's banged up enough to make it plausible."

I took a sip from my mug and pushed it away. Marta's coffee was strong, and I had to be up for school in the morning. "If we could find Paul's body—maybe he didn't die in a fall at all. Maybe he was dead before he went over. An argument, and Kevin whacked him with a hatchet or—" I winced. "He hunts. He's got guns. But *Tristan* asked for a lawyer. Maybe Tristan did his brother, on purpose or by accident, and then . . ."

I couldn't make it add up.

Tony shrugged. "Not my case, Cam. But you're right. It's interesting."

Marta came back into the room, babyless. "One thing you guys should explain to me, if you ever figure it out. How could Kevin have forgiven them, that gang of kids that murdered his brother? I mean, it's great to say he's a hero for what he's done for the boys, forgiving them and helping them and all . . . but honestly, how could he? Your brother is *family*." Her eyes narrowed. "If someone hurt Diego, Little Tony wouldn't—"

Antonio got up and put his arms around her. Buried his face in her black hair. I looked away, confused by their affection and by my own reaction. *Our envy of others devours us most of all.* Solzhenitsyn. I swallowed hard, ashamed. Marta and Tony were my friends. Pretty much my only friends. I did want happiness for them. I just wanted some for myself too.

Tony walked me to my car. "They're searching again for Paul, this time focusing on the area closer to where they found Tristan. Your theory's not bad, Cam. I don't think the kid could still be alive, but it sure would be helpful to examine the body."

I unlocked my car and got in, but Tony stopped the door with his foot. "Hey," he said, softly, stooping down. "When you gonna tell me whatever dark secret you're hiding? You know, I could just run you."

"Friends don't run friends," I said flippantly. "And besides, it's illegal to do a background without cause. You don't suspect me of any crime, do you?"

Tony's handsome face was grave. "Are you WITSEC, Cam?"

I made my expression as blank as possible. "What's WITSEC?"

He shook his head. "Never mind. Just know that Marta and I are friends, if you need us."

I didn't answer. Just slammed the door and drove away. But later, alone in my small bed in the cramped pool house, with Meme curled on a rug at my side and Vindi on duty by the door, I thought about Tony and Marta, their kids, their easy way with each other, the companionship and love they took for granted. Would I ever have that with anyone? It didn't seem likely. Relationships are built on trust, and there was no one in the whole world I could really talk to honestly, except my handler with the US Marshals. But I wasn't supposed to contact him except in case of real emergency, and he was a bit of a tight-ass, anyway.

I had once prized honesty above any other trait, and now every word out of my mouth was a lie, because Cam Baker didn't really exist. Neither did Audrey Smith or Serena Dutton or Juliet Gregory. I had had a name once, and a life. But that was gone. If I wasn't careful, the marshals would move me out of this placement too. I didn't know if they'd even let me keep my dogs. And it wasn't only the dogs I'd miss, and my job at Kennerly, and new friends like Tony and Marta. If I were to be honest, I felt a flicker in my chest every time I thought of that kiss in Kevin Delman's foyer. I knew that could go somewhere. I knew that could go somewhere very nice. Unless, of course, Kevin was a killer.

I took another morning off work and went to visit Tristan. I didn't want to think about what my paycheck was going to look like, but I was pretty sure Tristan needed visitors, and I knew I needed answers.

The same cop was on duty, but today she nodded as she waved me in. "I won't be here after ten," she said. "They're taking the guard order off."

Tristan looked a lot better than the last time I'd seen him. He was sitting up in bed intent on a little handheld Nintendo, awkwardly manipulating it with splints on one hand and a cast on the other. Consoles weren't cheap; I guessed Kevin had had it delivered to him to pass the hours. A stack of magazines—*Sports Illustrated for Kids, National Geographic, MAD*—sat untouched on the bedside table, along with an assortment of soft drinks and bags of chips.

Tristan looked up when I came in. Eyes like a cloudless sky in a face pinched and white with worry. "Hey, kiddo. How's it going?"

He shrugged. "You came before. When I was still asleep."

I nodded. "When you were waking up. You remember me from school, right? I'm Cam Baker."

Tristan nodded. "I remember you."

"Do you remember everything, Tristan? Kennerly and before that?"

He nodded.

"And after? The hiking trip? And what happened to your brother?"

His face closed. He looked down at the game player. "I'm not supposed to talk about it. I can only talk to the police and my caseworker."

"Not your lawyer?"

"I don't have one," he said candidly. "I guess I was a little mixed up when I said that, when I was waking up. I was—thinking about before, I guess. But Miss Jackson, she said I don't get a free lawyer unless I'm accused of a crime, and I'm not. There isn't any crime. Just the accident." He paused. "She said I can prolly go home really soon, to my real home. With my dad."

"You want to go back to Kevin?"

Tristan shrugged. "Well, yeah. That's where I live."

Relief flowed over me like a fresh breeze. If Tristan wanted to go home, Kevin was in the clear.

A nurse came in, smiling. "Well, young man, looks like you're good to go this afternoon," she said briskly.

Tristan looked up eagerly. "Home?"

The nurse smiled. "It's not up to me, but that's what I hear."

As if on cue, Kevin came into the room. "You hear correctly," he said. "Miss Jackson is on her way with paperwork as we speak." Tristan's eyes were on him, sober and intent. He reminded me of Vindi, when I'd first adopted her and her brother from their previous owner. Meme had settled right away, but Vindi had been wary. She'd been bounced around from racetrack to fosters to what should have been her permanent home, before she'd landed with me, and it had taken her a long time to trust me.

Now Kevin met Tristan's gaze. "Hey, son."

"Kevin!" Tristan's expression was hard to read. "Where were you? I've been waiting!"

Kevin smiled. "I know. It couldn't be helped. The police had to do their job, make sure everything was good. We can both understand that." He rested his hand lightly on Tristan's shoulder. "I'm sorry for everything, Tris. I just want to get you home."

As if he'd just noticed me, Kevin turned to me. "It's good of you to be here, Cam," he said. "You're a woman of your word. And if we could call upon you one more time—I could really use some help getting this guy home." He smiled and I remembered our kiss. I shrugged, but I thought of Ferdinand to Miranda. *The very instant that I saw you, did my heart fly to your service.* Kevin and Tristan had certainly weathered a tempest. We all had.

My phone buzzed and I went into the hall. Tony, texting to tell me the investigation was closing and Tristan was being released to Kevin's care. I stuck my head into the room to let Kevin know I'd be back by four, and then I headed back toward the street where I'd parked, and got ready for an afternoon assisting in the Kennerly chem lab.

It wasn't hard to get Tristan settled for the night. He had to have been exhausted. Even using the toilet was an ordeal, one that Kevin had to help with, despite his own injuries. A rotating shift of aides would start in the morning, but until then, Kevin was on call. He opened a bottle of crémant while I searched for flutes, settling finally for stemless glasses better suited to a red wine than a bubbly white.

"Sorry." Kevin clinked his glass against mine and motioned toward the living room. "Bachelor dad with two boys—not much call for proper wineglasses." He dropped heavily onto the beige sofa. "One boy. I'll have to get used to that."

I sat beside him and tucked my legs up under me. "It's no substitute for a brother," I offered. "I'm not suggesting that. But Tristan might find comfort in a dog. I certainly have."

Kevin put his glass down. Pulled me closer to him, wincing as he shifted his bad knee. My tattoo peeked out from my cropped jeans and he traced it with one finger. "Why, Cam? Why have you needed comfort? Since I've known you, we've been very focused on me. I feel as though there's so much to you that's still a mystery." He laughed. "Such as why you have a tattoo of Lucy on your ankle."

"Piltdown Man," I corrected. "Just kind of a reminder to myself. I'll tell you about it someday." I sipped my wine. "Other than that, no mystery. Just a normal, slightly boring life." I struggled to change the subject. As if on cue, there was a cry from Tristan's room. I was halfway down the hall before Kevin could struggle up off the sofa, grunting with pain.

"Hey, hey, hey," I said, flipping on the light. Tristan was wild-eyed, sitting up in bed, propping himself up on one hand with the other, still in a cast, held out before him as if to ward off some invisible demon. His hair and bedclothes were drenched with sweat.

"It's okay, buddy. You're all right."

Then Kevin took over, sitting on the edge of the bed, holding Tristan awkwardly against his chest as he murmured, "We're gonna be okay, Tris. We're gonna get through this. We're gonna get each other through it and we're gonna be all right."

"He's soaking wet, Kev," I said. "I'll get him a fresh T-shirt if you can get that one off." I found a shirt in the bureau and turned around. Kevin was easing Tristan's tee up over his head, careful of the splinted fingers. Tristan's chest was spindly and hairless, white except for the random stippling of purple and green bruises, and a ripe crescent of blue across his sternum. It would be easy for someone—even a doctor—to mistake the mark for just another contusion among all those he'd endured. But I knew what it was; I'd seen it before. The blue mark was the unmistakable print of the heel of a big hand. The kind of mark you'd get if someone had, say, shoved you really hard and knocked you off a cliff.

I tried to keep my face impassive but Kevin's eyes told me I'd revealed my shock. My phone was in my bag in the living room. I tossed the clean shirt to Kevin as I started to back away. "I'll get him some tea. Maybe we could all use some."

"Don't, Cam," Kevin said, shifting heavily on the bed. He lifted his bad leg and stretched it out before him. "Don't be afraid of me, please."

I could easily have outrun him, made it to the living room or just out the front door. But Tristan was trapped, both legs in casts, barely able to sit up unaided. I couldn't leave him.

"I won't hurt you," Kevin said calmly. "I wouldn't, first of all. But there'd be no point to it. I don't think there'd be any way to fool anyone. Not now."

Tristan looked up at him, fear in his face. "Don't tell her," he begged.

"Tell me what, Tris?" I asked. "That he pushed you and your brother off the cliff? I already know that. What is baffling to me is why you're covering for him. You've had so many opportunities—"

Tristan struggled, wincing with pain. "Just go away! Just leave us alone! You don't know anything!"

Kevin put his hand on Tristan's shoulder and the boy calmed. "Easy, son," he said. "The most important thing right now is for you to recover. Just focus on that. Let us take care of the legal stuff."

I nearly gagged. "Legal stuff! Kevin, you killed one boy and tried to kill the other."

"Shut up!" Tristan screamed. "Just shut up! We deserved it! Can't you see that? We deserved it for what we did, and now we're even! So just leave us alone!"

Kevin shrugged. "It's true," he said simply. "They did deserve it. But Paul has paid for what they did, and Tristan has suffered the same loss I suffered. We've each lost a brother. I'm willing to give him another chance."

He glanced down at Tristan with something like fondness. "And he's willing to give me another chance too. To be a real dad to him. No tricks. No subterfuge."

I knew my horror was reflected in my expression. *"The web of our life is of a mingled yarn, good and ill together,"* I whispered.

Kevin grinned. *"All's Well That Ends Well,"* he noted. "Fitting. Shakespeare's only play that's truly unclassifiable as either comedy or tragedy. Like real life, it's both."

"Please, Cam," Tristan pleaded. "Please just go away."

Kevin shook his head. "She can't, son," he said sadly. "She won't. She thinks she knows better than either you or I, the injured parties, what's fair and right. She will be our judge and jury."

"You will have a real judge and jury, Kevin," I said slowly. He was getting up with apparent difficulty, but I backed away, wary of those powerful arms.

"Yes." He nodded. "I've set things up for Tris. He'll go back into care, of course, but there'll be a trust for college." He tousled Tristan's blond hair where it hadn't been shaved. It was an awkward gesture and Tristan flinched. "And enough to finish the year at Kennerly, if Miss Jackson can arrange it. He'll have to go public after that." He hesitated. "Maybe you could help there, Cam. Keep an eye out, make sure he lands somewhere—stable . . ."

"Kevin, why? If you care so much about Tristan, why did you—"

He continued as if he hadn't heard me. "This house is free and clear, but that'll go to Lois and the girls. I'll handle my own defense, of course, such as it is. . . ." He smiled and I was struck again by the beauty of his brown eyes. "I wish it were otherwise, Cam," he said. "I feel like you and I—we could have been something."

Kevin reached for me, looked back at the boy. Hesitated. "I wanted revenge, yes," he said simply. "But not simple vengeance. I wanted them to *really know* what they'd taken. There was no way to convey—they were like animals. They murdered Mike like it was nothing! He crawled away and they were *laughing*, Cam! They laughed while he bled out and then they went and got snacks at the mall!"

Tristan was sobbing now.

"There was no way that simply locking them up—even taking their lives—would be justice, because they had no concept of what life could be, *should* be. They had no *concept* of what they'd taken from Mike and Lois and the girls. And me."

"So you decided to show them." I nodded. "You gave them everything—a home, wealth, education, fun—a father's love."

He nodded. "I wanted them to know, in those seconds before they hit the ground, exactly what they'd taken and what they were losing."

Tristan was curled tight against Kevin's words, rocking. "No. No. No. No."

I went to Tristan and put my arms around him. He was small for fourteen. Very thin. I tried to imagine him urging his friend to shoot the unarmed man they'd just robbed. Tried to imagine him laughing as that man crawled away, dying. But it was impossible. I could think only of his sea-blue eyes, his soft child's mouth.

"Paul's dead," Kevin said flatly. "Tristan checked."

"You lied about where they fell to slow the search," I said.

"Yes," Kevin said. "I didn't want Paul's body found, at least not immediately, because he almost took me over with him! He fought like a tiger. I'm proud, in a way. Paul wanted to *live*, Cam. They'll find handprints, a kick mark in the center of his goddamned back, fingerprints around his neck—and I'm proud of every bruise, damn it! That means I *gave* him something; I *taught* him something. His life was *worth* fighting for."

He sighed. "I suppose Tristan might as well tell the police where to look. We'll get Paul a plot at Forest Lawn so Tris can visit."

I stared at him. His handsome face. His cold eyes. "You never figured Tristan would come back. It must have been a double shock when you realized he wasn't telling what you'd done."

Kevin shrugged. "Not really. I thought—well, I thought maybe he'd had a change of heart. As I had. Because as soon as I pushed them, Cam, I was sorry. They had become something different from what they were when they killed Mike. They'd become human, and quite dear to me. I can't say I'm sorry Tristan is alive. I've forgiven him, for real this time, as he has me. The police cleared us, and if it weren't for you butting in . . . we'd be okay. We really would."

"It would never be okay, Kevin." I held Tristan a moment longer, then got off the bed. I knew Kevin wouldn't hurt him now. As I went past, he could have grabbed me, but he didn't. I heard him speaking softly to Tristan as I went to the living room and found my phone.

I left them alone together. It wasn't much, but it was all I could offer, those few moments of privacy to make whatever peace they could with one another. I finished my crémant, hesitated, then finished Kevin's too. I wondered if Lois would feel relief when she found out what her brother-in-law had done, or if she'd feel only a greater burden of sorrow. I wondered if Mike Delman's little girls would be happy that Paul Gates was dead and Tristan permanently wounded. I wondered if there was any end to our human capacity to cause grief, and to suffer it. John Milton wrote, *The mind is its own place and in itself, can make a heaven of hell, a hell of heaven.* Milton knew more suffering than most of us: deaths, divorce, illness, blindness, prison. I wondered which he'd chosen for himself in the end, a heaven or a hell. Then a sharp hard rap at the door brought me back to reality, and I got up off the sofa to answer it.

---

*"A Heaven or a Hell" is the fourth in my series for EQMM *about a librarian on the run after witnessing a gangland murder, with the eighth installment now in the planning phase. The first story, "That Which We Call Patience," was intended to be a one-off, but I liked the regretful, erudite, Shakespeare-quoting main character so much that I continued on, in the process learning that developing a believable fictional world means lots of fact-checking, back-and-forthing, and meticulous note-taking. It's fun to change the character's name and appearance regularly, but readers will call you on discrepancies between installments. If Cam's Piltdown Man tattoo is on her right ankle in the second story, it had better not be on the left in the third. Another challenge in constructing a series is to make the characters so compelling that readers are willing to overlook the implausibility of the basic premise—most people don't, after all, encounter and solve a murder every few months. I want readers to linger over the ending of "A Heaven or a Hell," confused—not by the plot, of course, but by their own emotions. If I've done my job well, they will feel genuine grief for Kevin Delman and Tristan Gates—cold-blooded killers, both.*

Ginny Swart *has done all those jack-of-all-trades things required for the background blurb for a great novelist. She's been a graphic designer, sold advertising, run an art school, been a journalist on a trade paper, produced newsletters for nine different businesses, worked as a maid in Australia, and tutored English in Hong Kong. She started writing in 2001 and won the Real Writers prize in 2002—the money paid for a holiday in the UK and after that she just kept writing. To date she has sold over seven hundred short stories, mostly to magazines but also anthologies and text books; she has written three very forgettable romances. The great novel is yet to come.*

BANG ON THE MONEY

Ginny Swart

MANDARIN HOTEL—TUESDAY, 16TH MAY

"Mister Marrick? Mister Marrick!?"

The seventeen-year-old hotel foyer busboy at the Mandarin Hotel, Singapore, continued to wander around the reception area, calling for "Mister Marrick!"—a dark brown envelope clutched in his white-gloved hand.

From a black leather armchair toward the rear of the foyer came the call: "Here." Which was followed by a raised hand.

The busboy immediately went over, relieved at finding the man so quickly. "Here, sir, a package for you." Before he was prepared to hand it over, Marrick had to sign the young man's docket as proof of delivery.

From a jacket pocket, Marrick took out a silver penknife and carefully slit open the thick envelope. Inside were two carefully cut sheets of cardboard, taped together, between which was a bronze colored key. The number 215 was impressed into the top.

Written on one of the cardboard sheets were the words "Changi—PP2509B—1530"

Marrick checked his watch—12:55.

He raised his hand again, calling "Here," and the attentive busboy appeared at his side. "I need a taxi in the next five minutes. Tell the doorman it's for Mister Marrick, room 1011."

The boy's enthusiastic "Very good, sir," earned him a $5 tip.

Five minutes later, to the "tock" Marrick got into the back of the yellow and green taxi. The smell of newly polished leather and canned air freshener was familiar but still irritating on the nose.

"Where to, sir?"

"Changi."

"No luggage, sir?"

"None at all. I'm going to meet someone. Do you have a card so I can get you for the journey back to the Mandarin?"

The taxi driver's smile said: *No waiting in the queue for a pickup this time.* "Here, sir. Ask at the booking desk and they will call for you."

And charge accordingly, no doubt, Marrick thought.

After he'd been dropped off, Marrick went through the terminal entrance, paused to get his bearings, then headed over to the large luggage storage lockers along the corridor wall between the TWA check-in and the executive lounge "curtained, for your discretion."

215 was easy to find, and with a medium sized suitcase now in hand, Marrick returned the key to the very pleasant woman manning the Airport Information stand.

From there he headed to the washrooms, found a stall, closed the door, and laid the suitcase on top of the toilet bowl. Two clicks and the case lid was thrown back, revealing a carefully folded white shirt, Collingdale Club tie, black shoes, and a sports jacket. After changing, Marrick opened the envelope tucked into the lid pocket, counted the money, put that into his inside jacket pocket, then extracted the dark blue passport and plane ticket (one way, Sydney). From the back pocket of his trousers he pulled another blue passport.

Tossing it into the suitcase, he said: "The king is dead. Long live the king." He clipped shut the case, opened the stall door, and made sure no one was using the facilities. From a trouser pocket he took a traveler bottle of talc, shook a small amount of the white powder onto his palm, then finger brushed it through his hair, changing it from professionally dyed dark brown to a more salt and pepper gray. Over by the mirrors and washbasins, he rinsed his hands clean in the end sink by the paper towel trash can, dried them, then Mr. Mike Carlisle left to board the 15:30 Singapore Airways flight to Sydney.

Back in the washroom, by the towel bin, was the medium sized suitcase—all that remained of the now-late Francis J. Marrick—waiting for someone to steal it.

LUCIANNA AVENUE, ROSE BAY, SYDNEY—FRIDAY, 19TH MAY

Casually he took a second walk past number 17. First time had been on the far side pavement to check for cars in the driveway, gardeners at work, or any other potential interference. This time he was on the house side, resisting temptation to look directly up the white stone driveway.

That's going to be a bugger if there's anything parked out front leaking oil.

He stopped the other side of the driveway and made a show of checking through his suit pockets. The "I forgot my keys" was always a good routine, because people didn't think twice when you went back and fished the spare key from its hiding place. Or, in this case, palming the recently cut duplicate from his shirt cuff.

Not that anyone was likely to be watching. 4:30 P.M. was always an ideal time. The kids had been back from school for almost an hour, so nannies were rushed off their feet, commuters still had to start their commutes, and generally everyone would be winding down for the Friday evening.

A double twist of the key threw back both the door lock and deadbolt, and the door swung inward silently. Pause, listen, then into the coolness of the hall and stairway, closing the door quietly behind him.

Again another pause, silently straining to hear any movement from within while putting on a pair of white cotton gloves and admiring the tasteful designer opulence on display. Not so much as to say gaudy—despite the large eighteenth century French gilded mirror on the wall—but enough to say never ever been strapped for cash. Not including the contents, he reckoned the value of the place alone would be around the $500,000 mark. The trouble was all the good stuff was far too big to drop into a pocket.

Thankfully, even with all that money, Mr. and Mrs. Constantine Tylor, were still too tight to pay for residential staff. Asset rich but cash poor? He doubted it. As he turned he caught his reflection in the mirror and couldn't resist a critical look at himself, smoothing his thick dark hair and awarding himself with a wide, confident smile. The practiced kind that crinkled his face into attractive laugh lines. *Still got it, Mike my lad, those gray hairs just add sex appeal.*

Satisfied that Mrs. Tylor wasn't in the house, Mike moved down the hallway and into the central lounge. A Harold Abbott original over the mock fireplace, cocktail cabinet by the wall, hardwood floors and a well-padded three piece suite with one of those geometric diamond designs—cushions to match. In front a wood and ceramic tile coffee table had several Art House magazines tastefully displayed on top.

Through one door off to the right was the study—wall to wall bookshelves, mahogany desk prominent. To the left, sunroom-cum-conservatory. The basement was the now obligatory entertainment room and wet bar.

Constantine, like Onassis, had started out an oil man, but had then diversified into finance.

The study would have a safe behind a bookcase—no doubt a key and combination affair—for all his bonds, papers, and ready cash. Probably a passport or two, for those incognito journeys. The safe was too much time, and no real chance of getting into it without the key.

No, as the song went: *The only way is up, baby . . .*

Plush carpet on the stairs kept everything silent, and on his way up he admired several photographs of Mrs. Patrice Tylor—Pattie Tylor as she was so often referred to in the gossip and social columns. Fashionably slim, athletic in some shots, bobbed blond hair and hazel brown eyes—she took a very nice photo—as did her jewelry. The sort of pieces that could easily fit into a pocket or two.

On the landing, spare guest bathroom, guest bedrooms 1, 2, and 3, and the master bedroom suite.

Inside the master—bed made and tidy by casual morning help—he resisted the temptation to draw the curtains. That was the kind of afternoon anomaly that could possibly attract attention. It was straight to the dressing table where, curiously, Mrs. Tylor's jewelry box was open and a four row white diamond bracelet was draped half over the front.

If you can't put your toys away, you really don't deserve them.

He picked up the bracelet and was about to drop it into his jacket pocket when movement in the dressing table mirror caught his attention.

It was Mrs. Tylor, standing in front of the now open walk-in wardrobe. She was wearing what looked like a Kym original "Summer Dress"—watercolor-style flowers on light cotton, white leather pumps, and an ever popular digital fitbit thing on her wrist. All that was missing was the large brimmed hat set at a slightly jaunty angle, and a tall glass of Pimm's No. 1. In place of the Pimm's was a decidedly unsociable blue steel 9 mm automatic.

Mike slowly raised his hands and carefully turned round to face her. It was obvious from her expression, and the steadiness of her hand, that she knew which end of a gun was which—and more importantly, how to use it.

He turned on his smile. "I can appreciate home defense, but don't you think that's a little excessive? I mean, can we not just talk about this?"

"What's to talk about? You're here attempting to steal my jewelry. If it wasn't for the fact that blood is difficult to get out of a wool carpet, I suspect I might have shot you before now. Not that the temptation has entirely left me."

"Well, I'll admit that I was attracted by the possibility when I found your front door open. But now I've seen the error of my ways, wouldn't it be for the best to just let me depart? I mean, do I look like a dangerous criminal to you?" He gave her no chance to answer. "No. I'm just a humble common or garden opportunist housebreaker. Harming anyone is beyond me—especially when they're as beautiful as yourself."

"I doubt that very much." She flicked the gun toward the open bedroom door—which gave Mike a clearer view of the weapon, and the fact that the safety catch was still engaged—"I think we should continue this conversation downstairs, Mister . . . ?"

"Tony. Tony Daniels." He extended a hand for shaking, but she just tilted her head slightly.

"Seriously? Look, let's go down to the lounge. It's got to be sunset somewhere in the world, and I know I could do with a gin about now. Also we need to talk."

Well color me curious. Knowing that the gun was no longer a danger meant he could relax and, hey, why not see what she wanted to talk about? "Okay. Should I lead the way?"

"Well, if you don't, I'll just shoot you in the kneecap. Any preference?"

He shook his head, smiled, then carefully walked down the stairs to the hallway. Pattie Tylor followed at a distance, and Mike found it a little unnerving to notice that the gun didn't waver from the line of his head.

In the lounge she pointed to the sofa. "If you'll kindly sit at the far end while I fix us a couple of tall ones." As he sat, she put the automatic on the coffee table, and their eyes met. She smiled. "If you want to check, the magazine is full of blanks. Oh, and the safety is on."

Over at the cocktail cabinet she set up two highball glasses with a strong Tom Collins mix, brought them over and sat at the other end of the sofa.

Mike tasted his—*heavy on the gin, or what?*—then set it down on the coffee table. "Okay, so what is it you wanted to talk about?"

Pattie took a mouthful of her drink, swallowed, and leaned back against the cushions. "Would you say, in your less than honest opinion, that you were a professional thief, rather than some lucky amateur?"

The question caught him by surprise. "Well, I . . . Er . . ." *What a way to start a conversation! He was good. More than good.* "Yes, I'd say I was very professional."

"Except when you get caught, like now."

Was it just an impression, or did Pattie Tylor remind him of a king cobra, trying to decide where to strike first?

She didn't let him answer, but carried on. "You see, Tony—if I may call you that?"

He nodded, then felt a touch embarrassed for not spotting her hint of sarcasm.

"Okay, Tony it is then. But you see, Tony, in my husband's line of work I've probably been introduced to dozens, possibly hundreds of very crooked businessman over the years."

"You must have been a child bride." *Any port in a storm . . .*

"Well, isn't that sweet—cloyingly so—so do be quiet until I've finished. These men believe themselves to be all powerful. They take what they want, and don't care who gets hurt in the process. I've decided I no longer want to be hurt anymore."

He nearly reached over to comfort her, but then thought better of it.

Instead he leaned back and took a longer sip of his drink. The Bombay Sapphire felt pretty warm on the way down. "So," he coughed into his fist. "Why don't you get a divorce?"

"Divorce? With all the lawyers Constantine has under his thumb? At best I would get less than half of what he'll say he's worth. He wouldn't be Constantine if he hadn't already squirreled away assets and properties via a shell company or two. We might not have slept together for years, but I do know him very intimately when it comes down to money."

"So . . . ?" Mike let it trail off in order to see how she'd react.

"So, I'd like you to kill him for me. That way everything comes to me, the poor grieving widow, regardless."

Mike's confusion was obvious. "Say what now!?"

"Kill him." She adopted a tone of voice she probably used when talking to very young children. "You know, make him deaded for me."

"Are you serious?" For some reason he felt as if reality had just had an earthquake.

"Of course I'm serious. Why else do you think I'm asking you to do it?"

He finished off his drink in a couple of gulps.

Pattie smiled at him. "Look, I'm going to make it easy for you." She picked up the 9 mm automatic from off the coffee table. "This is Constantine's Browning. It's registered to him, and he's flashed it around among friends—even at a dinner party, which was embarrassing in the extreme. So everyone knows he has it." She deftly ejected the magazine. "What everyone doesn't know is that it's only ever been loaded with blanks."

She showed Mike the top, giving him a clear view of the crimped ends—no metal projectiles.

"But why?"

"Because if someone gets to it before he does he's worried they'll shoot him with his own gun. Isn't that deliciously ironic? Being shot with your own gun. And now you have the chance to make that irony come true."

"What? There's no way–"

"Fifty thousand—pounds, not dollars." She stood up and went over to the cocktail cabinet. From behind the chrome shaker she pulled out a plain manila envelope and tossed it over to him. "You can count it if you feel you must. What do they say?" She looked thoughtful. "No honor among thieves?"

Mike didn't open the envelope—it felt satisfyingly weighty—but put it in his inside jacket pocket. He put an arm across the back of the sofa. Fifty large was not to be sniffed at. "So, you want me to shoot him with his own gun?"

"Most certainly." She walked back to him with the magazine carefully held between finger and thumb. "However, I've some 9 mm bullets in my wardrobe. A couple of months ago Constantine and his obsequious little sidekick, Paulo Stichi, took me down to some Country Club shooting range. Apparently it was supposed to be exciting and fun." She made a little scrunch of her lips. "They gave me a box of fifty rounds and basically left me to my own devices, so I divided the ammunition up equally between a Glock 17 and the pockets of my gilet."

She turned and headed for the door into the hall. "I'll go up and load this for you. Make yourself comfortable. Get yourself another drink, or you can pocket the cigarette lighter, you know, to keep your hand in. It's a good one—solid silver and made by Dunhill." Then she headed on up to the master bedroom.

Mike sat back and blew out a long sigh. The money—*oh, boy, the money!*—was very, very tempting. He'd have to adjust his plans, do some surveillance perhaps? Maybe Pattie would give him her husband's itinerary? His thoughts were interrupted by Pattie's return.

"There you are, all nice and deadly." She showed him the top round in the magazine—clean brass, and a small length of steel at the end. She picked up the Browning, then put it back down again.

"You know what?"

Mike was too stunned to reply, so she carried on.

"I think I'll keep this one," she slid the top round out of the magazine and looked at it for a couple seconds before she popped it in her dress pocket. "It'll make a lovely keepsake." Then she pushed the magazine back into the grip of the automatic.

Still aghast at her coldness, he said, "You're really serious about this."

"Of course I am. So, when can you do it? Tomorrow's Saturday, and Monday he's off to Malta, I think. How about Sunday, after church? Constantine is Greek Orthodox, but don't let that hold you back."

Mike shook his head. Things were getting out of his control. He'd come here to do a job, but it certainly wasn't this one.

"Look, something like this will take weeks—maybe months of planning."

Pattie put her hand in her pocket and pulled out a small square of paper. "Here's the address of his . . . Well, I suppose she's his mistress. He sees her every Thursday night." Again the thoughtful pause, then, "An extra twenty-five thousand if you shoot the pair of them when they're in bed together. The papers would love that. Maybe I could sell an exclusive as the first cuckold of spring?"

That had been it for Mike. He stood up from the sofa and snatched the automatic off the coffee table. Pattie stood up, surprise registering on her face. "What's going on?"

"I'm sorry, Mrs. Tylor, but your husband has already given me a payment to kill you. And as you know, Constantine is not a man you cross."

Then he shot her three times in the chest, almost point blank range.

As she dropped to the floor he looked over at her. It was sort of hard to tell where the bullets had entered her body because the watercolour flower design was mostly of bright red poppies.

Miraculously she started to move, putting her hand on the coffee table to help herself up, and Mike immediately pointed the gun at her.

Opening her eyes, she said, "Don't do that again."

In seconds she was back up on her feet. "I never realized how much that wadding would hurt. I know they use blanks in the theater, but even so."

Mike looked at the Browning in his hand, then back at Pattie. "Blanks?" His confusion was back, big time.

She brushed at the front of her dress where the three sooty powder burns were. "Looks like I'm going to have to say goodbye to this nice thing as well, as I can't see the dry cleaners being able to remove much of this. Nice grouping though. You really are a professional at this aren't you."

Mike sat down on the sofa again. "You switched live ammunition for blanks?"

Pattie reached behind the nearest throw cushion and came back up with a simple chrome revolver.

"There, that's better." She remained standing. "The whole thing is loaded with blanks, except for the one I took off the top. Oh," she pointed the revolver at his feet. "That little Walther you have in the ankle holster—the one you were supposed to shoot me with—you can put it on the floor now."

"How did you——"

"Well, Mike—can I call you Mike now? When you're married to an overconfident im-potentate, sometimes you become invisible. Constantine left the receipt for that little pistol under a stack of papers on his desk. That, and the fact I've had one of our bank staff provide me with monthly statements of his accounts—on pain of ritual castration, naturally. That's where I saw the money go out." She transferred the revolver to her left hand and her right danced over the touchscreen of the fitbit. "And now, of course, I have your incriminating confession recorded and uploaded to the Internet somewhere." The revolver returned to her right hand. "Isn't technology a wonderful thing?"

Mike leaned forward as he hitched up his trouser leg—hearing the loud click as Pattie thumbed back the hammer of the revolver. "Be careful how you take it out. Now put it on the floor and kick it over here." She put her shoe on it, then nudged it under the sofa, safely out of reach.

He looked at her. "So all that about killing your husband was a charade?"

"Good heavens yes. Why should I want him dead? He's got far too much earning potential left in him, and with your confession I have the perfect leverage."

"Blackmail?"

"Why Mister Carlisle, blackmail is such an ugly word. I much prefer demanding money with menaces. This recording will keep me in a nice monthly income for at least several decades—maybe more if I can get him to shed some weight and eat more healthily."

"And the money?" Mike's hand moved toward his inside jacket pocket—but Pattie flicked the muzzle of the revolver at him.

"Easy, tiger. No, you can keep the money. There's three thousand, in used notes, and the rest is all movie money—Hollywood jiggery fakery. There should be enough for you to pick up an airline ticket to Europe—though I'd make it several hops to help cover your tracks. As you say, my husband isn't someone you would want to cross, even accidentally. If you hurry, you should be able to make one of the late evening flights."

Mike stood and she followed him down the hall to the front door. Opening it, he walked out of the house, then turned as if to say something.

Looking at her now, he realized that not only was she was a very beautiful woman, but also intelligent, and as hard as a diamond.

He opened his mouth, but she just closed the door in his face. No wonder Constantine had wanted to see the last of her.

---

*The idea for this story, which is the first mystery I have written, just drifted into my mind one day (as all the best stories do). I liked the idea of the assassin sticking to the moral high ground and not falling for her extra inducement to do him in, when he already had a contract. On her.

Ellen Tremiti *studied creative writing and film at Emerson College where she was mentored by DeWitt Henry, memoirist, novelist, and founding editor of* Ploughshares. *Her memoir work produced during this time won an EVVY Award for Outstanding Nonfiction Prose. Upon graduation, she moved to Hollywood and pursued a career in the entertainment industry with reckless abandon. Her prose has appeared in* Alfred Hitchcock Mystery Magazine *and others. Her screenwriting includes a forthcoming action adventure series for ViacomCBS and a mystery TV pilot,* Gumheels, *that landed on Coverfly's Red List in 2021. She balances life as a writer with the bustle of the studio system, working as a script and story supervisor for feature films produced by Warner Bros. and DreamWorks Animation. While lawyers and judges run deep in her family, Tremiti is the first to unravel mysteries for storytelling purposes rather than legal proceedings. She recently completed her first novel. She and her husband, Aaron Waltke, reside in Los Angeles.*

THE INFLUENCER

Ellen Tremiti

1

Carol Clarke knew the light pink envelope carried the weight of her whole world within it. Even as she shuffled through the rest of her mailers, assorted bills, and the latest edition of AARP magazine, the corner of that pink, thick stock envelope poked out, calling out to her. Yelling at her, really. The walk back up her driveway to her California ranch home, as she shaded her eyes from the Altadena sunshine, felt like an eternity.

She dropped the mail onto her dining room table, pretending it meant nothing, and sauntered down the hall to get dressed for the day. Slacks, tucked in button-down shirt on her average frame, white hair pulled back. She looked in the mirror and puffed a little powder on her face and a light brush of mascara. She grabbed her gun holster and badge.

On her way out the door, she stopped and turned back to face the pile of mail. She sighed and relented, sifting out the pink envelope and noting the cute baby stamped on the flap. Clarke knew her daughter, Sam, had ordered the custom stamp with the name Eloise printed boldly beneath it, as if Sam's daughter would be a baby forever and she would always have a use for it.

Clarke tore it open and pulled out the confetti invitation card.

You're invited to Eloise's First Birthday! read the bold font. Below that, the address: the opposite side of the country in Wellesley, Massachusetts.

2

Are you a friend?

Every photo was personal. No matter what body part was featured, there was always the cluttered bedroom behind her. Old Comic-Con lanyards hung from a cheap lamp. Her bookshelf held DVDs, mostly action movies and B-level horror films.

Two discreet-yet-tasteful tattoos, a nose ring, four piercings in each ear, golden red hair, and a fair complexion graced the photos in various ways—a smile and a close-up on cleavage, abs against cotton, nerdy underwear, or nothing at all on Hump Day.

One picture posted daily to her social media accounts had the same message at the very bottom, accompanied by a generic motto: *Stay true to yourself, I love each and every one of you, thanks for being there for me.* Beneath it all, there was always the same question asked by Ginger Kelly.

Are you a friend?

Friends get exclusive access to me. I love everyone who follows me, but if you're a true friend, sign up for my monthly service and get to know me even better!

3

When Clarke walked into the bullpen, she watched the chaos with admiration. Cops bustling. Paperwork shuffling. It was a familiar din that hadn't changed much in her four decades on the force. From her time out on patrol as a rookie catching a peek into this room, to her last thirty years as one of them—first in robbery, then narcotics, then homicide—it always sounded the same. It was the sound of work, a sound she clung to as one of the first female detectives in the precinct.

"Cappuccino?" A newbie named JJ ran over with coffee outstretched in one hand, and Clarke waved him off. He nodded eagerly and skipped over to her desk, setting the coffee down. She worried JJ was a little too slick with his bright smile and need to please, but he'd been growing on her.

She headed straight for her boss's office, cutting right through the familiar sounds, and walked in without knocking.

"Bad time?" Clarke said.

Lieutenant Limon looked up from his computer. "Just the officer I was looking for."

Clarke shut the door and stood behind Limon's extra office chair. They'd known each other long enough that it was almost ritual: Limon would always offer she sit and Clarke would say she preferred to stand. Now, they skipped right past the pleasantries.

"It's time," Clarke said.

"Time for coffee?"

"You know what I mean, Jack."

Limon ran a hand through his sparse hair. "I'd rather we talk about this next year."

"At this rate, we'll never talk about it, and I'll work here until the day I die."

Limon shrugged. "All right by me."

"Most detectives don't stick around this long." Clarke paused. "I have a granddaughter now, and a daughter who needs me."

Limon waved a hand as if to swat the conversation away. "I know."

"It's time for me to retire."

There it was. The words her daughter Sam had said many times over, but she had never said herself.

"Hang up your spurs, collect a fat pension? Is that really you?"

"I wouldn't say it if it wasn't."

Limon eyed her, then rummaged through some files on his desk. "We'll start arrangements. I shouldn't have to say this, but this department won't be the same without you. These rookies, they have more spark getting French roast lattes for the office than they do detective work. But . . . I suppose that's my problem now. In the meantime, I have one last something for you. A favor, really."

Limon held up a file and waited for Clarke to take it.

"Missing person's case. Mother goes to my church."

Clarke opened the file and saw a beautiful, golden-haired young woman staring back at her with a cool, come-hither smirk and a hint of something else. Despair.

4

Clarke spent the first part of the day trying to make sense of Ginger Kelly. She was a minor Internet celebrity with twenty-five thousand Instagram followers and five thousand "friends," or paid subscribers, on her Devil's Darlings private page.

The Devil's Darlings website described itself as a space for alternative beauties and the men who appreciated them. Paid accounts received access to exclusive photos, videos, and first looks at national and international burlesque tours.

Clarke clicked through the site. The alternative pinup models had a mixture of unique tattoos and brightly colored hair, all posing with pouty lips, arched backs, and smoothed, photo-shopped skin. She scrolled to Ginger's page.

Five thousand friends. Clarke could count on one hand how many friends she had. The social media angle was giving her a headache. Maybe she simply ran off with an admirer. Maybe it was sinister. Either way, there was a never-ending list of suspects.

Clarke read over the missing person's report again. Ginger's mother had filed it forty-eight hours earlier: *Did not return*

home after a burlesque performance in downtown Los Angeles at the
Masondrie Hotel. Not typical for her to run away. Helps mother with
medication and chores. No other close family.

Clarke ran a finger over the listed home address for Ginger
Kelly and her mother, Aideen. Mid-City, below the 10 Freeway.
If she hurried, she'd beat the worst of the traffic. Clarke grabbed
her file and hurried out the door.

Mid-City was a small neighborhood by Los Angeles standards,
with most of its housing slapped together over a hundred years ago
by farmers and Old Hollywood hopefuls looking for a new life out
West. One by one, these ramshackle craftsmens would be bought
and flipped, turned into multimillion dollar homes. But still,
strip malls were more common than upscale restaurants. Bars on
windows, yellowed grass, and chain-linked fences commonplace.
Barbed wire sparkled under the LA sun.

The Kellys' home was no exception. It was in desperate need
of a paint job and a termite inspector. Clarke stepped up onto the
porch and knocked. A yippy dog barked, followed by the sound
of a latch being unlocked and then a dead bolt.

A small woman with dyed red hair cracked the door open.
"Can I help you?"

They sat in the living room, a cramped space with dark carpeting and beige walls. Knickknacks everywhere. Clarke pulled
out her notepad and crossed her legs.

"What was Ginger like the last time you saw her?"

"All dressed up for work, wearing my grandmother's emerald
hairpin. Ginger always looks so lovely when she wears it." Aideen
sniffed. "Gave me a kiss on the cheek and she left."

"She seeing anyone?"

"No. Has a lot of admirers though."

"Is it possible she was dating someone and you didn't know it?"

"Do you have children, Detective?" Aideen shifted in her chair.

"One daughter, about Ginger's age."

"Wouldn't you know if your little girl was seein' someone?"

Clarke's daughter had gone off to college across the country,
became pregnant her third year, dropped out, hid this for several
months, broke up with the man, and only then told Clarke.

"Not necessarily," Clarke said.

"Does she live at home?"

"No."

"Ah," Aideen said. "Ginger's always lived with me."

Clarke sensed a bit of judgment. As if my kid's supposed to live with me forever, she thought.

"May I see her room?"

Ginger's room was small with a twin bed and one lone window. Clarke took note of the sci-fi posters, video games scattered on the floor, and framed photos of Ginger in burlesque outfits, all geeky motifs.

"That's kind of her thing," Aideen said. "Classic looks like *Star Wars* and the like."

"Is there anyone she didn't get along with?"

Aideen touched Ginger's desk. "I wouldn't say she has enemies, but I know she doesn't like the Masondrie Hotel manager, where she does those shows a' hers. I think his name is Todd or something like that. But I have to admit, most of the time I don't know who she's talkin' to. Always on her phone, like a little portal to a world I know nothin' about."

Aideen looked around at all her daughter's things. "Detective, please help me. Something's wrong. I know it."

Clarke nodded as she followed her gaze and tried to picture Sam's belongings strewn about in the small room.

5

When Clarke returned home, she ate some leftovers from her fridge, poured herself a whiskey, then poured herself onto the couch. She sat alone, except for the case file waiting quietly across from her.

Lately, she had been feeling extra tired, but Clarke wasn't sure it was age. More like mental fatigue. Sometimes, all she wanted was a bourbon, neat, and to stay in bed all day. She felt like a cop cliché, if cop clichés applied to middle-aged women.

As if on cue, her phone rang. It was Sam.

"Hi, Mom."

Clarke heard Eloise fussing in the background.

"How's the little one?"

"She's moving constantly," Sam said. "How's work?"

Clarke knew that was a loaded question. "I told Limon today."

"Really?" Sam couldn't hide her excitement. "It's about time. You're in your sixties for crying out loud!"

"I am sixty."

"Molly's dad retired at forty-eight."

"I'm not Molly's dad."

"Okay, whatever. Eloise, are you excited?" The baby fussed more in the background. "Did you finally get your invitation to her birthday? We need to book your flight. And I thought afterward, we could look at a couple homes here in Wellesley for you. Just to see what's out there—"

"Sam, I—"

Sam's dreams were simple enough, and the fact that Clarke's throat tightened and a small knot had formed in her stomach made her feel guilty.

"I just picked up a case so I don't know for sure that I can make it. This weekend is cutting it close."

A long pause.

"Mom, you've known about it for months. It's one weekend. You're such a workaholic—"

Clarke could hear the frustration in her voice.

"I want you there," Sam said. "Someone can cover for you. One weekend."

Clarke didn't want to fight with her tonight. "Let's talk again tomorrow. Make plans."

"All right, Mom. Love you."

"I love you t—" But the call had already ended.

Clarke opened her laptop. She pored over Ginger's Instagram, taking note of the online comments. It was an odd mix of positive and positively offensive. She clicked on a photo of Ginger dressed for a performance and zoomed in on her updo. A large, emerald green hairpin adorned the side of her head. It sparkled under the stage lights.

Clarke didn't want online accounts of her own, but she had them. Sam showed her how, so she forced herself to post on her Instagram to her sixteen followers—usually photos of her garden, or perhaps a special occasion, like her sixtieth birthday or a holiday party at the precinct. She at least had to try, as Sam put it, to "stay in the know." But really, it only made her feel more disconnected from people. She didn't get it the way Sam or Ginger did. And yet, it was often the only way to see photos of her granddaughter, Eloise. And that was reason enough to keep the accounts.

Clarke hit refresh on her newsfeed and did a double take.

There it was.

A new photo posted from the screen name GingerKelly42.

PICTURE ONE

Letters cut from a magazine and pasted onto a sheet of paper, spelling out: "Here is Ginger's belongings. Pictures to follow."

6

"Inhale. Palms up, facing each other. Lean into the lunge . . . and breathe."

Clarke forced herself to go to six-thirty A.M. senior yoga at least twice per week at Savasana Yoga House. When she first set foot in this class and surveyed the gray-haired crowd, she felt extra old, a little embarrassed, and out of place.

"And bring your arms down into Warrior Two."

She liked the name of the yoga studio, at first. Savasana sounded relaxing, as most yoga positions do. When she realized the term meant "final relaxation" and literally translated to "corpse pose," her opinion changed. She was surrounded by death all the time. She didn't need a yoga studio named after it.

"Now, in your own way, find Savasana."

The death pose did feel great though. Lying flat on her back, feeling all the tension release from her spine and back muscles, seemingly melting into the floor, Clarke closed her eyes. She had to admit, she did belong here, and she was a grandmother, for God's sake.

Her mind went to Ginger Kelly—milky features against a black background—and then she heard the words in a voice that was not her own:

Are you a friend?

Clarke drew in a sharp breath and opened her eyes. Her heart jump-started, skipping a beat, thumping against her chest.

After class, she threw her hair up in a bun and headed to the office where she spent her morning going over phone records.

Triangulation of Ginger's cell phone led to a general area near the Masondrie Hotel as her last known location, but the phone had since died or been switched off. Clarke guessed the newest picture that was posted to her account—A threat? A taunt?—was from another device.

"Hello, JJ," Clarke said. She felt his presence looming behind her, waiting for the right moment to speak.

"Hey-yo!" he said. "Got your IP address that accessed Ginger's IG account."

Clarke turned and took the paper from him. "Thank you."

"Ya know, you need a subpoena to get the ISP to connect it to a physical address."

"I know that, JJ."

Sam taught Clarke that what JJ was doing was called "mansplaining." One of the many hilarious new words Sam had taught her. They were hilarious not only because they sounded silly, but because they created terms for things Clarke hadn't even realized she needed. Now she couldn't believe she went most of her life without them.

"Want me to help with that?" JJ asked.

"Nah. If you want, you can dig into Ginger's life. Workplace, schedule, et cetera. Let me know if you turn up anything useful. I *will* take a second coffee though, if you don't mind."

JJ paused, then smiled. "You got it, boss!"

Clarke sipped her coffee as she rolled her aging Honda Civic off the freeway and into the heart of downtown Los Angeles.

Downtown was the only place in LA that looked like a proper city. There were skyscrapers, a slew of courthouses, and iconic architecture of brazen steel, stone, and ironwork, like the Disney Concert Hall and the Bradbury Building. Despite its charms, however, downtown was still rough around the edges and oddly deserted at night.

It certainly had a dark history too. Clarke knew it well. The hotels in particular—poisonings, elevator accidents, suicides, unexplained deaths, ghost stories, and murderers in the room next door were commonplace over the last century, not to mention adulterous couples, prostitution, and drug smuggling. There was the haunted Cecil Hotel, where it seemed more residents checked in than ever checked out. And the glamorous Biltmore, which held the Academy Awards in the thirties and forties before it became known as the last sighting of murder victim Elizabeth Short, forever immortalized by another name: the Black Dahlia. Not to mention Hotel Barclay, which was killing ground for not one but *two* serial killers, slaying innocents in different decades in the same building: Otto Stephen Wilson and Vaughn Orrin Greenwood, aka the Skid Row Slasher.

Clarke had grown up hearing these stories, and after shaking off the horror of it all, they always fascinated her. It was as if these infamous crimes were somehow larger than life, like something out of a Hitchcock movie rather than history books.

It was partly why she became a cop.

Clarke approached the front desk of the Masondrie Hotel. The lobby was quite large. Sputnik chandeliers hung down from the vaulted ceiling, their dozens of thin crystal arms shooting out in all directions. Floor-to-ceiling windows along one wall let in a flood of light that splashed against the white marble floors and teak furniture.

She flashed her badge to a smiling receptionist.

"I'm looking for the hotel manager. Todd?"

"Oh . . . yes." The woman turned pale. She picked up a phone. "One moment."

A few minutes passed and then a booming, pleasant voice rang out.

"Hello! Welcome!"

The man was well-dressed, from his slicked hair down to his polished shoes. He was in an expensive-looking suit, though he looked rather young. Late thirties, Clarke guessed. He walked like he owned the place.

"Hello. Detective Clarke," she said. "Are you Todd?"

The man smiled. "No, I believe you're looking for Toriq Johnson. No Todd here. Toriq manages all our live entertainment, but doesn't come in until five. I'm happy to show you around in the meantime. I'm Laurent La Mener, the proprietor of the Masondrie Hotel."

So he does own the place, thought Clarke.

As they sauntered the hotel halls, Laurent gestured to various paintings and filigrees.

"Many of the touches throughout the hotel are original. The Masondrie was built in 1962 by my grandfather. For this area, that's relatively new. Most hotels around here were built in the twenties. They're more famous, you know. The Biltmore, for one—they've got an Academy dining room and Black Dahlia cocktail special. We can't compete! But even though the Masondrie has stayed under the radar, we've built up a reputation mostly by word-of-mouth."

Clarke admired the muraled ceiling.

"In '68, my grandfather had a French artist do the ceilings in the Baroque style. To imitate the competition."

Laurent led Clarke outside, around the manicured swimming area. The large lima bean pool certainly reminded Clarke of the 1960s.

Laurent pulled a pack of cigarettes and a lighter out of a jacket pocket.

"Would you like one?"

"No, thank you. I quit years ago."

Laurent nodded. "I'm sure I will—at some point."

They left the courtyard and stopped in front of a restaurant covered entirely in mahogany and heavy drapery.

"Obviously, we are very concerned when any of our employees is involved in any kind of . . . disturbing situation. We want her found safely and we are happy to help in any way we can. We just hope we can count on your discretion."

"Understood," Clarke said. "We will need security camera footage as soon as possible."

Laurent nodded. "Of course. Please stay for a late lunch. Tell them it's on me."

7

Clarke finished her plate of endive salad and sparkling water. Slowly, she noticed the entire vibe of the restaurant change. Music came on, lights dimmed, and more bartenders showed up, followed by a steady trickle of new patrons. She left the restaurant. Happy hour had begun.

Clarke asked around and found the entrance to the theater, which had modest seating and VIP tables in front. A handful of stagehands, dressed in black, ran back and forth across the stage with sparkly, fluffy, feathery props. Clarke walked backstage and down a hallway, fully expecting to be stopped by someone, but wasn't. She passed a few doors, then reached one that said, "Manager." Before she could knock, a man opened the door carrying a large box in his arms.

"Are you Toriq Johnson?"

The man nodded toward the office. "In there."

Clarke stepped inside the brick-walled space. It was tiny with no windows. Props strewn about. Toriq stood behind his desk going through papers. His sports jacket barely fit over his thick arms and square frame. Underneath, he wore a plain T-shirt with a gold chain that hung from his tanned skin.

"They told me you'd be stopping by," he said, briskly. "Ginger skipped out on us last couple nights."

"When she performed on Saturday, did anything seem out of the ordinary?"

"Not to me. One of the girls might be able to tell you more. They're not the brightest, but you're welcome to talk to 'em."

Clarke didn't respond.

"Yeah," Toriq cleared his throat. "They get ready down the hall."

"Did she seem like the type to run away?"

"No idea. She didn't hang after the shows. Me and the girls, we all get drinks. But not her." He shrugged.

Can't imagine why, thought Clarke.

"I'll go talk to some of the women."

"Knock yourself out."

In the staging area, a few dancers sat at makeup stations. Bright bulbs lit up their faces as they applied their blush and eyeliner. Clarke noticed one woman's vanity was a mess. Powder, blush, and glitter covered her mirror like a fine blood mist. In the corner, a bent photo of her and Ginger stuck out beneath a name scribbled in lipstick: Rowan Rodriguez. Clarke walked over and introduced herself.

"I can't believe she's . . . missing," Rowan sighed. She applied heavy eyeliner around her eyes, but Clarke could see right through to her black pupils. When their eyes met, she looked concerned. "She hasn't talked to me at all or answered any of my texts. Do the cops know what's up with that creepy Instagram post?"

"Can't comment on an ongoing investigation. Sorry," Clarke said. "Did she talk about going away? Start somewhere new?"

"No more than the rest of us."

"Is she seeing anyone?"

"Sort of," Rowan paused. "There's a guy who likes her a lot. Runs a comic book shop and comes to our shows. I think his name is Randy. His store is called Parallel Dimension. He always calls her 'his muse.'"

"Anything else come to mind? Places she talked about visiting?"

"She was here for a reason," Rowan gestured, indicating she meant more than the Masondrie, more than Downtown LA. Perhaps she meant all of Hollywood. "Be a star," she shrugged. "Like her idol, Kitty June. She's performing tonight, you know."

"Is that a big deal?"

"Oh, yeah," Rowan said, as if this was obvious. "You gotta see her act. You're staying for it, right?"

Clarke sat in her seat, waiting for the show to begin. She refreshed her phone and saw another photo posted to Ginger Kelly's IG account.

PICTURE TWO

A photo of Ginger's birth certificate and license.

8

The lights dimmed, music cued, and out popped a curvaceous, bubbly, blond woman. She had cellulite on her thighs, which surprised Clarke. She thought only the thinnest, sleekest women would be hired for burlesque. Women like Ginger Kelly. But as the woman moved with coy charm and confidence, she realized how wrong she had been. This first performer had a storyline, something about baking muffins, a housewife motif. It was funny, actually, like a scandalous comedy routine that ended with her wearing nothing but an apron.

This was followed by a black widow act, a woman drenched in faux diamonds, and then Rowan as a flamenco dancer. Rowan moved gracefully, balancing huge feathers that flopped high over her head. By the end of her act, the only feathers left were the tiny ones covering her breasts, revealing tattoos and a scar down the center of her chest.

The performers had an unapologetic attitude mixed with something she felt Sam would call "body positivity." Burlesque reminded Clarke of Old Hollywood. Of her favorite black-and-white films, movies she watched with her own mother. It gave her a feeling of nostalgia that she wanted to hold on to and never let go. It all felt very Los Angeles, and this was her home.

All at once, she thought of Sam. Sam wanted her to be someone without roots, with only her to cling to. Sam meant everything to her, but Clarke worried her daughter believed retirement would turn her into the grandma who wears an apron and bakes cookies, then sits and reads the local newspaper in front of a fire—an unironic version of domesticity that the burlesque dancer so easily mocked on stage. She worried that would never be her.

"Ladies and gentlemen, we have a special treat for you tonight," a hidden emcee announced, who sounded suspiciously like Toriq. "She's been all over the world on an international tour, dazzling thousands, and now she's back to perform for you all, *Miss Kitty June!*"

The stage went black and Kitty's footsteps sounded as she took the stage. Click, click, click. A quiet, pregnant pause and a spotlight lit up her poised figure. She was on the floor in the most balletic, elegant pose. Legs crossed, back arched, one knee up, hand hung over her head of dark, curled hair. A shawl of black lace with pointy ends, like a spiderweb, hung around her.

Her music was soft and ominous. For the first few bars, she looked like a statue until she moved in swift, purposeful arcs. The lace slid off her shoulders. She used her knee-high hose as props, pulling the silky fabric off her feet with so much show, Clarke was impressed. She felt the electricity in the air.

Smoke filled the stage and Kitty, her back to the audience, seemed to slip into the fog and disappear, only to materialize moments later, her spiderweb shawl held out in front of her. With a Matador's swoosh she flung the lace away, revealing that she had somehow slipped out of her black unitard and was now wearing vintage-inspired undergarments, garter belt, and pointed bra.

Instead of skipping off stage, Kitty bowed to her audience and exited with a whoosh of her spiderweb. The crowd exploded in applause.

9

The next day, a small package arrived with hours of security footage saved onto a flash drive. The Masondrie Hotel had forty cameras, including ones on either end of each of the sixteen floors. She told JJ to focus on the main floor and find the moment Ginger left the hotel after her shift. In the meantime, Clarke submitted paperwork for the IP address subpoena and got back into her car.

Parallel Dimension Comics was located in a strip mall in Van Nuys. In an area known as the Valley, a wide plain north of the Santa Monica Mountains, overlooked by historic Mulholland Drive, Van Nuys was most known for being affordable, especially compared to the mansions in Brentwood and Bel-Air.

Clarke took off her sunglasses and hung them on her button-down shirt. There was nothing glamorous about this location. Some of the stores' lettering was missing and the parking lot was cracked from the summer heat. The Parallel Dimension sign looked new, though, and Clarke took note of the store's tidy exterior.

A bell jingled as she entered the store. Rows of foldout tables lined the back wall where dozens of people were occupied, playing some sort of card game involving miniatures. Clarke strolled over to them, watching them midgame. They were immersed, and no one paid attention to her until she asked for Randy and flashed her badge. Randy was a tall man with long hair pulled back into a ponytail. He struggled to slip out of his bench seat.

They stepped into a corner of the store, in an aisle surrounded on either side by comic books. When Clarke mentioned Ginger, Randy's face paled.

"I heard she's missing," he said. "Crazy about those Instagram posts of hers, huh?"

"When's the last time you saw her?"

"At least a week ago. At another one of her shows—the Speak-easy Showcase, on Vermont? She does it every week. She's a muse of mine, see?"

Randy pushed aside some comics on a shelf and pulled one out that had a ginger-haired woman on the cover. She looked like a mix between a superhero and a figure skater.

"This is a trade from my indie press. We sell mostly online. E-books, Patreon. But I always keep a few copies in-store."

"You pay her for something like that?"

"No pay, just exposure." He pointed to the cover, as if Clarke needed further explanation.

"And where were you Saturday night?"

"Mayhem Fair in Pasadena. I had a booth Saturday and Sunday."

Randy pulled self-consciously at his ponytail.

"Do you have any documentation, tickets from the festival, anyone who can vouch for you?"

"Sure." Randy went behind the cash register and pulled out a Mayhem Fair badge. "I'll give you a list of people I know who stopped by my booth."

"Has Ginger contacted you in any way since Saturday?"

"No." He shook his head like a kid in class who was accused of cheating. "I promise you, she hasn't."

"How would you characterize your relationship?"

"Well," he grabbed at his ponytail again. This time, he pulled out the elastic and started putting it back up right away. "I obviously like her style, her vibe, her talent. Um . . . I'd say we're friends."

"But you wanted more?"

Randy turned red. "I don't know. Sometimes with a muse it's better not to break the illusion."

Clarke noticed a flat-screen TV behind the cash register displaying what looked like a Twitter feed. She did a double take. Front and center was a homemade missing person's poster of Ginger Kelly.

"What's that?" Clarke said.

"Oh, I run the comic book shop's RSS feed. Sometimes I play eighties movies."

"That poster for Ginger . . ." Clarke squinted. "*One hundred thousand 'likes,'* am I reading that right?"

"Yeah, I retweeted it from Alexis Matthews," Randy said.

"And Alexis Matthews is . . . ?"

"Big," Randy said. "Online, I mean. Oh, she's got a stage name too. Kitty June."

10

Clarke drove into the Hollywood Hills. The road wound back and forth, around and around, like a drunk snake. Finally, she pulled into the short driveway and admired the clean, well-kept front yard and midcentury modern architecture. Kitty's home didn't look very big, but Clarke knew bungalows like this one cost millions.

After she rang the doorbell, it only took a moment before Kitty came to the front door. She had on a silk robe.

Of course she has on a silk robe, thought Clarke.

Kitty made Clarke tea and they settled in at her kitchen table. Her hair curled around her, fluffy and dark. She had a full face of makeup on, almost like she was hiding behind it.

"So, Detective, my online poster worked? You're giving Ginger the attention she deserves?" Her voice was soft, melodic, and Clarke wasn't sure if she was putting it on.

"Actually, Miss . . . do you prefer June or Matthews?"

"Kitty is fine."

"Your post only made things a little more complicated. I'm here to learn what you know about her."

Kitty shrugged and her curls slid over one shoulder. "I just know she's missing. We're all a community out here. Most of us came from nothing, bought a one-way bus ticket, and showed up to make our way to stardom. We have to look out for each other. It's the least I can do."

Kitty smiled in an encouraging way, as if to say, *I'm just here to help.*

"Did Ginger mention anything to you, places she wanted to go, people she wanted to go away with? I'm trying to fully understand what Ginger wanted."

"Well, it's about wanting it all, you know? I started out trying to be an actress. I was a production assistant, a movie and television extra, I even interned at an agency, can you believe that?"

Clarke wasn't sure if she could or couldn't believe it. It sort of made all the sense in the world. Every year, hundreds, no, thousands of young people moved to Hollywood with their heads full of dreams, trying to wedge a foot into an industry's door that was more like a steel trap. If they could stick it out long enough, move from one low-level job to another, they just might find their own spot in it all. That, or they'd pack their bags and move back where they came from.

"Hollywood beat me down. Misogynistic cesspool," Kitty said grimly. "You know what they say. Fool me once, shame on you, fool me twice, shame on me."

"I'm not sure I follow," Clarke said.

"Oh, I was screwed over in my youth like everybody. But instead of giving up, I started booking shows all over the city. I had a blog right when they were becoming 'the thing to do.' I built up a cult following all on my own. Now, brands endorse me. I sell merchandise just by posting a photo with it. I made it . . . on my own."

Clarke had to give Kitty credit for that—sticking it out, finding her own crack in the door.

"Do you consider yourself an actress now, or a dancer, or a model, or—"

"Well, above all else, I'm an *influencer.*"

Clarke stared at Kitty, not comprehending. "Which means . . . ?"

"A social media influencer." Kitty pulled out her phone and showed it to Clarke. "See? Three million souls, all following *moi.* I sway their taste in art, fashion, makeup, fitness, even just motivation. I guide their lives, their identities, what they buy, how they think."

"I didn't know that was a job."

"A lot of people make a good living that way. It's all about becoming an expert in your field, or at least a popular one. It's about a persona, a narrative that you build for yourself and put out into the world. That's what I try to teach the girls, anyway."

"Anything else? Is there anyone who would want to hurt Ginger?"

"Not that I know of. I'm sorry I'm not more help, Detective."

An influencer. Clarke studied Kitty, who didn't seem to mind her gaze. Here was a woman selling products and dreams to anyone who would listen. She seemed open, but there was a hardness in her eyes, a wall behind the makeup. Perhaps it was the look of someone who really had made it on their own. As Clarke let herself out and said goodbye, she wondered who Kitty would be if she had a regular job, somewhere in the middle of America, but had trouble picturing it.

While snaking back through the Hollywood Hills, Clarke's phone buzzed.

"Hey-yo!"

"Hi, JJ," Clarke said. She was tired and not in the mood for his enthusiasm.

"Check it. Your IP address came in. Someone accessed Ginger's account at an Internet cafe near Kester and Vanowen."

"That's . . ." Clarke paused. "Van Nuys."

"Yep. Aren't you up there now?"

"Could you look up a residential address for me?"

11

Clarke pulled into Randy's apartment complex when her phone rang again.

"Mom, I know it's late but I haven't heard from you—"

"Sorry, Sam—"

"I found a red-eye flight for tomorrow night. Really decent price. What do you think?"

Clarke thought she saw a dark figure walk down a side alley toward the back of the complex. Was that Randy? A neighbor?

"I think . . . it sounds fine."

"We're really running out of time. You can pay me back—"

The figure disappeared behind the building. *Two days. Forty-eight hours.*

"Okay," Clarke said. "Book it."

Clarke noticed the complex didn't have a working security door. She walked inside and headed up the open-air stairs to Randy's apartment and pounded on it.

"Randy, open up! It's Detective Clarke."

No answer.

She banged again and to her surprise, the door came slightly ajar. Clarke pushed it open and stepped inside. She noticed a disheveled living room. She unsnapped her gun holster and surveyed a small, dark hallway.

Clarke walked across the carpeted floor, toward a light emanating from up ahead. She turned a corner and there, in the linoleum kitchen, was Randy's body, slumped against his fridge and lower cabinets. His back to Clarke. Red splatter flung across the kitchen cabinets. Ponytail soaked in blood.

Later, a crime scene photographer snapped pictures and a few deputies milled around, booties on their feet. A forensic tech held up a plastic baggie.

"Looks like molly, cocaine, assorted amphetamines. He has a stash. Weed too."

Clarke sighed. Randy hadn't told her he dealt drugs.

"Thanks," she said.

Clarke looked around and noticed an empty mug on the kitchen counter, tea bag inside. She stared at it, then stepped over to the microwave and using her sleeve as a barrier, popped open the door, revealing another mug. It looked like Randy had company.

"Think suicide's a possibility?" A deputy asked.

"No," Clarke said and shut the microwave door.

PICTURE THREE

Faded business cards and an address book with the initials MH on the cover.

12

Clarke was officially exhausted. She'd barely slept, and in the early morning hours, half-awake, she'd packed a bag for her weekend trip to see Sam and Eloise. It sat, waiting for her, in the trunk of her car.

In the bullpen, Clarke looked at a board with a timeline of events, Instagram posts, and pictures of everyone she had interviewed, when she heard someone approach behind her.

"What is it, JJ?" Clarke said without turning around.

"It's me, Detective."

Clarke turned to face the feminine voice.

Kitty was dressed in a khaki trench coat. Her curled hair pulled back with a head scarf.

"I need to speak with you."

Clarke led Kitty out of the bullpen. She could feel dozens of eyes watching them. They entered an interrogation room and sat at a metal table.

"So?"

"I know you probably don't like me," Kitty said.

"What does that matter, if I like you or not?"

"In my line of work, it matters a lot, but I want you to know, I was only trying to help."

"Help who? Ginger?"

"Yes."

"Help her do what?"

"Don't police say there's three types of motive? Money, sex, greed. There's certainly a fourth, Detective."

"And what's that?"

"Fame," Kitty said. "I suppose it's tied into money, but it's more than that. I had nothing, and now I have everything I ever dreamed of . . . and people *love* me. I just wanted that for the other girls too."

Clarke remained poised but instinctively glanced at the two-way mirror. Then carefully asked, "So what did you do?"

Kitty took a breath and fiddled with her head scarf.

"I told Ginger if she disappeared for a few days, I'd promote her missing poster online. She'd get a cult following, and we could drum up interest. Once she came back, she could use whatever story she wanted to help build her narrative. Your narrative's important, you know. It's how your fans understand you—how they *connect*."

"You're saying you and Ginger faked her disappearance to boost her Twitter numbers?" Clarke felt her ears burn.

"Yes, I am saying that."

"Do you know Randy Cohen is dead?"

"That's why I'm here. I heard about it through the Devil's Darlings. Something is wrong. I had nothing to do with that."

"Where is Ginger?"

"That's the other thing . . . I don't know. She was supposed to be staying at a motel down in Torrance, but I checked on her and she's not there. And those Instagram pictures. We didn't talk about that. I thought she was going overboard, but now," Kitty paused. "I don't think it's her."

"So you helped orchestrate her fake kidnapping, and now you're saying someone actually kidnapped her?"

"I don't know. It was supposed to be a simple plan . . . but—"
Kitty paused.

"I can only help if you tell me the whole truth."

Kitty took a breath, pressed her red lips together. "Toriq runs
an escort business out of the back of the Masondrie. Peddles
pills on the side with Randy. I think maybe she got mixed up in
something she shouldn't have."

"Excuse me."

Clarke exited the interview room and joined Limon behind a
two-way mirror.

"Do you believe this?"

"Maybe I'm getting too old for this job too," Limon said.

"I'm supposed to get on a plane tonight to see my daughter."

"Go," he said. "This is the best lead we've got. We'll check out
the motel and talk to Toriq. I'll cover for you. Let me do this.
We'll see you Monday."

Clarke watched Kitty through the two-way mirror. She sat like
a statue, unmoving, hands folded across her lap.

13

At Los Angeles International Airport, Clarke pushed her way
through the crowd to get to the check-in kiosks. She shouldered
her bags and headed toward security when her phone rang. Clarke
shuffled her items around.

"Detective Clarke," she said.

"Clarke, hey!" It was the unmistakable voice of JJ. "I did some
research on Ginger and the Masondrie like you asked. Found
something I thought might be useful."

"Limon's covering for me this weekend."

"Oh . . . sorry. Should I call him?"

Clarke checked her watch. "You have two minutes. Go."

"Cool, so the most interesting thing I found is that the hotel's
taken out a bunch of loans. It's failing, big time. The owners are
up to their eyeballs in debt."

"And?"

"Well, that's it. I thought maybe—"

"There's actually been some developments that point in a different direction. Limon has it under control, okay?"

"All good. Thanks for hearing me out. Oh, and I combed through the security videos. Couldn't find her leaving the hotel."

"All right. Thanks, JJ."

Clarke hung up. She put her phone away and stepped up to security. They waved her through the first checkpoint. She stood in the long line, edging forward step by step, but couldn't help thinking about Kitty June.

Kitty tried to make Ginger famous by faking her own kidnapping. Maybe someone knew their plan and used it against Ginger, but why? Was it really all about fame?

Of course it was.

It hit Clarke so hard it felt like a slap in the face.

PICTURE ONE

Letters cut from a magazine and pasted onto a sheet of paper: "Here is Ginger's belongings. Pictures to follow."

PICTURE TWO

A photo of Ginger Kelly's birth certificate and license.

PICTURE THREE

Faded business cards and an address book with the initials MH on the cover.

Clarke fumbled with her phone and opened a browser. She typed in "The Black Dahlia" and waited as the search bar loaded. She clicked on the first article that popped up.

The Black Dahlia went missing on January 9th, 1947 after her married lover dropped her off at the Biltmore Hotel in downtown Los Angeles. She was found, brutally murdered, six days later in a vacant lot in Leimert Park.

Clarke skimmed down to Evidence.

Evidence mailed to police days after her body was discovered was nearly identical to Ginger's Instagram posts: license, birth certificate, journal, the cut out letters, the message: "Here is Dahlia's belongings. Letter to follow."

"Next!" A security guard yelled.

Clarke handed her ticket and license over.

How many days was the Black Dahlia missing before she was found? Clarke put her items on the conveyor belt. Six days. Clarke counted in her head. Ginger had been missing for . . .

Six days.

She made it through security. Put her shoes back on and grabbed her bags. Gate sign to her right, exit sign to her left. There was no time to contemplate. She had to make a choice.

"Damn it," Clarke said and ran for the exit.

It took an hour to get from LAX to Brentwood, next to Bel-Air. Feels like a long shot but I have to be sure, Clarke thought as she pulled up to a gated driveway. The doors swung inward. Just as she parked in the roundabout, her phone buzzed.

Clarke was surprised to see a message from Limon:

Hey, Clarke! We found Ginger's clothing in Toriq's office. Matches the clothes she was wearing the night she disappeared. And get this, an IP address ID just came in for one of those posts . . . matches Toriq's smartphone. We'll keep the pressure on him to confess until you get back. Have a safe flight! We could not have done this without you.

14

Clarke slumped her shoulders. She had done what Sam told her not to do, what Sam told her she "always does." She put the job ahead of her personal life, ahead of the people who mattered the most to her in this whole world, and she didn't have to. Limon had it under control. She looked over and saw Laurent standing in his front doorway, a puzzled expression on his face. Clarke sighed and got out of her car.

"Laurent! Hello," she called out, sheepishly.

"Hello, Detective! Please come in. I heard Toriq's been arrested. Didn't know I'd get a personal visit from the police about it."

Clarke stepped inside the mansion and was met with marble floors, a cathedral ceiling, and a spiraling wooden banister.

"As you said, you wanted discretion, so I thought it would be best to go over what's happening directly with you," she lied.

Laurent led her into a study with high windows and lots of light.

"Would you care for a drink?" he asked, motioning to a liquor cabinet.

"Sure," Clarke said. "Scotch or whiskey. One of those days." One drink to settle her nerves and get her ready to call Sam and tell her what she had done.

Laurent poured two drinks and handed one to Clarke. She sipped it. The afterburn of the scotch was smooth and comforting. And obviously expensive.

"Thank you," she said. "I'd love a water as well."

"Of course."

Laurent left and reemerged with a glass of water. They sat on a Victorian couch, soft green velvet with dark wood trim.

"I have to admit, Detective. I always thought Toriq was trouble, but he got people in seats for shows, so . . ." Laurent shrugged. "I never thought he'd be capable of something like this."

"Did employees ever complain about him?"

"Not that I'm aware. I'm going to conduct a thorough investigation into our reporting procedures."

Clarke finished her scotch and picked up her water.

"Do you think Ginger is still alive?" Laurent asked.

"I really can't say. Catching Toriq is the best development we could've hoped for." Clarke finished her water and stood up. "Any other questions for me? Otherwise, I really must be going. I, well, I may have a plane to catch."

"You live a very spontaneous life."

Clarke walked toward the doorway and admired the heavy gold and green decor.

"I really appreciate you coming all the way out here," Laurent said.

"It's the least I can do," Clarke said.

Next to the doorway was a stone fireplace with a large impressionistic painting hung above it. On the end of the mantle sat a framed photo of the Masondrie Hotel. It looked like it had been taken in the 1960s. Next to it, on the edge of the mantle closest to Clarke, sat an emerald green hairpin. It glimmered under the evening light.

Clarke stopped. It took her half a second to process that this was Ginger's hairpin. Clarke reached for her gun and spun around just in time for a vase to come crashing into her forehead and nose, knocking her backward, off her feet. She hit the ground with a crash and a thud before fading into blackness.

15

Clarke's first thought was: No one will be looking for me for hours. She was on a plane to Massachusetts as far as anyone was concerned. Stupid. She should have told Sam, or Limon, or heck, even JJ. Her head pounded and she felt cool concrete beneath her. She let her eyes adjust to the greenish light.

There was a kitchenette on one side of the windowless room and an industrial shower stall on the other. Straight ahead of her was what looked like a dentist chair with . . . Clarke squinted.

A figure that looked like a woman. Small feet and wrists held down by something, perhaps zip ties or rope. Drip, drip, drip. Blood dripped over the sides of the chair, by the woman's ears, pooling on the floor.

"Ginger?" Clarke said.

A moan but no words.

Clarke felt her own bindings. Something like twine. They were connected to a metal ring in the wall.

A computerized lock whirled and the door clanked. Laurent looked just as he had in the Masondrie. Full suit, energetic expression, although now Clarke saw right through his friendly facade.

"Detective Clarke, how are you feeling?"

"What have you done to her?"

"The beginnings of her transformation. Let's say, her smile is a little wider now."

"The Glasgow smile. Same as the Black Dahlia. Why?" Clarke said. She was seething, angry—but she had to keep him talking.

Laurent paced the small room. He delicately took off his jacket and laid it on the kitchenette counter.

"The Masondrie has faded from the public eye. Our occupancy keeps declining. We need something big to put us on the map, something shocking that will make our hotel unforgettable like the others," Laurent said. "Just like in the good ol' days."

He fiddled with instruments, inspecting them one by one. "It hit me, late one night when I overheard Ginger and Kitty discussing their plans. See, the Biltmore draws crowds from all over, without a dime of advertising. They come for the history and its true claim to fame—a copycat killing now will do the same for the Masondrie. It'll be a media feeding frenzy. In this day and age, people will never stop talking about it . . . all thanks to this woman right here." He gestured at Ginger.

I should have gotten on that plane, Clarke thought. I could be hundreds of miles from this nightmare if only I had gotten on that plane. But just as quickly, she had another thought. Ginger doesn't deserve to die alone like this. This was Clarke's case. She belonged here. This was what she signed up for all those years ago.

But she didn't want to leave Sam and Eloise. She had to bury the hurt, to keep it from clouding her mind. She hoped they would understand. She hoped they would be proud of her. She hoped—

"People are looking for me," Clarke said. "My cell phone will lead them right here."

"Sure. That's where I've been. Driving your car and phone all over and then back to your place. That's where you're going to be found."

"Murdered in my home?"

"Suicide, actually."

"I don't think you've thought this through," Clarke said.

"On the contrary, I've thought this through very much."

Laurent moved toward Ginger, scalpel in hand.

"How did you frame Toriq?" Clarke said, quickly.

He paused.

"He's an idiot. Running drugs and pimping burlesque dancers in my hotel for years. All I had to do was take his phone, log into her account with a reset password, post the photos, and plant her clothing in his office. You know, I'm glad you came. It feels good to get this off my chest."

"You killed Randy. He must've figured out—"

"Came by to see Toriq after you visited him, caught me planting evidence. Said he wouldn't say anything, but I know he's obsessed with Ginger. In fact, I toyed with framing *him* . . . but not after he saw me. Couldn't leave any loose ends."

Laurent stepped over to Ginger. Clarke felt her entire body tense but there was nothing she could do. He slipped a hand around Ginger's neck and ran the scalpel along her jawline.

"I'll be back," he said.

Clarke watched him punch in a number on a keypad, but she couldn't tell what it was. Then he was gone.

Patience. That's what she needed right now. And a little luck. Clarke counted to ten. She listened. Nothing.

Clarke eyed Laurent's jacket sitting on top of the counter. She slid her arms under her feet, bringing her hands in front of her. She stretched herself out as far as she could and kicked the kitchenette cabinets. The clang shook them slightly.

The coat slid forward a little bit. Again, Clarke kicked the cabinets. They shook, and the corner of the jacket sleeve dropped over the edge.

Clarke stretched out on her back. *Corpse pose.* She hoped those years of senior yoga wouldn't let her down now. She reached a foot up. The toe of her loafer barely touched the sleeve. She tried to grip it against the countertop and slide it downward. Her foot slipped.

"Damn," she said.

This time, she reached with both feet and tried to pinch the jacket's corner between her two shoes. Clarke exhaled as her arms twisted over her at an awkward angle, body fully stretched out. *Pull.*

The jacket came down with a delicate whoosh. Now, for the moment of truth. With her hands still bound, she rummaged through the pockets, looking for . . .

"Yes!" she said.

His lighter, except it was not a lighter like before. It was a matchbook from the Masondrie Hotel. MH imprinted in gold across it.

Clarke sat up and held the book in one hand. She pressed a match against the striking strip. Nothing. Clarke took a breath and tried again. The light sizzled and glowed. She held the match under the twine that connected her bindings to the wall. Slowly, it began to burn.

She did it, again and again. That's when she heard it. A sound like footsteps. Clarke redoubled her efforts. She lit another match and another. The footsteps approached the door. She was out of time. With a mighty jerk she yanked her wrists apart and the twine snapped off at the burn point.

Clarke jumped to her feet, ran to the instruments, grabbed a small knife, then hid to the side of the door. The mechanical lock whirled and the door opened.

As soon as Laurent stepped inside, Clarke swung the knife as hard as she could, right into his neck. She twisted and pulled, hoping she hit the jugular. Laurent sputtered in surprise and dropped to the ground. Clarke leaned over him, by his ear.

"Don't worry, Laurent. You and your hotel will be very famous."

Clarke stepped over to Ginger and cut through one of her bindings. Ginger looked at her with a mixture of horror and fatigue. Her eyes widened and she moaned. Before Clarke could react, she was struck hard from behind. She stumbled sideways into a concrete wall. Clarke turned and kicked at Laurent, who was wobbly on his feet, blood soaking into his expensive shirt. He fell to one knee and Clarke kicked him in the chest. Laurent tumbled backward, followed by the sounds of choking, his lungs filling with blood. His legs twitched and then he went still.

Clarke felt nauseous. She touched the back of her head. It felt wet and warm. She kept her eyes on Laurent, willing herself to stay awake until she was sure he was dead. But she couldn't keep her eyes open and she gave in, letting them close.

16

She heard fussing. The sound was familiar. Eloise. Eloise jabbering about something. She thought she was dreaming, or perhaps this was the last thing she would hear before fading away completely.

"Shhh, shhh."

The sound of her daughter shushing Eloise. The combination was perfect. She felt so close to them.

"Mom?"

Clarke's eyes blinked open. She was in a hospital room. Sam held Eloise with one arm and put one hand on top of Clarke's.

"No one knew you were missing until you didn't get off the plane at Logan. I called Limon. They were looking all over for you. It was another guy, JJ, he had the idea to go to the hotel owner's house," she paused. "That's where they found you . . . and Ginger and Laurent." Sam bounced Eloise on one knee.

Clarke tried to talk but her voice was hoarse. Sam reached behind her and handed her a cup of water. She sipped it.

"You sure know how to upstage a one-year-old on her birthday," Sam said.

Clarke coughed. "Is Ginger . . . alive?"

"She is. She's recovering too."

Clarke looked over and saw Limon standing in the doorway, JJ peeking over his shoulder.

"Hey-yo!" JJ said in a loud whisper.

Limon had a small grin on his face that Clarke knew was a look of disbelief.

"Ready to retire?" he said.

17

A few months later, Clarke sat with Eloise on a blanket in her front yard. Dressed in a blue jumper and white hat, Eloise took shaky but confident steps around the blanket. Clarke couldn't believe how much she looked like Sam.

Sam came out the front door, a tray of snacks, seltzer water, and sippy cup in hand.

"Paperwork has been emailed!" she announced.

"Pasadena City College will be lucky to have you," Clarke said. "But are you sure you're okay with—"

"Mom," Sam said in her cautionary tone. "This is what I want. For Eloise and me to be close by. You'll be a great influence on her."

Clarke felt the warm Altadena sun on her back and the light breeze. It was all very perfect. A hat covered her scars, but she was almost completely healed.

Clarke's tablet dinged. She glanced at it. There was an email from Limon with the subject line, "Discussing your return date." Clarke dismissed the email. She'd deal with it later. Right now, she was with her daughter and granddaughter, enjoying a perfect day. Clarke picked up her tablet and opened the camera.

"Smile, Eloise!"

Eloise laughed as Sam scooped her up and jiggled her up and down.

Click. An excellent photo for her Instagram.

Clarke opened the social media app and pulled up the photo. She captioned it: *With my beautiful daughter and granddaughter, Sam and Eloise. Beautiful day!*

She hit send and the picture popped up at the top of her newsfeed. Just as quickly, the newsfeed refreshed.

Clarke found herself staring at a magazine cover featuring Kitty June and Ginger Kelly with the headline: TELL ALL! HOUSE OF HORRORS!

Ginger's facial wounds had healed, but the scars were visible.

The caption read: *Dear friends, Article out now! Don't miss it! Xx*

Clarke clicked on Ginger's profile. She now had over a hundred thousand followers. Her bio read, "Small town gal. Los Angeles Burlesque Dancer. Serial Killer Survivor."

Clarke took in the words for a moment and closed the app. She looked up at Eloise and held out her arms. "Come here, munchkin!"

On wobbly feet, Eloise marched toward her, laughing even as she tumbled forward, and Clarke caught her in her arms.

---

* *"The Influencer" was born at a metaphorical intersection in my life. I was on another IT phone call with my mother—for whom I am the de facto Internet guru—just as I was approaching the anniversary of a decade spent grinding away in Los Angeles. As we reviewed email phishing scams and stolen identities, my mind kept mulling over the generation gap between us, magnified by* *our relationships to social media. An online presence is like any other tool that might turn up in a criminal case—useful for innocuous purposes or just as easily weaponized. Unlike other evidence, a deleted Instagram post can't be bagged and tagged so readily. How does an accomplished detective like Carol Clarke fit into this changing landscape? Are we returning to the delirious amorality of classic noir, but exchanging postwar disillusionment for the post-truth deception of every curated tweet or heavily filtered image? It's a tangled web where the usual motives—sex, greed, revenge, madness—are hopelessly entwined, lost down a rabbit hole of paywalls and clickbait.*

This story was also an outlet, a pressure valve to release those ten years' worth of love and loathing for my imperfect city and the entertainment industry it was built on. I am eternally grateful to Linda Landrigan for selecting "The Influencer" for publication in Alfred Hitchcock *(my first professional sale). In Hollywood, they teach you to dream big (because what else do you have to get through those desperate days and seedy nights?). For anyone who, like me, is driven to push forward creatively, I hope you "find your own crack in the door" and pry it wide open.*

Joseph S. Walker *is a college instructor living in Bloomington, Indiana. He has a PhD in American literature from Purdue University. He is a member of the Mystery Writers of America, the Short Mystery Fiction Society, Sisters in Crime, and the Private Eye Writers of America. His stories have appeared in* Alfred Hitchcock Mystery Magazine, Ellery Queen Mystery Magazine, Mystery Tribune, Hoosier Noir, Tough, *and numerous other magazines and anthologies. He has been nominated for the Edgar Award and the Derringer Award and has won the Bill Crider Prize for Short Fiction. He also won the Al Blanchard Award in 2019 and 2021. Recent anthologies from small presses (which are helping to keep short crime fiction alive out of love and dedication, and are richly deserving of support) containing his stories include* Mickey Finn: 21st Century Noir Volume 2 *(Down & Out Books),* Monkey Business: Crime Fiction Inspired by the Films of the Marx Brothers *(Untreed Reads), and* Under the Thumb: Stories of Police Oppression *(Rock and a Hard Place Press).*

GIVE OR TAKE A QUARTER INCH

Joseph S. Walker

Ryan Vargas had been home for ten minutes when his phone buzzed with an incoming text. Tina, no doubt, with an explanation of why she wasn't there. When a man gets home after three weeks on the road, he has a right to assume his wife will welcome him. It's nice to feel you've been missed. Ryan took a deliberately long swig from the soda he'd opened before picking up the phone to see what her excuse was.

The message was from Tina's number, but it wasn't text. It was a picture of Ryan's wife in a chair. There was a strip of wide silver tape across her mouth and more wound around her arms and legs, holding her firmly in place. Her hair was unkempt, and her wide eyes had a pleading expression as she stared into the camera.

Ryan put his drink down. He was very aware of the sound of his pulse in his ears. He brought his hand up to the phone, but new messages began scrolling up the screen before he could begin typing.

3CY3YOUNG3. WE'RE WATCHING YOU.

"3CY3YOUNG3" was the password for the security system installed just last year. With the password and Tina's cell phone, whoever this was had access to every camera in the house. Ryan forced himself not to look at the one mounted over the fridge that covered the entire kitchen.

TWENTY MINUTES. GLEN OAK PARK. LOWER DIAMOND.

COME ALONE. CALL NOBODY.

Glen Oak Park was just a few blocks away. Ryan had donated the funds for its professional-grade baseball fields, where he played host to Little League tournaments played under banners with his name. He had money, plenty of money. He could pay a ransom. But the message didn't say anything about a ransom, and twenty minutes wasn't enough time to gather any cash. He stared at the screen, uncertain, and after a few seconds, a new text appeared.

YOU'RE NOT MOVING, RYAN.

He moved.

There were four baseball fields in different parts of the sprawling Glen Oak Park, all, thanks to Ryan, fully equipped with ample bleachers, real dugouts, and banks of lighting for night games. At the bottom of the long, wooded slope on the park's north end, the lower diamond was the most remote from the park entrance. There'd be a game there almost any weekend day and many nights during the week, but now, on a crisp Tuesday morning a month into the new school year, only one other car was in the parking lot. It was a dark blue Honda sedan, the rear end starting to go to rust. Ryan got out of his SUV and started toward the field. As he passed the sedan, he used his phone to snap a picture of the license plate.

A row of tall pines divided the parking lot from the field. He followed a paved path through the trees and came out behind the bleachers on the first-base side. A man sat on the edge of the dugout roof across the field, swinging a bat idly back and forth in front of his legs as though practicing golf swings. He was wearing track pants and a sleeveless black T-shirt, with a red baseball cap pushed far back on his head and a disheveled beard. His arms were thick with muscle and densely covered with tattoos, a web of symbols and words Ryan found incomprehensible. The man watched him coming across the diamond, his expression blank, the bat a metronome in front of him.

Ryan stopped ten feet away. "Where's my wife?"

"She's safe," the man said. Up close he looked a little older than Ryan had thought at first. Close to his own age. He held up a cell phone. "She's with a buddy of mine. As long he gets the calls he's expecting from me, and I say the things he's expecting me to say, she'll be fine."

"I want to talk to her," Ryan said.

"You know what they say about folks in hell and ice water. What you want isn't part of the game right now." The man's voice was deep, with just a trace of some kind of accent. Something Southern, maybe, but barely there.

Ryan crossed his arms. Absurdly he wished he had a prop, like the bat the man was swinging. Something to do with his hands. "Then let's talk about what you want. How much?"

"We'll get to what I want," the man said. He tilted his head back, inviting scrutiny of his face. "You remember me?"

Surprised, Ryan looked more closely. "No. Should I?"

"I'll give you a hint. My name's Mickey Loch."

Ryan's mouth went dry. He'd never been through a kidnapping before, but he was dead sure kidnappers didn't generally go around announcing their identity. "Why would you tell me that?"

"Thought it might spark something. I'd be surprised if you did remember, though. It was nineteen years ago. 1997. Your second Cy Young year."

"That's ancient history. What does this have to do with my wife?"

"I told you we'll get to it." Loch pointed into the dugout with the bat. "You want to sit down?"

"No," Ryan snapped. "I want you to tell me whatever the hell it is you brought me here to tell me."

"Man's in a hurry, I guess," Loch said. "Okay, we'll start the Wayback Machine. It was about this time of year, a game in Oakland that didn't mean a damn thing. You boys had already locked up your division, and Oakland was just trying to avoid losing a hundred games." Loch hopped down from his perch, put the bat on his shoulder, and swiveled into a batting stance. "Maybe you remember me better like this."

Ryan frowned. "I don't remember a Loch on the A's."

"I was only with them for one game," Loch said. "That game. Phil Jacobs was on bereavement leave and Hector Ruiz was nursing a sprained thumb. They just needed somebody who could stand in left field and look semiprofessional."

"And I suppose I was pitching."

"You were. I don't know why. You should have been resting up for the playoffs."

"I was trying to get to twenty-five wins. I had a bonus clause." He hadn't made it, but there was a big bonus for the Cy Young, plus playoff pay. 1997 was a good year. A bought-my-parents-a-house year.

Loch grunted. "Shoulda guessed. Anyway. I came up to bat three times that day. Three at bats, three strikeouts, nine pitches total. My career in the majors."

"Am I supposed to apologize?"

Loch kept going as though Ryan hadn't spoken. "Next day, I was on my way back to Triple-A. And the day after that, I was out on a run and landed in a pothole wrong. Broke my left leg in three places, shredded my ACL. X-ray looked like a damn jigsaw puzzle."

"Tough break. Are we getting to where my wife is anytime soon?"

Faster than Ryan would have thought possible, Loch darted forward, grabbed him by the front of his shirt, and shoved backward, at the same time sweeping his leg sideways to cut Ryan's feet out from under him. Ryan's back slammed into the ground. Before he could move, Loch was standing over him, holding the fat end of the bat forcefully against his throat.

"I been waiting to tell you this story for nineteen years," Loch said. "You mind shutting up for a minute and letting me do it?"

Unable to catch his breath, Ryan nodded. Loch stepped back, lifting the bat. Ryan, wheezing, rolled to his side and managed to sit up. He didn't try to stand.

"Team cut me, of course," Loch said when Ryan was breathing more easily. "First, though, they sent me to a doc who gave me pain meds. They were handing that shit out like candy back then. Cut forward six months and I'm unemployed, still limping, and hooked. Couldn't pay my dealer, so he told me I could work it off making some deliveries." Loch got into a batting stance again and took a couple of casual half-speed swings, staring out over the field. "I fell in with disreputable characters, is how my lawyer said it. Word of advice, Mr. Vargas. If you ever commit a felony, don't do it in Arizona. The guards are mean as snakes, and they don't believe in wasting AC on criminals."

"I'll keep that in mind," Ryan said. It took him two breaths to say it.

"Now, Oregon, they got some nice jails," Loch said. "But I guess I'm digressing." He crouched down to look Ryan in the eye. "Bottom line is, I want my fourth at bat."

Ryan looked from Loch to the pitcher's mound. "Here? Now? You're kidding."

"You saw the picture I sent," Loch said. "Seem like I'm kidding?"

"You kidnapped my wife so I'd, what? Lob one over the plate so you can say you went yard against a Hall of Famer? You're insane."

"Maybe. But I don't want any damn lob. I want you to try to get me out." Loch straightened and walked toward the dugout. "Doesn't mean anything if you're not trying."

"It doesn't mean anything either way," Ryan said. "For the love of God, man, I'm forty-five years old. I haven't thrown a pitch in ten years."

"That ain't exactly true." Loch stepped down into the dugout. He bent over and came up with a duffel bag and tossed it up onto the grass. "I was at that old-timers' game in Cooperstown back in July. You threw two scoreless innings, and you can still break ninety when you put your mind to it."

"Come on. That was against a bunch of other relics."

"Think I look like a spring chicken?" Loch bent again for a three-gallon bucket filled with baseballs. "So we've both lost a few steps. Just makes it a fair contest. I was in Indianapolis a couple nights ago, too, where you did that appearance at a minor league game. Watched you working with the pitchers. I'd say you've still got something."

"I'm a scout," Ryan said. "That's what they pay me to do now. Just how long have you been following me around?"

"Long enough," Loch said. He came up out of the dugout with the bucket. "On your feet, Vargas. One at bat. A real one. After that, I make a phone call, and this is all over."

Ryan pushed himself to his feet. "I'm not really dressed for this."

Loch nudged the duffel bag with his toe. "Tina picked out a few things from your closet."

Ryan felt the anger he'd been holding down surge. "Don't say her name."

"Whatever, chief." Loch bent over and unzipped the duffel. He pulled out a batting helmet and put it on, tossing aside his cap. "Get yourself ready. I'll wait out at the mound." He picked up the bucket and carried it out onto the field, along with the bat he'd been holding since Ryan arrived.

Ryan knelt by the duffel bag. He recognized it now, a relic from his playing days. It had been sitting on a shelf in his closet for years, untouched. Inside he found cleats and a cap, and some of his workout clothes. His second-best glove was in the bottom of the bag. His best glove was in a glass case in Cooperstown. He pushed his left hand into the glove.

There was a gun inside.

The tiny .22 Tina bought last year, at the same time the security system was installed, after she saw a strange man lurking around the yard and got nervous about Ryan's weeks-long scouting trips. It occurred to Ryan to wonder if the strange man had been Loch. Had he been planning this for more than a year?

Ryan felt the cool metal of the small gun with the tips of his fingers, imagining the scene. Loch getting into the house somehow, forcing Tina with a gun or a knife to get this bag together, telling her it was stuff Ryan would be using. Tina somehow finding a way to slip the gun in.

But what could he do with it? Loch had said his buddy was expecting phone calls at specific times. If Ryan shot him and he couldn't call, what would happen to Tina? Even if he just held Loch at gunpoint while he called, what code word would or wouldn't be said?

"Let's go, Vargas," Loch yelled. "Sooner this is over, sooner everybody gets to go home."

"Coming," Ryan said. He tipped the glove so that the gun fell into the bottom of the bag. As quickly as he could, he changed his shoes and traded his jeans and button-down shirt for a loose pair of shorts and a T-shirt. He shoved the clothes he had been wearing into the bag on top of the gun. Pulling a cap on, he picked up the bag and walked onto the field.

Loch was standing just to the third-base side of the mound. The bucket was between his feet, and the bat rested in the grass. He was tossing a rosin bag from hand to hand. As Ryan got close, he lobbed it to him. Ryan dropped the duffel in the grass and caught it.

"Forty warm-up pitches sound fair?" Loch asked.

"It's your carnival," Ryan said. "You tell me."

"I want this real," Loch said. "No excuses. I don't want you thinking later that your arm was stiff, and I don't want you hanging one over the plate in slo-mo. I want the best you can give me."

"Fine," Ryan said. "Forty's fine."

Loch nodded. "Go to it," he said. "I'll feed you."

Ryan climbed the mound. He kicked at the rubber, stretched his arms over his head, and bounced the rosin bag in his hand before dropping it to the back of the mound. "You bat left or right?"

"Right," Loch said.

Ryan nodded. Loch reached into the bucket and underhanded a ball to him.

Ryan toed the rubber and fell automatically into the stance he'd learned from his father four decades ago and had refined by the best pitching coaches in the world. Time slowed down. He felt as he always did with the ball in his hand, at home.

He lifted his left leg, still able to bring the knee nearly to his chest, and swung it down as his arm came whipping around at three-quarter speed. The ball split the plate in two but was chin level as it crossed.

"High and slow," Loch said. "You can do better than that."

"Gotta wake the arm up," Ryan said. He held up the glove. "Gimme another. This would be a lot easier with a catcher."

"I'll try to arrange more accomplices next time." Loch lobbed the next ball.

Twelve pitches in, Ryan could feel the blood stirring, the muscles growing loose and warm. Twenty pitches in, he started to work on location. For the twenty-fifth, he kicked into gear, unleashing a full-speed fastball that tore right down the pipe and, hitting the chain-link barrier between the plate and the stands, wedged itself into one of the squares and stuck there instead of bouncing back toward the infield.

Loch whistled. "That broke ninety, sure," he said.

"Gimme another," Ryan said.

Loch tossed it. "Lemme ask you something, Vargas," he said. "You ever watch the Hartman at bat?"

"I've seen it a few times," Ryan said. It was the first clip they showed at his Hall of Fame ceremony, the clip they would show on *SportsCenter* when he died. Game seven, bottom of the ninth, two-out, bases jammed and his team, the Tigers, clinging to a one-run lead. Sal Rodgers brought Ryan out of the bullpen on two days rest to face Jace Hartman, who'd won the Triple Crown that year. It was the only relief appearance Ryan made in his entire career. His shoulder was on fire before he threw the first pitch, and fifty thousand rabid Pirates fans were howling for his blood. It took eleven pitches, but he struck Hartman out.

Thinking about it now, he threw the cutter Hartman had missed for strike three and held out his glove for another.

Loch tossed it. "That second pitch," he said. "The one Hartman fouled straight back. You remember?"

Ryan grunted. He remembered. The crack cutting right through the crowd noise, the momentary sense of an abyss of despair before he realized where the ball was heading.

He stepped off the rubber and stretched his arms, feeling the fine sheen of sweat he'd built up.

"I figure he missed that one by about a quarter inch," Loch said. "Bat's a quarter inch higher, that's maybe a grand slam. No parade in Detroit, no third Cy Young. One-fourth of one inch. You ever think about that?"

"No," Ryan lied. He got back on the mound and threw. The ball skipped off the dirt two feet in front of the plate.

"Yeah," Loch said. "I guess not."

Ryan held out his glove. "Gimme another. Shouldn't you be warming up?"

"Spent most of the morning at a batting cage," Loch said. He tossed the ball. "Two more pitches, and it's go time, chief."

Ryan turned his back to the plate and looked out across the field, rubbing the ball between his palms. The fence seemed a lot further off in the old days. He turned back toward the plate and uncorked a beauty of a slider.

One more pitch—a fastball he deliberately put high and inside—and Loch nodded. "Okay," he said. "Batter up. Just remember, Vargas. You're not going to like what happens if I think you're teeing it up for me." He picked up the bat and walked toward the plate. "And if you're thinking about beaning me, remember I'm due to make a call soon."

For the first time, watching Loch walk away, Ryan noticed the minuscule catch in his stride, the whisper of a limp favoring his left leg. The ghost of one bad step, one moment of looking the wrong way. Off by a quarter inch, maybe.

He shook his head. He wasn't here to feel sorry for the man.

Loch got to the plate. He kicked aside the balls that had rebounded into the box, turned his shoulder toward Ryan, and screwed his back foot into the dirt. His stance was compact. Coiled. Ryan felt a distant tickle of memory. Maybe he did remember Mickey Loch.

He peered over the top of the glove for a second, picturing Vic Kelly, his longtime catcher, holding out a target. He dropped his hands to his waist, spun into his delivery, and gave Loch the best fastball he'd thrown in years, sizzling in just over the inside corner. Loch tensed as it came, lifted his left foot a fraction of an inch, but couldn't pull the trigger.

"Strike one," Ryan said. Loch stepped out of the box, looked like he was going to argue for a second, then nodded. Ryan got two more balls from the bucket, dropping one just behind the mound. He felt good. Loose. The way he had always felt on the good days. The ball was itching in his hand, begging to be thrown.

Ryan had always been a fast worker. Keeps the batter off balance. The Vic Kelly in Ryan's mind shifted slightly to the outside, dropped two fingers between his thighs. Ryan nodded to nobody, went into his windup, and produced a curveball that broke three laws of physics on its way to the backstop. This time Loch swung, but he didn't come within a foot of the ball. He stepped back from the plate, cursing.

Ryan didn't say *strike two* out loud. He turned and picked up the third ball, and rubbed it up and got set. If Loch had said anything about Tina at this moment, it would have taken Ryan a beat to remember what he was talking about. He was entirely absorbed in the feeling he'd had all those thousands of times, the feeling he'd almost forgotten, the sense that he was ten feet tall and bulletproof. He was gonna strike his man out.

The phantom Kelly held down a single finger. Back to the heat. Ryan nodded again, dropped his hands, and sent the ball screaming in.

He didn't see Loch swing. He didn't have to. The sound was enough, the solid, sharp concussion of wood meeting leather. Ryan let the momentum of his delivery carry him around to face the outfield, already knowing what he would see: the ball hurtling toward the wall in center-right, a solid line drive, fast and straight. The apparition outfielders weren't even trying to catch it, just head it off. The ball bounced once, hit the wall halfway up, and spun back onto the grass.

In the silence, he heard Loch's footsteps clearly. The man came and stood beside him, and they looked out together at where the ball had landed.

"Double?" Loch said.

"Probably," Ryan said. He didn't look at Loch. "I don't know how fast you were before you caught that pothole."

"Fast enough," Loch said. He took off the batting helmet and dropped it and the bat in the grass. He walked over to where he had tossed his hat, picked it up, put it back on, and walked back to the mound. Ryan was still staring out at the wall, his hands on his hips.

Loch pulled a keycard from his pocket and held it out. "Residence Inn," he said. "Room 327."

Ryan finally broke his gaze from the wall. He looked at Loch and slowly took the card. "327," he said. "What about your buddy waiting with her?"

"Isn't one," Loch said. "Oddly enough, I don't actually know anybody willing to commit a felony, so I could get my lifetime average to .250."

"But she's all right?"

"I imagine she's pissed," Loch said. "Scared. But yeah, otherwise fine." He crossed his arms. "For what it's worth, Vargas, I didn't say anything to her about the woman in Indianapolis. The one who shared your taste in bourbon."

Ryan clenched his jaw. "You want me to thank you? Or, what, not call the cops?"

Loch shrugged. "Doesn't matter. I'm already wanted in five states. Car I came in was stolen this morning. An hour from now, I'll be in a different one and across a state line."

"So that's it," Ryan said. "This really is all you wanted."

"It's all I've wanted for nineteen years," Loch said. "Guess I'll find something different to want now." He turned to face Ryan fully. "I don't suppose you'd shake my hand."

"No."

"All right. Goodbye, Vargas." He turned away. Instead of heading straight for the parking lot, he trudged out to center field, where he picked up the ball he had hit and stuck it in his pocket. Ryan watched him every step of the way. He might have been imagining it, but Loch's limp seemed a little more pronounced as he turned toward the right-field line and eventually disappeared through the pines.

I wanted to write about a kidnapping where the ransom was something other than cash, so I thought about what else might motivate a person to commit such a desperate act. For world-class athletes, the line between being one of the all-time greats and being an also-ran can be terrifyingly thin. That's true for a lot of people, but athletes act out their fates live, with thousands looking on. A good play at the right moment can become the foundation of a Hall of Fame career; a bad one can wipe out the memory of many good seasons. Ryan Vargas is on one side of that line, and Mickey Loch is on the other.

Many thanks to Rusty Barnes and Tim Hennessy of Tough, who gave the story a home and whose suggestions rendered it much stronger.

Colson Whitehead *is the author of eight novels, beginning with* The Intuitionist *and, most recently, the bestselling* Harlem Shuffle. *In 2016 he was given the National Book Award for* The Underground Railroad, *which won the Pulitzer Prize the next year; he was also given the Pulitzer Prize in 2020 for* The Nickel Boys. *Born Arch Colson Chipp Whitehead, at various times he used the first names Arch, then Chipp, before settling on Colson. He has written for* The New Yorker, The New York Times, Granta, Harper's, *and numerous other publications.*

THE THERESA JOB

Colson Whitehead

Carney took the long way to Nightbirds. This first hot spell of the year was a rehearsal for the summer to come. Everyone a bit rusty, but it was coming back—they took their places. On the corner, two white cops re-capped the fire hydrant, cursing. Kids had been running in and out of the spray for days. Threadbare blankets lined fire escapes. The stoops bustled with men in undershirts drinking beer and jiving over the noise from transistor radios, the DJs piping up between songs like friends with bad advice. Anything to delay the return to sweltering rooms, the busted sinks and clotted flypaper, the accumulated reminders of your place in the order. Unseen on the rooftops, the denizens of tar beaches pointed to the lights of bridges and planes.

The atmosphere in Nightbirds was ever five minutes after a big argument with no one telling you what it had been about or who'd won. Everyone in their neutral corners replaying KOs and low blows and devising too-late parries, glancing around and kneading grudges in their fists. In its heyday, the joint had been a warehouse of mealy human commerce—some species of hustler at that table, his boss at the next, marks minnowing between. Closing time meant secrets kept. Whenever Carney looked over his shoulder, he frowned at the grubby pageant. Rheingold beer on tap, Rheingold neon on the walls—the brewery had been trying to reach the Negro market. The cracks in the red vinyl upholstery of the old banquettes were stiff and sharp enough to cut skin.

Less dodgy with the change in management, Carney had to allow. In the old days, broken men had hunched over the phone, hangdog, waiting for the ring that would change their luck. But, last year, the new owner, Bert, had had the number on the pay phone changed, undermining a host of shady deals and alibis. He also put in a new overhead fan and kicked out the hookers. The pimps were OK—they were good tippers. He removed the dart-board, this last renovation an inscrutable one until Bert explained that his uncle "had his eye put out in the Army." He hung a picture of Martin Luther King Jr., in its place, a grimy halo describing the outline of the former occupant.

Some regulars had beat it for the bar up the street, but Bert and Freddie had hit it off quickly, Freddie by nature adept at sizing up the conditions on the field and making adjustments. When Carney walked in, his cousin and Bert were talking about the day's races and how they'd gone.

"Ray-Ray," Freddie said, hugging him.

"How you doing, Freddie?"

Bert nodded at them and went deaf and dumb, pretending to check that there was enough rye out front.

Freddie looked healthy, Carney was relieved to see. He wore an orange camp shirt with blue stripes and the black slacks from his short-lived waiter gig a few years back. He'd always been lean, and when he didn't take care of himself quickly got a bad kind of thin. "Look at my two skinny boys," Aunt Millie used to say when they came in from playing in the street.

They were mistaken for brothers by most of the world, but distinguished by many features of personality. Like common sense. Carney had it. Freddie's tended to fall out of a hole in his pocket—he never carried it long. Common sense, for example, told you not to take a numbers job with Peewee Gibson. It also told you that, if you took such a job, it was in your interest not to fuck it up. But Freddie had done both these things and somehow retained his fingers. Luck stepped in for what he lacked otherwise.

Freddie was vague about where he'd been lately. "A little work, a little shacking up." Work for him was something crooked; shacking up was a woman with a decent job and a trusting nature, who was not too much of a detective. He asked after business in Carney's furniture store.

"It'll pick up."

Sipping his beer, Freddie started in on his enthusiasm for the new soul-food place down the block. Carney waited for him to get around to what was really on his mind. It took Dave "Baby" Cortez on the jukebox, with that damn organ song, loud and manic. Freddie leaned over. "You heard me talk about this nigger every once in a while—Miami Joe?"

"What's he, run numbers?"

"No, he's that dude wears that purple suit. With the hat."

Carney thought he remembered him maybe. It wasn't like purple suits were a rarity in the neighborhood.

Miami Joe wasn't into numbers. He did stickups, Freddie said. Knocked over a truck full of Hoovers in Queens last Christmas. "They say he did that Fisher job, back when."

"What's that?"

"He broke into a safe at Gimbels," Freddie said. Like Carney was supposed to know. Like he subscribed to the *Criminal Gazette* or something. Freddie was disappointed but continued to puff up Miami Joe. He had a big job in mind, and he'd approached Freddie about it. Carney frowned. Armed robbery was nuts. In the old days, his cousin had stayed away from stuff that heavy.

"It's going to be cash, and a lot of jewelry that's got to get taken care of. They asked me if I knew anyone for that, and I said I have just the guy."

"Who?"

Freddie raised his eyebrows.

Carney looked over at Bert. Hang him in a museum—the barman was a potbellied portrait of hear no evil. "You told them my name?"

"Once I said I knew someone, I had to."

"Told them my name. You know I don't deal with that. I sell home goods."

"Brought that TV by last month—I didn't hear no complaints."

"It was gently used. No reason to complain."

"And those other things, not just TVs. You never asked where they came from."

"It's none of my business."

"You never asked all those times—and it's been a lot of times, man—because you know where they come from. Don't act all 'Gee, officer, that's news to me.'"

Put it like that, an outside observer might get the idea that Carney trafficked quite frequently in stolen goods, but that wasn't how he saw it. There was a natural flow of goods in and out and through people's lives, from here to there, a churn of property, and Ray Carney facilitated that churn. As a middleman. Legit. Anyone who looked at his books would come to the same conclusion. The state of his books was a prideful matter with Carney, rarely shared with anyone because no one seemed very interested when he talked about his time in business school and the classes he'd excelled in. Like accounting. He told this to his cousin.

"Middleman. Like a fence."

"I sell furniture."

"Nigger, please."

It was true that his cousin did bring a necklace by from time to time. Or a watch or two, topnotch. Or a few rings in a silver box engraved with initials. And it was true that Carney had an associate on Canal Street who helped these items on to the next leg of their journey. From time to time. Now that he added up all those occasions, they numbered more than he'd thought, but that was not the point. "Nothing like what you're talking about now."

"You don't know what you can do, Ray-Ray. You never have. That's why you have me."

"This ain't stealing candy from Mr. Nevins, Freddie."

"It's not candy," Freddie said. He smiled. "It's the Hotel Theresa."

Two guys tumbled through the front door, brawling. Bert reached for Jack Lightning, the baseball bat he kept by the register.

Summer had come to Harlem.

At Nightbirds, Freddie had made Carney promise to think about it, knowing that he usually came around if he thought too long about one of his cousin's plots. A night of Carney staring at the ceiling would close the deal, the cracks up there like a sketch of the cracks in his self-control. It was part of their Laurel-and-Hardy routine: Freddie sweet-talks Carney into an ill-advised scheme, and the mismatched duo tries to outrun the consequences. *Here's another fine mess you've got me into.* His cousin was a hypnotist, and suddenly Carney's on lookout while Freddie shoplifts comics at the five-and-dime, or they're cutting class to catch a cowboy double feature at Loew's. Two drinks at Nightbirds, and then dawn's squeaking through the window of Miss Mary's after-hours joint, moonshine rolling in their heads like an iron ball. *There's a necklace I got to get off my hands—can you help me out?*

Whenever Aunt Millie interrogated Freddie over some story the neighbors told her, Carney stepped up with an alibi. No one would ever suspect Carney of telling a lie, of not being on the up and up. He liked it that way. For Freddie to give his name to Miami Joe and whatever crew he'd thrown in with—it was unforgivable. Carney's Furniture was in the damn phone book, in the *Amsterdam News*, when he could afford to place an ad, and anyone could track him down.

Carney agreed to sleep on it. The next morning, he remained unswayed by the ceiling. He was a legitimate businessman, for Chrissake, with a wife and a kid and another kid on the way. He had to figure out what to do about his cousin. It didn't make sense, a hood like Miami Joe bringing small-time Freddie in on the job. And Freddie saying yes, that was bad news.

This wasn't stealing candy, and it wasn't like when they were kids, standing on a cliff a hundred feet above the Hudson River, tip of the island, Freddie daring him to jump into the black water. Did Carney leap? He leaped, hollering all the way down. Now Freddie wanted him to jump into a slab of concrete.

When Freddie called the office that afternoon, Carney told him it was no-go and cussed him out for his poor judgment.

⚬━✦━⚬

The robbery was in all the news.

HOTEL THERESA HEIST

BLACK HARLEM STUNNED BY DARING

EARLY MORNING ROBBERY

Customers carried rumors and theories into the furniture store. *They busted in with machine guns* and *I heard they shot five people* and *The Italian Mafia did it to put us in our place.* This last tidbit put forth by the Black nationalists on Lenox Ave., hectoring from their soapboxes.

No one was killed, according to the papers. Scared shitless, sure.

The robbery was early Wednesday morning. That evening, Carney locked the door at six o'clock and was almost done moping over his ledgers when his cousin knocked. Only Freddie knocked like that. He'd done it since they were kids, knocking on the frame of the bunk bed—*You still up, hey, you still up? I was thinking . . .*

Carney brought him into the office. Freddie plopped onto the Argent couch and exhaled. He said, "I gotta say, I've been on my feet."

"That was you with the Theresa? You OK?"

Freddie wiggled his eyebrows. Carney cursed himself. He was supposed to be angry at his cousin—not worried about the nigger's health. Still, he was glad that Freddie was unscathed, looks of it. His cousin had the face he wore when he got laid or paid. Freddie sat up. "Rusty gone for the day?"

"Tell me what happened."

"I am, I am, but there's something I got to—"

"Don't leave me hanging."

"I'll get to it in a minute—it's just, the guys are coming here. The guys I pulled the job with," he said. "You know how you said no? I didn't tell them that. They still think you're the man."

Before Miami Joe and the crew arrived at Carney's Furniture, there was time for monologues that ranged in tenor between condemnation and harangue. Carney expressed his rage toward, and disappointment in, his cousin, and proceeded to a dissertation on

Freddie's stupidity, illustrated with numerous examples, the boys having been born within a month of each other and Freddie's boneheadedness an early-to-emerge character trait. Carney was also moved to share, in emphatic terms, why he now feared for himself and his family, and his regret over the exposure of his sideline.

There was also time for Freddie to tell the tale of the heist.

Freddie had never been south of Atlantic City. Miami was an unimagined land, the customs of which he pieced together with details from Miami Joe. Miamians dressed well, for Miami Joe dressed well, his purple suits—solid, or with pinstripes of different widths—masterfully tailored, complemented by his collection of short, fat kipper ties. Pocket squares jutted like weeds. In Miami, Freddie gathered, they turned out straight shooters; it was something in the water, or a combination of the sun and the water. To hear Miami Joe expound on a subject—whether it was food, the treachery of females, or the simple eloquence of violence—was to see the world shorn of its civilized ruses. The only thing he dressed up nicely was himself; all else remained as naked and uncomplicated as God had created it.

Miami Joe operated in New York City for five years after departing his hometown in the wake of an escapade. He found work as a collector for Reggie Greene, maiming welshers as well as shopkeepers who were miserly with protection money, but he tired of such easy game and returned to thieving. At Nightbirds, Freddie had recounted to Carney some of Miami Joe's more recent capers—a trailer full of vacuum cleaners, the payroll of a department store. The flashy, efficient scores were the ones Miami Joe chose to advertise, though he alluded to a host of others he kept private.

Freddie and Miami Joe drank together at the Leopard's Spots, the last to leave, the nights unfinished until the pair had been converted into rye-soaked cockroaches scurrying from sunlight and propriety. Freddie never failed to wake with a fear of what he'd revealed about himself. He hoped Miami Joe was too drunk to remember his stories, but Miami Joe did remember—it was more evidence for his unsentimental study of the human condition. The day Miami Joe brought him in, Freddie had recently quit running numbers for Peewee Gibson.

"But you've never done a robbery before," Carney said.

"He said I was going to be the wheelman—that's why I said yes." He shrugged. "What's so hard about that? Two hands and a foot."

The first convocation of the crew was held in a booth at Baby's Best, on the brink of happy hour. In the dressing room, the strippers covered their scars with powder; blocks away, their faithful customers waited to punch out of straight jobs. The lights were going, though, spinning and whirring, perhaps they never stopped, even when the place was closed, red and green and orange in restless, garish patrol over surfaces. It was Mars. Miami Joe had his arms spread on the red leather when Freddie walked in. Miami Joe, sipping Canadian Club and twisting his pinkie rings as he mined the dark rock of his thoughts.

Arthur was next to arrive, embarrassed by the meeting place, like he'd never been in this kind of establishment before—or spent his every hour there. Arthur was forty-eight, hair corkscrewed with gray. He reminded Freddie of a schoolteacher. The man favored plaid sweater-vests and dark slacks, wore bookworm glasses, and had a gentle way of pointing out flaws in aspects of the scheme. "A policeman would spot that phony registration in a second—is there another solution to this problem?" He'd just finished his third stint in prison, thanks to a weakness for venal or otherwise incompetent comrades. Not this time. Arthur was the "Jackie Robinson of safecracking," according to Miami Joe, having busted the color line when it came to safes and locks and alarms, generally regarded as the domain of white crooks.

Pepper showed up last, and they got to business. "What about this man Pepper?" Carney asked.

"Pepper." Freddie winced. "You'll see."

Cocktails at the Hotel Theresa were a hot ticket, and Miami Joe often installed himself at the long, polished bar, talking shit with the rest of the neighborhood's criminal class. He took out one of the maids every once in a while, a slight, withdrawn girl named Betty. She lived at the Burbank, a once dignified building on Riverside

Drive that had been cut into single-room accommodations. A lot of new arrivals washed up there. Betty liked to stall before she let Miami Joe into her bed, which meant a lot of talking, and in due course he had enough information to plan the robbery. The idea of the job struck him the first time he laid eyes on the hotel. Where others saw sophistication and affirmation, Miami Joe recognized an opportunity, for monetary gain, and to take Black Harlem down a notch. These up-North niggers had an attitude about Southern newcomers, he'd noticed, a pervasive condescension that made him boil. *What'd you say? Is that how y'all do it down there?* They thought their hotel was nice? He'd seen nicer. Not that he'd be able to provide an example if challenged on this point. Miami Joe was strictly hot sheet when it came to short-term accommodations.

The hotel bar closed at 1 A.M., the lobby was dead by four, and the morning shift started at five, when the kitchen staff and the laundry workers punched in. Weekends were busier, and on Saturday nights the hotel manager ran gambling rooms for high rollers. Which meant bodyguards and sore losers—too many surly men walking around with guns in their pockets. Tuesday night was Miami Joe's lucky night when it came to jobs, so Tuesday.

He allotted twenty minutes for the takeover of the lobby and the raid of the vault. "Vault?" Freddie asked. It wasn't a real vault, Miami Joe told him—that was what they called the room containing the safe-deposit boxes, behind the reception desk. Since they were smashing the boxes open, Arthur wouldn't be able to use his expertise, but he was dependable, a scarce quality. He was cool with it. He cleaned his glasses with a monogrammed handkerchief and said, "Sometimes you need a pick, sometimes a crowbar."

Twenty minutes, four men. Baby, the eponymous owner, brought them another round, refusing eye contact and payment. The crew debated the details as the happy-hour trade grabbed stools at the bar and the music cranked up. Pepper kept his mouth shut except to ask about the guns. He focused on his partners' faces, as if around a poker table and not the wobbly Formica of Baby's Best.

Arthur thought five men was better, but Miami Joe preferred the four-way split. At the safecracker's gentle suggestion, they plucked Freddie out of the car and inducted him into the lobby action. It was only a few yards from the street to the hotel lobby, but infinitely closer to peril. Poor Freddie. Purple-and-blue lights sliding all over the place, this gun talk—it was unnerving. He didn't see a way to protest. Pepper glaring like that. The crew picked up on his hesitation, so, when Miami Joe said that his usual fence had been pinched the week before, Freddie gave up Carney as an offering, although he did not phrase it to his cousin this way in his retelling.

At 3:43 A.M. on the night of the job, Freddie parked the Chevy Styleline on Seventh, across from the Theresa on the uptown side of the street. As Miami Joe had promised, there were plenty of spots. The traffic at that hour was nothing. King Kong come running down the street, there was no one to see. Through the glass doors, Freddie could make out the night guard at the bell stand, fiddling with the long antenna of a transistor radio. He couldn't see the front desk, but the clerk was somewhere. The elevator operator sat lethargically on his stool, or was on his feet directing the cab up or down, depending. Miami Joe said that, one morning, forty-five minutes had gone by without an elevator summons.

It spooked Freddie, being in the night man's field of vision like that. He moved the Chevy closer to the corner, where the guard couldn't see him. It was the first deviation from Miami Joe's plan.

The knock at the window startled him. Two men got into the back seat and Freddie panicked, then he realized the disguises had thrown him off. "Settle down," Pepper said. Arthur wore a long, conked wig and a pencil mustache that made him look like Little Richard. Shaved twenty years off him—the time he'd spent in the joint refunded. Pepper was in a Hotel Theresa bellhop uniform, which Betty had stolen from the laundry two months ago. The night she grabbed it, she asked Miami Joe to put it on and say some dialogue before she permitted him to kiss her. It was all in the overhead.

Pepper had had the uniform altered. He hadn't changed his facial appearance. He had gravel eyes that made you stare at your feet. The aluminum toolbox sat on his lap.

Thirty seconds before 4 A.M., Arthur got out of the car and crossed the median. His tie was loose, his jacket rumpled, his stride erratic. A musician turning in or an out-of-town insurance salesman after a night in the Big City—in short, a Hotel Theresa guest. The night man saw him and unlocked the front door. Chester Miller was in his late fifties, slim built except for his belly, which perched on his belt like an egg. A little sleepy. After one o'clock, when the bar closed, hotel policy was to allow only registered guests inside.

"Perry? Room 512," Arthur told the night man. They'd booked a room for three nights. The clerk wasn't at the front desk. Arthur hoped Miami Joe had that situation in hand.

The night man flipped through the papers on his clipboard and pulled the brass door wide. Arthur had the gun in the man's rib cage when he turned to lock the door. He told him to take it easy. Freddie and Pepper were on the red carpet outside—the night man let them in and locked the door as directed. Freddie held three leather valises. A rubber Howdy Doody mask covered his face; the crew had bought two of them at a Brooklyn five-and-dime two weeks earlier. Pepper carried the heavy toolbox.

The door to the fire stairs was open. A crack. They were halfway to the registration desk when Miami Joe opened the door the rest of the way and entered the lobby. He'd been hiding in the stairwell for three hours. The Howdy Doody mask had come on five minutes earlier, but as far as he was concerned he'd been in disguise all night because he wasn't wearing a purple suit. There were no hard feelings about who got masks and who didn't. Some of the crew needed their faces revealed in order to do their jobs, and some didn't.

The arrow above the elevator door indicated that the car was on the twelfth floor. Then the eleventh.

For most of the day, the hotel lobby hummed like Times Square, guests and businessmen crisscrossing the white-and-black tiles, locals meeting for a meal and gossip, their number multiplied by the oversized mirrors that hung on the green-and-beige floral wallpaper. The doors to the phone booths by the elevator folded in and unfolded out, weird gills. At night, the swells congregated in the leather club chairs and on sofas and drank cocktails and smoked cigarettes as the door to the bar swung open and shut. Porters ferrying luggage on carts, teams of clerks at registration handling crises big and small, the shoeshine man insulting people in scuffed shoes and arguing for his services—it was an exuberant and motley chorus.

All that was done now, and the cast had shrunk to thieves and captives.

The night man was pliable, as Miami Joe had promised. Miami Joe knew Chester from his nights at the hotel; he would do as he was told. This was one of the reasons Miami Joe had covered his face. The mask smelled like piney ointment and pushed his breath back at him, hot and rotten.

Arthur nodded toward the bell on the desk, a signal for the night man to ding the clerk. When the clerk emerged from the offices, Miami Joe was upon him, one hand over his mouth and the other jabbing the nose of a .38 beneath the man's ear. One school held that the base of the skull was the best spot, the cool metal initiating a physical reaction of fear, but the Miami School, of which Joe was a disciple, liked below the ear. Only tongues went there, and metal made it eerie. There was an alarm with a wire to the police station, activated by a button beneath the desk where the guestbook rested. Miami Joe stood between the clerk and the button. He motioned for the night man to come around so that Pepper could watch him and the clerk.

"Elevator on four," Freddie said.

Miami Joe grunted and went into the back. To the left was the switchboard, where an unexpected visitor waited. Some nights, the switchboard operator's friend kept her company. They were eating pea soup.

The weeknight operator was named Anna-Louise. She had worked at the Hotel Theresa for thirty years, since before it was desegregated, routing calls. Her chair swiveled. She liked the night work, joking with and mothering the succession of young desk clerks through the years, and she liked listening to the guests' calls, the arguments and arrangements of assignations, the lonely calls home through the cold, cold wires. The disembodied voices were a radio play, a peculiar one in which most of the characters appeared only once. Lulu visited Anna-Louise at the switchboard every now and then. They had been lovers since high school and, around their building, referred to themselves as sisters. The lie had made sense when they first moved in, but it was silly now. No one really cares about other people when you get down to it—their own struggles are too close up. The women screamed, then shut their mouths and put their hands up when Miami Joe aimed the gun. To the right was the manager's office. "Get the key," he said. Pepper brought the clerk and the night man into the office area. Miami Joe stood by the wall of iron bars that separated the room from the vault, far enough away to cover both the men and the women if they tried anything funny. He didn't think that was going to happen. They were rabbits, quivering and afraid. Miami Joe's voice was level and calm when he spoke to them, not to soothe but because he thought it more sadistic. He felt the erotic rush he always got on jobs; it kicked in when the caper got going and dissipated when it was over, and then he didn't remember it until the next job. Never could get ahold of it when he wasn't thieving. It told him that his idea for the job and its practical execution were in harmony.

When the elevator door opened, its two occupants saw a lean young man in a silly mask at the desk, looking at them. He nodded hello. Arthur swept around, his gun out. He waved the elevator operator and the passenger out of the cab and directed them behind the registration desk. By now, Pepper had taken the key to the manager's office from the clerk and was conducting the four other captives into the room.

Rob Reynolds, the manager of the hotel, had arranged a nice refuge for himself. There were no windows, so he'd created some—tasseled curtains, identical to those in the finest suites upstairs, framed painted Venetian scenes. After the afternoon rush, he liked to imagine that was him under the hat, steering a gondola down salty boulevards in silence. An overstuffed sofa matched the ones in the lobby, though this one had endured less wear and tear; one man's naps and quickie fucks with past-due long-term residents couldn't compete with the weight of hordes. Autographed photos of famous guests and residents covered the walls—Duke Ellington, Richard Wright, Ella Fitzgerald in a ball gown, long white gloves up to her elbows. Rob Reynolds had

provided exemplary service over the years, the standard ameni-
ties and the secret ones. Late-night smack deliveries, last-minute
terminations via the Jamaican abortionist who kept two rooms on
the seventh floor. It was no surprise in some quarters when the
gentleman turned out not to be a doctor at all. In many of the pictures, Rob Reynolds was shaking hands with the Hotel Theresa's
celebrity visitors and grinning.

Miami Joe checked the desk drawer for a gun—this had just
occurred to him. He didn't find one. He asked the clerk where
they kept the cards that tracked the safe-deposit boxes. The young
clerk had gone by Rickie his whole life but these days wanted folks
to call him Richard. It was a tough haul. His family and those he
grew up with were a lost cause. New acquaintances switched to the
nickname as if they'd received instructions by telegram. The hotel
was the only place where people called him Richard. No defections
so far. This was his first real job, and each time he walked through
those front doors he stepped into himself, into the man he wanted
to be. Clerk, assistant manager, top dog, with this office to call
his own. He pointed to a metal box that sat on the desk, between
the phone and Rob Reynolds's nameplate.

Miami Joe directed the captives to the rug beside the couch:
Lie there with your eyes closed. Freddie covered them from the
doorway. Freddie wasn't a gunman, but Miami Joe figured he was
jumpy enough that he'd get off a shot if anyone moved; it didn't
matter if he missed so long as it bought the rest of the crew time
to put down an insurrection.

The team hit their marks. They wore thin calfskin gloves. Pepper,
in his bellhop uniform, took up his station at the front desk. Arthur
had unlocked the door to the vault, and now he and Miami Joe
stood before the bank of safe-deposit boxes. The brass-colored boxes
were a foot tall and eight inches wide and deep enough for jewelry,
bundled cash, cheap furs, and unsent suicide notes. Arthur said,
"This is all Drummond. You said they were Aitkens."

"That's what I heard."

Aitkens took three or four good whacks before there was enough
purchase for a crowbar. Maybe that was why they'd replaced them
with Drummonds, Arthur thought, which required six to eight

whacks. The take had been cut in half, if they stuck to the time-table. Miami Joe said, "Seventy-eight." Arthur got to work with the sledgehammer. The index cards recorded the box number, the name of the guest, the contents, and the day of deposit. The manager had sissy handwriting that was easy to read. Arthur got into Box 78 after six blows and started on the next while Miami Joe cleaned it out. The contents matched what was on the card: two diamond necklaces, three rings, and some documents. He put the jewelry into a black valise and searched the cards for the next box to hit.

If the banging rattled Pepper, he didn't show it. He'd been at the desk for one minute when he concluded that working registration was a lousy job. Most straight jobs were, in Pepper's estimation, which was why he hadn't held one in many years, but this gig was spectacularly bad. What with all the people. The constant yipping and complaints—my room's too cold, my room's too hot, can you send up a newspaper, the street noise is too loud. Fork over thirty bucks and suddenly they're royalty, ruling over a twelve-by-fourteen-foot kingdom. Shared bathroom down the hall unless they pay extra. His father had worked in a hotel kitchen, cooking chops and steaks. He came home stinking every night, in addition to his general sense of worthlessness, but Pepper would take that work over desk duty any day. Talking to these fucking mopes.

Bang bang bang.

Arthur attacked the safe-deposit boxes. Pepper got the first call about the noise five minutes later. The switchboard buzzed, and Freddie told the operator to get up and answer it. Anna-Louise put Room 313's call through. "Front desk," Pepper said. It was the voice he used when he was telling a joke and making fun of white people. He apologized for the banging and said that they were fixing the elevator but they'd be done soon. If you come to the front desk in the morning, he added, we'll give you a voucher for ten percent off breakfast. Negroes do love a voucher. The mezzanine floor was offices and a club room, shut now, and the Orchid Room occupied most of the third, or else they'd be getting a lot more calls. Mr. Goodall, in Room 313, had a voice like a chipmunk, whiny and entitled. Fry chicken all day in that kitchen heat over this goddam job.

"Tell her to stay at the switchboard in case there's more," Miami Joe said. Freddie stood in the doorway of the manager's office. He'd sweat through his shirt and into his black suit. The eyeholes in the mask made him think something outside his range of vision was about to clobber him. The men and women on the floor didn't move. He said "Don't move!" anyway. His mother did that all the time—tell him not to do something right before he was about to do it, like he was made of glass and she could see inside. But so many things lived in his head that she never suspected; he hadn't had that little-boy feeling in a long time. Till tonight. He'd jumped off the Hudson cliffs, but instead of hitting the river he kept falling. Freddie wasn't able to pull the trigger, so he hoped the captives would do what they were supposed to. At her station, Anna-Louise covered her face with her hands.

Bang bang bang.

The rug was freshly vacuumed, which suited the captives, who had their faces in it. The elevator passenger, the man from the twelfth floor, was named Lancelot St. John. He lived two blocks away, and his occupation was sitting at the hotel bar until he lit upon a suitable lady from out of town. If his quarry picked up on his euphemisms, Lancelot straightened out the money before he undressed her; if not, afterward he mentioned a present he wanted to buy for his mother, but he was a little short this week.

In the service industry, you shift your approach depending on the customer. Tonight's lady had flown in from Chicago to speak to a real-estate lawyer about a brownstone she'd recently inherited. Her mother had passed. Perhaps that explained the tears. He'd walked into robberies before—he'd be in bed soon enough. It was almost time for the Theresa to wake to the day, and the criminals had to wrap it up. The elevator operator had done time for stealing a car, and later that day, when questioned by detectives, he said he didn't see a goddam thing.

Arthur smiled. It was good to be out, it was good to be stealing again. Even if a quick glance told him that half the jewelry was paste. Half of it was real, fine-quality stones. He measured his prison time in terms not of years lost but of scores missed. The city! And all its busy people and the sweet things they held dear in safes and vaults, and his delicate talent for seducing these items away. He'd bought farmland in Pennsylvania through a white lawyer, and it was waiting for him, this green wonder. Arthur had put the pictures the lawyer sent him up in his cell. His cellmate asked him what the hell it was, and he told him it was where he'd grown up. Arthur had grown up in a Bronx tenement fighting off rats every night, but, when he finally retired to the nice clapboard house, he'd run through the grass like he was a kid again. Every hammer blow like he was busting through city concrete to the living earth below.

Bang bang bang.

They got two more calls about the banging. It was loud, rebounding on the vault walls, vibrating in the very bones of the building. The excuse about the broken elevator came about after they decided to keep the operator on ice in the office. How many people would call for the elevator between 4 and 4:20 A.M.? Maybe none, maybe plenty. How many would take the stairs down and be ushered by Pepper in his gentle way into the office with the other captives? Just one, it turned out, at four-seventeen, a certain Fernando Gabriel Ruiz, a Venezuelan national and a distributor of handcrafted crockery, who would never visit this city again, after what had happened last time and now this, fuck it. And how many guests knocked on the front door to be let into their rooms? Also one—Pepper unlocked the door and marched Mr. Leonard Gates, of Gary, Indiana, currently staying in Room 807, with its lumpy bed and the hex from the guy who'd had a heart attack there, into the back with the rest. Plenty of room in the manager's office. Stack them like firewood or standing room only, if need be.

Given that only two souls had intruded on their scheme, Miami Joe said "Keep going" when Arthur told him twenty minutes was up.

He wanted to push their luck.

Arthur kept swinging. Freddie became aware of his bladder. Pepper said, "It's time." It wasn't his visceral distaste for the front desk and the interaction it represented. You tell Pepper it's twenty minutes, it's twenty minutes. Arthur kept swinging.

Pepper could take care of himself if it went south. He didn't know about the rest of the crew, and he didn't care. When the fourth complaint about the noise came in, he told Room 405 that the elevator was being fixed and if they bothered him again he'd come up there and beat them with his belt.

Pepper permitted them to empty four more deposit boxes. He said, "It's time." It was not his white-boy voice.

They'd filled two valises. Miami Joe said, "Now." Arthur packed the toolbox, and Miami Joe put the index cards inside, too, to mess up the next day's sorting out. He almost left the empty valise, then remembered that the cops might trace it.

Pepper cut the wire to the police station, and Freddie yanked the office phone out of the wall. They weren't neutralizing the switchboard, so this didn't change their chances materially, but it was a show of enthusiasm that Freddie hoped would serve his cause in the postmortem. In Baby's Best, Miami Joe might mention it and affirm him. Those melancholy lights roving over him, red and purple. Miami Joe recited the names of the staff—Anna-Louise, the clerk, the night man, the elevator operator—and shared their addresses. If anyone so much as twitched before five minutes was up, he said, it was their job to stop that person because he knew where they lived.

The bandits were a mile away when Lancelot St. John sat up and asked, "Now?"

The thieves were overdue at Carney's store. Carney had a notion to turn out the lights and hide in the basement.

"And what do you expect me to do when they get here?" Carney said. "Check out the stash? Pay them for it?"

Freddie bent over to tie his shoes. "You always want in, in the end," he said. "That's why I gave them your name."

Carney stopped himself from saying what he'd been thinking the whole time: "You must have been scared." They weren't hoods. Freddie was a petty thief. Carney moved previously owned items on to their next destination. They didn't hold people hostage and keep lists of places to buy untraceable Howdy Doody masks.

But, as his cousin talked, Carney hadn't recognized himself in the innocents who'd been swept up in it, the switchboard operator and the rest. He'd thought about how he would have pulled it off. Most mornings, after all, he grabbed breakfast at the Chock Full o'Nuts on the first floor of the Theresa. One day, after he and Freddie had talked, he'd put down his Collins-Hathaway catalogue—"New Modular Living for Fall"—and found himself casing the joint. Through that door, you passed into the cocktail bar and then into the lobby. There were three ways into the lobby: the bar, the street, and the clothing boutique. Plus the elevators and fire stairs. Three men at the big front desk, guests coming and going all hours. . . . Carney stopped himself. He sipped his coffee. Sometimes he slipped and his mind went thataway.

He'd never robbed anything in his life, yet there he was. He was only slightly bent when it came to being crooked, in practice and in ambition. The odd piece of jewelry, the electronic appliances that Freddie and then a few other local characters brought by the store, he could justify. Nothing major, nothing that attracted undue attention to his store, the front he put out to the world. If he got a thrill out of transforming these ill-gotten goods into legit merchandise, a zap-charge in his blood like he'd plugged into a socket, he was in control of it and not the other way around. Dizzying and powerful as it was. Everyone had secret corners and alleys that no one else saw—what mattered were your major streets and boulevards, the stuff that showed up on other people's maps of you. The thing inside him that gave a yell or a tug or a shout now and again was not the sickness Freddie ministered to, more and more.

Fact was, he didn't have the contacts to handle the take from the Hotel Theresa. Neither did his man Buxbaum down on Canal. Have a coronary if Carney walked in with that kind of weight. The crew wouldn't be happy when they discovered that he was not the man Freddie had described.

The front door buzzed. The thieves had arrived.

"I got it," Freddie said. He rose.

Carney sat up and straightened his tie. He couldn't blame his cousin. He always said yes, didn't he? He'd been in on the Theresa job since Nightbirds, even if he didn't want to admit it. When they used to stand on the cliff over the Hudson, Carney had always eventually jumped.

The thieves buzzed again.

They took their places. The wheelman, the muscle, the safecracker. But it wasn't a heist until the fence stepped in. He got to work.

Michael Wiley *has written ten mystery and thriller novels, including three featuring Sam Kelson*—Trouble in Mind, Lucky Bones, *and* Head Case—*and the Shamus Award–winning Joe Kozmarski series. His short stories appear often in anthologies,* Ellery Queen Mystery Magazine, *and elsewhere. He is a frequent book reviewer and an occasional writer of critical books and essays. He grew up in Chicago, where he sets the Sam Kelson stories, and has lived for the past twenty years in Jacksonville, Florida, where he sets books that explore the dark side of the Sunshine State (*Monument Road *and the Daniel Turner thrillers).*

WHERE THERE'S LOVE
Michael Wiley

S am Kelson and DeMarcus Rodman stood in an alcove off the Cannella Jewelers showroom. Midnight had passed, and the store was dark except for pulsing green lights on the silent alarm box.

During business hours, Mrs. Cannella would stand in the middle of a circular glass case displaying engagement rings, gold necklaces, and ruby earrings. A chandelier hung from the ceiling. An open stairway rose to a second level, where a staff of jewelers with headband magnifiers worked in tiny rooms and a large safe occupied a room of its own. Mr. and Mrs. Cannella replaced the downstairs carpet twice a year so the lustrous pile made buyers feel they were floating into a rarefied space where the limits on their regular spending applied no more than gravity would a million miles from earth.

"Enough to give me a migraine," Kelson said.

"Hush." Years ago, Rodman had scored at the top of his class of police recruits. Then his little brother died at a cop's hands, and Rodman quit the academy. Now he went from one hustle to another, with sharper eyes than any cop on the beat. He seemed to know everyone and everything, from who scored big with three-card monte on the sidewalk outside Wrigley Field to who opened a Southside chop shop to strip apart stolen Mercedes-Benzes.

"Why should I hush?" Kelson said. "No one's here."

"Practice," Rodman said. "Pretend it's happening."

"You know that'll do no good."

"Pretend to pretend."

"You can't confuse me into being quiet." That was true. Ever since a coke dealer shot Kelson in the head three years earlier, he talked compulsively, especially when he was nervous. He was nervous now. "This job feels like a setup."

"Why would it be?"

"Insurance fraud?" When Mr. Cannella hired Kelson to provide overnight security, the request felt funny. *Why did Cannella want him for only one night? Why did he want him at all?*

"A shipment's coming in the afternoon and going out the next morning," the jeweler said, gazing at him over the top of his wire-rimmed glasses. "We're taking this one as a distributor, reselling parcels to other stores. A lot of people in the city will know we have the stones."

"Why not lock them up with the rest of your jewelry?"

The man's lips curled. "Last week, my grandson was playing upstairs. He managed to change the combination on the safe."

"Huh. Smart kid."

"A little rat. The safe is useless until we get a technician here. So we need a night watchman."

"Your voice sounds expensive," Kelson said.

"I'm sorry?"

"Couldn't you hire a guard from a security firm?"

The jeweler said he'd read a newspaper article about Kelson—a former undercover cop, shot during a bust-gone-bad, now struggling to reinvent himself as a PI—and was moved.

"I don't do pity jobs," Kelson said.

Cannella said he understood and wanted to hire him for his skill set.

Kelson heard irony. "I talk a lot, but I'm good at my job," he said.

"I'm sure you are." The jeweler's smile made Kelson think he believed that, with the frontal lobe damage, Kelson would have the skill set of a hamster.

"I'm not a hamster," he said.

"I would never mistake you for one," Cannella said. "Look, you can hang out and collect your check. Bring a book if you want. But no guns—I don't like weapons in the shop. This is a simple job."

Too simple. Kelson googled Cannella Jewelers and discovered that, three years earlier, the store had settled a claim that it sold a ruby brooch with an inflated appraisal. Two years before that, Mr. Cannella's name appeared on an industry list of jewelers under investigation for illegally sourcing gemstones. So Kelson invited Rodman to keep him company. Rodman was six foot eight and weighed almost three hundred pounds—better than a gun.

"I don't trust this guy," Kelson told him.

Rodman said, "Why would he hire security if he wants to rob himself?"

"He has a low opinion of me. If a burglar robbed the store after the owner hired a guard, no insurance company could fight the claim."

"Did he show you the paperwork for the shipment?"

"Paperwork?"

"At a fancy place like this, you should always know what they've got you on the hook for."

"I'm just a hired body."

Rodman leaned against the alcove wall. "Well, I'm guessing we'll have a quiet night."

"I'm guessing you're forgetting who you came with."

So Rodman put on a pair of earbuds and listened to his music while Kelson talked nonstop about Mrs. Cannella, who wore her artificially whitened smile like it was shiny jewelry, then about how strange it was that oysters made pearls.

A half hour later, Kelson yanked the earbuds from Rodman's ears. Rodman had closed his eyes in the dark, and, though he stood upright, he was breathing deep and slow, nearly snoring.

"Upstairs," Kelson said.

Rodman opened his eyes.

Upstairs—no, up higher, up on the roof—there were footsteps. Almost too quiet to be heard, but definitely footsteps.

"Hmm," Rodman said.

Then something thudded on the roof.

"Is there a ceiling hatch?" Rodman asked.

Kelson moved from the alcove into the showroom. "I didn't notice." He started up the stairs.

"Where's the crate?" Rodman said.

"Right."

Mr. Cannella had showed Kelson a wooden crate in a closet at the back of the alcove. "This is why we need you," he'd said.

Kelson came down the steps. He and Rodman moved back into the alcove and waited.

Rusty hinges stretched and screeched upstairs. Someone thumped lightly to the floor, followed by a second, heavier thump.

Kelson glanced into the dark showroom. The lights on the silent alarm had turned solid red. "Amateurs," he said.

"*Shh*," Rodman said.

"*Shh* yourself," Kelson said.

Footsteps crossed the floor above them. An upstairs light went on, casting a glow down to the showroom, then went off again.

"Idiots," Kelson said.

"*Shh*."

The footsteps came to the top of the stairway. Then two people came down, silent, slow.

"That's more like it," Kelson said.

"*Shh*."

The burglars—one of them tall and thick-shouldered, the other short and thin, both wearing cheap cloth masks—went to the display case and circled it. They shined penlights through the glass, paused, moved on. They whispered to each other like anxious shoppers. They passed a necklace with a sapphire pendant, passed an emerald-encrusted bracelet, and came to the ring display. Then, with startling speed, the short thief sprang over the case, vaulting into the space where Mrs. Cannella stood during store hours.

"Whoa," Kelson yelled.

The burglars swung around and aimed their flashlights at the alcove.

"Who's there?" the tall burglar said.

Rodman tried to silence Kelson.

"Sam Kelson," Kelson said.

The tall burglar fumbled at his waistband and found a black pistol. "Come out of there."

"Why?" Kelson said.

"I'll shoot you if you don't."

"You won't be the first." Kelson stepped from the alcove.

"What are you doing here?" the burglar said.

"Waiting for you. For a while I didn't think you were coming. DeMarcus thought we'd have a quiet night."

The burglar wiggled his pistol at him. "Who's DeMarcus?"

"You don't want to meet him. You've got a gun, but DeMarcus has something else. You could call it his skill set. The truth is, he's the gentlest man I know—and a real sucker for love—but he's huge and most people think he must be—"

"*Enough*," the burglar said.

"Probably not." Kelson glanced at the alcove. "Hey, DeMarcus."

Rodman sighed. "*Shh.*"

The burglars aimed their penlights at the alcove again. "DeMarcus is *here*?" the tall one said.

"You don't talk?" Kelson asked the little one.

Rodman hit a switch in the alcove, turning on the chandelier, then stepped into the bright showroom. He raised his hands to show he meant no harm, but the pose made him look like a grizzly working up an appetite.

"Holy crap," the tall burglar said.

"Told you," Kelson said.

But the little one vaulted over the display case as if to confront the enormous man.

"You don't want to do that," Rodman said, and lowered his hands.

Outside, a siren whined.

"Dammit," the little one said—with a girl's voice—and pulled off her mask. She looked about eighteen. Blond hair fell to her shoulders. She shook it to clear it from her face.

"Huh," Kelson said.

She went to the display case. "That one." She tapped a forefinger on the glass.

"Yes, ma'am," the tall burglar said, and smashed the glass top with his gun butt. He took a diamond ring from the display and offered it to her. "Will you?" he said, as a second siren and then a third joined the first.

"You're going to do this with the mask on?" she said.

"Oh." He pulled off his mask. He had the wide eyes and flat face of a kindly bulldog. He might've been twenty. "Will you?"

She smiled. "I thought you'd never ask."

"Aww," Kelson said.

"Aww," Rodman said.

The tall one slipped the ring onto the little one's finger, and the little one kissed him. "Let's split," she said.

They ran for the stairs.

"You're not taking the stones?" Kelson said.

The tall one stopped on the first step. "What stones?"

"In the closet."

"Shut up, Sam," Rodman said.

"What closet?" the tall one asked.

"In the—"

"*Shut up*," Rodman said.

The tall burglar came back down.

The little one, halfway up the stairs, said, "Don't be stupid, Lucky."

"Really?" Kelson said. "*Lucky?*"

"Listen to her, Lucky," Rodman said. "The cops will be here in about a second. If you want to get away, now's the time."

"Too late," Kelson said. "You're on video."

The tall burglar glanced around the store. A camera pointed back at him from the ceiling. He went to it and hit it with his gun butt. The casing could take more than that. So he shot it.

The girl on the stairs screamed. So did Kelson.

The tall burglar went to Rodman and pointed his pistol at his nose. "What stones?"

"Put down the gun," Rodman said, gentle.

"What closet?" the burglar asked.

"In the alcove," Kelson said.

The tall burglar lowered his pistol. "Check the closet, honey."

"Let's get out of here," she said.

"She's your smarter half, Lucky," Rodman said.

But the tall burglar went to the alcove and returned with the Cannellas' crate. He set it on the display case and pried open the top. There were twenty-five envelopes inside. He removed one, tore it open, and poured a dozen diamonds onto the glass counter.

The girl whooped like a bull rider, skipped down the steps, and scooped up a handful. She stood on her tiptoes and kissed Lucky again.

Outside the store, three police cars skidded to a stop, emergency lights flashing. More sirens approached.

"Uh-oh," Lucky said.

"Now Lucky's talking sense," Kelson said.

Rodman said, "Do you know how hard it is to get rid of hot diamonds?"

The girl said, "You ever heard of pawn shops?" She pulled another envelope from the crate and tore it open. She scooped a glinting handful.

Outside, a speaker crackled to life on one of the police cars, and an officer said, "Put your hands up and come out."

The girl yelled back through the display window, telling the officer what he could do with *his* hands.

"Technically, that's impossible," Kelson said. "I mean, biologically."

Rodman said, "You know that pawn shops give the cops daily reports of everything they buy? The reports include driver's license numbers."

"DeMarcus knows about this kind of thing," Kelson told the burglars. "He's an expert on stolen goods."

Officers climbed from their cars, drew their service pistols, and crouched behind their open doors. The man on the speaker repeated his demand. "Come out now."

Lucky looked confused, then said, "eBay."

Rodman said, "Because cops can't check eBay? You could make easier money shoplifting."

"That's how we met," the girl said. "He was coming out of electronics, and I was in the underwear aisle."

Another police car slid to a stop outside.

Rodman said, "Robbing a jewelry store's a loser score unless you have a fence."

"Maybe we *have* a fence," Lucky said.

Kelson snorted. "You're too dumb to have a fence."

"Who're you calling dumb?" the girl said.

"Who broke into a jewelry store to steal an engagement ring?"

"Nothing dumb about love," she said.

"Who's going to spend her honeymoon in jail?"

She grabbed the pistol from her boyfriend and pointed it at Kelson.

"You don't want to rile her," Lucky said.

The man on the speaker warned the burglars to do as they were told.

The girl held the pistol to Kelson's ear, led him to the front window, and yelled, "We have hostages."

A gun fired, and the front window imploded.

The girl and Kelson screamed. She dragged him back to Lucky and Rodman. They squatted behind the display case.

The girl yelled to the front, "You can't do that."

"Sorry," said the cop on the speaker. "Rookie error."

"We have hostages," she yelled again.

"That's us," Kelson yelled.

"Won't happen again," the speaker voice said.

Then, for a while, everything outside went quiet.

Rodman asked the burglars, "You came just for a ring?"

The girl said, "We thought stealing it would be romantic."

"Candlelit dinners are also good," Kelson said.

"I wanted to give her something nice," the tall burglar said.

"Ah, love," Rodman said.

"Funny story about a wedding I went to," Kelson said. "The bride's uncle—this old guy from Albania—toasted the couple at the reception. He said, 'Where there's love—'"

"Not the time for it," Rodman said.

Outside, a tactical van pulled up beyond the squad cars. Four men in body armor jumped from a sliding side panel. A square-jawed woman in plainclothes climbed out after them with a megaphone. She stepped between the cars and into the open, switched on the megaphone, and identified herself as Sergeant Angela Nguyen. She asked the burglars for their names.

The girl yelled back what Angela Nguyen could do with her questions.

"Biologically possible," Kelson said, "but sort of abstract."

"Do you *ever* shut up?" Lucky said.

"Nope," Kelson said.

Sergeant Nguyen spoke over the megaphone. "What do you want in exchange for the hostages?"

The burglars glanced at each other. "A helicopter?" the boyfriend suggested.

Kelson snorted. "What're you going to do with a helicopter?"

The man looked stung. "Go . . . somewhere."

"I don't want to go to anywhere," the girl said. "My grandma needs me."

"You have a grandma?" Kelson said.

The girl scowled at him. "*Everyone* has a grandma."

"She takes care of her," the tall burglar said.

The megaphone voice asked again, "What do you want in exchange?"

Kelson yelled back, "They're discussing it."

Then Lucky yelled, "A helicopter."

Kelson snorted again.

"Can't do a helicopter," said the megaphone.

The girl yelled, "We have hostages."

"No helicopter," said the megaphone.

The girl told the sergeant what she could do with the helicopter she wouldn't give them.

The sergeant asked, "Who am I talking to?"

Kelson yelled back, "His name is Lucky, believe it or not. Don't know about the girlfriend."

The girl shoved the pistol into Kelson's ribs. "If you don't shut up—"

"Cute couple," Kelson yelled. "Just got engaged."

"Put a cork in it, Sam," Rodman said.

"Lucky," the megaphone voice said, "what do you need to make this right? No helicopters. No jet packs or rocket-powered cars either. How do we do this so no one gets hurt?"

The girl and Lucky stared at each other again, as if hoping one of them would know.

"I just wanted to get married," she told him.

"That's all *I* wanted," Lucky said.

"Why'd you go back down the stairs?" she asked. "We could've been home by now."

Lucky glared at Kelson. "*He* started talking about stones."

"Don't blame *me*," Kelson said.

"I only wanted a ring," the girl said to her boyfriend.

"Yeah?" He mimicked her scooping up handfuls of diamonds and whooping like a bull rider.

"Kids, *kids*," Rodman said.

The couple looked despondent.

"We're screwed," the girl said.

"How'd you come in?" Rodman asked.

"Across the roof next door," the boyfriend said. "The 7-Eleven."

"Any reason you can't go back out the same way?"

The girl said, "They'll see us."

"They seem pretty focused on what's happening in this room right now," Rodman said.

The couple looked unconvinced.

"We'll distract them," Kelson said. "DeMarcus will go out."

"No thanks," Rodman said.

"If I go, I'll tell them what's happening," Kelson said. "They won't even need to ask."

"Ah, hell," Rodman said.

"Hostage coming out," Kelson shouted. "Heck of a good guy. He comes in peace. My only real friend—"

"Shut up, Sam," Rodman said.

He stood up behind the counter. He raised his hands over his head. He went to the front door, unlocked it, and stepped into the brilliant police lights. His shadow fell all the way back to the display case.

Sergeant Nguyen said over the megaphone, "Holy crap."

Another cop yelled, "Get down on the ground." Then all the cops were yelling—*On the ground—Get down—Now—Get down on the ground now.*

Rodman lowered to the pavement. Inside the store, Kelson crawled from the display case to the alcove.

Two tactical cops with ballistic shields shuffled over to Rodman and patted him down from his ears to his toes. They told him to stand, and all three retreated behind the patrol cars.

In the alcove, Kelson switched off the chandelier.

"Hey," one of the cops yelled outside.

"Go," Kelson said.

The burglars sprinted up the stairs to the second floor.

The cops shouted to each other. The tactical squad officers shuffled double-time behind their ballistic shields toward an alley at the back of the store. Cops crouching behind open patrol car doors swept their gun barrels across the front. A spotlight mounted on the tactical van shined through the shattered display window into the showroom. Kelson yelled, "Where there's love, there's no sin." The Albanian uncle's wedding toast.

The burglars pulled themselves through the ceiling hatch onto the roof. All the noise and commotion below seemed to belong to another world.

The girl kissed her boyfriend. "I love you, Lucky."

He kissed her back. "Love you too."

They sprang from Cannella Jewelers to the 7-Eleven roof. They crawled and kept crawling. As the tactical squad men kicked in the back door to the jewelry store and charged into the showroom, the burglars lowered themselves from the roof next door and disappeared into the dark.

An hour before dawn, Mr. Cannella arrived in a silver Audi. His wire-rimmed glasses glinted in the flashing lights of three remaining police cars. He ducked under the crime scene tape and went to a pop-up tent outside the jewelry store, where Kelson and Rodman were waiting for the robbery detectives to decide what to do with them. He thumped Kelson on the chest.

"I paid you to guard the store, and not only did you let *this* happen"—Cannella gestured at the shattered front window—"but the officer who called me said you let the thieves go."

"The best defense is a strong offense?" Rodman said.

Cannella gave him a confused look and turned back to Kelson. "*Why?*"

"They weren't much for thieves. Nice kids, in over their heads. Lovebirds."

Cannella said, "I'll have you arrested. For abetting."

Rodman said, "The trick is misdirection."

Cannella said, "Who are you?"

"DeMarcus Rodman." He extended an enormous hand. "Sam brought me along for the ride."

"DeMarcus kept the robbery from turning ugly," Kelson said. "No one hurt."

Cannella ignored the hand. His fury at Kelson was growing. "Did I tell you to bring a friend?"

"Distract and deflect," Rodman said.

"What are you talking about?" Cannella said.

"Ah, come on, we see through you," Rodman said.

Kelson said, "DeMarcus knows his stuff."

"I don't care what he knows. I hired you to—"

"Why?" Rodman said.

Cannella blinked at him. "Sorry?"

"Why did you hire Sam? He's good at finding missing people, snapping pictures through windows, that kind of job. But jewelry shop security?"

Cannella shook off the question. "I read a story about him in the paper. Ex-cop. Bullet in the head. I felt sorry for the guy. This seemed like something he could do."

Rodman said, "You hired an inexperienced guy to guard, what, a million bucks in diamonds?"

Cannella said, "If someone tried to take them, he just had to call the police."

Rodman said, "Where'd you get them?"

"I'm sorry?"

"Where's the paperwork? The . . . what do you call it—the certification."

Now Cannella smiled, as if Rodman was hitting with a broken bat. "We don't need any of that."

Rodman said, "If the stones are legal, you have papers."

"DeMarcus is an expert on stolen goods," Kelson said.

Cannella was sweating in his suit. "I don't *know* that they're illegal."

"I suppose the cops will be happy to hold the stones for a while as they figure everything out," Rodman said. "I suppose the news will be happy to run some stories about a jewelry store under investigation for dirty gems."

Cannella moved close. "What do you want?"

Rodman said, "You used to have a security camera in the store—"

"Used to?"

"You might be able to recover the recording. If you do, you'll see a couple of kids dressed up like Ninja turtles. Maybe that recording could disappear."

"No one's getting away with this," Cannella said.

"They're bonehead kids. Either they'll grow up and get smart or they'll stay boneheads and get caught."

"Why would you want to help them?" the jeweler said.

Kelson was eager to answer. "DeMarcus looks tough, but he's a sucker for love."

Cannella was trying hard to swallow his fury. He stared at the shattered front window. "I guess insurance could cover this."

"Or not," Rodman said.

"The adjustor will want to talk to me," Kelson said. "That might not work out so well for you."

"Maybe you could suck up the pain," Rodman told the man.

Cannella started to argue—but stopped when Rodman leaned over him. "That's it then?" he said. He looked as if he might cry. "You let the thieves get away. You wreck my store. You threaten me. Are you sure you don't want to torch the place before you go?"

"What do you think, Sam?" Rodman said. "Are we done here?"

"Almost," Kelson said.

"Ah, of course."

"What?" Cannella barely kept from whining.

"You can write Sam his check."

Cannella wrote the check.

The idea for Sam Kelson came to me a few years ago when I was eating lunch at a local diner with my wife and high school–aged kids. Like all good fathers, I embarrass my kids regularly—if usually unintentionally. I talk with the wrong people at the wrong times and with too little inhibition. At the diner, I was speaking to the server about replacing an egg salad sandwich that either was (in my opinion) or wasn't (my kids' opinion) spoiled.

"Just eat it," one of my kids said.

"Bad mayo?" I asked too loudly, drawing stares from other tables. "You're trying to kill me, aren't you?"

At this time, I was also looking for a new sort of character to lead a series of PI mysteries. I've always loved detectives who speak the truth, or their version of it, when facing powerful and dangerous antagonists. Their speech is full of tension and often is hilarious. But sometimes it's implausible.

What if, I wondered as I waited for my new egg salad, a detective really were incapable of speaking anything other than what was on his or her mind—the blunt truth, as this detective perceived it, in all of its dangerous, unseemly, and embarrassing detail? I knew that some people suffer from a condition of disinhibition, usually after experiencing a knock to the head. What if a person like this managed to become a detective?

The answer is Sam Kelson, a private investigator incapable of discretion, even when speaking out will land him in trouble. In "Where There's Love," he gets into—and then out of—trouble by saying too much during a jewelry store burglary.

BONUS STORY

Susan Glaspell *(1876–1948) began her writing career as a journalist, first in her home state of Iowa as a reporter for* The Des Moines Register *and then in Chicago, where she turned to writing fiction. Her first book, published when she was thirty-three,* The Glory of the Conquered *(1909), became a* New York Times *bestseller. She wrote eight more novels and more than fifty short stories, but it was as a playwright that she found her greatest success.*

Her background as a reporter provided invaluable material for her classic play, Trifles *(1916), the seed of which was planted at a murder trial that she covered. This ground-breaking one-act drama was immediately recognized as a masterpiece, as well as an important and influential feminist work.*

She founded what is generally regarded as the first modern American theater company, the Provincetown Players, where she is credited with discovering Eugene O'Neill, as well as working with Theodore Dreiser and Edna St. Vincent Millay. Her play Alison's House *(1931) garnered her a Pulitzer Prize.*

Trifles, *inspired by a real-life murder, in turn inspired her greatest short story, "A Jury of Her Peers," which originally was published in the March 5, 1917, issue of* Every Week *magazine and subsequently has been anthologized often.*

A JURY OF HER PEERS

Susan Glaspell

When Martha Hale opened the storm door and got a cut of the north wind, she ran back for her big woolen scarf. As she hurriedly wound that round her head her eye made a scandalized sweep of her kitchen. It was no ordinary thing that called her away—it was probably further from ordinary than anything that had ever happened in Dickson County. But what her eye took in was that her kitchen was in no shape for leaving: her bread all ready for mixing, half the flour sifted and half unsifted.

She hated to see things half done; but she had been at that when the team from town stopped to get Mr. Hale, and then the sheriff came running in to say his wife wished Mrs. Hale would come too—adding, with a grin, that he guessed she was getting scary and wanted another woman along. So she had dropped everything right where it was.

"Martha!" now came her husband's impatient voice. "Don't keep folks waiting out here in the cold."

She again opened the storm door, and this time joined the three men and the one woman waiting for her in the big two-seated buggy.

After she had the robes tucked around her she took another look at the woman who sat beside her on the back seat. She had met Mrs. Peters the year before at the county fair, and the thing she remembered about her was that she didn't seem like a sheriff's wife. She was small and thin and didn't have a strong voice. Mrs. Gorman, sheriff's wife before Gorman went out and Peters came in, had a voice that somehow seemed to be backing up the law with every word. But if Mrs. Peters didn't look like a sheriff's wife, Peters made it up in looking like a sheriff. He was to a dot the kind of man who could get himself elected sheriff—a heavy man with a big voice, who was particularly genial with the law-abiding, as if to make it plain that he knew the difference between criminals and noncriminals. And right there it came into Mrs. Hale's mind, with a stab, that this man who was so pleasant and lively with all of them was going to the Wrights' now as a sheriff.

"The country's not very pleasant this time of year," Mrs. Peters at last ventured, as if she felt they ought to be talking as well as the men.

Mrs. Hale scarcely finished her reply, for they had gone up a little hill and could see the Wright place now, and seeing it did not make her feel like talking. It looked very lonesome this cold March morning. It had always been a lonesome-looking place. It was down in a hollow, and the poplar trees around it were lonesome-looking trees. The men were looking at it and talking about what had happened. The county attorney was bending to one side of the buggy, and kept looking steadily at the place as they drew up to it.

"I'm glad you came with me," Mrs. Peters said nervously, as the two women were about to follow the men in through the kitchen door.

Even after she had her foot on the doorstep, her hand on the knob, Martha Hale had a moment of feeling she could not cross that threshold. And the reason it seemed she couldn't cross it now was simply because she hadn't crossed it before. Time and time again it had been in her mind, "I ought to go over and see Minnie Foster"— she still thought of her as Minnie Foster, though for twenty years she had been Mrs. Wright. And then there was always something to do and Minnie Foster would go from her mind. But *now* she could come.

The men went over to the stove. The women stood close together by the door. Young Henderson, the county attorney, turned around and said, "Come up to the fire, ladies."

Mrs. Peters took a step forward, then stopped. "I'm not—cold," she said.

And so the two women stood by the door, at first not even so much as looking around the kitchen.

The men talked for a minute about what a good thing it was the sheriff had sent his deputy out that morning to make a fire for them, and then Sheriff Peters stepped back from the stove, unbuttoned his outer coat, and leaned his hands on the kitchen table in a way that seemed to mark the beginning of official business. "Now, Mr. Hale," he said in a sort of semi-official voice, "before we move things about, you tell Mr. Henderson just what it was you saw when you came here yesterday morning."

The county attorney was looking around the kitchen.

"By the way," he said, "has anything been moved?" He turned to the sheriff. "Are things just as you left them yesterday?"

Peters looked from cupboard to sink; from that to a small worn rocker a little to one side of the kitchen table.

"It's just the same."

"Somebody should have been left here yesterday," said the county attorney.

"Oh—yesterday," returned the sheriff, with a little gesture as of yesterday having been more than he could bear to think of. "When I had to send Frank to Morris Center for that man who went crazy—let me tell you, I had my hands full *yesterday*. I knew you could get back from Omaha by today, George, and as long as I went over everything here myself—"

"Well, Mr. Hale," said the county attorney, in a way of letting what was past and gone go, "tell just what happened when you came here yesterday morning."

Mrs. Hale, still leaning against the door, had that sinking feeling of the mother whose child is about to speak a piece. Lewis often wandered along and got things mixed up in a story. She hoped he would tell this straight and plain, and not say unnecessary things that would just make things harder for Minnie Foster. He didn't begin at once, and she noticed that he looked queer—as if standing in that kitchen and having to tell what he had seen there yesterday morning made him almost sick.

"Yes, Mr. Hale?" the county attorney reminded.

"Harry and I had started to town with a load of potatoes," Mrs. Hale's husband began.

Harry was Mrs. Hale's oldest boy. He wasn't with them now, for the very good reason that those potatoes never got to town yesterday and he was taking them this morning, so he hadn't been home when the sheriff stopped to say he wanted Mr. Hale to come over to the Wright place and tell the county attorney his story there, where he could point it all out. With all Mrs. Hale's other emotions came the fear now that maybe Harry wasn't dressed warm enough—they hadn't any of them realized how that north wind did bite.

"We come along this road," Hale was going on, with a motion of his hand to the road over which they had just come, "and as we got in sight of the house I says to Harry, 'I'm goin' to see if I can't get John Wright to take a telephone.' You see," he explained to Henderson, "unless I can get somebody to go in with me they won't come out this branch road except for a price I can't pay. I'd spoke to Wright about it once before; but he put me off, saying folks talked too much anyway, and all he asked was peace and quiet—guess you know about how much he talked himself. But I thought maybe if I went to the house and talked about it before his wife, and said all the womenfolks liked the telephones, and that in this lonesome stretch of road it would be a good thing—well, I said to Harry that that was what I was going to say—though I said at the same time that I didn't know as what his wife wanted made much difference to John—"

Now there he was!—saying things he didn't need to say. Mrs. Hale tried to catch her husband's eye, but fortunately the county attorney interrupted with:

"Let's talk about that a little later, Mr. Hale. I do want to talk about that, but I'm anxious now to get along to just what happened when you got here."

When he began this time, it was very deliberately and carefully:

"I didn't see or hear anything. I knocked at the door. And still it was all quiet inside. I knew they must be up—it was past eight o'clock. So I knocked again, louder, and I thought I heard somebody say, 'Come in.' I wasn't sure—I'm not sure yet. But I opened the door—this door," jerking a hand toward the door by which the two women stood "and there, in that rocker"—pointing to it—"sat Mrs. Wright."

Everyone in the kitchen looked at the rocker. It came into Mrs. Hale's mind that that rocker didn't look in the least like Minnie Foster—the Minnie Foster of twenty years before. It was a dingy red, with wooden rungs up the back, and the middle rung was gone, and the chair sagged to one side.

"How did she—look?" the county attorney was inquiring.

"Well," said Hale, "she looked—queer."

"How do you mean—queer?"

As he asked it he took out a notebook and pencil. Mrs. Hale did not like the sight of that pencil. She kept her eye fixed on her husband, as if to keep him from saying unnecessary things that would go into that notebook and make trouble.

Hale did speak guardedly, as if the pencil had affected him too.

"Well, as if she didn't know what she was going to do next. And kind of—done up."

"How did she seem to feel about your coming?"

"Why, I don't think she minded—one way or other. She didn't pay much attention. I said, 'Ho' do, Mrs. Wright? It's cold, ain't it?' And she said, 'Is it?'—and went on pleatin' at her apron.

"Well, I was surprised. She didn't ask me to come up to the stove, or to sit down, but just set there, not even lookin' at me. And so I said: 'I want to see John.'

"And then she—laughed. I guess you would call it a laugh.

"I thought of Harry and the team outside, so I said, a little sharp, 'Can I see John?' 'No,' says she—kind of dull like. 'Ain't he home?' says I. Then she looked at me. 'Yes,' says she, 'he's home.' 'Then why can't I see him?' I asked her, out of patience with her now. 'Cause he's dead' says she, just as quiet and dull—and fell to pleatin' her apron. 'Dead?' says, I, like you do when you can't take in what you've heard.

"She just nodded her head, not getting a bit excited, but rockin' back and forth.

"'Why—where is he?' says I, not knowing *what* to say.

"She just pointed upstairs—like this"—pointing to the room above.

"I got up, with the idea of going up there myself. By this time I—didn't know what to do. I walked from there to here; then I says: 'Why, what did he die of?'

"'He died of a rope around his neck,' says she; and just went on pleatin' at her apron."

Hale stopped speaking, and stood staring at the rocker, as if he were still seeing the woman who had sat there the morning before. Nobody spoke; it was as if everyone were seeing the woman who had sat there the morning before.

"And what did you do then?" the county attorney at last broke the silence.

"I went out and called Harry. I thought I might—need help. I got Harry in, and we went upstairs." His voice fell almost to a whisper. "There he was—lying over the—"

"I think I'd rather have you go into that upstairs," the county attorney interrupted, "where you can point it all out. Just go on now with the rest of the story."

"Well, my first thought was to get that rope off. It looked—"
He stopped, his face twitching.

"But Harry, he went up to him, and he said. 'No, he's dead all right, and we'd better not touch anything.' So we went downstairs.

"She was still sitting that same way. 'Has anybody been notified?' I asked. 'No,' says she, unconcerned.

"'Who did this, Mrs. Wright?' said Harry. He said it business-like, and she stopped pleatin' at her apron. 'I don't know,' she says. 'You don't *know*?' says Harry. 'Weren't you sleepin' in the bed with him?' 'Yes,' says she, 'but I was on the inside.' 'Somebody slipped a rope round his neck and strangled him, and you didn't wake up?' says Harry. 'I didn't wake up,' she said after him.

"We may have looked as if we didn't see how that could be, for after a minute she said, 'I sleep sound.'

"Harry was going to ask her more questions, but I said maybe that weren't our business; maybe we ought to let her tell her story first to the coroner or the sheriff. So Harry went fast as he could over to High Road—the Rivers' place, where there's a telephone."

"And what did she do when she knew you had gone for the coroner?" The attorney got his pencil in his hand all ready for writing.

"She moved from that chair to this one over here"—Hale pointed to a small chair in the corner—"and just sat there with her hands held together and lookin down. I got a feeling that I ought to make some conversation, so I said I had come in to see if John wanted to put in a telephone; and at that she started to laugh, and then she stopped and looked at me—scared."

At the sound of a moving pencil the man who was telling the story looked up.

"I dunno—maybe it wasn't scared," he hastened: "I wouldn't like to say it was. Soon Harry got back, and then Dr. Lloyd came, and you, Mr. Peters, and so I guess that's all I know that you don't."

He said that last with relief, and moved a little, as if relaxing. Everyone moved a little. The county attorney walked toward the stair door.

"I guess we'll go upstairs first—then out to the barn and around there."

He paused and looked around the kitchen.

"You're convinced there was nothing important here?" he asked the sheriff. "Nothing that would—point to any motive?"

The sheriff too looked all around, as if to reconvince himself.

"Nothing here but kitchen things," he said, with a little laugh for the insignificance of kitchen things.

The county attorney was looking at the cupboard—a peculiar, ungainly structure, half closet and half cupboard, the upper part of it being built in the wall, and the lower part just the old-fashioned kitchen cupboard. As if its queerness attracted him, he got a chair and opened the upper part and looked in. After a moment he drew his hand away sticky.

"Here's a nice mess," he said resentfully.

The two women had drawn nearer, and now the sheriff's wife spoke.

"Oh—her fruit," she said, looking to Mrs. Hale for sympathetic understanding.

She turned back to the county attorney and explained: "She worried about that when it turned so cold last night. She said the fire would go out and her jars might burst."

Mrs. Peters's husband broke into a laugh.

"Well, can you beat the women! Held for murder, and worrying about her preserves!"

The young attorney set his lips.

"I guess before we're through with her she may have something more serious than preserves to worry about."

"Oh, well," said Mrs. Hale's husband, with good-natured superiority, "women are used to worrying over trifles."

The two women moved a little closer together. Neither of them spoke. The county attorney seemed suddenly to remember his manners—and think of his future.

"And yet," said he, with the gallantry of a young politician, "for all their worries, what would we do without the ladies?"

The women did not speak, did not unbend. He went to the sink and began washing his hands. He turned to wipe them on the roller towel—whirled it for a cleaner place.

"Dirty towels. Not much of a housekeeper, would you say, ladies?"

He kicked his foot against some dirty pans under the sink.

"There's a great deal of work to be done on a farm," said Mrs. Hale stiffly.

"To be sure. And yet"—with a little bow to her—"I know there are some Dickson County farmhouses that do not have such roller towels." He gave it a pull to expose its full length again.

"Those towels get dirty awful quick. Men's hands aren't always as clean as they might be."

"Ah, loyal to your sex, I see," he laughed. He stopped and gave her a keen look, "But you and Mrs. Wright were neighbors. I suppose you were friends too."

Martha Hale shook her head.

"I've seen little enough of her of late years. I've not been in this house—it's more than a year."

"And why was that? You didn't like her?"

"I liked her well enough," she replied with spirit. "Farmers' wives have their hands full, Mr. Henderson. And then—" She looked around the kitchen.

"Yes?" he encouraged.

"It never seemed a very cheerful place," said she, more to herself than to him.

"No," he agreed; "I don't think anyone would call it cheerful. I shouldn't say she had the homemaking instinct."

"Well, I don't know as Wright had, either," she muttered.

"You mean they didn't get on very well?" he was quick to ask.

"No; I don't mean anything," she answered, with decision. As she turned a little away from him, she added: "But I don't think a place would be any the cheerfuller for John Wright's bein' in it."

"I'd like to talk to you about that a little later, Mrs. Hale," he said. "I'm anxious to get the lay of things upstairs now."

He moved toward the stair door, followed by the two men.

"I suppose anything Mrs. Peters does'll be all right?" the sheriff inquired. "She was to take in some clothes for her, you know—and a few little things. We left in such a hurry yesterday."

The county attorney looked at the two women they were leaving alone there among the kitchen things.

"Yes—Mrs. Peters," he said, his glance resting on the woman who was not Mrs. Peters, the big farmer woman who stood behind the sheriff's wife. "Of course Mrs. Peters is one of us," he said, in a manner of entrusting responsibility. "And keep your eye out, Mrs. Peters, for anything that might be of use. No telling; you women might come upon a clue to the motive—and that's the thing we need."

Mr. Hale rubbed his face after the fashion of a showman getting ready for a pleasantry.

"But would the women know a clue if they did come upon it?" he said; and, having delivered himself of this, he followed the others through the stair door.

The women stood motionless and silent, listening to the footsteps, first upon the stairs, then in the room above them.

Then, as if releasing herself from something strange. Mrs. Hale began to arrange the dirty pans under the sink, which the county attorney's disdainful push of the foot had deranged.

"I'd hate to have men comin' into my kitchen," she said testily— "snoopin' round and criticizin'."

"Of course it's no more than their duty," said the sheriff's wife, in her manner of timid acquiescence.

"Duty's all right," replied Mrs. Hale bluffly; "but I guess that deputy sheriff that come out to make the fire might have got a little of this on." She gave the roller towel a pull. 'Wish I'd thought of that sooner! Seems mean to talk about her for not having things slicked up, when she had to come away in such a hurry."

She looked around the kitchen. Certainly it was not "slicked up." Her eye was held by a bucket of sugar on a low shelf. The cover was off the wooden bucket, and beside it was a paper bag—half full.

Mrs. Hale moved toward it.

"She was putting this in there," she said to herself—slowly.

She thought of the flour in her kitchen at home—half sifted, half not sifted. She had been interrupted, and had left things half done. What had interrupted Minnie Foster? Why had that work been left half done? She made a move as if to finish it,—unfinished things always bothered her—and then she glanced around and saw that Mrs. Peters was watching her—and she didn't want Mrs. Peters to get that feeling she had got of work begun and then—for some reason—not finished.

"It's a shame about her fruit," she said, and walked toward the cupboard that the county attorney had opened, and got on the chair, murmuring: "I wonder if it's all gone."

It was a sorry enough looking sight, but "Here's one that's all right," she said at last. She held it toward the light. "This is cherries, too." She looked again. "I declare I believe that's the only one."

With a sigh, she got down from the chair, went to the sink, and wiped off the bottle.

"She'll feel awful bad, after all her hard work in the hot weather. I remember the afternoon I put up my cherries last summer."

She set the bottle on the table, and, with another sigh, started to sit down in the rocker. But she did not sit down. Something kept her from sitting down in that chair. She straightened—stepped back, and, half turned away, stood looking at it, seeing the woman who had sat there "pleatin' at her apron."

The thin voice of the sheriff's wife broke in upon her: "I must be getting those things from the front-room closet." She opened the door into the other room, started in, stepped back. "You coming with me, Mrs. Hale?" she asked nervously. "You—you could help me get them."

They were soon back—the stark coldness of that shut-up room was not a thing to linger in.

"My!" said Mrs. Peters, dropping the things on the table and hurrying to the stove.

Mrs. Hale stood examining the clothes the woman who was being detained in town had said she wanted.

"Wright was close!" she exclaimed, holding up a shabby black skirt that bore the marks of much making over. "I think maybe that's why she kept so much to herself. I s'pose she felt she couldn't do her part; and then, you don't enjoy things when you feel shabby. She used to wear pretty clothes and be lively—when she was Minnie Foster, one of the town girls, singing in the choir. But that—oh, that was twenty years ago."

With a carefulness in which there was something tender, she folded the shabby clothes and piled them at one corner of the table. She looked up at Mrs. Peters, and there was something in the other woman's look that irritated her.

"She don't care," she said to herself. "Much difference it makes to her whether Minnie Foster had pretty clothes when she was a girl."

Then she looked again, and she wasn't so sure; in fact, she hadn't at any time been perfectly sure about Mrs. Peters. She had that shrinking manner, and yet her eyes looked as if they could see a long way into things.

"This all you was to take in?" asked Mrs. Hale.

"No," said the sheriff's wife; "she said she wanted an apron. Funny thing to want," she ventured in her nervous little way, "for there's not much to get you dirty in jail, goodness knows. But I suppose just to make her feel more natural. If you're used to wearing an apron—. She said they were in the bottom drawer of this cupboard. Yes—here they are. And then her little shawl that always hung on the stair door."

She took the small gray shawl from behind the door leading upstairs, and stood a minute looking at it.

Suddenly Mrs. Hale took a quick step toward the other woman, "Mrs. Peters!"

"Yes, Mrs. Hale?"

"Do you think she—did it?'

A frightened look blurred the other thing in Mrs. Peters's eyes.

"Oh, I don't know," she said, in a voice that seemed to shrink away from the subject.

"Well, I don't think she did," affirmed Mrs. Hale stoutly. "Asking for an apron, and her little shawl. Worryin' about her fruit."

"Mr. Peters says—." Footsteps were heard in the room above; she stopped, looked up, then went on in a lowered voice: "Mr. Peters says—it looks bad for her. Mr. Henderson is awful sarcastic in a speech, and he's going to make fun of her saying she didn't—wake up."

For a moment Mrs. Hale had no answer. Then, "Well, I guess John Wright didn't wake up—when they was slippin' that rope under his neck," she muttered.

"No, it's *strange*," breathed Mrs. Peters. "They think it was such a—funny way to kill a man."

She began to laugh; at sound of the laugh, abruptly stopped.

"That's just what Mr. Hale said," said Mrs. Hale, in a resolutely natural voice. "There was a gun in the house. He says that's what he can't understand."

"Mr. Henderson said, coming out, that what was needed for the case was a motive. Something to show anger—or sudden feeling."

"Well, I don't see any signs of anger around here," said Mrs. Hale, "I don't—" She stopped. It was as if her mind tripped on something. Her eye was caught by a dish towel in the middle of the kitchen table. Slowly she moved toward the table. One half of it was wiped clean, the other half messy. Her eyes made a slow, almost unwilling turn to the bucket of sugar and the half empty bag beside it. Things begun—and not finished.

After a moment she stepped back, and said, in that manner of releasing herself:

"Wonder how they're finding things upstairs? I hope she had it a little more red up up there. You know"—she paused, and feeling gathered—"it seems kind of *sneaking*: locking her up in town and coming out here to get her own house to turn against her!"

"But, Mrs. Hale," said the sheriff's wife, "the law is the law."

"I s'pose 'tis," answered Mrs. Hale shortly.

She turned to the stove, saying something about that fire not being much to brag of. She worked with it a minute, and when she straightened up she said aggressively:

"The law is the law—and a bad stove is a bad stove. How'd you like to cook on this?"—pointing with the poker to the broken lining. She opened the oven door and started to express her opinion of the oven; but she was swept into her own thoughts, thinking of what it would mean, year after year, to have that stove to wrestle with. The thought of Minnie Foster trying to bake in that oven—and the thought of her never going over to see Minnie Foster—.

She was startled by hearing Mrs. Peters say: "A person gets discouraged—and loses heart."

The sheriff's wife had looked from the stove to the sink—to the pail of water which had been carried in from outside. The two women stood there silent, above them the footsteps of the men who were looking for evidence against the woman who had worked in that kitchen. That look of seeing into things, of seeing through a thing to something else, was in the eyes of the sheriff's wife now. When Mrs. Hale next spoke to her, it was gently:

"Better loosen up your things, Mrs. Peters. We'll not feel them when we go out."

Mrs. Peters went to the back of the room to hang up the fur tippet she was wearing. A moment later she exclaimed, "Why, she was piecing a quilt," and held up a large sewing basket piled high with quilt pieces.

Mrs. Hale spread some of the blocks on the table.

"It's log-cabin pattern," she said, putting several of them together, "Pretty, isn't it?"

They were so engaged with the quilt that they did not hear the footsteps on the stairs. Just as the stair door opened Mrs. Hale was saying:

"Do you suppose she was going to quilt it or just knot it?"

The sheriff threw up his hands.

"They wonder whether she was going to quilt it or just knot it!"

There was a laugh for the ways of women, a warming of hands over the stove, and then the county attorney said briskly:

"Well, let's go right out to the barn and get that cleared up."

"I don't see as there's anything so strange," Mrs. Hale said resentfully, after the outside door had closed on the three men— "our taking up our time with little things while we're waiting for them to get the evidence. I don't see as it's anything to laugh about."

"Of course they've got awful important things on their minds," said the sheriff's wife apologetically.

They returned to an inspection of the block for the quilt. Mrs. Hale was looking at the fine, even sewing, and preoccupied with thoughts of the woman who had done that sewing, when she heard the sheriff's wife say, in a queer tone:

"Why, look at this one."

She turned to take the block held out to her.

"The sewing," said Mrs. Peters, in a troubled way, "All the rest of them have been so nice and even—but—this one. Why, it looks as if she didn't know what she was about!"

Their eyes met—something flashed to life, passed between them; then, as if with an effort, they seemed to pull away from each other. A moment Mrs. Hale sat there, her hands folded over that sewing which was so unlike all the rest of the sewing. Then she had pulled a knot and drawn the threads.

"Oh, what are you doing, Mrs. Hale?" asked the sheriff's wife, startled.

"Just pulling out a stitch or two that's not sewed very good," said Mrs. Hale mildly.

"I don't think we ought to touch things," Mrs. Peters said, a little helplessly.

"I'll just finish up this end," answered Mrs. Hale, still in that mild, matter-of-fact fashion.

She threaded a needle and started to replace bad sewing with good. For a little while she sewed in silence. Then, in that thin, timid voice, she heard:

"Mrs. Hale!"

"Yes, Mrs. Peters?"

"What do you suppose she was so—nervous about?"

"Oh, *I* don't know," said Mrs. Hale, as if dismissing a thing not important enough to spend much time on. "I don't know as she was—nervous. I sew awful queer sometimes when I'm just tired."

She cut a thread, and out of the corner of her eye looked up at Mrs. Peters. The small, lean face of the sheriff's wife seemed to have tightened up. Her eyes had that look of peering into something. But next moment she moved, and said in her thin, indecisive way:

'Well, I must get those clothes wrapped. They may be through sooner than we think. I wonder where I could find a piece of paper—and string."

"In that cupboard, maybe," suggested to Mrs. Hale, after a glance around.

One piece of the crazy sewing remained unripped. Mrs. Peter's back turned, Martha Hale now scrutinized that piece, compared it with the dainty, accurate sewing of the other blocks. The difference was startling. Holding this block made her feel queer, as if the distracted thoughts of the woman who had perhaps turned to it to try and quiet herself were communicating themselves to her.

Mrs. Peters's voice roused her.

"Here's a birdcage," she said. "Did she have a bird, Mrs. Hale?"

"Why, I don't know whether she did or not." She turned to look at the cage Mrs. Peters was holding up. "I've not been here in so long." She sighed. "There was a man round last year selling canaries cheap—but I don't know as she took one. Maybe she did. She used to sing real pretty herself."

Mrs. Peters looked around the kitchen.

"Seems kind of funny to think of a bird here." She half laughed—an attempt to put up a barrier. "But she must have had one—or why would she have a cage? I wonder what happened to it."

"I suppose maybe the cat got it," suggested Mrs. Hale, resuming her sewing.

"No; she didn't have a cat. She's got that feeling some people have about cats—being afraid of them. When they brought her to our house yesterday, my cat got in the room, and she was real upset and asked me to take it out."

"My sister Bessie was like that," laughed Mrs. Hale.

The sheriff's wife did not reply. The silence made Mrs. Hale turn round. Mrs. Peters was examining the birdcage.

"Look at this door," she said slowly. "It's broke. One hinge has been pulled apart."

Mrs. Hale came nearer.

"Looks as if someone must have been—rough with it."

Again their eyes met—startled, questioning, apprehensive. For a moment neither spoke nor stirred. Then Mrs. Hale, turning away, said brusquely:

"If they're going to find any evidence, I wish they'd be about it. I don't like this place."

"But I'm awful glad you came with me, Mrs. Hale." Mrs. Peters put the birdcage on the table and sat down. "It would be lonesome for me—sitting here alone."

"Yes, it would, wouldn't it?" agreed Mrs. Hale, a certain determined naturalness in her voice. She had picked up the sewing, but now it dropped in her lap, and she murmured in a different voice: "But I tell you what I *do* wish, Mrs. Peters. I wish I had come over sometimes when she was here. I wish—I had."

"But of course you were awful busy, Mrs. Hale. Your house—and your children."

"I could've come," retorted Mrs. Hale shortly. "I stayed away because it weren't cheerful—and that's why I ought to have come. I"—she looked around—"I've never liked this place. Maybe because it's down in a hollow and you don't see the road. I don't know what it is, but it's a lonesome place, and always was. I wish I had come over to see Minnie Foster sometimes. I can see now—" She did not put it into words.

"Well, you mustn't reproach yourself," counseled Mrs. Peters. "Somehow, we just don't see how it is with other folks till—something comes up."

"Not having children makes less work," mused Mrs. Hale, after a silence, "but it makes a quiet house—and Wright out to work all day—and no company when he did come in. Did you know John Wright, Mrs. Peters?"

"Not to know him. I've seen him in town. They say he was a good man."

"Yes—good," conceded John Wright's neighbor grimly. "He didn't drink, and kept his word as well as most, I guess, and paid his debts. But he was a hard man, Mrs. Peters. Just to pass the time of day with him—." She stopped, shivered a little. "Like a raw wind that gets to the bone." Her eye fell upon the cage on the table before her, and she added, almost bitterly: "I should think she would've wanted a bird!"

Suddenly she leaned forward, looking intently at the cage. "But what do you s'pose went wrong with it?"

"I don't know," returned Mrs. Peters; "unless it got sick and died."

But after she said it she reached over and swung the broken door. Both women watched it as if somehow held by it.

"You didn't know—her?" Mrs. Hale asked, a gentler note in her voice.

"Not till they brought her yesterday," said the sheriff's wife.

"She—come to think of it, she was kind of like a bird herself. Real sweet and pretty, but kind of timid and—fluttery. How—she—did—change."

That held her for a long time. Finally, as if struck with a happy thought and relieved to get back to everyday things, she exclaimed:

"Tell you what, Mrs. Peters, why don't you take the quilt in with you? It might take up her mind."

"Why, I think that's a real nice idea, Mrs. Hale," agreed the sheriff's wife, as if she too were glad to come into the atmosphere of a simple kindness. "There couldn't possibly be any objection to that, could there? Now, just what will I take? I wonder if her patches are in here—and her things?"

They turned to the sewing basket.

"Here's some red," said Mrs. Hale, bringing out a roll of cloth. Underneath that was a box. "Here, maybe her scissors are in here—and her things." She held it up. "What a pretty box! I'll warrant that was something she had a long time ago—when she was a girl."

She held it in her hand a moment; then, with a little sigh, opened it.

Instantly her hand went to her nose.

"Why—!"

Mrs. Peters drew nearer—then turned away.

"There's something wrapped up in this piece of silk," faltered Mrs. Hale.

"This isn't her scissors," said Mrs. Peters, in a shrinking voice.

Her hand not steady, Mrs. Hale raised the piece of silk. "Oh, Mrs. Peters!" she cried. "It's—"

Mrs. Peters bent closer.

"It's the bird," she whispered.

"But, Mrs. Peters!" cried Mrs. Hale. "*Look* at it! Its *neck*—look at its neck! It's all—other side *too*."

She held the box away from her.

The sheriff's wife again bent closer.

"Somebody wrung its neck," said she, in a voice that was slow and deep.

And then again the eyes of the two women met—this time clung together in a look of dawning comprehension, of growing horror. Mrs. Peters looked from the dead bird to the broken door of the cage. Again their eyes met. And just then there was a sound at the outside door.

Mrs. Hale slipped the box under the quilt pieces in the basket, and sank into the chair before it. Mrs. Peters stood holding to the table. The county attorney and the sheriff came in from outside.

"Well, ladies," said the county attorney, as one turning from serious things to little pleasantries, "have you decided whether she was going to quilt it or knot it?"

"We think," began the sheriff's wife in a flurried voice, "that she was going to—knot it."

He was too preoccupied to notice the change that came in her voice on that last.

"Well, that's very interesting, I'm sure," he said tolerantly. He caught sight of the birdcage.

"Has the bird flown?"

"We think the cat got it," said Mrs. Hale in a voice curiously even.

He was walking up and down, as if thinking something out.

"Is there a cat?" he asked absently.

Mrs. Hale shot a look up at the sheriff's wife.

"Well, not *now*," said Mrs. Peters. "They're superstitious, you know; they leave."

She sank into her chair.

The county attorney did not heed her. "No sign at all of anyone having come in from the outside," he said to Peters, in the manner of continuing an interrupted conversation. "Their own rope. Now let's go upstairs again and go over it, piece by piece. It would have to have been someone who knew just the—"

The stair door closed behind them and their voices were lost.

The two women sat motionless, not looking at each other, but as if peering into something and at the same time holding back. When they spoke now it was as if they were afraid of what they were saying, but as if they could not help saying it.

"She liked the bird," said Martha Hale, low and slowly. "She was going to bury it in that pretty box."

"When I was a girl," said Mrs. Peters, under her breath, "my kitten—there was a boy took a hatchet, and before my eyes—before I could get there—" She covered her face an instant. "If they hadn't held me back I would have"—she caught herself, looked upstairs where footsteps were heard, and finished weakly—"hurt him."

Then they sat without speaking or moving.

"I wonder how it would seem," Mrs. Hale at last began, as if feeling her way over strange ground—"never to have had any children around?" Her eyes made a slow sweep of the kitchen, as if seeing what that kitchen had meant through all the years. "No, Wright wouldn't like the bird," she said after that—"a thing that sang. She used to sing. He killed that too." Her voice tightened.

Mrs. Peters moved uneasily.

"Of course we don't know who killed the bird."

"I knew John Wright," was Mrs. Hale's answer.

"It was an awful thing was done in this house that night, Mrs. Hale," said the sheriff's wife. "Killing a man while he slept—slipping a thing round his neck that choked the life out of him."

Mrs. Hale's hand went out to the birdcage.

"We don't *know* who killed him," whispered Mrs. Peters wildly. "We don't *know*."

Mrs. Hale had not moved. "If there had been years and years of—nothing, then a bird to sing to you, it would be awful—still—after the bird was still."

It was as if something within her not herself had spoken, and it found in Mrs. Peters something she did not know as herself.

"I know what stillness is," she said, in a queer, monotonous voice. "When we homesteaded in Dakota, and my first baby died—after he was two years old—and me with no other then—"

Mrs. Hale stirred.

"How soon do you suppose they'll be through looking for the evidence?"

"I know what stillness is," repeated Mrs. Peters, in just that same way. Then she too pulled back. "The law has got to punish crime, Mrs. Hale," she said in her tight little way.

"I wish you'd seen Minnie Foster," was the answer, "when she wore a white dress with blue ribbons, and stood up there in the choir and sang."

The picture of that girl, the fact that she had lived neighbor to that girl for twenty years, and had let her die for lack of life, was suddenly more than she could bear.

"Oh, I *wish* I'd come over here once in a while!" she cried. "That was a crime! Who's going to punish that?"

"We mustn't take on," said Mrs. Peters, with a frightened look toward the stairs.

"I might 'a' *known* she needed help! I tell you, it's *queer*, Mrs. Peters. We live close together, and we live far apart. We all go through the same things—it's all just a different kind of the same thing! If it weren't—why do you and I *understand*? Why do we *know*—what we know this minute?"

She dashed her hand across her eyes. Then, seeing the jar of fruit on the table she reached for it and choked out:

"If I was you I wouldn't *tell* her her fruit was gone! Tell her it *ain't*. Tell her it's all right—all of it. Here—take this in to prove it to her! She—she may never know whether it was broke or not."

She turned away.

Mrs. Peters reached out for the bottle of fruit as if she were glad to take it—as if touching a familiar thing, having something to do, could keep her from something else. She got up, looked about for something to wrap the fruit in, took a petticoat from the pile of clothes she had brought from the front room, and nervously started winding that round the bottle.

"My!" she began, in a high, false voice, "it's a good thing the men couldn't hear us! Getting all stirred up over a little thing like a—dead canary." She hurried over that. "As if that could have anything to do with—with—My, wouldn't they *laugh?*"

Footsteps were heard on the stairs.

"Maybe they would," muttered Mrs. Hale—"maybe they wouldn't."

"No, Peters," said the county attorney incisively; "it's all perfectly clear, except the reason for doing it. But you know juries when it comes to women. If there was some definite thing—something to show. Something to make a story about. A thing that would connect up with this clumsy way of doing it."

In a covert way Mrs. Hale looked at Mrs. Peters. Mrs. Peters was looking at her. Quickly they looked away from each other. The outer door opened and Mr. Hale came in.

"I've got the team round now," he said. "Pretty cold out there."

"I'm going to stay here awhile by myself," the county attorney suddenly announced. "You can send Frank out for me, can't you?" he asked the sheriff. "I want to go over everything. I'm not satisfied we can't do better."

Again, for one brief moment, the two women's eyes found one another.

The sheriff came up to the table.

"Did you want to see what Mrs. Peters was going to take in?"

The county attorney picked up the apron. He laughed.

"Oh, I guess they're not very dangerous things the ladies have picked out."

Mrs. Hale's hand was on the sewing basket in which the box was concealed. She felt that she ought to take her hand off the basket. She did not seem able to. He picked up one of the quilt blocks which she had piled on to cover the box. Her eyes felt like fire. She had a feeling that if he took up the basket she would snatch it from him.

But he did not take it up. With another little laugh, he turned away, saying:

"No; Mrs. Peters doesn't need supervising. For that matter, a sheriff's wife is married to the law. Ever think of it that way, Mrs. Peters?"

Mrs. Peters was standing beside the table. Mrs. Hale shot a look up at her; but she could not see her face. Mrs. Peters had turned away. When she spoke, her voice was muffled.

"Not—just that way," she said.

"Married to the law!" chuckled Mrs. Peters's husband. He moved toward the door into the front room, and said to the county attorney:

"I just want you to come in here a minute, George. We ought to take a look at these windows."

"Oh—windows," said the county attorney scoffingly.

"We'll be right out, Mr. Hale," said the sheriff to the farmer, who was still waiting by the door.

Hale went to look after the horses. The sheriff followed the county attorney into the other room. Again—for one final moment—the two women were alone in that kitchen.

Martha Hale sprang up, her hands tight together, looking at that other woman, with whom it rested. At first she could not see her eyes, for the sheriff's wife had not turned back since she turned away at that suggestion of being married to the law. But now Mrs. Hale made her turn back. Her eyes made her turn back. Slowly, unwillingly, Mrs. Peters turned her head until her eyes met the eyes of the other woman. There was a moment when they held each other in a steady, burning look in which there was no evasion or flinching. Then Martha Hale's eyes pointed the way to the basket in which was hidden the thing that would make certain the conviction of the other woman—that woman who was not there and yet who had been there with them all through that hour.

For a moment Mrs. Peters did not move. And then she did it. With a rush forward, she threw back the quilt pieces, got the box, tried to put it in her handbag. It was too big. Desperately she opened it, started to take the bird out. But there she broke—she could not touch the bird. She stood there helpless, foolish.

There was the sound of a knob turning in the inner door. Martha Hale snatched the box from the sheriff's wife, and got it in the pocket of her big coat just as the sheriff and the county attorney came back into the kitchen.

"Well, Henry," said the county attorney facetiously, "at least we found out that she was not going to quilt it. She was going to—what is it you call it, ladies?"

Mrs. Hale's hand was against the pocket of her coat.

"We call it—knot it, Mr. Henderson."

THE BEST MYSTERY STORIES
2022
HONOR ROLL

Additional outstanding stories published in 2021

Mike Aaron, Business Travel
Mystery Tribune (March–April)

Nancy Bourne, American Girl
The Briarcliff Review (Volume 33)

S. A. Cosby, An Ache So Divine
Jukes & Tonks, ed. by Michael Bracken & Gary Phillips (Down & Out)

Talia Deitsch, The Famous Patient
North Dakota Quarterly (Fall–Winter)

John M. Floyd, Everybody Comes to Lucille's
Jukes & Tonks, ed. by Michael Bracken & Gary Phillips (Down & Out)

Dana Haynes, The Waiting Game
Alfred Hitchcock Mystery Magazine (July–August)

Kristen Lepionka, Remediation
This Time for Sure, ed. by Hank Phillippi Ryan (Bouchercon)

Bennett Sims, Unknown
The Kenyon Review (November–December)

H. K. Slade, The Last Gasp
Black Cat Mystery Magazine (Volume 10)

Lucas Southworth, We Could Have Been Kids Together
Conjunctions (Volume 77)